Vampire Valley:
An Anthology of the Vampire Valley Novels
By
Carl Reader
Including:
The Hostage of Vampire Valley
Resurrection in Vampire Valley
The Haunting of Vampire Valley

All characters in these novels are purely fictional. Any resemblance to any person, living or dead, is strictly coincidental.

Vampire Valley: An Anthology of the Vampire Valley Novels

Carl Reader

Published by Carl Reader, 2024.

This is a work of fiction. Similarities to real people, places, or events are entirely coincidental.

VAMPIRE VALLEY: AN ANTHOLOGY OF THE VAMPIRE VALLEY NOVELS

First edition. November 7, 2024.

Copyright © 2024 Carl Reader.

ISBN: 979-8227917584

Written by Carl Reader.

The Hostage of Vampire Valley
ONE
Climbing the Walls

When all was supposed to be eternal peace and silence, a scratching on the other side of the bare white wall startled her awake. She had almost drifted off to sleep, which meant she had almost drifted from life forever. Now that she realized she was still alive, Maggie gulped in air greedily to encourage consciousness.

She lay in bed trembling at midnight with her long hair covering her like a blanket, and then she pulled up her hair to cover every part of her face but her eyes. She didn't dare doze off again, lest her step-parents creep into her room and murder her, just as they had murdered her parents. She lay on her back half-awake, still not believing they had not come in the room yet, her heart racing, trying her best not to doze and therefore to live. She hoped her long hair would protect her from them, from what end they had in store for her, but it did not protect her that first night in Montana from fear. Fear boiled up in her and caused an awful silent storm of words to break into her skull as though a dam broke on a dike. The garble of words washing over her brain rose inside her as the servants of fright, a flood of fear. The word drowned into her thoughts like sheets of water from a hurricane, leaving her mind to drown in madness. Floods of words are much the same thing as nightmares, and waking nightmares are the worst of all.

Then the words subsided for a moment, and there was just one voice.

2

"You're right to wake up. If you stay in bed, you'll die. They will kill you. Come out into the night with us, your friends, and you'll live. Stay with them and you'll die. You were meant to be with us and live."

All at once a thousand screams flooded back into her mind at a greater volume, none of them making sense, louder than a volcano and as incomprehensible, flowing over her mind and crushing her thoughts as a rock-strewn mudslide crushes sheep. The screams would have split open any normal human skull, but Maggie's skull was not normal. Once the voices screamed at her she thought they might further split apart even her already shattered mind, overwhelm it and break it into yet smaller pieces. Someone unseen invited her to get up out of bed and live in the night, to flee from her step-parents to life. It was not normal, she realized, to hear voices without sounds, but again she was not normal, being used to a life that called up such things as screams inside the head at midnight. The thousand voices crying out, now like burning tortured cats, continued that first night in her new house in the mountains and they went on and on and on and on.

At first she watched horror movies on TV to keep her eyes wide open in case her step-parents crept into her room. She didn't have the courage to close her eyes when the movies bored her, so she watched as clouds partially scrubbed by moonlight raced by her window and the voices without sound screamed at her. Spring dirtied the air, and its pollen rushed in through her open window screens and brought on her allergic reactions. She sneezed and sneezed and that helped to keep her eyes wide open as the painful silent screaming continued, as though transferred from the horror movies to the inside of her head, there to drown the remainder of her sanity. Any rest but death would have been welcome, a soothing friend when all of her old friends were left far behind two thousand miles away in Manhattan. Instead of rest she heard again the loud silent screaming voices seemingly crying out from somewhere deep inside her own head, wrestling with each other behind her eyes for attention, demanding it. The voices came from below, and yet they seemed linked to the dark clouds above that were scrubbed by the moon and floating in those awful odors, all within the bowl of this mountain valley. She was not certain she liked her new home in Montana all that much, and was very confused and frightened by it, especially by the words that came as nightmares when she was startled awake. Montana was proving not to be the fresh, natural place of romantic imagination, but instead a weird spot with unseen creatures screaming at her about walking the night.

"Come with us," the solitary voice said suddenly, very clearly, at another pause in the screaming. "You know what will happen if you don't listen to us."

She knew that if she slept she would not live. The voices seemed to know that, too. At least someone was talking to her, a friend who was concerned for her welfare, and it planted an irresistible impulse in her to sit up in bed. Maybe someone in this weird, violent world wished her well. Maybe someone would save her.

"Where are you?"

"Down here, come down to us. We know that it's blood you want, and blood we have, so that you can live."

Still groggy and fearful, she could make little sense of the offer of blood, although the word itself brought a strange, coppery taste into her mouth. Why would they offer her blood? It seemed so silly when what she needed was safety and rest.

"If you made sense, I would listen to you," she said, talking to the air. "I thank you for keeping me awake, but most of the time I don't understand what you're saying and all you are is a lot of babbling. I'm not afraid of you, so make some sense and I might listen and come to talk to you."

With the offer to talk further, the babbling tumult of thousands of voices inside her head lifted to a painful crescendo that extended far past mere seconds and into several minutes, as though the offer brought on that awful excitement. All the voices vied for her attention now and made her feel as though her very brain was being diced to bits. They all wanted her to come to them, and screamed at her to do so. It was a pleasant possibility, that someone might need her, but the screaming of all those voices all at once left her tilting again toward madness. It was only fair to listen to beings who screamed so loudly and hurt her so, for beings who screamed loudly did so because of two reasons: one, they were mad and howled at mere trifles like breezes and clouds; or, two, some great injustice had been committed against them and they cried out for fairness in a dark world. The impulse to descend to them was a compulsion she had to agree to, since she was so weakened by her torture and compelled by her needs.

"Make sense! At least make some sense! And stop talking all at once! I'll come down, if you only make sense!"

"Then come down, Maggie Long Hair. When we see you, we'll make sense, it will all make sense, we promise," one voice managed to say, above the rest.

With that, those words, the screaming stopped and she was on her feet, the floor creaking beneath her weight and her heart thumping wilding with the prospect of escape from her step-parents. When she was on her feet, her long hair trailed behind her down to the tops of her legs. She was a girl so desperate for a friendly touch that she would do anything and go anywhere, except she didn't know where down here was and exactly what it was she was doing in her attempt to make friends.

Down was obviously down, silly girl, but it seemed a far distance to go to the shining oak stairs just outside her bedroom door and she was exhausted and frightened, if not intrigued by the voices that made friends with her at midnight by screaming inside of her head. Still, she definitely was the girl who would do anything, absolutely anything, and anything she was about to do, if it meant the voices would settle outside her mind and communicate to her as rational friends, company to loneliness and fear and despair.

"Come down," one deep sonorous voice of a boy said again, reminding her of what she was to do. "Come down."

"You don't have to tell me again. I understand you. Wait for me. I'm coming, boy."

The voice was as pleasant as the depths of the sea.

"I am not a boy, but an old man. Come down to me."

The pleasant ocean of his words washed over her, but lies were everywhere, and she suspected she knew a boy's voice when she heard one, like this one, this boy's voice pretending to be an old man's. She was very certain it was a boy talking under some disguise, speaking in disguise for a reason she did not know, but she knew the boy called to her and she must go, if only to escape the death that awaited her if she remained in bed.

"Come down and open the door. Spit to the wind with us, it's glorious, spitting, and then let us out and all of us will be free."

Again, they were making no sense, but she was already up and too afraid to return to her bed. What did they mean by asking her to spit with them? What did they mean by that? She might as well have been walking on ice as those carpetless oak floors, still bare but with Persians unrolled against the walls, too lazy to open out in battle and cover the floors with the ice of their bodies. Persians invaded Greece, but not those floors.

6

All the floors were ice, as cold as the centuries-old dead, from her bedroom into the hallway where her murdering step-parents slept uneasily together behind the closed door of their bedroom. She moved as quietly as possible, in an agony that they might discover her. Her feet waked on icy floors down through hallway and the living room until finally there was some warmth under her when she opened the door to the basement and stepped onto the oddly toasty bare wooden steps there to go down. It was as though those steps had the temperature of life in them, or brimstone below them. The screams were transformed into murmurs during her trek down, almost unbelieving murmurs of joy that she would listen and descend toward them, barely able to control themselves from screaming at her again. She is doing it, she is doing it and coming, they murmured, but then they began screaming again in a crescendo when her foot first hit that first step to the basement and they knew she was coming to them for certain, she was coming, she was coming for sure, to their pure joy. Again, they nearly split apart her head.

"Come to all of us! We are all here, not just him. Yes, come! You dear one, dear girl who will do anything for us, come to us and let us be free again! We will never leave you, and he will be here, too, for your love! You will be safe with us!"

They would kill her with their uncontrolled screams if her step-parents heard them, but she would die pleasantly and be below with them, forever with them in their basement where she would call with them to others to join them, as soon as she found them and him and joined with them. Anything was better than lying half-awake in her bed waiting for her step-parents to kill her. She wished to find him most of all, whoever that was, and end the pain of the screaming and simply be with him and safe. She flicked on the light switch at the top of the stairs and hurried down the steps and soon was with them. From the ice of the upstairs floors she now stepped onto a lake of fire in the basement, as though the heat from the souls burning below and calling her inflamed the concrete. Then, to her surprise and as far as she could tell, she was still alone, just fevered and delusionary. The souls of her feet were scorched in agony so that she fell to her hands and knees. They too were scorched in agony but still she did not see the voices calling her although she cried out to them now in her pain. She had been tricked again and was as lonely and vulnerable as ever.

"Where are you? I'm here, but you're not. I came down to you, but you left. Where is he? Help me, please. Where are you? I can't stand being alone here without you, and my step-parents will know where I am soon."

"You are just above us. Open the trap door. Open it! He is here for you. You are just above us! We are almost with you, and he wants you!"

She grappled with her pain to do as she was told to do, to enter hell and more pain but no loneliness, but as she crawled across the floor there was no trap door anywhere in the basement, no relief to the burning concrete that the ultimate pain of hell would give, and finally she had to admit to herself that she could not tolerate for a minute more this earthly pain in order to find the final pain and relief of hell.

"You're no where! I am a fool again. You called to me, but you're no where, nothing but an illusion off of fire. What have you decided to do, pretend you are in my head to end it? Why would I end it if I have to stand alone again with more lies?"

"We are just beneath you! Trust us! We called to you because we want you! We are as honest as the sun! Come to us! We desire you more than life itself! He desires you!"

She could not. All she wanted now was to rise. They, too, had lied to her and she was still alone and in danger. She would not be with them because they were not here. They lied. Devils lie. She crawled in desperation back to the stairs as the screaming inside her skull worsened to the loudest noise possible among stars, the loudest a noise could be anywhere, even in the great silence between the stars, but as she lifted a burning palm onto the first stair the stair was ice, and it burned her with cold, and she shrieked with agony, but it was not as though that mattered. She barely gasped at the pain, barely felt the searing of her flesh, so desperate was she, but instead ascended the stairs like an animal, like a dog, quickly loping upward on all fours, and she was a dog or an animal by the time she reached the corridor of shining floors beyond the open door to the basement, so loud was the crying out inside her head. The world was utterly ice now that she had run. She evolved, a little more human, when upstairs, rising to her burned feet, but only because on her feet she could run from this world. She could run with the speed and reason of complete panic and now she ran outside through the kitchen door and into the night, where the world might be a little bit normal, anywhere but inside this house of screaming voices. Outside, it was as though a wall had suddenly been erected before her eyes. She ran into it and could go no farther. Trapped, even more desperate now, she scratched at the outside wall of her screaming home and clawed at it, since she could not them, and the kind of animal she became now was a monkey, climbing. She discovered she could rise by clawing the wall with her hands and feet, some special being now that those devils who screamed inside her head motivated her: she was capable of climbing up walls with hands and feet that stuck to the siding. She pulled herself up and up, past the porch, moonlight lighting her path like a pure wan frost on the stucco walls, and she passed her bedroom window where her bed lay rumpled and disordered, skewed, her sheet pulled partially off the bed to expose the shoulder of the mattress and the covers swirling on the floor in whirlpools. She would climb to the stars if she possibly could. Never that night would she enter that room, ever, for there was the real danger. She climbed upward because that was where the lying voices were not, it was up there she was as far away from the basement as she could be, since her world walled her off and she could not escape in any way but upward from those who taunted and lied. She was clumsy then, as she swung a leg up and clung to the gutter at the base of the roof to pull herself onto the rough shingles, another grind to her poor flesh, as she scraped her knee and bloodied her palms clambering to that place closest to the silent stars, on a rough slant now in the darkness. She closed her eyes with the relief of it, nearly limp, close to the sky, nearly wanting to fall to the ground in the great calm that overcame her, but the roof was rough and held her, unlike the icy floor that had nearly given way beneath her.

"Is she here? I can sense her. I thought she had left us, but it's not so. She's come closer to help us climb out the pit! Help us climb out the pit now! Spit to the wind!"

And then the screaming got still louder, and she knew she would never escape it until she gave in to it. The screaming was up and the screaming was down and it was everywhere but she could not know where it truly was.

"You're right, she's out there! We sense her, too. She is not a bad person, not the bad person we thought her to be when she left but a good one, one who will be with us out in the world, one who will give us her hand to pull us out and spit to the wind."

Then she saw what she had been looking for in the basement, her way out, the place were the voices came from. It was a large circular silver vat sunk in the roof like a hot tub, reflecting the moonlight in its cover, and it contained the voices that assaulted her thoughts. The home of murderers had an entrance to hell in the roof. The silver shining trap door leaked a sick, blue-grey light from its edges, the fetid, rotting blue blood of demons, for the light did not simply leak from the openings around the trap door, but it emanated out a short ways into the air and then fell like a waterfall onto the roof, where it flowed in a sheet toward the edge of the roof and then disappeared into the darkness. It was rotten, and it smelled rotten as all the piles of all the dead smell rotten. That was where she was going. She was going to open the door to escape to death, she was certain she was going to do so now. She was about to end it all with the great relief that comes in the embrace of friendly demons.

Maggie stepped into the sick, blue-grey light flowing over the shingles and felt a tingling rush of excitement, as though mice danced on her feet, as it wrapped around her. The awful blue light had a sweet and a fetid smell that traveled up her legs and wrapped around her, so that she glowed blue-grey as she reached for the handle of the trap door.

"Spit! Spit more! Spit as much as you can! She's opening it! She's opening the door! Spit! Spit!"

When she opened the trap door, a dozen panicked but delighted eyeballs, sunk in hollow skulls, suddenly looked up with joy and bore into her from below the frame of the open vat. Each of the six sickly emaciated demons below her, made mostly of bone, was spitting out the blue-grey light in liquid form with great hacking coughs. It congealed into a deep pool that sank them up to their necks, as though they were ill with a deadly blue-grey flu and spit its remnants out all around them in an ever-deepening flood. They were drowning in a silver tank in their own sickly excretions. A blue gob shot out toward her from an inconsiderate mouth and struck her shoulder, but its disgust was limited by its airy, light-like nature and it evaporated into the atmospheric demon-spit that already encased her, failing to become liquid.

"Come down and spit with us. You'll be safe here."

"It doesn't look very pleasant, but I might as well."

"No! Wait! Make her pull us out! We all want to be out of here and no longer have to spit."

"Don't say that. She has to come down to us, for her own safety."

"But I want to get out."

"No, you're right. We shouldn't have to spit any longer. Let's go out into the world where the real blood is."

With that, one of the hacking demons lifted a hand made exclusively of bone and blue spit, no flesh on it, toward her for her assistance in escaping the pit. She bent and reached down for the bony fingers, but at the last second both hands shot back to their owners as though they had touched horrible heat, fires of a thousand degrees.

"What are you doing? Grab her. You could have pulled her down to us, for her blood. Now she won't come down. Take her hand."

"There's something strange about her, I'm afraid of her, and you said you didn't want her down here. You said we should get out into the world again. She might hurt me with her strangeness."

"Of course we want her down here, and she's not that strange. That's what we wanted, to have her spit with us. We really don't want to get out of here, do we?"

With that the confused demon raised a sickly smile to her, baring red teeth, and motioned with his bony but hesitant fingers for her to come down to them. Her hands tingled at the invitation, ready to reach for the bony fingers and enter that world of blue air and liquid, any other world where she did not ever have to see or ever hear from those killers in the house below her, for they were worse demons than these and blue spit might be a better fate than that which awaited her with her step-parents below the demons. All six demons were reaching upward for her eagerly and smiling with their red teeth, friends now.

"Come. We've been waiting for you. You'll never have to fear again."

No, she thought. She sensed there was something very false about them, just as they sensed there was something strange about her. She did not need false friends.

She slammed shut the demons' door as they cried out, "No!" and "Please!" and "Come to us, lovely one!"

After that, all was silent, even deep inside her anguished mind. The mice no longer danced on her feet. She lay on the slope of the roof, feeling safer up there than anywhere, in the wonderful night silence, with stars for friends, and immediately fell into a deep sleep.

She had never known how wonderful a dawn could be when waking up after a safe night's sleep watched over by demons. She saw the sun rise above the red rim of the earth, the blue-spitting demons barely a memory, and perhaps only a dream. She thought she would have to do this dream again, after the sun settled below the opposite horizon and night came on and she had once again to escape her step-parents or die.

Perhaps being with demons was the solution to all her problems.

TWO
A Boy on a Bike

The orange juice was sour as old ground stones. She drank it anyway to wash away the remaining memory of blue spit on her tongue. The juice was always sour, like old stones, just as all mornings when she came down from her bed for breakfast with her murdering parents were curdled and sour and full of fear. She no longer avoided these moments when fully awake, no longer concerned herself that the next moment with them might be her last, for what was there left to live for? Blue-spitting demons? More endless nights on the roof? Yet compared to this painful dialogue with the bloody death that she knew her step-parents would bring to her, the taste of the demons' airy blue spit on her tongue was sweet. Her murdering parents sat together at the kitchen table, disgustingly sweetly together, like two sweet rolls in chairs, while she stood silently in the room by the mammoth laboring refrigerator and lifted the glass of stone-sour orange juice that had been set out for her, perhaps as an end that had been foretold for her now coming with her first sip of the juice. She let her long hair down in front of her, a protective flag, as she drank the bitter brew. Poison had the sickly sweet taste of rotten almonds, she knew, and she tasted none of it now, but she breathed a different poison every day, breathed it every day with the first sight of these extraordinarily beautiful but humble but deadly people who were now her parents. Sweet hypocrites who spoke lovingly to her but planned the worst of all possible death for her, that's what they were. So lovely were they both it was difficult to look at them and not fall in love with their perfects faces, round and smooth-skinned and clear, with a luminescence and good cheer to them, but that was if you didn't know what they were and what they had done. They practically cooed to each other with love, their eyes moist with tenderness for each other. Both were tall and slender and blond with piercing blue eyes of an other-worldly cast, both perfectly proportioned as a man and a woman are supposed to be in the world of advertised lust displayed on television commercials, and each was perfectly calm and confident, in the ridiculous and unrealistic way people are depicted on television. It was false, television love, Maggie thought, and these were silly but deadly people. Perhaps they were so calm and confident because they had gotten away cleanly with murder, which also made them confident as they hunted her. Both were dressed in immaculate and stylish exercise suits, ready for their morning jaunt to work. Every day was like this, silent and perfect. She knew it was and would be for a long time, even in this new house and new Montana life, until they finally decided the time had come to rid themselves of her. Her fingers trembled and sent shudders up through her arms and to her shoulders so that she was a shaking mass, stricken with the fear she hated, so shaken and afraid of the stone-sour orange juice that she had to set it down on the table until she could compose herself. Yes, the demons' blue spit looked appetizing compared to what they offered her. Her step-mother actually wore make-up, as though about to go out to dinner on a Saturday night, rather than to a sweaty day at the store. Maggie was trembling with defiance of them, in their perfect running suits and coifed hair, and in love still with the memory of how her parents had been so different, so authentic. Her legs nearly collapsed beneath her with the memory of their grisly deaths. Her true parents had been groggy and disheveled in the mornings, not absurdly perfect and hypocritical, but they had died, killed by these two phony people.

"Sleep well, dear?"

Her step-mother had finally decided to acknowledge her presence in the room. Maggie literally jumped at that sweet voice, over-confident and syrupy. The sudden movement was unseen by her parents who were engaged in their steaks and eggs benedict and deep gaze into each other's eyes. Maggie got tight control of herself again, recovering from the quivering mass she had been, and steeled her nerves and focused her hatred on them once more. Her step-father gently lifted a stray strand of blond hair from her step-mother's forehead and replaced it behind her ear, his smile for her so saccharine and loving it disgusted Maggie. It disgusted her completely, this phony sweetness, and it only made her need to defy them more overwhelmingly intense.

"I slept on the roof," she broke in. "There are demons up there. I wanted to be among them and not down here with you perfect, hateful people."

A worried look passed between her step-dad and step-mom, a break in their confidence, and with it she understood that they were concerned her mind might have clouded and cracked again in this thunderstorm of misery. She realized it was the wrong thing to say immediately, for they might think seeing demons was good reason to destroy her at once and then they might resort to more effective means than curdled orange juice with the grit of stones in it to do so. The kitchen was filled with knives waiting for her blood, and her need for defiance turned to fear.

"Demons?"

"Blue-spitting demons with love in their hearts."

"Oh, Maggie. You really didn't see demons, did you, dear? There really aren't any demons on the roof, or anywhere in Montana, you know."

Her mother tapped her fingers on the tabletop, as though in a nervous warning, but Maggie could not stop herself. She simply could not live with this sort of phoniness.

"Hundreds of them. I saw hundreds of demons!" she screamed. "They filled the sky!"

Again, that knowing and worried look crossed between the two people who would kill her brutally without an ounce of terror or remorse.

"Your door was locked when we came to say good-night. We didn't see –"

Just the sound of her mother's voice was enough to set her off again, call up the screeches of the dead blue-spitters inside her mind. Her hands clamped down on her head, her fingers digging into her skull. She nearly screamed. She clamped closed her eyes and held both hands against the sides of her head and buckled at the waist. When people who have killed your real parents and are not punished but instead are free to eat eggs and steak for breakfast, they should simply eat their ill-gotten food, and not enjoy the benefits of a real love, or of torturing children, as these step-parents of hers seemed to do, so in love with each other that no small kitchen with all its knives could contain it. It was only with regret at the disturbance she presented that they turned their attention to her now.

"Maggie?"

It almost sounded like real concern, authentic love. From inside her confusion came the ridiculous memory of the demons whispering to her, *Come spit with us*." She heard them again.

"Sit down and eat something," her step-mother said to interrupt the demons. "You never eat anything."

She straightened up, her eyes wide open with anger and the absurdity at their phony care and concern for her. Sarcasm would be best here.

"I'd love to, mother. Normally, I wouldn't have anything to do with you, but today I'll have a steak, uncooked. It's what most demons eat, and I realized today that's what I am, a demon."

She practically spat out the words, as the blue-spitters spat out theirs. Her step-parents looked down to their steaks in unison, crest-fallen and beaten by her angry words.

"A steak? At last," her step-father said. "At last you're eating something."

"Oh, I'll eat, I'll eat like no one you've ever seen. I'll eat blood, that's what I want, a big, bloody steak, with mostly the blood. Just the way you eat them, with red blood dripping out of them."

Her step-mother looked horrified.

"Let's give it to her," her step-father said, leaping up ridiculously and sliding a big butcher knife from its block on the granite counter. "A bloody flank steak. Or maybe a cut from the leg. This makes me excited."

A handsome man being silly is all the more silly, since beauty is serious business. Stephanovich Emory brandished the big butcher knife at her, waving a blade that was not burnished and bright but darkened and stained and rusted, certainly dirtied by dried blood. She let out a little cry, and thought of some way to do away with herself quickly, before her step-father could sliver her with the blade. She should have tumbled into the vat of demons when invited to do so, she thought. She should never have allowed them this chance to kill her. At least she wouldn't be standing here, waiting to be butchered by this fool, if she had relented and dunked herself in blue spit. Some flecks of fresh blood glistened on the dark sharp steel that Stephanovich held, the only brightness on the blade, as it swished by her throat, and Maggie had the sudden, awful thought that this was the knife they had used to kill her parents, each in turn, her mother killed first by Stephanovich and then her father murdered by Elsa, so that they could be together in lust, her beautiful new parents, in this beautiful new kitchen two thousand miles from what had been her beautiful home with real parents. The meat locker was behind her, but she did not think of that as he came at her with the knife. She thought only that the knife that had killed her parents was to be plunged into her now. She surrendered suddenly to her fate and thought how comfortable it would be to die in the same way her parents had, murdered by the same knife that had killed them, and what difference would it make if they murdered her or she killed herself or died with blue-spitters? She wished for her end, any end, but for an instant she thought existence in a vat on the roof with a bunch of blue-spitters might be preferable to what was to come now, that terrible pain. She stiffened. Pain was welcome, and it would be over in a second. She didn't recall the meat locker especially built on to the side of the kitchen in the weeks before they moved in and its sides of beef and cuts of pork and lamb cooled and kept fresh in it. She thought instead this was the end. Her step-parents were prodigious eaters of flesh, but she didn't think of that now, being preoccupied with her own death. She thought only of how her own flesh was to be butchered, sliced and slivered, as had been her parents'. She closed her eyes and waited, but she sensed Stephanovich moving past her, a light breeze brushing by her off his large presence, and then her utterly fatigued and damaged brain remembered the meat locker and in her twisted mind were airy visions of the sides of beef and legs of mutton and the flanks of pork hanging above pools of red. She heard the door to the meat locker open and then a moment later close with the sucking sound of a tight seal. When she opened her eyes, a slab of red beef, dripping blood, hung from her step-father's fingers directly in front of her nose. He grinned hideously behind the meat.

Almost immediately, before she could snap at it with her teeth, it dropped onto a hot black iron frying pan her step-mother had placed over high heat on the top of the range. A sizzling of fat and flesh cried out to her immediately from the steak, as though it objected to its torture, but also a wondrous fragrance reached her nose as the meat burned on contact.

"Don't ruin it," she protested, her mouth already salivating with the thought of the blood inside it. "Just a few seconds on each side, and then give it to me. I want it raw."

An overwhelming hunger accosted her not just in the belly, but deeper inside her, an aching for food similar to the aching for love she felt, and Stephanovich, knowing instinctively how to cook her steak, flipped it over with a spatula for another few seconds. She was starving at the sight of blood oozing from the top of the steak, nearly mad for it. Her step-father lifted the steak out of the black iron frying pan with the spatula and slid it onto a gleaming white plate.

Suddenly, she heard a voice call out from above her head, "Me-eat ..."

She knew the voice came to her without the benefit of a body attached to it, from somewhere off the wind and out of this world, out of the deep, dark sky beyond morning, the deep endless night of the universe where the spirits not allowed on earth lived. She knew it was not a good voice that invaded her ears. She snatched the steak off of the plate before the voice could become a presence and steal it from her, and she ripped into it with her cutting front teeth, feeling the heat from it singe her fingers and the blood from it delight her tongue. Her eyes rolled back in her head. She had not eaten in three days.

When she opened her eyes, as she chewed, she noticed that her step-parents were staring at her with delight, pleased she was finally eating again, but still a little worried at her strange behavior. Stephanovich again had picked up the butcher knife again from its resting place on the countertop, gripping it tightly and holding it just below his chin. The knife made it appear as though his head was a large round piece of blond cheese skewered on a toothpick and grinning maniacally. The truly crazy idea that her step-parents might not just kill her but eat her, too, when she was fattened up, came into her head when they continued to stare at her longingly. They might be fattening her up, they might, after she had refused to eat for three days before the move to Montana. She could not refrain from tearing into the steak with her teeth, but the thought she might be eaten made her wish to flee, like a dog running from other dogs who were after what fleshy prize she had, and then that is exactly what she did. Once again ripping into the steak, she turned from this odd form of murder her step-parents were inflicting on her and rushed in a panic outside with the steak. She did not go alone. The dark voice from above followed her, repeating the obvious fact to her that she had meat, but then muttering something garbled about its wanting meat, too. "I want my meat your meat meat." It would make little sense to her to hear voices from above if she had not already experienced the blue-spitters on the roof, but this voice seemed even stranger than theirs had been the night before. She licked the blood from her lips. Once again, despite the utter joy of eating again, she felt nauseated by the memory of the blue-spitters and their disgusting habits, in their tank just above her head. Yet they were the only friends she had left. As she chewed, she glanced upward, and was awarded with the knowledge her adventure of the night before had not been a delusion, for she saw the lid to the tank in which the demons stewed gleaming in spring's sunlight on the roof. She breathed in a lungful of fresh air and turned in a half-circle as she bit into the steak again, taking in the encircling panorama of the mountains of the Bitterroot and Sapphire ranges. Snow still capped the Bitterroots to the west, while the Sapphires to the east were clear of it. Her head, too, was clearing of its dark thoughts, like melting snow on a mountaintop, liberated by the mountains and air, when she saw a boy circling on a bike at the end of the cul-de-sac, a small boy no more than five years old, who appeared to have an unnatural interest in her. He stared at her as he rode, his eyes glued on her and his head pivoting unnaturally toward her as he rode away. The dark voice repeating meat meat meat resumed in her head and she wondered if it originated with the boy. He stared at her as he rode in circles, practically twisting his head off as he rode away from her in the circle and then snapping his vision back to her when he came around toward her. Her heart flew into her throat and blocked her swallowing as this dangerous boy with the owl's head stared at her. She stood with a mouthful of chewed meat staring back at the boy who might be her lost younger brother while the screaming of meat meat meat grew louder in her head. Tommy. Her brother had found them, found them in Montana. Tears filled her eyes as she forced herself into motion and quieted the voice and walked quickly to the end of the driveway to make certain it was Tommy, the boy who had disappeared, the only person in the world who was her flesh and blood and the only person she could still love. She was trembling with hope, her heart beating fast that her agony of loss might end now. Oddly, in the boy's second circle of the cul-de-sac, he grew from a five-year-old who could be her bother to a larger ten-year-old, and then to a still larger fifteen-year-old in his third circle. In the beginning of his fourth circling of the cul-de-sac, he was fully sixteen-years old, and now rode in a straight line for her, another delusion who had been her lost brother, her lost love, and now was not.

"Have you been hearing a voice?" he asked, as soon as he braked the bike before her.

Her heart momentarily stopped racing, but then continued to race at the presence of this strange boy, who seemed so magical in his abilities to change and grow and twist his head in circles, and then she could swallow again. Staring at the boy still made it difficult to do so, for he glared at her accusingly and with narrowed dark slits that barely revealed his bright blue eyes, from beneath a thick mop of straight black shining hair and a narrow bony forehead. Her heart raced so fast it was about to burst. The boy, too, seemed in the same agitated condition as she was, but then he gave her a quick, charming smile to comfort her. It was as though the sun had turned black clouds to mist. He had been practically hyperventilating with anger at her as he waited for her to speak, leaning with one foot down from the bike, but now the smile was like a sunrise, further melting the snows of loss. He had high cheek bones and a small, pursed mouth that was unnaturally red, and he was nearly as pale and emaciated as she was. Instead of answering him, she narrowed her eyes to complimentary slits and glared back at him while tearing off another chunk of dripping red meat and chewing it.

"Ew."

"What?"

"You eat like an animal," he said, insultingly.

"So what? You're act like one."

"Maybe I am on."

"I wouldn't be surprised."

He laughed, throwing back his head with amusement, instead of being insulted, and then his eyes narrowed further as though deepening in anger, serious again. Then a twinkle of amusement returned to his gaze as it opened with understanding and humor. Both of his feet settled onto the pavement and he turned from stiffness to softness before her, calming, just as he had gone from a five-year-old to a boy to her age, magically in the circle at the end of the road.

"I'm sorry. I should have said hello and told you who I am. I was an animal not to say hello first and be polite."

She simply tore off another chunk of meat and chewed, instead of answering.

"It's very dangerous what you're doing," he said. "I'm here to tell you that."

"Eating meat is dangerous? It's not that bad for you."

"Eating raw meat outside. You heard his voice, didn't you?"

"Whose voice? I hear lots of voices."

"A voice from nowhere that keeps repeating the same thing, over and over. He's obsessive that way."

"Who is?"

"Karel."

"Oh, Karel. That clears up everything. Now I know. Karel. Karel repeats everything. Now I know how dangerous what I'm doing is because of Karel."

"That's not what I meant?"

"Then say what you mean."

"You saw the blue-spitters last night, didn't you?"

She stepped back and held the meat by her side. The boy had been watching her, stalking her. He appeared poverty-stricken in shabby clothes but yet strong and proud, with ripped grungy jeans and tattered sneakers and a determined look in his eyes, the eyes of a stalker and killer. He had bony elbows and shoulders beneath his black hoodie, she noticed, but with the mention of the blue-spitters she refrained from her continuing assessment of him to stare into his eyes again, which were once again narrow black slits over blue irises, threatening eyes. The more she looked at this beautiful boy, the faster her heart raced, despite the threat.

He could be her friend, but she was afraid he was rude and perhaps odd.

"How do you know about the blue-spitters?"

"You climbed up on your roof and opened one of their tanks. You saw what they have to do in there."

"What do you mean, one of their tanks, and what do they have to do in there? And who are you?"

She was impatient again, and anger was ever-present within her. With a wave of his hand, without telling her who he was, the boy gestured to the curving row of development homes ending in the cul-de-sac. She saw what he gestured to immediately. On top of each of the homes, which were backed by the hulking panorama of big-shouldered mountains, was a roof with a silver vat and closed silver lid on top of it, each the same and each holding blue-spitters, she knew now. She nearly dropped her breakfast to the pavement with astonishment. Hers was only one of many houses with blue demons as residents on top. Blue demons were evidently everywhere. The roofs and gleaming tanks disappeared toward the horizon of mountains, each holding blue demons. It was a shock to her that each of the houses in the development had a built-in tank of silver, real silver, and demons, real demons, for the tanks gleamed with a beauty only fine jewelry had, jewelry that was found shining next to diamonds in a necklace or bracelet or ring in a fine store on an exclusive street, a 5th Avenue in New York City or the Ramblas in Barcelona. They were a long way from New York and Barcelona. Every home had a silver prison for demons as a built-in feature, and in total there must have been thousands of blue-spitters on the roofs. It was a few seconds before she commenced chewing again.

She turned back to him at a loss for words, blood dripping from the corner of her mouth.

"You see?"

She nodded.

"I put them there. I captured all of them, and I'm here for you."

What did that mean, that he was here for her? Was she to be entombed in a silver tank? There was little pride, only a kind of weary bitterness, in his gaze as he let his eyes wander over his work, the vats packed with blue demons on the tops of the dozens of houses in the neighborhood she was only now becoming familiar with. But why was he there for her? Was he going to trap her, too?

When he turned to her again, he was suddenly trembling again with anger.

"You almost helped them get out. Or, worse, they almost dragged you in to make you one of them."

At first, she thought she might apologize now that she knew he did not intend to imprison her, but the boy's anger was so out-of-character for him that she thought no mere boy was going to yell at her and get away with it. She sensed she should yell back at him, but she regretted it, for he had said he was here for her, maybe here to help her, and that softened her. She was alone in the world, for all she knew. Tommy was dead, too.

"How do you know I almost let them out? How do you know even if I was up on the roof or what I was doing up there?"

"I know because I was there with you, and so was Karel. He could have killed you in an instant."

She laughed at the absurdity of it.

"So you're telling me I was in danger. That's ridiculous. I didn't see anyone. I didn't see you or Karel."

"Do you think a vampire is going to let you see him before he kills you?"

That stopped her in her tracks. It took her a moment to recover.

"So now I was in danger from a vampire I didn't see. I don't care. I'd do it again, I'll do anything. I don't believe you, not one word of what you say. Tonight I might just climb back up there and visit with my demons again. I just don't care."

"You might not care now, but Karel was right behind you, and I was right behind him to make sure nothing happened to you. Do you think this is funny? If he'd pushed you in with the others, then that would have been the end of you and him, because I would have made sure he followed you, but not in one piece."

The front door opening behind them suddenly silenced them. Out stepped Maggie's step-parents, still dressed in their ridiculously expensive work-out suits and gleaming with all the self-priming and self-importance that arrogant, self-righteous murderers have. Each had every blond hair perfectly in place and each wore that perfectly pressed and cleaned workout ensemble with the word "Nike" emblazoned on their chests. And each had a just perfectly white smile of just perfectly formed teeth when they saw Maggie with the boy. It disgusted her so completely that she could not take another bite of her steak and threw it aside onto the lawn for the ants.

"Maggie? We have to go now. Who's your friend?" Elsa asked.

"How should I know? All he does is talk about demons and how they're out to get me. I think he might be one."

Her step-parents walked directly up to her, but stared at him, confused as usual by their daughter, reluctantly smiling at the boy.

"Hello. So far, Maggie hasn't had much nice to say about you."

"My name is Mabin. I was just having a conversation with your daughter about the people in the neighborhood."

At least she knew the boy's name now, and could assume he didn't possess any of the unsavory habits of the beings trapped in her roof. He appeared to be terribly polite, while they weren't.

"It's nice to meet you, Mabin."

"I feel the same way about you. Hello, Mr. Emory." Her step-father showed surprise and then distrust at the use of his name and the extension of Mabin's hand, but Mabin was quick. "I saw you name on the mailbox."

Stephanovich glanced at the mailbox at the end of the driveway.

"How about that? The builder must have put it there as a courtesy. We certainly haven't had time to introduce ourselves to the neighborhood. Anyway, it's nice to meet you, too, Mabin. I'm glad Maggie finally met somebody."

He extended his hand, and the boy shook it with a grave calm.

"Well, we've got to get to the store. The first day is the biggest one. You two have a nice time."

"I had other plans," Maggie snapped.

So quickly did Stephanovich and Elsa climb in their Infiniti SUV, as though in relief, and then completely ignore her and drive off that it seemed they disappeared by magic, and as soon as they had driven around the corner Mabin's eyes widened in fear and suddenly his arms violently gripped her around the waist and drew her to him with a force that snapped back her head. "Look out!" he screamed, and she screamed in reply as he pressed his body up next to hers and she thought desperately for some way to fight him off, to make him loosen his grip on her. Then she realized if she did so, she might die. Somehow, they had shot straight up into the air and were floating hundreds of feet above her house, the sight of her parents' tiny Infiniti SUV already in the distance at a stop sign and the streets of demon-topped houses winding away toward the mountains. Now he simply held her by the hand, keeping her aloft by doing so, as though both of them were filled with helium, and despite herself and this assault she took in the incredible panorama below her, the houses dotted with demon pits and the endless mountain range to the west extending all the way into Idaho, like a vast bumpy plain of furniture covered with green and brown and white sheets. She was speechless at the beauty of it. , and she was a thousand feet in the air with nothing supporting her but the gentle touch of his fingers on her palm. They were like two dancers on the air in a minuet with the great mountains and blue-spitters below. If it was safe, she would have pushed him away so that he could not touch her at all, but she realized that if she did that, she would miss him terribly and also most likely fall to her death.

"What are you doing to me? I didn't ask to be up here. What did you just do?"

"You'd be dead down there. You said you were the girl who would do anything, so when I saw Karel I thought this might be the safest place for us to get away from him."

"Karel? I didn't see anything. I saw no one. Why do you keep talking about people I can't see? What am I supposed to do now? Just stand here on the air?"

"He was right behind you. He knows he needs you now."

"On the ground? He was behind me?"

"Yes."

"What does he need me for?"

"I can't say."

"Well, he's not behind me now, I'm certain of that. Why are we still up here?"

"You're not frightened, are you?"

"No. I'm never frightened. What's there to be frightened of?"

"Look over there. You'll see."

Mabin pointed to a dark stain in a vast white billowing cloud hovering in the distance over the mountains to the west, something very foul in the pure white of the cloud, and oddly, the sight was terrifying in itself. The strangest storm she had ever seen was rushing in from Idaho, an endless tumult of clouds rolling toward them for miles. The black spot in the huge cloud was like a terrible dark rotten fungus on a wedding dress, a rancorous and festering threat of ruination on the natural world and beauty, and as they stared it grew darker and darker as if it was growing ranker and ranker, roiling with anger, and now the sulfurous odor of rotten eggs rode on the wind from the dark riotous spot to her nose, assaulting it with no consideration at all for her. So far, it was one rotten smell after another in Montana, with this being by far the worst of all.

"He could engulf us in that. That is Karel."

Maggie let out a little laugh.

"He doesn't look like much, and he could use a shower."

Mabin's eyes narrowed, as though the danger was so great he could not laugh at her simple joke. As if hearing her, and angry at what she said, the black spot in the cloud cracked with thunder and then lit with an ominous golden glow inside, about to unleash its fury. Out of the golden aura inside it, the ugly black spot spat a bolt of lightning into the earth far below, and then a hideous thick black rain, like tar, fell from the dark glowing spot in the cloud, draining the darkness out of the cloud but fouling the side of a mountain with a black slime that oozed down into a mountain stream. With Karel gone from it, the cloud was pure white again. So perverse was this unnatural display that Maggie unconsciously inched closer to Mabin, for the first time in months feeling just a little secure, despite their heady perch on thin air and the threat of Karel. With a smile, he took her free hand, so that he held both of hers, and they descended slowly and gently from high in the air, her gaze caught in his, and landed just where they had departed from moments before, but with a far different feeling toward each other. From the cold heights, they descended into warmer air. Blinking and staring into her eyes, Mabin gently let go her hands, speechless at what he saw in her eyes. For the first time in months, since her parents were murdered, she felt the chill leave her hands, and a magical word entered her mind: love. She didn't dare speak it, but she thought it. Love.

"I ... thank you," she said.

"If I leave right away, I might capture him," Mabin said quickly. "Will you stay indoors until I get back?"

"You're coming back?"

"Of course. He knows you're here now, and I have to be with you. It wouldn't be safe for you outside."

"Can't I go with you? I want to be with you, too."

"That really wouldn't be safe. Please. Just stay inside."

He left. She didn't know how. In an instant, he was simply gone, as though she had dreamed him.

THREE
Daytime of the Demons

As the morning warmed, she heard the blue-spitters on the roof sloshing around in their tank, as though dirty clothes had come alive in a washing machine that had stopped. There was a low murmuring of the demons that reached her ears down below, but the blue-spitters were generally quiet and well-behaved as the day wore on, not nearly as loud and raucous as they had been when midnight struck the previous night. She still felt Mabin's warm touch on her fingers and in the palm of her hand and she thought of how strange it was that the warmth from his touch could linger for hours. Of all the strange things she had experienced so far in the Bitterroot Valley, the strangest was that simple human warmth he had shown her, and she missed it terribly. She hadn't felt much of that sort of kindness and warmth for many months, and for her it was even odder than anything she had seen so far in her new neighborhood. She had survived her first night in the Bitterroot Valley, but just barely, and had even experienced a touch of kindness and a look of tenderness.

She thought she had been brought here only to be killed, far away from anyone for whom that might matter. She would die here before long, she knew, with or without Mabin's kindness and gentle ways. She didn't know what sort of strange ritual death her step-parents had in mind for her, and she had been unable to discover the reasons for the perverse rituals with which her true parents had been murdered, since she had been kept from the courtroom at both of her step-parents' trials, and, oddly, the court records had been sealed. She always believed that if she had known more about her parents' murders by her current step-parents, she would have been able to ascertain how she would die and why, for murderers rarely deviate from their *modus operandi*. Learning the reason her true parents had been killed might have given her a clue as to how she would be destroyed, but the only records she could obtain were the initial newspaper reports of the crimes. At first, there had been nothing very sensational about her mother's murder, for her death by asphyxiation had barely been reported, until its odd nature came to light. Her true parents had been divorced and her real mother, Dr. Ellen Ant, had been living with her new husband, who was now Maggie's step-father, Stephanovich Emory, when she had been found sealed in a Mexican herb factory in Newark, New Jersey, tied tightly face-down with metallic cords to the steering wheel of her black Ford Explorer, the back of the Explorer filled with trees of jalapeños, bags of onions and sacks of garlic. The last thing her mother had said to her was, "Be ready for us. I'll see you at dinner tonight," but she never had. The Explorer, with her mother's dead body inside, had been found sealed tightly in a cleansing room where the produce was meticulously washed before going to market. The Explorer's motor was sputtering but still running when the workers found her. The oxygen in the room had been reduced to nearly nothing as it was consumed by the Explorer's V-8, and the emissions from the poorly tuned motor had reduced her mother's life to nothing. The sweet smells of peppers and onions and garlic still managed to overwhelm the carbon monoxide when the workers opened the door and dragged her mother from the vehicle. Maggie could not see a black Ford Explorer pass by, or view a TV ad for one, without becoming violently ill with the memory of her mother's end. She could not eat for days after seeing a black Ford Explorer, then or even now. In contrast, her father's murder had been sensational from day one. Before the Twin Towers had been knocked down on 9-11, he had been found tied on the roof, also with the same metallic ropes, the kind used to build suspension bridges, on the South Tower, seven stakes driven through his body. His left eye, his heart, his liver, his left leg, his right arm, his right shoulder and his right foot all had sharpened oak stakes of various lengths pushed through them, and it was estimated he had been dead for two weeks before he had been found. He also had been re-married, to the woman who was now Maggie's step-mother, Elsa Emory, but perhaps the oddest thing of all happened once his spectacular murder was splashed all over the New York tabloids. After the initial reports of his gruesome end had been detailed in the tabloids, all information from police and prosecutors ceased flowing to the media, even the legitimate press. There was simply silence about it, as though it had never happened. The New York Times could learn nothing more of why Dr. Alan Ant was found murdered high on top of the World Trade Center, all the blood drained from his body as though he had been embalmed. He had been dead so long before he was found the tabloids assumed the blood had simply drained out of his wounds and evaporated without a trace in the high dry atmosphere atop the South Tower, his internal fluids the victim of an unforgiving nature. It was odd, but odder things happened later at the Twin Towers.

And then her little brother disappeared.

Tommy Ant was all she had left after her true parents' deaths, and the agony she felt at losing her parents in the dual killings was alleviated only in his presence. She clung to the one shred of her previous life she had remaining, knowing there was no one but her to take care of him now, and he clung to her.

"I have nobody but you, and you have nobody but me," he said to her. "We can't ever let that change."

She was lifted out of her grief a little when his inquisitive, deft mind explored the murders of their parents on his own, trying with reason to piece together why both parents had met such odd and unexplainable ends. His determination to investigate the murders of their parents gave her a reason and the will to live, a determination to leave grief behind and plunge into action, but then grief returned. She felt alive only when she and Tommy were working on clues to solve the crimes. Then things became odder still when both Tommy and Maggie, as minor children, were awarded into the custody of Stephanovich and Elsa Emory, acquitted murders, who were married as soon as Elsa was acquitted, even this unusual and damning event of matrimony going largely un-noticed in the press. Why, Tommy asked, had the two people suspected of the murders of their parents suddenly fallen in love and married, when it was very clear in doing so it deepened and legitimized the original suspicions against them? She barely understood what he was saying at first, and she was astonished that a child's mind many years younger than hers could be so keen. Then she understood that for them to marry, their respective spouses would have to be eliminated, and it was clear that was what they had done.

"I'm as sure they killed our parents as you are," Maggie said.

"I'm surer of it than anything," Tommy answered. "And they're creepy, besides."

"We have to prove it."

Tommy nodded eagerly.

"The key is the steel ropes used to bind them both," Tommy said, as they whispered together in the dark their first night as captives of the Emorys. "If we can find the steel ropes around here, we can tie Stephanovich and Elsa to the murders. Darn them. We could still have our parents if not for them. We wouldn't be alone with just each other."

It broke her heart to hear of his broken heart, but they had little luck in finding any evidence, despite turning the house upside-down with their secret examinations, searching through the basement and attic quietly but extensively, looking for just one strand of steel. They found nothing. Tommy even searched old newspaper articles in the downtown library and on the Internet, looking for stories detailing thefts of such material or vandalism to bridges that would yield it, and still nothing came of it, and still their parents were dead and un-avenged.

Then one day Tommy came to her so white in the face it seemed all the blood had been drained from him, that the information he now had obtained had murdered him but he hadn't yet died. She understood at once he had discovered something new.

"It's not the steel ropes," he said, anguished in the knowledge. "It's not the ropes! We were looking in the wrong place. Come with me. I know what happened now."

He took her to an upstairs bedroom and lifted a corner of the carpet, his little hands and thin arms straining with the effort. He had pulled off the baseboard with a hammer and tugged out the staples holding the rung down earlier. Now all he had to do to show her the evidence was lift the heavy carpet and hold it up, trembling as he did so.

Even to her untrained eye, it was clear that under the carpet a number of oak floorboards had been replaced with pine.

"The stakes that killed our father were made of oak," Tommy said, an incredible sadness coming over him and tears falling from his large round blue eye as he looked up at her from under his thick mop of auburn hair. His voice broke. "They did it. Stephanovich and Elsa murdered our parents."

She knew what he was thinking, that this discovery was also the end of them.

"Now they have only us to get rid of," he said.

"It won't happen. I'll do anything for you," she told him. "Don't worry. I'll do anything to keep you safe and alive. They'll never get anywhere near you, from now to forever."

"And I'll do anything for you, too. You're my best sister ever and you're all I have left in the world."

But that was the end of Tommy, after that discovery and their embrace and mutual promise of protection. When she came home from school that day, Stephanovich and Elsa informed him that her little brother was missing, and she let out a shrill cry of despair, unable to hide her feelings any longer. They told her almost with a note of satisfaction in their voices, smirks on their faces. She wondered why they waited to kill her. The police made a cursory investigation and turned up nothing, and Maggie could not believe that, given her step-parents' past, they did not suspect them immediately. Maggie freaked out, running out into the street, desperate to get away, knowing she was next to be killed but not knowing when, but she was captured when she ran headlong into a yellow cab, rendering herself unconscious. Little attention, again, was paid to the story in the news, and soon after Maggie was informed the family was moving from Manhattan to Montana to escape all the bad memories and negativity surrounding them in the city. She hadn't given up on finding her little brother somewhere in the maze of the metropolis, once she was healed of the wounds suffered in her collision with the taxi and released from the hospital. She protested violently, thrashing out at her parents' murderers when they visited her and escaping from the hospital one night to rush to the police with the story of the missing floorboards. "It was the floorboards! The floorboards prove it!" She was hospitalized again and then put on anti-psychotic medication and while in restraints was thrown on a plane headed to Missoula.

Where was Mabin when she needed him so desperately? Where was the one kind person on earth? The sun had traveled past noon in the sky, inching through the blue as though mocking her, and he was nowhere to be found. She longed to tell him the story, longed to tell him why she climbed the walls on her first night in Montana to find new friends on the roof and instead found blue-spitters, who for her, in her condition, were just as good as friends. With a family like hers, demons did not live up to their name. She longed to tell him all the good reasons why she was possessed, psychotic, and why blue-spitters appeared as friends to her, and she was so agitated by her time alone all day with her dark thoughts, she believed anyone would do for a friend now, even the demons. Her step-parents most certainly could have killed her brother, too, and that possibility more than whispered to her. It shouted in her shattered brain the way the voices had the night before.

"It will always be just you and me," Tommy had said to her tearfully at their father's funeral, his little hand in hers. "There's no one else we can trust but each other. Always be my friend, won't you?"

That memory did it. She couldn't stand it, couldn't be alone any longer. She found her medication but refused to take it, preferring to be as coherent as possible when her step-parents murdered her, at least to put up a fight when no one else would fight for her. She heard giggling from above, a single, high-pitched outburst, like the squealing of an insane child, from the vat of blue-spitters on the roof, and she gave in to her impulse to befriend someone, anyone, rather than be alone with the dark and dangerous thoughts she had. If her new friend Mabin was going to leave her alone, she'd seek companionship elsewhere, anywhere. She wanted more than anything not to be alone with these hideous thoughts of hers.

"Come visit us," a voice said to her, as though in a joke. "Come spit."

It was as though they read her mind, and mocked her, laughed at her, but even that didn't matter. The demon's joke brought on a chorus of giggling in response from his fellows.

"Yes, yes, tell her to come down to help us spit out this blood."

"Tell her to come at once. But tell her not to open the lid."

"No, don't ever open the lid in daytime."

"Oh, no."

"No. Never in daytime. Never open the lid in daytime."

Then a demon voice rose above the others.

"You will come down to us, won't you, Maggie Ant? We'll tell you things about your Tommy that you don't know, special things, wonderful stories of where he is."

She stood straight up, alert now at the mention of her brother, and shouted at the roof.

"What do you know about him? Where is he? Tell me!"

"Oh, she's shouting now," a voice mocked.

"Yes, she's shouting."

"Shouting is good for us."

"It's good she's shouting at us, good for her and us."

"We make her mad."

"Yes, mad. She is mad."

"Shout more."

Again, it was as though they mocked her.

"Come down to us and you'll know everything," an authoritative voice said, still only half-seriously. "We'll tell you about your poor little brother and all his woes."

She was trembling and felt she was about to collapse again. At first, she believed they might know something about Tommy, that Stephanovich and Elsa hadn't killed him but had dragged him to Montana in the same way they dragged her out here, but then their hideous giggling made the fact they didn't even know where they were more obvious, that they believed they were in the basement, as she had at first, when they were really on the roof. She knew telling her they knew where her brother was most likely a ploy, for if they didn't know where they were, how could they know where her brother was? It was too much to be alone with such voices and not respond, and she had to take any chance she could, even dangerous ones, to find her brother. She opened the back door and lifted her eyes upward as a precaution, in some way aware there was a danger above that could swoop down on her now that she was outside and exposed, but she had great courage and greater foolhardiness. The two combined would not let her stop. There would be no detour into the basement as there had been the previous evening in a fruitless search for the voices, for she knew where they were and how to reach them. In an instant, she was climbing the walls again. Her feet and fingers stuck to the vertical surface as she climbed, and she could easily navigate around the windows and over the cornices, surprised at how simple such an impossible feat was now that she was practiced in it. With mastery came lack of fear. Soon, she was on top of the house again, the clear open air washing over her. The slope of the roof presented no obstacle, and as soon as she was next to the vat of blue-spitters they sensed her and broke out in a barrage of voices inside her head.

"No, not now!"

"Don't come here now, you fool!"

"Come back at night. You won't open the lid now, will you? We need you to come back at night when we can get out with your help and fly off for blood."

"Help us fly out at night for more blood," a pitiful voice said. "We haven't flown through the night in so long."

"Get us out of here. Spit with us."

"Don't open the lid!"

"It's daytime!"

"No, don't open the lid."

"We want to fly!"

"Don't open the lid! It's daytime! Don't let her do it!"

The barrage of voices assaulted her immediately, as though in a panic at what she might or might not do. No blue steam seeped from around the silver lid, and the voices were merely inside her head, but she knew the blue-spitters were huddled inside the vat and speaking to her in some other-worldly way.

The calm, authoritative demon voice took over.

"Maggie will help us fly out," it said. "She's come in friendship, and will come again tonight, when she can help us fly. We know this, don't we?"

A chorus of voices immediately agreed.

"I know it."

"I know it, too."

"Yes, yes, oh, yes. A friend of the spitters, she is, who wants to see us fly again."

Maggie was firm in her next demand.

"No. I came here because you told me you knew where Tommy is. Now tell me and stop this."

"Of course we know where he is," the authoritative voice said, to soothe her. "It's just ... we're trapped, and how can we show you where he is when we're trapped. We need your help in getting out and then we will take you to your brother."

"At night."
"Yes, not during the day."
"Help us!"
"Tonight help us."
"We want to fly."
"We want your blood."
"Quiet! She will help, won't you, Maggie?"

These demons were annoying creatures that had their own agenda ruled by anguish, it was clear to her.

"Why did you make me climb up here if you don't know where Tommy is? I won't be a fool. Where is Tommy? That's the only reason I came. You can stay inside there forever for all I care, if you don't tell me where Tommy is."

"But you like spitters," a pitiful voice objected.
"Yes, you like us."
"You like us very much."
"Come spit with us."
"Not now."

"Be quiet. Let me talk to her. Now, Maggie, you know we know where Tommy is, don't you, friend? Now promise to come back at night to help us out of here, and we will take you to him. We will need a rope soaked in human blood for us to climb out, or a ladder from a slaughterhouse of humans. Make sure everything you bring is bloody, bloody with human blood, and then we can climb out and fly and then we will be your friend and we will happy to take you to your Tommy, for your friendship."

It sounded like the most absurd thing she had ever heard.

"Do you think I'm a fool? I won't be thought a fool. You're not going to do anything for me, are you?"

"No! No! We don't think you're a fool! You are no fool, but the flower of our love."

She knew desperation made them ridiculous and dumb, made them want to escape from their captivity at any price, even the price of self-respect, but still her blood boiled at their taunts and the insult to her intelligence.

"You're just trying to fool me into thinking you know where Tommy is. All I want is my brother, and I'll help you escape. I hate you for teasing me like this!"

And then the chorus of voices made a fatal mistake: it answered anger with anger.

"Oh, really? You hate us."

"I hate you more than anything."

"Oh, you do? Then we hate you, too, and will not do a thing for you. You should not talk to us in that way, for we will take your blood so swiftly your end will come in a few seconds of panic, a wispy moment of a death for you. I will drink you dry in an instant."

"I don't care about that. I want my brother."

"Try us no longer with your silly desires for your brother, but do what we say and make that the end of it. Come back in the darkest dark of the night. Let us climb out on a bloody rope when you come, or we will take your blood in the most painful way possible."

"I want her blood!"

"Let's take it now!"

"We can't!"

"We do what we want. She can't stop us."

"I can taste is, the blood of this girl. I will taste it, and then will no longer spit and I will fly through the night again."

"Drain her dead!"

"Take all of her blood in pain!"

"Great pain for her!"

"Shut up! All of you, shut up! I just want my brother!"

"No! We will kill him, too, if you don't give us what we want! Do what we tell you, or we will take your blood and kill your brother!"

"Then do it!"

With that, with her anger boiling over irrationally with far more force than all of the demons combined, she threw open the lid to the silver vat and for just one second saw their anger and hate for her as the sun struck their faces, before their anger and hate turned to horror and fear and ignited. In that one second before they ignited and burned, they were not as she had seen them the previous night, emaciated and disgusting beings constantly spitting out blue liquids, but were normal men dressed normally in business suits, and they were not immersed in blue liquid. But so twisted were they with evil emotions that even the mere instant they were exposed to the sunlight before they burned shocked her into a realization: she was just as twisted with rage and hate as they were. It did not burn her, though, but left her whole. Just as they had threatened to drink her blood in an instant, draw all of the life out of her without giving her a chance at redemption, so did the sun instantly burn them as their loud cries escaped the vat. Their screams rose in a column of sound from the silver vat and spread across the sky like bats on fire, and then dissipated immediately. The sounds ceased as though they had never existed. Looking down, she saw nothing left of the blue-spitters but blackened corpses reaching up for her, upright ashes in human skeletal form, their faces and hair now burned to black ash but with their mouths still contorted with hate for her. Then even the standing ashes collapsed into separate mounds of black dust on the silver floor. The wind whipped up some of the ash, stirred it into a whirlwind broth, and blew it around her and into her nose. She coughed it all out, and they were gone. They had finally escaped, but not in the way they had wished to. She gasped at the utter finality, and futility, of it. The silver vat was completely empty.

A low growl caused her to turn around.

"What have you done to my friends?"

The same foul odor that had assaulted her earlier in the morning assaulted her now. Ten feet away from her, its hair standing on end, an immense black wolf was talking to her, its fangs bared and its yellow eyes glowing with hate as it spoke. It was at least a dozen feet in height. It stood on the peak of the roof above her, so that it was backed with nothing but sky, and the impression of pure black on clear blue it made on her made her cry out in terror. Nothing she had ever experienced called up such fear in her, not even the butchering of her parents and not even the death of her younger brother at the hands of fiends. She had never experienced the fear that such a gigantic presence called up.

"I asked you, what have you done to those who did you no harm?"

The question was delivered with a deep growl, but it was not a so much a question but a threat, since this creature obviously knew what she had done and was using the low growling inquiry to intimidate her. The black wolf paced around, twisting closer toward her, and when it did, she saw that the immense beast, saliva dripping from its jaws, was not simply huge, but deformed, too. Its front legs were bent and twisted so that its paws faced each other as though the wolf was pigeon-toed, but worse than that, its back half was missing so that it stood only on its front legs like a two-legged person racked with a bone-twisting disease. There was an angry agony in its yellow, sick eyes. As she backed away, it turned and slinked toward her. A rope of intestine fell from its insides and dragged along behind it, and she realized the half-wolf creature's body was open at the gut to its interior organs. It jumped at her, dragging its intestines behind it, but she instinctively leaped for cover behind the silver lid of the vampire vat. It came to a sudden, frightened halt two feet short of falling in the empty tank. It stared into the silver vat as though utterly terrified of its emptiness and demon-dust, but then raised its eyes again at her with renewed anger. It circled toward her, intending to deprive her of the protection she now enjoyed behind the tank's silver lid by forcing her out into the open, but before he took a second step, he halted and glared with hatred at someone behind her. There was someone behind her, and she hoped it was Mabin. Her heart sank when she realized it was breathing as heavily as the black wolf was, and she thought, oh, no, not a second one, not a second black wolf. She turned slowly, and to her relief saw that there was Mabin. He was not the same boy she had seen that morning, though, for he was terribly dirty, practically wrapped in wet mud, and larger still, grown to over six feet tall. He also was terribly bloodied with claw marks across his scalp and left shoulder, and the blood and mud combined in a terrible admixture and was smeared over his ripped shirt and bared chest. His breathing was has hard and forced as the wolf's, and he paid no attention to her but locked eyes with the torn creature facing him.

"She opened the lid in daytime and let them burn," the wolf said. "She should never have done that."

"She didn't know what she was doing, and if they had left her alone she wouldn't even have known they were here."

"She shouldn't have done it, it was the worst of things she could have done. She should never have burned them, and she will pay for it."

"She didn't know what she was doing. Leave her alone and deal with me."

"She's in this now and will suffer as they did."

"No, it's you and me, as always. She has nothing to do with this."

"She has everything to do with it now, and I will make her burn, I promise that. It is me and you and her now," the wolf said, raising a black paw to point at her. It stepped toward her threateningly, but Mabin pushed her behind him and the wolf halted at his intercession.

"You know I could be something else next time," the wolf said. "But she won't know it's me, and it's then she'll find out what it means to burn vampires. If you burn my brothers, I will burn you, girl."

Before Mabin could answer, the wolf turned so quickly he was little more than a blur. With a few steps he was at the roof's edge, and then he flew off in a giant arc over several houses toward distant ground, his guts trailing behind him and the light falling on his insides to reveal blue and pink and white bloody organs.

Maggie regained the ability to speak before Mabin did.

"Who was that?"

"Who do you think it was? I told you Karel was loose and you shouldn't come out of the house."

"This morning Karel was in the clouds. He didn't look like that."

"You don't think a vampire can reveal his true form in daylight, do you? You see what happens to them when they do."

Mabin kicked at a pile of black ash that had flown out on the wind to land on the roof.

"He was awful. Why was he like that, on just two legs? What happened to the rest of him?"

Mabin's eyes narrowed so that they became slits.

"We fought in the mountains. I tore him in half. He did this to me."

Mabin gestured to his bloody, matted hair. Maggie's eyes rested on the deep slashes in Mabin's scalp and shoulder, the results of Karel's attacks on him, and she felt strangely attracted to the mess of black mud and the red oozing out of his wounds and covering his clothes. She moved closer to him and touched the wound on his scalp tenderly and felt a tingle as her fingers rested on the bloody mud. His eyes quickly locked on to hers as though in fear. Suddenly, they were kissing, and it was as though they were not twenty feet off the ground on that dangerous roof, but again a thousand feet up in the clouds and completely and utterly safe.

He broke away.

"I have to go."

"Why?"

It was so stupid for him to leave now. She was covered in mud and blood from being so close to him, and an odd tingling, like a low current, emanated from the mix and seeped deep into her soul.

"Karel's vulnerable. If I go after him now, I might capture him. We do have an empty vat to make a home for him."

With a smirk at the joke he had made over what she had done to the blue-spitters, Mabin looked down at her. He touched her lips and then suddenly made the same gigantic leap off of the roof Karel had a moment earlier.

"Take a shower now or you'll end up like him," he yelled back at her, as he leaped.

She had no idea what he meant, but she immediately went inside and did as she was told. She showered away all the mud and blood and threw her clothes into the trash, feeling a strange regret and exhilaration as she did so. She didn't know why she'd become like Karel if she didn't shower, but with the way things were going on her first day here, she didn't question she could be cursed. She didn't question that anything could happen to her here.

But that didn't stop her from going out that night to look for Mabin.

FOUR
Looking in the Mirror

The demons did not wait until midnight to enter her head. She braved a family dinner of steak, pot roast, lamb, veal and chicken with her step-parents, finding that once she had eaten meat in the morning it called up a vast hunger in her, an emptiness that demanded attention, the way loneliness demands attention. Added to the trying events of the day, the spark of hunger ignited into a raging feast at night, while she fidgeted in fear with Stephanovich and Elsa nearby holding carving knives and stabbing forks and cutting the meat inches from her eyes. She sat eating with her chair to the wall and her plate on her lap, with furtive glances at the two murderers. She could not eat enough meat, and Stephanovich and Elsa appeared unable to cut enough as they worked with the knives constantly within a few feet of her. She survived the meal, which left a little curve in her belly that hung over her low-slung belt, and then quickly retreated to her room and locked herself in, feeling more and more like a trapped animal, before her step-parents could recall she needed murdering, too. She had expected that a good meal and the absence of blue-spitters on the roof, spitters that were burned to ashes now, thanks to her, along with the presence of Mabin, might make her less nervous at her precarious circumstances, but the thousands of other demons did not wait until midnight to cry out to prevent that comfort. She lay on her bed, exhausted that she had to fight so hard for her life, and as soon as the sun abandoned the earth the first cry of despair went up from a holding vat just down the street. It was a loud cry, but it reached the inside of her head almost as a whisper.

"They are dead. Our friends are dead from sun. We are trapped here, spitting. Where is that girl who would spit with us? The one who killed our friends?"

A disgust rose in her at the many hundreds of screaming blue-spitters and their activities where the emptiness inside her had been, but it was only a distraction, for after the first blue-spitter cried out in the night, an entire chorus of them rose in the neighborhood, all whispering of despair and loneliness and offering an invitation.

"They are gone. Come spit with us. Help us get out with the bloody rope. Throw us a blood-soaked rope. Help us as you were going to help them."

Their insistent whispers were like a thousand mosquitoes attacking inside her head, all so confused that they flew into each other and stung their own kind in the attempt to get her attention. A mass murder of clarity and sense was perpetrated inside her skull by the voices, and finally she had to sit up and scream.

"Stop it!"

There was a shocked silence for a second, and then the sting of their insistent whispers began once again with an increased volume and frequency inside her brain.

It made no sense, this world made no sense. She rolled from side to side on her bed like a man woman. At midnight, the occupants of the holding tanks had been vile demons regurgitating a blue-gray froth relentlessly, but when she had burned the occupants on the roof of her house, they had been normal vampires, standing trapped in a dry tank with a human appearance. Only the personalities that demanded blood remained the same. She had so many questions, but with the stinging whispers of the demons confusing her, she could barely form them. Why were the occupants of the tanks blue-spitters at night and vampires during the day? When was her end coming? Why did Mabin leave her and fly off after an opponent he had nearly killed when she so very clearly needed him, and where did he get his immense power, a power great enough to tear an gigantic black wolf in half, if he was not a vampire, too?

A scratching at the window made her leap to her feet, her heart beating fast like clock wound too tight, as though her death might come flying through the window in a noisy shower of glass. She thought for a moment she saw a blue-spitter staring in at her, but it turned out to be only her own distorted reflection in the glass. A branch of a tree blew in the wind and scratched the glass again. It was nothing, but she did not like being alone in her room with these distortions and random noises while so many difficulties surrounded her. She had to take some action to end them. Once again, there was a scratching at the window out of the dark. She threw the window wide open, ashamed at her fear and driven again by loneliness and fear to get out of there.

"I climbed the walls last night because I thought I had no choice. Let's see if I can climb the walls tonight just because I want to."

She felt an itching in the tips of her fingers, as though her hands longed for action, and she leaped up onto the wall and climbed. The tank that had held the blue-spitters was as empty as she had left it, with just a whippoorwill of black ash blowing up in the moonlight when she lifted the lid to see if they had been replaced by others of their kind. The ash swirled and settled at the bottom of the tank like stray burned newspapers burned to dust. The sting of the whispers inside her head had continued as she had climbed up the walls, but it hadn't added any difficulty at all to the climb: it had been as easy as walking upright along a street. It seemed second-nature now for her to climb the walls, clinging with her hands and feet effortlessly. The moon had risen from between the dip between two mountains to the east to a point halfway at the top of the sky. The voices inside her head were totally nonsensical again and completely annoying and painful, and the moonlight did not help the situation, as it cast illusions on the land from behind scudding clouds. The demons' chorus of whispers grew to a chorus of screams echoing in the bowl of the mountain valley as she stood on the roof holding her head and wondering what to do next. Stop it, stop it, stop it, she screamed again and again. Perhaps she should visit the blue-spitters on the house next door, just to quiet them. She laughed at the idea. She remembered how easily Mabin had risen with her to a great height, and she wondered if she could do the same on her own. She dared to think that perhaps she had soared into the heavens on her own, flown on her own. It seemed trite and bothersome to climb down the walls of her house, walk across the yard and then climb up the walls of the house next door. It would be so much easier to fly.

"You should come see us spit," a voice said clearly from the tank of demons next door, and she understood they were reading her mind. "It's been quite some time since we've had a visitor, and it's not right for you to leave your friends alone."

Friends, she thought. My friends. Even the word was a lie it was a comfort. The distance separating the two houses was not far, and the moonlight reflecting off the slant of her roof made a path for her from house to house. She did what she was not supposed to do and looked down, only because she was not supposed to. It was a fall of twenty feet, but what did it matter? She would do anything to escape the fearful loneliness of living with murderers. The impulse to risk everything to escape her situation was too strong. She lifted her foot over the chasm and watched the moonlight touch her toe, and then she was off. With incredible speed, she whisked from one roof to the next and found herself planted on the opposing slant before she could blink. She reached down to cling to the shingles, but it was not necessary. She stood firmly in place. It was as though she had thought herself from one roof to another, and it was exhilarating. You never know what you can do until you attempt your foolish impulses.

"You've come."

In an odd way, this demon's voice was friendly and welcoming, full of warm tones and pleasurable notes, like a song, not at all like the harsh gasps of the demons last night or the hypocritical kindness of her step-parents. It was relaxed, friendly, like distant music on a summer night, but muffled by the lid of the holding tank. She lifted the lid without a second thought, half-mad and driven by the impulse not to be alone and vulnerable one minute longer. A scene much like the one she had witnessed the night before presented itself to her. Five demons huddled together and spat out the blue liquid filling their lungs and stomach. The friendly demon was standing apart from them, smiling up at her, but he also seemed to be choking on the blue spit dribbling out of the side of his mouth. He appeared to be holding back the regurgitation that would expel the liquid from his stomach and lungs out of politeness and as demons go, he was not that bad looking. He was emaciated as all the demons in the tank were, but he had a shock of dramatic black hair combed back and fine fair features, a delicate look to him that still allowed his masculinity to show through. It's always a pleasure when you encounter someone who is handsome and happy to see you, and it was very evident this demon was very happy to see Maggie. He could not suppress the overwhelming need to regurgitate any longer, and vomited up a thick shower of blue spit.

He wiped his mouth delicately with his sleeve.

"I'm so sorry," he said. "Where are my manners? Excuse me. I certainly didn't mean to do that in your presence."

"That's all right."

He wiped his mouth with the back of his hand, his sleeve not that effective for the task. He raised his eyes toward the dark night over her shoulder.

"Look at that," he said, allowing his eyes to wander upward toward the stars. "I'm so surprised. I haven't seen the night sky in so long. What a glorious sight to one as tired as I."

He had to drink in the sight for a few seconds more, but then he quickly set his eyes on her again and welcomed her with that warm smile. His teeth, too, were red, but even that made him attractive, for they shone with health and were well-formed and strong.

"How did you get us up on the roof?"

"I didn't bring you here. You've always been up here. I had nothing to do with it."

"I'm confused then. I thought we were in the basement, so I have to apologize again," he said. "You were so kind to come here and show me the sky again after I have spent so long a time deprived of it. I can finally look at the sky and its magical stars again, and I would, if a more beautiful vision hadn't presented itself to me."

He gave her a shy, charming smile with the compliment, but immediately a knot of blue liquid shot up from his stomach and doubled him over. He spat it out into the pool of blue-gray liquid reaching up to his knees. The five other demons on the opposite side of the tank were also vomiting up the blue liquid, holding on to their throats and stomachs as they did so.

"Would you like me to come down and keep you company?" Maggie asked, her heart weakened by pity. "I'm all alone, too, and I don't feel safe."

"Would you?"

"I feel I don't have a choice."

"Better yet, allow me to come up there and keep you company."

"All right. That might be nice."

"Have you brought the bloody rope?"

"No. Why would I?"

A darkness passed over the handsome demon's visage, like an ugly sudden storm on a spring night.

"Don't trifle with me. You know if I'm to come up out of this pit and be your friend I can only do so up a bloody rope. It's the only way I'd have the strength to do so. Do you have the rope or not?"

A shadow from behind her crossed over his face, and then settled on her and the entire tank of demons, a dark shadow from moon. She was aware someone was behind her perched on the peak of the roof. A look of great joy and relief passed over the handsome demon's features when he saw who it was. She believed she knew who it was, too.

"You, girl, might as well forget the bloody rope. We won't be needing it," the demon said, betraying his lie of friendship. "In fact, you might as well forget everything. You won't have need of anything in your absurd little life in a few seconds more."

A sneer from the demon accompanied a great rushing of wind, as Karel leaped down toward her off heights of the roof. She knew immediately what to do, leaping straight up in flight without thinking about it and then coming down behind the raised lid of the vat. Karel landed exactly where she had been, but she had moved with such speed he was frustrated in his attempt to crush her and then tear her broken body to pieces.

My powers are growing, she thought.

A horribly loud and shrill jabbering rose from the open vat as the six spitting blue demons celebrated Karel's arrival and their impending release, and the hope in that jabbering immediately raised a chorus of similar noises from all the vats throughout the development. It was as though all the birds of hell had cried out in joy upon seeing the devil, and the noise nearly overcame her, overwhelming her from all sides. She had to cover her ears. Karel was still the immense black wolf he had been earlier, jaws dripping rabidly with white saliva, as his glistening narrow eyes stared at her, and she noticed his guts still trailed behind him, dragging along on the shingles as he moved. Since speed and surprise hadn't worked to capture her, he now moved slowly as he circled the silver vat, frustrated in not trapping such easy prey as Maggie. He was salivating frothy, sticky torrents of rabid liquid to vent that frustration. The froth stuck to the fur of his chest, making him look as though he had a wet white beard.

"When did you learn to fly?" he asked.

"It's just something I picked up along the way."

"Are you going to get us out of here? We've been waiting so long for you just to get us out of here."

Karel paused to glance down at the handsome demon in the vat, just as another glob of blue-gray liquid erupted from the demon's mouth and splattered against the silver side of the vat. Karel stepped back in disgust. The five other demons followed suit with the handsome demon and regurgitated in unison into the growing pool of blue-gray saliva rising up beyond their knees.

"I have to deal with the girl first."

"Help us now!"

"Yes! Get us out! We haven't had fresh blood in months and we need a good meal. We'll help you with her. Let us take her blood."

So this was how they were going to treat her, Maggie thought. She had been confused and foolish enough to think they were her friends. She had been foolish to live by desperate thoughts. They would treat her as a meal in payment for her friendship. She felt a rising anger originate in her stomach and travel up her throat. It did not continue out through her mouth as the demons' globs of blue spit and bile did but settled into her arms. Karel was not the only one who had unmanageable anger issues when crossed. Her eyes burned with it. Her anger caused her to make bad decisions constantly, and her anger now was directed toward the blue-spitters who betrayed her, without a thought of its consequences. Just as her neurotic fears of death and need for friends had led her to this roof to talk to the demons, so did her anger cause her to push closed the silver lid of the vampires' holding tank. It left her unprotected from Karel.

"There. You won't be getting out any time soon," she said, with a laugh.

The action assuaged her burning impulse of anger, but what she saw then made her realize she might have made a mistake in giving in to the impulse for revenge. Karel stood glaring at her from just ten feet away, an easy leap after which he could wantonly rip her to pieces. She had given up the protection afforded her by the open silver lid, out of spite, and now her laughter seemed futile and foolish. Karel glanced down at the closed lid, and then up at her again.

"You know I can't touch that. I can't get them out by myself."
"I suspected as much."
"But you know what I'm going to do to you now, don't you?"
"I hadn't thought about it, but I don't care."

"You don't care?"

"Not a bit."

"Are you so confident you can get away that you risked this, the mutilation I'm going to do now?"

"What are you waiting for? I don't really care what you do, not one bit."

"I don't believe this. What I have in mind for you is horrible, even by my standards. I wish you would explain this to me, why you feel this way."

"It's none of your business."

An angry snort from Karel, accompanied by a burst of saliva, flew over her like a gust of wind laden with a foul sheet of thick rain. The goo he spat over her carried so wretched an odor, and sickened her to the pit of her stomach so effectively, that she realized she did care very much what he did to her. Something far less pleasant than what he had already done to her could be in store for her. What it might be came easily to her imagination. Hers was only a brave front. If his saliva was so utterly disgusting, his plans for her had to shift to a more horrible end of the spectrum, be far worse than rotted saliva. She shifted on her feet uncomfortably, worried now. It occurred to her that her impulses were completely untrustworthy, and she reminded herself to resist them in the future, if she had a future. To do something simply for the fun of vengeful self-satisfaction simply hadn't worked for her. She saw Karel's reflection in the silver like of the vampire vat.

"I still want to know why you don't care if you're mutilated," Karel said, obsessed with the idea, almost confused by it. "I've never heard of such a thing, and I've mutilated a lot of people."

His desire for this sort of knowledge led to the undoing of his plans. The aspect of the night changed suddenly and radically, in a way even she did not know it could. She felt the world give a slight shudder, a suppressed hiccup in space and time, before Karel tired of waiting for an explanation from her and took action. With a snarl and a leap, he was upon her, but as soon as he slashed at her, he was not really there. She turned away from the slashing paw as it passed through her only to see the same scene she was engaged in on the roof of the house next door. There, Karel was set upon a girl, her, but this time she was not really there, for he could not grasp her in that vision, either. Frustrated, he slashed again and again at the girl, until he realized she was like a hologram and looked up. He was looking into a mirror, and so was she, and with one mirror faced to another, the two characters replicating themselves toward infinity. There were an infinite number of Maggies on one roof after another, and there were an infinite number of Karels, an infinite number of victims and vampires, whose images did show up when reflected in a second and third and fourth mirror, as though something was wrong with the entire legend. Karel did not know which girl to kill, and wildly tore at the reflection he thought he had in his grasp, until he realized the futility of it. That night on the roof of the world, she saw the world reflected in the images of the two of them struggling mightily in reflections of what they were in reality. Karel leapt to another roof and another Maggie, but Maggie had sense enough not to leap to a different roof and different vat, since she might leap into Karel's grasp. He was foolish enough to believe he could defeat an infinite number of images, and would go mad from the effort. Maggie saw that while she had the chance, she should take it, and she quickly slipped off the roof just as Karel was about to pounce on another of her images. She saw what he planned to do to her then, and she was happy she was just a reflection in the mirror as he sunk is teeth into her false image. She climbed back down the walls and into her bedroom window with every fiber in her being quivering, strings struck with panic.

"You should have waited for me to come back."

She had been re-introduced to another kind of fear on the roof and carried it down into her room, and despite her fierce claim she would do anything, she was learning its lessons. Fear had an effect even on her unstable mind. Now, the voice in the candlelit twilight of her room startled her, as it occurred to her that it could be Karel's, until she realized who it was. On the floor, Mabin lay on his side, with two glinting mirrors in his hands. He was using one mirror to catch the candlelight and reflect it to the other mirror and then onto the ceiling and walls. He was clever and deft in manipulating the mirrors, so that first one wall and then another and then the ceiling sparkled with reflected light. She relaxed into a sigh.

"It was you."

"It is me. Who else can I be?"

His play with words frustrated her.

"Don't toy with me. That's not what I said. I mean I know it was you who pulled that trick on the roof."

Mabin stood quickly and shrugged, as though agreeing he was guilty of the sleight-of-hand that had saved her. His hands were empty now, the mirrors hidden.

"I was a little surprised you went back up on the roof, after your previous experiences up there."

"I told you. I'm crazy. I'm almost as crazy as those blue-spitters. I don't care what happens to me."

"I'm not so sure of that. It's wrong to think like that, and you're not wrong."

"Well, you should be sure I'm crazy, but there has to be somebody in this valley who can hold a normal conversation."

"You won't find him in the vats."

"I don't know that for sure. You said there were hundreds of them."

"And you won't find one demon in them who wants to do anything but get out of his prison and take your blood."

"What did you do with the mirrors? What was that trick?"

He grinned.

"I don't know what you're talking about."

"I saw you playing with the mirrors in here, but out there the mirrors were gigantic and reflected things to infinity."

"Were they that big?"

"Don't mess with me. I warned you."

"What people see is always inside their minds."

"Oh, please! You are messing with my head!"

"Maybe you are."

"You know, I think maybe you should go. If you can't see how upset I am, then you're not the person I thought you were. I am crazy and upset. I know that, and I don't think you should try to make it worse for me. I'm trying the best I can to get out of this by being as crazy as possible, letting it go on and maybe hanging out with some weird people and thinking that maybe it'll just go away, but you're not helping me by making me look into one mirror reflected off of another mirror reflecting back into that mirror. How can that help anybody?"

She was quivering with her eyes stuck to the floor where Mabin had been, but now he was beside her and gently touched her cheek.

"I'm sorry. I had to do it. This is hard on me, too. If you think that wasn't Karel out there, then you're wrong."

"I know he was there. I know it. I'm not that crazy."

"You don't know what he would have done to you if I didn't make you both see what it was you were doing a thousand times over."

Now when he touched her cheek she let her eyes rise up to meet his, and she was crying.

"It was a really weird thing to do, and I was scared."

"I just don't want you going anywhere near the demons without me. Promise me that?"

For some reason, she didn't take this as concern on his part, but thought he was patronizing her, looking down on her as though she was stupid as well as impulsive. On impulse again, terrible impulse, her anger flared up at him as it flared up when anyone crossed her, or seemed to cross her. She became someone she was not again, confused, obsessed, torn apart. She little understood he was trying to help. She burst into emotional flames, angry and ill-tempered, when all she wanted was for him to hold her and stop playing games.

"I told you to go."

"In a minute."

"I burned the other blue-spitters, and tomorrow morning, as soon as the sun's up, I'm going to burn the demons that crossed me tonight. I just wanted a little friendship and warmth, and they wanted my blood."

"Maggie ... please."

"That's all I wanted from you, too, but it's too easy to burn them. Anybody can do it. You just expose them to the sun, and they burn up. They're evil, so why shouldn't I do that if they toy with me?"

"Please don't."

"Are you taking their side now?"

"I'd never do that. I hate them more than anything, and believe me, I'm on your side, I really am, but if you burn them, it just becomes more difficult for me. All their powers go to Karel when they die."

"You don't seem to have any trouble with them. You'd have burned them all by now if you had the courage. I have the courage."

"It's not courage, and it's not the smart thing to do."

She was stomping around the room now, throwing her hands in the air wildly.

"Smart? You're telling me what's smart now? Am I so stupid I don't know whether or not to burn demons?"

"It's not a matter of being smart, or burning demons. I'd burn all of them, if I could, but I know that's the wrong thing to do. Tommy is in one of those vats. Your brother is in one of those vats."

As quickly as her anger had flared, it disappeared, and in its place was a stunned silence that rendered her incapable of movement or thought, as though the demons had succeeded and managed to drain all the blood out of her. Her legs fell out from under her and she crumbled to the floor. He fell down beside her just as the tears streamed out of her eyes.

"Tommy's alive? You're sure?"

"I've seen him."

"I can't believe it. That's all I wanted, to be with him. Now I have to find him. He's all I have. You have to understand that. He's all I have and all I live for."

"I know."

"We have to find him."

"If you burn all the demons, you might burn him. That's why I don't want you going anywhere near them without me."

"Are you saying Tommy is a demon now?"

"I hope not. I don't think so. I don't think he'd ever drink blood."

"They don't have any blood. How could he drink blood if he's in there with them and they don't have any blood?"

"They sick creatures, and the silver of the tanks make them worse. What do you think they're spitting up, Maggie? It's blood, blood they've taken from their victims and can't digest now, because of the silver. Every night, when normally they'd be out taking new blood, the silver makes them sick, and they regurgitate the blood they've already taken. Every morning, when the darkness goes away, they drink their own blue vomit, and the cycle begins again."

A real queasiness arose in her stomach.

"And Tommy's in with them?"

"If he ever gets so hungry he ever drinks in what they spit out, then he's a vampire, too."

Again, she had no place to put her fury but on Mabin.

"How could you let him stay with them? I don't believe you let him stay with them. We have to get him out of there."

"That's what I've been trying to do."

"I don't believe you let him stay in there with them. Why haven't you gotten him out of there?"

"I've tried." Mabin threw up his arms in frustration with Maggie. "He's been in there for four days, and time is running out, and I've looked almost everywhere. I don't know how he can stand it."

She let out a cry at the vision of Tommy alone with the demons.

"I can't stand this! He's all I have. What are they doing to him?"

"I promise I'll find him, but you have to promise me you're not going to burn anymore of them. They were human once."

"I won't burn them. I promise, but you have to do more. At least I know he's alive now, so all I want is to find him."

"I know, Maggie. I've been looking for him every night, but they're clever. They're hiding him, but I will find him, I promise."

His determination made what she said next almost pointless. But she still felt desperate over Tommy's situation, and she felt compelled to let it out.

"You have to."

Before she knew what she was doing, her head still spinning with the craziness of the situation, another strong impulse overtook her, and she stared in Mabin's eyes and then suddenly grabbed him fiercely and kissed him. She was shaking violently as she held on to him, finally close to someone, nearly unhinged by the information she had taken in, unable to do anything but hold tight to Mabin.

They broke apart, as Mabin pushed her away by the shoulders.

"I have to go. Karel is waiting for me, and I don't know what damage he'll do if I'm not there to stop him. He's trying to prevent me from finding your brother with all sorts of tricks, but he won't."

Maggie was still quivering, still held back by Mabin, impelled to grab him once again but unable to move, still a little dizzy and crazy. Mabin suddenly stood up.

"Find Tommy," she said.

"I promise I will."

And then he was gone, as the first crack of thunder resounded in the mountains. He flew off so suddenly she barely recalled what had happened, barely remembered he had been in her empty arms seconds before, and she sat on the floor in confusion, rubbing her temples and sobbing.

Her step-parents' shouts broke her out of a trance that had lasted several moments.

"Maggie, would you like some more dinner? We still have a roast and some ribs, plus some chicken if you want it."

Even the threat of being killed by her step-parents couldn't bring her out of her confusion. The trance fell over her again, since eating more was far behind on her list of priorities now that she knew Tommy was alive. Mabin had once again left her, and the great intolerable loneliness descended on her once more. She couldn't acknowledge anyone who wasn't going to help her find her brother, even those who might kill her, at least until she figured out just what was going on.

It was not impulse that led her now but something much stronger. Without a second thought about replying to her step-parents, she rose and walked over to the window.

She opened it and felt the strong night wind from the coming storm tumbling through her hair, like thick rough unseen fingers. She'd do her best to go out among the blue-spitters' abodes and find Tommy herself, rescue him from some truly unsavory company, even if there were a million real Karels out there, instead of a thousand false vampires reflected in glass.

FIVE
A Light Is On

Several cracks of thunder and nervous bolts of lightning splitting the sky out over the mountains greeted her as he climbed the walls outside her bedroom window intending to search through the vats of blue-spitters for her brother. It didn't matter what Mabin said: she was going to find Tommy tonight. The sky was dark and the stars were gone, masked by castles of clouds, as her fingers lightly touched the siding and somehow lifted her toward the roof. The towers of heavy thunder caps, clouds so think and high they could have enveloped the moon, had rushed in from Idaho over the Bitterroots again, carrying the distant slivers of lightning that fidgeted in their bellies. The intermittent flashes filling the heavens brought daylight to the night and sky, which were utterly devoid of light until they cracked alive in the clouds. She crawled across the roof by feel and found the empty vat on top of her house by the glint of its silver lid twinkling in the dark, somehow a source of a weak light, a dying flashlight. She threw open the lid and waited until a flash of lightning showed her it was still empty, devoid of even a trace of the blue-spitters she had burned in daytime. Obsessed with her mission to find her brother, she wanted to make sure he had not been imprisoned in the empty vat while she looked elsewhere. She would search everywhere, in each vat, all through the night, until she found him. The thought of the little boy trapped for days with the vile creatures she had discovered, creatures condemned for all eternity to vomit up the human blood they had taken, nearly made her faint. She had been so wrong to think they could be her friends, so wrong it verged on madness. She gasped in a heavy dose of the light mountain air deliberately. The swimming in her head lessened immediately, replaced by an even greater determination to find Tommy, even if she had to do it alone, without Mabin. This would be his last night among blue-spitters, she promised herself.

The hundreds of houses in the newly built development presented themselves into her sight with the next flash of lightning. They were strung out in curving rows on the plain just outside the tiny town of Victor, dwarfing the village by their numbers and informing Maggie of the magnitude of her task. She would have to visit each house and each holding tank until she found Tommy. She would have to deal with thousands of blue-spitters and endure millions of pleas from them to get them out, and she would have to be deaf even to their insults and move on. She had a soft heart, and then she joked to herself that she had a soft brain, too, and it might just make her accommodate one of the vampires, if she liked him, or if he would help her. She steeled herself, determined she would do no such thing if she could help it, do nothing but liberate Tommy, despite the fact that Mabin had told her to go no where near the spitters without him. Mabin did not know what it was like to lose everyone you loved except the one tiny light of your life. Tommy was the only thing on her mind as she inched toward the edge of the roof ready to visit the handsome vampire imprisoned in the next house. With the next flash of lightning, she leaped and flew easily to the next roof, landing right next to the vat of blue-spitters there.

She lifted the lid to their prison.

A look of utter surprise from the handsome vampire greeted her from the eerie glow inside the vat, followed by a smile of pure pleasure, just before his stomach erupted and he spat out a thick rope of undigested blood, reminding her of what he was. She had no patience for the charming smile he then gave her once again, remembering how he had thirsted for her blood just a little while earlier. She got right to the point, so that he would have no illusions concerning the reason for her visit.

"Where's my brother?"

"It's still night. You can get us out with the bloody rope now," he said eagerly.

"That not what I asked you. I asked you where my brother was."

"And I told you to free us, now. You wouldn't have come back if you weren't going to free us, for love of us. You like me, admit it. You like all of my friends."

"I don't like you. I don't like you at all, or anyone else in there. I just want my brother returned to me."

"Oh, you care for me all right. How could you not? That is why you came back. I know you and your type. The only way you can be with me, though, is to get me out. I know you want very much to be with me."

Maggie gasped when she was caught in the vampire's gaze, admitting to herself that she was entranced by the handsome monster, charmed, but she gathered her strength and snapped out of it, realizing just how creepy his come-on was.

"The only time I want to be with you is at dawn, when the sun comes up and I can open this lid again and burn you. I love burning vampires. I would love to burn you, and I will, if you don't tell me where Tommy is."

He even smiled at this.

"I certainly don't believe that. You'll be back, night after night, no matter what I do. I know it's me you've come for."

"I don't think so. I think I've proven to myself that visiting a fool twice is two times too many."

She gave a quick look to each of the other five blue-spitters to make sure none of them was Tommy, and then she flicked the lid with her fingers and it flew down and slammed closed heavily due to its own weight, much to the surprise of the charming vampire, who appeared shocked he was not escaping that night.

"Good-bye. Pray I don't come back in the morning."

She laughed because she knew he heard her, and he wondered how he liked the threat and his prospects for the morning.

She focused once again on her task for the evening.

If she was going to rescue Tommy, she had to avoid the confusion of checking the same vat time after time for his sweet face, which meant she had to institute a system of marking off those vile holding tanks she had visited so that she would not duplicate her efforts. She decided to simplify things by going street by street, beginning with her house as the jump-off point and working first the right side of the street and then the left. Her house was in the middle of Empire Road, and she had burned one group of blue-spitters and threatened another. No Tommy. She had to move on quickly. The night would not be long, and when the storm arrived in full force it would be a difficult task she had assigned herself, as the winds thrashed her and the lightning threatened her. Another flash of lightning illuminated the next house in line, and with the flash of light she was off through the air once again, this time giving in immediately to the impulse to fly that would help save her brother, another impulse she accepted without thought. She landed beside the next tank of captured vampires and wasted no time. She had to find the boy before it was too late, and since she landed directly in front of the vat of blue-spitters bent at the knees from the force of her landing, she simply gripped the edge of the lid and threw it open by standing up. The familiar blue-gray glow from inside enveloped her in its spooky mood.

"Tommy?"

The trapped remnants of what had been six female teenage vampires were engaged in the same horrifying and degrading activities of disgorging undigested blood in the form of blue-gray saliva and bile that their many compatriots in the other vats were engaged in. Each was dressed in a period outfit, four from the eighteenth century and two from the sixteenth century, all long skirts and lace, and as soon as the lid flew up, they raised their arms over their eyes to protect themselves from what they thought could be daylight and cowered against the sides of the vat. The young women still had beauty in the faces, the softness and skillful confidence of youth, but they were still vampires and had dark circles around their eyes, a bluish hue to their skin and sharp red teeth. Maggie would have none of their tricks, tricks she knew all vampires would play, and asked them what was on her mind immediately.

"Are you hiding a little boy in there?"

"Sister! Good evening. Have you come for us?"

A particularly lovely girl with a mass of blond curls and rouged cheeks stepped toward her and raised her arms, imploring Maggie for help.

"Help me first! Please, help me to escape this place before all the others!"

The effect of the gesture was negated by the blue bile and saliva around her lips and the red teeth she showed.

"Step aside!"

Another of the young female vampires pushed her aside.

"No, help me first! I deserve it more!"

Then a chorus rose from them all in one voice. It was odd the way they all said the same thing, in exactly the same words.

"Help us! If you're our sister, you'll help us from our torture."

Maggie simply stared down at them, a little surprised they could speak in one voice so perfectly. It was a chorus of youthful stupidity.

"She has finally come! We're saved!"

Several could not resist the urge to vomit, and it stained the long skirts of the women opposite them and then drained down to the floor, where it accumulated in a pool of blue-gray liquid. The girls wiped their mouths with lace handkerchiefs.

"I came for my brother, and if you have him you had better hand him over. If not, I'll be back with daylight."

"It's not daylight, it's night, and what a wonderful sight the stars are, and how wonderful it is to see a sister. I thought we were underground."

"Give us your hand," the lovely blond vampire said, in her own voice.

"Will you answer my question? Is Tommy in there?"

"Tommy?" all six voices said.

"Do you have the bloody rope, sister?" the blond vampire asked on her own, without the chorus of fools. With the mention of the bloody rope the woman's red teeth showed, not in a smile, but in a sneer.

The girls spoke all in one voice again:

"Give us your hand. We have no Tommy. Give us your soft flesh, our sister, to bite."

"I want my brother. You're of little help to me."

"Give us some blood! It's the taste we want."

"We have no boy here. We are –" the lone blond girls said. She stopped to salivate at the sight of Maggie's white neck.

That was all Maggie needed to know. She brusquely slammed down the lid on the vampire girls in lace, disgusted with their pretensions and communal voice and bad habits, knowing what concerned her now was time, the time her brother spent imprisoned with such awful creatures. He could not survive much longer. If she wanted false friends, she had only to return to Manhattan. These girls might have entranced her in her naïve days, but she had no time for such silly vixens now. She had to move on to the next vat of blue-spitters as quickly as possible, and when the lightning flashed over the mountains again, she was in the air once more for a split second, en route to the next house and next vat of blue-spitters.

She had barely thrown open the next holding tank when the blue-gray glow from inside it mixed with a flash of lightning that landed nearby and mingled with it like smoke to form a continuing illumination that engulfed the entire roof. It was as though the air had ignited and glowed now, suspended around her like gelatin, or the lightning had hesitated in mid-flash and turned into an eerie bubble of light encasing her activities in the night. She could see everything within the bubble of light. She had no time to question the blue-spitters in the vat or even look down to determine who they were. As usual, they were babbling about the bloody rope and her reaching down and extracting them from their hell. With a shudder, she saw the form of the immense black wolf, Karel, still torn in half, in outline on the peak of the roof, with something in its mouth and its intestines hanging down the slope of the roof over the shingles. It caught her gaze in his, narrowed its eyes, and then dropped the thing in its mouth onto the roof so that it rolled a few feet toward her.

When it stopped, she was staring into Tommy's blue eyes.

"Do you want him?" Karel asked.

The black wolf lorded over him, close enough to prevent any escape attempt. Maggie was about to rush toward her brother, but Karel anticipated that and stepped forward so that he claimed possession again over the boy by his towering presence, menacing him and dripping white saliva from his mouth onto the roof next to him.

"Leave him alone!" Maggie said.

"Maggie! Get this stinking, ugly dog away from me! He smells worse than anything I ever smelled and I hate him worse than anything I ever hated!"

"I'll get him, Tommy. In a minute."

"Hurry up! He put me in with these other goons in a disgusting little tank. Maggie ..."

He reached for her, still covered in the blue-gray slime his captors had immersed him in, and then he looked up with scorn at his captor. "You stink!" he shouted at the wolf. He coughed uncontrollably and nearly vomited as he reached back for her and implored her with his eyes to come to him, but nothing erupted from his stomach or lungs as he sat there choking at the black wolf's feet and reaching for her. He must not have eaten in days. His face was emaciated and taut, his T-shirt and jeans filthy with vampire vomit, the liquid drying and caking on his hands and face. He rose to one knee, but Karel immediately stomped down on him with an immense black-clawed paw and pinned him to the roof. Tommy grunted and then punched out at the paw, but his fists were one-tenth its size and his face contorted with the weight of the wolf on his stomach.

"Get off of him!"

"I asked you if you wanted him, and you never answered. Do you want him, girl?"

"You have no right to treat him like this. He's only a boy. Get your paws off of him, or I'll do something you –"

"Not worth the tiny amount of blood in him, is he?"

Maggie narrowed her eyes in anger at the threat from Karel to take her brother's blood.

"Is that why he's still alive? Because there's not enough blood in him? Is that why you haven't turned him into one of you?"

"I couldn't care less if he lived or died or joined us or spent eternity in a silver tank. He's a snack, nothing more. I have him because you have my friends, who are much more valuable than he is, immortal. You've already burned some of them, for no good reason other than you felt like it, so why shouldn't I do something as bad to him? If I have him, I have you."

"If you want me, you can try to take me. Just try it. I told you, he's just a boy. He's not anything like your creepy friends."

Karel pressed his weight down on Tommy, his paw pinning him to the roof, and it made her brother gasp and grimace again in pain.

"Maggie!"

"They are my friends you're holding," Karel said.

"And I could burn all of them."

Karel narrowed his eyes at her in hate.

"I doubt it. Not before I bled your brother to death. It makes me more powerful when you burn them, since I get their powers, but I need them, and sometimes I get tired of doing all the work, and want them for the harvest. You're almost as pitiful as he is. You can't do anything but keep my friends from me."

That was enough. She threw caution away with a cry that vented all her pent-up rage, rage for the murder of her parents and rage for the loss of her brother, rage for this mad move away from her true friends to this mountain valley of vampires, and it was pure rage that motivated her as she bent at the knees and leaped through the air toward Karel, intending to knock him down and fight with him for as long as it took for Tommy to escape from under him. In mid-air, she suddenly questioned the foolish angry impulse that had led her to this rash act, the sort of impulse that she had realized earlier was extremely unhealthy, and understood this might be the unhealthiest impulse she had ever given in to. It was too late now. Karel opened his dripping jaws so wide they were like a dirty trash can opening to consume her, but she dodged his teeth and aimed for his mid-section, to knock him off-balance. She braced for impact, but then found herself impacting nothing. She landed with a thud on the peak of the roof, not understanding what had happened.

When she turned around, Karel was grinning at her, amused at the futility of her attack. She had passed right through him.

"You're not the only one who can play with mirrors," he said.

She reached out, intending to pull his leg out from under him, but her hand passed through the hologram.

"I asked you if you wanted your brother, but you responded by attacking me," Karel said, pretending to be hurt. "You should have known I wouldn't have risked encountering Mabin again. I wanted to deal with you and you alone, but you attacked me. Let this be a lesson to you. Your brother is going back to be with my friends again in that dirty, ugly prison of theirs."

"Wait a minute."

"No waiting. He's gone to them. She doesn't want you, Tommy."

With that, the hologram, an illusion of the immense black wolf and her tiny brother sent from someplace she could not discern, bent and lifted Tommy in its mouth again. Tommy kicked out at the wolf, but he was helpless. Karel's eyes glowed red and wide with the flow of blood that the excitement of having a victim in his mouth gave him.

"Maybe next time you won't be so rash. Maybe next time you'll listen to me."

Tommy was kicking out desperately, crying and pleading for her help.

"Don't let him, Maggie! I don't want to go back into that tank ever again. Don't let him take me back there to those things! Can't you do something, Maggie? Stop him! Please! Stop him!"

The lightning flashed again out in the mountains, and this time it struck dry earth like a match thrown down into straw. A group of pine trees ignited on a slope of the mountain, just as the glow from Karel's presence dissipated. Tommy was gone into the dark, carried off by the monster.

Maggie sat on the peak of the roof breathing fast in frustration from the pain of her failure. Karel had been right. She was helpless against him, but still felt she wanted to twist off his huge stinking head with her bare hands. The eerie light he had brought faded and left her in the dark. Now, only the equally eerie but weak light from the vat of blue-spitters remained. She might be helpless against Karel, but she was not helpless in finding her brother. She would continue to look for him. She knew he was back in one of the vats, dunked in the spit and slime of trapped vampires, and she would never relent in her search for him, no matter what Karel did. There were tears in her eyes as she rushed over to the open vat on the roof, the vat she had not yet looked in. It would be just like Karel to attempt to fool her into closing that vat when Tommy was hidden inside.

Karel had not fooled her. Inside the vat were six male vampire children, all baring their red teeth fiercely when her face appeared over the rim of the tank.

"Drag her down to us!" one shouted out immediately, in a ridiculously childlike voice. "Drip her blood into our mouths!"

"Go for her neck," another screamed. "Jump to the vein in her neck where the good blood is!"

"Drink it all! We can finally drink blood again!"

The tiny, evil creatures leaped and leaped toward the stranger who still had real blood in her veins above them, but they barely left the floor of the tank before they had to bend over and spit out the undigested blood of those they had taken as victims earlier in their youthful careers.

Maggie gently closed the lid, almost feeling sorry for them, and quickly leapt toward the next roof, her tears for her brother falling to the ground from mid-air as she flew.

SIX
Steak Béarnaise

She pushed herself to the end-limit formed by the bright Bitterroot dawn, the rise of the sun over the Sapphire Mountains, when six demons sizzled and cried out as she lifted open the lid to their vat. That was the end of the night's adventure in search of her brother. She dropped closed the lid to allow them to live. After all, as Mabin said, they were human beings.

Flying from roof to roof, lifting one silver lid after another, had not yielded the one loving person she still had a connection to on this earth. A single beam of sunlight shot from over the mountains through the crack she created under the lid of that last vat when she lifted it, and the smell of the vampires' burning assaulted her with much greater strength than did the normal stench inside. She had dropped the lid quickly enough so that they did not die, as she gasped at the acrid smell of their burning, but they still had screamed in agony at the touch of the sun. The cursing that rose from the vat, directed at her, informed her they were still alive and now drinking their own excretions after she darkened their prison. She understood that if she had incinerated them, Tommy would be in greater danger, much greater danger, buts she reluctantly ended her search. The thought that her little brother would have to spend one more day trapped in a tank of vampires nearly halted her heart in mid-beat. She hated to live under such a threat, and hated what they had done to him, but Karel held Tommy and that was threat enough for her to modify her behavior and spare the vampires, despite her great reluctance to do so. Nothing would have given her more pleasure than to burn them, despite Mabin's comment that they were once human. After all, they had made the decision to drink blood of their own free will, it seemed, and she simply hated them the more she thought of it. She must have been mad to think she could have been friends with such creatures, but then she was mad, she told herself. After closer contact came an understanding as to whom those demons were and she did not like it, although she was still as desperate as ever for friends, any friends, any understanding. Her anger was so great she had to remind herself again that they had once been human and deserved compassion, no matter what.

At dawn, she found it more difficult to climb the walls of her house and slip in her bedroom window than it had been the previous night to climb out. The night's work had exhausted her, and as soon as she heard her step-parents leave the house for work at their outdoor attire and equipment store, she collapsed onto her bed behind her locked door, believing they could not murder her if they were no where near her. Thoughts of the night still haunted her wakefulness and would not allow her to rest or to dream. In her memory, she saw each demon's face and the many hordes of them all spitting out their blue-gray bile in the scores of tanks she had examined. The horror of it would not leave her mind. Tommy's predicament would not leave her mind. She could not rest, and now a great hunger raged in her, since the previous night's efforts had depleted all her stores of energy, even the neurotic energies forced into her by living under the threat of imminent death at the hands of her step-parents. She hadn't eaten for days prior to moving to the Bitterroot Valley, but now she found she had to eat if she wished to remain conscious. She had to eat meat. The great need was deepened and intensified when she smelled the frying of fat and red flesh wafting up from the kitchen below and immediately imagined the meat sizzling and leaking blood into the pan in the kitchen below. She bolted upright. Maybe her parents hadn't left for work, her confusion and anger made her fear, but that was not possible. She had peeked out her window to see them climb in their Infiniti SUV and drive off. She rushed to her bedroom door, unlocked it and ran downstairs, thinking if she surprised them they would be less able to surprise her with an attempt on her life. She burst into the kitchen with little attempt to remain quiet, preferring to rush in on them with a sudden, furiously loud entrance. She screamed as though out of her mind as soon as her foot hit the kitchen tile and she screamed and screamed, letting out the all horror of what she had seen and all the fear she had had to push down deep inside her. So swiftly was there a knife at her throat that the utter silence of shock possessed her immediately. The knife came away.

"It's you," Mabin said. "I'm sorry, but you did come in here like a demon. I thought it might be one of them."

She stepped back, breathing hard at her near-death experience, and regained her composure.

"I didn't burn any of them, just as you told me not to. I wanted to, but I didn't, because you told me they were once human. And I didn't find Tommy."

"I didn't find him, either. Of course, I was busy trying to keep Karel from burning down the mountains."

"I saw him last night. He played the same trick on me with the mirrors that you played on him."

"He learns fast."

"What do you mean you were trying to keep Karel from burning down the mountains?"

"He's setting the forests on fire. He thinks if he creates enough smoke and fire and mayhem I won't be able to see what he's doing and he'll be able to free his friends. Come look at this."

There were two steaks frying in a huge pan on the stove. Mabin flipped them over before taking her hand gently and leading her to the door. He led her outside. To the west, a huge plume of thick white-gray smoke was rising into the sky over the Bitterroots. It rose a thousand feet and then bent over, like an actor taking a bow, and then the smoke fanned out and extended horizontally over the valley. Farther south, over Darby, three more huge plumes of smoke, barely made smaller by distance, rose from the mountains. Unlike actors, these plumes rose straight up as though three giant Indians had set their cooking fires near each other.

"Remember that first day you saw him? When he looked like that black ooze in a cloud?"

"I remember."

Maggie smelled the meat cooking and could barely contain herself. She wished to rush back in the kitchen and lift a steak from the pan with her bare hands and tear into it. Her mouth was salivating like a demon's as she stared at the ghastly plumes of smoke.

"He wants to burn the entire valley. He'll hide in a cloud and instead of dripping down out of the sky as he did that first night you saw him, he'll shoot out a bolt of lightning, hundreds of bolts of lightning, to set the forests on fire. Last night, there were one-hundred-twenty-eight strikes recorded around Darby alone. Three caught fire."

Almost unconsciously, Maggie moved closer and closer to Mabin until he wrapped an arm around her shoulder and pulled her to him. She was desperate to be close to someone, anyone, and now finally was. Closeness to him was the only thing that assuaged her hunger. They watched the plumes of smoke fill the sky in silence, embracing.

"Why is he doing this?"

"He thinks if he burns everything down, the entire valley, he'll somehow be able to set his friends free. Who knows what such a creature think? That's why we have to –"

"What?"

"Come inside. We have to eat. This is ridiculous. We don't have a moment to ourselves to eat, and now this fool is doing something as ridiculous as burning down the valley. The bigger the fool, the dumber the action."

Worse than cutting himself off before he told her why Karel was burning down the mountains was the fact that he removed his arm from around her shoulder. She felt lost and alone as soon as he did so. Not only was she starved for food, but she also was starved for affection, any sort of closeness, to anyone, she realized again when he let her go. It was an agony not to be next to him, holding him. It was a crazy thought, but she understood that was why she had been willing to move in with the demons when she was even crazier than she was now, just a few short hours ago. She was utterly and completely lonely. He went back inside, seemingly not understanding her need, and she followed. The steaks were still cooking, and their smell brought up that almost uncontrollable hunger in her again. Instead of grabbing one for himself and throwing one to her to gnaw on, Mabin found the butter and eggs in the refrigerator and expertly separated the whites of the eggs from the yolks in a bowl. He squeezed in some lemon juice with the yolks and then melted a stick of butter in a pot on the stove, while she stood by, haplessly lonely and violently hungry, on the verge of collapsing.

"Do you have tarragon?"

"Tarragon? What's that?"

"A spice. Do you have any?"

"How should I know? What's do you use it for?"

"The sauce."

"What do you need sauce for?"

"It's sauce béarnaise, for the meat. You didn't think I'd just throw a steak on a plate for you, did you?"

"I guess not."

"Oh, I'll need some fresh ground red pepper and I'll also need to chop up some shallots."

Watching him work to prepare the steaks and sauce, and smelling the aromas his work filled the air with, made Maggie forget about the huge plumes of smoke outside, the demons, her murderous parents, her loneliness, her missing little brother. She settled into a kind of comfortable exhaustion, a trance, finally with someone who cared for her, at least a little, she knew, but someone who was putting just a little too much effort into showing it with a kind act of making an elaborate sauce for their steaks and not physically demonstrating it. She wished he had his arm around her again. She wished he had two arms around her and was very close to her with no inclination to go anywhere. She was trembling with hunger and desire and could barely wait for both to be satisfied. The béarnaise sauce was thickening to a delicious yellow with an aroma that combined with the aroma of the sizzling steaks was nearly impossible to resist. She was salivating so heavily she had to swallow again and again, simply to avoid looking like a fool.

"I never wanted meat as badly as I have the last few days," she said. "I never ate it before. Now it's all I want."

"This valley does that to you."

"I'm so stressed out I have to eat meat. What do you mean, the valley does that to you?"

"They don't call it Vampire Valley for nothing. It's either blood or red meat, that's the choice here. You really are what you eat here."

She laughed and stepped closer to him and the sizzling meat, and she didn't know which she wanted more.

"So if I drank your blood I'd be a vampire?" she joked.

"Of course. You know that. You're already one now, but just the good meat-eating kind."

She gave a little laugh at what she thought was also a joke. She envisioned the sick creatures just a little ways above their heads, creatures tricked into believing up was down but still trapped in their own vile habits and made so ill by them they retched all night long. He couldn't mean she was one of them. She dipped her finger into a pool of blood topping one of the sizzling steaks and stuck the red finger in her mouth to tease him.

"There. I'm a vampire now."

When was he going to put his arm around her again?

"I know. You have been for quite a while. You are as sick as everybody else. You just didn't realize it."

There was something so serious in the way he said it that she was sorry she made the joke, was sorry she had tasted the blood. It did give her an elation she hadn't felt in months, as though she was rising out of the dark pit of depression her parents' deaths had driven her in to and was lifted into a bright, cool, clear sky. It was as though he read her mind.

"Don't worry. It's animal blood. I know you'd never drink human blood. None of the good ones ever would. None of us would."

She lost patience with him.

"I'm not a vampire!"

He continued to stir the béarnaise, unconcerned with her shout.

"Right. Then what are you?"

"Just a crazy girl, nothing more."

He stopped stirring and turned toward her.

"Haven't you thought it was just a little strange, the things you can do already, after just one day here. If you think about it, not many girls can climb walls or take a step off of a roof and fly."

"That's just ... it's just ..."

"You can't really explain it, can you?"

"It just seemed natural. I didn't have to think about it. I just did it."

"Of course, but crazy girls don't fly, so that proves it. You're a vampire." He hesitated. "And so am I."

She stood next to him, confused and quiet, not quite knowing what to make of him.

Her lifted the steaks one by one out of the frying pan and placed each on their separate plates. He dribbled the béarnaise sauce over the tops of each, and then slathered it across their surfaces, while she stood struck dumb by her new identity. It slowly occurred to her that he was right, as though acknowledging what was true made her more comfortable. Understanding brought peace. Maybe she was a vampire. He garnished each plate with a sprig of parsley. He turned and placed the dishes of steak béarnaise on the kitchen table.

"Here, eat. It's what good vampires do."

She simply stood there, staring at the steaks, now not knowing if down truly was up, or up truly was down.

"I thought you said you were hungry."

"I am, but I'm a little surprised."

"Let me show you something. Sit next to me."

Lowering herself to settle in beside him on the chair beside the kitchen table was as natural as stepping off the roof and flying had been the night before. A whiff of pine smoke, seeping in from the fires outside, caught her nostrils and momentarily broke her concentration. He had the most beautiful, luminous eyes. The sweet smell of the destruction of the forests caught his nostrils, too, and he was also momentarily distracted, a worried look crossing his face. He grabbed hold of the steak knife beside his plate so firmly it startled her, since she was convinced anyone who grabbed a knife in that way in such close proximity was about to use it malevolently against her. He sliced off a piece of the nearly raw meat, freeing the juices inside to run onto the plate, and then he dipped the sliver of beef in its own blood and lifted it to his mouth.

"This is what we need to do now," he said, after chewing and swallowing the beef. "Karel can't cause much harm during the day. If he showed his true form he'd burn up like the rest of them, and has to change his shape and that weakens him. The fires he sets will still burn, but in the daytime, we can rest. This is how it's meant to be."

He put his hand on hers, and she didn't know which was more irresistible, his hand or her hunger. He removed the hand, so she gave in to the hunger. It seemed natural simply to pick up the steak and rip it to shred, but instead she did as he did and cut off piece after savory piece and ate, touching it to the sauce on her plate first. They were so close their legs touched. She let them, and moved closer. The two sensations, of touch and taste, were so keen she trembled. The béarnaise sauce imparted a wondrous flavor to the meat, a flavor that she thought could never exist in this world, and the boy she had close to her was someone she now knew was not of this world, but of some world of forgotten dreams, the dreams she had had before all the trouble of this world had been loosed and had come down upon her. The pleasures of eating and love were so great she could not consume them fast enough, and within a few minutes their plates were empty.

"I think you're ready," he said.

"I know I am," she whispered to him.

"Come on."

He stood and took her hand as she raised herself to be beside him, a warm glow in his touch moving up her arm and settling in her chest and from there expanding through her. She recognized it was the flow of good and warm fresh blood rushing through her, not the bilious and vile stuff of those creatures on the roof. She and Mabin had not taken that blood from others, but made it from the feelings they had for each other. He walked her to the door and outside to the hot spring day, where the fires were. It was as though the flames glowed from the mountains onto her, and she felt a great warmth on her face and bare arms.

"We'll be together today," he said. "Nothing can stop that, but tonight we have work to do."

It was almost too much to bear, to have such great good feelings so suddenly thrust upon her when for months all she had felt was hate and misery. A floodgate opened, and the bad feelings washed out of her. He was behind her with his hands on her shoulder, speaking softly to her, and she wanted to be close to him so badly she simply answered that need and backed up so that she pressed against him. She reached back and took his arms and wrapped them around her, settling them on her stomach, and felt the temperature of the warm blood they shared glow hotter.

"It's how it was meant to be," she said.

"I knew you were coming."

"Did you?"

"I knew it with all my heart."

"I knew nothing about it, until you came. Now I know everything."

He leaned down to speak softly into her ear.

"Can I say something?"

"Of course."

"Tommy."

With the one word the memory of her brother and his tortures came rushing back in a flood of bad feelings. She brought her hand to her mouth and cried out.

"Why did you say his name?"

"I don't want to ruin things, but I don't want you thinking too much about him today. We can't forget him, though. I promised you we'd set him free, and we will, but I mentioned him to you to make that promise again. We won't forget about your brother, but we have to think about our needs, too."

"All right. It's hard, though. I'll just think about us today."

"I promise you we'll find him. We have to work together now."

"Always together."

She settled against him again.

"Those fires, they're dangerous," he said. Mabin gazed out over the mountains. "Karel can't do a thing during the day, so we're free to be with each other, but I tell you tonight we have to work together to get rid of the demons."

"To get rid of them?"

"It's getting too dangerous to keep them where they are. Do you see that mountain over there? It's called Saint Mary's Mountain."

"I see it."

"That's where we're going with them. We're checking each vat you and I didn't check last night for your brother and then we're taking the rest of the demons to Saint Mary's Mountain before Karel can destroy what we have here."

"Could he do that?"

"If he burns the entire valley, yes. He's not beyond that. He controls the lightning."

She turned and pressed up against him.

"I'll do anything you want."

They stared for a moment at one at the mountains rising high to the west and saw the smoke rising in plumes and smelled the strong pine odor the burning released. She pressed up against him and he tightened his hold around her waist.

"It's time to go inside," he said. "The sun is high, and the heat is beginning. We have a big night ahead of us."

"And a better day? Tell me we can at least have one good day."

"We'll have a good day. It will be a wonderful day."

He released her waist and took her hand. Inside, the house was dark and cool and they didn't bother with the dishes. They didn't bother with much for hours, except each other.

SEVEN
Saint Mary's Mountain

A mountain on fire grows smaller in the dark. The trees are ablaze, and at night each tree is a candle in the distance, and unless the entire forest covering the mountain is ablaze, the individual fires shrink the imposing size of the giant, since the fiery trees are all you see, each standing out and making the mountain insignificant. In the daytime the mountains grow large again and stand out as the challenges they are, blocking the way and daring anyone to pass.

Mabin made four meals of meat that day, all creative creations using the pork and beef and chicken and duck in the Emorys' meat locker, but their ravenous appetite barely showed a difference in the amounts of flesh stored in the near-freezing room. Maggie hadn't eaten so well or often for months, and in just that one day of feasting and love she felt the meat come back to her bones, and she watched it come back to Mabin's, too. Her step-parents spent the day and night making a living, keeping their athletic apparel and equipment store open until nine, so the house was theirs. She locked her bedroom door behind them after their last meal of the day at eight in the evening, and still the dark had not come on and still her step-parents were not home and still the mountains loomed as challenges in the twilight. Above them, in the waning daylight, the demons had nearly finished consuming their regurgitated blood. When the dark came on they would begin again the patterns of gagging and sickness brought on by the silver vats and bloodless darkness they suffered. The dry thunderstorms, filled with crackling thunder and shivering lightning, filled the smoke-thickened air even before night came. The fires grew during the day in the tinder-dry forests, especially to the south around Darby, where Karel's touch was spectacularly effective. Dozens of forest fires ignited at his behest, sending firefighters in their yellow uniforms and helmets from all the towns of the Bitterroot scurrying southward to fight them, while the smoke drifted north and choked the entire long length of the valley. His work successful in the south, Karel rushed north to ignite the forests surrounding the other towns – Hamilton, and Corvallis and Victor and Stevensville and Florence, all of which were shrouded in smoke. He paid particular attention to the Mormon polygamist community of Pinesdale near Corvallis, dropping his bolts of fire in great proximity to their homes and barns, so that the firefighters had to rush up-valley again to save the Mormons from destruction. Karel appeared north near their town, Victor, in the shape he had already shown Maggie, the immense black wolf, but this time he came as the whole creature, or nearly whole. When Maggie caught a glimpse of him running through the mountains, she saw he had retrieved his back half from the draw in which Mabin had thrown it after tearing his enemy into two pieces. The two halves of the shape-shifting vampire had not re-united, and the back half trailed the front half by a few feet as one followed the other and loped through the mountains. The back half occasionally tripped on the trailing intestines of the front half, comically stumbling as it tried to catch up.

"There he is," Maggie said, pointing to him in the darkening evening. "Karel's back on earth, running up that mountain."

Mabin's gaze scanned the horizon and caught sight of his rival.

"I see he's found his better half. He wants us to know he's here."

It would have been hard for them to forget anything about Karel, since what he had done to the valley and Maggie's brother remained so firmly in their minds. The vision of that beast holding little Tommy in its mouth suddenly ignited in her, like a flash before her eyes, and her heart cramped up and nearly stopped in agony. She choked on mere air. They had been able to do nothing during the day, necessarily leaving the boy to his fate, and now she remembered how awful that fate was.

"What's he done with my brother?" she cried. "Something awful?"

"He probably did what he said he would. He probably put him back in a vat."

"We have to find him as soon as we can. I'm so afraid for him. Promise we will?"

"I promise."

"Tonight?"

"If we can. It's going to be a big job to move all the vampires and we have to be careful now with Tommy hidden in one of the vats."

"Has Karel stopped igniting the forest fires?"

Maggie was worried Karel had some sinister ideas involving her brother and those fires. He was not beyond burning an innocent child. He might even relish it.

"No, he'll start again. He can't do much else but burn the valley to stop us, and he wants us to know he's not going to make it easy for us."

Mabin bit his lip and waited anxiously for the last vestiges of daylight to drain from the western sky, and when the rims of the mountains had lost all their red and orange outlines and turned to black he glanced at Maggie, who was waiting anxiously by the window for the darkness to fall.

"You know it's time."

"I know. Tell me what we have to do and I'll do it."

"We're not going to walk through the neighborhood and we're not going to climb the walls anymore. I think you're ready. I can see it in you. You're leaping out of the window after me and we're going to fly as far and as fast as we have to. I think your powers have reached that point."

"What happens if I can't do it?"

"I'll help you, but once you make the leap you'll know you can."

With that, he opened the window pane and disappeared through the opening and into the night air so quickly it was as though he was smoke up a chimney, and even before she consciously leaped she followed, all without thought, smoke herself. He had been right. It didn't take thought; it took action. She saw him just ahead of her flying so fast in the smoky dark that the buildings passed in a blur, and then she realized the buildings were a blur because she was flying just as fast as he was. With an increased effort, she caught up to him, just as he slowed and landed on the first house on the next street over. The lights were off, and the house appeared quiet, except for the gagging of the captured vampires, which had begun with the darkness. She settled quietly next to Mabin on the roof.

"Listen, they've started."

"I hear them."

"Is Tommy in there?"

"I don't know. He could be, but we have to look in each vat we take before we take it. No matter who's in there we have to deal with them now that Karel is burning the entire valley."

With that, he flipped open the lid and the demons screamed immediately, fearing in their backward and confused notions that it was still daylight, despite the fact that they were sick and gagging. They were that foolish and uninformed. They had spit up only small amounts of stolen blood, blood taken from who-knows-what innocent victim, and the glowing ruminations provided the only illumination in the dark. It pulsed with light, a thin film on the bottom of the silver pit, as though the floor of the vat was smeared with smashed blue fireflies, and as soon as the lid opened there was a crack of thunder and a bolt of lightning as a response from Karel from above. Maggie was staring at the demons, but she could not make out Tommy's form when the bright light flashed around her. The bolt landed a hundred feet away in a stand of Ponderosa pines and immediately set them ablaze. Maggie jumped, startled at the closeness of the lightning, and she trembled with fear. Karel was up in the clouds again, doing his dirty work. In an instant of light, the flash of lightning had revealed six very old demons. They were bent with age, their joints swollen with arthritis, and their flesh hung loose on their arms and faces.

"Give us a drink," a crackling voice begged. "Something good."

The creature meant Maggie should lean close, exposing her neck to him, but she barely paid attention to the request. He lifted a crooked finger to her, indicating for her to come near.

"Tommy's not there," Maggie said.

"Are you sure? I didn't think I saw him, either, but there wasn't much time to look."

She felt her heart sink, but she was certain none of these ancient demons was her brother.

"He's not here. I'm sure of it. Tommy!" she shouted into the night, looking away from the vat.

There was no answer.

"All right, we have to get them out of here then. Grab that end."

"What do you mean?"

"Grab the handle on that end of the vat. We're taking them to Saint Mary's Mountain before Karel can burn the place down and free them."

With that, Mabin flipped the lid down on the gagging demons, frustrated as Maggie was that they had not found her brother. When he did so, she saw the handle, opposite the one he leaned down to grip, and she wrapped her fingers around it. A great gust of wind whipped over them as the thunderstorm intensified and blew harder, sweeping over them with cracks of thunder and mere heat flashes of lightning, but still no rain. Another bolt exited a cloud and flashed into another nearby stand of Ponderosa pines, igniting those dry trees and sending an explosion and grand illumination up from the torches the trees immediately became.

"Here we go!" Mabin shouted, above the noise of the strike.

Again, there was no thought to it, or effort or attempt on her part. She simply rose deliriously into the darkness while holding on to the silver handle, with Mabin doing the same opposite her, rising as easily as air. The shining silver vat reflected the orange and red flaming trees, distorting their agony into glorious gleaming portraits as they burned nearby. Rapidly, they left the portraits behind. They flew toward the mountain. Again, the night air above Victor was black and smoky with Karel's rage, and Maggie had no idea what they were doing or how to get where they were going.

"It doesn't matter," Mabin said, as though reading her mind. "Just do what I do."

There was no need to think at all extensively of what she was doing, since it seemed just to happen, as though she truly was half-awake and could neither go to sleep nor wake up again. They rose a thousand feet into the air within seconds, with Maggie not understanding it or realizing it until she was rushing over the thin air high above the burning valley, looking to the south as they flew and seeing the bumpy mountain ranges surrounding Darby with massed red and orange flaming pines in the dark. Several considerably smaller fires lit the night directly below, the trees like giant candles sending their heat and smoke up toward them, where it dissipated at their toes. Karel struck again and again with lightning from the clouds, sometimes igniting a fire in the thick forests and sometimes missing, the lightning hitting below them with no effect but a wisp of smoke that disappeared into the darkness. They flew directly through a plume of swirling thick smoke, but once inside it realized it was not just smoke but ash and embers, too, so hot that the remains of the burnt trees rose in it as though bursting from a large-bore canon on the ground.

"I can't see!" Maggie said, her eyes burning, and when she said it she realized she couldn't breathe, either, and choked on the ash and embers.

"Over this way!"

Mabin nodded to the right, and they flew that way. In a moment, they were clear of the smoke and ash but still gagging on the refuse remaining in their lungs and clearing their eyes of similar noxious materials. Another plume of smoke and debris loomed ahead, but this time they veered around it, tilting the silver vat on a slant and feeling the demons inside it slide across the floor and bash into the wall with a thud. Saint Mary's Mountain was just below. They slowed down and descended, and it was only then Maggie realized they had been flying at a tremendous rate of speed, perhaps in the hundreds of miles per hour, but now they eased down slowly toward a clearing in the forest three-quarters of the way up the southern slope. The land was open and flat and packed down for just this purpose, landing vats of demons. They came to rest, their eyes acclimated to the dark. In the side of the mountain was what looked like another larger lid to a larger demon vat, silver glinting with reflected star light, and the air was fresh and clear with a wonderful whiff of pine. They were still hacking and coughing to clear their lungs of the pollution they had descended through to get to the mountain.

"You can set you end down now," Mabin said.

Maggie hadn't realized how light the heavy tank of captured vampires felt to her, or perhaps it was that she was extremely strong now. She didn't know. She was doing things she had never dreamed of doing and doing them naturally and without much effort, merely thinking and they happened, in that dream-state that harsh effort brings on. She wondered what else was possible in her new life of living with vampires in Montana, but her mind had little else running through it. She set down the demons on the soft forest floor of pine needles.

Suddenly a soft blue-gray glow, like that in the interiors of the vats of blue-spitters, lit up the clearing, and with the light she saw Mabin had opened the lid in the side of the mountain, exposing a large round tunnel lined with silver boring downward into the mountain endlessly. The silver reflected the glow, which seemed to emanate from all the way down the sloping tunnel.

"Do you see that?"

"What is it?"

"That's where they're going," Mabin said.

"Down there? What's down there?"

She peered into the heart of the mountain through the blue, glowing tunnel, which glowed like neon in the surrounding blackness.

"The same thing they're in now, but in a much-bigger version. It's an old silver mine I found that wasn't nearly worked out. It still held tons of silver, so I lined this shaft with it and built their final prison down there and used the rest of the silver to make the vats."

"What are we going to do now?"

"Help me with the lid. It slides off once it's open."

He flipped open the top to the vat of blue-spitters, exposing them to the night, and then the two of them slid it off its hinges to the right and set it on the ground. She heard the vomiting and spitting inside, and smelled the awful odor of the old, rotted blood they stood in, but she did not look at the ancient creatures inside the vat. She had seen enough of them.

"All we have to do now is dump them out, and go get some more."

"Dump them out?"

"Help me tilt the vat toward the tunnel and we'll slide them down it."

"What the heck. Okay."

"Are you sure Tommy is not in there? Once they're down inside the mountain, there's no getting out."

"I'm sure."

"Here they go, then."

Once again, it was as though she had been made for this work, since the ease with which she and Mabin tilted the vat made the task simple. The first gagging demon exited on an angle, sliding into the silver shoot while still spitting, and a bit of the regurgitated blood from his mouth hit the pine needles on the forest floor and set them on fire. Mabin stamped out the small fire immediately, twisting the sole of his shoe over it as though putting out an errant cigarette butt. Two more blue-spitters slid out of the vat, exiting neatly and shooting down the slanted tunnel into the mountain at a tremendous speed. The last three spitting demons were fighting their extradition into the mountain's base, doing all they could to hold on to the bottom of the vat, but in the end the silver had so weakened them they could not resist gravity at all and went flying down and down and down with a suddenness that shocked her. It was as though the vat was not a vat but a gun that had fired them downward into their doom. For a moment, they stood in complete silence on the dark mountainside, pondering what they had done.

"This is just the beginning," Mabin said.

He gazed at her trembling with hope.

"Of what?"

"We're going to send everyone who's drunk blood down into that pit. This valley will be rid of the spitters once and for all. They'll stay down there forever, or at least until we can find a cure for them."

It sounded like a joke, curing vampirism, and she laughed until she saw Mabin was serious about what he said. She was a vampire. He was a vampire. And as far as she could see, everyone else was a vampire. If he thought they could cure that, he must know a lot more than she did. She simply believed that some were strong enough to live on their own merits while helping others and some had to steal life from others to succeed.

"We're working on it," he said, again as though reading her mind about the cure. "Help me with the vat. We have to store the empty ones in the forest. We might need them again."

They replaced the lid on the empty vat and dragged it into the forest, finding a home for it among a stand of tall pines, and then Mabin leaped up out of the forest toward the smoky sky without a word, brushing the soft branches of the trees above as he flew by and leaving them shaking. She followed immediately, without hesitation, brushing the same soft tree branches, and soon found herself rushing along beside him in the smoke and fire-debris, balanced high in the air over the valley, her long hair trailing behind her, coughing once again to clear her lungs but feeling she had met the sweetest boy in the world.

"You don't know how difficult it was to bring all of them here," Mabin said, "and how long I worked."

The smoke surrounded them, and the wind was rushing by.

"I didn't hear you," Maggie said, clearing her hair away from her face. She removed a dying ember from her hair, flicking it out into the night air. She watched it fall toward the fires swirling below.

"It took months, and I had to gather them from all around the world. The places I've been and the things I've seen, just to gather all these vampires, you wouldn't believe it. I've traveled to every continent, almost every country, gathering these poor creatures one by one. It's been a long time away from home, too long, and I only wish one thing."

"What's that?"

"I wish I had you with me all that time, that we could have been together all those months. I wouldn't have been so lonely then."

"I wish I had been with you, too. I wouldn't have had to go through what I had to go through, either. I was lonely, too. It was just awful without you."

"We've known each other forever."

He held her hand tightly, and she felt the sinews and strength of his grip, and that grip was like a promise, for she knew he would never fail her. For that moment holding his hand, she felt awed just being beside him, being beside such a magical creature who fought so hard against the blood-takers, someone who had done so much to bring them here and yet had the compassion to dream he could cure them. He had hinted he could cure them but had left that as a mystery for her imagination to solve. How could anyone think they could cure vampires? Such a person was very special, unusual in his goodness, and she flew as close as she could to him, close enough to take his hand and smile at him warmly, for in this odd sky flying over this odd valley she felt true comfort for the first time in a very long time. She felt it with him, and she leaned in to give him a kiss on his soft, willing lips as they flew. She had been left totally alone, bereft of family and friends, and suddenly to have another person working with her and caring for her was almost too much to bear. Tears of joy came to her when the kiss broke off, but the tears had little time to wash her face of the blackening ash of the smoke and fires, for their speed was so great it returned them to another roof and vat of blue-spitters within seconds. They still have nearly endless work to do, Mabin's dream to accomplish with more great efforts. The thunder crashed and the lightning flashed to the ground out in the mountains, but Karel could do nothing more to vent his rage. They were going to fly away and dump out this vat of demons into the mountain's belly, once they checked it make certain it did not contain her brother. The blue glow lit the night dimly, as Mabin opened this vat's silver lid. Its hinges creaked as though in objection. Maggie immediately poked her head over the rim to the vat to examine its contents.

"Is he in there?"

She leaned further over the vat's edge to peer in.

"Tommy?"

The long fingernails of a leaping blue-spitter nearly tore into her face, and his hideous grimace rose toward her, his fangs bared and the five other blue-spitters below squealing with delight at his attempt to capture her and rip into her flesh.

"Tear with the fangs and taste with the tongue!" one screamed.

"Yes, tear her and taste her!"

Unable to rise very high, the jumper fell back into the cesspool of rotted blue blood with a splash, his weak energies expended, and he immediately gagged violently with the effort he had made to sink his fangs into her. Furious, Mabin leaned over the rim of the vat and screamed down at the demons with a quivering anger.

"Anyone who does something like that ever again to her will see daylight as soon as the sun rises! Mark my words, you will see daylight if you try to harm his girl in any way again, and you will not like it!"

The jumping demon's only answer was to gag and then snarl and whimper, cowed by Mabin's loud warning. He snarled again weakly, which called up a gaggle of weak, half-hearted snarls from his cohorts, who cowered against the silver walls.

Mabin turned to her.

"Are you hurt?"

"He almost got me."

"He did. They never give up. Don't turn your back on them. They might not be much once they're captured in silver, but they can be lethal if they get out, and they'll never stop trying for your blood. Once they're that sick, they only want more and more and more blood."

Maggie's hope to find Tommy inside the holding tank was already dashed by the jumper's attempt at her life, but with Mabin beside her, she cautiously peered down again into it to search for her little brother. She called out his name, but her effort was wasted, for inside this tank were six of the most undistinguished vampires she had ever seen. So sudden had been the attack on her that she had been unable to recall the details of their appearances. Each was a middle-age male with brown hair wearing a button-down plaid shirt and tan slacks, the uniform of the uninspired, but each had succumbed to drinking blood and now had to pay the price. They gagged their rotted feasts onto their penny-loafers. Tommy would have stood out like a rose among weeds in a vat of such insipid men. With disappointment, she told Mabin Tommy was not there and they closed the lid and quickly flew off with them and disposed of the bland blue-spitters in the mountainside. Cowed by Mabin's rebuke, they had made no attempt to escape or attack during the entire process.

"That was easy," Maggie said, once they were aloft again.

"They might be the most dangerous kind of vampires," Mabin said, as they flew directly toward yet another roof and its vat of blue-spitters.

"They looked so normal."

"Awful things become normal when normal people do them. Then no one has any feeling about them anymore. They just seem to be the thing to do. Don't be fooled by how normal some vampires look."

When with Mabin, who looked so sleek and determined flying next to her in the sky, the clear night sky above the smoke was her favorite place, black and full of stars, with one kiss after another. "If we keep kissing like this, we'll never get done," he teased her. When they flew a course that avoided crashing into the smoke and ash entangling them from below, even the fires in the forests beneath them seemed to take on the majesty of rebellion against evil, the same rebellion they were engaged in. It was as though the fires defied Karel's disastrous intent by turning his strokes of anger and destruction into gorgeous and glorious ends for themselves, ends of light and fire and passion when he had intended the fires do his destructive bidding to save the tainted vampires. There was that rebellion in the fires, until the forests turned to smoke and ash in the effort for good, and the more Maggie flew by Mabin's side to remove the malicious blue-spitters from doing harm forever, the more she felt the majesty of their cause. She could barely believe the change in her from just twenty-four hours ago, when she had been so desperate and alone that she had been willing to crawl down into a vat with demons, just to relieve her heartache. Now she had a lover, and now she was flying high above it all with him, to save her brother and save the valley from sinking further into blood corruption and wanton violence. The more blue-spitters they entombed in the mountain, the more efficient they became at it and the faster they could work together. It took only moments now to lift a lid on a silver container, examine its contents of vampires, fly with it off to the mountain and dump its contents into the bowels of the earth and return for another. The blue-spitters came in all forms. They were men and women and boys and girls and young and old and rich and poor and black and white. Anyone could become evil. Just the taste of blood would do it. Everyone had the potential for darkness. Six at a time, the blue-spitters left on a tilt from their vats of silver, sliding down the tunnel into the mountain, their slide lubricated by the blue vampire vomit left behind by their predecessors. A thousand vampires were dumped from their holding tanks into the mountain in a desperate rush by Mabin and Maggie to liberate the valley and find Tommy before Karel could destroy their efforts with fire. If he burned the houses, the vats of blue-spitters would melt and fall to earth and release their contents on the world. Tommy would die. More and more bolts of lightning struck in the night, sometimes flashing by so close to them in the sky that Maggie could see their rough ragged edges and feel their searing heat and static electricity, and it would take all her courage and will to hold on to the vat of blue-spitters they were carrying and not drop it into the night below. The forests became vast roiling carpets of fire below them, following the ups and downs of the mountains and valleys, as the flames twisted in the wind and moved closer to one town after another and the firefighters scurried with their trucks and equipment to ward off their destruction.

"Can we get them all in one night?" Maggie asked, frightened when a huge wind kicked up and rapidly pushed the flames below toward Victor like a giant hand.

"I don't think so. The dawn's coming, so Karel has to stop soon. If these fires come too close to town, we might have to burn the rest of the vampires rather than let him have them. I hate to do it. It'll make him stronger if he takes their powers, but we'll have to deal with that if it happens."

"What worse can he do?"

"A lot worse. You can't imagine."

"What about my brother? He still has my brother. We can't burn anyone if my brother's still missing."

"We'll find him soon, I promise. I don't know what he could have done with him, and why he'd do this to a little boy. We should have found him by now, but there are a thousand more to go."

Maggie set her jaw, as Mabin gripped the dark air with his free hand in an expression of helplessness and frustration.

"I'm not stopping until I find him," she said grimly.

"I'm not stopping, either. We might have to work tomorrow night, too, if the town survives the night."

A great crashing noise below them made them look down. Another tall stand of burning pines tumbled over onto the earth below, sending a cascade of embers upward before the sparks halted in mid-air and then scattered back down to earth.

"He's burning everything!" Mabin said. "Why does he have to burn everything?"

"I don't know what he's doing. It's as though he's making no sense on purpose, just destroying for no reason."

"There won't be a thing left. Hurry up. Come on. We can get a few more vats before the sun comes up, and then he'll have to stop."

A long narrow lip of red sat on the eastern horizon and whispered dawn was coming, but if things continued the way they were, it might be the worst dawn ever, with the valley in cinders and hundreds of captured vampires teetering on the verge of freedom. So many fires sent so much smoke and ash into the atmosphere that Maggie and Mabin could barely navigate a clear path through the columns of smoke to Saint Mary's Mountain with their cargo of blue-spitters. The mountains on both sides of the valley below were seas of fire, and in their desperation they pushed themselves to fly faster and work harder, deliver one payload of demons after another, all while greater and greater frustration set in. They quickly dumped their current charge of blue-spitters into the mountain, and flew back in an instant to the last house on Heathen Lane to collect the final tank of the evening for disposal of its contents. They lifted it, feeling weary but proud of the good work they had done that night, and with the sun threatening to cast its first flickering fingers of light over the land, they flew together faster than they ever had to Saint Mary's Mountain, landed in their familiar spot and opened the tunnel to the blue-spitters' dungeon once again. Gasping for air in the smoke swirling around them, they opened the vat and tilted it so that the demons sloshed forward and tumbled out.

"Did we –"

The words were barely out of Mabin's mouth before Tommy's cries split the early morning light with shock and fear.

"Hey! No! No! What are you doing? Where am I going now? No! Don't do this! I can't go down there! Maggie! Help!"

She barely caught sight of Tommy's face and tiny figure as he cried out to her. He was entangled in the mass of blue-spitters tumbling down the silver tunnel. His panicked eyes caught hers and he reached out for her desperately with a tiny hand before he disappeared into the darkness below. With a strength she didn't know she possessed, she pushed the empty silver vat aside and rushed toward the entrance of the tunnel.

"My god, we forgot to check this vat before we dumped it!" she cried out. "We were in so much of a hurry we forgot to check it! Tommy was in there! How could we do that to him? I've got to get him out!"

"We can't get him out."

"What do you mean, we can't get him out? We're getting him out. We have to. Do you know what they'll do to him down there?"

"There's no escape from inside the mountain."

"I don't believe that! There's got to be a way out!"

She was the girl who would do anything, and now she proved it by diving into the tunnel head-first, landing on her stomach on a glob of blue vomit stuck on the downward incline. It proved extremely slippery and it rocketed her into the darkness below as she cried out, "Tommy! Tommy!" She seemed to slide down in the dark forever, screaming for her brother, before a faint blue glow signaled to her she was about to end her descent. She gained tremendous speed as she slid on the blue goop toward the glow, and she screamed again and again at the utter madness of it. She heard her name called out below her and above her, as Tommy cried to her from below and Mabin flew down the silver tunnel above, calling for her to come back. She heard a sound below like several heavy boulders falling into a lake and knew Tommy and his vile companions had reached their destination. Then, suddenly, she was in mid-air, but not for long. She splashed down into four feet of the glowing blue liquid and closed her mouth and eyes and held her nose as she fell through it and crashed onto the silver floor. Even though she held her nose and closed her eyes, she thought she had never smelled anything as foul as that old, digested blood. She found her feet and stood up, gasping, but not for long. Something smashed into her and she tumbled back down into the blue vomit of regurgitated blood, this time barely able close her mouth and eyes and hold her nose before it rushed in. Again, she found her feet and stood up to see Mabin beside her, as covered in the blue slime as she was and as disgusted and gasping as she was.

"Why did you do that?"

"Do what?" he asked.

"Crash into me!"

"I had no choice. You dove down here and I couldn't do anything but follow you."

"Why? Why did you have to follow me?"

"Because where you go, I go, and I want you to live."

His gentle voice, and what he said, softened her. She wiped away old blue blood from her face, as she looked around desperately for Tommy.

"Well, you shouldn't have run into me."

"You shouldn't have dived down here."

She was still wiping the blue slime off of her face and searching the dark tank for Tommy when she realized this was no time to argue with Mabin.

"I had to. I had to follow my brother. Do you see him?"

"Tommy?"

"Yes."

"I don't see him."

"Tommy!"

Calling out, and hearing the calls echo in the cavern, made her realize how desperate their situation was. In the dim glow, the lake of blue vomit extended off into the far distance, and in the lake were standing the multitudes of blue-spitters they had dumped here, some bent over and spitting and vomiting and others cupping the blue liquid in their hands and raising it to their mouths to drink. They were up to their chests in the vile blue liquid. Aside from a hushed mumbling from a few of the spitters, there was utter silence hanging over the blue-gray glow inside the mountain. A rounded silver dome ceiling was barely visible twenty feet above them in the dark, and in it was the opening to the tunnel, which glowed with the light of dawn.

"As soon as we find him, we're flying out of here," Maggie said.

"Well ..."

"Well, what?"

"I'm not so sure of that."

"Why?"

"We can't."

"What do you mean, we can't?"

"I mean we're just like them down here and don't have many powers when trapped in silver. We belong up there, Maggie, in the light." Mabin pointed to the surface. "There's not much we can do to escape. Our powers don't work this far down in the earth, surrounded by the silver."

"I don't believe that. Why should that be true? Look."

With a sudden leap up, Maggie attempted to fly toward the opening, but she simply rose a few inches and then settled back down heavily into the lake of vomited blood. When she settled again up to her chest in the thick blue liquid, there was a look of despair and hopelessness on her face that quickly turned to panic. Mabin was right: they were powerless now. Desperate, she wiped the glowing blue gel off one arm and then the other as though knocking off crushed slimy bugs.

"Oh my god."

She wiped off more and more of the blue liquid in disgust, panicking as she realized their situation, and Mabin raised his eyes to the light of the tunnel above as though longing with all his heart to be once more in the sunshine. Then he, too, lowered his gaze in despair to the lake of blue surrounding them. Off to the side, there was a splashing sound that made them look up in unison. Just above the surface of the blue lake, out of the circle of light formed by the rays of dawn shining down from the tunnel, they saw the head of a small boy struggling to remain above the bloody vomit. Tommy was doggy-paddling toward them, too short to stand without being covered by the four feet of blue liquid but too defiant simply to stop swimming and sink below the surface.

"Hey, hey, Maggie ... hey ..."

"Tommy!"

"Help me! I'm drowning!"

They practically leaped toward him, sending a wave of blue across the surface that splashed up another obstacle for him. He had to raise his chin and swim harder, closing his eyes and mouth tightly to avoid swallowing as the wave of blue washed over him. When she saw him in such distress, Maggie couldn't help but see a movie flash through her mind of all he had endured in his days trapped with blue-spitters. He had choked on the smell of them and their spitting and vomiting, and he must have been half-mad with fear as they threatened him, and he had never been able to find respite in sleep. The wave washing over him subsided just as they reached him, and she saw the dark circles around his eyes and blue vomit caked in his hair and she saw the fight in his eyes. She got to him first, and she lifted him with her hands under his arms and held him to her.

"Tommy! I never thought I'd see you again."

He was gasping so hard for air he nearly hyperventilated and could not answer her for a moment. He wrapped his arms around her.

"I missed you so much."

"I missed you, too, really a lot."

"They told me at first that you were dead. Stephanovich and Elsa told me that you had to be."

"Yeah, well, I'm not, and what do they know, anyway?"

He was still fighting for air and was defiant enough to respond with scorn to the bad information their step-parents had given out. Mabin moved close and helped support Tommy on the lake of thick blue gel, his hands just below Maggie's.

"Who's that?" Tommy asked. "He's not one of them, is he? Get your hands off of me, you creep."

"No, he's one of us."

"I'm Mabin."

He moved closer and supported more of Tommy's weight.

"He's my boyfriend."

"You're Mabin?"

"I am."

"Those things talked about you when I was shut up with them in that tiny tank. They were really afraid of you. Nice to meet you, dude. If the vampires hated you, I have to like you."

Tommy held out a tiny hand and Mabin shook it, grinning.

"Nice to meet you, too, dude."

Tommy returned the grin but then released his grip on Mabin's hand and held tight to Maggie, finally breaking and letting his feelings go and sobbing with relief. "Maggie ...It wasn't any fun these last few days. It was so horrible."

"I know. It's all right now, though. It's over."

Maggie, too, cried with relief when she finally held her brother in her arms again. She tightened her grip, her arms taut around him, and laid her head on his shoulder, feeling the comfort of her own flesh and blood, knowing she had rescued him. Then she looked up. Sunlight was streaming down from the opening in the tunnel, but they were still stuck far down below the surface, a billion pounds of mountain on top of them. It was strange, she thought, that this mountain had looked so small when she and Mabin had flown high over it so many times the night before, but now, holding Tommy with Mabin standing beside them quietly, in this hopeless situation, Saint Mary's Mountain loomed above them monstrously, very large and imposing and dark indeed.

Trapped, it was then she truly felt like Maggie Ant, a tiny, tiny Maggie Ant.

EIGHT
Vengeance of the Blue-Spitters

The lake was receding around them. Hungry after a night of gagging and vomiting, the blue-spitters were busily engaged in drinking the regurgitated blood they had expelled the previous night, and the slurping sounds of their activities were echoing all around them. It went on for hours and froze Mabin and Maggie and Tommy in place. The drinking of old blood sent the level of the lake down and down, until the hundreds of spitters were on their hands and knees lapping up every last drop of digested blood. The blue slime dripped off of Maggie and Tommy and Mabin, slippery in nature and pulled down to the silver floor by gravity, until the three of them were practically free of it. The spitters ventured into the fringes of the light near Maggie and Mabin and Tommy, very cautiously yet greedily, hungry for the fresh blood the three of them held but singed by the slightest touch of sunlight, and they had to be satisfied, for now, with whatever blue slime they could lick off the floor. They scrambled back wildly on all fours, in pain, when the weak rays of light surrounding the three non-vampires touched them. Many stood and burped when they had consumed all the thick blue liquid they could, and there seemed to be a chorus of bad manners of burping and belching deep inside the mountain. Soon, the buzz of low and secret conversations rose among the blue-spitters and reached Maggie's ears, and then they were shooting glances the way of the three free humans standing in the well of light on the silver floor. Maggie had put Tommy down when the level of rotted blood receded, but he still tottered weakly, so depleted by his continuing ordeal with the blue-spitters that he had to hold Mabin's hand just to remain upright. Their fresh blood, a tonic for vampires, was out-of-reach as long as it was in the sun, but the vampires were never satiated and hovered as close as they could to the light without getting burned. Maggie knew they were trying to figure out a way to get to her and Mabin and Tommy, tear open their flesh, without the inconvenience of being incinerated. She knew it was only a matter of time before the long day ended and night shut off the beam of saving brightness from above and they would be in great peril. The gigantic cavern rose above them like a coliseum of silver, and Maggie knew all-too-well what mayhem happened in ancient coliseums.

"That wolf told them not to drink my blood when I was trapped with them," Tommy said. "Do you think they still won't?"

Mabin set his lips and narrowed his eyes at the mention of Karel and didn't answer. It seemed his adversary had won.

"I think they were more afraid of him than anything," Tommy went on. "They kept up that disgusting spitting and vomiting all night, and then drank everything they vomited during the day. They kept whispering they would drain me dry, but they were too afraid to do it. They thought the wolf would get them and kill them if they did."

Tommy hadn't been difficult to hold up in her arms out of the lake of rotted blue blood, Maggie thought, since he hadn't eaten anything during his confinement with the spitters and was terribly thin. To her, he weighed no more than an envelope, and she knew her strength had multiplied ten-fold since she had been in Montana. What awful things he must have suffered, she thought, and put her arm around his shoulder. A spitter caught her eye and snarled at her, an odd snarl, something like a taunting smile. She ignored him.

"It must have been terrible for you. I'm sorry we couldn't find you sooner," she said to Tommy.

"That's all right. I know you tried. If you had to look among all these vampires, I'm surprised you found me at all."

"There are still about twice as many out there as down here now," Mabin said. "They're up there, trapped, and we have to bring them here before they can escape and begin killing again."

"Then I guess I'm pretty lucky," Tommy said. "That one, over there, he was one of the ones in my tank."

Tommy pointed to an emaciated elderly vampire bent at the waist, his eyes riveted on the floor, still looking for rotted blood to slurp up. His fingernails were as long as carrots and twisted and bent and dirty, and his sparse white hair was swirled on top and unkempt, like a map of a hurricane.

"Hey!" Tommy yelled at him. "Remember me?"

The vampire's head snapped up and he sniffed the air for blood. He snarled at Tommy, baring his red teeth. He stepped toward them, barely venturing out of the dark, but he immediately squealed in pain when the light brushed him. He scurried back into the dark like a whipped dog.

"That's what'll happen if you come near me now," Tommy yelled at him. "You freak. You creepy freak. You picked on me all the time, and now I'm going to pick on you."

Tommy had pulled free from Mabin's hand, and when he ran toward the vampire in the dark Maggie panicked and quickly followed. He had nearly reached the limits of their circle of light and entered the darkness when she caught him.

"Tommy, you don't want to go into the dark." She grabbed his shoulders and saw the glow of several eyes in the blackness as she did so. She pulled him back into the safety of the light.

"I guess not. I just hate that one in particular. He's a punk. He dunked my head in that blue junk whenever he could and told me to drink it."

"Come back over here with us. It's safer."

"Okay. Hey, how long does it stay light outside here?" Tommy asked.

"For a long time."

"But for how long?"

"Maybe until ten at night."

"Because I was thinking that maybe we ought to get out of here before the night comes."

"That's what we were thinking, too. I don't know if we can, though."

"I want to kick that punk's butt before we go."

Maggie laughed Tommy's threat, but then suddenly remembered what had gotten them here, how she had neglected to check that last vat of blue-spitters before they dumped it into the tunnel, and she broke out sobbing.

"I'm so sorry. I was so careless, and I messed up, I'm always messing up. I just didn't see you inside that tank with the others. I should have been more careful."

A tear fell from her eye onto the silver floor of the cavern.

"Ah, that's all right. Don't be sorry. You saved me, and I know we'll get out of this. It's not your fault. It's theirs."

He tilted his head toward the vampires with a look of scorn for them.

"I promise we'll be home soon."

"We can go back to New York?"

"If you want to."

"Good. So far, I hate where we are. It's sick, everybody here is sick. Is everybody in Montana a vampire?"

"Mabin says they are."

"Then they must be. This place is a scab on the face of the earth. What's wrong with these people?"

"I don't know."

"It's creepy here, really, really creepy."

"I know."

"Hey, it's going to be light a while, so can I lay down and get some sleep? I'm really tired. I mean, you won't let them get me while I'm sleeping, will you?"

"Never. You can sleep as much as you want."

"All right. Let's go back to where Mabin is. I haven't slept for a couple of days."

Maggie let Tommy lead her back to Mabin, his soft hand in hers, into the brightest part of the circle of light, but before she did so, she checked the rim of the circle of darkness surrounding them and saw the glinting of several pairs of eyes, aligned in a row as though the vampires were intently watching their every move, intent on pouncing. She spun around and saw that they were encircled by the glinting eyes of the vampires, all waiting for night. She shuddered and followed Tommy, glancing over her shoulder again and again. The blue-spitters had done an excellent job of licking up their vomit. The floor of the immense silver tank was sparkling and clean. Tommy examined it, just in case, before he sat down and stretched out to sleep.

"Hey, buddy, you don't want to go too near those guys," Mabin warned him. "No matter what they say, they're not your friends."

"I know. I hate them. That guy wasn't my friend. I just wanted to make fun of him. I hope they come after me while I'm sleeping, because I want to fry them in the light."

"They're pretty bad, the way they are now. Maybe we can teach them something better," Mabin said.

"That'll be the day."

Tommy stretched again, his tiny arms reaching up into the light. So exhausted was he that without another word he blinked and fell fast asleep.

Mabin raised his eyes to her, and Maggie saw something in them she had never seen before.

She saw fear.

"What are we going to do?" he asked, in a whisper, as though Tommy might hear. It appeared as though he was having a hard time standing, as though he was so affected by their predicament he might topple over. Maggie was astonished that he, of all people, appeared weak.

She felt the same helplessness that made him whisper.

"I don't know. What can we do? It seems we're just normal in here, and can't do anything wonderful. When I think how great last night was, when we could fly all over the place and I could kiss you up in the sky ... I felt so strong."

"It seems those days are over, except for the kisses." He leaned in and touched her lips with his. "All of our days might be over. I can't believe I failed."

He glanced down at Tommy with regret and frustration.

"Your poor brother."

"You didn't fail. I messed up," Maggie said. "If anybody failed, I did, but I don't think we've failed yet. We'll think of something."

Maggie moved close to Mabin, and he took her in his arms and held her gently. He was the only bit of warmth and comfort in this cold, cold cavern of silver. Mabin had built this, Maggie thought. He had built this massive structure deep within the mountain and gathered up all the spitters to imprison here. That was not failure but wild success beyond what anyone she had ever known could do.

"I'm exhausted," she said. "Do you think it's safe if we sit down next to Tommy?"

A scream from the vampires made an answer they did not wish to hear. Out of the corner of her eye, she saw something large and dark hurtling toward them, a thing thrown up into the air by other vampires, but it did not remain dark for long. It was one of the spitters, tossed aloft by several of the others to burn in the light.

"Look out!" Mabin screamed.

The vampire had ignited in the air above their heads as soon as it flew into their circle of light, and a second prolonged scream issued from its burning throat, and then the flaming mass fell with a thud at their feet. Completely engulfed in flames, the vampire was still alive as it kicked and wiggled on the clean silver floor next to them and twisted in mad agony as it burned, a victim of its friends.

"Help! Shove me back into the dark! I am –"

Tommy screamed at the sudden intrusion, woke up and jumped to his feet, the vampire burning to ashes beside him so quickly it lost its ability to speak in mid-sentence and was silent. It another few seconds, it was reduced to a line of black cinders and ash with no resemblance to the human being it had once been.

Maggie spun around, ready to face any other blue-spitter who leaped out of the dark at them.

"What are they doing? Don't they know what will happen to them if they come into the light? Are more of them attacking?"

Mabin was calm and knowing, his eyes set on the dark beyond the column of light. His toe poked at the pile of ashes.

"I don't think they're attacking."

"Then what is this? Why did he fly in here?"

"He didn't fly of his own free will."

Maggie was horrified at what she had just seen, and backed away from the pile of ashes at her feet.

"He didn't?"

"They threw him in here. It was revenge. I think they're killing their own. It's what they're like. They must have thought he did something wrong."

Tommy was listening intently as Mabin spoke.

"I wish they'd throw the creep who messed with me in here," he said, staring down at the black pile of burned vampire on the silver floor.

As though in answer to a prayer, another dark screaming hulk flew out of the blackness and burst into flames above their heads, a twisting torch. It crashed into Mabin, screaming loudly in as much agony as the first burning vampire, but Mabin swiped at it with his left arm and easily knocked it to the ground. Maggie gasped and ducked and nearly panicked, her eyes wild at the scene of the second flying, burning vampire. The second vampire's screams did not end when it landed. It writhed in great pain, begging as the first vampire did, asking them to push him back into the dark, and for the short time it remained recognizable, they saw it was Tommy's former roommate, the vampire with carrot-long fingernails and hurricane hair. Tommy gasped and his eyes widened at the burning horror at his feet. He barely had time to recognize his tormentor. The vampire was simply there burning and shaking and crying out in the agony of the flames, and then gone. That instant, two more dark forms hurtled out of the blackness over their heads, and of course they, too, burst into flames as they fell into the circle of light. These were extremely obese demons, round and plump as elephants, and their fat bodies sizzled at Maggie's feet as they fried and took all of five seconds to be reduced to two more weighty piles of cinder and ash. This time, Maggie's screams accompanied their violent immolation. Tommy rushed out of the way, holding his head. "What are they doing?" he screamed. "It's not right to burn up all these people!" Maggie, too, was still screaming at the sight of the flying obese bodies. She screamed louder then when the flames climbing up from their bodies nearly engulfed her and Mabin and Tommy. She grabbed her brother and pulled him away to safety.

"I knew them, too! They were in the tank with me, too, the fat ones."

While several small flames lingered within the ashes of the obese demons, tiny burning spirits of what raging fires they had been, another final shadowy hulk arced out of the darkness above their heads, also igniting like a match and screaming when it came into the light. It fell into the ashes already on the floor, so that it slid across the shining silver screaming with pain and begging for the dark, until it mingled its ash with the others' in an instant and was silent. Maggie and Tommy and Mabin stood with the black remains swirling around their feet in little whirlpools, shocked at the sudden deaths of all these vampires.

"Hey, that was the last guy in my tank. What is going on? They burned them all."

"It's what you asked for, isn't it?" a voice interjected from the dark beyond the light.

Maggie felt a chill run up her spine at the voice's calm, cold, cruel tone of authority. It had a malicious quality to it, like an executioner's voice with a torturer's heart, and it was filled with irony. With her eyes acclimated to the light, it was difficult to see beyond their circle. In that darkness, she could barely distinguish the mass of captured vampires, creatures she and Mabin had sentenced to their present situation, arrayed in a circle around them, but she could feel the bulk of their numbers pressing around them, down on them, ready to burst in on them, and she sensed their malevolence. The cruel, self-possessed voice led her to look to her right, where its owner was standing in the forefront of the demons, clearly in the dimmest portion of the light and suffering from it. He appeared to be boiling from the effects of the light on him, as though in a pot of roiling hot water, but he resisted his pain and fought hard to remain where he was, refusing to retreat when he had something to say. She could tell he had something to say. He was itching to speak.

"Thumbs down on those vampires," he said, turning his thumb toward the floor and looking behind him for a reaction. Several of the vampires snickered in the dark, amused at the incineration of their friends. "Thumbs down for what they did."

The vampires standing in the edge of the light was a small, slender man with erect posture, his hip slung out to the side. He had maintained a tiny pot belly on blood. He was dressed in a waistcoat and ruffled shirt, and had a shock of dark hair combed back dramatically, along with large, catlike eyes. His very large eyes had very black pupils of the deepest black, and his skin appeared damaged and coarse and pock-marked. With his thumb still pointed toward the floor, he held his head in the air haughtily and sneered at regular intervals as he stared at them, baring his red teeth, as though a sneer had to accompany each painful breath he took in the light. Just from the looks of him, and his attitude, Maggie sensed he might be the most awful man she had ever encountered, in love with pain, his own and others, but she was oddly fascinated by what he said.

Tommy took a few quick steps toward him, and the pleasant surprise of it, the surprise of having a potential victim nearly come within his reach, brought a small smile to his face. He dropped his arms to his sides but then reached out one small, rough hand toward her brother.

"That's right. Come to me boy."

"Tommy! No!"

Maggie rushed to her brother's side, and Mabin soon followed, but the demon remained in the dim light, suffering but too proud to move or be intimidated. His flesh was blistering from the light, and his hand dropped to his side again when he saw the boy failing to come within reach.

"This is what I'd like you to do," he said to Tommy, baring his fangs and chomping on the air like a dog biting nothing.

"What's that mean?" Tommy asked. "What do you want us to do?"

"Come to us."

"Don't do it, Tommy!"

Mabin laughed.

"Look at you. Why would we ever do anything you wanted us to do?" he said quickly, nearly spitting out the words. "We'll never do what you want us to do, because you're just another fool who drank blood and is suffering now because of it."

The vampire tilted his head in offense, but went on.

"Oh, yes you will come to us. Eventually, you will come to us. They all do."

"Not all. Millions never did."

The blue-spitter pointed to the circle of light emanating from the tunnel above. This vampire had an arrogance to him, but also a lightness, as though he was made of pastry and didn't know he was flimsy.

"Look up there. Eventually, all the light will die out, and that's when mere demons cowering away from the light like us once again become vampires. All of us will be vampires again, hundreds of us, and you are only three. You will be ours when the dark comes."

"We'll be long gone by then."

"You yourself made escape impossible. You built this place so that it's impossible for us to escape. We'll see how you fare, trapped in your own prison."

"You don't see much."

Tommy pointed a small hand at the haughty blue-spitter.

"The same thing will happen to you that happened to those creeps who were in my tank with me," Tommy threatened. "You'll burn."

The demon broke eye contact with Mabin, turned to the side and moved two steps to his right, where he spun around back to them and stared with ferocity at Tommy.

"So you think I'll burn, do you, you stupid little boy?"

"Yeah, like all those others."

"Oh, them. We did that to them, sent them flying out of this cool darkness into the light to burn. Lovely, wasn't it? We burned your friends for you, Tommy."

Tommy stepped dangerously close to the vampire.

"They were not my friends, but why did you do that? It was really a mean thing to do."

The blue-spitter gave out a choking laugh, with residue from the night still in his throat, and he had to clear his throat of blue spit before responding.

"We burned them because, little boy, they wouldn't eat you. All that time in the tank with you, and they refused to eat you. We can't tolerate that kind of behavior from vampires, and we made an example of them. They paid the price for refusing to be what they were and not eat you whole."

Tommy's eyes widened with the information and he was shocked into silence.

As he stepped closer to them while speaking, one of the blisters on the demon's forehead came to a bubbling boil and popped. He screamed and shuddered and closed his eyes from the pain and suddenness of it, gasping as he reached up to feel the clear liquid dripping down his face from the tattered wound, his eyes widening in surprise.

"Damn this light."

Still, he would not step back into the dark, would not surrender his pride as a vampire. He raised his eyes to them.

"Well, Maggie Long Hair, I take the name of Noah, for I am going to lead you two-by-two into our world. You and your brother can come be one of us, but that thing can not."

He pointed angrily to Mabin with a quivering arm, snapping his arm toward him, his eyes narrowing, but he had to withdraw his arm immediately and step back into the dark, since his jacket had caught on fire. He screamed in pain and slapped out the flames with the help of his brethren, and once the fire was out defied his pain once more by stepping again into the dim light, agony still painted on his face.

"You'll have no rest while the light lasts," he warned. "It is the only thing keeping us from you, and rather than let you sleep, some of us will die. I will decide which ones and we will throw vampires at you all day long."

He gestured to another vampire behind him, making a throwing motion without looking back, and immediately another dark form, dressed in a plaid wool jacket and blue shirt with a red tie, came hurtling toward them in the air, with the predictable result. It screamed in terror and pleaded, "No, have mercy! Please! Not me!" but then ignited with a loud cry of agony once it reached the light. It arced down behind them onto the hard silver floor, there to burn and beg for the darkness and die in ashes within seconds, its face contorted with agony. It barely had a chance to object to its fiery and sudden death.

"Yuck," said Tommy.

"This is only the beginning. There are many of us who have failed as vampires, collaborated with you and been captured and tormented in those terrible vats of silver, and then there are those of us who have resisted. Karel wants to save us all. I do not agree with him. I have resisted, and I want the weaklings who submitted destroyed, for they caused our capture, and we will destroy them with a purpose, to destroy you. By the end of the day, when darkness comes, you will be so feeble it will be easy for us to come take your blood. You, Mabin, will be torn to pieces. The girl and the little boy will become like us."

It was too much for Mabin to endure. He turned away, realizing the truth of what the arrogant vampire said, and understanding that it would very likely come to pass. He saw no way out, and he crumbled to his knees suddenly, clutching his chest as though in pain. When he did, another blue-spitter, this one in a serape and sombrero and cursing in Spanish, was hurled out of the darkness toward him and transformed to a flaming, screaming ball of flesh in the light. The catapulted vampire descended with a flaming heaviness on top of Mabin. It knocked him to the floor of silver, and he had to scramble to avoid the flames, which reduced the Mexican blue-spitter to ashes quickly.

"I can't believe this is happening," Mabin gasped, nearly losing consciousness.

"This is my sentence on you!" Noah screamed, pointing at Mabin. Then he spun around to face the darkness. "And it is my sentence on you, all who did not fight those who imprisoned us and collaborated with the humans! You will burn today to weaken those we have captured. Your bodies will be sacrificed as punishment and so that true vampires can once again taste blood, their blood!"

Noah stepped toward the dark and pointed a finger skyward in a gesture of triumph, drunk on his own thoughts and waiting for the cries of joy and assent to rise from the blue-spitters.

Instead, Tommy spoke up.

"Ah, screw you," he said.

There was complete silence, complete as the darkness, in the cavern. Tommy's defiance had silenced the mass of vampires. His moment stolen from him, Noah spun around toward Tommy, furious, and stared at the little boy. He gestured for another hapless blue-spitter to be sent aloft and turned to flames, and the pitiful screaming creature, in some way shamed for not being enough of a vampire, rose into the air, headed for Tommy. It was one of the arrogant young girls attired in period dress Maggie had seen earlier, her frills and lace in flames as she arced through the air. Tommy quickly stepped aside and the burning little girl blue-spitter slid across the floor and ended in a pile of ashes. The disgraced girl barely had time to scream out before she was gone.

"As I said, screw you," Tommy said, his voice choked by a note of sadness for the young vampire who had died at his feet. "You missed. None of you ever does anything right. So, I repeat: screw you."

NINE
As the Light Dies

To fight off the bombardment of the blue-spitters, Maggie wrapped herself in her hair, as she did when she slept, out of the habit of cocooning within it to protect herself. She stood with her back to Mabin and Tommy while each watched for the next flaming blue-spitter to be hurled toward them out of the darkness, like a bale of burning, screaming hay.

As the hours passed and she dozed between attacks, her eyes drifted lazily up toward the tunnel in the ceiling, where the day's light constantly changed its intensity as the clouds passed by high above and the sun shifted its position in the sky.

She suffered greatly from her fatigue, but not as much as Tommy, who had been awake for days, and Mabin, who seemed to be falling apart before her eyes. Being trapped in his own prison seemed to drain Mabin worse than any of them, and he seemed sick and disoriented. Something strange was going on inside the cavern. Tommy managed to call out from his post whenever a burning hulk of flesh was about to fall on them and disintegrate, turn to ashes, but it was as though Mabin was drugged or drunk, and she could barely rely on him to warn them when a burning spitter was about to descend on them from his quadrant. He wobbled on his feet constantly, fighting to remain upright but failing often and tumbling to the floor out of exhaustion. For the eighth time, she rushed to him when this happened yet again as another blue-spitter, an old man in overalls, came screaming and burning in the air above them. The spitter came to rest at the edge of their circle of light, thrown short, but he was still consumed in a second by the bonfire of light. Maggie lifted Mabin's head off the silver floor, for he had fallen as the latest bale of fire streaked over his head. He could barely speak, and seemed to be fighting with his tongue to do so.

"I don't know ... why ... I am ... so weak."

"You're not weak, and we will get out of here. No one could have done everything you've done."

"I'm going to ..."

A whiff of the burning vampire at the edge of their circle reached them. Maggie gave out a little cough at the obnoxious odor, but the smell brought on a coughing fit that had Mabin convulsing in her arms in obvious agony. She held him tightly, fearing she might feel the life exit from his body. Finally, Mabin's convulsions eased and he laid back, his head resting on her shoulder.

"It's strange."

"What is, love?"

"I don't know what's wrong with me."

She stroked his head gently, feeling the moisture there that indicated sickness.

"Is that better?"

He gasped soft, gentle words into her ear in a husky voice.

"It's better when I'm next to you. It's all right if I die next to you."

She gave out a little cry and held her fingers to her mouth in a panic.

"You're not going to die. You can't mean that. You can't."

Maggie felt a hideous set of eyes on her. She noticed that Noah was watching them intently from the edge of the darkness, concentrating on each movement they made as a general watches a battlefield, pacing back and forth, probing for weaknesses in his enemies, a self-satisfied smirk accompanying his every agitated move. He had seen Mabin collapse and appeared to be in a fevered state of great excitement when he saw his foe fall to the floor. His pacing quickened to a furious back-and-forth walk, and he made a rapid gesture into the darkness.

"Prepare three more to be thrown into the light," he ordered, to the cadres in the darkness behind him. "Hurry!"

"Tommy, watch for more of those things flying in here," Maggie said. "Mabin's hurt badly."

"What's wrong with him?"

"I don't know, but you have the watch now. I don't think he can help us."

"Why? Is he bleeding?"

"He's not bleeding."

"Then what's that? It looks like blood to me."

Tommy pointed to Mabin's chest, where a dark patch of red stained his shirt. She cried out but touched it, and immediately a kind of excitement flowed up through her from her fingertips that she had never experienced before, something like a pleasant shock of electricity and an intoxicating explosion of light in her brain. She wanted to taste the blood. What Mabin had said was true. She was a vampire, too, and her nostrils flared in anticipation of the feast.

He could barely breathe, but he spoke, realizing what she was feeling.

"Don't ... do it."

"I ... don't know what you're talking about."

"You want to taste my blood."

"You ... Well, you might say that, but I don't, really. No, I don't. I love you. What happened to you?"

It was all she could do to keep her bloody quivering fingertips from her mouth.

"I love you, too. Do you want to be like them?" Mabin gasped. "Do you want never to see the sun again, or daylight?

The wind through a field of wildflowers? If you taste it, all those things are gone. You'll become a creature of the night."

"Why are you bleeding? You're making this so hard for me!"

She was quivering all over with the feelings of blood-lust she was forced to resist, and with the panic she felt at Mabin's injury and fading consciousness.

"I'm sorry. I ... didn't know I was ... bleeding."

"Open up his shirt. See what's wrong with him," Tommy said. "What's the matter with you, Maggie? Do something! He's the one who's hurt, not you."

She had been so confused by the sight of blood on this boy she loved, not knowing if she should hold him and cry out in pain or lift her fingertips to her mouth to taste him that she hadn't thought of the obvious thing to do. She hadn't thought of discovering the source of the wound. She unbuttoned his shirt and immediately she heard Noah cry out from the darkness.

"It's done! I got him!"

He had been watching this scene and now saw what they saw.

"Hurl them toward the light now!" he screamed. "All of them! I want all of the vampire sinners thrown at the girl now!"

A narrow shaft of silver protruded just above Mabin's heart like a large nail, except this silver shaft had no head on it but only a bloody narrow flat end.

"She's found it! Throw them now!" Noah screamed.

"It just takes one taste, Maggie. Don't." Mabin insisted weakly.

The words were barely out of Mabin's mouth when the first of the flaming blue-spitters descended upon them. Out of the darkness, screaming as had all those before him, came the hulk of the burning vampire, a fat man twisting in the air to escape his agony but on target. He crashed directly on top of Maggie but then bounced off to the side after the impact. He hit the floor so hard that he shattered, simply broke up, and left several pieces of burning flesh on the floor next to her.

"Pull that thing out of his heart!" Tommy screamed. He had ducked as the fat flaming blue-spitter flew over his head.

Mabin looked down at his chest.

"Silver stinger," he said dreamily.

Then it seemed as though the entire sky was filled with screams and flames as four more burning vampires descended like flaming meteorites toward her. Another overweight vampire, a woman, landed on top of her, and this time she had to push it off and onto the floor beside them as it burned, singing her hands, but almost before she could push it away, another extremely skinny female vampire landed on the floor and skidded toward her, instantly disintegrating into ashes. She kicked the ashes aside. Two more, a cowboy and a businessman in a blue suit, fell at once on top of her and knocked her to the floor beside Mabin. She could not move or fight under their weight. They screamed in agony and wriggled desperately at the pain of their burning, and they cried out so loudly on top of her that she nearly went deaf. They turned to ash without igniting her, but covered her in their black soot, the same black soot that all the burned vampires left as a residue. Tommy grabbed her hands and tugged on them, extricating her from the pile of vampire ash but not giving her a moment's rest.

"We've got to pull that thing out of Mabin," Tommy said. "That's what they're trying to prevent. They want him dead. That's why they're throwing so many vampires at us."

She struggled to her feet and found Mabin covered in ash on the floor. His shirt was still open, but the blood had caked in the ash, covering the wound and the shaft of silver stuck in his chest. He was unconscious and barely breathing.

"What are you waiting for?" Tommy yelled. "Pull the thing out!"

Maggie was staring at the new blood seeping from the wound in Mabin's chest, mesmerized by the tiny gusher of red pumped out by his still-beating heart, so Tommy pushed her aside and brushed the wet ash and blood off of Mabin's chest. As Maggie watched, he examined the surface of his chest carefully and felt around on it, finally finding the tip of the silver shaft. He gripped it between his thumb and forefinger, squeezing hard on the quarter inch of silver that was exposed, and then pulled out an eight-inch sliver of shining metal from Mabin's heart. Mabin shuddered, still unconscious and bleeding. He gasped, shuddered again and then settled motionless on the floor. Maggie froze out of the fear that something terrible had just happened. Tommy had the presence of mind to slip the silver dagger into his pocket rather than let the blue-spitters obtain it again and perhaps use it again. Maggie's thoughts were reeling in fear for what might have happened to Mabin as the final flaming vampire in this barrage, another businessman in a blue suit, came hurtling out of the darkness toward them and ignited in the light. The smell of it and the closeness of the fire on its flesh and its screeching pain deepened the dizziness she felt, and she collapsed onto her knees next to Mabin on the floor, in despair, for he was still motionless and pale.

"Oh, no, friend, this can't be your end, our end. What has happened? Don't end this way."

The latest vampire thrown into the light burned away to nothing a few feet from them, his life wasted, his death having no effect. Tommy pulled Mabin's wet shirt closed on his chest, but it did not alter his condition. He remained as still as death, his eyes wide open, staring at the tunnel of light above.

With a snicker, Noah stepped out of the darkness into the dim twilight at the edge of the circle of light, once again stepping into the burning pain the light inflicted on him. The pain he suffered shot through him as badly as ever, but again he endured it with a masochistic stoicism. Noah shuddered as his flesh sizzled, but still he resisted his agony. In fact, he appeared to love his pain, as though he reveled in it. He grinned in its presence.

"One of you is gone," he said, gasping in agony. "The worst one of you is gone."

"He's not gone!" Maggie screamed, tearing at her face.

"He is gone. No one survives my sting. He'll be torn apart once we have you. And once the light fails, we will have you."

"What if he's not dead?" Tommy asked the vampire. "Then what are you going to do?"

He moved closer to Maggie and leaned over Mabin. He slowly reached into his pocket and removed the shaft of silver and slipped it into Maggie's hand.

"Does he look as though he has one ounce of life in him?" Noah asked, sarcastically.

Maggie broke out sobbing, her body shaking all over.

"He doesn't."

"Then I would say he's dead. A fact is a fact, you agree. Learn from it. Mabin is dead."

Maggie sobbed uncontrollably, lifting Mabin by the shoulders to embrace him, her tears falling onto the blood and ash on his face and streaking down his cheeks. Angry now, she nearly cursed herself for even considering tasting his blood.

"You might as well come to us now," Noah said. "You're too weak now to do anything about us. I promise we can end all your suffering, once you come to us and we escape this place. Oh, we will have glorious fresh blood this evening!"

Noah put his hands together as though in prayer and raised his arms toward the light above in ecstasy at the prospect of drinking blood again and once again the light blistered his face and boiled his skin. The pain didn't seem to bother him very much, as he danced around in triumph, loving his agony now that he had triumphed.

Maggie stood up suddenly. She lifted her eyes to Noah and tilted her head to the side. She had a crazed look in her eyes as she stared at him and held one finger, the finger with Mabin's blood, before her face.

"This is his blood. It's mine now, since I have tasted him. I suppose that means we will come over to you."

"Taste it again to show your faith me."

"No! Maggie! No! Don't do it!" Tommy said. "Look at him. Do you want to be like him?"

Before Tommy could stop her, Maggie planted her finger in her mouth, her eyes rolling back in her head and her entire body shuddering with the taste of the blood. Her eyes snapped open and she snarled at Noah as he had snarled so often at her, and a diabolical smile rose to light her face.

Noah smiled in return at her good work and extended a hand to her.

"It's done, then. I'm glad at your decision. Come to me. I'll drain you of all but just enough blood to let you live. Soon, you won't be able to tolerate the light."

Maggie's eyes once again rolled back in her head as she took the first steps toward Noah. She staggered, but then regained her footing on the slippery silver floor and raised her arms high above her head in ecstasy. She danced sensually a few feet in front of Noah, barely lifting her toes from the floor, her long hair flying, as though in celebration.

"Come. We'll return for the boy after we take your blood."

Her eyes widened and she stared directly into Noah's.

"I'm coming to you."

Maggie's right arm suddenly shot down and the sliver of silver flew in a straight line toward Noah. It landed with a thud in his chest, surprising both him and the knot of blue-spitters that had gathered behind him in anticipation of Maggie's arrival and her provision of fresh blood. So great had been the force of her throw, powered by rage, that the silver disappeared into Noah's chest without a trace, just as it had disappeared into Mabin at some secret time without a trace. Noah collapsed to his knees, reaching out for Maggie, who stood emotionless, staring at him. Her entire body shook.

"You ..." he said, and fell toward her. "... did not tell me the truth." He crawled a few feet into the light, catching fire as he did so, screaming but making it far enough to grasp Maggie's ankle.

"Why did you lie to me?" were his last words to her.

Then the light did its work. Within seconds he was reduced completely to ashes.

"So much for that creep," Tommy said.

Maggie turned solemnly and returned to the center of the circle of light, walking as a nun walks after prayer, her arms stiff at her sides. She knelt again next to Mabin and lifted him in her arms, covering him with the blanket of her hair. Tommy knelt also and hung his head in sorrow.

"I promised you never to drink blood and I didn't drink yours," she said to Mabin. "What should I do now?"

He did not answer, his lifeless eyes pointed skyward. Above them, the evening light was fading and night was coming on.

They were frozen in the circle of light.

TEN
Rescue

Maggie knew it was not in the nature of any of the blue-spitters to care for one another. At Noah's order, without hesitation, they had thrown their fellows into the light for the most horrible of deaths. While she sat holding Mabin's body in her arms and the light failed, caring for him now that he was dead more than she had ever cared for anyone, there was not a single expression of sorrow for their lost leader from the hundreds of captured vampires. With all memory of him gone, they waited with one thought: to take fresh blood when the night killed the burning light. Noah had lived a tainted life, and now he was nothing, not even a faint trace of remembrance in any blue-spitter's mind. No one cared, but the blue-spitters did still care about the new blood that was about to become available in their midst. When the darkness came inside of Saint Mary's Mountain, the fight among them for who would drink and who would be left with nothing would commence and degenerate into a riot of vampires, like rabid dogs fighting over two small pieces of bleeding steak. Both Maggie and Tommy knew this, and their silence with each other confirmed the dangers of falling before this pack of sick dogs were real. The vampires had no sense of human kindness or caring and each was forgotten as soon as he died, with not a single memory of what he had been in any of those twisted minds.

Maggie wept as she held Mabin in her arms and rocked back and forth, now and again glancing up to the circle of light shining down on them and remembering how it had been to live in the light, to fly, to love. He had been with her for such a short time, yet in that time they had experienced things that few people ever had, and she knew that once she understood all about what had happened, understood why he needed to trap the blue-spitters in this mountain and why the great enterprise had ended this way, she would have a great thing to ponder for the rest of her life. She would know a great thing from her association with him, and she stroked his still-warm cheek with the thought and murmured she loved him. It was all she had left of her time with Mabin, that hope of understanding. Maybe in the future it would be something great to know, a wonder to remember what it was to do something out of love, but for now she had only sorrow. Understanding she should at least make an attempt in her grief to recall the best times, she had tried to recapture alone what she had had with him and what she had been. She tried to lift herself up and fly toward the light with his body, with Tommy trailing behind holding her hand, but the power to suppress her attempts that the silver inside the mountain held was too great. She never rose an inch off the floor, and she felt the entire weight of the mountain pressing down on her. It was pressing down with the weight of his death, but also with the weight of hers, which she knew was coming soon.

"Did you love him?" Tommy asked.

"Yes. I loved him all of a sudden and at once, as soon as I saw him."

"Who was he?"

"I don't even know that."

"I liked him a lot, especially if you loved him. He was a good guy, you could tell. If it wasn't for him, those things would have killed me a long time ago."

Tommy pointed toward the circle of vampires closing in on them, and as he did so, they jumped back in fear. Crowds are cowards and act that way even when they don't need to.

"Wait a minute. Do that again," Maggie said.

"Do what?"

"Raise your hand toward the vampires."

"Like this?"

Once again, when Tommy raised his hand toward them, the blue-spitters retreated in fear.

"Did they ever do that before?" Maggie asked.

"Are you kidding? All they ever did was torment me, dunk my head in that blue junk they loved so much to slurp up like pigs and tell me when the time was right they'd drink my blood."

Maggie gently laid Mabin's head down on the hard silver floor and then stood up. She remembered something Mabin had said to her, that if one of the blue-spitters died, his powers passed to Karel. It was a frightening thought, for now that Noah had killed so many of his own kind in the attempt to get to her blood, all of those blue-spitters must have passed their powers on to the black wolf above them. There was that even darker side to this disaster inside the mountain, but there was also another side to it, she believed now.

"Did you ever think you could fly, Tommy?"

He thought she was joking and said, "Like this?"

To his amazement, he elevated a foot off the floor and hovered there. Out of the dark despair of mourning, a spark of joy and hope rose in Maggie's heart. Tommy looked more surprised than anyone that he hovered in mid-air, attached to nothing.

"What am I doing?"

"You're flying. Mabin told me something once. He said that if one of these vampires died, his powers were taken by the most powerful among them. You were the one to pull the spike out of Mabin's chest."

She looked down at the still figure below her on the silver floor, and her tear fell onto the silver floor beside him and she shuddered with regret. Even good news has no effect when a loved one has died.

"Wait a minute. He was a vampire?" Tommy asked.

"Everybody in this valley is. He told me that, too, but he was good and never took the blood of another."

"So that means I'm a vampire, too?"

"I think so. I'm not quite certain of that, or what all of this means."

Tommy dropped to the floor.

"Oh, man. What next? Now I'm a vampire."

"Can you fly any higher than you did? Maybe we can still get out of here."

"I guess I can try. Why would I want to be a vampire? I never did anything to deserve it. I don't even really believe I can fly."

"That's not how these things work. I never had any idea I was one, until I started climbing the walls my first night here."

"So you think I could fly all the way up there?"

Tommy craned his neck to look at the circle of light above them and then raised his arm to point to it. At the gesture, the vampires gasped in fear and retreated once again.

"I think you might be able to do it."

"Okay. I'll try it. Here goes."

Just as he was about to make the attempt, there was a small thud on the floor beside them, and both of them jumped off to the side in the twilight, startled and expecting another burning blue-spitter to disintegrate in flames on the floor beside them. Instead, there was a thick knot at the end of a rope, and with the sight of it a thousand things, fragments of fear, went through Maggie's panicked mind at once.

The bloody rope ... Karel's power is increased ... he's here and going to free them all ... all of the world is in flames ... Mabin was right ... We have lost ...it's the bloody rope ...

She expected the blue-spitters to close in on them now and clutch the rope to climb to freedom in a world ruled by those like Karel, blood-takers. She expected they'd pause only to slash open their throats and take what they'd longed for all this time, their fresh blood.

Instead, a voice called out to them loudly.

"Maggie ... Tommy ... grab the end of the rope. I'll pull you out of there. One at a time, grab the end of the rope!" the voice shouted.

Whoever it came from, the voice echoed inside the silver cavern as though amplified, booming off the smooth walls and floor and ceiling, and in an instant Maggie's heart soared from fear to hope. She thought for a second it might be a trick, a ruse that Karel would use to get them in his power, finally to defeat them, but then that seemed absurd to her, since she and Tommy already were in his power and he had only to wait a short time until the light faded before he could kill them and free the other vampires. It made no sense that Karel would attempt to save them. Around them, the light was fading, and soon the stars would be twinkling above this grave of theirs if she did not make the correct decision immediately. The circle of blue-spitters was closing around them as the darkness crept into the remains of twilight protecting her and Tommy. They were ten feet away, and then eight, some with sizzling skin that caused them to press back but all with a hunger for blood that compelled them to push forward again, their eyes all focused on Maggie and Tommy in a sort of perverted stare, a thousand perverted stares out of the dark. In their lust for blood, they had no individual identities, only the one communal thought of a group intent on their destruction, and she had only moments. She made the only decision that gave them a chance to survive.

"Take a hold of the rope."

"You go first."

"Tommy, grab the rope!"

"Both of us should go."

"He said one at a time. Nobody could pull both of us up at once. Now grab it and jump, before neither one of us can get out of here."

Tommy's eyes widened in fear at the prospect of never escaping the inside of the mountain and he reached up and took hold of the rope a foot above his head and twisted his arm around it to secure the grip. He grasped it with his other hand and before he could leap the fisherman above gave a mighty tug and he rose into the air. His power assisted the ascent, making him light as a sparrow and nearly as adept at flight, and he rocketed skyward while the blue-spitters groaned at the loss of half their feast. They covered their eyes with their arms as they watched him disappear into the light. The rope dropped again with a thud beside her and she heard Tommy scream from above.

"Come on, Maggie, they're almost on you. Grab the rope and let's go."

She smelled the rank breath of the spitters closing in on her and heard their whispers so close she nearly froze in fear. One screamed as the light burned him, and her head snapped up to see him blistering in the weak glow from the tunnel.

"No. I'm not leaving Mabin's body. I won't let them have him. I can't stand thinking of what they'll do to him."

"Maggie, come on! You have to leave him!"

"No! I won't!"

She grabbed the end of the rope and slid it under Mabin's motionless form, just under the arms, and then pulled it up and around to form a secure knot. Something brushed her hair, and she turned to see a blue-spitter so greedy for her blood that he had entered the circle of light and touched it. His skin was sizzling and there was the agony of his burning and the lust for her blood fight painted on his face. His blue oxford-cloth shirt burned to tatters instantly and his pants and penny loafers smoked, about to ignite. He retreated a few steps with a snarl for her, unable to endure the pain of burning to obtain her fresh blood.

"Pull on the rope!" she screamed. "Pull him up now!"

Mabin's head rolled over to the side as he rose toward the light, and she watched him ascend slowly, his body utterly still and twisting in the light, an ascent to safety by a dead man that took forever. While she watched his body ascend into the light of the tunnel, she felt something brush against her hair again. Not just one blue-spitter, but a second touched the flag of her long auburn hair now, as they could no longer wait for the light to fade but had to drink her now. She spun around, thrashing at them to drive them off, and then she found what she was looking for on the floor, the sliver of silver that had killed both Mabin and Noah, and wrapped her fingers around it. What had killed them could save her. She stood and spun around again in desperation in a great circle with the spike held out before her, the horde of blue-spitters pressing toward her out of the dark, just an arm's length away, many now with their skin blistering and sizzling, but overpowered by their lust for her blood. "Get away!" she screamed. "Get back!" Her words had no effect. She thought she would save the thin silver shaft for the first demon who attacked her, plunge it into his heart and then deal with the others. She spun around and raised the silver spike for all to see as another touched her hair, and they pressed back against the hordes pressing forward in a fight between blood lust and the pain brought on by the burning light.

"Come over," an old man bent over with age croaked to her, groaning in agony as the surface of his skin burned. "Noah said you would be one of us. Come over, and you can be with us. We just want enough of your blood to live, not all of it."

"Get away!" She swung out the hand that held the silver spike. "I won't do it, ever. Mabin wouldn't want it."

They retreated with fear at the mention of his name, but then pushed forward again.

"Then we tear with the fangs, and we taste with the tongue, and you die. We will taste you till death."

"Tear her, tear all of her. Oh, taste her."

She slashed out with the silver spike again, and as she did, the knotted end of the rope hit one of the spitters in the head, breaking open his blistered skin and sending the water inside the blister running down his face, causing him to yelp in pain. The rope settled on his shoulder and she saw the only chance of survival she might have. She rushed toward him, screaming as loudly as she could in desperation, and kicked out at his chest, sending him tumbling backward, the rope falling to the floor in front of her. From behind, another of the spitters dove toward her, grabbing her ankle, and she slashed downward with the spike and tore open his wrist, freeing herself and wounding him mortally. She leaped to grasp the rope at as high a point as possible and when she had it she slashed out blindly with the silver spike in her other hand as the blue-spitters converged on her.

"Pull up the rope! Get me out of here! They have me! They have me, Tommy! They're all over me!"

She felt the rope move up an inch, but then there was an arm around her waist and she knew the spitter would try for the back of her neck, to tear it and bleed her. Blindly, she slashed over her shoulder with the silver spike and her instincts were right. The spike tore into something soft, and the clinging vampire cried out in pain and dropped off of her. The rope moved another few inches upward and her feet left the floor, but now there was another blue-spitter with his arm around her waist and another gripping both feet. She had only one hand holding tightly on to the rope, and she felt it slipping. She buried the point of the silver spike in the arm around her waist, and with a hissing noise the vampire let go and fell to the floor. Somehow, she was still rising, slowly, but still rising. A blue-spitter tugged on her hair painfully, and she screamed, but its grip was weak and he could not hold her. The vampire with his hands gripping her ankles was rising with her, and then the darkness fell, utter and complete darkness, the sun gone to rest, and she could see nothing. She was six feet off the floor with only one blue-spitter holding her down, and then suddenly he coughed, choking as the spitters did every night on their stolen blood. She felt one of his hands slip off her ankle, and he gave out a retching sound. She felt his fingers slip, and then he vomited and he had to let her go as his guilty convulsions were uncontrollable. He fell onto the heap of vampires crowded below her, and once again the blue-spitters commenced their uncontrollable night-time hacking and spitting. Their curse had freed her.

"You let her go!" a spitter cried out at the last vampire who had a hold on her. "You should never have let her go. Now we have nothing!"

She could only imagine what they would do to him.

She was as light as a feather and alone in the dark rising toward more darkness, knowing what she had escaped and thankful for that escape, and now that she was free her heart soared and raced wildly with relief as her destruction fell away below her.

"Thank you," was all she could murmur. "Thank you."

But she didn't know who she was thanking.

She was free. She was flying when she thought she never would again, and she felt the wind from above entering the tunnel and lifting her spirits. She raised her eyes toward the opening of the tunnel with the hopes of seeing all those glorious rays of starlight in the gorgeous night sky, with her only regret being that Mabin would not be there to see them along with her.

ELEVEN
Escape

At the bottom of the tunnel, just above the gigantic cavern holding the blue-spitters, they secured Mabin's body and began the ascent, pulling themselves hand-over-hand by the rope up the incline, still a thousand feet away from freedom. In the dark, Maggie could feel Mabin's stillness in her heart as she left him behind, but she knew she had to climb to escape without him, that his stillness would forgive her until she could retrieve his body. She was wrong about never seeing starlight again with him. She saw it in his still-open eyes.

She was as determined as ever not to leave him behind, to save his body from the vampires, but she had to extricate herself from the situation first and then reclaim her lover. If there had been a light above it would have been easier to climb, easier to reach for that goal, but instead the darkness had taken complete possession of the night and forest above. Neither the man who saved her nor Tommy had said a thing once they pulled her out of that pit of vampires in the bowels of Saint Mary's Mountain. Exhausted, they had tied Mabin to the end of the rope and begun their ascent without speaking, silenced by the presence of death, the man wearing a thick wrap around his head like an Arab and Tommy so weak from his long ordeal that his knees nearly buckled with every step. Each of them was secured to the rope with the kind of tie rock-climbers use around their waists, and the progress to the surface was slow and difficult and trying, with each of them gasping for air, sapped of energy, but each of them knowing they could not quit, given what was below. There was no choice but to endure every agony of every step that the climb demanded.

In the last twenty feet, Maggie smelled the sweetness of the burning pines and saw the light of the forest fires at the end of the tunnel. Instantly, the pleasant fragrance, plus her impending freedom, lifted her heart and eased her exhaustion. She could feel the oppression of the pit flee as she rose to regain her strength in the world where light ruled and darkness was only temporary, and as soon as she had entered the world of light again, she turned without hesitation and pulled on the rope, dragging up hand-over-hand the loving dead weight she had left behind so far below. Once escaped from the silver tunnel, a tremendous rush of energy and strength returned to her, as though the poisoning effects of the heavy metals of the cavern were washed away by the freshness of burning pine and the fierceness of freedom. Tommy had collapsed on the floor of the forest after the climb, next to the man who had saved them, and now he lay on his back staring at the night sky, his chest heaving. He seemed to glow from the fires' light. When he saw what she was doing, he jumped to his feet, grabbed the rope and made the same effort she did to bring Mabin back to the surface. His tiny figure beside her, working so hard and suffused with the same energy that drove her, astonished her, since most boys who had been what he had been through wouldn't have been capable of much aside from tears and madness and hysteria.

"It's all right, Tommy. I can do this. Why don't you sit and rest?"

"We've got to get him out of there, no matter what. If it wasn't for him, we'd all still be trapped in there, vampire meat. We can't leave him to those things."

Together, their hands flew over the rope, more powerful than a machine, raising the Mabin's body up the steep slope so quickly it appeared in minutes. They had dragged him to the surface faster than they had been able to clamber out of that pit, due to their renewed strength at their escape, and as soon as his body appeared, Maggie untied the rope around him and sat embracing him on the ground, his limp body across her lap and her long hair covering him like a shroud. She wept again for him as she held him tightly on the pine needle floor of the forest, the blood dried now on his wound and shirt, his limp hand trailing among the pine needles as she rocked him back and forth in mourning.

"Oh, Mabin, it's my fault this happened to you, it's my fault. I should have been more careful, sweet boy. I'm always too quick to do a thing, Mabin, too quick to do anything. I was rushing to find you, Tommy, and I was not careful."

She let out a cry, tears streaming down her face, when the man who had saved them from the blue-spitters rolled over on the ground, groaning. He was dressed in combat fatigues and army boots, his head still wrapped like an Arab's. He sat up, one hand rising to his head as though it pained him, and then he slowly unwrapped the cloth. Stephanovich Emory, her murdering step-father, emerged from under the head wrap.

"Maggie! Get up! It's him! It's him!" Tommy yelled. "He just wants to kill us!"

Stephanovich was too groggy to react very much to what Tommy was yelling. Instead, he stood shakily, wobbling as though he might fall, and again held his head.

"It took every inch of rope we had in the store to get you out of there," he said. "It's worth it to have you back, but I don't feel well. I don't. I just don't have the same powers you two have."

Maggie felt herself recoiling from the man who had murdered her mother, all the confusion she felt before meeting Mabin returning to fluster her, and her eyes instantly raced over Stephanovich for any evidence of a knife or gun or other weapon. She and Tommy had escaped the vampires only to fall into the hands of their original tormentor and she had no idea of what sick plan he had for them. She found the silver spike in her pocket and gripped it firmly, wondering if it could kill a mere human.

"I'm so sorry about Mabin," he said.

"We know what you –"

"Why did you get out us out there?" Maggie snapped at him, interrupting Tommy. "Are we going to become your victims now?"

The question appeared to confuse him.

"I had to get you out. You're my children and the vampires had captured you. I've been fighting for months against the vampires, and they had my son and daughter."

"I'm not your son!" Tommy screamed.

Again, Stephanovich appeared confused by such a lack of gratitude.

"Yes, you are, and I love you both very much. I know some bad things happened in the past, but once I figured out what had happened, I knew this was the only place you could be."

"You knew all along what they were doing to us," Tommy said.

"What sick thing are you going to do to us now?" Maggie yelled.

Again, Stephanovich appeared confused and exhausted, looking from one to the other.

"Why, nothing. I don't have your powers. I can't do a thing to you."

Now it was Maggie's turn to look confused, as the anger drained from her. Stephanovich seemed so harmless, and spoke so gently, that it was hard for her to believe this was the man who had so ruthlessly destroyed her mother, heartlessly ended her life. She clutched Mabin's body close to her, as though it could still protect her, and rocked back and forth again. Tommy stood beside her, as though he was going to protect her, even though his fear and anger were transparent. Stephanovich collapsed to the ground again, sitting there cross-legged, still confused and overcome with fatigue as though he had received a blow to the head.

"I can't believe I climbed all the way down there and back up," he said. "I just can't believe it. I've never done anything like that before in my life."

It was as though he was talking to himself, as though he was stunned by his trip down the silver shaft to the pit of vampires, stunned by what he had seen there and astonished by the rescue of his children. He was not a creature made for adventure. Maggie stared at this handsome, hapless man, so feeble yet so strong in his determination to extricate them, to do the things he did in climbing down into the pit and pulling them up to safety, and she was surprised that he had succeeded when both she and Mabin had believed they were doomed. She remembered her first night in Vampire Valley when the voices had told her down was up and up was down and thought maybe Stephanovich's personality was an odd mixture of good and bad traits that easily confused anyone who was not careful to read him accurately. He had saved them, but he had murdered her mother. How could those two contradictory actions exist in one person?

"I still don't know what you intend to do to us," she said.

"I'm going to take you home and love both of you. We'll have a big meal and rest. I know it must have been awful for you these first few days in Montana. The vampires haven't made it pleasant for anybody."

The wind whipped up, sweeping away the remnants of smoke hanging over the peak of Saint Mary's Mountain, but then it died down again and a thick blanket of smoke blew in to settle over them like a memory. Maggie didn't quite know what to make of her step-father's talk of loving her and Tommy. It made no sense for him to murder their mother and love her children. She didn't know if it was designed to confuse and blind her in the same way the smoke from the forest fires did, but when the hazy air settled over her and she felt Mabin in her arms she remembered again that night transporting the blue-spitters to this mountain, how she and Mabin had soared over the valley together while Karel struck with lightning and fire and smoke below them, how the entire valley seemed to burn with his anger, the trees all matchsticks. A movement in the forest out of the corner of her eye caught her attention. Something large was lurking among the giant soaring pines. When she saw it she realized she had no time for memories. She saw a second giant black form slip between two tall trees and hide, and then she was dead certain they faced a greater danger than they had ever faced before, when Mabin was alive and could protect them. She had thought Karel would have transformed into a storm and begun his strikes on the valley at this time of night, igniting more gigantic fires and burning more virgin forest, but she realized it made more sense for him to attack his enemies where they stood, now that Mabin was dead and they were weak, rather than attack in an indirect manner and burn the forests in an attempt to free the blue-spitters. Karel had lost the element of surprise when Maggie caught sight of him, and she wanted to make certain he knew he had lost it. She wiped Mabin's hair from his forehead, kissed his lips and then stood.

"Where did you park the van?" she asked Stephanovich.

"It's at the trailhead. Elsa is waiting for us there with it. Why?"

"Because we're going to have to run for it. There's a vampire in the forest, the worst one of all of them."

"A vampire? Where ..."

Stephanovich did not have to finish his sentence to find out what she meant. Before he could, the towering black wolf stepped out of the forest and into the clearing, still just one half of what he had been before Mabin tore him in two, but then his second half stepped out of the trees behind him. From both halves the insides of the creature leaked, guts trailing behind the first and tumbling out of the second as it walked. Karel seemed even larger than he had that night on the roof, and Maggie remembered what Mabin had told her about the increase in a vampire's powers by the death of other vampires. Many had died inside Saint Mary's Mountain, burned in the rays of daylight streaming through the tunnel, and Karel must have assumed their strength. Looking up at him was like looking up at a mountain from its base. He stepped off to the side, wary of her, too, for Karel knew the same rule and knew that if Mabin was dead, someone had assumed his abilities.

"Not again," Tommy said. "Not him again."

Stephanovich was frozen to the spot, just as his words were frozen in the air by the sight of Karel. He stared up at the huge wolf, stuck dumb and silent.

"I'll take that body now," Karel said.

"You're never going to so much as touch it," Maggie replied at once.

She held up the silver spike, and Karel stopped in his tracks.

"So you have that?"

"I do."

"Then I don't care much what the three of you do tonight," he said. "All of you are insignificant, and since I know how weak you are, I can take you anytime I want. For tonight, the three of you can go, if you let me do to him what he did to me. Give me the body to tear to pieces and you three can leave, for tonight."

"She said you couldn't have it," Tommy chimed in. "Are you stupid, or do you just not listen to smart people?"

Karel glanced at Tommy.

"Hello, mouthful. Did you say something?"

"Yeah, I said stay away, or else."

If such a creature as Karel was capable of mirth, he would have shown it at Tommy's threat.

"Maggie, what are we supposed to do?" Stephanovich whispered.

Karel immediately swung his gigantic head toward them, his hearing so acute whispers were like shouts to him.

"You can't do much of anything," he said. "Now give me what I want and you can leave, or suffer the consequences. He did this to me, so justice says I must do the same thing to him, only worse."

"You think that is justice?"

"I know it. Give his body to me!"

Maggie turned to her step-father, while watching Karel out of the corner of her eye.

"Pick up the body, Stephanovich," she said.

"You want me to pick up the body? With him here?"

"That's what I said."

"If you touch it, you will be the first one I dismember."

"Pick it up, Stephanovich. Don't worry about him. I'll take care of him."

"You?"

Stephanovich hesitated, looking first at Maggie and then at Karel, but then he stepped toward Mabin with trepidation. The black wolf leaned toward him, threateningly, as if about to pounce, and Maggie stepped between them.

"Get out of my way, little girl. I won't tell you again."

"It's you who are in my way, because anywhere I go with Mabin is my way. You are in my way. You get out of my way."

She held up the silver spike and as though by magic it twinkled with the light of a dozen stars.

"So you think you can spike me? That might prove to be a little more difficult than spiking a spitter. In fact, if you try it, you will die at once."

Maggie crouched and pinned her gaze on Karel, waiting with a burning concentration for the move he would make to take Mabin from her and carry him off to dismember him, and the gigantic black wolf narrowed his eyes and raised his upper lip in a snarl, intent on doing just that. Behind Karel, his severed back half was less conscious of the combat about to take place between Maggie and his forward parts, and Tommy was keenly aware of the unconscious nature of Karel's posterior. While Karel squared off against Maggie, his attention focused with great malevolence upon her, Tommy quietly worked his way behind the black wolf's back legs, and it was then Maggie heard his voice.

Don't bother to think of it, Mabin seemed to say. *Just do what you have to do.*

A quick glance at the boy's body told her he was still dead and could not possibly have spoken to her, and with that knowledge she quivered with the pain and injustice of it. Still, she believed the dead boy knew what he was talking about. She could not think of what she had to do if she was going to do it properly, for thought brought fear and any move against Karel had to depend on pure speed of movement, a radical slashing of the beast without fear. She was hearing voices again, but they were the voices of reason in her head, not the voices of chaos from the vats of blue-spitters. When she shot forward, Tommy moved at the same instant, but her move was so swift she was on Karel immediately, with no time to see what her brother planned. She slashed with the silver spike at Karel's giant paw, as big as a serving plate, before the wolf could think, intending to disable him rather than kill him at that moment. She did not believe she could have killed him at that point. The black wolf roared with agony as Maggie's thrust the spike into his foot. She was too savvy to drive it all the way into him, knowing it would impede her if she did and knowing she would need it for further combat. Instead, she raked the point across the foot to do as much damage as possible. Karel stumbled. He nearly toppled over but then regained some control of his damaged paw, despite the pain, and managed to remain upright, limping off to the side toward the forest with an annoyed growl. It was then his ears pricked up and his eyes widened as he saw what Tommy was doing. Her little brother had the Karel's back half in his grasp, both of his tiny hands wrapped around the beast's immense left rear leg, and he was dragging the two back legs toward the tunnel. Maggie knew at once where he had gotten the strength for this feat, from Mabin, he had inherited Mabin's strength, and with a powerful pull, Tommy brought the pair of legs down to the ground and continued to drag them toward the pit. Karel saw that his back half was about to disappear down the tunnel and he let out another great roar, greater than the first, and leaped toward Tommy. It was too late. The little boy tossed the black wolf's hind quarters through the opening of the tunnel, where they disappeared down into the mountain, sliding down to the blue-spitters. Maggie leaped toward Karel, this time flying over his head and slashing down with the silver spike to tear open his ear, and just as the gigantic jowls of the wolf were about to wrap around Tommy, the pain from the spike pulled up his head like a tug on the bridle of a horse, halting him. Tommy scooted off to the side safely and after a moment there was a huge splash as Karel's back legs fell into the vomit of the blue-spitters far below.

Karel turned quickly to Maggie, who had landed at the edge of the forest.

"It's the boy, isn't it, not you?" he asked.

She feigned ignorance.

"I don't know what you mean."

"I mean he has Mabin's powers, not you. You have the silver spike, but he's the one who pulled it from Mabin. He's the one I have to contend with now, not you."

"Oh, you'll have to contend with me. You'll have to contend with us both."

Maggie moved off slowly to the side, pretending to be frightened of Karel, so that his eyes would follow her and not see what was happening behind him. As soon as Stephanovich knew it was safe, he picked up Mabin's body and slung it over his shoulder. He quietly disappeared into the forest with it, heading down toward the trailhead where his wife waited for him in the van, while Tommy sneaked up behind Karel. Maggie waited to see what Tommy was going to do and stood quivering in fear before Karel, just five feet from his mouth, easy prey. For some reason, Karel hesitated in snapping her up into his jaws. Perhaps he was not quite certain he could destroy her. When she saw Tommy had stepped on the end of Karel's intestine, which trailed on the forest floor behind him, she knew she had to run. Tommy smiled and nodded at Maggie, and she was off, streaking into the forest in a blur, just ahead of Karel's jaws, which finally snapped down, nearly catching her trailing long hair. Frustrated that she had been so close and he had not been able to capture her, Karel leaped forward, only to feel the searing pain of his intestines being pulled out behind him, as they were pinned to the forest floor by Tommy's foot and he was rushing forward. He roared once again, and had to cut short his pursuit of Maggie into the woods while he turned to see why he was in such great violent pain so suddenly. Now he roared at Tommy, and that roar was all the inspiration Tommy needed to lift his foot and flee into the forest behind Stephanovich. He moved so quickly he was no more than a tiny blur, but Karel was able to keep the blur in sight, and immediately loped after him, entering the glowing forest where the boy had, his giant head moving back and forth as he scanned the trees for his fleeing quarry. Below them, as they fled through the woods with Karel in pursuit, the tops of the tall pines were engulfed in flame, Karel's handiwork from the night before, and the light from the flames lit the forest with a golden light and illuminated the four figures rushing downhill toward the trailhead. Stephanovich was still in the lead in the race, with Tommy just behind constantly glancing back over his shoulder. Maggie ran down the hill off to the side, but closed quickly toward Stephanovich, and Karel was making his way through the forest behind them, slowed by his size but still gaining on them. Ahead, a giant torch of a tree cracked in the middle. Its flaming head crashed to the forest floor, sending a shower of sparks into the night air directly ahead of them. Maggie caught up to Stephanovich just as he cut to the left to avoid the mass of flame that had fallen from the sky to ignite the forest floor. He was breathing hard in the smoke-obscured and flame-filled forest, but he had a firm grip on Mabin's body and was making good progress downhill toward the parking area at the trailhead.

"Are you all right?" she asked.

"I'm fine, but I can't move fast enough. I know he's going to catch me before I get there."

Maggie took to the air, again unconsciously, as her front foot simply elevated her upward rather than down again onto the pine needles of the forest. She swung around in the air, flying faster than any of them could run, toward Karel, who was just twenty feet behind Stephanovich.

"Whoa, look at her!" Tommy said, pausing to tilt his head up as his sister flew over.

In the bright glow of the firelight, her long hair was like a burning flag trailing behind her, and Karel had no difficulty seeing her coming. He side-stepped to avoid her as she flew over, and as he did so he raked his claws over the side of a tree, sending a shower of sparks up into the air. She flew directly through the sparks, closing her eyes as she did so, and when she opened her eyes again, she had to halt suddenly to avoid crashing into a tree. She turned in mid-air and caught sight of Karel again. He had continued in his pursuit of Mabin's body, blinded by his blood-lust for revenge. Maggie set off again after him holding the silver spike in front of her, intent on driving it into him now to finish him off once and for all. Karel caught up to Tommy. Instead of sinking his jaws into him, he simply brushed him aside, sending him tumbling down the mountainside in a ball. He wanted Mabin's dead body and was made insane by his anger and his hatred for his dead foe. The giant wolf was just two steps behind Stephanovich when Maggie descended on him, wondering if it would work, would kill him, if she drove the spike into his skull. It's too late now to know, she said to herself, as she crashed into him, both hands in front of her aiming for the point between the wolf's two ears. The impact sent them tumbling to the ground as Karel howled in pain and she grunted with the impact on the forest floor. She stood quickly, knowing the wolf's first move would be to pounce on her if she simply lay there, and she discovered she still held the silver spike. It had grazed Karel's head, opening another wound and dazing him, blood running down into his eyes. He did not pounce immediately, but slowly rose to his feet, wobbling and unsure of himself, until he caught sight of Maggie standing before him defending herself with her shining weapon held in front of her.

"Long Hair, you're on fire," he said.

She glanced at her shoulder, and it was true. The sparks Karel had raked into the air when he saw her flying toward him had caught in her hair and ignited. Still holding the silver spike with one hand in front of her, she quickly patted the flames on her shoulder with the other, smothering the fire. She shook her head in case any other embers were stuck in her hair.

"I'm not on fire," Karel said.

It sounded odd and foolish for him to say such a thing, but then Maggie realized how dazed and confused the blow to his head had left him. Again, his feet nearly slipped out from under him, and he staggered off to the side. His eyes caught hers, and as he tottered she thought she saw a stupid grin come to his face. He blinked, his eyes so heavy they nearly closed for good.

"Got to get away," he murmured. "Got to get away from the girl."

It appeared for a second he had fallen onto the pine needles of the forest floor, but then Maggie realized he had melted, just as he had that first night Mabin had pointed him out in the clouds. Karel had shape-shifted into a puddle of black ooze at her feet, but he did not remain there. As liquid as water, he flowed downhill quickly and came to the base of an unburned tree. With great rapidity, instead of flowing farther downhill, he shot in the form of the black ooze up the trunk of the tree, reaching its top in an instant and then disappearing into the clouds. A bolt of lightning crashed down and landed far ahead of her.

She cowered, keeping her eyes on the sky in case he would come back. When she let her eyes settle back down onto the earth again, she saw that below her Tommy and Stephanovich were still running toward the parking area in the glow of the firelight, picking their way through the dark trees backlit by the fires. Once again she looked to the sky. The thunder cracked and the lightning flashed, but after another moment she thought it was finally safe and followed her brother and step-father downhill to the van.

TWELVE
The Destruction of the World

"What's wrong with Mabin? What happened to Mabin?"

Elsa was in a panic and rushed from the van when she saw Stephanovich and Tommy exiting the burning forest carrying Mabin. Stephanovich was so exhausted from the long run down the mountain that he could barely hold Mabin's body as he staggered onto the parking lot, and Tommy had to run beside him propping the dead boy up on his step-father's shoulders. Stephanovich collapsed onto the dirt parking lot, letting Mabin down softly on top of him as he did so as though he did not wish to injure him further, and Tommy helped the body come to rest without further injury. Maggie was two steps behind them, hurrying to catch up and help them.

"Don't drop him," she said. "Lay him down on the ground gently."

"He's just sleeping, isn't he?" Elsa asked. "There's nothing wrong with him, is there?"

An agonized look from Stephanovich, who was on his hands and knees on the forest floor overcome by exhaustion, told her there was something very wrong with Mabin. Tommy bit his lip in silence and stared at the body on the ground, while Maggie slumped down next to Mabin, her eyes as moist as a doe's eyes, and stroked the dead boy's forehead.

"Oh, no," Elsa said. "He's not, is he?"

No one answered but instead they hung their heads.

"How did it happen? It didn't really happen."

A sudden loud explosion just up the hill startled them from their grief, as another lightning bolt from Karel's hand struck just twenty feet away from them, sending a splatter of pine needles and sparks and wood flying up into the air around them. The concussion from the explosion settled in a few seconds, covering them with debris, but then an odd gurgling sound rose in the forest where the bolt of lightning hit and in the soft glow of the forest fires Maggie saw a thick red liquid coagulating in a pool formed by the lightning strike. A narrow stream of the red liquid broke out of the pool, trickling downhill toward them, and then Maggie realized what the red liquid was. It was blood. Tommy saw it, too, and stood up in awe and disgust, his mouth dropped open in wonder, until he shook his head and rubbed his eyes as though they itched.

"It can't be."

All questions about what the liquid was were answered when another bolt of lightning struck just behind them. Instead of a shower of pine needles and sparks, they were instantly splattered with blood. The blood stuck Stephanovich and Elsa in the face, while Tommy and Maggie felt it hit their shoulders and the backs of their legs. Even Mabin's face suffered a splattering of red splotches, and the dry ground around them was pitted with red, as though raindrops of red had fallen in the dust. Elsa and Stephanovich were wiping their faces when another strike hit at the front of the van, again throwing up a shower of red, but this time the blood drenched the van, filling the air with the sounds of metallic pings, as though a cascade of stones had hit the vehicle. Without wiping off the dead boy's face, Maggie quickly lifted Mabin by the shoulders to his feet.

"We've got to get out of here!" she screamed. "He's tempting us! If we don't get out of here, we'll be covered with blood and unable to resist it."

Elsa let out a cry of grief and immediately ran to the van and swung open its back doors, while Tommy and Stephanovich helped Maggie drag Mabin's body across the blood-soaked earth and into the van. They leaped inside, as another bolt of bloody lightning shot down from the sky. It struck precisely where they had been recovering from their exhaustion on the ground, again sending up a large spray of red that fanned out over the van again, just as they were closing the back doors. Elsa and Stephanovich clambered across the floor of the van to the front seats and immediately started the engine, while Maggie and Tommy sat in the back with Mabin's body. A huge red flash exploded in front of the vehicle, engulfing it in a tidal wave of blood that rocked it back and forth and nearly stalled the engine.

"Get us out of here, Elsa!" Stephanovich yelled out. "I can't take this! I can't take the blood!"

The engine roared to life as Elsa stepped on the gas and turned on the windshield wipers at the same time. The wipers stalled at first at the thickness of the blood they were asked to remove, but then whisked the red lumpy liquid aside so that the glow of the forest fires and the road down from the mountain came into view through the two clear arches on the windshield. The van leaped forward and struck a pot hole full of blood, sending another splash up to splatter the side window of the vehicle. Maggie screamed and jumped back, thinking irrationally that the blood was about to strike her face, but then the van hit a clear, straight stretch of road and leaped forward, raising a trailing cloud of dust behind them. Karel aimed for the van but hit the dust, as the next bolt of blood from the sky crashed down just behind them. Elsa pushed down hard on the gas pedal again and the van flew in a straight line on the unpaved road toward the highway. Two bolts of red lightning struck simultaneously on the left and right of the van, but it was moving too fast now for Karel to strike it with any accuracy, or splatter with more blood. They raced fast toward the highway, the skies clear now.

Almost without slowing down, Elsa turned the blood-soaked van onto the highway and raced toward home.

"Is it stopping?" Elsa asked. "Has he given up?"

A flash of lightning and a crack of thunder behind them told them Karel hadn't given up, but instead had retreated into a previous mode of attack, once again hurling hot white lightning down onto the earth to ignite the forests. The van hurtled into a thick bank of smoke, so thick that Elsa had to ease off the gas pedal and slow to a crawl, just to gain a few feet of visibility in front of her. Several more explosions behind them shook the vehicle. The smoke screened them from Karel's attacks but it slowed their progress so greatly that it took nearly a half-hour to creep through the dark and smoke and reach home. Home was barely recognizable to Maggie, more like a castle on top of a foggy mountaintop than a development house, and even though she had spent so few days calling it her home, it could not have been a more welcome sight. The grinding noise of the garage door opening automatically suggested safety was just ahead, but once they had crept through the garage door opening and parked inside, the grinding closed of the garage door reminded her once again how dangerous her step-parents could be. Now she and Tommy were trapped inside the house with them. They opened the back doors of the van and all four of them took part in silently sliding Mabin's body out of it, holding it aloft, keeping it from touching the concrete floor as though it was a religious artifact that would be defiled if allowed to touch the earth. They had to work their way with the body around two large black drums near the door that led to the kitchen, and once inside they carried Mabin directly to the dining room table, where they laid him out under a golden candelabra. For the first time, they saw fully the price he had paid for his adventures of the night before, his torn and bloody clothes, his disheveled hair and the dried blue caking on his arms and legs and face.

"This never should have happened. The strongest among us died. What are we going to do?" Elsa asked. "He was the last protector."

Her question had no answer. Maggie and Tommy had no idea what she meant by that, that he was the last protector, but their step-parents' grim depression seemed to match the way she and her brother felt and looked. She and Tommy were just as battered as Mabin appeared to be, with disheveled hair and various substances splattered over their clothes and faces. Tommy wiped the hair out of his eyes and touched Mabin's face gently. Maggie felt herself weeping, along with Elsa, and even Stephanovich had moist eyes that dropped tears onto the walnut tabletop.

"Did he say anything before he died?" Elsa asked.

"He said he failed and that was the worst part."

"Failed? He didn't fail, but I knew he'd think like that at the end. He was that good."

"He didn't fail," Maggie said emphatically. "We have half of the blue-spitters trapped in Saint Mary's Mountain, and we're going to make sure we trap the rest of them there."

"You're going to take them?" Stephanovich asked, staring directly at her.

"Tommy and I are. Right, Tommy?"

"If you say so. If that's what we're supposed to do. I'd really like to do to them what they did to me."

"I don't know if you realize what you're facing if you try to do that alone."

"She's not going to do it alone," Tommy said quickly. "She's doing it with me."

"But you're not protectors, or I don't think you are," said Elsa. "Karel is far worse than anything you're seen so far, and you can't defeat him without Mabin. Stephanovich and I are helpless against him. We have no powers. If you try to do what Mabin did with the blue-spitters, he'll kill you."

"I threw half of him into that hole in the mountain. How bad can he be? Kids at my old school in Manhattan were worse than him."

"Were they vampires? Did they take for themselves all the powers of evil a vampire can take for himself?" Stephanovich asked.

"They were just bad."

"And some of us are worse than others. Some vampires enjoy what they do, taking blood, and think their lifestyle is the only lifestyle there should be in the world."

"Once they start, it's the only way they can live, off of others," Elsa added.

"Maggie and I can stop them."

Stephanovich bit his lip and was silent for a moment. Then he raised his eyes to Maggie with great determination.

"I think it's time you understand what's going on here in Vampire Valley. Come with me."

Without another word Stephanovich turned from them and headed through the kitchen and back out to the garage, where the blood-soaked van was parked next to their immaculately clean SUV. Maggie and Tommy and Elsa followed silently but quickly, each realizing that time was essential, that all of them had to move quickly and with great effect to defeat Karel. There were hundreds of vats of blue-spitters still to be moved to Saint Mary's Mountain, and only a little boy and a teenage girl to do it. Stephanovich was pulling up the lid on one of the black barrels, straining with the effort of removing it, but by the time Maggie and Tommy reached him, the lid was off. They moved closer, and then they saw what was inside and they did not like it.

"That's disgusting," Tommy said.

"Why would you keep a barrel full of blood in the garage?" Maggie asked. "Wouldn't that only attract more vampires?"

"It's not blood," Stephanovich said quickly. "It's the antidote."

"What's that?" Tommy asked. "The antidote?"

"It's why Mabin collected all the vampires and why he was taking them to Saint Mary's Mountain. It's the cure. He was going to return their health and well-being to everyone, and would have succeeded if things hadn't gone wrong."

"You mean if we hadn't come along," Tommy said.

"I didn't mean that."

"We can cure vampires?" Maggie asked.

"It cured us," Elsa said. "It can cure you, when you're ready."

"Wait a minute, I'm not convinced I'm a vampire," Tommy said. "I'm not sure my sister is, either."

"After what you've done you don't believe it?" Stephanovich asked.

"No. If we were vampires, we'd be drinking blood all the time like the rest of them."

"That's not the only thing we do."

"What else is there for a vampire? Drink blood, sleep all day, kill at night."

"There's more," Stephanovich said. "Come with me."

With that, he topped the barrel with the lid and banged down on it with his fist, sealing it tightly with a single blow.

"What a minute," Tommy said. "What's in the other barrel? More antidote?"

"I'll tell you later. Right now, I want you to see some technical data. It's important you see this data."

Once again, without another word, Stephanovich led the way as they traveled from the garage, through the kitchen and the dining room and into the living room, hurrying as though their lives depended upon getting to the low coffee table fronting the couch, where Stephanovich sat and immediately opened a drawer filled with papers. He collected the papers into a neat, thick stack, placed them on the table and rifled through them, intent on finding a particular one. There were printed and hand-written sheets of paper, but Maggie could make no sense of what any of them said, until Stephanovich pulled from that chaos of information a yellowed, ancient sheet of paper and handed it to Maggie, seemingly pleased he had found it.

"That paper begins the history of the vampire virus," he said, triumphantly. "It's the virus we all have now."

As soon as the sheet of paper touched her hands, Maggie knew from the feel of it that there was something odd and wicked about it, that its crinkled surfaces, splotched and stained and covered with strange, twisted characters, simply felt threatening, as though the information it contained could leak into her fingertips and inflict harm on her with its evil intentions.

"Wait a minute. There's a vampire virus?" Tommy asked.

"There is, and we all have it," Stephanovich said.

"All four of us?"

"No, all of us, everywhere. Every human being on earth."

"Every human is a vampire?"

"Every human has the potential to be a vampire," Stephanovich corrected. "It's blood that brings out the evil in us, when we take the blood of others. People like you and Tommy and Mabin are a little different and somehow have tremendous powers without drinking blood. It just works that way, I don't know why."

"How do you know that?" Maggie asked, challenging him.

She could barely tolerate the feel of the paper on her fingers, and she certainly could not read the strange language on it, but she held on to it hoping it might tell her something, some secret.

"That paper records the beginning of the Transylvanian Mystery, as the church called it," Stephanovich said, indicating the document Maggie held. "That sheet of paper tells the story of the beginning of what we're trying to end today, what Mabin gave his life to end. All of these papers document the research that went on here in the Bitterroot Valley at the Rocky Mountain Laboratory of Viral Research to discover why people drink blood, and why it gives them such immense strength and seemingly supernatural powers."

Maggie felt as though the piece of paper might burn through her fingertips, that it was attacking her in a devious way. She had to reach out and hand it back to Stephanovich before she went mad.

"I can't understand anything this paper says. I can't hold on to it any longer," she said, distressed. "There's something wrong with that piece of paper. Take it. Please."

She yelled the last words, which made Stephanovich reach out and quickly retrieve the yellowed sheet from her.

"You'd have to be an expert in ancient Slavic languages to understand it," he said, "and it does have blood on it. Did you touch this old, dried patch of blood?"

"I don't know, but I don't like that piece of paper. I never felt anything so creepy, not even the blue-spitters."

"I should have warned you about it. Other people have had the same reaction you did after touching it. Some of them never regained their sanity."

He put the yellowed sheet of paper on the tabletop. Even when she looked at it, it troubled her, seemed to threaten her.

She blinked several times and then forced herself to turn away from it.

"Mabin was bothered just as much by it as you are, when he first saw it," Stephanovich said. "It's a good thing, really. It shows you understand without really knowing what the paper says."

"It shows I understand what?"

"Everything. Everything else these papers tell us. I knew you'd comprehend this from the very beginning. You probably sense what's in the rest of all this, all these papers that took so many years of research. You understand them without reading a single one of them, and it makes me think you have the same great powers he had."

Maggie let her eyes fall to the papers on the tabletop, but she got no sense of foreboding similar to the one she had when she allowed her gaze to rest on the yellowed sheet of paper marked with odd characters again. She shuddered and had to close her eyes and turn away from it before it did make her utterly insane.

"I don't understand anything you're talking about," she said, confused and frustrated. "They're just papers."

She waved her hands wildly in the air to vent the pain and frustration she felt in the presence of the paper detailing the Transylvanian Mystery.

"But the research? You understand the research, don't you?" Stephanovich asked, almost in desperation. "You understand what your mother and father had to do with this, don't you? They must have told you something about it."

"Why are you bringing them up? I don't want you talking about them. All I know is they were murdered."

"But you don't know why?"

"No, but you seem to know a lot about it."

"Yeah, why do you know so much about it?" Tommy asked suspiciously.

"Because they started all this, all the chaos in this valley and around the world. They drank blood."

Maggie let out a scream, and Tommy stiffened so much and shook in anger so badly it appeared he might break in two.

"No, no, no. That's not what I remember about them," Maggie said. "They weren't like that. They were decent. They were doctors and they helped people. That's what they always told us, and if they couldn't spend a lot of time with us, it was because they were busy helping others. I know they were good people, even though at the end they weren't there for us all the time. You're lying to us now. Why would you lie to us?"

Maggie's face was contorted with anger and pain.

"I don't know how else to tell you this. They were doctors, and they helped people once, but in the end, they drank blood. We sent them all this research asking for their help, and instead they misused it to increase their own powers."

"You just shut up about them!" Tommy said. "You don't know anything about them! They were good people!"

"I'm sorry. I thought you might have figured this out by now. At first, they agreed to work on the vampire virus antidote with us and then they became frustrated and weak and just decided their work was pointless and life would easier if they simply gave in to the virus. They knew that it did its worst when activated by human blood, that it gave a vampire all these incredible, evil powers like the power to change shape and the power to fly and live forever, but they also knew drinking blood made the vampires terribly allergic to heavy metals, like silver and lead and gold, that that it made it impossible for them ever to live in daylight again. They weighed the positives and negatives, and they came to the conclusion that it was pointless to deny people the powers they always wanted, pointless to deny themselves, so they drank blood and figured out a way to dispense the virus through an aerosol spray worldwide. They infected the entire world."

Maggie felt the blow of a sledge hammer that struck her but did not wound her, the sledge hammer of disillusionment, and she stared at an antique grandfather's clock that had belonged to her parents and now stood in the corner of the living room. She watched its pendulum swing back and forth after the blow to her head and dignity and concentrated on nothing but the motion of the pendulum, hypnotized by it, not wanting to hear what Stephanovich was saying. But she had heard it. She made her mind a complete blank out of desperation. As calm as she was at the news of what her parents had really been, Stephanovich was at the opposite end of emotions, so agitated and pacing fretfully now that it seemed he might collapse from his agitation. His face was red and he was hyperventilating. He was muttering and throwing his arms wildly in the air in a way she had never seen anyone do. Spit was flying out of his mouth without his control as he spoke. The horror of her parents' vampirism nearly made him insane.

"They wanted to destroy the antidote that they had created. All of this work ..." Stephanovich paused to sweep the papers off the table and onto the floor with one motion of his arm. "All of this work, they wanted it to go for nothing, once they drank blood. They lost their minds, and then –"

Stephanovich paused here and stopped to stare at Maggie helplessly, now seemingly calm and focused on her. She finished his sentence for him.

"And then they infected you."

"Yes."

"So you killed them."

Stephanovich froze for a second, staring at her.

"Maggie, what else could we do?"

Maggie covered her face, but before she did, she saw Tommy staring at Stephanovich with the kind of horror he reserved for tombs and blue-spitters.

"Yes, what else could we do?" Elsa repeated. "They were killing everyone, drinking blood every night and not regretting any of it. We had to do it. They were as bad as any of the other vampires, or worse. They killed Mabin's parents and drank their blood, but they didn't count on the powers they unleashed when they infected him, too. They thought that a mere boy couldn't hurt them and that they were invulnerable, but they weren't. Mabin would have stopped them if we hadn't killed them first."

"They weren't really aware of what they had unleashed, but they loved it, loved the power they had," Stephanovich said. "We trapped them at twilight, and then –"

"You killed them," Tommy said. "We know how you killed them."

"Yes, we killed them. We separated them and killed them."

"So now you're going to kill us," Tommy said.

"No! Why would we do that? You're the only ones left who can protect us. Once we took the antidote, we were powerless, but we weren't going to drink blood. Mabin had more powers than any hundred of them combined, but now look what's happened to him. We thought he'd fix all this, deliver the antidote to the blue-spitters, but now –"

"Now the job's only half-done," Maggie said.

She moved next to Tommy and put her arm over his shoulder and he turned to embrace her, weeping at what he had learned about their parents.

"What do you want us to do?" Maggie asked grimly.

Stephanovich was silent for a moment, hesitant to answer, but then spoke calmly.

"We've got to get the rest of the blue-spitters into one place. We've got to get them to Saint Mary's Mountain and deliver the antidote all at once."

Maggie took a deep breath.

"Come on, Tommy."

"Where are we going?"

"We have to go back to the mountain."

"Tonight?"

"We have no time. The valley's on fire. Soon, we won't be able to see a thing, with all this smoke, and soon the fires will reach all the houses and burn them down, and we don't know what else Karel has planned. The blue-spitters will be free if we don't do this. Then Karel would have won and Mabin really would have lost. We all would have lost."

Stephanovich and Elsa had fallen onto the couch next to each other and sat there weeping and embracing each other, exhausted by their tale and full of regret at what they had done. Maggie led Tommy through the dining room, pausing to look at Mabin's still form in the dark and touch his face gently, and then she walked with Tommy toward the kitchen door.

"Do you think you can climb walls yet?" she asked. "You're going to have to learn to, really fast. You're going to have to learn that and a lot more."

THIRTEEN
Back to the Mountain

The night air was so fouled by the burning of the pine forests on both sides of the valley that Maggie and Tommy coughed at once and in unison as soon as they stepped outside the kitchen door. Maggie hadn't seen the sun in days. Now she knew what Mabin meant when he talked about missing daylight, missing the sun, as one of the worst parts of becoming a vampire. The night was terribly dark, unnaturally dark and ugly, and since there was so much smoke fouling the air, the dark had weight to it, like cheese, that they would have to fly through if they were going to deposit the rest of the blue-spitters inside Saint Mary's Mountain. Karel's fires had had another day to spread and burn the forests and blanket the valley with smoke. Maggie remembered what a great difficulty it had been at first for her to lift each of the vats of blue-spitters up into the air and then navigate through the sky with Mabin to the spitters' place of imprisonment. She remembered the columns of smoke and burning ash that had risen from the earth after Karel's touches of fire, and how she and Mabin had had to find ways around them in the sky, all while carrying each vat with its full complement of blue-spitters to the mountain. How she and Tommy were going to lift several hundred vats of vampires and fly them into the sky, navigate in the thick smoke, avoid Karel's blasts of lightning and deposit the demons in mountain by dumping them down the silver tunnel was beyond her understanding, a challenge to her confidence. Just do the thing, Mabin had said to her. Mabin had been an expert at fighting vampires, while she had been a novice, and they had experienced extreme difficulties while flying the first several hundred demons to the mountain. Now, she had reached an intermediate level in vampire combat, but Tommy was below a beginner's level in that art and it was just one more reason to miss Mabin, her love.

"The first thing we have to do is climb that wall," Maggie said.

"What do you mean, climb that wall?" Tommy asked, coughing in the foul air. "Who climbs walls?"

"Grab onto the wall with your hands and feet and climb up it."

"You're kidding, right?"

"I had to do it the first night here, and I didn't have anyone to tell me how, or even what I had to do. I just did the thing. Watch."

With a speed that surprised even her, Maggie leaped onto the wall and stuck to it by her hands and feet. She did it so quickly it was as though the wall had pulled her onto it of its own accord and she was stuck there by suction in her hands and feet she didn't comprehend.

"Whoa. I don't know if I can do that, Maggie," Tommy said. "It appears fairly difficult to do for a normal person."

"You're in Vampire Valley now. You're not normal anymore."

"I'm not?"

"No. Do your hands feel sticky?"

"A little."

"That's good, then. That's the way mine felt at first. Don't leap onto the wall the way I did. Just walk up to it and start climbing. I bet you can do it. I'm sure you can."

Tommy had the natural reluctance of the novice, and Maggie knew that if you didn't accept your powers, you couldn't use them. She had to explain them to him, patiently and in as much detail as time would allow. She had to let him know he had them, and then tell him how to use them. She knew Tommy had all of

Mabin's abilities after withdrawing the silver spike from his chest, but she guessed would be years before he would discover all of them, dig deeply into his own soul far enough so that he could find them hidden there. She'd keep the lessons simple for now, reveal only those powers he needed to get through the night, and help him realize what great things he had in him before they could use them. Even a small thing like climbing a wall appeared to be a challenge to him, but it was essential to the success of their mission.

"Is this what I do?" he asked, reaching up to grab for the wall. "What do I do with my other hand and with my feet?"

There was no need for further explanation, since natural ability took over. With one hand on the wall, the other grasped it as though it had its own intelligence. It was the same with his feet. Tommy scurried up the wall like a little spider, seemingly without knowing what he was doing, for a startled look came to his face before a smile of pleasure replaced it.

"Whoa! I can do it!"

"I told you."

He turned from her and scrambled toward the roof, so fast even Maggie had difficulty in keeping up with him, and he climbed over the gutter and onto the shingles without any difficulty at all.

"How did I do that?" he asked, when Maggie clambered up beside him. "I did do what I thought I just did, didn't I?"

"Yes, you just did it. All the best things come naturally. You just do them without thinking about it. They happen without intention."

Standing on the roof of their house again gave Maggie an odd sensation, a sort of sweet remembered queasiness. As soon as she felt the wind blowing the smoky air over her, and saw the thousands of burning pine trees in the distance through a break in the smoke, it was as though it was her first night in Vampire Valley again, and she imagined she had all the experiences she had already had ahead of her. It was as though she was about to discover the blue-spitters for the first time and wonder if she should join them. What had she been thinking? How lonely had she been, to contemplate befriending the demons? With Tommy there on the roof, it was as though she was about to fly for the first time, too, and about to meet Mabin. Then, without knowing it was coming, she shivered uncontrollably.

"What's wrong?" Tommy asked, when he saw her staring out over the valley.

"It's nothing. I was just looking at the fires and thinking about what's happened to me here. Come on, you have to learn to fly now."

"What?"

"Don't worry. You already know how. You climbed the wall, didn't you? You almost flew when you were inside the mountain."

"Climbing the wall was going up, and this is going down. Down is dangerous. Just because I can climb walls it doesn't mean I can fly."

Maggie walked to the edge of the roof, quickly and confidently. She wanted to show Tommy how easily it could be done, to show no fear at all, but she also wanted to escape from the memories of Mabin that would prevent her from doing her job. If she was to fly again, if she was to do the work that had to be done and get the blue-spitters into the mountain while Karel attacked them, she had to forget. Without letting Tommy see it, with her back to him, she wiped away a tear. Then she stepped off the roof and floated in midair. She turned around to face him and hovered there with a smile.

"That's how you do it."

"No, that's how you do it. If I did that, I'd fall like a rock."

Tommy glanced down over the edge of the roof. Maggie remembered when she had done the same thing before the first time she had flown.

"Tommy, you know you're a vampire. You can't be afraid of the things you have to do. Watch this."

With that, Maggie shot up into the air, flipped over in mid-flight, and then flew down again to hover in front of Tommy. Her long hair settled around her like a robe.

"You mean I can do that?" he asked.

"If you want to. Just step off the roof. Humans who aren't infected with the virus can't do this and shouldn't try it, but vampires like us can. We know now you're infected with the vampire virus and are a good person, so you can fly like this."

Maggie smiled at her little brother while she continued to hover in the air just a few feet in front of him, her long hair lifted by the wind. She held out her hand to him, inviting him to fly to her. He reached for her hand, but then withdrew his.

"I don't know about this."

"I won't let you fall. All you have to do is take the first step. You know what you are and what we have to do to make this place safe. You have to fly, Tommy."

A worried look crossed his face, but he raised his hand to her and lifted his foot. He held his foot in mid-air, and then stepped off the roof.

"Ooops."

He dropped several feet, but then suddenly rose to hover beside her, again seemingly without intending to. It just happened. He was flapping his arms as though that helped him maintain his position in the smoky atmosphere beside her, but once he realized it was not necessary to flap like a bird he raised a fist in the air in triumph.

"Yes!"

"I told you you could do it."

"It's easy, and kind of neat. Maybe being a vampire isn't so bad."

"Don't get any ideas, Tommy."

"Don't worry about that. I've seen what drinking blood does to people."

"Are you ready now?"

"I guess so."

"Then let's go."

With that, Maggie turned and shot in an arc across the sky. She knew exactly where she had to go, the house where she and Mabin had left off in transporting the vampires from the roof tops to the mountain dungeon. To give Tommy confidence, she didn't look back but instead flew directly toward the first house in the next rooftop row of blue-spitters to be lifted and carried off into the sky on their way to Saint Mary's Mountain. If he fell behind, or even if he fell to the ground, she knew it would be an experience he would learn from, and she was certain nothing bad would happen. But if it did, she knew it would only increase his understanding of his powers. It was a short flight, a short flight being best for a first-time flying vampire, but that did not mean it was an easy flight. Flying just one street over through heavy smoke, with Karel above hurling lightning bolts into the forests, was a frightening enough project in itself, but doing so with a heavy heart made it difficult for Maggie. The flashes and crashes coming from the sky increased as they flew, and she knew Karel had seen what they were attempting and would do whatever he could to prevent them from transporting the second convoy of blue-spitters to the mountain. She felt one rain drop, and it gave her hope that a normal thunderstorm would drench the valley and undo Karel's work, but she was not justified in that hope.

It would be another dry thunderstorm that night in vampire valley, with plenty of thunderbolts and it would be another night of hell for them. She landed on the first rooftop in a long row of rooftops, the familiar eerie blue-grey glow from the vat of blue-spitters engulfing her feet, and if Tommy hadn't landed beside her immediately, she might have lost heart. Seeing him succeed on his first flight gave her the courage to believe that she had the power to do what she had to do, even without Mabin, but it was with Mabin in her heart that she promised to herself to defy everyone who opposed her, to the death, no matter how difficult or awful the night became. She would defy them all to the death if they attempted to prevent her from doing Mabin's work.

"Well, we're here. What do we do now?" Tommy asked.

Maggie was staring at the eerie light engulfing her feet, set on her task.

"I think you know that, too, without thinking about it. You know what Mabin and I did to get all those blue-spitters to the mountain. Now you and I have to do the same thing."

"What happens if the wolf comes?"

"I don't think he will. He's busy trying to burn down the valley, and he might be a little afraid of us by now. He thinks if he makes it difficult enough for us by burning up everything, we won't be able to get the demons to the mountain."

"Well, he's wrong about that."

"I know he is."

"Should we look at them?"

Without giving her time to answer, Tommy bent down and lifted the lid to the vat of blue-spitters. As always, the sight was disgusting, with all six of the demons bent over and spitting and vomiting their blue bile at their feet. One saw Tommy and leaped up desperately toward him, his eyes wide with the possibility of getting out, while still gagging on the regurgitating blood.

"The bloody rope! Give me the bloody rope!" he cried out. "I want to get out of here!"

Tommy dropped the lid of the vat to let it fall closed heavily before the blue-spitter could tear into him.

"Whoa."

"What did you do that for?" Maggie asked.

"I don't know. I wanted to see them, that's all. I won't do that again."

He stepped away from the vat, and Maggie pointed to the opposite side of it. Now that Tommy was free, it was completely unnecessary to open any of the vats.

"There's a handle over there, and one here. Why don't you go grab that one and I'll take this one, and then we'll fly off with them over to the mountain."

"I guess I can do that."

"I did it. I know you can."

As soon as Tommy touched the handle, a tremendous torch of lightning, as wide as a freight train, bolted to the ground fifty feet from the house, sending up a hail of sparks and blasted soil that splattered the house like a thousand rocks shot from a canon. The strike had been so powerful that the crater where it had struck glowed brightly, like molten lava. Maggie jumped away from the vat and Tommy cowered near it, hunched over as the debris showered down on him. He didn't let go of the handle. The air smelled of sulfur and earth. Several of the sparks settled onto the roof but did not set fire to it. Maggie returned to the vat of blue-spitters.

"He almost hit us with that one!" Tommy said, still hunched over.

"He won't hit us. We're too close to the spitters. He knows that if he hits us, he kills them. I don't think he can hit us anyway. He's just not that good."

"Come on then. What do we do now?"

"We hold on to the handles, no matter what, and we fly."

"How do we know where the mountain is, in all this smoke?"

"We'll figure that out as we go."

"Got it. Just do the thing. Come on. I'm ready."

There was a rumbling in the sky like indigestion in a giant's belly as the clouds rolled along above them in the wind, flashing lightning as though about to belch fire to the earth again. Tommy grunted with the effort as he and Maggie slowly rose in the air with the vat of blue-spitters, inching their way up from the roof, and after a minute they were only thirty feet above the house. Even at that height, the air was thick with smoke almost to the point of being opaque. It was impossible to see more than a few feet in front of them. Tommy's determination to carry out his task could not overcome his caution over the newness of it. He was being overly careful as he held tightly to the handle and flew up slowly into the smoke. He glanced over to Maggie time and again as though asking her what to do.

"I know this is hard," she said, "but we have to go faster than this. We have over three hundred more of these things to carry to the mountain, and we have to get them there before dawn."

"All right, but how fast can I go? I don't know how fast I can go because I've never done this before."

"It doesn't matter. You can fly almost as fast as lightning."

Tommy's eyes widened at the knowledge of his vast ability to navigate the skies, but it appeared at first he did not believe her, but then after a few seconds something came into his eyes that told Maggie he did believe her. He nodded to her, and with that she looked away from him and closed her eyes, sensing where the mountain was, not knowing through all the smoke where it was, but sensing it. She had a feel for it and could go on nothing but impulse now. Her impulses had led her terribly astray before, but now she had to trust them. Again without thinking about it, she shot across the sky going as fast as she could and then shot up on a steep diagonal in an attempt to rise above the smoke. After several hundred feet of climbing, she looked back to see Tommy hanging on to his silver handle for dear life, grimly flying but barely keeping up. She slowed suddenly when she saw him in distress, but slowing so suddenly had a disastrous effect. He did not slow down, but continued to fly on just as fast until he realized what was happening. The vat of blue-spitters tipped over, the lid flew open, and one of the creatures tumbled out. The demon tried desperately to grasp a hold of the lip of the vat, but he was in such a weakened condition that his fingers slipped and let go, and he tumbled down through the smoke toward the ground. Maggie immediately righted the vat of blue-spitters so that the lid slammed shut, but Tommy tumbled over her head now and she realized his grip had faltered and he was flying free above her.

"Tommy!"

She worried he might fall to earth, but there was no need for that. Tommy flipped over as she had when demonstrating how to fly at the house, and he knew immediately what to do. He flew in a half-circle through the air to the bottom of the vat of blue-spitters and threw up his arms to support its weight.

"I've got it! Go get him!" he yelled to her.

"Can you hold it?"

"Don't worry. I've got it. Go get the blue-spitter."

She really had no choice in the matter, since one free demon meant all the demons would be free eventually. She let go of her silver handle and immediately hurtled down after the falling vampire, falling through the smoke so quickly she sensed the earth was about to meet her head-on all-too-soon, and then she caught sight of the tumbling blue-spitter. She still did not know how far they had fallen or how high they still were, but she was about to find out. Since he had been free only a few seconds, away from the toxic effects of the silver, the blue-spitter had not regained his powers but was still making a weak attempt to fly, resisting the pull of gravity as best he could but succeeding only in slowing his descent. Maggie shot down toward him, mindless of how close they were to the earth, and caught him securely by the collar and dragged him skyward just as his feet brushed the ground. He immediately attacked her, baring his fangs with a snarl and lunging in mid-air toward her neck, but she had a firm grip on him and held him off at arm's length. He twisted and turned violently like a fish on the line, his strength increasing with every breath of night air, but he was still no match for her. She pulled him skyward by the collar, worrying if Tommy was all right, flying as fast as she could through the thick smoke.

"Your blood will be sweet, little one, like candy, when I take it," the vampire said. "Give me just a taste of my sweet candy now, and you can go free, I promise."

She wouldn't dignify the request with a response. She caught sight of what she was looking for, that reflected speck of light in the sky. The silver vat was no more than a sparkling dot above her, but it was still aloft and in place, which meant Tommy was still holding it there with all his strength. In another instant of shooting skyward with the struggling vampire, she reached the holding tank, lifted its lid, and unceremoniously tossed the blue-spitter back into it, where he belonged.

"Sweet blood, give me your sweet ..."

She slammed closed the lid.

"Are you all right?" she asked Tommy, flying down to hover beside him.

"Sure. That was quick. This was no problem at all. I guess I really do have powers. I'm a pretty strong little kid."

"I told you."

"I almost feel like I could do anything."

She flew beside him, lifting her arms up to the bottom of the vat to take some of the weight off of him, and then they worked their way to the sides of the vat, walking with their hands on it through the air, still holding it aloft as they did so, and then they worked their way up the sides of it, holding the weight, until they reached the silver handles and grasped them.

"Are you ready?" she asked. "This time we're going to go as fast as we can. We have too much work to do to stop again or slow down at all."

"I'll watch you to see what you're doing. Go as fast as you want. I can keep up."

With that, Maggie nodded and bolted off through the thick smoke toward Saint Mary's Mountain, her grip firmly on the silver handle and Tommy in place opposite her true to his word, flying as fast as he could. The skies above them flashed again and again ominously, the flashes so huge they lit the smoky sky like daylight, but unlike daylight they offered no hint where Saint Mary's was. It made little difference, since Maggie was certain she could sense the cavern holding the blue-spitters, as though she had some sort of radar for them, and she flew straight toward them in the direction she sensed. It took only a few seconds before she realized the mountain was below them and began the ascent toward the drop-off point, with Tommy trailing behind flying with a tight grip on the spitters. They broke through the smoke and into the clearing above the landing platform, hovering for a moment before setting down just in front of the lid closing off the tunnel to the blue-spitters. The platform was splattered with a thick caked substance the color of rust, and although Maggie knew silver did not rust she thought something was wrong as the vat of blue-spitters came to rest on top of it. When they opened the lid to the tunnel and the soft blue-gray glow of the spitters below lit the scene, she realized the rust was dried blood, left over from the bloody lightning Karel had hurled at them earlier, and she saw that it was everywhere. It was in caked patches on the ground, stuck in the pine needles, and on the side of the mountain. It splattered the tree trunks and branches, and it covered the rocks. She felt a strange excitement when she brushed some aside with her foot, and inside the silver holding tank the spitters were extremely animated and agitated with the nearness of their favorite food.

"Be careful of that," Maggie said.

"It's that bloody stuff the black wolf threw at us, isn't it?"

"I think so. There's something very strange about it, though. I have a bad feeling about it."

"Me, too. Why's there so much of it?"

"He threw a lot of bloody lightning at us. I guess it just doesn't go away. Hurry up. Let's get these spitters inside the mountain."

With that, they flipped up the lid to the vat of blue-spitters and immediately turned it over to send them sliding down the silver tunnel to meet their friends. The spitters slid quickly down the steep incline, snarling and snapping their jaws as they went in the blue-gray glow, until they splashed down among the others after free-falling out of the bottom of the tunnel. Maggie slammed shut the top of the empty vat and turned to Tommy.

"I'll show you where we keep the empties in case we need them again," she said. "It's over –"

When she looked at her brother, Tommy's stunned expression and gaping mouth made her stop in mid-sentence. He was staring at something at the edge of the landing pad, his eyes raised upward to a point that seemed to end at the treetops. She heard a rattling and realized before she saw it that it was a rattlesnake, but for an instant she didn't understand why Tommy wasn't looking at the ground instead of toward the sky. He seemed to be staring at a rattlesnake in the sky, but then when she turned toward it, she understood.

"Oh, no."

"I don't like that thing very much," Tommy said.

The snake was reared up ready to strike, its head eight feet off the ground with the rest of its body coiled behind it, a rattle two-feet long shaking its warning at the tail end and its mouth wide open, its fangs on display. Its body was as fat as a man's body and its glistening red fangs were as long as Tommy's arms. It was covered with the same sort of blue slime that lined the vampire's holding tanks, and its red fangs, as red as the teeth of the blue-spitters, made Maggie think that this was a vampire snake, something related to the blue-spitters. She made the connection immediately between all the dried, caked blood covering the area and the possibility that the snake that grown to its unnatural size by drinking it.

"Recognize me?"

Maggie stepped back. The voice coming from the snake's mouth startled her almost as much as its sudden appearance. There was something familiar about the voice, but at first she could not say what it was.

"Do you mean you don't recognize me? You don't, do you? I rained down from the sky with the bloody lightning."

There was the inspiration of madness in the way the snake said it, spoken in the way an over-excited preacher would speak, as though the words were so crazy they couldn't possibly be true.

"So what does that mean?" Tommy asked, sarcastically. He, too, realized the snake was a vampire and therefore not worthy of respect.

Instead of answering, the snake struck out toward him, opening its mouth as wide as it could but stopping just short of devouring the boy. Its mouth was so cavernous it could have devoured him with a single bite.

"You missed," Tommy said, not moving an inch.

"I meant to miss. I thought you should know who it was who bit you and tore you to pieces before I did it. You still don't know me, do you?"

"I guess I'll never admit knowing you if you're going to kill me afterwards."

The rattler swung its head from side-to-side above them, blood dripping from its fangs, and the rattle at the end of its tail shook fast in agitation.

"It's a smart thing to say, but not smart enough to prevent what's going to happen to you. You killed me once, but you'll never kill me again. I refuse to die a second time, but I guarantee both of you will suffer the experience for the first and final time."

The way he spoke, and the quality of his voice, made it dawn on Maggie just who the snake was, or rather, who he had been. Before she could say the name, the snake turned and set his small eyes on her.

"You know me don't you?" it said, as though it was reading her mind.

"Yes. You're Noah."

The name rolled off her tongue with a bitter taste, while the fact that she knew him seemed to please the snake. It rocked back-and-forth with pleasure and a hint of a smile seemed to turn up the corners of its mouth. An anger bubbled up in Maggie at Mabin's killer that would have blackened the night further if she let it out, and she reached for the silver spike in her pocket, her eyes narrowing with hatred for the creature that had ended Mabin's life. She had the spike within her grasp but her hand shook so violently with anger and loathing she doubted she would be able to grip it firmly enough to remove it from her pocket and stab the beast.

"I told you I came with the bloody lightning. Karel took my powers when you killed me with the silver spike, but he gave my soul and my powers back to me in the lightning he threw to earth. This snake took me in when he drank the blood Karel threw at you, and he and I became one. We became what you see before you. It's most unfortunate for you it happened this way, but I rather like being a snake."

With a hatred seething in her that made her eyes red and narrow, Maggie caught Tommy's eye. His look seemed to say to her what she already had running through her mind, that the snake would die if she spiked it once again, but she shook her head, realizing the beast was too gigantic and powerful now for her to bury the silver into its chest with any precision. She would have to plant the spike directly in its heart while she grappled with it, and she did not even know where a snake's heart was located, or even if it had one. Tommy nodded at her insistently, but she shook her head at him with greater insistence at the impossibility of spiking the snake. A thought of escape occurred to her, for escape appeared to be the only logical possibility when confronted with such an overwhelming foe. With a barely perceptible look to the skies, Maggie indicated to Tommy what they should do, and with an equally imperceptible nod, Tommy indicated he understood what the plan was. She removed her hand from her pocket and grasped the handle of the silver vat nonchalantly, noticing that Tommy did the same with his handle, and she held on tightly as she turned toward Noah again.

"I don't know what you'd want with us when there is so much more fresh blood all around you, free for the taking, on the ground," she said. "Look. It's all over the place. Karel's been hurling the bloody lightning at us all night."

She waved her hand over the panorama of forest and hillside, and lightning flashed above them. A nearby stream even seemed to glisten with red as Karel's bloody lightning seeped into it from the ground.

"That's where you should drink."

"I'll drink my fill once you two are dead. All I want now is to kill you and avenge my own death."

"You'll have to wait a long time for that," Tommy said.

Noah ignored him, fascinated with the blood draping the landscape, covering the rocks and mingling with the earth and water.

"It's all old and dried, not a fresh drop among it, although it's still very tasty. I've drunk enough of it, and it won't compare to the sweet freshness of the blood I'm about to take from you two young ones."

Maggie pointed to the stream.

"Are you saying that's not freshest, coolest blood you've ever seen? Most vampires would kill for blood like that."

Noah could not resist the nearness of fresh blood, and the mention of it made him turn his head on impulse, eager to collect it. It was all the opening Maggie and Tommy needed. As one, they shot toward the sky carrying the vat up with them, and it was lucky they took the silver vampire container with them. Noah leaped toward them and would have snagged at least one of them from mid-air, but the vat obstructed his strike so that his powerful jaws slipped off its surface. The bite had been aimed at Maggie. His mouth clamped shut and his head brushed her feet, knocking her off-course, but as he fell back to earth she righted herself and continued to rise into the sky. A second strike by Noah had him hurtling toward them again in the sky, his mouth wide open and his fangs bared, but it was clear this attempt was going to fall short. He snapped closed his jaws several feet below them, realizing his failure, and fell back down to the blood-soaked forest. After rising another twenty feet into the sky, they stopped to hover above him as he curled up on the earth below.

"I know you'll come back," he shouted up to them. "You have no place to take the blue-spitters but here, and I'll be waiting for you. There's no escape. If you come back now, I'll let you live and allow you to be one of us."

"Forget it! No deal!" Tommy screamed down at him. "You're too creepy!"

Angered at the insult, the snake leaped up toward them again, but came up far short and fell in a heap back down to earth. He curled round and round himself at the entrance to the tunnel, tightly coiling his plump body as one circle inside another and another.

Tommy was moving his feet as though walking on air but he was going no where.

"It's a good thing vampire snakes can't fly," he said to Maggie.

"Are you sure they can't?"

"It looks like this one can't, and that's good enough for me."

"Come on. I'll show you where we keep the empty vats and then we have to go back for the next tank of spitters."

"What about him?" Tommy asked, indicating the snake below. "How are we going to dispose of the next batch with him here?"

"We'll think of something. It is a vexing problem, but we can't stop working now. If we don't get all the spitters into the mountain by dawn, it might be too late. Karel's just about burned down the valley, and if he comes up with anymore tricks like this one, we might be finished."

The smoke from the forest fires was so thick, and getting thicker, that flying another fifty feet up completely obscured the earth below. Maggie stared down at what she could not see, hating the snake all the while and thinking hard of what she could do to destroy it. They could not see Noah, and he could not see them. They flew quietly off to the side of the coiled snake and then descended to the spot Mabin had showed Maggie where the empty silver vats were stored, with Maggie thinking and thinking some more of the solution to her problem. Her hate seemed to get in the way of her thinking, so she knew she had to calm herself and think rationally to succeed. There was a time for reason and a time for impulse. They deposited this empty vat without a word to each other and then shot off up into the thick smoke again, with no indication that Noah realized they had been just a short distance from him. Tommy stayed close by Maggie's side, uncertain of just where they were in all the smoke but confident in her ability to navigate their way to the next rooftop of blue-spitters. They flew low and fast, even faster than Maggie had flown with Mabin, and with the night and the smoke so deep and thick they flew nearly blind, with only an occasional glimpse of the burning forests and streets and houses below. There had to be some way to lure that snake away from the entrance of the tunnel, she thought, but then she realized they couldn't simply draw the snake away, no matter what trick they might come up with, to let them work. They had to kill it, since it had proven its ability to return again and again to life. Maggie knew exactly where they were going, directed by a strong sense of direction that she did not comprehend or understand. It was simply inside her, another impulse, something she felt so strongly that it could not be wrong, something made stronger by the urgency she felt to kill of Noah. She flew silently, her jaws clenched, understanding that the vampire she had killed once in revenge inside the mountain was back, a problem returned in a larger, more lethal form, and that it would be even more difficult to kill him this time. His nasty personality remained, and was encased now in a more lethal body. She alighted on the correct rooftop, the house next in line from where they started removing blue-spitters that night, with Tommy landing beside her simultaneously, and suddenly, as if a light had come on in all this darkness, she realized what the solution to her problem was. It was so clear to her now how to kill Noah that she spoke quickly and emphatically, with great certainty.

"We have to go as fast as we can," she said, without explaining further.

"I know. You already said that. I still don't see how we're going to dump of any more of the blue-spitters into the mountain with that snake there."

"I told you. We're going to go as fast as we can."

"So? I still don't know what you mean by that. Just because we can go fast doesn't mean we can kill him."

"Yes, it does. Speed kills. Come on. We'll kill him with speed."

She gripped the handle on her side of the vat, a kind of focused fury animating her so deeply that she shook with rage, unable to contain the great anger at Mabin's killer that grew stronger and stronger the longer she hesitated in killing the snake. She couldn't stand that it was still alive. Everything about it was wrong. That it could live at all was wrong. Mabin should still be alive. It, Noah, should still be dead, instead of perversely risen as a new monster, and now that she understood how to kill it she knew it was no longer necessary to think calmly. She could be as angry as she wished to be. Thinking calmly would only obstruct them now.

"Whoa, Maggie. You look a little crazy. Are you all right?"

"I'm all right, but I am a little crazy. I can't stand that thing and what it did to Mabin. I hate it. Come on, let's go, and no matter what, don't stop or slow down."

She barely let Tommy grip the silver handle with his tiny hand before she shot off into the sky carrying the next vat of blue-spitters aloft, with her brother struggling to keep up and the vampires inside sloshing around in their own liquid. It was nearly impossible to soar across the sky as fast as she did, as impossible as flying to the stars by closing your eyes and wishing for it, but she was operating not on a wish but with a nearly uncontrollable rage that forced her to amp up her effort, to fly faster and faster. Miles and miles of sky flashed by with nothing to mark them but a blur of smoke and heat. In an instant, they reached the spot high in the sky above the tunnel leading down into Saint Mary's Mountain, but instead of slowing, Maggie immediately pointed them straight down and dove with the vat and Tommy toward the tunnel, increasing their speed manically with the free-fall, in a suicidal descent that was beyond their control now. The smoke thinned near the ground to reveal the giant sleeping snake still coiled at the entrance to the tunnel, unaware of what was about to happen to him. They had only seconds.

"You're crazy, Maggie! What are you doing? Stop! Slow down!"

"Never! No! No!"

The earth was coming up so fast it would soon flatten their faces.

"All right! Let go now!" Maggie screamed.

"Let go?" Tommy asked, still confused by what they were doing and watching the ground rush up to into their eyeballs.

"Let go! Now!"

They released the vat of blue-spitters not ten feet off the ground, with the snake suddenly waking up just before it smashed into him. They heard a thud as the vat crashed into Noah's thick body and tumbled over, spilling out the blue-spitters but still crushing and pinning the giant snake under its weight. Tommy and Maggie arced up out of the dive, brushing the pine-needle floor of the forest with their cheeks, but both knowing they had to dive down again immediately to retrieve the vampires before they escaped into the forest. Despite his present form, Noah let out a scream worthy of the worst of any living vampire when he was crushed, the cry echoing through the woods and splintering several trees. He was thrashing around, crushed by the weight of the silver vat, attempting to free himself from under it, his rattle working furiously in anger, but his body smashed and broken by the speed and weight of it. His giant head thrashed from side to side in pain, as he was dazed and still uncertain of what had happened to him, until he caught sight of a blue-spitter lying half-conscious and confused on the ground beside him. In his distorted mind, Noah must have blamed the vampire for the attack and immediately snatched him up in his mouth and swallowed him, just as the spitter came to and screamed in terror. Another blue-spitter was standing at the entrance to the tunnel, wobbling and barely able to maintain his feet, as dazed as the first blue-spitter Noah had swallowed, and then he disappeared down the snake's throat in the same manner as the first. Maggie grabbed two blue-spitters off the ground at once by their collars, and Tommy lifted the door to the tunnel. Noah snapped at her as she flew past him with the spitters, but she was out of range of his bite, since he was pressed into the ground by the weight of the silver vat, and she threw the two vampires into the tunnel immediately, watching them slide down it until they disappeared into the dark.

"You did this," Noah hissed at her, looking back at his broken body and realizing what had happened, and understanding he was going to die once again. "You are the one who did this."

It was as though he couldn't believe she had killed him once again, but she was too busy to pay any attention to him, since both of the remaining blue-spitters had come to after the crash, just a little stunned now but on their feet. Tommy swooped down to grab one of them by the collar, just as Maggie had done with the two vampires she had captured earlier, and he dragged him through the air kicking and screaming to the entrance to the tunnel, where he threw him in. The spitter disappeared into the bottom of the mountain with a cry. They heard him splash down below in the pool of vampire vomit. The final blue-spitter flew directly at Maggie's throat, his mouth agape and his red fangs bared, but she flipped over in the air, ending up behind him, and captured him by the collar, her long hair covering them both for an instant. She struggled to drag him through mid-air to the tunnel, like a big fish on a hook, and when she was near the entrance, she dropped him and then kicked him through the opening with both feet and watched as he slid down into the darkness.

Noah was still pinned under the weight of the open vat, with blue vampire vomit splashed over his head like paint, his tongue flicking out to clean himself of it and bringing it into his mouth to swallow. Even now, while dying, he couldn't resist blood. His small eyes had followed Maggie's progress, watching for a chance to strike, as she and Tommy cleaned up the mess the crash had caused and deposited each of the blue-spitters into the mountain.

"This makes no difference," Noah said in a hoarse voice, when the final spitter of the batch was inside the mountain. "You still have to get by me before you can imprison any more of my friends, and I won't let you by easily before I die."

Tommy was unmoved.

"Do you always eat your friends?" he asked, hovering just a few feet in front of him.

"Often," Noah answered immediately, turning his gaze to him. "Would you like to be my friend? Or my next meal? No one needs friends like you two do. It's your great weakness and it will be your undoing."

"We've still got each other," Maggie said.

"And I think I'll drop a few more vampires on you," Tommy said.

Noah snapped out at Tommy. It was a weak, half-hearted but violent strike that didn't come close to him. Tommy shot off to the side and up into the air and then flew around behind the giant snake to escape. Noah watched him as Tommy circled around behind him for as long as he could, being pinned to the ground by the silver vat and unable to move, and then Maggie dropped down onto the ground ten feet in front of the snake. She stood there facing him and leveled a steely gaze upon him. It was a hot gaze that said her hatred for him had not cooled a bit.

"You killed Mabin once," she said. "It might have been the worst day of my life."

"So sorry. It was one of my best days, except for the fact that you then killed me."

"Don't laugh about it."

"I can't help but laugh at you. You are a simple, pitiful girl."

The snake deliberately let out a sick hissing giggle, and his giant tongue slipped in and out of his mouth. Maggie stared at him and then pulled the silver spike out of her pocket, her steely gaze set upon Noah.

"I thought we were done with you, that killing you once was enough, but now you came back, so I see killing you once wasn't enough. It's going to take a second time to make things right. The same thing's going to happen to you again, for what you did to Mabin, and it's going to happen in the same way and I'm going to do it."

She held up the silver spike so that Noah could see it.

"Killing you twice is not enough for what you did to Mabin, but this time, please, don't even think of coming back. I will kill you as many times as it takes."

"You might regret what you're –"

Before Noah could finish, Maggie raised the silver spike before her and flew fast with it pointing directly at the snake's giant jaws, not caring what was about to happen to her but intent only on driving it into the snake and killing it. Noah hissed and snapped out at her, extending toward her as far as his crushed body would allow, and finally opening his mouth wide to engulf the foolish girl who flew toward his mouth. At the last moment, Maggie halted in mid-air, the snake's gaping mouth inches away, dripping blood. She flipped the spike into the air above Noah's head, where it hung for an instant before Tommy flipped over the silver vat, as he had been taught, and caught it in one hand. Without hesitating, from just four feet above the snake, Tommy dove down, the silver spike extended before him as Maggie had had it extended before her when she flew toward the snake, and he drove the spike into Noah's head, between the eyes, where it slipped into his brain. Instead of letting it go, Tommy stood on the head and stomped down on it with his foot to drive it deep into the thick skull, and Noah collapsed onto the forest floor, dead. The snake's mouth snapped closed and the giant head settled onto the forest floor, its eyes still open but glazed and cloudy.

Tommy straddled on top of the snake's head and stood looking down at what he had done.

"That was crazy, but fun," he said. "Are there any other vampires around we could do that to?"

"I hope not."

Maggie was still apprehensive at the dangers of Tommy standing on the giant snake's head, wondering if some new trick was in the works.

"I don't know if you want to do that," she said, cautioning Tommy where he stood. "Is he really dead?"

"Sure, he's dead. I do good work."

"It was good work. Thanks."

"You're welcome. He deserved it, for what he did to Mabin."

A set of headlights, like large twinkling stars, appeared on the access road leading to the area, flashing through the trees as the vehicle made its way toward the tunnel in the mountain. After what they had just been through, Maggie and Tommy grew silent and calm and a little alarmed, not knowing what was coming next but readying themselves for another fight. The headlights drove directly toward them, leaving the access road and entering the forest to climb up the mountainside, until they saw it was Elsa at the wheel of the family SUV, bumping over the rough surface of the forest floor. She waved to them when she parked a few feet away, and then she got out of the truck carrying a picnic basket.

The sight of the large, dead snake stopped her in her tracks.

"Oh, dear, what happened here?"

With Maggie and Tommy too stunned to answer, she walked with the basket around the dead giant snake's head, watching it all the while, until Tommy flew down off the beast and landed beside her.

"This snake got in our way while we were bringing the blue-spitters to the mountain," he said. "We crushed it and then we killed it."

"I guess that tells the tale, all right."

Elsa put the picnic basket down and touched one of the red fangs.

"You certainly did kill it, didn't you?"

She turned her back on the snake and looked at Maggie.

"It wasn't easy," Maggie said.

"I guess not. You two have had quite a night so far, and I thought you might be hungry," she said. "I know you haven't eaten in a long time, so I brought you some wonderful things."

She bent down and opened the basket, and as she did so a final breath blew out of the snake's nostrils, a wet, putrid breath of dead air. Then the beast's body relaxed into the ground completely, no hint of life remaining in it at all. Elsa leaned away as the rank air flowed over her, and then she turned to the snake again to make sure it had expired. She blinked and looked from Maggie to Tommy, after her concerns were alleviated by the motionless body.

"Don't worry," Maggie said. "After what we did to it, that snake's never going to threaten anyone again."

"Nope, never. I guess I am really hungry," Tommy said. "I hadn't thought about it, I was so busy."

Elsa looked shaken, but she turned around again to face them.

"You two need to take a break," she said, bending to the picnic basket, her voice breaking. "It's not healthy to go for so long without food."

Maggie had twitched nervously when the giant snake let out its final breath, and now she stared at it, knowing it was dead but uncertain of everything and anything after what she had seen on Saint Mary's Mountain so far, despite what she told Elsa. Noah had come back to life once. It could do so again if some odd circumstance arose again, like the bloody lightning, and Maggie knew better than to relax.

"I don't know about eating," she said. "We've got so much more to do tonight. I don't know if we have time to take a break."

Elsa laid out a blanket on the ground a little distance from the dead snake, snapping the blanket in the air first and then smoothing it out with her hands.

"We have everything you like. We have roast beef, fried chicken, steak, lamb, sausages and a pork roast. It's just what you need, after all this," she said.

"I don't know," Maggie said. "I –"

She felt her teeth grinding together, anger still burning inside her and tears nearly flowing out of her. She kept an eye on Noah's immense dead body.

"Maggie, we could use a break," Tommy said. "Come on. Relax. We've gotten this thing out of the way, so we can take a few minutes to eat."

Tommy sat on the ground and picked up a piece of fried chicken and hungrily bit into it. Maggie was still quivering inside with hatred and fear at the beast that lay dead nearby, unable to forget what it had done to Mabin.

Then suddenly she closed her eyes and forced herself to let everything go for a moment, all the fear and anger, and let out a sigh of relief.

"All right," she said. "We should have something to eat, I guess. I forgot about eating completely, too, I was so busy, but I guess we can take a few minutes, just a few, and then we have to get back to work."

The roast beef looked awfully good, and Noah's bulging eyes were completely lifeless, and Maggie had to admit she was very, very hungry and relieved.

She sat down on the ground, feeling like a human being again.

FOURTEEN
Karel Returns

They ate until they were full, quickly and with a purpose. They were starving, but they had not known how hungry they were until they ate, for the things that had preoccupied them were things they could not ignore, dangers that encased and erased hunger and made them forget all of their needs. In the think smoke hovering over the mountain, and with the dry thunderstorm kicking up the rousing wind and thrashing up prickly pine needles all around them, they ate hurriedly and with the great purpose of regaining their strength and their well-being, for both of them knew they were frazzled already but still had a long, fitful night ahead of them. When they were done, when the picnic basket was empty and Elsa had carried it back to the SUV, they lifted the crashed silver vat off of the giant snake and flew with it to the storage point in the forest a short distance away, and then they returned to drag the snake's body from the site. It was a massive task. The several hundred pounds of dead flesh did not move easily, and even with Elsa helping, tugging at the back end of the body just above the three-foot rattle, it moved only a few inches. Finally, Elsa backed up the SUV and tied a rope to the trailer hitch. She wrapped the other end of the rope around the body just below the snake's head, secured it with a figure-8 knot, and then started the truck. The truck growled with the effort, but she managed to drag the beast off the landing pad and into the forest a short ways, the snake's tongue still hanging out of its mouth as if to confirm its demise as the body bumped over the forest floor. With that work done, Maggie and Tommy said good-bye to their step-mother and flew off into the sky again immediately, feeling much better after the food but still grim and determined. They saw the SUV below making its way slowly and carefully down the treacherous mountainside to the access road.

"I'm not tired. Are you?" Tommy asked.

This high up, in the thickest part of the smoke, they could see very little but an occasional glimpse of the fires below consuming the pines. They could barely distinguish one another. Tommy flew close to Maggie's side to make sure he was going in the right direction.

"I'm not tired at all," Maggie answered. "I was just a little sad and angry back there. I'm sorry. I just wanted to get this work done and go home and be with Mabin again."

"What did you say?"

"I said I wanted to be with Mabin again."

"I know. I feel really bad about what happened to him, too. You can't really be with him again, though. You know that, don't you, Maggie?"

She bit her lip as they flew through the sky.

"I know. I just really wanted to say good-bye again, to say good-bye forever. I wanted to tell him something, that this wrong never should have happened."

"You're right. It never should have. We'll do the best we can to fix it."

"I wish –"

"What?"

"Forget it."

Tommy grew silent for the last few seconds of the flight to the next rooftop of blue-spitters, and Maggie understood that his silence meant determination, a determination as great as hers, to end this travesty of vampires and bring some sort of normality to the Bitterroot Valley. They went about their work quickly and efficiently, lifting the next vat of vampires into the air without a word to each other and flying off to the mountain with it so fast it was as though they blinked and found themselves landing again next to the giant dead snake. During the flight, the lightning had flashed in the distance and the thunder had roared far away, and on the return trip to the housing development of blue-spitters, their silence continued and the work went on uninterrupted. It was as though Karel knew he could do nothing to prevent his demons from being imprisoned in Saint Mary's Mountain and had retreated to sulk and burn more of the forest. As they worked, emptying the rooftops of the development of their vampires, Tommy got more and more of a feel for the routine. He could fly as fast as Maggie now, and he seemed to gain strength as the night wore on, nearly lifting the vats by himself and emptying them out into the mountain with very little assistance from Maggie. The food had done both of them a great deal of good. But there was more to it than that. Both felt their powers increasing and both seemed to sense that the completion of the job was eminent, that all of the blue-spitters would be entombed in the mountain by the end of the night and life could commence again normally, and that gave them the inspiration to go on. One vat of blue-spitters after the other rose into the air out of the housing development and shot across the sky to Saint Mary's Mountain. They worked as blurs in the smoky night, sure of themselves and their powers and not worried about Karel. He had done his worst, they believed. They moved each piece of cargo to its destination in less than a minute, time after time, all in silence. Karel did not dare show himself and could do little but drop lightning into the forests and clap with thunder and frustration. They could see dawn would come soon, and with it, the end of their labors.

Then, with just one street of blue-spitters to remove to the mountain, they landed at the tunnel-site and noticed the empty black metal barrels.

There were three of them, but neither Maggie nor Tommy thought much of it until they tipped over this vat of captured vampires and watched them tumble down into the mountain. They heard their six splashes below and then turned to each other before flying off for another load of blue-spitters.

"Did you see those barrels?" Maggie asked.

"The three of them, over there?"

"Yes."

"Were they there before?"

"I don't think so. I don't remember them."

"What do you think they are?"

"I don't know. Let's go look."

They closed up the tunnel and flew the empty silver vat to its storage area before flying back over the treetops to examine the barrels. They landed a few feet away from them and approaching them cautiously. They were carelessly discarded, lying on their sides with their tops scattered about, one here and one there, and Maggie could see each was empty but she felt a great need to examine them. She felt drawn to them as though they had once held souls. She walked closer and saw the remains of what they had contained.

"These were filled with blood," she said.

"Real blood?"

"Yes."

"All of them? All of them were filled with blood?"

Maggie stared at the mountain with a blank look.

"He's feeding them."

Tommy instantly understood her and turned to her with his eyes wide with amazement. They simply stared at one another for a moment. They had no idea of what to do next.

"Karel has gotten a hold of a blood supply and is dumping it in these barrels down into the mountain to feed the blue-spitters. You know what fresh blood is to vampires. You know how strong this will make them."

"You mean strong in the way we've been getting stronger?" Tommy asked.

"Yes, but there are more of them. They might be able to overcome the effects of the silver and get out once they're strong enough. I don't know what to do."

"We have to stop the wolf."

"But he's not going to show himself while we're here. When we fly away, he brings more blood to the vampires. We have to keep flying them here, but if we do, he'll keep feeding the spitters when we're not here. We can't win."

"Unless we stop the wolf."

"How?"

"We just do. We keep bringing the blue-spitters until they're all in the mountain. We're almost done. When we are, we'll have to fight the wolf. He'll be the last one we throw into the mountain."

"Do you think we can, I mean, beat the wolf in a fight?"

"We have to, Maggie. Just think what happened to Mabin. That was all his fault, all of this was his fault. Think about it. Think what happened to Mabin and then tell me we can't beat the wolf."

Maggie remembered that when they were trapped inside the mountain with the blue-spitters, Mabin had lost heart momentarily after being spiked, that he had felt the weight of the mountain on top of him and believed he had lost the fight, been defeated by chance and carelessness. It had astonished him then and weighed on him, breaking his heart when he did not know he had been spiked and weakened by that, and now Maggie understood what he had felt. She knew what defeat felt like, what a silver spike to the heart felt like, and of course Tommy was right. There was nothing left to do but carry the remaining vats of blue-spitters here to the mountain and then fight Karel when he came to collect his vampires and rule the world. That's where all this was leading, to that fight, to the end of everything. It had been far too easy that night, and they had become too adept, too good at their jobs, and it had misled them into believing the contest was over and that they had won before the final decision was in. Over-confidence in its worst form had afflicted them.

"Here's what I think Karel will do," Maggie said.

"Okay. What?"

While Maggie spoke, Tommy turned his eyes to the black barrels scattered over the forest floor and scanned the pine needles for blood.

"I think Karel is going to let us bring the rest of the blue-spitters here and then I think he's going to try to release them. That's when I think we're going to have to fight him."

"I'll fight him anytime he wants."

"I don't think he'll show up before we've collected all the vampires in one place. He's letting us do his work for him, and then he'll try to free them."

"Do you need the spike?"

Without waiting for an answer, Tommy quickly flew up on top of the giant snake's head and leaned down in an attempt to pull the silver sliver out of Noah's brain.

"I can't get it. It's pushed in too far."

"Don't worry about it. I don't know if it would work on Karel anyway. He's too large and he's too fast and he has too many powers. We're going to have to figure out something else."

Maggie estimated that they might have a half-hour or forty minutes to come up with a plan to defeat Karel, since there were only about thirty vats of blue-spitters remaining that had to be brought to the mountain and deposited inside it. They had become so fast and proficient it that it too only a minute or so for the roundtrip from here to the development. Dawn was at least two hours away. Dawn was the time they would have the advantage, since they had not drunk blood and would not be bothered by the light. Karel had shown his ability to shape-shift in the light to avoid the sun's usual effect on vampires, but she believed it was in the light that they had the best chance. They had been in a hurry to collect all the blue-spitters in one place, thinking Karel would destroy the valley or obscure his efforts with smoke to confuse them, thereby leading to the release of his demons, but maybe they had been too quick to fall into his trap.

"Let's take a break," Maggie said.

"Why? We're almost done."

"I think Karel wants us to finish quickly."

"Yeah, but they've had blood down there now. Don't you think if we wait the blue-spitters will get more and more powerful?"

"You're right. Whatever we do, we're going to have problems. I was hoping for the dawn to come soon."

It was as though they were trapped in a situation without a solution, that if they hurried their work the dark would be to the advantage of Karel and if they waited for the light the growing strength of the vampires would also be to the advantage of Karel. He was clever as well as powerful. Tommy rose to hover above the dead snake's head and Maggie could not resist the impulse to fly. She rose up to hover next to him.

"I guess we've got some real problems," he said.

"There's got to be something we can do. We killed the snake together, didn't we? We can figure out something to kill Karel, too."

"I say we finish what we started and bring the rest of the vampires here. What else can we do? Karel's still has to defeat us, too, and I don't care how many of his friends he brings up here to fight on his side, that's going to be hard."

"All right. Let's slow down a little, though, and wait for the light, and see how things go."

"Agreed. That's the best course. Right in the middle."

Once again, they shot off into the sky, flying as fast as thought flies out of habit, and arrived at the next rooftop of blue-spitters within seconds. With the anticipation of what was ahead, the final end to their work and their confrontation with Karel, the blood pumped fast through Maggie's heart and she could not help but think of Mabin and of the vampire virus coursing through her veins. It was the virus that gave her these powers to do what she was doing. It was the virus that enhanced her natural talents so that they were inflated into powers she could only have dreamed of, and she couldn't help but wonder where all of this would lead and if it was right. Mabin had made it right by the way he lived, but she had yet to learn how to live in a way that would make living the right thing to do. Mabin had died, been murdered, been defeated, and she wondered if the same fate was waiting for her. Karel could do anything, he would do absolutely anything, and just as Mabin had been surprised by the silver spike, Karel could have some other deadly surprise waiting for her. While she was thinking, she stared off into the sky, not seeing anything because the smoke obscured the stars.

Her thoughts led her mind to other images, images of the future and what it held and what might happen to her and Tommy. What she imagined the future to be if Karel won did not paint a pretty picture in her mind.

"Maggie?"

"Yes? I'm sorry. I was just thinking about things."

"Are you okay?"

"There's nothing we can do but what we've been doing, is there?"

"I guess not. We have to do it. Think of what would happen if we didn't."

"We'd all be sick little creatures, like them."

With the blue-gray glow emanating from the holding tank and engulfing their feet, Tommy knew exactly what she meant.

"Come on. We'll go slower, I guess, but I don't think it matters how long it takes to get the blue-spitters to the mountain. We just have to get them there and then see what happens. Whatever happens to us happens. We can't stop the world."

There were four more hideous black metal barrels emptied of blood and scattered over the forest floor when Maggie and Tommy returned to Saint Mary's Mountain. They settled down in silence with their vat of blue-spitters on the landing pad before the silver tunnel, their eyes on the empty barrels, knowing what had become of the blood inside and aware of how insecure its deposit into the mountain could make their future. They exchanged grim glances. In preparation for dumping this latest batch of vampires into the mountain, Tommy lifted the door to the tunnel and immediately saw the effects the fresh blood had had on those below. A few feet down the tunnel, a blue-spitter was clawing his way up toward them with difficulty, refreshed and empowered by the blood Karel had fed him, but still struggling to climb the slippery silver sides of the tunnel. He looked like a simple, middle-aged man in work clothes and work boots, balding and pock-marked in the face, but his fangs were out and he was choking, spitting and hacking, on the blood he had recently ingested. As soon as he saw Tommy, he hissed and snarled at him, redoubling his efforts to climb the slippery silver surface to get at the boy's blood but sliding back a few feet.

"Hurry up, Maggie! Let's dump these guys. One of them has nearly climbed out!"

Expertly now, they threw up the lid of the holding tank they had flown in with and immediately dumped the new load of blue-spitters down the tunnel. All six crashed toward the escaping vampire, who was still struggling to climb the slippery slope, knocking him backward, and this time there were seven splashes as the blue-spitters hit bottom after screaming down to the bottom of the silver tunnel in a heap. As soon as Maggie and Tommy turned from their work, they saw a large shadow lurking in the forest, a dark form that slipped away into the blackness and smoke covering the mountainside.

"He was watching us," Maggie said.

"I saw him. Let's try something different," Tommy said. "Let's go as fast as we can and try to kill him the same way we killed Noah. Maybe he'll get careless, like Noah did."

"So you think that maybe we can do the same thing to him that we did to Noah. Is that what you mean? Crash into him?"

"It's exactly what I mean."

They pushed the empty silver vat off to the side, not bothering to fly it to the spot in the forest where the other empties were stored, and returned to the development for yet another container of blue-spitters. They did not speak, they did not hesitate and they did not slow down. Instead, they barely set foot on the roof of the next house in line before grabbing the handles of its silver holding tank and flying back toward the mountain at a speed that astonished even them. They knew what they had to do. Without slowing down, without hesitating, they crashed through the smoke hanging over Saint Mary's Mountain, unable to see where they were going and uncertain they were even in the right spot. At the last second, the smoke cleared and there was the giant wolf below, pouring a barrel of blood down the opening to the silver tunnel. They were flying so fast they barely caught sight of him before they had to let go of the tank of blue-spitters and pull up before crashing into the mountainside. The silver vat descended like a bomb toward the wolf, but Karel had sniffed something, raising his nose to the air when Maggie and Tommy let go of the vat, and in an instant he shot off to the side in a blur, as fast as they were but with a sharper sense of danger. The tank of blue-spitters landed exactly where he had been standing, crushing the empty black barrel, and opening as it tipped over. The coughing vampires within were dumped directly into the opening with the force of the crash and were gone down the tunnel in an instant. They splashed into the blue vomit below all six at once, sending the huge splashing sound up to the surface in a wave just as Tommy and Maggie landed.

"We missed him," Tommy said, turning away from the opening. "We missed him!"

"It was our one chance with him. He'll know to be a little more cautious now."

"How did he know we were coming?"

"I think he saw what we did to Noah and was watching for us. He didn't want to make the same mistake Noah did."

"We won't make the same mistake again, either. We almost got him. If we see him down here again, we can drop blue-spitters on him even faster."

Karel had used a ten-foot wooden pole to prop open the door to the tunnel, since he was still highly allergic to the damaging effects of the silver on his kind and unable to touch it. Maggie removed the pole, closing the door with her other hand, and then snapped it in two, as though it was no more than a rotten twig. Tommy picked up a piece of it and with equal strength snapped it in half and threw the pieces into the forest, before picking up the second section of the broken pole and doing the same with it. Karel had disappeared into the smoky forest, but they felt his presence near. Just off to the side of the landing pad was another black barrel, this one full of fresh blood, and when Maggie saw it she immediately walked over to it, tore off the lid and tipped it over with her foot, dumping the contents into the stream flowing downhill. There was a howl in the forest as Karel watched his blood disappear into the stream and flow away, wasted to the vampire. They heard him running off into the distance, crashing through the underbrush and kicking up the debris on the forest floor. Tommy pushed aside the empty silver vat and then picked up the crushed black barrel and tossed it into the woods toward the fleeing black shadow. The barrel landed near the scattered pieces of the broken prop.

"Don't come back!" he yelled. "The same thing will happen to you that happened to Noah!"

Maggie scanned the area, turning in a circle, for any glimpse of Karel.

"What should we do now?" Tommy asked.

"I think we should take our time, some of the time. Other times we should go as fast as we can. Karel won't know what to do. He won't know if it's safe for him or if he's about to be smashed. He'll have to go slowly now if he wants his vampires to drink blood, and he'll have to be cautious. We've made our point."

Karel must have transformed himself then and risen into the sky, for once again when they shot upward and headed toward the development to continue their work, the smoky atmosphere was filled with crashes of lightning and claps of thunder, but no rain. Then sensed it would be very unhealthy for them to waste time during the return flights to the development, since if they didn't fly as fast as they could he might strike them with a bolt of lightning from high above and end their endeavors, for that was their only vulnerable time. They returned to the mountain with another load of blue-spitters, and then another and another, and still there was no sign of the blood-drinking wolf. The forests were quiet, except for the immediate area where there had been blood dumped. There, strangeness hung over mountain, as though the souls of those from whom the blood had been stolen had seeped into the forest with the blood and taken life in the trees and rocks and soil. Tommy thought he saw a tree move once, uproot itself and travel to a new spot, and Maggie swore rocks had piled themselves. The bloody stream whispered to them and then murmured in many voices, and even the smoke had fingers that reached out and touched their skin. The blood gave new life and consciousness to everything, but no more reached the vampires inside the mountain to do the same for them. When Maggie and Tommy made their final flight back to the housing development for the last complement of blue-spitters, the final six of thousands, they could not help but feel an exuberant confidence take flight with them. It remained with them on the return flight to Saint Mary's and heightened to exhilaration when they opened the door to the silver tunnel one last time, tipped over the vat of blue-spitters and sent them sliding down into the mountain. They had done what Mabin had set out to do. They had finished his work. Their work was done, and he was not a failure. Now what?

Now Karel came out of the forest.

He did so silently, seemingly unnoticed by them, and he did so as if domesticated now, calmly and with no intention of harming them. He settled down by the giant snake, resting on the shaggy knees of his front legs, several feet shorter than when he stood at his full height, and he licked the snake's huge head with a tongue as big as a large front door. Both Maggie and Tommy felt his presence and knew he was there, but they did not turn around to face him, realizing any chance they had of surprising him lay in his mistakenly thinking he had surprised them. He yawned, and that slight noise was enough to startle them into turning around. If he was about to leap on them, they might was well no longer pretend that they did not know he was there.

"Did you bring them all?" he asked.

"We brought all the vampires," Maggie answered.

Tommy sensed something was wrong and still had a bitter edge to him.

"Why do you care? You're the one that's going to be down there with them in a minute," Tommy said.

The small boy glared at Karel with steel in his eyes, and in response Karel let his tongue hang out of his mouth playfully, panting as a dog would pant while playing with its master.

"I was so foolish at first, and it made me waste a barrel of blood," he said. "I was trying to feed your guests before all of them had arrived, which wasn't logical. Once you nearly crushed me the way you did Noah, I came to my senses. The logical thing to do was to wait until all my friends were here, and then let them feast on blood. I have plenty, so I have to thank you for your efforts."

He gestured to the edge of the forest with a nod of his head, and in the dim light glowing out of the silver tunnel, rows and rows of black barrels containing blood were lined up like legions of liquid soldiers.

So that was what he was waiting for, Maggie thought, for us to finish bringing the blue-spitters. He was waiting for us to do all his work for him and then he'd unleash all the vampires after he fed and strengthened them.

"So?" Tommy said.

The one word held all the defiance her little brother could muster. The black wolf glared at him, no longer playful.

"You're not going to get to use it," Tommy added. "When we're done with you, we'll return the blood to where it belongs."

"Oh, I'll use my blood for my purposes, little boy, after I use yours. Look at the two of you. There's nothing to you. You're just a boy, barely bigger than my toenails, and you're just a girl, not much stronger than all this smoke. You've done what I wanted you to do. You can fly away now if you think you should, but I'm sure you won't, because you know I'll be free then to feed your friends and bring them back to real life, a vampire's life. I know you want to fight me now to prevent that."

"So what are you waiting for?" Tommy asked.

"The question is what are you waiting for?" Karel responded. "You're waiting because you know you have nothing that can harm me. You have no strength, you have no claws and you have no teeth worth mentioning. You don't even have that silly little silver spike anymore. You failed to crush me when you could have, and you don't even have any ideas on how to kill me, not a single one. In short, you have nothing. You are silly children."

Maggie thought that never in her life would she agree about anything with the black wolf, but with a glance at Tommy, she had to agree with him now. Her little brother looked so helpless, standing there with his fists clenched, staring at Karel in the blue-gray glow from the tunnel. It was as though the boy was standing next to a dark skyscraper, one looming over him and about to collapse on top of him. She knew she was just as helpless. Without Mabin, they were helpless. They had been duped.

"Oh, let's just wait another minute, then," Karel said sarcastically. "I can see you're speechless, and if you don't want to fight me at this moment, let's just wait a short time while I prepare myself for you."

Karel sneered at them with disrespect but then, once again, he changed expressions and panted at them like a playful puppy, looking from Maggie to Tommy, toying with them and waiting for their response to his challenge, and when one did not come, he lunged forward. Both of them shot off to the side like blurs, but it was not them Karel was lunging toward but the body of the giant snake. His upper jaw flew up, like a bridge rising to let a ship pass, and he slammed his red teeth closed on Noah's immense head, chomping down on it to crush it, as his eyes rolling back with the pleasure of eating the dead beast. It was tough meat, and Karel had to grind his jaws together to break up the bones and sinew repeatedly. He had bitten into only half of the snake's head. He chewed and then chewed some more and then shook his head violently, and with the motion the snake's body snapped through the air like a whip and then smashed down next to Maggie, throwing up pine needles and dust. She flew black a short ways up the mountainside to avoid being knocked over by the force of the blow on the earth. She watched in a panic, wondering what she could do, if anything, as Karel chewed the bloody half-head he had in his mouth and then finally swallowed it. He looked from Maggie to Tommy, his eyes like slits, as though threatening them, as though saying, this is what I can do to the snake. Imagine what I can do to you. He turned back to the snake. With one motion the bridge of his jaws opened wide again and he leaned down and bit off in the remainder of Noah's gigantic head. He chewed on that contentedly, shifting the food from one side of his mouth to the other to break it up, and swallowed again, the lump traveling down his throat. He licked the snake's blood off of his lips and calmly let the food descend into his stomach, looking once again from Maggie to Tommy threateningly. Then, as though sucking in a piece of thick spaghetti, Karel slurped downed in the remainder of Noah's snake-body, without chewing it, with the rattle disappearing last of all.

"Now to wash it all down with something to drink," he said.

Karel pulled the lid off of one of the barrels of blood with the claws of one paw and tossed it aside, watching it roll away through the forest. He closed his mouth over the barrel and lifted it high in the air by tilting back his head and drinking, much of the blood not reaching his throat but instead running out of his mouth and dripping in currents down the black fur on his neck. It appeared at first to Maggie that he had drunk poison. She watched as he emptied the barrel of blood with gusto and then shook his head and let out a roar that reverberated throughout the forest, a roar of pain and agony, it seemed to her. Her heart soared with hope as he crashed onto the forest floor, his huge tongue rolling out of his mouth, his two remaining paws suddenly pointed toward the sky.

"He's dead! Is he dead?" Tommy asked.

In answer, there was a cracking sound, as though a tree had split in two, and then there was a crashing sound, as though the tree had fallen heavily to earth. Something was happening to Karel, and it was making a terrible noise. From just behind his shoulders, where his back half had been torn off by Mabin, there emerged the giant snake's rattle, intact and shaking its warning, slowing emerging, but the transformation did not end there.

The remainder of the back end of Noah's body slid out behind Karel, now part of his body. Karel had merged his front half with Noah's back half, creating a giant creature that was half-wolf and half-rattlesnake. Completed now, Karel rolled over so that his front paws rested on the earth and Noah's back half extended out behind him, balancing him and rattling, and Maggie saw that the transformation did not end with merging of the two vampires. Instead of the usual fangs of the wolf, Karel now had the gigantic fangs of the rattlesnake, and they were dripping with venom. Leaving his feet, Karel rose in the air on the strength of the huge snake-body and hovered above Maggie and Tommy. His eyes, too, had become small red snake-eyes, and they glared down at the two tiny creatures below.

Now things seemed even more impossible to Maggie.

"Remember what you did in daylight, Maggie Long Hair?" Karel asked.

Even his voice had changed, becoming more like a hissing sound of ill-formed words, but there was no mistaking what he meant. His meaning was very clear.

"I burned your friends," Maggie answered calmly. "I let them see the sun, and they burned. It would never have happened if they hadn't drunk blood."

"Yes, they burned," Karel hissed, towering above them and slowly moving from side to side while watching them. "Did you ever think you would know what it was like to burn slowly from the inside out, simply because some fool rained sunlight down on you?"

"I would never drink blood, so I would never know."

"No you wouldn't drink blood, but you're going to know now what it's like to burn. I will keep my promise to you."

Without explaining himself further in words, Karel let his action demonstrate how he intended on burning Maggie and

Tommy. Rearing back even higher, he opened his mouth wide and hissed loudly. He spat out two torrents of thick white venom from his fangs, the venom spraying over their heads and crashing into the mountainside above them. It immediately ignited as though shot from a flame-thrower. The pine needles on the ground caught fire with a thumping sound, and the trees ignited as huge torches, crackling with the sudden blaze. The inferno behind them forced Maggie and Tommy forward in desperation to escape the heat, toward Karel, who watched them stumble forward without moving, waiting for the correct moment to spray out his venom on them and end their desperate flight. With two short bursts, he sprayed venom first to his left and then to his right, igniting the ground on both sides of them and forcing them together. They came together and embraced as the fire closed in around them.

"We can fly out," Tommy said.

"It's too late. He'd burn us in the air."

"Good-bye," Karel said.

He reared back high above them, opening his mouth wide and baring his fangs in preparation, and as he did so Maggie saw a sudden light come on, perhaps the light of the fire that was about to consume them raining down on them before destroying them. There was a sudden thwacking sound that knocked Karel off-balance. Something had hit him in the neck. Then there was another thwack, and another, and Karel staggered off to the side as the flames rose up higher around Maggie and Tommy. Karel crashed to the ground, but then rose up again on his snake's body, opening his mouth wide again in preparation for spraying them with the thick fiery white venom, but now there was a whooshing sound and another thwack, as Karel was hit yet again with a missile flying through the night. He staggered back again, allowing Maggie and Tommy to rush out of the opening in the flames that he was formed when he staggered back and fell to earth, and again he struggled to rise up over them but could not. His massive head simply settled onto the earth and did not move. Two more missiles whooshed through the air and impacted his snake-body, sending a shudder through him, and then he was completely still.

"What was that?"

"I don't know."

"Is he dead?" Tommy asked.

"We can hope he is."

"We didn't have to do a thing to kill him. What happened?"

Maggie thought she knew, but she had to make sure by turning around to the source of the light. Between two trees, the headlights of the family SUV cut through the night and illuminated the scene. From out of the dark beside the two trees stepped Stephanovich and Elsa holding two crossbows aloft at their shoulders, pointed straight at Karel, their eyes set on his dead body but not taking any chances. They walked forward carefully, stepping gingerly and keeping their eyes on Karel as though uncertain he was dead, the crossbows loaded with the kind of silver shafts they had shot into the vampire.

Stephanovich dropped his crossbow to his side and walked up to Tommy and laid an arm over his shoulder.

"Are you okay, buddy?"

Tommy embraced his step-father. His arms and legs were shaking now that he was finally safe.

"I think I am. I don't think I got hit by any of the venom."

Stephanovich looked Tommy up and down, scanning him for the fiery liquid, but he saw none.

"You're clean."

Elsa dropped her crossbow to her side and came to stand next to Maggie.

"And how about you?" she asked. "Are you all right? Have you had enough to eat tonight?"

"I'm fine."

She felt the same sense of relief that Tommy did, and felt as though the tears were about to come, but she thought of Mabin and somehow that stopped the flow. Silently, she spoke to him and let him know they had done what he wished them to do.

"How did you do that?" she asked Elsa, when she returned from her talk with Mabin. "How did you kill him? You said you had no powers, so how did you kill him?"

"I said we were powerless, not helpless," Stephanovich said. "A human can always find a way to kill a vampire, if he thinks about it enough."

"I'm so glad you came. We did as much as we could. I don't think we could have killed him without your help."

"Ah, we had him," Tommy said.

"Sure we did."

"We better check, to make sure," Stephanovich said. "Wait here."

He raised his crossbow loaded with the silver bolt and inched his way carefully toward Karel's corpse, the crossbow held at his shoulder ready to fire. He circled around to the front of Karel's head, staring at him until he stood just before the beast's open jaws, and then he raised the crossbow to sight it and fired a bolt into the mouth, sending it flying into the back of the beast's throat. The silver missile thudded into Karel's head but had no other effect. He did not move from his death-pose.

"I think we're okay," Stephanovich said.

He turned his back on Karel and returned to the family circle.

"I know you're tired, but can you help us with the last thing we have to do?" he asked Maggie.

"What do you want us to do?"

"Help us carry out the antidote and administer it to the vampires. We'd got it in the back of the truck."

"Can I help?" Tommy asked.

"Sure, you can, that's why we asked," said Elsa. "You've done so much already and we knew you'd want to help with this, too."

The two barrels that had waited for this moment in Stephanovich and Elsa's garage were carried one at a time by Maggie and Tommy and their step-parents from the back of the SUV to the landing pad. Stephanovich pried open the lid to the first one, his hands shaking in anticipation of the moment he had waited so long for, and then he asked Maggie to open the door to the silver tunnel in Saint Mary's Mountain.

"I hope this works," he said. "We went through all this trouble to find a cure for these people, so I hope it works."

"It will," Elsa said. "It's got to."

Once again, the four of them lifted the barrel containing the antidote and poured the contents down the shaft of the tunnel. When they were finished, they rolled the barrel over to the other barrels that had contained the blood that was to be fed to the vampires.

"Aren't we going to dump in the second container?" Tommy asked.

"One barrel should be sufficient. It's powerful stuff."

"Don't you want to make sure?"

"It doesn't contain any antidote," Stephanovich said.

"Well, what's in it, then?" Tommy asked.

"It's the bloody rope."

Stephanovich pried open the top of the barrel to reveal a tightly coiled, thin rope in red liquid.

"That's disgusting."

"It's not really a bloody rope," Stephanovich explained, "but the vampires think it is. Remember how they always said they needed the bloody rope to climb out? Well, once they've drunk the antidote and it takes effect, I'll lower this rope saturated with more antidote down into the tunnel. If they're cured, they'll all be able to climb out. If not, they'll burn."

"So that's the bloody rope," Maggie said. "I wondered what they meant by that all this time."

"It is. All the vampires knew about it. Elsa and I will finish up here. You might want to go home and rest."

"Are you sure? We can still help you."

"You've done more than enough. Are you well enough to fly home by yourselves?"

"I guess we are."

"We'll see you there once we've lowered the bloody rope into the tunnel and given the vampires a chance to come out as human beings again. Okay?"

"I'm fine," Tommy said. "Bring on more vampires."

Maggie laughed and then said she was okay to fly off on her own, too.

Just as they were ready to take off, the first rays of the sun rose over the horizon. They waited as the sun rays walked down the fires and unburned trees of the mountainside, happy that they did finally get to see sunlight again and transfixed by the beauty of the sun coming up over the eastern mountains through a break in the smoke.

The sunlight hit Karel, and they watched as first the snake's body smoked and ignited and then the flames spread to the wolf's black fur. He was burning as he intended to burn them. In death, Karel's shape-shifting could no longer hold, and he went through one last transformation. He became what he had been. The huge black wolf returned to his human form, an ancient emaciated man with a completely bald head and very thin shoulders, but a man still attached to the burning body of the rattlesnake. A full, intense ray of the sun hit him: the flames shot up from his flesh and in an instant he was reduced to ash and smoke.

"I guess we don't have to worry about him anymore," Tommy said.

"I wonder who he was," Maggie said.

"We know who he was," Tommy said. "He was a vampire."

Maggie stared at the pile of ashes that had been Karel.

"Let's go," Tommy said. "I'm hungry. Are you?"

Maggie said that she was. They waved good-bye to Stephanovich and Elsa and rose into the sky for the final flight home. They flew through patches of smoke into columns of sunlight, weary and flying slowly but finally safe and together. The smoke and sunlight alternated as the fires were dying and the sun was rising. Just below them they saw their home. From the west, another thunderstorm was approaching, flashing lightning and crashing with thunder, but this was not another of Karel's dry thunderstorms, but a huge billowing cloud full of water. They descended toward home, and as they did so they felt the first few drops of a storm that would finally douse the vampire fires with a tremendous, day-long downpour of rain.

FIFTEEN
The Hope of Saint Mary's

It took twenty-four hours for the antidote to work and the blue-spitters, now human again, to climb out of their prison in Saint Mary's Mountain. Far from avoiding the light now, they lined up in the pit of the mountain to climb hand-over-hand up the rope toward it, wishing to escape the pool of blue slime, the blood of thousands of innocent victims that remained festering in the silver cavern at the bottom of the tunnel. They emerged into the sunlight individually after their long climbs, each blinking at the light but warmed by it as though it was an embrace of a loved one. Not one was burned by the sun. Men, women and children each made their long climb out without a single misgiving or misadventure, as they all remembered what a horror they had been and what misery the vampire virus had made of their lives. Stephanovich was waiting at the entrance to the tunnel, his crossbow slung over his shoulder just in case the antidote didn't work for some individuals, but he never had to use it. Each of former blue-spitters emerged into the sunlight contritely and took Stephanovich's hand, one by one, so grateful they nearly broke out in tears, and each said almost the same thing.

"I'm so sorry for what I did and what I was."

"You were sick. It's not your fault."

"But I never should have drunk blood. It was wrong. I couldn't resist it. I was weak."

"It's over now. You can start living again."

They came back into the world as refugees, in a hopeless situation, with no place to go and no means of support, homeless and jobless and many without family, but all that had been taken care of. Elsa and Maggie and Tommy waited behind Stephanovich with mugs of coffee or hot chocolate to warm the former vampires in the mountain's chill morning air. They had blankets to throw over their shivering shoulders, taken one after the other from large stacks of them on a table, as one former blue-spitter after another passed by and received a hot drink. As the morning wore on, the crowd of refugees grew so that it nearly covered the mountainside, with some standing and some sitting on the pine needles and many talking over the horrors of their experiences, and when the last former blue-spitter emerged from the mountain, Stephanovich said it was time take everybody home.

"We're going to take them home with us?" Maggie asked.

"Where else would they go?"

"But where are we going to put them all? There must be nearly three thousand of them."

For a moment, Stephanovich appeared confused by the question, as though he hadn't thought of where the refugees should go to live, or that Maggie had asked a very foolish question.

"Didn't you notice, Maggie? Every house in the development is empty but ours. We're taking these people home to be our neighbors and friends. The houses where they were imprisoned on the roofs will be their new homes."

When everyone had a little more time to adjust to their freedom outside the mountain, to breathe the air and look to the clear sky without fear of suddenly going up in fire and smoke, Stephanovich led the trek down through the forest to the access road and then out to Route 93, the main highway. Behind him, the thousands of former vampires followed quietly, with the dignity of having regained their humanity, their heads held high, each determined to make this a better life. They had quite a bit of work to do. On both sides of the highway, Karel's fires were still smoldering in the wreckage of the forests covering the mountainsides. The rains of the previous day had put his fires out, but one mountain after another was a blackened disaster, a huge hump of charcoal with the remnants of thousands of trees standing only as branchless stumps. The caravan of former vampires stretched for miles down from the mountain outside of Stevensville, along the highway toward Victor and then over the dusty, unpaved side roads leading to the new development, with Stephanovich, Elsa, Maggie and Tommy at the head of it, leading the way. Once they had reached the outskirts of the development, there was no need to direct anyone to their new homes. Each refugee remembered their nights imprisoned on their rooftops in the silver vats, and each one along with his or her roommates or family headed immediately toward their houses without further direction or encouragement.

"Do we have to do anything else?" Maggie asked.

"All the houses are furnished and fully stocked with food," Stephanovich said. "It's up to them now what they make of their lives."

They took lawn chairs out of the garage to watch the progress of their new neighbors and friends in re-populating the development. They sat in the sunshine with cool drinks of lemonade and ice tea as the former vampires went into their homes, showered and changed and made dinner. Maggie was silent, nearly overcome at the scope of what had happened, staggered by the change of circumstance that was taking place for thousands.

After a few hours of watching those thousands re-establish their lives, Stephanovich stirred in his lawn chair.

"There is one more thing we have to do," he said, seemingly uncomfortable as he turned toward Maggie.

"What's that?" Maggie asked.

"We have to take care of Mabin."

She was afraid she knew what that meant. They had to bury him. They got up, again in silence, and went in their dark, cool house through the kitchen door, a quiet funeral procession, Maggie thought. They passed through the dining room and came to the living room, where Mabin was laid out in a coffin surrounded by flowers. He barely looked dead. Maggie saw the same lovely face she had seen that first morning when he rode by her on his bike, his skin rosy and fresh, and if his eyes hadn't been closed, she might have thought he was merely resting for a moment. He was dressed in a black suit and a tie, and his mop of dark hair was neatly combed and his bony face appeared to be at rest. She brought her hand to her mouth to suppress a sob as she stared at him.

"There's one more thing I have to ask of you, Maggie," Stephanovich said.

She thought he was about to ask her to help with the burial, and of course she would do that, with a heavy heart.

"I hesitate in asking this. It's not pleasant."

"I know. You can ask me anything. I'll do anything for him."

"I need your blood."

A jolt of horror and the terror of exactly what he meant by that shot through her. So this was not over, the vampires were still out there and in power. In fact, they were in her own house.

"You stay away from her," Tommy said in a panic, stepping in front of her to protect her. "If you come near her, I swear you're dead."

"No, no, it's not like that," Stephanovich said quickly. He reached into his pocket and removed the familiar yellowed sheet of paper that he had told them contained the Transylvanian

Mysteries. He quickly waved it in the air. "I don't want your blood for me. I want it for Mabin."

"For him? Are you sure? Are you sure you're not still a vampire?" Tommy asked.

"I told you. We're cured. We don't have a single power, not one, but I do know things. I was reading the mystery earlier and discovered something new in it, something we can do for Mabin."

"I thought you said you had to be an expert to read the Transylvanian Mysteries."

"No. I'm not an expert, but my name is Stephanovich and my family originated in that area and I know those languages. I can read this. I thought it said here that we can revive a vampire if the sweetness he knew in life is given to him again in death."

"What does that mean? Does it mean if I kiss him, he'll revive? That's just silly, but I'll do it anyway. I'll do anything for him."

She turned again to the coffin.

"That's what I thought it said at first, but then I read it over and over and over and I remembered that these are vampires we're talking about here on this paper and it didn't really say sweetness. That's what I thought it said, but it didn't really."

"Okay. What did it really say?"

"They're vampires. When they said sweetness, they meant blood. They meant the blood of the beloved. I need your blood for him, Maggie."

Again, Maggie stood shocked into silence, unsure of how any of this worked, or if it was wicked. Of course she would give her blood to him, but how could she possibly believe such a thing as reviving the dead was possible? It was simply absurd. She had little time to think this over, for Stephanovich reached into the coffin and removed a large hypodermic needle from beside Mabin's body. He held it in the air for her to see, his hand trembling.

"There's more," Stephanovich said.

"What more could there be?"

"I have to take the blood from your heart."

The hand with the hypodermic needle dropped to his side suddenly and he closed his eyes and continued to tremble. Tears steamed down his face at what he was about to do.

"You can say no if you want and I would understand. You should say no. It says in the Transylvania Mysteries that I have to take the blood from the heart of the beloved and inject it into the heart of her lover. It could kill you, Maggie. It really could, and I shouldn't do this."

"But you said it could bring Mabin back. If it stands any chance of bringing him back, I want to do it. I want to."

"Think of it, though. This paper ... maybe it's just an old paper and doesn't mean anything. You really could die if I do this, Maggie. You could die."

Maggie looked into the coffin at the terrible stillness inflicted on the only boy she had ever loved, even for a day. She touched her heart, and then laid her hand on his.

"From my heart to yours," she said. "My blood is yours. You can have my blood."

She turned to Stephanovich and opened the top button of her blouse and pulled down the fabric to bare the flesh over her beating heart.

"I'm the girl who would do anything," she said. "I'll do anything for him, even if I die."

"This is real, Maggie. If I do this to you, it really could end for you. I want to make sure you understand that."

"I know. I understand completely. You said that already. Just do it quickly, Stephanovich. Tommy ..."

She held out her free hand to her little brother, smiling down at him, and he took her hand in his to comfort her. Then she returned her gaze to Stephanovich. The tears were still rolling down his cheeks as he lifted the needle to point toward her. Then his hands dropped to his sides again as though it was an impossible task for him.

"Maggie ..."

"Please just do this quickly."

Stephanovich let out a sound that was a combination of a sigh and a groan and lifted the needle and pointed it toward her. He took two quick steps to her, still sobbing, and pressed the needle carefully into her flesh over where he thought her heart was. With a sudden, violent movement he slammed his hand onto the back of the needle, sending the point deep into her flesh. She closed her eyes as she felt the thin sliver of stainless steel puncture her skin and enter her heart and hesitate there for a moment. So this is what Mabin felt when he died, she thought. Darkness swirled around her and she heard Tommy calling out her name again and again and she felt herself drifting away, leaving this earth. Then Stephanovich drew out her blood. She felt it drained from her heart as though drawn through a straw from a beating jar of flesh, and then she fell to her knees. The needle slipped out of her chest, and when she looked up she saw Stephanovich holding the hypodermic full of her red blood.

"Is it okay? Did you heart stop?" he asked.

"Are you okay, Maggie?" Tommy asked.

"Maggie? Did your heart stop?" Stephanovich yelled.

"Maybe for an instant," Maggie managed to answer. "I think I'm all right."

"That's good. The paper said the beloved heart should stop for an instant. Can you get up? You need to watch this."

"I have to watch?"

"Yes, the blood has to go into Mabin immediately, and you have to watch, or it might not work."

Maggie struggled to her feet, her vision blurred and her head swimming. Stephanovich did not hesitate at all. He turned with the needle full of her blood, hovered with the point down toward Mabin's chest over his heart and then jammed it into him. He pushed down on the needle to empty the blood into his chest, and that instant Mabin's body shook violently and then settled back and Maggie thought she saw his eyes flicker open. Stephanovich withdrew the needle and slammed closed the coffin's lid.

"What did you do that for?" Maggie asked. "He was coming to."

"He can't come to now. It takes a year."

"A year?"

"Exactly one year, or he could die for good, and we have to get him out of here, now!"

"Why do we have to get him out of here now? Why can't we wait?"

"Because the mysteries very specifically say he has to be buried as quickly as possible in a place free of vampires and left in the ground undisturbed for a year. More than that, he has to be buried by the one who has his powers. Then he has to be dug up a year later by the beloved who gave him blood. That's how it works. Tommy has to take him back to Saint Mary's Mountain, and exactly one year from now, you have to dig him up. The mysteries are very clear on that. We have to take him to a place free of vampires and wait one year for him to revive."

Stephanovich took a trenching shovel from behind the couch and laid it on top of the coffin.

"Tommy, hurry up. You have to do this. You have to bury him as soon as possible and remember the exact time the last shovelful of earth goes on him. You can do that, can't you?"

"I think so."

"Then let's take him outside. You have to fly him back to the mountain and remember exactly where and when he's buried."

Too confused and shocked to do anything immediately, both Maggie and Tommy stood stock still while Elsa and Stephanovich carried Mabin's coffin out the back door. Elsa shouted for them to follow and they both slowly moved along behind, Maggie still weak and confused and disoriented after the blood was taken from her heart and Tommy not quite understanding what he had to do. Maggie staggered outside, the bright sunlight hitting her eyes and making her feel the same way the needle in her heart had made her feel.

"Can you fly away now with him, Tommy?" Stephanovich shouted urgently. "Are you strong enough? Can you do this?"

"I think I can. I'll try really hard. Help me."

"Wait a minute. Take my watch."

Stephanovich unstrapped his watch from his wrist and stuffed it in Tommy's pocket.

"Remember, you have to write down the exact moment on this date you throw the last shovelful of earth on him. You can remember to do that, can't you?"

"Yes, I think so. Please, help me lift the coffin on my back."

"Hurry!"

Maggie could barely see or hear the situation around her, knowing only that her little brother was about to take on a terrible responsibility with the task of burying Mabin in exactly the right place at exactly the right time. The world was swimming in a blur around her and she could barely stand. She was vaguely aware of the coffin rising into the air above her, on top of Tommy back, while he held the trenching tool. Again she heard a voice inside her head, but this time it was only one voice, Mabin's voice.

See me in a year. Come to see me in one year. We'll be together in a year.

She slipped down onto the ground, her legs folding beneath her, and raised her eyes to the sky. High above her she saw Tommy flying away, a small dot struggling with a large coffin on his back, headed to Saint Mary's Mountain. She heard someone shouting in the house next door to open the window and let in some light and air.

THE END

Next is ...
Resurrection In Vampire Valley

1

In a panic, Stephanovich Emory peered at the yellowed, musky document held just inches from his eyes. His cheeks were red and pinched and his breathing came so hard it nearly blew the trembling paper out of his hand. His fingers shook and his eyes blinked as the sweat poured into them from his forehead. He clutched the document so tightly in frustration that it crumpled and tore in his hands.

"No, no, I love the boy too much for this, more than life itself," he murmured. "This can't be. I can't do this. Never!"

Tommy lay on the floor screaming as the black blood ate like acid into his skin. Stephanovich did his best to concentrate on the task and not to hear the screams of his son. He brought the Transylvania Mysteries closer to his eyes and peered once again at the odd squiggled writing. Fingerprints etched in ancient brown blood on the mysteries, but that blood didn't matter now, it didn't matter at all. A few more seconds of this torture of his son and he would hyperventilate into unconsciousness at what the mysteries were telling him to do.

"What does it say, darling? Hurry. Tommy's not going to last much longer. How do we save him? What can we do?"

"I can't see! There's no light down here. No, I can't see what it says. I can't see! It's no good! I can't read it!"

"You have to! Only scripture can save him now, and I know you can read it, you just don't want to! Tommy is dying! Do something to help him! Do what the mysteries tell us to do."

"I can't stand this pain!" Tommy screamed. "Whatever you have to do, do it now!"

A little cry broke from Stephanovich, like a pitiable peep from a stricken bird in a net. He spun around like a mad monkey in a cage and lifted the paper above his head to throw light on the tiny, cryptic, foreign characters written in fading black ink on the yellowed sheet, on the Transylvanian Mysteries. He wished to make absolutely sure of his instructions.

"Oh, no. Oh, no, no, no! It does say that. It says what I thought it said."

"What is it? What does it say? Hurry!"

Stephanovich threw his hand down to his side and shook in anger.

"I can't do this! I can't do this no matter what! I won't do it! I love this boy. I love him more than my own life. It has to be wrong!"

"You have to do what it says. No matter what it is, you have to do it! We live by the mysteries, and without them we're done."

"It says we have to cut off his head. Only that will save him."

In the dark basement of their new house, with the unseen mountains of Montana beyond the dank walls of the basement seemingly mocking them with brightness and light and life and joy, they fell into that peculiar awful silence that is the quiet of the soon-dead. Motionless, in great fear, and seemingly eternal, that quiet gripped them so tightly it squeezed the breath out of them so that no air passed into or out of their lungs for several seconds.

Elsa and Stephanovich simply stared at each other, as though not believing their lives had come to this.

Only when Tommy screamed out in agony from the floor again did they come back to an existence they no longer wanted. The little boy was in such great pain now he was beyond speech, beyond reason, and yet they would not, they could not, kill him as the mysteries dictated.

"Are you sure you read it correctly?"

Stephanovich partly crumpled the parchment in his hand, forming a tight angry fist around them.

"It says, 'The victim of this black affliction of blood dissolution must be hung upside-down like a savage wild pig and his head cut off from his body, before the black blood dissolution washes over him completely and tears the hair from his head and dissolves the skull shielding his brain in a flooding agony of pain. Then it will be too late for him, it will be too late to make the victim whole again, if the brain is gone, and he will wash away into the ground and his spirit will wither and die and never reach eternity.'"

"Good god! It says that?"

"I can't do this sacrifice, not to one I love so much. Let me kill myself first."

Stephanovich looked around desperately for a knife to slit his own throat.

"No! Stand him up! Good god, stand him up and gather your courage for this!" Elsa screamed. "The black blood is trickling up the back of his neck!"

The boy was bound in a straightjacket, his feet tied together so that he could not kick or move but only scream in agony. In a pool of his own black and red blood on the concrete floor, he thrashed in agony, the two-colored blood seeping out of his flesh in an uncontrollable flow until he looked like little more than commingled black and red liquid somehow formed into the shape of a boy.

He could still scream, and only out of desperation at what Stephanovich said must be done to him could he still talk.

"I heard what you said! I heard it! You want to cut off my head! You want to cut it off and think that will make me better, but no, don't do it! Don't cut my head from my body! It won't help me at all. Please, please don't do it!"

Almost roughly, and certainly grimly, they grasped the little boy's dissolving arms in their rubber-gloved hands and pulled him to his feet and stood him on what used to be his feet. His legs would not hold. Elsa had to support him while Stephanovich tied the rope around the bloody bones of his ankles. Grasping him close as he thrashed and cried out, they felt the black blood splash by them, and tears flowed from their eyes as they prepared to do this horrible thing to their son.

"Hold him! Hold him!" Stephanovich yelled out, his voice breaking with the agony of what he was doing.

"I'm trying. He's slipping away. He's slipping away, and dying! Whatever you do, do it quickly!"

"Hold him tighter."

"I am holding him tightly. He's dying. Don't you understand that?"

Again, a cry of agony broke from Stephanovich's throat. He sobbed so loudly Elsa's legs nearly collapsed beneath her, but he shot to his feet and in one motion threw the loose end of the rope over a wooden beam above their heads. He caught the other end and was pulling on it hard before he regained his composure and roared out instructions to his wife.

"Let him go!"

She could hardly hold him, and her heart told her she must not let him go, as the fierce tug on the rope tore the little boy's body out of her grasp and upward, upside-down, to swing as a man executed by hanging would swing in the wind. In her agony over the coming murder of their son, she grasped the body feebly until it slipped out of her hands and swung away. She gave out a piteous cry, and the body flew further skyward, like a savage thrashing pig's, until it hung over a large silver vat. Even before it stopped swinging Stephanovich tied off the rope on the sturdy handle of the vat and picked up a machete off the floor.

"Don't do this! Not this!" Tommy screamed. "I want to live! Fix me somehow, but not this!"

"The blood is washing over his hair!" Elsa screamed out, stricken with grief. "He's done! He's finished!"

"This is going to kill Maggie, to lose her brother, too. We are all dead after this."

The little boy's body was disintegrating already, falling in small pieces to the bottom of the silver vat.

"Just do it!" Elsa screamed. "You must do it now! Cut off his head! Save your son from more pain."

With hot tears streaming down his face and washing his son's red blood away from his cheeks in white streaks, Stephanovich drew back the machete in a full arc and screamed out so loudly the noise blew open the basement's casement windows with hurricane force.

Outside, the happy, sun-drenched mountains felt the fierce power of the scream wash over them. They could understand nothing of the animalistic horror of that scream, or what it meant to everyone who lived in peace in their shadows.

To the mountains, it was a scream that meant nothing.

2

Maggie walked barefoot through the mountains for several hours each day. Her trips sometimes lasted until sunset, on summer days, that is. When the winter snows covered the Bitterroot Mountains, her pilgrimages were curtailed by Stephanovich and Elsa out of concern for her survival. The mountains were unforgiving and fierce in the winter and would surely kill her. Since Mabin had died, she had little use for her powers, even for survival, and she ignored the magic within her to wait for his return. She did little with her life but wait for him to live again, as was promised by the mysteries. With little concern for herself or understanding what she was doing, she closed off her mind and would have walked in the cold but for her step-parents' concerns. So in winter she paced barefoot inside the house while staring out the windows at where she thought Mabin was buried.

"It's up there where my sweet love lies, calm and at peace," she'd say, in a sing-song musical way, talking to the mountain as though it would answer. "Keep my sweet love warm and well, mountain, until the day he steps out of his grave and walks into my arms, for it is said he must return to me, according to the truth of the mysteries."

There were strange ideas twirling around in her head, tiny dancers of hope. He was to come to life again just one year after he was murdered by the vampires who were now recovered and living normally as her neighbors and friends, free of the lust for blood. She and Tommy and Mabin and Stephanovich and Elsa had saved those tortured souls and brought them back to a normal life, and to further develop the community, Stephanovich and Elsa were making plans to begin gold-mining operations on the mountain and employ hundreds of the saved from the town. Stephanovich had already blasted several exploratory shafts into St. Mary's mountain to discover where best to do the mining. The souls they had rehabilitated from their monstrous habits and made human again were alive and well and soon to prosper due to their efforts, but Mabin was gone, at least for this year. Yes, he was to come to life again, be resurrected, Maggie knew, by her blood. She waited for that and that alone. Maggie was not recovered from any of her earlier adventures in fighting the vampires, and simply lived these days in wait for Mabin's rebirth, which she believed would make her whole again. During all those months of waiting for love to flourish, like the green buds of spring, she walked barefoot through the house staring at the mountains, mumbling to herself. She lit up brightly whenever she saw Tommy. Tommy was going to save Mabin and her. He alone had that power, since he would perform Mabin's final resurrection.

"You remember where you buried him, don't you? You remember what day you have to go out into the mountains to dig him up, don't you?" she'd ask. "It's exactly one year after he died that you should go to the mountains and bring my love home to me."

"I remember. Here, I have it written down, the date and the time and the place, on this piece of paper in my pocket. See? I know the mysteries say I'm the only one who can exhume him up and revive him, so I'm really careful with the exact location and time."

"I don't know what I'd do if you can't save him. I might wander through the mountains forever without him, or eat the earth, or live in a tree and stare at the sky all day."

"Ew, gross, Maggie."

"Or I might do worse to myself."

"Maggie, come on. Don't be a dorky jerk about this love junk. You know I'll do what I have to do to bring Mabin back. You're saying these things again like your brain is all messed up and scrambled. I don't know why they come out of you. They make me think there's something wrong with you."

"I think there is something very wrong with me, Tommy. It's all wrong."

Tommy would produce the crumpled sheet of paper from his pocket, carefully open it and hold it in front of her gray sparkling eyes, which danced at the sight of it. Her eyes had dark circles around them, and the bones of her cheeks stuck out alarmingly, for she had nightmares and lost sleep and weight. She would scan the boy's scrawl and she would smile adoringly at the writing on the paper, as though it was scripture. She'd nod, shiver and hug Tommy and say, "You'll tell me you're going on the day you dig him up, won't you? I can't come with you, according to the mysteries, but I'll wait here until you bring Mabin back home to me. You have to tell me when you're going to do it, though, so that I can be happy that day and prepare to love him again. You know I can't be happy until that day."

Sometimes, Maggie collapsed to the floor out of sheer exhaustion when pestering Tommy about when he was doing to bring Mabin back from the dead, and he'd have to help her into bed and make her rest until she was well. He'd serve her chicken soup he made himself.

"Just get better," he'd say. "You can't be like this when Mabin comes back. He wants to see the same beautiful girl he loved when he died, not a sick girl."

"I promise to be beautiful for him. I promise to get better, if he thinks I should."

Although he was several years younger than Maggie, Tommy was a mature and confident boy, more confident and mature than Maggie ever was, and he was every bit as tough as she was. He'd hold her lovingly, comforting her, and stay with her through her fits of anxiety. She had lost her lover, and Tommy had only been captured and held and tormented by the vampires. He had been saved, she and Mabin and Elsa and Stephanovich had saved him, but Mabin had not been saved, and had been killed, and it made her sad and mad and a little crazy to be alone. How is it that the best and strongest among them had died? The only thing that kept her going was her little brother and his promise of bringing about Mabin's redemption. Tommy understood that once the year was over Mabin would be healed in the ground by the blood that had been withdrawn from her heart and injected into his heart. Then Tommy would be there to dig up her lover, who would be bright and sweet and as loving toward her as he had ever been, and the vampires could never harm them again with strong Mabin at her side. The blood from her heart was in the grave with him, she thought as she lay sick in bed, and her blood was healing him and making him whole again. It made her feel she was with him.

Still, it had been a sad, lonely year, and she had many twisted thoughts of what could go wrong. Secretly, she feared her blood could not cure him, that it was not good enough, and he would never live again.

When winter passed, she returned to the forest to wait for her lover.

In the woods where she walked, she noticed certain spots on the ground held pools of black blood, blood leftover from the bloody lightning that had been hurled at them by Karin after the vampires had killed Mabin and he could no longer protect them. In other places, blood was leaking out of the mountain. Much of the blood simply dried up and disintegrated, becoming part of the forest and nature, but other pools bubbled up and hissed, as though freshly seeping out of St. Mary's mountain. The mountain itself seemed to be bleeding, while Mabin lay dead in it. In waves that lapped the edges of the pools, this active blood seemed to want to break the bonds that trapped it. In places, the black blood had broken through the surrounding walls that held it. It had seeped out in streams, only to be frustrated again when the ground wrapped new walls around it and held it in check. Maggie knew better that to touch the black blood, and she hated it. It was a contagion, and evil, the same sort of contagion that had destroyed Mabin, and it was best simply to let it dry up and die, be transformed into something good in nature by the forest's beneficent forces. She noticed it was leaking out in places all over the mountain.

"The black blood can not harm you," she sang to herself. "I walk over blood, and laugh at blood, and know you are better than it."

"Maggie!" Tommy would yet at her. "You're doing it again. Let's go home before you make yourself sick in the head again."

Stephanovich had told her what she little she knew about the black blood, that it held sickness and disintegration for any living person who touched it, but that it healed the dead. That only made her crazier as she walked among the standing lakes of blood in the forest. They were like dark mirrors of wickedness, and she would stare at her image reflected in that wickedness. Evil never left the blood, even when vampires were cured and the black blood left them.

She thought she found Mabin's grave on one of her walks through the forest, and the strange thing was the grave was covered by a pool of the black blood.

Maybe she was wrong, maybe this was not the place where Mabin lay buried under the mountain forest's healing soil, maybe this was not the place where he was beating death with the blood withdrawn from her heart reviving him after Stephanovich injected it, her blood, into his heart. The black blood was bubbling up like thick tar over the spot she thought was Mabin's grave, but it was contained in a pool there. She wondered, *should I break through the wall that holds the blood in its pool and let it flow out so that he will not be harmed?* Maybe this is not the place he is buried, she thought. *Oh, why is he dead? Why not me instead?* Maybe it was just another pool of blood in the forest where there were many pools of blood, and maybe he was still safe. She lifted her toe carefully, about to dip it in the blood and then push it through the wall of soil that held the blood in place.

"What are you doing?" Tommy had screamed at her, so alarmed he ran to her from next to a huge Ponderosa pine. "Are you crazy? Don't you know what that is?"

"It's black blood. I know black blood, and black blood knows me. I know it could kill me, but I'm afraid Mabin is in there in the black blood."

"He's not! He's not, no! He's somewhere else. I buried him somewhere else. If you touch the black blood it will destroy you the way it would destroy any of us if it gets out!"

She drew back her toe but continued to stare at her reflection in the dark pool. That does not look like me, she thought, as she stared at her own image. What if I am not me anymore? Will he still love me?

"Ah, well, if that's the case and Mabin is not in there, then I won't touch it," she said suddenly, just so that Tommy would not yell at her again.

She stood staring down at the pool of shimmering black, and still saw her contorted image in it. Her image was speaking lying words to Tommy.

"Get away from it. Don't worry. Even if that is Mabin's grave, I'll take care of it. We just have to wait for the whole year to pass and your blood to revive him and things will be as they were with the two of you."

"I love Mabin," she murmured, seeing her lips move truthfully in her reflection. "I love you, too, Tommy."

So Tommy had taken her by the hand then and led her away from the grave with black blood, for something in her little brother's manner told her it was Mabin's grave and he was in terrible danger from the viscous blood. If it was seeping down into the grave, it could do terrible things to him, and she could not let that happen. She loved her brother and Mabin too much for anything bad to happen to either one or the other. If she lost Tommy, too, she would lose it all.

"Wait."

"What?"

"Is he in there? If he is in there, you have to tell me," she said, very calmly. "I won't lose him again to the black blood."

"I told you, I'll take care of it. I'm good at this stuff, saving people. Now let's go. It's not close to a year yet. We don't want to disturb his recovery."

"Good-bye, Mabin. Good-bye, my flower."

Tommy grabbed her by the hand and pulled hard on it to get her moving toward home and she skipped through the forest with him.

Her walks on the mountain did not end with Tommy's warning to stay away from Mabin's grave, and Tommy did not forget what his sister proposed to do. In a way, he did not trust her, and he thought she was more than a little crazy. He did not trust the way she was now, with as many wispy goblins in her head as there were real vampires in the world. He accompanied her on her walks after that, watching her carefully and steering her away from the area where she believed the grave of her lover to be. Her memory was so poor now. Her mind had holes in it. She could not remember the place where the grave was. She thought it might be better that way, since she knew in her heart it was best to stay away from the grave, for she would spend all of her time there if she could. Her memory was so clouded, and it always seemed her mind was in a fog, or missing parts of itself, and she had so hard a time just living without Mabin.

Then one day she turned around while walking through the forest and Tommy was not there.

Her heart pounded when she thought he had never been there, that he was imaginary and unreal, along with everything else, that he was someone she made up in her insanity to drive away the goblins from her thoughts. Tommy had never been with her in the forest, she imagined, feeling more than a little crazy, and she nearly collapsed on the ground when she realized what that meant, that her little brother was dead and that Mabin was dead and they were all death and never coming back. The vampires had won. They had taken both, and it was only an illusion she had lived by for this entire year, that she would love again, that Mabin would live again. They had not killed the vampires, and she never even had a little brother.

"Tommy? You should be here but you're not here. What's wrong? Did I do something? Are you mad at me? Why won't you talk to me?"

Before she knew it, she was running away so fast from the demons in her head that she thought she was in some other world, a world of blurs and incense and smoke and brittle claws reaching out to scratch her arms as she ran by. They scratched her arms to get to the blood inside her, and she felt the warm trickles of blood dripping down her arms as the trees scratched her.

Then someone said inside her head that the black blood had reached the town of Victor.

She reported that to her step-father.

"My god, what are they talking about now?" asked Stephanovich. "The blood is isolated in the forest, it's trapped there and can't come here. We've stopped blasting the mountain, in case that's what has opened the cracks in it. Who said there was black blood in Victor?"

"Pamela Perashunet. She said she saw a lump of it crawling across her lawn and leaving a trail behind her," Maggie said. "I went to her house. It was there. The trail of blood was there. I saw it."

"Who is this Pamela Perashunet?" Stephanovich asked. "I don't know anyone by that name."

"I know her well. That woman hasn't recovered yet from her time as a vampire," Elsa broke in. "Some of Karin's victims are still a little wobbly. She's one of them."

"I saw the trail of blood."

"Maggie ..."

"It was headed for our house."

Stephanovich blanched when he heard that. He appeared as though he had swallowed something very large and it was caught in his throat and blocked his speech.

"Where's Tommy?" Maggie asked. "He should know about this."

"I haven't seen Tommy."

"I haven't seen him for days."

Stephanovich turned away with such pain gripping him that he bent at the waist and grimaced in agony. He wrapped his arms around his center and leaned so far forward he nearly collapsed.

"My head ... my head is going to crack open," he cried, grasping his skull. "I am going mad."

"Doesn't that worry you, that we haven't seen Tommy?" Maggie asked, barely noticing her father's condition in her preoccupation with her own.

"Please, don't ask us about Tommy now," Elsa said, with such a strange, twisted expression on her face that it seemed she had gone mad, too. "You don't know ... Tommy needs some time to himself."

"Why? I need Tommy to myself."

"Stop asking, Maggie," Elsa yelled, grasping her head as Stephanovich was grasping his. "Please. He needs time to himself, that's all. Look what you're doing to your father. Please just let it go and don't ask about Tommy again."

"Well, if you don't care about him, I do. I'm going to the woods to look for him. He's my brother and I love him."

"Don't you think we do?" Stephanovich screamed, frothing at the mouth. "I love that boy more than god."

"Don't go in the woods, Maggie," Elsa said.

"Why? What's wrong with dad?"

"It's not safe. And Tommy is not there."

"Then you did see the black blood. It was here. What happened to – "

"It's still all over the forest. You know what happens if you touch it."

"Mabin's in the forest. He's all alone, buried in the ground with all that around him. Can you imagine what that must be like for him? I have to go to him and stay with him through the night."

"You'll endanger us all. You'll kill yourself."

"If he stays in the ground one day too long, it will be the end of him, and Tommy is – "

"Don't talk about Tommy!"

"Mabin has your blood in his heart. That will protect him. Don't worry about Mabin. Tommy has things under control."

Maggie calmed down with that thought of safety, a warm feeling rushing into her heart at the idea that Mabin had her blood within him, injected into his heart, so that nothing could harm him now. Her blood was coursing through his heart and veins, so he could never be lonely, and he could never be harmed, and soon he would be alive again and with her.

Her brother Tommy would save her lover Mabin. She knew that to be the case now.

"I'm going to find Tommy," Maggie repeated, walking toward the door as though in a trance.

Stephanovich fell to the floor with a crash, unable to resist the agony the mention of his dead son's name gave him.

"You touched it!" Maggie yelled. "That's what's the matter with you! You touched black blood!"

"No, it's not ... that. I did not do that," Stephanovich managed to say. "Tommy ... "

He wept and groaned pitifully from the floor.

"Then what is it? Where is Mabin? Is he here? He brought the black blood into this house, didn't he? I know you'd hide him from me if he was here and wasn't right."

"It's not even the day to dig him up," Elsa said wearily, tears streaming down her face suddenly. "Look what you're doing to your father with this crazy talk. Do you have a heart at all?"

Kneeling beside him, Elsa caressed her husband's soaked forehead, and then she sobbed with agony herself, biting her lip and covering her eyes with her free hand.

"I can't live like this."

"Something's wrong."

"There's nothing – "

"Don't lie to me. Things haven't been right this entire year, for it has almost been a year since Mabin was killed and we buried him with my blood to resurrect him."

"It will all work out," Elsa said. "Just trust us. Things might seem bad right now, but trust me they will work out."

Stephanovich let out a wail as he curled up tightly on the floor, pulling his knees into his chest.

"Look at him. Does he look normal? Don't try to tell me everything will be all right while dad can't even stand or talk."

"Tell her," Stephanovich whispered from the floor. "Tell her what we did."

"Tell me what? What did you do?"

"We can't tell her."

Stephanovich's voice was barely audible.

"We have to tell her. Tell her what we did."

"I can't!"

Now Elsa collapsed to the floor next to her husband, sitting down suddenly on her haunches and staring off into space with a dead look in her eyes. She was frozen in horror, and then she trembled slightly.

"I can't tell her what we did unless I did it to myself first. I must take revenge on myself for what we did."

Stephanovich gripped his gut tighter and closed his eyes so that he could not see the words he was about to utter.

Nothing was going to stop him from admitting what they did, from admitting his guilt.

"I cut off Tommy's head. It's in a cooler in the cellar, along with the rest of him in a silver vat."

Then there were three on the floor as Maggie collapsed beside them. She fell down hard when her father admitted he had killed his only son.

"Why did you do it?" she screamed. "To Tommy ... why ... to Tommy?"

"Because the mysteries told us we had to," Elsa yelled. "They are sacred. We had to do their bidding. They told us to cut off his head."

"His head? His head?" Maggie held her own tightly. She got to her knees. "Would you kill me if the mysteries told you to? Would you do that? Cut off my head?"

Elsa and Stephanovich exchanged glances helplessly with horror. They could not say a single word in answer.

"Cut it off! Go ahead! Cut it off! I don't have a single thing to live for, so you might as well kill me, too! Do it!"

3

As she screamed, Maggie entered an even stranger state of mind in which she thought she was a reflection of herself in a mirror looking back at herself but unable to see anyone there. She felt flattened-out and shimmering, and trapped within two dimensions and unable to understand or see anything real. A man with a good heart who is broken down by grief and guilt can only babble the story of the horror he's done, and when he has beheaded his only son out of necessity the only coherent thing he can say is, "I'm sorry. We live and die by the mysteries. I love my boy, I love him, and he was dying. We had to kill him to save him."

It was not good enough for Maggie.

"That's ridiculous!" she screamed.

It did not seem possible that such a good man as Stephanovich could do something so heinous as cut off the head of her little brother.

Yet he had admitted it.

"The black blood had gotten him," Elsa managed to say, seeing the strange way Maggie was looking at everything, as she thought of herself as only two-dimensional. "The mysteries told us it would save him, but nothing good came of it."

How could they have thought anything good could come from such an act? Stephanovich was a sweet man with a loving heart, and Elsa was a good woman, but the only message Maggie received from her parents' wails and babble as they writhed on the floor were their expressions of sorrow and self-revulsion after doing something they could not justify. She stopped listening. Everything was unreal to her, existence inside a mirror from which she could no longer see herself. To make it worse, a plethora of indistinguishable words poured out of Stephanovich like the words of a madman. It was as though the mysteries were speaking their ancient languages through him, and the only clear thing he said was that he was sorry, and sorry, and so sorry. Stunned, Maggie still could not much comprehend anything of what he said or what she saw, for as troubled and incoherent as he was, she was just as stricken. She understood at once that her little brother was gone, but she could not believe it, for she could not see such a thing ever happening. It was a great blow to her since he was one of the two loves of her life, but she also understood with dread that his death also meant the other love of her life was as good as dead, too. Mabin could never recover now, never grow again to be the lover he had been to her while buried underground with her blood in him, and the great cure promised in the Transylvanian Mysteries would never come about. Brother and lover were gone.

There were no images of this world she could still recognize.

"We should drink blood," Elsa said.

Again Maggie seemed divorced from any sort of reality, unable to comprehend such babble.

"Are you insane?"

Stephanovich sat bolt-upright and turned to his wife.

"No!" he screamed in her face. "No! Never! That will solve nothing."

Suddenly, he was awake and alert and glaring at his wife.

She did not flinch, but her eyes tossed around in their sockets as though they had thoughts of their own.

"Why not? Why shouldn't we? Ha, ha. I'm tired of this, of always losing the things we love most, just so we can say we're good people, just to live by our sacred mysteries. We've held out all these years and lived by our sacred texts what has it gotten us? We have been upright, uptight even, while everyone else has given in to their desires for fame and immortality, and what has it gotten us?"

"We're still human. That is quite enough."

Stephanovich was clear-spoken and calm in his opposition, still glaring at her, when Elsa suggested they taste forever.

"Look what it's gotten us," Elsa repeated. "I see nothing good in this world right now."

Maggie was curled up into a ball, groaning, and if a cup filled will blood infected by the vampire virus was offered to her now, she would not have hesitated but would have done what her step-mother suggested.

That might have made her seem real to herself again.

"This only seems insane. We can work this out," Stephanovich said. "There's no need to fall victim to the weakness and failings of others when we have the mysteries on our side."

"My dead boy ... Only blood, and forgetting, could make any of us feel alive again. Maybe drinking blood would make him come back to us."

"Bad blood is what took him from us."

Elsa seemed crushed by those words, and tumbled over and lay on the floor in the same fetal position that twisted Maggie's body with agony.

Maggie thought of the one thing that could make the world real to her once more.

"I want to see Tommy," she said. "If all has gone wrong, maybe this is our time to turn. Maybe it would save him."

Stephanovich turned to her with horror, trembling again and about to collapse into the same incoherent agony that had consumed him moments ago before revulsion brought him back his dignity.

"We can't. We can't show him to you. We can't stand what we've done. I can't look at it. I can't let my eyes rest on the thing we've done to our son."

"If we showed you, we'd have to drink blood," Elsa said. "We'd be as terrible as those we oppose. But, oh, if we ..."

"It wouldn't bring him back."

"I have to see Tommy. Show me what you've done to him."

"No!"

Now Elsa seemed to have come back to her dignity, seemed to have understood what she had suggested would fix nothing. It was as though the image of what Tommy was now, once brought back to her, showed the futility of corruption.

"What good would that do, Maggie? We've told you what we did, and the best we can do now is survive the guilt that's tearing us to pieces, making us mad. There eventually might be a way out of this in the mysteries. We still trust them. We have to put our hopes in them."

Maggie's mouth gaped open, and she stared at Elsa in disbelief, but Elsa with clear wide eyes turned to Stephanovich and nodded.

Stephanovich could not bear to look at his wife, and turned to Maggie.

"Then translate the part of the mysteries that will tell us what to do to save Tommy," Maggie said. "Then we can save Mabin, too."

"I can't translate it."

"Why not? You're the language expert. You can translate anything. Get them to tell you how to fix this."

"I can't translate that section of the mysteries because it's still writing itself in ways I haven't seen before."

"What does that mean?"

"It means the mysteries are as alive as you and me, and that old piece of parchment containing the mysteries is a sentient, growing being. It's taking nourishment from the lives around it and reacting in words to the situations we find ourselves in. It knows Tommy has been beheaded. It told us to do it. It's part of a greater plan."

"A plan to destroy us?"

"Perhaps."

"No. That's impossible."

"Waiting is the only thing possible. The Transylvania Mysteries have a soul, and it is contained in the words it writes when it understands the world around it and instructs us on what to do next."

"That parchment is alive?"

"Why shouldn't it be?"

"Because it ... I don't know. It's parchment."

"It is made of sheepskin, which was once and is again alive whenever we consult it. We've been waiting for days for more words to inscribe themselves on it so that we would know what to do. We haven't told you about Tommy because we were afraid and horrified and paralyzed with grief. We're helpless to repair our wrongs until it tells us what to do."

Maggie shot to her feet.

"I'm not waiting. I want to see the mysteries."

"It won't do any good. We check them several times a day. We've checked them everyday, all day, since Tommy ..."

Stephanovich broke down again with a sudden outburst of tears that found him covering his face in shame and dread at what he had done. His face was so red and bloated and soaked with tears that it seemed every tiny blood vessel in it would burst from the pressure.

"I think I can read them."

"You can't read them, Maggie. You don't know the language. You've never been able to read them."

"I think I can read them now. I can feel it. I think I'll know what the mysteries want to say once I have them in my hands. I just feel it."

Stephanovich stood so still, staring at Maggie, that it seemed he had frozen in time and might never move again. The paralysis had taken over his mind and would not let him move or think or respond. Then his jaw twitched and his eyes softened. He had learned never to question Maggie's powers, for she was able to do more sober of blood than anyone he knew who had imbibed. He shivered, and then moved quickly toward a drawer in the cabinet, hesitated there staring down at it, but then pulled the drawer open and removed the ancient parchment containing the Transylvanian Mysteries. He crossed the room to hand the parchment to her.

"What do I do?"

"Read it."

"How do I do that?"

"It has to become your mind. It feels your mind. What you see in front of you has to become your mind."

In a strange way, Maggie understood what he meant. As soon as the mysteries were in her hands, she felt them soften from a stiff, unyielding document to a cloth-like softness. At the top of the parchment, she saw characters that were no more than scribbles lined up from side to side, with others walking wildly up and down the page, all across the page. If this was her mind being probed ... She stared at the squiggles until they began to move coherently, to re-form themselves into something intelligible, like black worms twisting across the surface to become sentences. Somehow, she understood what one word meant, then another and finally the last two, even though the writing came in no language she comprehended.

She dropped the parchment to the floor.

"Oh, no, what did it say now?" Stephanovich asked. "I can see from your reaction something is wrong. It can't be more horrible than what it told us to do."

"It repeated what it told you to do."

"It repeated?"

"It said to me, 'Cut off his head.'"

Stephanovich gasped, staring down at the document, and Elsa rushed forward in tears and leaned over and roughly swiped up the mysteries off the floor.

"That's it! I've had enough. I can't stand it. Let's get rid of this awful thing. How much more awful can things get? What other horrors must we endure because of it? Drinking blood can't be worse than this."

With his hands trembling, Stephanovich gently pulled the mysteries from Elsa's hands. She let them go, but then hung her head and wept.

"You know you don't mean that. Here, Maggie. Go ahead, read it. Try again to understand."

He handed the parchment to her.

"I don't want to. Why did it tell me to do what you already did?"

"Maybe because you're reading seriously for the first time. Concentrate. Think seriously of what you want to know. It won't disappoint you. It's clear to me now that you can read scripture. It's a great gift."

Maggie grasped the ancient document, once again coarse when it reached her hands, but then it softened again when she lowered her eyes to it. As soon as she did, black characters formed one at a time on its surface, making a word that made no sense to her, one she could not understand. Once the word was formed, its strange characters migrated across the surface, leaping over or under each other, until they stood still and Maggie comprehended what it was saying.

"What does that mean?"

"What did it say?"

"It said, 'tomorrow.'"

"That's all?"

"That's it. Just 'tomorrow.'"

In frustration and anger, Maggie lowered her eyes to the mysteries once again, and to her surprise, more inky characters were forming across the page. Each was more exotic than the other, resembling nothing she had ever seen but each imparting in her a sense of promise and hope that she felt in her gut. Quickly now, the characters seeped out from the sheepskin one after the other, and then spread in similar martial formations across the surface, leaping over one another or ducking beneath each other. Within seconds, there was a line of the exotic characters across the page. Their movement stopped.

With a quick glance, Maggie read the words she had never seen, and then her hands trembled. Her face turned white.

"What is it?" Stephanovich. "Did it repeat itself?"

"Yes. It says, 'tomorrow.'"

Maggie's hands were trembling as she held the mysteries.

"You told us that already."

"I know, but it added something I don't want it to say. It says, 'Tomorrow. Come back tomorrow after a night in the woods. Both have black blood in them. If you survive tonight, you will die tomorrow.'"

Elsa collapsed to the floor hysterically.

"Now our daughter? They're taking our daughter now? The mysteries want to kill her, too. It's too much, too much. I won't do it!"

Stephanovich angrily tore the parchment from Maggie's hands to read it for himself. His eyes danced across the page intensely, and then he too dropped to the floor, resigned to the new horror.

"It's true. That's what the mysteries say. If Maggie doesn't die tonight in the woods, she'll die tomorrow in some way we don't know."

Stephanovich raised his eyes skyward and opened his arms in an embrace of the heavens.

"The mysteries see Maggie dead, also. It can not be. Stop this! Stop it, stop it, stop it!"

Now Maggie felt her mind swimming out of control as she stumbled backward into the cabinet and held on to it to keep herself upright.

"It wants me to find Mabin in the woods tonight," she said. "That's what it means, that's all. It's not that the mysteries want to kill me. Tommy is dead and can't dig Mabin up, but I can. It's telling me to exhume Mabin up and save him, and then I might die."

She flashed a wry smile at Elsa and Stephanovich and her gray eyes sparkled strangely.

"It's all right. It's what I want. I wanted this all along."

Then she blacked out and collapsed to the floor beside her parents, who embraced her tightly in tears until she woke up and remembered what she had to do.

She stepped out of the mirror and back into reality.

4

It was as good to go out at twilight to die as a real person as it was to go out later in the black of night to find death as a mere reflection of herself. There was clarity and purity to the late mountain light and freshness to the evening mountain air that braced her for what she had to do, go die for Mabin. Death could as soon come early as late, as long as she found Mabin first, as long as she lived life with as much reality as possible, and brought her lover home.

The sun had sunk behind the mountains and it was time to go while there was still light.

Try to be brave and die without thinking of yourself, she thought. Think of your brother, and think of Mabin, and then you will be able to make things right with yourself. Always make things right with yourself first.

Elsa was fidgeting by her side but silent, as though she wished to speak but thought she should not.

"Why not stay home?" she finally asked, frightened, as Maggie was about to leave. "Please, every minute counts. Stay with us at home for just one more night. We know you can't avoid what's going to happen to you, but if you have the choice, why not put it off for one more night?"

"Elsa, Maggie is not going to die," Stephanovich said. "I'm certain of that. I'm sure that's not what the mysteries meant for her."

Maggie shook her hair and looked at her reflection in the window. She no longer resided in the mirror and would not exist as a mere reflection, she told herself. She would do what real things needed to be done.

"It doesn't matter, except to me," Maggie answered, as if she had not one care in the world. "If I don't go into the mountains, we know it's the end for Mabin. If I do go, it's the end of me tonight. If I don't go tonight, it's the end of me tomorrow. So what does it matter if I live a few more hours? I would simply be putting off the inevitable without saving anyone, for the mysteries say it's tonight in the forest I die or tomorrow in some way I don't know about."

Elsa's answer was to turn to Stephanovich and repeat her earlier solution.

"Why can't we drink blood then? Then we could at least keep Maggie alive, if the three of us turned. What harm will it do to keep Maggie alive, or even better, immortal? And we can stay with her forever and never lose another child."

"It's not a choice any parent should ever have to make, so we won't make it," Stephanovich said. "That's final. We are living our lives as human beings, and that's final."

"I'm thirsty, I'm thirsty," Elsa whined. "I want her to live. It could save her."

"I'd like to see Tommy one more time before I go," Maggie said.

"No, you wouldn't," Stephanovich snapped, turning to her, alarmed. "You should not see what he looks like in his present condition. Your mind would snap and you would not be able to do now what you have to do. Instead, remember the way he was the last time you saw him, and think you will see him that way again if things work out."

"Then I guess I'm off."

She kissed Elsa on the cheek, and then Stephanovich.

"We'll check the mysteries every day for a solution to what ails Tommy. If, in some way, you don't – "

"I will. I can feel it. All of us will survive in some way, if only in each other's minds."

Elsa let out a wail and tears flowed down her cheeks as she embraced Maggie so tightly she thought it might be the end of her, too.

There was a gurgling sound that froze the two of them just as Stephanovich was about to throw his arms around them both to join in the hug.

"What's that?"

The noise came from the edge of the forest, just twenty feet away. In silence, the three of them walked toward the gurgling, and when they had reached the first trees, they saw a flow of thick black blood tumbling between two rocks and inching toward them. They instantly recoiled in disgust.

"Good god, the blood's making its way out of the forest now," Stephanovich said. "I don't know if we can stop it before it breaks through and overwhelms us all. It's flowing out of cracks all over the hill."

He ran in a circle around the flow until he came to the other side of the rocks and looked down. His eyes followed a course up into the forest until his gaze settled on a point fifty feet up the hillside.

"It's a flow, a stream," he said. "Soon, it'll be a torrent. It's coming from far up there, from somewhere near Mabin's grave, I believe, but it's moving very slowly for now."

"It's my path to follow," Maggie said, staring up the mountainside as though she was in a trance.

"What do you mean?"

"The blood will take me to him."

"Why do you say that?"

"Because I know. Something in my head told me. I'm to follow it up into the mountains toward Mabin."

"Don't touch it!"

"I know. It's telling me that, too. Mabin's telling me that touching it killed Tommy."

"It's just blood, Maggie, and it's not going to stop right here," Stephanovich said, leaping down off the rocks in a panic. "It's coming for the development. It's coming for everyone. For all of those who used to be vampires. It wants them all back again. How did we get things so wrong when we cured all these people? It's coming for them, and I have no confidence they'll be able to resist it."

The black blood barely had moved from the base of the rocks, but it was creeping toward town as slowly as the hands on a clock move, just as Stephanovich said. As though it had a life of its own, the blood suddenly leaped in the air in twin towers eight feet tall, as though it had hands, toward Stephanovich's throat. It came within inches of him, but all the physical training he had done in his life made him too fast for it, and he leaped back to avoid its grasp. He stood staring at the pool of black blood that had attacked him, panting and blinking fast, and backed away from it an additional three steps.

"How do you kill a thing that does that? I never saw it do anything like that before. We are fighting a special foe here today."

"What ... I don't understand what just happened," Maggie said.

"Now you see now what it can do, Maggie, and what you have to fear."

"I saw, but why is this happening?"

"That was close. It's not something we can understand until we live it."

"Move away from it, dear," said Elsa, grabbing Maggie by the arm. "You know what happens if it touches you. Poor Tommy found out what – "

Elsa broke off her warning and sobbed again, trembling over her entire body.

"Can't you stay?" she wailed.

"We should tell you something," Stephanovich said quickly, turning to Maggie.

"I know what the black blood can do. You don't have to tell me."

"It's not that. It's something about Tommy."

"What about Tommy? Is he all right?"

"Maggie, you know he isn't."

"But he will be, right?"

"I don't know. We will do our best to bring him back once the mysteries reveal the procedure."

"Then what's going on? Why are you acting so weird?"

"Well ..."

Stephanovich stared at Elsa, until she turned her head away and tightly pursed her lips.

"What about Tommy?" Maggie insisted.

"He caused all this."

"What do you mean?"

"The blood, I mean, the black blood escaping was his doing. He went for Mabin early. He dug up the corpse before it was ready to live again, and the black blood took him in the process. I might have opened cracks in this mountain with the blasting for gold, but he dug directly into the spot where the blood was thickest."

Maggie paused for a moment to stare at the dark pool near her feet, as though it would tell her what it all meant.

The blood was calm and mute.

"But he was so sure of himself. He said he knew exactly where Mabin was buried and what day he had to exhume him. He said it over and over."

Stephanovich pulled Maggie away from the blood by the arm and stared into her gray eyes intently.

"He did it for you."

"For me? What does that mean, he did it for me? Didn't he know the day Mabin would come back was the only thing I was living for? Didn't he know how much I love him?"

"He didn't think you would last the full year. None of us did. He thought you had gone crazy."

"I'm here. I was waiting. I'm not crazy but I am strange and I had all my hopes pinned on my little brother."

"And he knew that. It was too much pressure, Maggie, and you were not helping by acting so – "

"What?"

"Acting the way you were. We all thought you were going insane from waiting and thinking of what happened to put Mabin in the ground. We all knew Mabin was not just going to sleep comfortably in the warm earth for a year and then wake up normal and refreshed. You knew what he was going through as one of the departed dead who must come to life again. It was a year of agony in the earth, a rebirth in pain for him."

"I don't understand. Why did Tommy do this? All he had to do was wait for the day. I could have waited."

"No, you couldn't. You were going insane. We all saw it. He couldn't stand the thought of you going crazy, so he went early to the grave without asking us and waded into the black blood covering it to dig up your lover. Mabin needed the black blood, and your blood to heal, but he required more time. Tommy disrupted everything, the entire process, for you, for what he feared might happen to you."

"Then it is my fault."

"It's bigger than that, much bigger. You were a small player who had difficulty reading her part. It's not your fault. He shouldn't have done what he did, but we damaged this mountain, too."

"I know Mabin's out there now. If he didn't come to me after Tommy dug him up, I know he couldn't. Things went wrong. The process went wrong, and I'm going to him now. He needs me, for something is wrong with him. I don't need the mysteries to tell me that."

"Maggie, the mysteries said you would die if you went into the mountains tonight."

"Won't you stay now, now that you understand?" Elsa asked.

"The mysteries said I'd die alone and in misery if I don't go. I'm going."

Maggie stepped away from them in case they attempted to stop her.

A world that has fallen to pieces does not come together again simply by waiting a year for your lover to recover, she thought. She had had enough of being led around by ancient rules and methods, ragged writing on parchment and thoughtless submission. Let me die if I have to. Something had to be done, and she had to do it. So Tommy had ruined the process. She had ruined it, too, by loving too hard when she should have been waiting calmly and patiently while in love, and Elsa and Stephanovich had done their parts to ruin things. Now she had to fix the disaster all of them had created. Maggie flashed her gray eyes at Stephanovich and Elsa, and both of them knew better than to argue with the fire in those eyes. She turned from them to stare at the black blood bubbling up from the stream slowly rolling down the mountain, and it was too dumb to respond to her but she knew that it understood what she was doing and was waiting for her, waiting for her to make a mistake. She had this horrible sense that it understood her. It understood her in some silent way that shook her. Perhaps it understood too much, and would trap her as it had trapped Tommy. It had some life in it beyond its utter still malevolence that seemed to know nothing beyond that malevolence but in truth knew all. None of that mattered. She had to act.

"Good-bye," Stephanovich said weakly.

His voice was so shaken that she knew he thought he was not going to see her again. Elsa was frozen to one spot, staring after her. If the black blood wished to have her now, she could have done nothing but allow it to take her.

"Good-by, Maggie," she whispered, her eyes saddened with utter resignation.

Maggie saw her trail of blood straight ahead like a shining path wending its way down St. Mary's mountain, for the stream of black blood inching slowly for the town was catching the last rays of sunlight and blinding her with its brilliant, shifting reflections. Why these Bitterroot Mountains held such horrors disguised in such great beauty Maggie could not say, but her heart caught at the sight of that beauty and the knowledge that what was ahead of her was stunning as well as deadly, but at least it would be real. It almost seemed to make her fate worthwhile, if she could die in the midst of such maleficent glory while doing something real.

"Good-bye," she answered quietly.

The stream of blood was not going to get her just yet, she thought, no, it won't, not while I have to save Mabin, not while I still have hopes for Tommy. She strode up the mountain following the path the blood made for her, but hiking at least five feet away from it at. She thought when the dark came she might not be so lucky as to have the reflections of the setting sun lighting her way on the black blood's surface. She thought it might have its way with her then and she would never make to up the mountain to her lover's side. When the dark came, she would deal with it. She would not die without seeing Mabin, for that would only extend the darkness in which she had been living for a year, and she was tired of that darkness, tired of living inside a mind that did not work. She climbed the side of the hill quickly, knowing the light would last only so long and that then she would have to rely on her powers to find her way in the dark. She would have to leave normal sight behind and reach deep inside herself for what had died in most of us eons ago, that ability to live by the primeval instincts that guided us deep into the darkness and to safety. With a sudden insight she understood that was what the black blood was doing, living by the instinct of the past when blood was only blood and not yet human. She shuddered with the knowledge of the person she must become, for it was not a person at all. It was the hidden one. It was the person of the blood-knowledge hidden deep inside her. For a second, she wanted to turn around and tell Stephanovich and Elsa what she had to become now, but she knew it was always wrong to turn around and look back at the beginning of a quest, that nothing good could come of it but a surrender to the past instead of continuing on with the will to conquer. Yet her blood, the black blood inside her she could not acknowledge, seemed to grab her by the throat and spin her around.

She thought at first the dark figure was Stephanovich coming to follow her, and the words telling him to return to the safety of the town were on her lips when the figure's watery form collapsed and fell down into a pool just a few feet behind her.

It had taken the shape of a man in a cloak, but it could not hold the form once her gaze fell upon it.

The black blood behind her had been human for an instant, but now it was simply liquid once again.

She told herself it was madness to think she had seen what she had seen, and rejected it. It was simply another idea out of her mirror-self, and not real. At least she hoped it was not real.

Maggie pushed on up the mountain hurriedly. Now I know I'll have company on this quest, she said to herself, even if it's imaginary company.

She saw the light in the forest failing all around her.

She could not let the light inside her fail.

5

"Is she gone?"

Elsa asked the question a few seconds after Maggie disappeared into the trees at the base of the mountain. The black blood was gurgling up around their feet, and Elsa stepped back instinctively.

"Hurry. We don't have much time," Stephanovich responded. "We have to get the boy and take him where he told us to take him. We have to get there before she does."

"Stephanovich ..."

"What is it?"

"What if she doesn't make it? The forest at night is not a place for a girl alone, especially around here."

"She'll make it. She has far too many powers for us to question her, and it's our part to save Tommy. That's what we have to do."

For the past year, Maggie was not the only one troubled by the madness brought on by their gruesome past in vampire valley. Elsa and Stephanovich had suffered, too, but they had the strength of experience to help them resist it, and they could fight it with that experience. Mabin's voice and form had come to them in dreams nearly every night. His voice whispered to them, whispered in the late twilight of their bedroom when they turned in to sleep, and then after they had tossed and turned with the difficulty of drowsing while living such a life as they lived, his spirit and visions of him came to them, too, into their dreams, as clearly as though he was standing before them. He was covered in the black blood, but flicking it off him with disgust, and he always asked the same thing.

"Is she all right? Has she gone mad yet?"

For weeks, each of them retreated into the silence of their troubled sleep to keep their visions from the other, but it turned out Mabin was visiting them both at once, and saying the same thing. No one responds to a dream with words if that person knows it's a dream of someone you love. They respond only with longing, and when it is a nightmare that comes to you when you sleep, you think it's best to endure the nightmare and let it fade away at first light. That is what each of them had done for a long time. Yet Mabin returned night after night to both of them, at the same hour, and he persisted with the same question, and yet they did not tell each other what he asked or that he had been a visitor to their slumbers, and they refused to answer him.

"Is she all right? Has she gone mad yet?"

The repetition of the same question, night after night, to both of them, at the same time, wore on them like nightly water torture, for despite the belief that Mabin's appearance was simply a nightmare, and normal for people under such stresses, they could not get the vision of the repeating image and its plaintive question out of their heads when dawn came. They worried that both Tommy and Maggie were having the dream, for they slept poorly and it showed in their physical degeneration, their black eyes and loss of weight. Coming to them night after night after night after night, the dream wore them down with a madman's persistence. They barely had the strength to drag themselves from under the covers and live the day, and they wore down emotionally as Mabin's question stayed with them all day and they had no idea of how to answer it. Each lost weight, wasting away, and became haggard and weak, and darkness encircled their eyes and nested inside their chests.

"Sleep well?" they'd ask Tommy and Maggie in the morning. They would never get an answer.

Nothing could be right in their world until Mabin returned to it, until he threw off the black blood and became human again. He could not be human again until he stepped out of both his grave and their dreams.

Then one morning they came to understand that it was not a nightmare that was visiting them as they slept. It was Mabin's spirit itself.

"Is she all right? Has she gone mad yet?"

This time, it was not Mabin's voice that asked the question but Elsa's. She was buttering toast she would not eat, since she could not overcome her nausea. She was buttering it simply to occupy her thoughts while the question burned in her mind, and she did not realize she had babbled out loud. She dropped the toast onto the table and her fingers quivered.

"What did you say?" Stephanovich asked.

"Nothing," Elsa muttered. "I was buttering toast and babbling. Buttering toast. Just buttering toast. And babbling."

Her head nearly fell down onto the table with fatigue and wear and grief.

"No, I heard you. You asked if she was all right, and if she had gone mad yet."

"No ... I don't ... whatever it was."

Stephanovich pulled out an empty chair violently and sat down quickly beside her.

"No. I heard what you said. Your exact words were, 'Is she all right? Has she gone mad yet?'"

"I guess I did say that."

"Those are the same words I've been hearing night after night, month after month."

Elsa's head rose slowly until she tilted it and stared into Stephanovich's eyes.

"I knew it!" he burst out. "Mabin's been talking to you, too, at night. He's come to us both at night, and wanted to know about Maggie. I thought it was a nightmare that came at the same time every night. It was exactly 3 a.m. he came, every night, night after night, for all these months. I know, because I forced myself to wake up and look at the clock when I had the nightmare, and it was always 3 a.m. I thought I was going insane."

Elsa let out a sob.

"Do you think he came into Maggie and Tommy's dreams, too?"

"No, he would never do that. He knows they could not handle it if he did."

"It was always 3 a.m. when he came to me, too, because I forced myself to wake up and look at the clock, just to keep myself from going mad. We've been having the same nightmare at the same time every night."

"No!"

Stephanovich shot to his feet.

"It was not a nightmare," he said. "It was Mabin. I'm convinced of that now. Why didn't we talk to him? Why didn't we answer him? He came to us for help and we let him down. We can't do that with the children. We can never let them down."

"The boy ... is going through death all alone. We should have answered him. He was lonely and came to us and we did not answer. He just wanted a reassurance that Maggie was still ... sane."

"It won't happen again. I didn't know. I didn't know he had come to us for help and assurance."

"We couldn't have told him about Maggie. We couldn't have told him what she's like now."

"If he comes again, we'll talk to him."

"I want him to come. I didn't know, I didn't know he was lonely."

Now they looked forward to what they had thought was a nightmare, for now they could speak to him when he came in the middle of the night, for they knew it was not simply a trick sleep and fear played on them but a true visitation, the speech of a dead boy insisting that they tell him of the world of the living and the girl he fretted over and loved. Most of all, he wanted to hear of Maggie and how her mind had endured the horrible adventures they had undertaken together, adventures that ended with his death.

"Is she all right? Has she gone mad yet?"

Both Elsa and Stephanovich were deep in sleep when he asked that question at 3 a.m. that night, and they blurted out their answers in their sleep at the same time.

"She is hanging on, but she misses you and loves you so much."

"She can't wait until you return. Can you stay and talk with us? Why not talk to her in her dreams?"

"She would not know it was me," Mabin said gently, a tender smile crossing his lips after finally getting an answer about Maggie. "I want her to be well, and you should always say you believe I'm well when she asks you, but don't tell her I come to you at night in dreams. She might be upset to see me this way, the way I am now."

Mabin disappeared back into the darkness of his dark world at the mention of his own corruption, for he was corrupted as well as any several months in the grave could corrupt him or anyone.

"Come to us again," Elsa said, as he disappeared. "We'll look forward to it."

It was both easy and difficult to talk to Mabin in the ensuing nights in their dreams once they found out his presence was real, for it was a great relief to see him again but it was also a great effort to converse sanely in dreams with a purgatorial soul, with both of them talking at once and Mabin doing his best to answer each of them. He was not the handsome, loving boy he had been when he had been killed but had all the misfortunes of an early death painted on the vision of his spirit that came to them. He arrived every night at 3 a.m. and asked first of all about Maggie.

After Tommy botched Mabin's resurrection and died in the attempt, they did not have the heart to tell him that she wished to go out into the woods with the black blood threatening her to find him and bring him back to life herself.

Then their sleep at night grew crowded with spiritual visions, for Tommy arrived one night at midnight and asked about Maggie as well.

"Does she know I died?"

This time, both Elsa and Stephanovich had the sense to answer the new intruder to their dreams. Simultaneously, while sleeping, they broke out into tears to see their dead son, even if he came only in a dream.

"She knows now. We can't figure out what to do with her. She wishes you were still with us. We wish you were here. We miss you so much."

"Is she mad at me for ruining Mabin's resurrection? I did it for her."

"She knows that. She forgives you, and knows she shouldn't have pushed you to work magic that wasn't ready to be worked."

"Can you help me?"

"We will do anything we can, but the mysteries aren't speaking to us about it. They told us what to do when you got sick, but we don't know what to do now, how to bring you back to this world."

"They told you to cut off my head."

"Yes, but if we knew what to do next to make you live again, we would have done it at once with all our heart. You have to believe us."

"I believe you, and I know how it must be done."

"You?"

"Yes, I learned it here. This is a place I do not want to stay, but I learn things here."

"Then we'll do it," Elsa blurted so loudly she almost woke herself up. "Just tell us what we have to do, and we'll do it. Please. Just tell us. We love you so much, and if we can just get you back again, I know everything will work itself out."

"I love both of you, too. I have to inform you where Mabin's grave is, and you have to take my remains there. The grave is empty now, but the powers that were saving him are still there, although they can't help him anymore now that I've broken the spell they had cast over him."

"Tell us exactly what to do," Stephanovich said. "I promise we won't fail you this time."

"What do we do at Mabin's grave?" Elsa asked quickly, confused at what she thought she heard.

"You must put my remains where Mabin once slept in death. Boil a pot of the black blood at the gravesite and pour it over my remains. Then cover the grave and leave it at once, for what happens next might kill you."

"But what about you? How can we do such a thing to you?"

"We'll do it tomorrow," Stephanovich said. "We'll do it as soon as we wake up in the morning."

"No!" Tommy screamed at them.

He had never screamed at them in his life.

"But why not?"

"Maggie can't see. I don't want her to see what happens to me then. You have to do it when there is no chance she can see what happens to me when you do it."

"If you say this will work, we'll have to try it. I can't tell you how awful we feel for what we had to do to you. It's been like death for us every day."

"Soon it will be over, I promise you that."

Elsa and Stephanovich had prepared for their journey into the woods with Tommy's remains as soon as they woke up the next morning, so they were ready to do as he bid as soon as Maggie disappeared into the woods that night. They had loaded up their new Humvee with a large pot and camp stove for the boiling of the black blood, and had set into their GPS unit the coordinates Tommy had given them in their dreams. They had protective suits, goggles and rubber gloves to protect them when dealing with the black blood. When Maggie disappeared into the woods, they ran to the cellar doors where they had locked in the large silver vat that contained Tommy's blood remains and the cooler that held his head. They struggled with the silver vat first of all and barely found room inside the Humvee for it, but then Elsa rushed back into the cellar for the cooler and ran to the Humvee with tears streaming down her face, nearly overcome with the emotion she felt at what she transported. She tenderly placed the cooler at her feet on the passenger's side of the vehicle and screamed at Stephanovich to go, go, just go!

"Let's get this over and done with, so we can have our children back with us."

"Do we have everything we need?" Stephanovich asked, and pushed the key into the ignition. "I just don't want to forget anything important. We can't make anymore mistakes."

"We have everything we need but time. Time will take everything from us if we don't rush and beat Maggie to the grave."

Without answering, Stephanovich switched on the GPS unit and set it for the coordinates of Mabin's grave.

"I hope Tommy is right about these," he muttered. "I have a feeling – "

"What does the GPS say?"

"It's taking us up the access road and then onto an old logging road. Good. We should be able to make it pretty quickly up the mountain and to the grave and get there before Maggie does."

"Then go as fast as you can. I don't know if I can stand being in here with this, with Tommy like this at my feet. My mind is going, it's going, I tell you."

As she spoke, a wave of black blood crashed into the windshield of the Humvee, turning the twilight into night and making her scream as though a knife had been pushed into her spine. The black blood oozed down the glass and seemed to search in streams for an opening to the interior of the vehicle, as though the vampires that once held the blood were still part of it and informing it as to what to do. Elsa screamed wide-eyed again as she watched the fingers of blood through the clear glass. Stephanovich understood what the blood was doing at once and pushed closed the vent that allowed in fresh air. The blood seemed to be leaking from every opening in the mountain, every crevice and crack. He quickly hit the ignition and the engine roared to life, and he choked on something that came up his throat from his stomach. Still his fingers flew over the controls. He turned on the windshield wipers and then the windshield washer, and once the windshield washer fluid hit the blood it curdled and retreated as though in pain. Elsa was frozen in place, her eyes still wide, as the blood washed away.

"It has life in it," Elsa said. "It's as though there is a life of its own in it. The vampires are still in it."

"Look at that, what the wiper fluid does. That's good to know," Stephanovich said, ignoring her in the attempt to comfort her. "It wants nothing to do with the wiper fluid."

"I don't care!" Elsa screamed angrily. "It's bad enough it seems to know what we're doing and wants to prevent us from doing it, but now more of it is oozing out of the woods. Soon the entire town will be awash in it. What's its intention? What does it want to do to us?"

"I think it just wants us."

"You mean we're its intention?"

"Us and everyone. It wants everyone in town. You see what it did to Tommy. That's us, if we don't stop it."

"It's sickening. I can't, I can't."

"You can, and we will. Hold on! We are going to do this."

Stephanovich threw the Humvee into gear and tromped on the gas pedal to send it lurching toward the forest. As soon as the truck veered off to the side to avoid the creeping black blood on the ground, the blood turned in its course and followed them, like a stream changing its direction in pursuit of quarry, but too slowly. The Humvee charged up the hill, and the blood lacked the strength to follow, still too weak to do much but flow downhill. It painted the hillside everywhere the Humvee's headlights turned.

"I think we've gotten away," Stephanovich said.

The Humvee went crashing and bouncing across the rocky inclined earth, and Elsa's head seemed to bounce with it, as though it had lost its attachment to her neck. Stephanovich felt compelled to reach out gently and place his hand on the back of her neck as he drove. That steadied her head, but she had so lost control that saliva dripped pitifully from the side of her mouth. Embarrassed, she wiped it away with her sleeve, and groaned and then sobbed quietly.

"Why do we have to do this?" she asked in a small voice. "Who would make us do the kinds of things we have to do now? Anyone who would make us do these things is evil, and nothing more. Just evil."

Stephanovich hesitated a moment, staring ahead at the old dirt road on which they had embarked, reluctant to say anything but knowing he had to.

"I am trying to hold myself together."

"How? How can you hold yourself together when things like this are happening?"

"There is no explanation but that evil things are as they are and will forever be with us, but so will people like us always be here to prevent evil."

"But Tommy? Look what we have of him now. How can that be anything but madness? It's as though the world is nothing but mad, and I'm going along with it into my own insanity."

"I promise you we'll make things right with him. The mysteries know. They understand what is going on and will tell us what to do."

"Even if we do make Tommy whole again, what then about Maggie? Now we're told she has to die tonight or tomorrow. Is that right? Does saving one make the end of another any easier?"

The Humvee passed over such a huge rock that the steering wheel nearly twisted out of Stephanovich's hands, but he tightened his grip on it and, set his gaze on the deepening twilight outside the vehicle and pushed the accelerator farther down toward the floor. The Humvee leaped forward into the coming darkness.

The cooler on the floor had flown up after hitting the bump, loosening the lid, and with a sudden impulsive movement, Elsa pushed down on the lid to make certain Tommy's head remained safely inside. She retched, turning her head aside, and then wiped her lips with her trembling fingers.

"We'll do what we have to do," Stephanovich said. "We've never failed our children, and won't now."

"I don't think my brain is attached on the inside anymore," Elsa said. "I can feel it moving around inside my skull."

She was gazing wide-eyed out into the night, and she hugged the cooler to her chest, her chin resting on the lid.

Stephanovich turned on the headlights and surrendered to the temporary quiet of the unavoidable madness inside the Humvee.

He drove over the black blood, and hated it so much that he got a perverse pleasure out of running it over mercilessly and with utter hatred.

6

Maggie believed that the higher she walked on the mountain the greater the amount of light there would be in the world.

The set sun still tossed its rays over the top of the summit, and some of that light spilled down its sides so that it lit the slope Maggie climbed. There was the light from the sun, but there was also the light she could imagine that would illuminate the hill once she found Mabin. He was her way, and her light. He was out of his grave, she knew, pulled from it too early by Tommy's desire to help her maintain her sanity. She also knew Mabin had survived. She would not. To bring him all the way back into this world she'd have to leave it, said the mysteries. She believed that was a fair trade: it was simply the way things were. Sometimes, she told herself, it's better to die than live on the way she was living on.

She stepped around a large rock just before tripping over it. It was so dark she nearly stepped into a pool of the black blood hiding behind it. The blood hissed at her, the gas beneath it escaping all at once from the center, and she nearly laughed.

"No yet, my friend," she said. "No mistakes yet. I can still see."

There would be a fight before the trading of lives was consummated. She could feel that inside her, and she could feel it coming on as she climbed toward it away from the pool of blood. It was nearly impossible for her to believe how much blood St. Mary's mountain had leaked out. Something like that pool of blood was hovering above her on the summit, squatting like a complicated fool intent on ridding the earth of her, and there were other things all around her in the dark that would like to have her before the large fool on top of the mountain had her. As practice, she closed her eyes and continued walking, for once the light was gone, her vision would be all but gone, and she would have to summon every power she had just to find Mabin and trade her life for his in all this darkness.

"I'm not on top of the mountain, I'm here now. The top of the mountain is where I'm going," she said to herself, as though repeating a mantra. "It's on top of the mountain that I'll die."

The sudden intrusion of a voice where there was no shape or form made Maggie spin around, and her heart beat wildly. It sounded as though it was behind her, but when she turned to face it, there was nothing.

"Give up your life to his grave now," the voice said, sarcastically mimicking kindness. "There is no point in climbing farther. You can't bring him back. I have him."

The voice seemed to be behind her again, but when she spun around quickly once more, there was no one. She thought she saw a small circle of fires hovering among the trucks of the pines, like the floating wicks of a dozen candles, but then it was gone. She knew, in some way, that everything depended on her quickness, and if she did not respond quickly to the formless voice, things could go badly. Her blood boiled in her. It was not from anger but necessity that she readied herself. She did not know what she would do once she faced this thing, but she knew she would do something. She had to.

"That foolish little boy."

The lights appeared again among the trees, floating ten feet above the ground in the dark twilight air, and the voice was mocking her with Tommy's failure, she thought. She wasn't going to answer the voice and play its game, for she knew that in some way the voice was inside her head, while living outside her as those dozen small flames dancing together in a circle above her. When she looked directly at the circle of small flames, it flickered out. Now she saw and heard nothing. It was part of her madness but part of the world, too, to think she saw things when they were only in her head, for everything had to exist in her head and outside it to be real.

"The stupid little boy, your brother. If only he had listened to what the mysteries told him to do, you wouldn't be here now, and I wouldn't have you, and we could have all the blood we wanted."

That angered her, and she rushed toward where she thought the voice was. She saw the circle of small fires floating in the air to her right and up the mountain, and she rushed toward it but stopped. She did not say it, it took all of her will power not to say it, but she knew whatever was talking to her, it did not have her, not by a long shot. It was goading her along, making her climb harder, trying to make her forget herself, and then it might take her at the top of the mountain. There she might meet her end at the hands of this thing that teased her. She sensed she was fighting something that was there but in another way was not there. She had to find the part of the thing that was there, and fight that, not the thing that was not there. Fighting the part of the thing that was not there would mean she had lost.

"What a thought," the voice said. "I can find you, and read your mind, but you can't find me. I've already won."

Oh, I will find you, and you will regret it, she thought, remaining calm and concentrating on her task of saving Mabin.

"Not until you're dead will you find me," the voice answered her. "Then you will find me, and regret it, and then it will be too late."

You're on top of the mountain, Maggie thought, speaking to the thing with her mind. It can't make me think you're here if you are not.

She spoke to it with her thoughts, and it read them again, because it was in there, inside her head, and it knew she wasn't going to fight it inside herself, but outside, when the time came. It knew it, too. Whatever the thing was gasped at her thoughts, but then it laughed.

"Splash," it said.

The black blood. She leaped back, thinking the single word portended a jet of the black blood shot at her in some way. The thought had only to move an inch through her mind before she reacted to it.

"Oh, hell," she said out loud, when she saw the threat made manifest before her eyes.

There was a column of blood that had collected itself to a height of six feet just in front of her, and now it threw itself at her with all the force it could muster. Maggie hadn't leaped into the air to fly since she had been with Mabin. She thought she had forgotten how, but at the word "splash" she understood at once what the thing that was both here and not here was doing. The black blood was doing its bidding, and as soon as Maggie understood that she was in the air and soaring above the forest floor. She saw the column of blood below her tumble over, having missed her. With a kind of whimper, it seeped into the ground where she had stood and disappeared.

What have I done? Maggie asked herself. There are better ways to occupy myself than with these mad thoughts.

It was as pleasant as anywhere she had ever been, there in the tops of the pines, for it reminded her of her time with Mabin. She had soared with him, and then when he died she had sunk back to earth, so far she almost sank into it. The night was pleasant because she had gotten the dark thoughts out of her mind by manifesting them and then escaping them through flight. It was so dark she knew it mad little difference if she kept her eyes open or closed them, for she was mind-walking now. Somewhere, far off to her left, an owl hooted. With her eyes closed, the sound was many times more pleasant than when her eyes were open. She kept her eyes closed, and listened to the owl.

Whatever had intruded into her head was gone now, and she was safe hovering in the treetops listening to the owl.

She would have stayed there forever, if she could have.

Only saving Mabin would be in her thoughts now. Every other evil thing would have to wait.

It was time to return to Earth.

Reality beckoned, and she would live only by her reality now, not by the thoughts and illusions awakening and dying inside her head, and especially not with the black blood wrecking havoc on her soul.

When she came back to earth, there were a dozen of the small circles of light, wreaths of pink and orange candlewicks, lighting the way up the mountain.

As she walked, the orange and pink circles of light kept pace ahead of her, illuminating things so that the black blood would not attack her again.

There was something very pleasant about the glow in the forest the circles of light provided. She knew then that they had nothing to do with the black blood, and that they had not threatened her, but only seemed to, since they had appeared when the blood spoke to her.

Perhaps they were there to help her find the way to Mabin.

It was a comforting thought, and she decided it was true, for she needed all the help and comfort she could get.

*

When they found Mabin's grave, it was totally dark, dark only in the way it can be dark at midnight in the forested mountains. Both Stephanovich and Elsa were crying quietly, their tears lit on their faces by the dashboard lights and the light from the GPS.

"You have arrived at your destination," the GPS said.

"Shut up!" Stephanovich screamed at the device.

"We know that, damn you," Elsa chimed in. "Why? Why so soon? I still don't know if I can do this."

She stared at the GPS unit hard, as though her eyes could melt it, but then a cry broke from her as she thought of why they were there. She threw open her door and leaped out of the Humvee onto her knees in the dark. As though mirroring her, Stephanovich threw himself against his door and then tumbled onto the ground, sobbing.

"This is too real. It's too much for anyone."

"Why this? We can't do this."

"I'm so sorry, I'm sorry, Tommy."

"We must get through this horror to bring our son home."

Elsa let out a wail that echoed through the forest for so long it seemed it would never stop echoing.

Then there was complete silence, one that neither Stephanovich nor Elsa wanted to break, because if they did, that meant they would have to do what they had come here to do. Suddenly, the silence was shattered by the loud bubbling of the black blood in Mabin's grave. The unexpected intrusion in their grief and horror silenced them, and they froze in place, as if they knew there were further objections to their mission by the black blood, different objections for different reasons. A slow anger welled up in Stephanovich in defiance to the bubbling blood, and Elsa trembled with rage at the hunger of that open pit for her son. It seemed to say to them that their emotions were of little matter and they should get on with it, get on with the surrender of their murdered son to its hunger for him. What the results of surrendering Tommy to the whims of the black blood would be they could not say, but they knew they could not allow things to go on as they were now. The dreams and the mysteries had pointed to a way out for them, but unfortunately that way dictated Tommy be sentenced to a commingling with the same forces that had taken him in the first place. The blood wanted what it wanted, and because it didn't acquire the boy the first time around when he had been so foolish as to challenge it, it wanted him now all the more.

Still, Stephanovich knew that the black blood cured the dead but killed the living. So it is written, he said to himself.

Elsa was the first to surrender to the ghastly duties of resurrection. Gathering herself together, she stood and stared at the pool of bubbling blood without emotion. First clearing her throat, she reached in to the Humvee and gently lifted the cooler off the floor.

"Wait," Stephanovich said.

"What?"

"We do that last. First, the remains of his body are sacrificed to the blood."

She understood immediately. She closed the Humvee's door quietly and placed the cooler on the ground.

"I'm glad it's dark," she said. "If I saw or thought about what we are doing, I'd go mad."

"We can barely see. That's good."

"If only I couldn't see this in my mind."

Stephanovich nodded at his wife, and she at him. Both nodded at the other again, but then realized they could not delay any longer or they would fail. In silence, they walked to the back door of the Humvee and lifted it to reveal the silver vat that held Tommy's worldly remains, the melted remains of the boy who had once been but was no more after the black blood reduced him to what pieces of his being were in the vat. They struggled to pull the silver vat from the van, nearly growing ill at the sounds of sloshing it made, but managed to remove it from the truck without allowing it to touch the ground. Struggling to hold it aloft, tears streaming down their faces, they carried it to Mabin's open grave where the excited black blood was bubbling frantically at the feast in which it was about to indulge. Little did it know that feast could lead to its end. The black blood shone in the scant light of the mountain night, its smooth surface constantly interrupted by bubbles like a strange evil hot drink that had been fermented and poured into the pit. Elsa was struggling to remain on her feet as she carried the silver vat, and Stephanovich was sobbing quietly.

"I know this is witchcraft, but what else can we do?" he asked, as they approached the pit. "This is the only chance we have, our one and only chance."

"It is set in scripture. I believe it. We must do what the mysteries and our dreams say," Elsa answered in a monotone that broke into a cry at the end of the sentence when she could not contain her horror.

"Set it down at the edge, here," Stephanovich said, quietly, to calm his wife. "All Tommy's dream said to me was to pour in his remains, then lower in his head. Is that what they said to you?"

"As I remember it, yes."

"Then so be it. We do this first."

Stephanovich grabbed the handle and side edge of the vat to tilt it over the bubbling blood, and Elsa mirrored his efforts on his opposite side. Grunting, with a sudden effort, they tipped the vat all the way over, not looking at what was inside but hearing it slosh down into the pit. They nearly retched at the horror of it. Stephanovich groaned after the effort, but even as he looked down to see its effects he was sightless, for the night was too dark to allow any vision but a minimal sloshing of the remains down into the pit. The black blood barely acknowledged reception of Tommy's damaged body but simply continued to boil and bubble as it had, and then there was a barely visible whirlpool in the blood draining the blood down and down.

"Nothing. He's not returned to us yet."

"It knows we're not finished."

"Do we have to do the rest?"

"It wants his head. The dream said that would bring him back. Tommy said it to us in the dream."

"I don't know if I can."

Stephanovich stepped back from the pit and stared down into it as the blood whirled around and around.

"I'll do it."

He went to retrieve the cooler from beside the Humvee. In a moment he had returned to his wife's side and placed the cooler on the ground. The black blood bubbled slightly faster in excitement, and Stephanovich lifted the cooler's lid. He was about to reach inside when Elsa grabbed his arm.

"It is up to me. I'll do it."

"No, dear, you don't have to. It doesn't really matter who does it."

"I said I would do it."

"I thought you couldn't. You don't have to, and shouldn't have to. No mother should have to do this to her son. Let me. I did this to him."

"This might be the last I'll ever see of him. I want to hold the one thing we have left of him one last time."

"Believe," Stephanovich said passionately. "Believe and things will be as they should."

With that, Elsa reached into the cooler and gently lifted out Tommy's head by his curled hair. She did not wish to, but something made her look on his face one last time, some motherly reflex that she would have been better off without but was too powerful to resist. There was no response from the boy's head. His eyes were closed and there was an expression of utter peace and tranquility on his face. Without hesitating, but still weeping, Elsa leaned down and slowly lowered the head toward the bubbling black blood, whimpering as he did so. Stephanovich stood by her as she performed the awful thing she had to do, watching the process. Elsa leaned farther and farther over the pit until Tommy's head touched the black blood. Then with a groan she dropped the head into the thick black swirling liquid, which showed no sign of what had happened but simply continued to bubble on and swirl without concern. Tommy's head quickly disappeared into the circling wet dark darkness.

"Is that it?" Stephanovich asked. "Is that all?"

"Oh ..."

"What is it?"

"Nothing's happened."

"Perhaps it will take time."

"What if the dreams were wrong?" Elsa asked. "What if we had the same false dream and we did this for nothing?"

"Oh, my god," Stephanovich screamed. "We've been tricked!"

As soon as he finished speaking, the sides of the pit moved slowly toward the center, and in alarm both Stephanovich and Elsa stepped back away from what they had done. The ground around the pit was closing like a wound quickly healing, and within a few seconds the pit was completely closed. The forest floor at their feet where the pit had been was the same as it was anywhere around them, and they had difficulty discerning where Mabin's grave had been.

"He's gone."

"What happened? Did this work? Was it a trick? What was supposed to happen? It simply took him from us."

"It took him."

"Was that supposed to happen? I don't know. Should we have trusted our dreams?'

"What if all this is wrong?"

"It can't be. No. We have to believe. Look what happened. Mabin's grave closed up. The black blood is gone, and it's taken our son. I'm wrong, it's not a trick, it can't be."

Elsa wailed again, and once again the wail echoed through the forest as though it would never end. Stephanovich draped his arm over her shoulder to comfort her, and she raised her eyes to him.

"When do we get Tommy back?"

"I don't know, I don't know. Somehow it will happen."

Stephanovich removed his arm from his wife's should and wrung his hands together and then grabbed his head.

"What parent should have to do this? What have we done wrong but try to love our boy and listen to the good in our lives and live by the truth of the mysteries?"

Elsa dropped to her knees, staring at the grave and scratching her cheeks in agony. The covered pit simply stared back at her. Stephanovich, too, simply stood without movement as though paralyzed by the foolhardy madness of what they had just done. Both stared at the closed grave that contained their son and their daughter's dead lover, but the grave was so quiet and calm it shouted its evil indifference to their agony, mocking them with the brutal eternity they had surrendered to.

"What should we do now? Is Tommy simply gone? What will Maggie do once she discovers what we've done? She might have known what to do to bring Tommy back, if we just hadn't listened to our dreams, our mad dreams. We're fools, damn fools to do these things."

"We're not fools. We believe as we must. Maybe we should go home and wait," Stephanovich said. "I don't know what else there is to us after this."

Elsa stared at the ground, stunned.

"It simply took him."

"We didn't get to boil the black blood."

"Did we do something wrong again? I didn't even think about the boiling of the blood."

Before Elsa could break out into a wail again to shatter the quiet of the forest's night once more, an odd sort of illumination appeared twenty feet away between two hulking pines. It was not a flame, or a flashlight or a lantern, but an outline of fire in the shape of a figure in a cape. Only on the edges of the figure did the fire glow in a shimmering outline like many small overlapping candles flickering and lapping those edges, flowing in line from the head to the shoulders down the sides to two legs and feet. The flickering flames even burned in outline beneath the feet and up the insides of the legs, subject to the slight breezes that fanned the thin delineation of orange fire. It was as though the figure had just been lit in the darkness as a cigarette lighter is suddenly lit in darkness, but this figure was composed of dozens of cigarette lighters. Then thick eyelids snapped open to reveal two burning red eyes with black pupils in fiery coals in a very shadowy angular face. The figure's mouth opened, another small cavern of fire, and they felt the heat off the figure from twenty feet away and heard a quiet, gruff voice answer their question.

"Next, I need the girl."

"What are you talking about?" Stephanovich said.

"Who is that?" Elsa yelled out. "Who are you? Do you have Tommy?"

The flames outlining the figure flared up and out to burn a foot around the figure, but then just as suddenly the flames died down and flickered. Inside the outline of flames, the figure was as black and empty as the night. It was as though the night air flowed through the figure, as though there was nothing inside the outline of flames.

"I want and need the girl ... now."

Both Elsa and Stephanovich became aware of a sudden flourish of great heat that flashed over them like an unseen airy wave, heat emanating off the figure outlined in fire. The intense warmth seared the flesh of their faces until Elsa screamed and Stephanovich fell to the ground writhing as though he had been engulfed in an inferno. In an instant, they went from burning to freezing, for now the light from the outlined figure suddenly and inexplicably died and they were plunged into complete darkness. The cold only made their burning worse, for their flesh was damaged and blistered from the attack of immortal heat. Throwing icy air on their agony only made it worse.

"What was that? What did it mean? Have we gone mad because of what we've done?"

"Did we really see anything? Did we make that up in our minds? Are we insane?"

"I think we are insane. We can't be anything but insane after the things that have happened to us."

Elsa and Stephanovich spun around looking for the departed outline of flame, but it was gone.

"I saw a light in the forest and walked toward it."

In their confusion at the intrusion of a new voice, Elsa and Stephanovich spun around in different directions, each looking for the figure outlined in fire but bumping roughly into each other. Their senses told them that figure was up to no good, and should be guarded against, but the new voice was familiar and soft, like music, compared to the harsh tones of demand the empty figure had imposed on them. The figure outlined in fire was still imprinted on the backs of their eyes when they blinked, and the dark was so complete now that they could see nothing else.

"Why did you come?"

It was Maggie, and Elsa and Stephanovich recognized her then by her soft charming voice and her slow amiable movement, a figure of light in a black night. Still, they trembled after what they had just seen and what they had just done. They were caught. They had hoped to escape her detection once they had performed the heinous duty their dreams had inflicted on them, but now they were caught and deemed guilty and should suffer at her hands.

"Maggie, we had to come," Stephanovich burst out. "We couldn't let you do this alone. Now. Let's go back home and not think about what the mysteries said must happen to you. We shouldn't stay in this place for another minute."

"But this is where I'm to find Mabin's grave," Maggie said. "Yet the earth looks so smooth. Where is the grave?"

"It closed," Elsa yelled suddenly, in a panic.

"How did that happen? Is Mabin here? Did he make it out?"

"It was that way when we got here," Stephanovich lied. "I'm sure things are going to be fine, but we should get out of here now. You should forget about sacrificing yourself for him. There's no point in staying when everything's gone wrong."

With her eyes adjusting further to the darkness, Maggie at first listened to what they were saying but then looked upon what they had done and understood they were uttering nonsense just to get her out of there. The evidence of their crime was on the ground around them. The silver vat was positioned at the edge of what had been Mabin's grave, and although it was silently gleaming silver, it was speaking loudly with its silence. She knew what those silver vats were used for. They could capture vampires but also hold the remains of the dead.

"Is Tommy in there?"

"God, no."

"If he's not in there ..."

Maggie could not believe the conclusion she reached from seeing the empty vat. She looked further and saw the cooler that had held Tommy's head beside the vat. Gasping, she looked first into the empty vat and then bent to see the cooler also was empty.

It was not difficult to reach the conclusion about what had transpired in the dark of the forest by the grave.

"You got rid of Tommy? You buried him?"

"No, no, Maggie. Let us forget what happened here tonight, and leave before other evil things happen," said Elsa. "We just saw something, some strange lights. We don't know what's in these woods, or ... down there."

"No! You know why I came here, and now there is no grave. I saw the lights, too. There is no grave and no Mabin and there is nothing I can do about it but wonder why you brought Tommy's remains here."

"That's why we have to leave. The point of coming here is gone. There is no point in staying. There is no point in anything here."

"What did you do to the grave?" Maggie demanded to know. "I have to know if I wasted my time in coming here after Mabin."

Stephanovich closed his eyes and leaned back his head so that he stared sightless at the black sky. He sighed, realizing there was no way to hide from Maggie what they had had to do.

"We had dreams, terrible, awful dreams," he said. "We each had the same terrible dream with Tommy in it, and he told us what to do to bring him back to us. That's all we ever wanted to do, bring Tommy back to us."

"Is Mabin free? Did you do what the dreams told you?"

"We did."

"And what was that?"

Stephanovich dropped his eyes to where Mabin's open grave had been and stared at the ground there. His entire body shook, down to the fingertips.

"We're complete fool!" Elsa wailed, falling to her knees.

"Our dreams told us to pour Tommy's remains into Mabin's grave, that he would be revived again if we did."

Now a wail broke from Maggie and she spun around and dropped to the ground. Elsa could not control herself and wailed on and on, as though she had lost her mind.

Maggie stood up and spun around to face them again.

"Then where is he? You poured in his remains to bring him back to life, and you believed it would work, so where is he? Tommy? Are you here? Tommy!"

"We might have been fooled," Elsa said. "We are such abject fools."

Her eyes were wild and fiery and she drooled.

"Fooled? You've been fooled?"

"We might have been," Stephanovich said. "That's why we have to leave as soon as possible. We saw a creature here. We don't know what it was, but it came once we had done what we had to do. The grave closed up without Tommy returning to us, so we thought something might be wrong. We didn't know what to do, and then this creature showed up over there, and he – "

"He did what?"

"I don't want to say."

"Tell me! I have to know if I'm going to be able to help save them."

"He said he wanted and needed you next. We have to get out of here before he takes you. You understand, don't you?"

"Yes, that's why we have to get out of here at once," Elsa chimed in. "This creature closed the grave and said he was taking you next. Please, we have to leave here as soon as we can. We can't have him take you, too."

"What about Mabin? And what about Tommy? Do we leave without them? I don't care about me if they're gone."

"There is something here we don't understand," Stephanovich said. "Let's go home and consult the mysteries. We're helpless without the mysteries, and I don't know now if we're dealing with white magic or black magic. Please don't let them take you, too."

"I don't care about that. I'm not leaving without my little brother and my lover."

While they had been speaking, the darkness slowly lifted, as though sweet dawn had come to their single small portion of earth. In the forest it was as colorful as sunrise, orange and pink, and while they had been engaged in the passion of their arguments about what course to take next, they barely noticed the light that allowed them to see each other fully. There had been a noise, too, as they argued, a creaking and quiet clashing and roiling of rock and stone, and the dank smell of the inner earth came to their nostrils all at once, as though a million dank mushrooms had grown up around them. The light came again from small dancing flames, but this time the light illuminated not a figure of a stranger but the outline of a grave, Mabin's grave. A thousand tiny flames outlined the open grave, free now of the black blood but with orange and pink lights at its bottom, far at its bottom. While Maggie and Stephanovich and Elsa had seen just a few of these creatures of tiny lights before, there were now many of them, all nothing but small inexact circles of flickering flames, but with a presence that said they were alive and the grave was alive.

"I'll take her now," a sad voice said.

Elsa instinctively grabbed for Maggie, for it was the voice they had heard, but she was too slow. Maggie side-stepped quickly to the edge of the grave, where the flames burned. She looked inside without moving, mesmerized by what she saw there. Below there was a lovely light cavern at the bottom of the grave. She smiled at them in the circles of flickering flames, thinking she had reached her destination, and then lowered her eyes into Mabin's open grave again.

"Both of them are there," the voice said. "Go to them. You're next for purification."

Shivering, Stephanovich, too, heard the voice and recognized it as that of the creature that had been outlined in fire, but he did not know which one of the many flaming circles around the grave contained the voice. He rushed toward Maggie, for the saw the grave was deepening with an orange and pink glow at the bottom and inviting the girl in, but she tore her arm out of his grasp and instinctively leaped over the grave, over the light, to the other side. She stood staring first into the grave and then at Stephanovich, and then back into the grave, the pink and orange light from the deep cavern below flickering on her face.

"Good-bye," she said.

"It won't do any good," Elsa pleaded. "That voice was the voice in our dreams. Don't trust it. We thought it was Tommy, but it was that voice, that thing, and look what it made us do. Don't follow it, Maggie, don't."

"Is Mabin in there?"

Maggie asked the grave the question, and in answer the flames outlining it leaped up enthusiastically and its interior glowed even brighter.

"So he is," Maggie said. "My lover is down in there."

She did little at first but stare into the grave, trembling, while the orange and pink lights washed over her. She slowly lifted her eyes toward Stephanovich, and then toward Elsa.

"You should come with me."

Maggie shook violently, and while staring in Elsa's eyes stepped forward and plummeted down.

She was gone instantly.

It was not a shallow grave or a grave similar to any other. Maggie fell very far very fast, as Elsa and Stephanovich watched. Then, like waves rolling together, the dirt and stones at the sides of the grave rolled together, closing the opening through which Maggie had fallen, while the flickering circles of flames around the grave followed the dirt and stones in a whirlpool until they met in the middle and extinguished themselves with popping sounds. The lights too fell down into the sacred rent in the hillside as they went out.

The earth smoothed itself over. It was as though there had never been a burning tomb of flickering lights secreted on the forest floor, just the forest garden, as it had been forever.

"Maggie!" Stephanovich screamed at the forest floor.

"What has she done? Maggie? Oh, my god, what has Maggie done?"

"She did what she came here to do," Stephanovich answered, and fell to his knees. "We couldn't have stopped her. We were in the way. We lost Tommy, because we got in her way. She knows far better than we do what has to be done."

"We were desperate. We did this because we were desperate. No one could stay sane after what we've been told to do."

"We did that thing to Tommy to save him and it was all a ploy. A ploy! She would have known better. We didn't know, we didn't know it was all a ploy, and now they've taken them all from us."

"Something wanted them all. Evil tricked us. We should have jumped with her."

Stephanovich stared at the dark forest floor.

"We can't now, but we won't make this mistake again. At least now we know there's more to this than black blood. There is someone in there with our Maggie and Tommy. Someone did this, and somehow we have to get our children away from them."

"Should we start digging?"

"Dig? How can we dig? This is not a matter of simply moving earth, but moving spirits. If we opened the earth here, I doubt we'd find the place she disappeared to. We've done enough evil work for one night. It would be a mistake to dig. From now on, we listen to nothing but the mysteries. Our children are gone, our dreams are gone. If another dream comes along, we wake up. It's about time we wake up to what is happening in this town with all its vampires. We need to be harsh."

"Just give me a minute."

"Of course. I think I have an idea of what happens next," Stephanovich said. "It isn't good, but at least we know now whom to trust."

Elsa slowly dropped to her knees next to Stephanovich on the dark forest floor. She reached out and smoothed the dirt and rocks over Mabin's grave and sobbed quietly. She lifted a handful of dirt, and then let it fall through her fingers.

"We trust no one but the ancient Transylvanian Mysteries," Stephanovich said. "Even them we'll question. We'll never be such fools to do again what we did to Tommy tonight because we dreamed it."

"And Maggie," Elsa added, in a very quiet voice. "And Maggie. What have we done to Maggie?"

"What have we done to our children?"
"Bad things. We've done bad things."

7

Maggie was surprised that she had fallen through Mabin's grave into neither fire nor earth, but straight down into cold, clear air, along with wondrous lights, the orange and pink lights of the tiny circles of flames she had seen on the surface. They followed her as she fell, surrounding her with their flickering lights in the darkness, like thousands of sparklers descending with her through the air of the cavern.

She had expected Elsa and Stephanovich to leap into the grave after her, but thought it might have closed too quickly for them to do so.

It was like no grave she had ever imagined. For a moment, falling through the cool crisp air, she was glad she had jumped, for soon she'd see him, see Mabin, and it was beautiful here, with the tiny flames accompanying her on the freefall down.

There was a strange sort of happy feeling here, in the midst of the tiny tumbling lights. This was not a grave but huge empty cavern through which she was falling, with miniature flames flashing all around her.

"Elsa? Stephanovich?" she called out, still hoping they had followed her but she had not seen them. "Are you here?"

There was no answer but the soft pitter-patter of liquid falling into liquid. It was as though she was falling through stars.

"I wish they had come with me ... Are you anywhere here? I guess they didn't jump in, although I don't blame them."

After a short fall through the gorgeous illumination, her descent was broken by a soft landing on a cushion of rock. It was strange, for this rock was not hard but like a soft sponge. It yielded to her and ended her descent easily. The constellations of tiny flames that had accompanied her down died out, extinguished after lighting her way to the floor of the cavern. She took two quick steps forward as soon as her feet hit, for she had the good sense to realize something or someone who wished her no good might be expecting her, and she did not wish to be taken unawares by anyone or anything, now that it was dark. Despite the clear, multicolored, pleasant atmosphere, she comprehended that she was still in a grave, a very lovely grave, but still a grave.

"Is Mabin here?" she asked, but then realized the cavern was empty and she was talking to the rocks.

She shivered, feeling abandoned by Elsa and Stephanovich but realizing there was nothing she could do about it now. With her tiny stars gone, she held her breath and looked around carefully, trying to understand her situation. She didn't know what this place was, but she knew this was where she would have to defeat death with love. It was the only weapon she had.

It was not too soon to feel that love, but it was too soon to ask about Mabin, for there was no one to talk to and no response but the silent dripping of the rocks. The two steps she had taken were enough to make her realize the rocks were not dry but sodden. She looked down and saw her feet had left imprints in the surface behind her, and the imprints were filling with red. She glanced at her feet and saw that her weight had pushed her feet down into the rock a few inches. More blood outlined her shoes, seeping up out of the rock as her weight pressed her down. It was a place of blood, and she did not understand what that meant yet.

She spun around quickly in a full circle, to see what her new world offered or threatened, and she missed Elsa and Stephanovich again and wished they were here. "Hello?" she called out to them. She saw more of the same, spongy rock in fantastic formations, arches and pillars and columns and hills, and shimmering orange and pink light. She heard dripping, much dripping all around her, and farther away she saw a smooth surface, like a small lake at sunset, but she knew what the lake was, despite the shimmering orange and pink reflections in it. And she knew what was dripping all around her. She shivered, because where there was so much blood to be had for free, there would be those types who wished to take it at any price.

"I don't know why this happened," she said to herself. "If Mabin is still in the grave, I should be, too. I will find him and Tommy and get out of here as soon as possible. That's my course of action."

She expected an answer, for she still couldn't believe Elsa and Stephanovich hadn't leaped with her. There was no answer. For no reason, her feet slipped out from beneath her. She fell on her backside and commenced on a long slide down a rock-face that inclined steeply toward the shimmering lake below her, not daring to scream since it might alert someone she was here. It was as though she had been standing on a table, and the table suddenly tipped. She screamed silently with the suddenness of it. She threw out her hands to slow her slide, but she continued to slide downward without any loss of velocity. True rock would have cut and bruised her, but this rock merely provided a slippery, porous surface on which to lose control. A slide of fifty feet landed her in the same situation in which she had begun – upright on soft, bloody rock, with a view of a lake in the distance. There was no sky above, simply dark earth for a ceiling, but otherwise it was as though she had landed at another spot in the same world of bright colors and spongy rocks and fantastic forms and dark blood.

Looking to her right and then her left, she noticed a path between two large rocks, and since it was the only indication of which way she should go, she took it. Rivulets of red seeped out of the rocks at her sides and continued on until soaked up by the rocks at her feet.

"I can't trust this place, I can't trust this place, I can't trust this place," she repeated to herself, because it was so lovely and quiet yet existed as some sort of realm of the dead awash in blood. "It can't be trusted here. Beauty must earn your trust."

She jumped nervously when a rock fell into the lake in the distance, fallen from the ceiling, startled with the deep plunking sound of it.

Above, a light flickered on, and she was quick enough to raise her eyes and see a ring of flame just below the surface of the earth, her sky. The ring of flame disappeared, like a match being blown out, or rather a circular array of matches being blown out, when she was all right, and she saw it as not much more than a curiosity. Yet it was uncomfortable to discover there were invisible things above her head that lit themselves like matches and perhaps dropped down rocks.

"I can't think about that. Maybe the tiny flames are watching over me. In a place like this, where would Mabin be?" she asked herself out loud, forcing herself to think. "I can't answer the question. I don't know the place, so I don't know where in it he would choose to be. This might be more difficult than I thought."

Then she admitted something to herself: "I jumped on impulse."

The only thing to do was to move on, since moving on would lead to some sort of investigation, at least, and also to discoveries. Hopefully, if she explored she would find the way to Mabin, for she was just below his burial place and it had only been a few days since Tommy had desecrated the grave for her benefit, to raise her resting lover. Would he have moved far? Mabin could have moved a great distance in this underworld of black blood, but she did not even know if he was alive or partially revived or finally dead. He could be in another grave under one of the large sponge-rocks of blood, someplace she would never find him.

And she did not know of a way out after her precipitous leap.

"Is anyone here?" she asked in a loud voice.

She noticed another flickering of light above her head at the sound of her voice, and then another and another, and she lifted her eyes just in time to see the same phenomenon she had witnessed a few seconds ago. Like fireflies, the rings of flames came to life and then died above her. When the lights died out, they left a smell of burning matches.

These creatures of flame had lit her way into the grave and were lighting her way through this underworld now.

"Discoveries already," she said to herself, staring upward at the flickering rings of flame. "I learn something new each second."

Each light blinked out, leaving the dark earth as her sky again.

She kept glancing around carefully, trying to find out where she was and what was happening in this place. Tommy, too, was down here someplace after Stephanovich and Elsa had been foolish enough to listen to the voices of their dreams, although from the tales her imagination told her of his end he would be in far worse condition than Mabin. The boy would need her far more than Mabin. It occurred to her that she had no idea of what she had to do to bring her brother and her lover back to the surface, or back to life to begin with, but she knew such things could be done. She had leaped into this mountain underworld without thinking, without a plan, yet anything could be done, she believed, if you knew the mysteries and they knew you. Despite their disagreements, she wished again she had Stephanovich and Elsa beside her with their copy of the mysteries to guide them. She would have felt much safer with the two of them by her side.

"Why didn't you jump with me? You should have jumped in with me. At least we could have been together. I'm alone now, I'm all alone."

The lights above her flickered on and off sporadically as she spoke. They are listening to me, she said to herself. It was like an airy dance of fire, dozens of floating flickering dances, like empty fireflies, set against the dark underbelly of the earth. It made her shudder. In the darker spots along the path, the lights were a welcome relief, for they illuminated the shadowed corners of the rocks. The outlines of flickering lights almost seemed friendly, but why would they be friendly in such a place as she was now? It didn't make much sense to imagine any good beneath the surface of the earth where the dead normally resided. Her path was dry and easy to walk, and she had no choice but to walk it, for it was the only place she could move forward or see clearly. She realized she had not heard a single thing since she had broken through Mabin's grave and entered this place. She realized that because she heard the first sound she had ever heard underground. It was a cross between a groan and a cry of pain, and it was pitiful but not self-pitying, for the sound had a quality of strength to it, and she knew what it was as soon as she heard it.

"It's him," she whispered to herself. "Mabin?"

She stopped in the returning silence to listen for more.

Perhaps she had not spoken loudly enough.

"Mabin?" she asked again, just above a whisper, but again only the silence answered her.

The stillness gave her no answers, but excitedly she picked up her pace, the outlines of light above flickering faster and faster and providing her more and more light along the path. She went twenty feet in the blink of an eye, pivoted around a rock to follow the curving path, and then walked another twenty feet in a straight line. She entered a shadowy clearing in the path surrounded by columns of rock. The outlines of light congregated above her and illuminated the open space before her. She heard the sound of the groan and the cry of pain, and she saw him sitting at the far end of the clearing on a long, spongy, bloody rock. He had a black hooded cape covering him as he slumped over, and he rocked forward and back as he groaned in agony.

"Mabin?"

She spoke in a normal, hopeful voice, and for a third time he did not answer. He stared off into space and would not look at her, no matter how much she wished he would.

"He doesn't know me," she whispered to herself. "He doesn't know I'm here. Is he senseless still? Or is death forgetful? He should know I'm here."

She hesitated before rushing to him to throw her arms around him. The thought struck her that since he had been dead for so long he was still more of a spirit than a boy, half-dead and half-alive. But he is living, at least in some way, she screamed inside silently with joy, for it had been promised to her that he would live again with her blood in his heart but she had been forced to accept the fact that he was dead for this past year. There was a finality to that that made her question what she was seeing. I know there are many tricks in the world of the dead, she told herself. Maybe this was some other thing in her lover's form, or an empty illusion of the black blood. Maybe she should not disturb it, if it is a false thing. She thought of what she would say to Mabin, the words that would not surprise him too greatly with her presence, and settled on his name again, simply his name, when she was close enough for him to hear it. She had it on her lips when he suddenly spoke first, his head still hung down and covered by the hood.

His voice made her freeze in place, for it was deathlike and very cold, like ice thrown over a corpse.

"They said you were coming."

That was all. No love, no kindness, no hope. He still stared off into space without looking at her. His voice, the voice she had wanted to hear for so long, was not as it had always been, warm and deep, attentive to her. It was like a stone talking, and it surprised her into silence, for the stone sounded distant and disappointed and indifferent to her. She was shaking inside violently because it was not right he had died, it had never been right, and now he was different but was here and they were still very far apart. Death still divided them with its cold hands, pushing them apart at arms' length.

"Do you remember me, Mabin? Do you know who I am?"

"I know you. You shouldn't have come," he said without looking up. "Never, never, never. You shouldn't have come for me. I'm not right yet. Why did you come when I am not right? It's so wrong to see you here now while I'm like this. You might not like what you see of me."

If he knew her feelings, how could he say such a thing?

"I don't care what I see of you or what you've become. I came for you. I don't care if you're not right yet, or different. One day you will be."

"You should think more about what death does to a person. You should know what it does. You know I would have come back to you when this was over, and now you're making this more difficult. You should have waited. This is the wrong place for us. And the wrong time, and I am still wrong and unhappy with what I am."

"I couldn't wait. Tommy tried to raise you too soon because he knew I couldn't wait. Did you see him here yet?"

"Tommy? Why would he be here?"

She covered her mouth: he did not know about Tommy's death. She forced herself not to speak, but then grew angry with the way the conversation was going. It should have been a loving and warm conversation and it was merely cold questioning and aloof recriminations.

"He's here because the black blood got him," she explained, sounding cold and angry herself, but suddenly understanding he had to know all. "It got him when he was digging you up, because I was impatient to see you again. Blame me. Elsa and Stephanovich saw no way to revive him but to bury him in your grave."

Mabin groaned.

"My god."

Maggie took a quick step toward him.

"Can I come sit next to you?"

"No! Get away from me!"

Mabin screamed his answer so aggressively Maggie nearly stumbled backwards. Then he slumped over further and rocked back and forth.

He spoke in a softer voice.

"Tommy must be on a much lower level. He would have needed purification on all five levels if he died from the black blood."

"Purification? Five levels?"

"That is what this place is, I was told by those lights, the things above us. They're called –"

"The lights can talk?"

He ignored her, and went on.

"We are inside a top-secret facility, the National Emergency Blood Bank, the repository for blood taken from dead vampires that is piped in and undergoing purification before being reused to give others life."

Maggie was so disturbed by Mabin's informational tone and lack of affection that she burst out in questioning.

"A blood bank? What ... Why are you being like this? I don't care about any national blood bank. I came for you, and my brother. Look at me. Who told you I was coming?"

Mabin pointed up to the flickering lights near the ceiling.

"The Outliners. They said you wanted to come, and I'm like this because oddly enough I've been dead for nearly a year, if you've forgotten. So. There you have it. You have all your reasons why I'm like this."

Her heart caught, and skipped a beat. He was right, and he had good reason to be the way he was, made so cold by the grave, but to be so icy with her just did not feel right. This was not how she remembered their relationship to be. She loved him, and would do anything for him, even jump in his grave, and he could not even be civil to her. Above, the rings of fire were still dancing and burning, flickering out and then coming to life again. When she raised her eyes toward the earth's floor above, Maggie shivered at the sight of them, for now she knew there was something more than alive about them. And they had a name. Outliners. They were spirits, and they had a function – to protect this place and its blood ... and Mabin.

She could control herself no longer. She rushed up to Mabin and fell on her knees before him. She was about to embrace his legs when a wail broke from him and he leaned away from her desperately.

"*Noli me tangere!*" he screamed out. "Do not touch me!"

Shaking and injured, Maggie rose and backed away from him quickly, stricken and with tears flowing down her cheeks. She stood quivering before him, feeling betrayed. He no longer wants me. After waiting for him all this time, loving him for all this time, he would not touch her or let her embrace him. He no longer wanted her. His feelings were dead. The grave had quenched their love. He had allowed it to quench their love, and he was a thousand miles from her.

"You can not touch me because if you do you will be polluted, too," Mabin quickly explained in a soft voice. "What happened to Tommy will happen to you if you touch me: the black blood kills the living and heals the dead. You can still climb to the surface and live. You haven't been polluted yet, so climb up and live far away from me."

"I can't! I can't do anything like that, and I don't care about living up there anymore. I don't care about being without you. I'm not leaving you again. How much worse can it get, if I can't touch you? How much worse can things get than they've been for the last year? I'm an insane woman, utterly crazy because of what we went through together."

"It can get very much worse, unless we all get very much better," Mabin snapped, again in a cold voice. "There is only one way to do that, to get better, and it is the way down. If we go down together through all the levels we can get better."

"So I won't be crazy anymore and you won't be cruel?"

"You are not what you say you are, and I am not what you see I am."

Annoyed with him, Maggie simply stared at him, thinking he was as crazy as her. Her thoughts still condemned him, for he appeared upset with her, nervous, and he was speaking spooked nonsense. He spouted Latin, a dead language, when she came near, and told her not to touch him in an old dead thoughts, and talked of levels and recovering from death. She thought that's what he had been doing all this time, recovering from death for the last year, when she saw now it was a sham. He was simply running away from her. Recovering from death was a sham, and she had spent nearly a year loving a ghost, a memory different from this twisted creature, and now that ghost was mad and in this hell and staring back at her and telling her the impossible could happen if they descended levels together. The mistrust that was in her gray eyes reflected in his when she stared into his face.

"You don't know where you are," he said softly. It was the sort of softness she wanted to hear. "I know what you think of me, but it's true, what the mysteries said is true, I swear it. I could have recovered and returned to you the same person I was after Stephanovich injected your blood into my heart. It was the blood of my beloved in my heart, and it would have healed me if it had had the full year of death to do so. You know I loved you once."

Maggie stepped away from him, backpedaling to sit on a sodden red rock facing him. She sat limp and empty, confused and suddenly tired from the disappointment of seeing her lover in this awful state again. He had said his love for her was in the past.

"You expect too much of me," Mabin said, as though reading her thoughts.

"I expected too much of me."

"Do you still have feelings for me? Does this place make a difference?"

Even this he asked with cold, icy, indifferent words.

"I don't know. I don't know what I'm feeling now."

"Do you see those things up there?"

Mabin pointed to the ceiling of dark earth, where the Outliners were still blinking on and off.

Suddenly, this cave seemed a hideous neon hell, a wicked square in a rotted underground village or city.

"I saw them before, but I didn't think much of them. I thought they might be some sort of exotic insect, or gas flickering on and off."

"They're much more than that. Don't be confused by their appearance."

"They seem empty things, small fires linked in necklaces that die too easily."

"You're right about one thing."

"What's that?"

"They're dead. They are dead. They've died. They are the souls of dead vampires, empty immortal things that had so little purpose in life that they've been given the greatest purpose after life. They are vampire souls, or the remains of what once had been human souls, and they are here to watch over the place and make sure the process goes correctly, and they're here to help any human who's foolish enough to come here."

"What process are you talking about?"

"The process of purification. This blood, this black blood, is what's left of what once coursed through their veins, what was stolen from others and now has to be made pure again before all those they killed can move on. This is their hell. They make their blood useful to others."

Maggie could not look at Mabin as he spoke. She was too confused and disappointed in him. Where were the fireworks she had always thought would go off once they were finally reunited? Stop thinking of yourself. The thought occurred to her that that was all she had been doing. He droned on, but as he talked what he said seemed to make more and more sense to her – the flickering lights with emptiness inside, the lake of blood and rocks saturated with it ... all of that seemed a fit redemptive underworld for vampire souls. She stared across the red lake to where it ended in a dark horizon and saw more of the Outliners hovering above it aimlessly. Dead souls. Old souls. Old vampires. Empty now but for the flickering energies they somehow gathered to show off as the guardians of black blood.

Was Mabin one of them now?

"I think that maybe anyone who hasn't done what they've done can be made whole again. Then they'd have to find their way out of this place. At least that's my understanding."

With the realization of what this place was taking from her, and had taken from Mabin, Maggie had descended into silence and contemplation. But what is broken can be fixed. Mabin can be fixed. Maybe I can be fixed. She was tired of the madness of thinking only of herself, and saw that she had a bigger task with Mabin than she expected.

"And Tommy? Can he live again?"

"I don't know. I didn't know he was coming, and I don't know the circumstances of his death. First, we have to find him."

"What about us?"

"When you've been killed by a vampire, as I have, coming back to life is a long road. You haven't been killed, but there was something ... taken from you. We don't belong here. Tommy doesn't belong here. I don't know what's going to happen to us, if this place can fix us."

Maggie felt a sharp pain in her heart, at the place where the long needle had been inserted to draw out her blood to then be injected into Mabin's heart. The pain radiated up her left arm and up her neck. She closed her eyes to endure it, but it was so intense tears welled in the corners of her eyes.

"I would stay here with you, but I want us to leave together and things to be as they were," she gasped, the pain knifing through her side.

Mabin stood, and the suddenness of his movement caused the hood of his cape to fall back, revealing a scalp that appeared singed and burned, as though by fire. His hair gone, his head was as smooth and barren and blackened as a dome of polished stone. He quickly grabbed the back of the hood and pulled it forward over his disfigurement.

"I'm sorry."

Maggie gasped at what she saw, and Mabin near fell over after getting to his feet so suddenly. So this is what he meant when he said he had not healed. She rushed toward him, but his raised hand stopped her in her tracks. She froze. The flesh was burned away from his face, leaving only red and raw scars. He was only partially healed by his year in the grave nurtured by her blood: she wondered if his scars covered his entire body.

"So now you know about me," he said.

Maggie jumped up and rushed toward him. She knew touching him would only increase his agony, for it was as though he had been burned at the stake.

"I don't care. As long as I can be with you, I don't care what you look like, how bad it is. Things have to get better."

"Don't!" he yelled at her, stopping her in her tracks after she took another few steps toward him. "If you touch me, I'm done. Mortality, your mortality, can end me, and it would be an end of agony. I'm not of your world now, and all this would end if you touch me. You would end."

Maggie burst out in tears.

"Why?" she screamed.

"Don't you notice something odd about me?"

"Many things, Mabin."

"I'm not breathing."

She stared at the cloth over his chest and saw it was true. His chest neither rose nor fell, and the air was still and stagnant around him. She could do nothing but stand two feet away from him, staring at him. She sobbed until there was nothing inside her, no feeling or energy or strength. He truly was not a living, breathing being, but something else, and he did not want her. He could not.

He turned from her and walked into the shadows.

"Follow me," he said. "If you think we have any chance at life, follow me."

Crestfallen, she shuffled her feet forward, across the slippery spongy surface that pretended to cure so many ills. The shadows, the utter darkness, closed around her as she moved until she felt she had no use for her eyes or heart or soul and closed all. Her shuffle propelled her forward, but she did not know where she was going or why she was following him. She was simply following in darkness, feeling nothing and thinking nothing. Love was lost. All was lost.

Mabin had no breath. He was not alive.

And she doubted if she was.

8

By the time Elsa and Stephanovich returned home, the black blood had coagulated and dried in the wound in the sloping side of the mountain in their backyard. Stephanovich snorted in disgust at the sight of it on his lawn. They drove the Humvee across the backyard directly to their back door, feeling the crunch of the blood beneath their tires. The ride down the mountain had been rendered silent with the frustration and horror of losing their children to Mabin's grave, while thinking they were saving them by their actions. Their horror commingled with guilt and anger, for they should have understood their dreams meant little if they did not correspond with reality in some way, whether symbolically or actually or through a true flight of night-time fancy. The crunching blood beneath the Humvee relieved them in a way. It was no longer flowing, so it was no longer a danger. It could come after no one if it was static, in place, dead again. It could infect no one. It could only disgust.

"I'm going to have to blow the top of the mountain off," Stephanovich said, staring grimly into the dark when he parked the Humvee at the back door and turned off the headlights. "I'm going to load all the dynamite for the gold-mining operation into this truck, plant it on the mountaintop and blow the whole thing to smithereens."

"With the children trapped inside?" Elsa asked. "That's madness. You're not thinking clearly."

"I can do it without harming them. I can do it if I plan carefully and plant the charges above Mabin's grave. I doubt they've fallen anywhere but down from the gravesite, and if we blow off the top of the mountain, we can start to dig, or find the caverns they've entered, and get them out."

"The entire mountaintop? You're going to remove the entire mountaintop to find Maggie and Tommy?"

Stephanovich slumped in his seat. He held his head and then ran his hands through his hair in frustration.

"It does sound ridiculous when you put it that way. What else can we do?"

"We need to understand what just happened. We need to consult the mysteries and find out what they have to say. We can't simply blow up the mountain and hope to pick up the pieces."

"It's what I feel like doing. I'm so angry. I'm so hurt. I thought we could be happy here once Mabin came home. I thought we were through fighting vampires and now they've taken our children from us and I see no way to get them back."

"We can still be happy. We have to be careful, too. We can fix this and bring the children home."

"It goes way beyond that."

"How?"

"The mysteries. How can we trust them anymore?"

"Do we have a choice?"

"They've begun writing themselves again. It's been hundreds of years since they've done that. Someone might have co-opted the process, figured out how to make the mysteries speak for them instead of the mysteries speaking their own truth."

"Let's see if that's so. It's our only choice. Let's go inside and consult them at once."

"Why didn't they warn us we couldn't trust our dreams?"

"I don't know. We should have known better. Let's give them a chance to explain themselves."

In the dark, Stephanovich felt his face flush with the anger and aggravation of not understanding his situation, of being forced to confront the fact that the mysteries might be false or corrupted. What had always been true for him, scripture to nourish his soul, might have been misshapen into lies by a force they did not understand.

"If they're false with us, I'm blowing up the mountain. I don't care. And I'll blow up the mysteries, too, and this entire state."

Stephanovich's face was red and his cheeks were puffing in and out as he hyperventilated.

"Turn on the headlights, dear. I can't even see the back door in the dark."

Stephanovich found the switch for the headlights and twisted it violently, as though taking out his anger on it. The lights filled the backyard like a sudden bolt of sunrise, and in the light, something jumped off of all fours and shot toward the dark edges of the night. Once it was in the air, the figure landed on two legs and ran hissing and howling into the dark. It was the form of a man, but not a man. It wore a plaid shirt and khaki pants and penny loafers but it had been on all fours with its face pushed into the earth. Stephanovich lunged toward his door, his anger flaring, and flung open the door and jumped out.

"Who the hell was that? What was it?"

"Yes, what was that?" Elsa asked.

"You know what it was. It was eating the dried blood. I bet they're all out here eating the dried blood in the dark."

Elsa shuddered at the thought, and peered out into the night. At the edges of the headlights' beams, there was more hissing and howling, so much more hissing and howling it seemed a dark stadium full of the fans of the black blood had formed around the house. The headlights had driven them into the dark away from their meals and they were not pleased. The chill of the mountain night sent shivers through Stephanovich, but he stiffened his spine and stared directly into the foul noises at the edge of the light.

"We have another situation to deal with. Get out of the truck on this side," he said resolutely to Elsa. "It's not safe to get out on your side of the truck. Get inside the house and turn on all the outside lights, then turn on every single inside light. I'll stay here and keep them away until you have the house as bright and threatening as it can be to them."

On her hands and knees, Elsa crawled across the driver's side seat and jumped to the ground behind Stephanovich. She stood close behind him for protection and hesitated to stare into the darkness once more. She could just make out dozens of dark shapes, both men and women, and when they ventured forward and the light struck them, they screamed and scurried back into darkness.

"They're vampires again."

"They gave in. After all we did for them, they gave in and drank the blood."

"Hurry, get inside."

"But I know who they are," Elsa said, with great sadness. "I recognized so many of them, our neighbors and friends. We've been living among these people for a year. They were our friends, friends we cured."

"Not anymore. I couldn't see all of them. Who are they?"

"They're our neighbors, the Westons and the Smiths and the Davidsons and all the others. All the people we cared for and nursed back to health. They've regressed to the blood again, after all our efforts to save them. It's disgusting."

"Get inside!" Stephanovich screamed. "This damn mountain of blood ... Turn on the lights and we'll be safe. You know what we have to do to them now that we recognize who they are. We can't let them exist, and we can't let them get to us, for it's us they want now."

"But we were so kind to them. I feel so bad for them."

"Believe me, they don't return the kind feelings, as much as I wish they would. They've betrayed us for this dirt on the ground. Get inside."

Elsa managed to overcome her soft feelings for the recidivist vampires, their former friends and now their tormentors, and slid her key into the back door's lock and pushed the door open. She stepped inside and fumbled around, stumbling out of her regret and hurt at the betrayal of her neighbors. Stephanovich called to her to turn on the lights, quickly. "They're getting closer!" he said. "The headlights are dimming!" With the treachery of their friends, Elsa was so confused she could not remember the switch for the outside lights was right beside her, next to the door. She stood still, unable to move, until she saw the two tiny red lights across the room. The red lights blinked off, then on again, and off again, and then on, and then the two tiny lights moved toward her at eye level. Heavy, rasping breath fouled the still mountain air, and she could not breathe out of fear. Slowly, she realized the red lights were eyes boring into her own for no good purpose. Soon there would be hands crushing her neck and throwing her to the floor for the warm blood that coursed through her veins, and it was then she remembered where the light switch was. The red eyes were close, and illuminated two fangs in the mouth below them. Elsa reached out for the light switch and the eyes glowed bright red in anger at her, rushing toward her now, and she could not find the switch. She braced herself as the thing was about to knock her to the ground, but then a bright beam of light flashed on over her shoulder directly into the face of Harkin Davis, or what had been Harkin Davis. Mr. Davis squealed as the light from the bright torch Stephanovich held burned into his eyes, and he spun around in agony as his flesh sizzled. "Turn it off, turn it off! I beg you!" he screamed. "You're begging me, after what you were about to do?" Stephanovich yelled. "It's me, Harkin. Turn off the light!" He stumbled across the room, alternately squealing and gasping and pleading, until he saw the dark shimmer of the window over the sink and with a giant leap flew up and then through the glass, shattering the panes and frame of the window with the force of his exit. Stephanovich quickly flipped on the inside lights and then the outside flood lights. There was more squealing as the light hit the vampire neighbors congregated outside their house, and then the creatures scurried off in all directions into the darkness. Most disappeared up the hill onto the forested mountain.

"I can't believe Mr. Davis would do that. He was so –"

"We're turning on every light in the house," Stephanovich screamed. "Pray there's no power failure."

Just as he evoked prayer to keep the lights on, they flickered low to a sickening yellow. Gasping, Stephanovich slammed closed the back door and locked it tight. He glanced through the door's windows at the well-lit backyard, empty now, but still holding their neighborly enemies in the forest beyond the light.

"We can't go out at night anymore. We'll be stuck inside this house without our children forever."

Elsa spoke the words in a flat monotone, disappointed and staring straight ahead.

"Oh, we'll go out at night again, but they won't," Stephanovich warned.

"I loved the night sky here when it was empty of vampires, and now we can't go out at night," Elsa said, as though she had not heard a word her husband said.

"We'll think of something for them, something appropriately awful," Stephanovich said, as though he enjoyed the idea. "The mysteries will tell us what to do."

"But we're so alone now. Everyone in town has turned. I can sense it. Everyone! All our friends, they've gone back to drinking blood and are outside in the dark waiting for us."

"Somebody's resisted. There has got to be somebody who's resisted. We have to have some friends left."

"I'm afraid we have none."

As though in answer, there was a heavy thud above, and then another and another and another. The vampires were landing on the roof, where it was dark, dozens and dozens of them. The dim roof was a place to roost once the dried blood on the ground was all taken, and under that roof was the only human blood within close proximity – the blood of Stephanovich and Elsa. They could smell the two humans, and the two humans knew it. Stephanovich and Elsa could sense them smelling their blood.

"I think it's time to consult the mysteries," Stephanovich said. "They should help. They will help."

"I hope they have something helpful to say, or we could be done in the way our children are done in. Imagine ... I never imagined we would end like this."

"We're not ending. If they don't leave, we ..."

"Yes, I'm sorry. We have to be optimistic about the future, and not imagine what might happen to us inside this house tonight."

Elsa seemed to have regained some sort of crazy courage just in time to push her husband along toward the living room. She pushed him and then nodded at him for encouragement and closed the curtains over the windows of the back door, checked the lock and pulled on the door handle to make certain the door was shut tight. She pushed him again, but he barely moved. Stephanovich extracted two kitchen knives from a drawer under the counter and handed one of them to his wife, who took it without question. Elsa touched the point of the knife with her fingertip to check its sharpness, but accidentally pricked the skin to allow a drop of blood to exit and form in a small bulb on her finger. The vampires on the roof squealed with delight at the scent they picked up. There were more thuds on the roof as the vampires continued to land in the dark, heights above, planning their next move and squealing with excitation at the smell of blood.

"They know what you did to yourself," Stephanovich said. "That little hurt, they smelled it."

"This?"

Elsa held up her finger.

The vampires let out a raucous volley of squeals from above.

"Let's put a band aid on that, quickly," Stephanovich said. "Damn it, they're as strong as ever if their senses could detect just one drop."

A band aid from the drawer covered the wound, and the squealing above temporally quieted.

"Now let's get to the mysteries to figure out what we have to do now," Stephanovich said. "Somehow, we have to free Tommy and Maggie first of all, but I think we might have our work cut out for us before that, just to survive."

Stephanovich pointed upward.

"The children ... we can't forget about the children, though," Elsa said. "Those poor things, underground in who-knows-what situation. They have it worse than us, don't you think? They have it worse, don't they?"

Above, the vampires on the roof calmed down after their feast in the backyard and temptation on the roof, and Elsa and Stephanovich moved into the living room for a long night of reading.

They pulled the manuscript of the Transylvanian Mysteries out of the drawer and to their consternation saw that the parchment was blank.

9

Maggie's powers seemed to multiply with intensity as she walked in what she sensed was a spiral path circling downward. It was as though she could feel her strength and clarity coming back to her as she walked. She had to sense the path, since it was so dark, utter blackness, with the purifying blood dripping all around her in quiet pitter-patters. The increase in her powers to what they had been before going crazy had begun as she walked up the mountain to Mabin's grave. It made her think she had to care about something to be powerful, and now she cared only about restoring Mabin as she herself regained control of herself. She felt a kind of perspiration developing on her face, as though the humidity of the caverns increased as they descended. The wetness was so thick she had to swipe it away from her forehead with her fingers. She had to sense Mabin, too, since he was as silent as the dead, which seemed too real to her since she had discovered he was no longer breathing. She stopped when she heard sloshing up ahead in the dark that ceased quickly, and when she moved on she found herself walking through an unseen stream that crossed the path. Although she could not see the liquid she walked through, she knew what it was. She sloshed through it as had Mabin before her, feeling its purity, and although she understood what flowed over her feet, she could do nothing but walk on. Yet something in her wanted to bend down and drink. This blood was no longer black but fresh.

"It's part of it," Mabin said.

It was such a relief to hear his voice that she nearly cried out with joy. She composed herself before replying.

"Part of what?"

"This process. You know where we are. We have to cover ourselves in the good blood to heal. It's natural we do so. Just don't move off the path. There are things ..."

"What things?"

"You don't want to know, but I've seen them. We're not the only ones using the blood for purification. Sometimes I think they're not even human."

She stopped mid-stream to sense what might be around her, but her heightened senses told her nothing. No one was there, and Mabin was moving on without her. After what he had just said to her, she realized he was not quite coherent, either. There was no one chasing them.

After crossing the stream and stopping again, they were on the second level in the caverns of purification. A faint glow in the utter darkness caused them to look up. At first, there was what seemed like nothing more than the light of a small candle illuminating what looked like a ceiling far above them, but then the weak glow seemed to break apart into many dots of light, with one dot following the other. The dots traveled in a circle above them, gaining power as they circled around and around hundreds of feet above, and then one dot broke the circle and began a downward spiral toward them. The other dots followed, and as they dropped down in the darkness both Mabin and Maggie recognized them as the Outliners, the souls of the dead vampires and caretakers of this place. The fires that composed their rings burned pink and orange and they seemed to travel the same path Mabin and Maggie had traveled down the spiral path from the first level. Maggie moved closer to Mabin, but she felt him stiffen as though frightened of her.

"We need to undress," Mabin said. "Our clothing is soaked, but we needed the second-level blood on our flesh before the ritual will work. They will remove it, along with some of our difficulties."

Maggie barely saw Mabin's outline in the near-darkness, and she thought her heart would break if she had to see his scarred and torn body. What he was saying still made little sense to her. She heard the sounds of Mabin gently lifting his shirt over his head, and she felt the blood rush from her brain so quickly she grew faint. She gathered her top at the waist in two fistfuls of cloth, squeezing the blood out of the shirt as she did so, and after she pulled it over her head and dropped it on the ground, her hand flew out and brushed Mabin's shoulder. He screamed in agony at her touch, for only the touch of the living can injure the dead with a memory of life, and he staggered away in the dark, his bare feet splashing across the porous rock.

"I'm so sorry," Maggie said. "I didn't mean to touch you."

He gasped in pain. Instead of screaming at her, he seemed pleased.

"It's all right. I needed to feel something, even pain. Pain from you is not so bad."

"I'm so sorry," she repeated. "I didn't know I could hurt you. I didn't mean to hurt you."

"You don't know how happy it made me that you touched me," he said. "I gasped in pain when you hurt me. Air came out of my lungs when it hadn't for nearly a year. It means this place is working. As soon as I can breathe, I might begin getting better."

"I won't do it again."

"I hope you will, when the time comes for that ritual."

The darkness was still so absolute that they could see little of each other, nothing complete of each other, and nothing of their surroundings. Maggie felt she was living in a riddle, and then the dripping commenced from above, drops falling from the ceiling in a slow shower, as if the blood knew what to do, as the ancient vampire blood continued its journey of purification from the top level of the cavern toward the bottom. A kind of pure animal pleasure overcame her, as though she wanted to run through this place naked and yelling. Without knowing how he understood what to do, Maggie sensed that Mabin was tossing aside the rest of his clothing, and she followed in doing the same, in the animal pleasure of it. She shivered in the delight of animal ecstasy. The warm liquid falling through the darkness above settled over her flesh in a comforting shower, caressing her as Mabin's hands had once caressed her, and she tilted back her head in rapture and felt the blood ever warmer and warmer as it flowed over her body. Now she gasped, and she saw the glowing Outliners above continuing their journey down toward them, growing ever larger and brighter but still unable to cut through the darkness enough for them to see each other. She waited for them, waited for sight to satisfy her with a real vision of her lover. She moved her eyes from the Outliners to where she thought Mabin was, eager to see him again in the light, eager to see his healing. She saw and heard nothing of him. He was still wreathed in the darkness as the purifying blood dripped over them.

Now the Outliners spiraled down toward them faster and faster, their fires growing brighter and warmer as they followed the path down to the second level. Maggie's heart beat wilder and harder at their approach, as she watched them for a short time. She turned her gaze to where she knew Mabin was, longing to see him again. The Outliners were very close now, just a few feet above their heads, but still their light could not cut through the blackness of the second level. Then suddenly one of the Outliners flew down and encircled her head with a blinding light. It was as though a ring of the most intense fire burned just in front of her eyes, scorching her sight as though the sun rose a foot in front of her, but it had a pleasant warmth and soothing heat, and just before the ring of fire encircled her completely, she saw that another Outliner had descended and encircled Mabin's head, giving her a fleeting glance of him before the brilliant light blinded her. Her heart nearly stopped at the sight of the damaged dead boy, at how horribly death had disfigured him, and she flailed wildly, trying to free herself from the vision, not knowing if she was about to be tortured and killed, turned into what Mabin was now. The first circle of light then dropped down to her shoulders as she fought hard to save herself, and with eyes still nearly singed from the first Outliner's burn, another Outliner encircled her head and as it did, she saw that a second Outliner was descending over Mabin, too. This might be the end, an end in fire and blood. The downward spiral of Outliners was breaking its line in two to descend over Maggie and Mabin one after the other, flooding over them with warmth and heat and fear, and giving Maggie glimpses of Mabin as one ring of fire after another dropped over her. Several of the Outliners had dropped near the floor to a third spot, seemingly encircling a dark rock on the floor of the cavern, but with the endless line of the flashing Outliners dropping down over her she could do very little but gasp in the orgy of light. She could not move her limbs, was paralyzed by some force, and could only stand and wait to burn. She saw little as light and darkness alternated around her, as though she was staring into the sun and then into the darkest of caves. She screamed out, but then the sensation was complete ecstasy when the final Outliner dropped down over her and she seemed to bask in the heat and glow of the souls of the former vampires. Greater and greater grew the heat and light, and she shook and cried out in her burning purification, so deeply immersed in the healing spirits of the dead that her mind was wiped clean, purified and empty. She collapsed in the circle of light and fainted. The blood that had showered over her was cleaned away by the Outliners' light and heat, and her flesh was as fresh and clean as though an icy waterfall had roared down over her.

She lost consciousness, just slipped away into the darkness, as she reached out her hand and called to Mabin.

Within seconds she was awake and curious, all the light dissipated but with the warmth of the dead souls' embraces remaining in her, as she glowed from within. Her clothes, fresh and dry now, covered her, and she was on her feet. They had clothed her. She knew Mabin was near, for she could feel the heat coming off of him and sense the purity that had been burned into his soul, too, and she wanted him.

"Can you breathe?" she asked. "Come close. I don't hear your breathing, but did it work for you? Is there any life in you?"

"I think my heart is beating a little," he said. "I have no breath. It's not with me yet, but I feel so well. It's like something I haven't felt since last I saw you."

In the complete darkness, Maggie stepped toward him, nearly weeping with relief. Finally, he had given her a kind word. Her lover was coming back.

"Don't!" he yelled out at her, sensing what she was about to do.

She stopped where she was, no more than a foot from him.

"Why not? You said your heart was beating again. You must feel something again, so why can't I come near you? I want to touch you, to hold you."

"I want ... It's ... not right yet. I feel ... I want you, but I feel this great pain when you come near. I ... think something is still very wrong. When you're near, I feel as though I'm burning inside, burning with nothing but pain."

Maggie raised her hand to her mouth to suppress the cry of her hurt and disappointment at the agony she was causing him, and then she lifted her hand him but did not extend her arm. He was gasping as though her presence was an iron stake thrust through him. She let her fingertips merely reach out in the dark to a spot near his chest and softly beating heart. A lump formed solidly in her throat, a soft rock, and she dropped her hand to her side. Loving a dead boy as he was forced back to life was more onerous than she had thought it would be when she had jumped so hopefully into his grave to retrieve him. She listened in the silence of the utter darkness for a breath, hoping it would come after enduring the embrace of the vampire souls, but the air did not move, for she was holding her breath, too. The dripping of the blood in the darkness commenced again, and as the drops hit the floor they splattered throughout the cavern but did not touch them. That part of the ceremony was done.

She let out an exhalation.

"I guess we should get moving," Mabin said, matter-of-factly. "We need to find the third level for the next purification, and I don't have a clue how to get there."

As though in answer to him, one of the Outliners encircled an opening in the distance, firing a ring around it and illuminating the first few stairs of the interior. The edges of the Outliner flickered brightly in the gloom, but the center of the soul was as empty as space.

"Here," it whispered, hoarsely.

"Did it speak?" Maggie asked. "Can they tell us what to do?" She walked toward it, curious.

"I think it did say something."

"I am Natas," the Outliner said in a hoarse voice so low it could not have been heard anywhere but here, beneath the earth's great silence.

"Natas, you say?"

"Yes."

"Is this the way?" Mabin asked. "Should we follow you, Natas? Is there anything we need to know?"

"I am your guide. Step through me and you will find the place you need. But know that when you come close to me it brings me as much pain as the girl brings you when she comes close. The memories of life are the most painful things for the dead."

"We'll stay as far away as we can."

"And the others, too, please. They will fear you if they feel too much pain in your presence. Step through me now."

"Where are the other Outliners? I never saw you before," Mabin said.

"It is time for me to take your hands and lead you. The third level is the most difficult yet, and it is far away. So hurry. I can not burn for long around this opening with you so close. The other Outliners are waiting. I am in agony."

Maggie looked back for Mabin, and then spun around.

"Tell me you feel something and this will end soon. Tell me you love me."

"I ... can't." He seemed confused. "It's not in me to say such a thing."

Utterly frustrated by his response, Maggie raced across the spongy, soaked rocks toward Natas, desperate to make things right in this underworld of nothingness and frustration.

"Maggie ..." Mabin said. "Wait!"

It was too late. She leaped through the ring of fire and onto another downward path. Without hesitating, she continued on her hike, full of determination to complete this quest and find out if love could exist again once a lover has died and with it his love. She heard Mabin rushing toward the opening but still did not look back. She heard the Outliner groan when he leaped through the ring of light and she could hear his first few footsteps behind her hurrying to catch up. Then the Outliner Natas blinked off, so that they were in total darkness again, unable to see where they were going or where they had been.

All they could do was continue on the path down, ever downward toward spiraling hope, using their instincts and intuition to find the third level of purification.

"I didn't like his name," Mabin said, when he caught up to her.

"It's obvious. No one would be that obvious," Maggie answered, not wanting to let her bitterness enter her voice but hearing it there anyway. "It means nothing, but I hope he is the opposite of what who he told us he is."

"Natas is Satan backwards."

"I know. I don't think he's steered us wrong so far. No one would make up a name like that and expect anyone to trust him."

"Do you trust me?"

She did not answer, but pushed on.

It was so dark, and so quiet, with the path continually sloping downward, that it was as though Maggie had lost her own breath and heartbeat. It would be very difficult and pointless to go on if Mabin could never love her again.

She existed as little more than darkness floating in darkness, and she wondered if she was losing her life as she proceeded onward, instead of gaining it back.

If she could not have Mabin again as he had been, then she might as well die.

She hurried on again through complete darkness. Her heart was not broken yet. He had not yet broken it, although he seemed to be trying.

10

"Do you think we should call Montana Power and Light?" Elsa asked.

"I think our problems are bigger than our utilities."

"What about the lights? If our lights go out, we're at their mercy."

"I think we're all right there. We can fight just as well in the dark as they can. And we love each other. They don't love anybody, so they are at a disadvantage."

The lights were flickering as Stephanovich stood in the living room clutching the Transylvanian Mysteries and staring at the blankness on the parchment, waiting for the mysteries to write themselves again. The mysteries would tell them what to do, how to get out of their predicament, but they were silent on the issue because it seemed they did not know what to do but promise to protect each other through love. The vampires, once their neighbors, were still on the roof, having insinuated themselves a little too closely to the only fresh blood left in the town, Elsa and Stephanovich, but still the mysteries were silent on their predicament. Their blood was blood the vampires would have great difficulty in obtaining, for both knew how to deal with their type and were adept at it. As the night wore on, it was clear that the vampires had little idea of what to do, for they simply remained on the roof. Perhaps they had lost the skills necessary to be successful in their condition. Before dawn, they'd have to fly away and leave, and dawn was not that far away, yet they made no move.

"We have to inoculate everyone with the antidote again," Stephanovich said.

"It worked once. We should be able to do it again. We can inoculate them and settle them all in their houses again."

"The only problem is the formula is written in the mysteries, and they're not speaking it. I don't remember it, it's complicated."

"Why are the mysteries blank?"

"I don't know. If they remain blank all night, we'll have to try something else. We have to get Maggie and Tommy out of that mountain first, and I don't have a clue of how to do that. These creatures did that to us, took our children from us, and I don't quite know what to do because of that."

"Maybe you're right, dear. Maybe we need to kill them all and blow off the top of the mountain to get the children out."

"The mysteries are worthless now, and I feel like killing them instead of healing them after what they did to us and the children."

Stephanovich threw up a hand in frustration, and the mysteries trembled in his hand as though objecting to their worthlessness.

"It will all work out, dear. The mysteries will speak to us again, but if we have to kill them, we will."

Stephanovich threw the yellowed parchment onto the coffee table in utter frustration. His face reddened in anger.

"We've always done everything right. Why has this happened to us? One little mistake by our boy and now we're stuck in this situation, not that it was his fault. We have to be perfect if we're going to save them, but no one is perfect. It might be easier to kill them all and then save the children."

"Let's have some coffee and wait for the dawn. Coffee will clear our heads, and then maybe the mysteries will have something to say to us."

"All right, but stay away from that broken window in the kitchen. They can reach us through that, and I don't want to get careless."

Carefully, his eyes peering out into the backyard with the help of the outdoor floodlights, Stephanovich filled the coffee pot with fresh water and poured it into the coffee maker. He knew who was out there in the shadows. The Smithsons, who gardened for a living, and the Avrils, the family of five who home-schooled their own children and tutored others. The Rumsons, who built a Little League field and coached boys and girls, they were there. All of those people were there. He thought all of them were friends, but now he knew better. Soon, the enticing smell of freshly brewed java wafted through the air, and with it Stephanovich and Elsa's hunger returned. They had to have something fleshy and bloody as their frustrations with their vampire neighbors grew, and Stephanovich remembered there were thick cuts of steak in the refrigerator. He placed an iron frying pan on top of the gas range and turned on the flame to a high heat.

"We'll sear the steaks on each side for a few seconds and then eat them as raw as possible," he said, walking to the refrigerator. "I can't believe how hungry I am."

"Me, too. Make them bloody red on the inside. They aren't the only ones who gain strength from blood."

Stephanovich was reaching for the refrigerator door when there was a banging beneath his feet. He stopped and stood stock-still, staring at his shoes. Elsa, too, froze with her eyes on the floor, just as she was about to pour a cup of coffee. Both stared at the floor for a few seconds more until the noise repeated itself.

"Did we turn on the lights in the basement?" Stephanovich asked, in a whisper.

"I didn't. Did you?"

"No. How could we have been so stupid? Every light outside and inside the house is on, except for those in the basement."

"They're down there."

"Get the hammers and silver spikes," Stephanovich said. "Stun them with a blow to the head, and then spike them through the heart. I don't think I can take any more of this. I can't stop thinking of what they did to the children."

"I remember that. You're not the only one losing patience with our friends, and this isn't the first time I've done this."

Elsa removed two claw hammers and a handful of silver spikes from a drawer next to the dish washer. She handed a hammer and the fistful of spikes to Stephanovich and then wrapped her fingers around another handful of spikes for herself.

"Let's go," she said. "They've decided for us what we're going to do. Not only have they taken our children, but now they're invaded the safety of our home. It's intolerable."

Stephanovich tip-toed across the floor so that the vampires would not know he was coming, and Elsa followed in the same careful way. He slowly swung open the basement door but halted when it squeaked on its hinges. With one quick motion, he pulled the door open and reached for the light switch on the wall and threw it on. Nothing happened. The darkness in the basement into which he peered was as complete as the darkness of midnight in the forest.

"Of course," he whispered. "They unscrewed the light bulbs. Next they'll throw the breakers to plunge the house into complete darkness. It's lucky we got to the silver spikes before they could do that."

"Go down. We can't have vampires in our basement. We'll show them what we do to rude monsters that steal our children and break into our home."

Stephanovich descended the stairs, his senses heightened by the fact the vampires knew they were coming. He had a spike ready in one hand and his hammer lifted in the other as he walked down into the dark. Elsa mirrored him, hammer in hand and spike ready to drive into a vampire's heart. As soon as they got to the bottom of the stairs, they saw three sets of red eyes glaring at them from the dark near the furnace. The vampires did not move but continued to stare at them. Stephanovich spun around, thinking their motionless gaze was a trick to confuse them and thinking there were more vampires behind them. Elsa had her hammer raised toward the three sets of red eyes, ready to pounce.

"We only want to talk," a voice said.

"Since when did a vampire only want to talk when he saw fresh blood before him?" Stephanovich asked. "Are you hungry? Come on. Try me."

Stephanovich raised his hammer higher in the air as though aiming a blow at the trio of vampires.

"I could have taken your blood at any time when I was in the house before," the voice said, and both Stephanovich and Elsa recognized the voice as that of Harkin Davis. "I don't care about drinking you at all, not one bit."

"None of us do, now," another voice said.

"Ester?" Elsa asked. "Is that you?"

"Yes, it's me. You know, I always hated you," the second voice said. "You've always been so holier-than-thou."

"But why? We've been friends for years, we –"

"Shut up!" Harkin Davis screamed out. "No one cares about your petty little spats. Let's get what we came here for and then leave."

"I wouldn't drink her blood if it was the last blood in Montana."

"It might be," said the third voice.

"Oh, god, you, too, Selma?" Elsa said. "I'd recognize your voice anywhere. At the club we used to –"

"We don't care about taking your blood," Harkin Davis roared out. "It's insignificant. It's nothing. We want you off this mountain, so that we can have the blood inside it. That's what we want."

Before he could think of what he was doing, Stephanovich let out a little laugh at the absurdity of it.

"You want something you can never get to," he said. "That mountain is sealed tighter than Mars, and just about as difficult to get to. You'll never get into that mountain."

"But we know Maggie got in, to save that boy of hers. We want you to get us in the same way she did. We want our blood returned to us, and then you can leave Montana in peace."

"You think it's your blood?"

"Yes, it's our blood. It's our birthright."

"That was never your blood. Other vampires drank it of their victims. It was never your blood."

"It is ours! Once the mountain leaked it out and we drank the black blood it became ours. We will never settle until it is fully ours, all of it, and you are settled somewhere in Iowa, or some-such other place."

"The mountain is sealed and will stay that way. You're why we lost our children, and if they're anyone leaving Montana, it's you, as black ash."

"That is not what I heard you say about the mountain being sealed. You said you have dynamite and would blow off the top of the mountain, just to get to your little dead boy and that girl with the beautiful gray eyes, who is also dead now, I presume. You can have gray eyes and the boy, if he lives, but we want Mabin for our revenge."

Stephanovich laughed and pointed a silver spike at Harkin Davis and raised his hammer again.

"Are you ready, Elsa?"

"You take down Mr. Davis, and I'll take down the other two ladies."

Suddenly, the three sets of red eyes darted off to the side, and stopped there before Stephanovich and Elsa could pounce on them.

"Open Mabin's grave for us," Harkin Davis demanded, when they were settled at a new point in the dark at a safe distance. "Maggie got in that way, and so can we."

"We don't know how to open the grave. Some other power opened it to take Maggie from us."

"Then give us the dynamite and we'll do what you threatened to do. We'll blast and blast until we find the caverns of blood."

"You'll never find what you need to open the mountain. I would never be so foolish to let dynamite sit around."

"You have until tomorrow night. If the mountain is not open by then, we'll not be kind to you, and we will find the dynamite. Think on it."

With that, all six red eyes closed, there was a flapping of wings and with a rush of wind the three vampires flew out the open cellar doors as bats.

"What do we do now?" Elsa asked.

"Close the doors."

"I meant about their offer. We can't give them what they want, but we have to get Maggie and Tommy out of there. They know that. They'll be watching us."

"This only makes it more difficult. I suppose we will have to kill them."

Stephanovich walked across the basement floor and reached up and pulled down the cellar doors.

"We didn't think enough," he said. "We could have been killed because we forgot to turn on the cellar lights. We can't be so careless again."

"They'll be watching us every step of the way. We don't have any idea of how to get Maggie and Tommy out of the mountain, but if we have to get shovels and dig, we're getting them out. When we do, they'll be there to get in to the blood."

"I have a few ideas of what we can do to stop them," Stephanovich said. "And the mysteries won't be silent forever."

The light from the kitchen above illuminated the top steps leading down to the basement, and now that his eyes were accustomed to the dark, Stephanovich saw the light bulb above his head had been unscrewed. He reached up and turned it so that the 100-watt bulb flooded the basement with light.

"There. That should take care of that," he said. "Are you hungry? We should eat before we go out at dawn and kill them all. That's all that's left to us, our only choice. They have to sleep once the sun comes up, and I'm in no mood to spare any of them this time. No more antidotes for them to bring them back to human form. They're all going to die, and then we figure a way to get Tommy and Maggie out of that mountain as quickly as possible, if they're still alive."

"Don't say that. I have to know they're all right before we go on our killing spree."

"If anybody can handle what's inside that mountain, the children can."

Stephanovich and Elsa climbed the stairs in a grim silence. Soon, two thick steaks were sizzling on the red-hot griddle. Blood seeped out of them into the pan immediately, evaporating in the red-hot heat, so Stephanovich turned them over at once, barely before the first side had darkened to charcoal. Then he let the second side of the steaks sizzle in the escaping blood for just a few seconds.

The vampires were not the only ones hungry for a quick transfusion. The steaks were dropped onto their plates, still leaking blood, and both Stephanovich and Elsa lifted their dishes and tilted them so that they could lean down and drink the blood that flowed out copiously from the nearly raw meat.

Hope and blood were the only two things that gave them the strength to carry on.

11

Mabin and Maggie had to trust their instincts in guessing they had arrived at the third level of purification, since they were still plunged in total darkness.

They were traveling down through the mountain without their sight, with only instinct to guide them.

Little had changed from the trek downward through the black night inside the mountain when they stopped, only the grade of the rocks beneath their feet, as the surface of the spongy rock was flat instead of inclined. This had to be the third level. It was impossible to tell, aside from the leveling of the floor and their feel for the place, for the gloom was unchanged and the dripping of the purifying blood through the rock and earth continued without alteration. Although they could not see it, there seemed to be a vast open space surrounding them, as though they stood in the middle of a great plain in a still wind. This felt right, or as right as coming to rest in such a place could feel.

In silence, anxiously sensing each other only feet away in the vastness, they stood hoping for some sign that the next ritual was about to begin, perhaps in a sudden flicker of light from the Outliners. Previously, they had been followed down a level by the flickering souls, but if the Outliners were near at this level, it was not apparent. Maggie hoped that at any second the familiar circles of glittering fires would ignite and float above, showing her Mabin's form, for then they could continue their purification, finish with the resurrection, and return to real life on the surface as lovers. She wanted more than anything to see how much he had healed and if life had made any progress in awakening the boy to become what he had been.

"Are they near?" Maggie asked. "Mabin? Can you sense them?"

"I sense darkness. There's not much else. This place seems vast."

"I sense only you. It's almost as though I'm touching you without touching you. Why are you silent? Tell me you feel better."

"The dead are always silent."

Maggie's first instinct was to flare up in anger and remind him how difficult it was to love a dead boy whose heart had lost its pulse and whose breath was abated. He had to stop thinking of himself as dead, now that she was with him. Further, loving someone with the cold silence of the grave still on them was nearly impossible for any normal nature, for how do you converse with the half-dead?

Instead of burning suddenly hot in speech like an Outliner, she decided to be diplomatic with the boy who seemed barely able to leave behind his own destruction.

"You know, I don't have to tell you how I feel. I tell you because I thought it might help bring you back to life, that's all. Maybe I was wrong. Maybe we should wait and be ready for what comes next and talk about us later. The important thing is to wait, and be ready."

It sounded wrong to her, as most fabricated excuses always did, but talking to Mabin in this state was like talking to a wooden post. She ached for the true Mabin she had known in life. But his death was a reality she had to face and the only solution was to endure this difficult purification to bring him out of himself, of this underworld, and then live and love on the surface as they once had lived and loved. The solution was to endure and hope, and to purify herself, too. She could not push him too hard to take up life once again.

The wooden post spoke.

"Do I seem different to you?" he asked.

Even his voice was odd.

"Yes."

The word was out before she could think of a diplomatic answer, and she regretted it immediately.

"Who loves the dead?" Mabin asked, as though he read her thoughts. "Only a crazy person would love the dead. Is it true you're crazy, Maggie?"

She felt him turn away in disappointment. But why? Why?

"I love the dead. I love you."

"And that only proves you're mad."

He said this with such pain in his voice that she knew this wasn't sincere.

"You are dead, and if loving you is madness, then I am certainly insane," she snapped back at him.

She was barely been able to stand after answering. He was being so hurtful, and she felt stunned that he would be so blunt, so hard with her. She recognized that the situation demanded the cold reality of truth, but splashing that cold reality into her face was anything but pleasant, and it was cruel to point out to a crazy person she was crazy. She had been driven insane by his death and perhaps she remained that way this entire year, but attempting to fix what she had broken was a sign that her madness did not persist and did not run deep, for it meant she at least recognized what insanity was. She had come here to bring him out of this place and back to her, and her leap into his grave meant she knew exactly what she wanted and what she was doing. That is not insanity.

"This will cure me, too," she said, calmly. "The Outliners know it. That's why they're treating me, too. You aren't the only one who needs this. I wish you understood how much I need it, too."

His hesitation meant he truly was having difficulty understanding her, that maybe the blood was not yet flowing to his brain, despite the fact that his heart had restarted on the previous level.

She heard a laugh break from him.

"Maybe I'm one of the walking dead now. Maybe we both are. Oh, this is such a cruel place. It's cruel to treat each other like this."

"It is not cruel if it works."

"It is cruel. Only with cruelty can the living bring the dead back to life. Force me back, Maggie, please. I can't do it myself."

The dangerous possibility of what he said was not what she took away from his answer. She ignored his meaning. She heard only his laugh, which she had not heard in a very long time. It was a warm wind on a very cold night, that laugh. It was something to hold on to. It meant something was going right inside him, that laughter was a sign that not only his heart was healing but also his soul. Forget what his words said. Good things were happening to them despite how difficult they felt their situations to be. The two of them were stuck in the middle of a vast, dark place, with no clue of which way to go or what to do, and that sense of infinite darkness surrounding her suddenly made her shiver. Maybe this was cruelty. If only he would come near with that warmth of soul she remembered so well. He could still be lost in that infinite darkness, she could still lose him forever in it, if she did not do the things that her madness told her to do to heal him. Yes, it was her madness that had led her to this place with him, and it was madness that would heal them both. Madness lit the way, for now there seemed to be light. Above, an Outliner flickered to life, hovering over them with a weak circle of light that barely illuminated a pool of pink twilight around them. The weak light increased the sense that they were trapped in an immense darkness that rolled on an on to an unseen infinity.

"It was not easy to find you," the Outliner said. "No soul knows all of this place, even if that soul has been here for a millennium."

Maggie recognized the Outliner as Natas, the backwards Satan they had counted on for help. If he hadn't been providing them with the only light they had seen for a long time, she would have been leery of his intrusion, but light was light when the darkness is complete, and it is welcome.

"It's lucky I found you. I might not have."

"Are we still inside St. Mary's mountain?" Maggie asked.

"You are and you aren't."

"What does that mean?"

"Every place has an inside and an outside. Decide in which of them you are living. The go toward that place."

There was no point in pondering that riddle, or even pondering what Natas implied. She saw Mabin just a few feet from her, standing tall and straight, his eyes lifted toward the light and glowing. There had been a remarkable transformation in him since the last time she had seen him in the light. His hood was pulled down and he looked like the same boy she had known on the surface, the sweet, long-haired, handsome, dark boy she had longed to see while he had been recovering in his grave and she had paced the surface impatiently waiting for him. Her heart nearly flew out of her chest at the sight of his physical recovery, of what he looked like, for he looked like the same beautiful boy she had dreamed of. She longed for him, she longed to step into his arms, but his arms were not yet open to her, and he appeared confused as he stared up at the soft light. His body might have regained the beauty it once had, but his mind had not regained its beauty. His mind was barely functioning, it seemed to her.

Natas floated over Mabin and descended to speak to him.

"You have something of hers," he said.

"What is that? I have nothing. The dead have no possessions."

"You have her blood."

Mabin's eyes blinked nervously, looking up into the dim light, as Natas flickered above him.

"Yes? It healed me. It kept me hoping for a year."

"Then there is something you must do."

"What's that?"

"You must return her blood to her. You must give it back before you can continue. Her blood has kept you alive, but now it's driving away the things you had that should be inside you again, the forces you own and should own again, and it's keeping her power from being hers. It's making her weak and mad not to own her own blood. And it's making you foolish and timid."

"I would return it without question."

"Then do so."

"But how?"

"The same way it was given to you, but in reverse. Give it from your heart to her heart, just as it was given to you from her heart to yours."

"My blood has just begun to flow. How can I give hers back? Aren't our bloods mixed?"

"Your wound has not healed. Her wound has not healed, inside or out. Both wounds need to heal. Lift off your hood and you will see the wound is open. Her wound is open. Give her back what is hers in an embrace. You owe that to her."

With a sudden movement, Mabin flung his hood and cape up over his head and dropped them to the floor. It was as Natas said it was, for in his chest, just over his heart, a circular opening in the flesh was exuding the first drops of the blood Maggie had given him to begin his resurrection nearly a year ago. Natas flickered above them, momentarily plunging them into darkness again, but then his fires lit and his circle glowed above them.

"Let him do what he must do," Natas said to Maggie.

"He's hurt. I can't take back my blood if he still needs it."

"It's done the job it was meant to do. And your wound is open now," Natas said to Maggie.

With that he was gone, and the darkness and chill returned to cover them.

"Come close to me, Mabin."

He did not move.

"Come close."

Still he did not move.

Maggie knew she could not hesitate, for she understood the intention of the vast black cavern around them now. It intended to swallow them if they did not comply with its intentions. It would separate them, for it was so empty and vast and they would have eternity to spend here in separation if she did not respond, which meant they would be estranged in this infinite dark, never to unite again. She pulled her shirt over her head violently and felt the cold of the great cavern, and it was as Natas had told her, for her wound was open and empty, longing for a return of the blood that was in Mabin's heart. She had no time to lose. She knew where he was in this blackness and rushed to him, pushing her breasts into his chest and sighing with the contact to his flesh as he groaned. The two wounds seemed to seek each other out as though some instinctual magic guided their hearts toward each other. They could do nothing themselves, for the instinct of the heart took over as the wounds locked together. Mabin gasped as Maggie's blood pumped from his heart, and

Maggie screamed in pain as it returned to her body, feeling it pushing and throbbing into her again and again with each beat of Mabin's heart. When all of her blood had returned to her body, the wounds did not separate but remained locked together. Slowly, the flesh retreated. Their bodies separated. The edges of Mabin wound were healing, and then Maggie's wound knitted together slowly, as she panted and groaned. Pressed up against him still, she kissed his neck and then his shoulder and then the wound. The flesh over it was smoothed under her kiss, and then it was as if it had never existed. Mabin finally embraced her, pulling her close to him with immense strength. He kissed her hair, her forehead and her mouth.

"It's suddenly so different. You're so warm now," she said to him. "This is all I ever wanted."

"We're as close together as we can be with the exchange of blood."

"It's the first time I felt this in so long. Maybe we can get still closer."

"Count on that warmth from now on. And the closeness."

Maggie felt the tears flowing down her cheeks. His kind words were what she needed.

"We're almost back, aren't we?"

"We could leave here now and be together forever if we knew how."

"Yes. We could leave together, if we knew how."

Maggie looked around, but it was utterly pointless. The darkness persisted, and suddenly she shivered at the thought that they were buried alive, for they were alive now and it seemed they were buried, too. And there appeared to be no exit anywhere, with darkness strangling hope.

Suddenly, she heard someone scream for help, and she thought she knew the voice but then everything crashed down around them, drowning out the call for help. Instead of emptiness, they were in the middle of a huge cascade of debris. It was all around them, rocks and earth and dust and even the Outliners flickering on and off in the landslide, and before long it pulled them apart from each other and sent them tumbling through a very large hole beneath them. Just as they had come together again, they were torn apart. Maggie screamed as Mabin was pulled away from her by the crashing debris all around them, and he reached out for her, calling her name.

"Maggie!"

"Maggie!" another voice screamed out. "Maggie!"

"Mabin!"

Something struck her in the back of the head, and now the darkness had no chill or vastness or sense that there was someone there, someone she loved, to share it with her.

It was complete darkness, without sound or touch or sight.

She thought she had heard Tommy's voice while she tumbled downward endlessly through the landslide.

12

Stephanovich could not believe their great good luck as day broke.

It looked like it would be a very good day, a fine day, to kill their enemies.

As soon as the sun had risen, he and Elsa finished their coffee and raw meat quickly and rushed outside into the protective rays of light shooting straight across the earth to send the recidivist vampires scurrying back into hiding in the darkness. None of them dared face the harsh melting rays of the sun or the wrath of the living, few though they may be. But it was almost as though the vampires had forgotten they were vulnerable to other dangers while taking their daytime naps, for they had gone straight home to bed after their first night as reborn immortals, drinkers of the black blood.

Elsa and Stephanovich had not.

They had thrown their three gas cans into the back of the Humvee and driven into town to the hardware store to purchase more. While the door to the store was swinging open and a sign on it advised them the business was, too, there was no one in attendance to assist them in their haste to rid the valley of the vampires. They waited a short time, ringing the bell on the counter several times, and then concluded the workers at the hardware store had drunk blood, too. All in town had drunk blood. They helped themselves to all the gas cans in stock and headed for the local service station, being careful to leave the exact amount of cash on the counter to pay for their purchases.

Victor was a ghost town. Not one soul appeared on the sleepy streets filled with heat mirages or peeked out their shuttered windows or stood in their bone-dry yards with their dogs yawning as the pooches did their business.

"Look at this. This town has ceased being human," Stephanovich said. "I knew it. The shops are empty. The houses are shut tight. They've all turned, but not for long. Fool me once ... and I'll kill you the next time you try it."

"It's horrible, but maybe the only way we can get the children back is to become one of them, but not like them, good vampires instead, not like they are."

"Are you utterly insane?" Stephanovich screamed. "After what they did to our children, you want to become like them?"

Knitting his brows in anger after his outburst silenced his wife, Stephanovich looked away from her and pushed down on the accelerator. The Humvee jumped away from the curb.

"Why is it that nearly every morning after breakfast you have second thoughts about remaining human?" Stephanovich went on as they drove down the street, his face red with anger and his brow tight and drawn. "It's distressing. Every morning you feel the same confusion about your role as a human being. What is it about mornings that make you think of drinking blood?"

"I ... not really. I don't want to turn," Elsa answered, deliberately widening her eyes and shaking her head. "I just haven't awoken, and I've been so upset. They've all turned, though, that's all, every one of the people we knew. This is going to be very difficult, given the circumstances and their great numbers, what we have to do now. If we reclaimed our powers –"

"We are going to kill them all!" Stephanovich screamed. "And we're not drinking blood to do it. Strong coffee and meat are good enough. We're going to burn every damn one of them to a crisp, and then somehow we're going inside that mountain to get Maggie and Mabin and Tommy out as soon as possible. After that, we're going to live normal lives as before. That's the end of the debate."

Elsa's eyelids drooped, and she settled her head against the window. She cried quietly, and Stephanovich thought he had gone too far in berating her for her weakness. She was suffering just as much as he was. She simply became confused, and allowed herself to consider the wrong solutions.

Stephanovich set his eyes on the road, accelerating in anger, and reached a top speed of one-hundred-and-five miles-per-hour before the service station came into view. Elsa, uncomfortable now that she again had let out her secret desire again to become an evil immortal, sat squirming and awake. Stephanovich's reckless speeding nearly frightened her to death. With the service station just fifty feet ahead on the right, he slammed on the breaks, sending the Humvee squealing with its tires smoking up and over the curb, where the truck bumped to a stop beside the gas pumps. Elsa had snapped forward, held back by her seat belt, but nearly slammed into the windshield.

"Stephanovich!"

"What? Are you awake now? Have you forgotten your desire for blood? Am I going to have to do this by myself?"

"You drive too fast for your own good."

"Ha! What's the difference? Are you worried about danger? There are vampires everywhere, so maybe we should worry about them, not my driving. Everybody in Montana drives too fast for their own good anyway. Now that you're awake, do you still want to become an immortal?"

"Look, I'm sorry," Elsa said. "I don't want to be a vampire, and the coffee just kicked in. I just have a little craving for blood in the morning sometimes. It passes. It always does. You don't have to take it out on me just because I think of how fine blood would taste sometimes, instead of coffee and meat every morning."

A huge smile crossed Stephanovich's face. It was as though he had not heard her, or not listened.

"I can not believe our good luck," he said, ignoring her, with wonder in his voice.

He was staring at the side of the service station. Its bay doors were open as though the attendants had left in a hurry to join the other vampires, and beside the station, a large tanker delivery truck was parked. It sat there peacefully staring out at the mountains, the fluid inside it not nearly as valuable to the vampires as the fluid coating St. Mary's mountain. It had no value for vampires: they left it.

"If that thing is full, we won't need all these gas cans," Stephanovich said.

He shut off the engine, removed his seat belt, threw open his door and stepped out of the Humvee. His feet had barely hit the ground before he was running toward the tank truck. He climbed up on the running board to see if the keys were in the ignition and giggled when he saw they were. Then he jumped down again and took a few slow steps toward the back of the truck. He tapped on the side of the tank as he walked. The tank responded with deep low sounds, and then he grinned to himself.

"It's full!" he screamed. "Ha, ha! We can burn every one of them in Victor with this!"

Elsa hurried to his side.

"Let me see."

She tapped on the side of the tank, and her tapping repeated the low sound of a full load of gas.

"I was thinking we'd hear echoes," Elsa said. "I was willing to bet they had off-loaded the gas into the below-ground tanks and we'd hear echoes, but that tank is definitely full. The fools!"

"We should return to our development and burn it first, burn all our neighbors first, the ones who betrayed us the worst," Stephanovich said. "We built all those wonderful houses for them, cured them, and then they revert at the first chance they get. Curse them! I'm sorry we have to wreck such a nice neighborhood as ours, though, but it has to be done."

"We gave them a second chance. The proved they don't deserve it. It's their own fault if we kill every last one of them."

"I guess some of us can't change."

"Or don't want to."

"So much for second chances."

"Screw second chances for vampires."

Stephanovich climbed up into the driver's seat of the tank truck, and Elsa rushed around to clamber into the passenger's seat. Their moods had changed from anger and fear to joy within the space of a few moments of luck. They brought the old beast of a truck to life with a twist of the key and turned back onto the highway, where Stephanovich did not relent from his intent desire to immolate those who had so betrayed them. The old dark green tanker had a great deal of life left in its engine, and Stephanovich pressed hard on the accelerator to drive it down to the floor. Soon they reached seventy miles-an-hour, and then eighty. The old truck shook and coughed, the steering wheel shaking mightily in Stephanovich's hands, but he was leaning forward and glaring at the road, oblivious to the fact that speed was about to pull the old truck apart. Luckily, their development was only a few miles from town center. They reached their street within minutes.

"Go inside and get as many of those boxes of matches we use to light the fireplace as you can," he said. "The long ones that keep your hands safe, get them."

"I can't believe what idiots our neighbors are," Elsa said. "Look at that. Every house on this road has its curtains drawn on every window, bottom and top floors. They might as well put up a sign: 'Vampires live here. Darkness required.' What idiots."

"Hurry. Get the matches."

"Yes, yes."

"The Jones vampires live next door. They get it first."

The sun rose so quickly it was as though it conspired with them to destroy the nests where the vampires reposed. It lent its light and heat to the morning, restricting the vampires' movement into day and adding its flames to the ease of setting the dry houses afire. Elsa jumped from the truck and ran into the house, while Stephanovich drove the tank truck across the lawn, which the sun had baked hard and the clouds had refused to water. The lawn was an ugly brown patch and as solid as the highway. Stephanovich parked the truck by the Jones' big picture window. Knowing exactly what he was doing, he pulled the tanker's hose down from the side of the truck, found a rock and smashed the picture window with it by tossing it through the glass. He picked up the hose, inserted the end of it into the house and turned on the valve to get the gas flowing, making sure to saturate the curtains. After just a few seconds, he shut off the valve, nearly choking on the gas fumes, his heart pumping blood through his veins in excitement as strongly as the hose had pumped gas into the house.

"Now we pay you back for taking our children," he said, talking to the broken glass and gasoline smell.

Elsa ran up to him with four large boxes of fire-starting matches.

"Is this enough?"

"Did you ever see gas burn? One match, one ignition and then an uncontrollable blaze. They're done, all these vampires are done. There won't be a single one left by the end of the day."

"Can I light up the first house?"

"No, it's too dangerous. Give me the matches and drive the truck next door to the Leukowicz house. We have to be careful. If we keep the truck parked here, the gas is so explosive it'll send out flames to the truck and then you'll really see a blast. When you have the truck safely parked on the Leukowicz' lawn, I'll light a match and throw it in the window."

"Got it."

Understanding the importance of moving the gas away from the flames immediately, Elsa ran around to the driver's side, climbed in and cranked the engine to life. Without waiting a second, she jammed the truck in gear and gunned the engine, so that it sent a cloud of dust into the air from the dry lawn. The hose dragged along behind the truck in the dust, but it was a short distance to the next abode of vampires and the hose was not damaged. Elsa brought the tanker to a stop right where it should be, in front of the Leukowicz' picture window.

"Get ready!" Stephanovich screamed, removing a match from its box. "All of you, get ready to die! Elsa? Ready?"

"Yes."

As soon as Elsa looked away and pulled on the parking brake, Stephanovich lit one of the long-stemmed matches and threw it in the broken window. The burning match head brushed the burgundy curtains and immediately set them ablaze in a wild flash of cleansing fire. Stephanovich took to his heels and ran toward the Leucowicz house, hoping he would make it before the explosion took place. He had just crossed the property line when the flames from the curtains dropped onto the floor, where the gasoline had pooled. With a whoosh, the gasoline there ignited and sent a huge flame licking out the picture window, hungry for air. The Jones house, framed out of dried pine, was an eager host for the flame, and it welcomed it in and encouraged it to burn, burn, burn everything, burn it all! Within seconds, barely before Stephanovich reached the next victims' home, the entire first floor was ablaze at the Jones residence. Stephanovich allowed himself a fleeting glance at the fire next door, but then picked up the tanker's hose, threw a rock through the Leukowicz' picture window and shoved the hose into the window and turned on the valve to get the gas flowing. After a few seconds, he shut off the valve and removed a long-stemmed match from its box.

"Take off, Elsa!" he screamed. "We don't have a second to waste. Drive next door to the Cranston house while I burn these Leukowicz bastards. Go!"

Again, Elsa pushed the accelerator to the floor with gusto, sending up another cloud of dust swirling up from the hard dry Leukowicz lawn. She headed for the Cranston home to park the tanker just in front of their picture window, which now looked out upon their deaths. Stephanovich dragged the long-stemmed match over the match box and it jumped into a flame, as eager as he was to get this next fire going. Sensing the enthusiasm of the flames, he threw the match through the broken window while taking his first quick step away, and it is lucky he did so. The match immediately ignited an immense blast of flame that shot out through the picture window as though to grab Stephanovich in burning fingers and pull him inside into the inferno. Stephanovich needed no more encouragement than that to run at full speed to the Cranston home. Before he lifted the hose from the ground and picked up a rock to throw through the front window, he glanced back, sensing a presence, and saw a second-floor window open on the Jones residence, which was completely engulfed in flames. The roof above the window was ablaze, as were the walls around it, but inside it Mr. Jones had already made his choice. He would burn outside in the sun in flames as a vampire rather than die in his sleep in his burning home.

"You did this to me!" he screamed at Stephanovich, as he leaned out the window and his flesh ignited.

"And you took my children!" Stephanovich answered. "I'd do worse to you if I could."

In flames, Mr. Jones leaped from the window, but death in the sun turned out to be the worse choice, for as soon as he was in midair in the light of day, he ignited completely, his human form disintegrating in fire so completely that it was nothing but a pile of ashes by the time he hit the ground. Mr. Jones had been squealing as he jumped from his window and he had continued to squeal as he dropped to the ground. It was only when he lay in a pile of ashes that his squealing stopped, although his cries remained in Stephanovich as an echo of what the man had been. A final circle of flickering flames rose up off of his ash, but dissipated in the hot morning air.

"Stephanovich!"

"What?"

"What are you doing? Why are you just standing there looking back? We have to push this enterprise forward!"

"One of them jumped. Mr. Jones jumped and burned in mid-air from the sunlight and I told him how happy I was to see he was burning."

"So why aren't you burning more of them? If you keep looking back, the vampires will stay one step ahead of us. We're going to have jumpers. Just ignore them and do your work."

Stephanovich was about to answer when another upper-story window shattered, glass flying everywhere, while

Mrs. Jones rocketed out of her home on fire. She, too, was squealing while the sun ignited her entire being in an instant, turning her to ash that scattered and blew in the wind, drifting upward, and falling downward and sideways. She let out a little circle of flickering fire when her ash hit the ground, as though her soul rose in fire. It floated upward and away before disappearing in the bright air.

"This is horrible," Stephanovich muttered to himself, "but I love it."

"Why are you just standing there again?" Elsa yelled at him. "We're killing them all, aren't we?"

"Yes, we are."

"So kill them then."

She was right. There was no time to waste on sentiment. She had certainly awakened from this morning's flirtation with drinking blood to the realization of her hatred of vampires, the ones responsible for the loss of their children. These were true vampires, and they were true vampires who would do the greatest harm to them if allowed to live. They had taken Maggie and Mabin and Tommy, and would take them, too, if they were not destroyed. With a violent heave and guttural grunt, Stephanovich threw a rock through the Cranston's front window and then pumped in the allotted quota of gasoline and dropped in another long-stemmed flaming match. He was about to run when a horrified face suddenly popped up in the picture window. Mr. Cranston had been sleeping on the couch under the picture window and had been the first item in the house to catch fire. He sat up soaked with gasoline and on fire, his eyes wide with terror and horror. He sneered and bared his fangs at Stephanovich, just as his hair, slicked back with gasoline, caught fire. He reached out a burning, clawed hand at Stephanovich while screaming, but he did not come near to grabbing the pyromaniac. Then he fell back onto the floor, a squirming and screaming torch that ignited the living room rug and then set the entire household aflame as he rolled across the floor.

"We're all finished because of you!" he screamed in his agony. "What did we do? What? We were simply hungry!"

Somehow, a few of the vampires had gotten word while sleeping that Elsa and Stephanovich were rampaging through the neighborhood with a gasoline tanker truck and matches. Before the two humans reached their home, these few desperate ones leaped out of their bedroom windows before Elsa and Stephanovich could get to them, with predictable results. Many transformed to bats, and attempted to escape that way, but simply burned up as smaller versions of themselves. Vampires up and down the street were leaping out of their windows into the thin air in an attempt to fly from danger, but they had barely exposed themselves to sunlight before they burned up, squealing in pain.

Not one made their escape through the air.

Elsa had pulled the tanker truck up onto the next house in line, the home of hardware store owners, the Martellis, when she and Stephanovich first spied the desperate suicides taking place up and down the block. They had been concentrating so hard on their work they had not bothered to look ahead.

"They're doing our job for us," Elsa yelled with joy, pointing out several flaming vampires turning to ash in mid-air just down the block.

"Good, but there are still too many of them, hundreds," Stephanovich said. "These suicides won't put a dent in them. We're going to be busy all day, and possibly part of the night. Most of them are too cowardly for suicide."

"We better get them all. If any remain, they'll know we mean business, and it could be a difficult night ahead for us."

Stephanovich paused to throw a large rock through the Martelli's front window, and then opened the valve on the hose and stuffed it in the front window. He spilled gasoline on the front of the house and lawn, making a mess of what had been a neat effort on his part up until then.

"Darn ... that's enough gas for this house. I think we underestimated how long this would take. I don't see us being done before dark."

He shut off the valve and the gas stopped flowing into the house.

"What about the children?"

"Don't worry about that, we're paying them back for the children. We have to do this first to save them from more danger. We'll do the best we can and hope they last until we're done. Pull up to the next house honey, hurry."

Stephanovich waited until Elsa had driven the truck across the lawn and all the way up to the front of the next home with its curtains shut tight. He stepped back, lit a match and dropped it on the gasoline-soaked ground. Immediately, the flames burned hot and followed the path Stephanovich had made of gasoline up the wall and into the Martelli house. He turned and ran without looking back, feeling the flames lick hot on his back, and soon there was more squealing and more vampires vaporizing in the sunlight.

"Who lives in this house?" Elsa asked, when Stephanovich had caught up to her.

Before he answered, he rolled up the hose and hung it on the truck, making sure the valve was shut off. Then he quickly hopped up into the passenger's seat.

"I think Mike Malvois lives here alone," he answered, out of breath. "We're going to spare him for the moment. I've got an idea."

"What's that?"

"Drive to the community center. If we see the curtains closed on it, we'll know the vampires have taken refuge inside, maybe dozens of them. If we catch them there, it might speed this process along."

"Good idea. Ha, ha. A wonderful idea."

Before Elsa could put the truck in gear and take off for the center, there was that squealing above that was becoming so familiar to them, as Mike Malvois had chosen the coward's way out and leaped from his bedroom window into the bright sunshine. His dust settled onto the hood of the truck and blew up against the windshield prompting Elsa to turn on the windshield wipers. As she did so, a circle of flickering flames rose from Mike Malvois' ashes and disappeared into the brightness above.

"What were those flames? That circle of flames that flies off of them?" Elsa asked.

"I don't know, but I've been seeing a lot of them rising out of the vampire's ashes."

"I hope they all continue to burn in hell."

"They will, believe me, they will."

Elsa put the truck in gear and headed for the community center, which was at the end of the street with a circular lawn surrounding it. The curtains were closed tightly. Tall trees lined the street before the center, so Elsa had to navigate up the driveway and then onto the lawn.

"With this, I think you should drive around the building slowly, while I open the valve and hold the hose and we encircle the place with gasoline," Stephanovich said. "Once that's done, I'll break a window and pump in a few gallons of gas. Then you drive away, and I'll light the match."

Stephanovich jumped out of the truck and prepared to set the community center ablaze. He had just begun pouring gasoline on the ground next to the building, with Elsa driving ahead slowly, when a face peeked out from behind the curtains.

It was Len Stevenson, with deep black circles around his eyes and fangs so long they hung down nearly to his chin. The sunshine struck his face, burning him through the glass, and he had to draw back quickly.

Stephanovich had seen him, but had no mercy.

"You made your bed and now you have to sleep in it, Mr. Stevenson," he said. "And soon that bed's going to be burning."

"Damn you, Stephanovich," the vampire cried out from behind the curtains. "If I ever see you at night, the outcome will be different. All of us should have attacked you last night when we were on your roof and had the chance."

"You won't have that opportunity ever again. You'll never howl at the moon again, ever, or even see it, or taste blood again. Ha, ha!"

Elsa and Stephanovich worked slowly around the perimeter of the building laying down the circle of gas as several of the vampires inside peeked out now and then through the curtains, sneering at them and screaming indistinguishable curses. As he said he would do, Stephanovich broke a lower window and pumped in several gallons of gas. Elsa drove away several hundred feet, and then Stephanovich lit the match, dropped it on the gas on the ground and soon the building was surrounded by flames. The fire leaped inside through the broken window, and the squealing began as the dozens of vampires inside caught fire.

Not one leaped out a window.

By then the monsters knew there was no escape and chose to die where they belonged – in the dark.

"Good job," Elsa said, when Stephanovich jumped in the truck to drive to the next victims' house.

"No time to congratulate ourselves," he answered. "Let's deal death while the sun shines."

"It's going to be a bad day to be a vampire."

13

Maggie thought she had never felt such a warm, pleasant dawn.

She was not yet awake, but a pink and orange light caressed the inside of her closed eyelids, as though a gorgeous sunrise was muted by those eyelids. Her body was warm, with a pleasant moisture seemingly caressing each part. I was as though she was in a tepid bath of salt water. She stifled a yawn, but could not stifle stretching, except she could not stretch.

Instantly, she understood she was in no pleasant bath free to move as she wished, but in a kind of prison, where she could not move at all. She attempted to stretch again but was as frozen in the packed earth as if in a grave, and now she understood what Mabin had felt for nearly a year. He had been in an uncompromising prison of earth, his only comfort that blood of hers injected into his heart. Now that she could not feel him near and understood what the loneliness of the grave was, she felt tears come to her eyes, and she wept. Still, there was that light caressing her eyelids, and as the tears welled up, she opened her eyes to see her situation was not as dire as she had thought it to be. She could perceive light through the rock and debris covering her. One of the Outliners hovered over her in the air, flickering in the darkness of the cavern as though to mark the spot where she lay buried.

"Can somebody get me out of here?" she asked. "Hello ... I'm in here. Mabin? Where are you? Are you there?"

No one answered.

She attempted to move again, initially believing it was pointless, but then found that the sensation of being buried alive had been a dream, too, for she could flex her arms and legs. She struggled to be free, as a swimmer struggles to break free from a current. The warm dank earth, rocks and debris fell away from her. She dug herself out, up toward the light, and as soon as she had reached the surface she saw Mabin several feet away doing what she was doing, digging himself out. Another Outliner hovered over the spot where he had been buried, overseeing his effort to free himself, like a chandelier over a macabre dance in a dark hall. She saw Mabin's face was stained with the blood that was dripping from above and seeping down into the earth, and reached up to feel that her face, too, was stained. She reached up to wipe it away, but her fingers and hands were smeared with a mixture of blood and earth, which smudged her face with the main elements of this place. Mabin saw her. There was such shock on his face at the sight of her that she understood he thought he would never see her again, but most of all never expected to see her in her present condition. Then a wave of pain and relief crossed his features, and with a violent thrashing of his arms threw off the last vestiges of earth and rock that imprisoned him. He called out her name, "Maggie!" and jumped to his feet and ran to her.

When he was close, she called out to him with tears in her eyes.

"You came for me."

"Yes. How did we get out? What happened?"

"I don't know."

He reached down and took her by the hand to pull her to her feet.

"I didn't know how things collapsed around us," he said. "I was afraid I was in the grave again when I woke up, that you hadn't come for me yet, and that I might never see you again."

She flew into his arms, using his force to rush to him as he lifted her. She embraced him. It didn't matter that they were covered in blood and dirt.

"I had the same dream. I thought we were finished and would never see each other again."

"It was a bad dream."

"A very bad dream. Let's never have that dream again."

He kissed her, and held her to him, and the Outliners above them danced and flickered in the air.

He held on to her for a while and then stepped back and looked up.

"Natas?" he asked.

"Yes?"

"What went wrong?"

"What do you mean?"

"I thought we were finished with the third level and on our way to the fourth level when the ground fell out from beneath us and nearly killed us."

"This is the fourth level."

"How did we get here?

"Just as you were supposed to get here."

"By crashing through the earth?"

"By understanding that everything you thought you knew and counted upon could be taken from you in an instant."

Mabin blinked, and looked over at Maggie, confused.

"So the ground was supposed to crash out from under us and bury us, just to make us understand?"

"It was preparation for this level."

"How?"

"By emptying you of your beliefs and presumptions and presuppositions and readying the empty vessel for the re-insertion of your soul."

Mabin was shocked into silence at what was about to happen to him.

"And Maggie? Why did Maggie have to go through this? She's not dead, and never was."

"It was healthy for her to understand that all could be lost in an instant, for she is undergoing purification, too. Since she still has her soul, she can skip this level and go down to the fifth level, but it's good for her to know that as difficult as this is, it is better than the life she had before she came here."

"I'm staying with Mabin," Maggie said.

Natas flew over her, as though caught in a breeze.

"As you wish."

"I didn't realize I had lost my soul when I died."

"You were pulled apart from it, as you were separated from all things inside you. Remember your heart, and understand you had to be re-united with it."

"To Maggie?"

"Yes."

Mabin held her hand tightly in his.

"How do I find my soul?"

"It found you."

With that, Natas moved to the side, and the second Outliner hovered closer to Mabin, burning brighter and brighter as it moved nearer to him. It was a blue soul, not the orange or pink of the other vampire souls. Mabin reached out to his particular soul, but his hand passed through it. He tried to grasp it again, but again his hand broke the ring of flickering fires and he could not. He brought the hand to his side and turned to Natas.

"How do I re-unite with my soul?"

"It is not easy. The soul leaves the body through the mouth at death. Remember all the dead you've seen. Just at the moment of death the mouth opens and the soul flees, chased out by death."

"Does it return as it left?"

"No. That is impossible."

"Then how?"

"It returns the way it originally entered the body, through the navel."

"The navel is not an opening. It is tied off, closed."

"Then we untie it. It is a careful process, for we can allow only your soul in again, since there are many here yearning to enter a body again and will jump at the opportunity to do so. If another enters your body, a monster is created and all is lost."

As though understanding what was about to happen, the ceiling of the cavern lit up with a dozen Outliners, all flickering in anticipation of entering a body once more. Then there were a dozen more, and a dozen more, and more and more, until the cavern glowed brightly with souls eager to live again through the dead boy. They hovered in the air above, with Natas and Mabin's blue soul closest of all.

"Take off your shirt and prepare yourself," Natas said. "This can be difficult and painful."

With his eyes raised to the Outliners, his face glowing in their light, Mabin first removed his hooded cape, and then his shirt. With his flesh exposed, the Outliners flickered with excitement, and Maggie moved close to him to protect him from an unwanted intrusion from an insistent soul. She pressed up against him to cover his navel and watched as the Outliners congregated around them like fireflies.

"Your breath will drive them away," Natas said to Maggie.

She glared at him as though insulted.

"I beg your pardon."

"That is not what I meant. The breath of a living human reminds them of how they left their bodies, on its last breath, and they must back away, pushed by it, like a sailing ship before the wind."

It sounded curious to Maggie, so she tried it. Pursing her lips, she let out a breath at the nearest Outliner. Sure enough, it fled as though in a panic, traveling all the way up to the ceiling.

"The navel is a knot most can not untie," Natas said. "It would be nearly impossible for Mabin to untie it himself and keep the other Outliners away with memories of their deaths. That is why you're here. Only a chosen woman can take the place of the woman who originally gave Mabin his birth and his soul. Only a chosen woman can re-open the navel and return his soul after it is lost. Is she your chosen one?"

Mabin's soft gaze settled on her.

"Yes."

Maggie felt her hands trembling with anticipation of the task she was about to perform. To begin with, she had no idea of how to untie a navel, or how to return a soul to one who has lost it, and her fingers felt thick and clumsy.

"What do I do?"

"It is a ceremony. It is felt, not understood. Feel the Ceremony of the Re-Opening of the Navel and you will be able to do it."

Just as Natas said, when she decided to begin the ceremony, feelings on how to commence came to her in the way that light comes to the eye, instantly and without effort. Her hands moved from Mabin's shoulders to his navel and she felt its small tight fleshy knot and searched for an end, as you look for the end of a shoelace. It was smooth and not at all clear where its end was, and then she realized it did not have an end but had become like the terminus of a finger, simply round and soft. She knew, with the thought coming to her as the thought to move her hands to his navel had come to her, that untying the navel might not be a literal event. She let her eyes rise and let her hands simply feel the knot at his waist, hoping that feeling would tell her how to perform the task. The Outliners were hovering close in anticipation of entering Mabin's body, so she picked out the one that had been pointed out to her as Mabin's soul and then drew in a long breath and let it out, spraying the unintended souls with air to drive them off. They flew away as though in a panic, programmed to leave on a whiff of death, and Mabin's soul dropped close to her hands. Then she felt it. This was the end of the knot, a hard point she noticed only now. She closed her eyes so that she would not have to see Mabin's pain at what she did next. Natas had said this could be difficult and painful, and she knew now it would be. She could not avoid it. Frustrated that the knot would not give, she opened her eyes and tore at the small hard spot with her fingernails, ripping the flesh and seeing Mabin's soul hovering just by her hands, flickering on and off with excitement at the life that was about to open to it. With a great tearing effort, she rent the soft knot, ripping it open. He screamed and stiffened, his legs nearly giving out, and he trembled to stay upright. The Outliners above dashed downward for the open navel, and Maggie held the wound open as Mabin's soul returned to its place behind his stomach. Quickly, after his soul had re-entered his body, she formed another knot to tie off the entrance, her hands awash in Mabin's sticky blood, and pulled it tight. The dozens of Outliners stopped short. Their lights burned so brightly that it was as though the sun had come close. Then when they saw the omphalos tied off, their brightness flickered and diminished and they disappeared back into darkness, the intended abode of dead vampires. There would be no live body for them to enter and pollute.

 His soul safely inside him, Mabin fell to the ground. His eyes were closed but the eyelids quivered in pain. Then, suddenly, he slept, and all was calm. His breath came deep and full and his expression was serene.

"It is done," Natas said. "The shock of becoming complete has worn him down."

"How long will he sleep?" Maggie asked.

"Until you both wake up."

"What does that mean? I'm not sleepy. I'm well. This ceremony is done, Mabin is himself again and we should move on. I will protect him until we do."

"You are not yourself."

"Then who am I?"

"For a living being with a broken heart the fourth level appears easy, but it demands of the living being one very difficult thing."

"What is that?"

"That you make peace with the past so you can live only for the now."

This sounded to Maggie like a riddle, and she paused to consider it.

"I never wanted anything but that, to forget. It's why I came here to resurrect Mabin. The past had its teeth into me and its hands around my neck and had invaded my mind because he died. I know my mind was unwell. Now that Mabin is whole again, I think we're done here. I have never been more satisfied."

"So you think you're well?"

The question made Maggie uneasy, for she didn't know the answer. A girl half-mad doesn't know which half is sane and which half is disturbed, but she lives out of both halves. Maggie didn't know in which half she existed.

"I can see you're troubled. That's why I said you can travel down to the next level when you wake, for it's in sleep on the fourth level that a distressed one recovers. Fourth-level sleep is the most curative rest you will have. Lie down beside Mabin. It's where you are supposed to be, with your lover and at rest."

As her knees folded, slowly bending, the suggestion to lie beside Mabin seemed to be the only reasonable and necessary thing to do. Her eyelids were heavy. He was breathing the peace of the recently born, recovered from a difficult rebirth and preparing for a new day without concern. She was drowsy, so drowsy she tumbled down, breaking her fall by reaching out for Mabin and letting her arm drape across his chest. Her eyes were closing, and she fought it for a while, hoping to draw out the pleasant feeling it gave her to rest her head on Mabin's shoulder, her arm around his waist.

But her eyes were closing, closing, and she could do nothing about it.

Yes, this was where she was supposed to be.

Just before she drifted off, she thought she saw a diminutive figure with his shirt off reaching down to his navel to begin the ceremony they had just completed.

It might have been a dream, brought on by a sleep she had fallen into without realizing she was asleep, but then several of the Outliners lit up high above and she knew those souls were looking for the remains of themselves that they had lost long ago.

They wished for a second chance in another body.

She thought she had seen Tommy, but she was closing in too fast on unconsciousness to make certain of what she had seen.

She mumbled his name as she fell asleep. The last thing she saw was another small blue soul drifting above the diminutive figure struggling to untie his navel.

14

By the time their lunch break came around, Stephanovich and Elsa had burned half of the town. Much of Victor lay in smoldering ruins. They had been slowed by the necessity of returning to the service station to refill the tank truck from the underground storage bins, for destroying a village completely takes more fuel than can be carried in one truck. It was a tricky process, pumping gasoline from underground up into the truck, and it was time-consuming and tiresome and demanded concentration. Still, they worked with great determination, always remembering what was at stake and how dangerous it would be once night came.

Despite the high cost of tarrying, they stopped before noon, famished and tired from the excesses of their work. Returning to their house meant navigating through streets consumed in the conflagrations they had initiated and encouraged, and that had to be done carefully with a tanker again full of flammable liquid. The black dust of the burned vampires who had leapt from their homes to avoid the flames wafted through the neighborhood, dancing in evil whippoorwills. In places the black dust of the dead was as thick as chimney soot.

"You're finished in Montana," Stephanovich said to several of the whippoorwills, as they raced by on the wind. "Accept it and leave us alone."

"There is nothing here for you," Elsa shouted, talking to the air. "You'll never get to the blood of the mountain."

Stephanovich asked Elsa if she would cook lunch and then retired to the living room to consult the mysteries. Their children were uppermost in his mind, and although their first priority had to be destroying the vampires to make the world safe again for Maggie and Tommy and Mabin to live in once they emerged from the mountain, it disturbed him that the three of them were still underground somewhere in St. Mary's mountain experiencing who-knows-what? The mysteries had always helped him in determining his next step in his confrontations with vampires. He was worried the ancient manuscript was still blank, but then he was very much relieved when he was approaching them and saw there was a single line of cryptic letters, written in an ancient language few understood, across the top of the parchment.

He quickly translated the sentence and then laid the document back down on the coffee table.

"Huh," he said to himself.

"Was there anything written on the scripture?" Elsa asked, when he returned to the kitchen.

The lunch burning on the stove was comprised of the same things that they had burned for breakfast. Two thick steaks sizzled on the griddle, and when Elsa turned them over, blood dripped out of them. They were salivating with hunger at the sight of the blood.

"The mysteries are writing themselves again," Stephanovich answered, after smelling the meat and blood, his hands shaking with hunger.

"What did they say?"

"They weren't much help. They advised something we're already doing. When I translated the single line, it read: KILL THEM ALL. We know that. It's what we've been doing all morning. Weren't they aware of what we were doing?"

"Was that it?"

"That was it. We've killed a great many vampires here, but maybe it's telling us to continue our work in other places, too, rather than attempt to rescue the children."

"I don't know. I don't feel right spending so much time on the vampires, especially elsewhere, and not trying to rescue the children."

"We have no understanding of why the grave took our children. The mysteries might be telling us they can handle themselves inside the mountain, so maybe they're not in any grave danger."

"Stephanovich, they've been buried alive, or at least Maggie has been. I don't know if Tommy and Mabin even ..."

Here Elsa broke down in tears at the thought that she might never see her son and her daughter's lover again. She might never see Maggie again. It was too much for her.

Stephanovich took her in his arms.

"Maggie is as tough as they come, and being crazy makes her even tougher," he said. "I know we might have made a mistake with what we did to Tommy, and what Tommy did in digging up Mabin too soon, but Maggie makes very few mistakes, even while unstable. If anyone can bring the two boys back, she can."

"I'm not so sure. She's been so ... crazy ever since Mabin died. She's not herself. She can't function the way she used to."

"She'll find a way. She is more expert at this work then any of us."

"So you think the mysteries are telling us they're okay?" Elsa asked eagerly. "That we should keep burning the vampires and not worry about them?"

"That's what they said. KILL THEM ALL. It can only mean we should continue to do what we're doing now."

"I feel a little better now after talking this through. Eat your steak."

"The mysteries are telling us we're doing the right thing. I'm convinced of it. They're saying kill them all, and then find a way to save the children."

The lovely summer mountain air was fouled by the smoke of so many homes in flames and polluted by the ash of the numerous burned vampires. It was as though a great volcano had erupted and spewed ash all over the countryside. Alternately, the fresh air off the mountains and then the thick smoke and ash blew in the open windows. With a silence that came with an understanding of the importance of their work, Stephanovich and Elsa ate hurriedly and without conversation. Their silence might have saved them. They had hacked their ways through the bulky slabs of meat with sharp knives and consumed it hungrily, and then they tipped their plates to drink the blood that had seeped out of the beef. They were sipping their coffee in preparation for a return to work, waving away the smoke when it blew in the broken kitchen window, when Stephanovich cocked his head to the side, as though listening for something.

"Oh, no."

"What is it, dear?"

"Did you hear something in the basement?"

"I think I did."

"I think I did, too."

"These damn ... We can't even finish our coffee in peace. Did we leave the basement lights on?"

"I don't know."

"We didn't think of it, but our house would be the perfect place for them to hide. We'd never think of looking for them here."

"Let's go after them then. We can't avoid a confrontation with them if they're in here. Bring the flashlights from the closet. I'm sure if they're down there, they've unscrewed the light bulbs so they have the advantage of the dark."

After grabbing the two brightest torches from the closet, Elsa and Stephanovich flipped the switch at the top of the basement stairs in the attempt to turn on the lights below. Just as they expected, nothing happened. Tiptoeing down the stairs with the flashlights on, they walked with only the two beams they carried lighting the way.

"I thought they couldn't come out in daylight," Elsa whispered.

"They might have been down here all night. Maybe we missed them before."

Suddenly, the batteries died in Elsa's flashlight.

"What just happened?" she asked, panicked. "What happened to my flashlight?"

"The batteries, when was the last time we changed them?"

"I can't remember."

"Well, that's what happened. The batteries died."

Elsa dropped her flashlight and huddled behind Stephanovich at the bottom of the stairs, shivering with fear. Then his flashlight flickered, but the light did not die but turned a weak yellow. That mustard light barely cut through the darkness in the basement.

"I don't like being in this deep gloom with the likes of who I believe is down here," Stephanovich said. "It perplexes me. I'm very perplexed."

"I thought we killed most of them."

"The mysteries said, KILL THEM ALL. Maybe that meant we didn't and the mysteries were telling us more were in the basement. Maybe it was a warning we had more killing to do."

Stephanovich, despite his misgivings, stepped forward into the darkness, and Elsa grabbed a handful of his shirt to make sure she stuck close to him. The rancid smell of the burned vampires had sunk down into their basement. They held their breath as they walked, and then suddenly Stephanovich spun around and screamed out.

"Who's there?"

"Natas."

It was not a name either Stephanovich or Elsa put much trust in, for they understood its derivation at once. Thinking backwards is a very useful skill to have, and they had cultivated it in their long years of fighting vampires. They froze in their tracks.

"What do you want? Don't pretend to be someone you're not."

"I came to warn you."

"Of what?"

"Of something I'm going to show you. Don't be frightened. First, I'm going to let you see me. I'm ten feet directly in front of you, so don't be surprised when I appear."

"All right. This better not be a trick."

"No trick. I am what you will see."

Slowly, one flickering light at a time, Natas lit himself into a circle hovering in the air before them, as if a sphere from the wicks of candles were lit one at a time, only just the wicks. The tiny lights seemed wavering and unstable when the circle closed, as though they might go out at any time. When he was fully alight, his soft glow reached into the corners of the basement, so that Stephanovich and Elsa could see there was no other intruder.

"It's that thing we saw at Mabin's grave," Stephanovich whispered.

"What have you done with Maggie?" Elsa screamed suddenly, losing control.

Natas' lights flickered from the force of her shout.

"I did nothing to her, but only allowed her to do what she wanted more than anything. She's fine, and will be whole again soon."

"You've been inside the grave with her?"

"Yes, and inside the mountain."

"And Tommy? And Mabin? What about them?"

"All will be as they were. I did not come about your children."

"That's all we're interested in. We don't care about anything else," Stephanovich said. "Tell us about them."

"Tell us what you did with our children!"

"You need to listen to me, for time is short," Natas said. "In just a few moments, if you stay here, you will die."

"Are you threatening us? We don't compromise. We don't have anything to exchange for our children, so don't think we'll compromise."

"You will die if you stay because of this."

With that, Natas increased his luminosity, glowing as brightly as the broken light bulb above his head would have if it had not been shattered. He moved backwards, floating away from them, until he came to a spot another five feet away and halted.

"Come close," he said. "Look up."

Warily, Stephanovich and Elsa moved toward him, alternately staring at him for any trick and craning their heads upward.

When they came within five feet of him, both halted and gasped.

"They knew you would be home at noon for your lunch. They're on a timer, and will explode in three minutes. It's lucky you came home early for your break."

"My dynamite!" Stephanovich yelled, staring at the tied bundle of ten sticks above. "They got to my dynamite."

"I'm afraid they have all of it," Natas said. "This is not much of it. They stole it from this basement where it was hidden under the floor."

"Damn them!"

"As you wish, but it's not time to think of their end, but yours. There's no time to damn them or disarm the bomb, and I have no abilities in that area. They decided to do to you what you are doing to them. You must get out now."

With that, Natas flickered off, immersing them in the dark, save for what weak yellow light emanating from their flashlight.

With a rush of wind, he disappeared up the stairs and out through an open window in the kitchen.

"Run!" Stephanovich screamed.

He spun Elsa around and pushed on the middle of her back. She needed little encouragement but that. She stumbled quickly toward the staircase, with Stephanovich close behind holding the light to point the way. They ran up the stairs and into the kitchen and Elsa headed for the back door. Stephanovich turned toward the living room.

"Where are you going? We don't have time!"

"I'm not leaving without the mysteries. We have no chance without the mysteries. Go. Start the truck. I'll be out as soon as I get them."

There was no time to argue. Elsa pushed open the door and disappeared, while Stephanovich rushed into the living room, didn't see the mysteries where he had left them and quickly scanned the room, desperate to find them.

"Where are they? Where are they?"

He had looked in every corner, counting the seconds until the explosion, and then stooped to find the Transylvanian Mysteries under the coffee table.

"Are you hiding?" he asked, grabbing them and running for the back door.

They had been blown to the floor by the fouled mountain air rushing through the windows.

The mysteries were writing themselves furiously, the strange curlicues forming as Stephanovich raced outside. He did not have time to stop and read. He ran for the tanker truck, realizing that if the house blew up now the nearby truck full of gasoline would most likely blow, too, and their escape would be foiled. Elsa had opened the passenger's door for him, anticipating that every second saved could be a second that saved their lives, and she had the truck running and in reverse. As soon as Stephanovich had climbed up onto his seat, she floored the accelerator and let out the clutch, without even allowing him to close his door. The truck lurched backwards and she spun the steering wheel around to race desperately in reverse down the street. She was twisted around, her head out her window, watching where they were going, but Stephanovich was facing forward when he saw their home blown to pieces. The blast was so tremendous in its noise and power that it temporarily blew the sense out of Stephanovich. He could not believe what he was seeing. His house was nothing but flying debris. It was as though they had driven into the center of a tornado. A massive fireball was expanding and rushing toward them, with bits of their home and possessions mixed in the blast circle.

"Faster!" he screamed. "This truck will blow up if the fire reaches us!"

"It's floored! We can't go any faster in reverse!"

Debris showered down on them, but the fireball reached out for them but could not grab them. It dissipated in frustration just at their front bumper as they were fleeing, and then it gave up and retreated into nothingness, having done its work.

Elsa kept her foot pressed to the floorboard, the engine screaming in protest, while they rushed away backwards as quickly as the truck could travel. When they had raced away another five hundred feet, she stopped, her heart beating quickly to look back at what had happened.

She saw a huge hole in the ground where their house had been.

Instead of gasping at the destruction of the house, Stephanovich was staring down at the piece of parchment held in his hands, seemingly unconcerned with the disaster they had so narrowly averted.

"Do you see what they did? Did you see what happened to our house?" Elsa shrieked at him. "They destroyed our home!"

Stephanovich continued to stare at the piece of parchment.

"What are you doing? Do you know we almost died?" Elsa yelled. "How can you be reading at a time like this?"

In answer, Stephanovich turned the piece of ancient parchment toward her.

On it, in English, was written, over and over, KILL THEM ALL, KILL THEM ALL, KILL THEM ALL, KILL THEM ALL, KILL THEM ALL ... until the entire sheet was filled with the commandment.

"They never spoke in English before," Elsa said.

"No, never."

"Why now?"

"I think they want to be very clear about what we should so," Stephanovich answered. "They want to leave no doubt."

"I think it's clear. I think it's very clear. I think it's very clear what we have to do now. Let's get on with it. We should never have stopped for lunch. We could have killed another dozen in the time it took to eat lunch."

Instead of backing up, Elsa put the truck in first gear and drove forward toward the remaining homes of the development.

There were fires of hatred burning all around them, but also in their eyes.

15

By the time Maggie awoke, she had forgotten nearly everything that had transpired in the recent past. She did not fail to remember that she had fallen asleep with her arm draped over the boy she loved. In the first instant she came back to consciousness, it was distressing that her arm was flat against the soft spongy rock and her face pressed into it. Mabin was gone. Her eyes snapped open, like a doll's eyes. Several of the Outliners were lazing above, barely burning, but the light was sufficient to let her know she was wrong about being alone. Mabin sat nearby on a rock, watching her sleep, and she saw something she had not seen in a very long time.

His smile.

The return of his soul meant he could smile again.

His smile meant everything to her, for it was an honest smile, the same she had seen over a year ago when she had met him as a boy riding a bike, a boy who was a shape-changer and a magician and fierce fighter, someone who was a match for any of the vampires and strong enough to defeat a dozen of them. That boy had died saving her on their adventures, and she had come to him again in this place, in the grave, but he had not been the same boy in the grave that she had met that day riding his bike. The boy she met in this place was broken and piecemeal, a person with his soul and his heart torn out. This magical dark place had given him back both his soul and his heart. She had helped with that, traveling down the layers of his resurrection. In return for her efforts, the boy she had known and loved was given back to her. She could tell he was back.

He had smiled at her and looked directly into her eyes with a soft dance of a gaze.

And he kept smiling at her.

"How did you sleep?"

"I slept best when you were here, when I had you in my arms. It's not a good sleep now that I'm up and you're not in my arms."

"But then if I was still in your arms, we'd still be asleep, and I couldn't see you."

"Then would it be better to be asleep?"

"No, it would be better to be in your arms and awake."

"Then what are you waiting for?"

Mabin had never let his smile abandon him as they talked, but now the smile grew brighter, just as the Outliners grew brighter as their interest grew, and he slipped down off the rock and lay beside her, his arms around her and hers around him. Above, several more of the Outliners flickered on, lighting the cavern with a soft pink glow and drifting down to hover in the air above them like bright sunrise clouds. Maggie did not wait for him: she kissed him very hard and eagerly, some of the madness still in her at not having him for so long and motivating her to kiss him hard, desperate to kiss him as hard as she could. She ached to kiss him hard. If she could not kiss him hard, he might not really be there, alive and well, and if not for that hard kiss telling her he truly was there, and his answering hard kiss, she might be convinced of her insanity again.

"It has been worth it."

"Worth the whole year of sadness? Of being alone?"

"Worth it to be able to forget that."

"We have forgotten, haven't we? We don't have to think of that time alone ever again."

"No. Never again. Never again to think of that, just to be together."

Now he kissed her again, and all her sleepiness left her as she pushed up against his body, stiffening as she felt his warmth, warmth that she had missed and not felt until now as she traveled through the spiraling grave with him. Without letting him know it, thinking it would ruin the pleasure of the moment, she cried silently, her eyes closed. She knew his eyes were closed, too, with passion, so that he could not see she was crying with relief and release, but then she felt what seemed to be a sob break from him. He was overcome, too. The sob shook him briefly, but then he softened into the warmth and she knew he felt the same relief and release she did, only ten times as strongly, for he had been dead and now he was alive and she had only been insane with grief. For him, this year in hell, or whatever this was, had been far more difficult, ten times more difficult. She felt him pulling away and wondered why, oh why, would he do that now and pulled him back to her with as much force as she could.

"Why would you leave me now?"

"We're not alone."

"Who is here but us?"

"The Outliners ... they're coming closer."

"Indecent Outliners. Old souls who don't know better. Go away from here."

With that, she waved her hand in the air as though shooing flies. Remembering what Natas had told her to do to drive them away, she puffed up her cheeks and blew out her breath at them.

As they scurried away, back to the ceiling, Mabin laughed.

"Kiss me," she said. "I don't care about the Outliners. I don't care if we're indecent in front of them."

He kissed her, and she draped a welcoming leg over him to let him know what she wanted. She rubbed herself savagely against him, and groaned. He groaned in responsive passion, and was almost as savage pressing up against her. Panting, she thought she had fainted, for the cavern closed down into darkness as though a light switch had been turned off. But how could the light be gone, when there was so much heat now in this place?

Kind Outliners. Decent souls.

They understood, the Outliners understood, for even the souls of old vampires were elegant enough to remember the poetry of darkness and love and to leave the lovers alone when passion was re-ignited inside the grave.

*

Hours passed before the lights came back on.

Then, shy as stars, the Outliners twinkled near the cavern's sky. Slowly, the orange and pink luminescence returned where there was already much heat.

"Do you think it's day?" Maggie asked.

"I think it's night. There are stars up there."

"They're Outliners, silly boy."

"No, they're stars. There are only stars when I kiss you."

"The day wouldn't dare return while we're kissing."

"No, it wouldn't have the courage."

"Then let's kiss again and make it night."

"Yes, let's make night."

The stars took their cue.

Decency returned to the cavern sky as the Outliners and twinkled out into darkness.

*

The boy walked alone down the long ramp to the final level, the fifth level, where the purifications ended. He was hobbling along on wobbly legs, still recovering from the re-insertion of his soul and his own resurrection, but he was moving with determination, sure of himself and confident he was about to arrive at his final destination, at last fully alive and intact.

"The stars are in the sky," he muttered to himself in a sing-song voice, mocking good-naturedly what he had seen on the level above. "When we kiss, the stars are out ... It's lucky I got out of there when I did or I'd have to put up with all that goofy stuff. Who wants to see junk like that as soon as you come back to life?"

Despite hobbling along in pain, the boy walked fast, pulled down the slope by gravity and his eagerness to find a way out of the caverns. Then the ramp leveled out to a flat plain of several hundred acres with rounded perimeters backed by sheer cliffs, like a gigantic half-bowl. As large as the plain was, the dark russet lake shimmering just beyond it was larger, seeming going on and on toward a horizon that could not be there, since the boy knew they were inside a mountain. It was a very large mountain, and larger at the base than above, but not as large as an island or a continent. The lake of blood has to end somewhere in here, the boy said to himself. I just can't see it. Everything has an end, and this has to be it for me and the lake.

"I wish they'd hurry up," he said out-loud. "Who wants to stay in a place like this for one minute longer than they have to?"

He wasn't going to shout for Mabin and Maggie to get a move on. He wasn't going to wait, either, now that he knew the lovers were all right. He looked around for an exit, an archway with light at the end or a tunnel or another ramp or an opening in the floor covered by a manhole. He'd see them on the outside, after they were done with the gushy stuff. He had had about enough of all this darkness and being dead in the darkness and longed for the light of a normal day, where he could sit outside in the grass or go hiking or sit trout-fishing by a clear crystal stream of real water. He wanted to be someplace he could work up an appetite and then go home and eat real food, delicious stuff, steak and eggs or Danish pastries or a General Tso' salad full of chicken and greens and sesame seeds. He was about finished with this being dead stuff.

"I really wish I could find my way out of here," he said loudly, thinking no one could hear him. "I don't know if Mabin and Maggie want to go home just yet, but I sure do. Now where is the exit from this dump?"

He had wished someone was around to help him out of his predicament, but he hadn't expected an answer to his question. He'd have to find the way to freedom himself.

"It's always that way. I always have to do things for myself if I want them done."

Still hobbling, but becoming stronger by the second, the boy set off on a hike around the right-hand perimeter of the plain, walking toward the red lake. When he came to the sheer cliff bounding that perimeter, he saw that the cliff was oozing purified blood, blood that had seeped through the clean earth to become whole again. It could be put to good use by good people, but had once been put to bad use by bad people but now was immaculate. The clean blood was collected in a stream by the wall that flowed down and emptied into the lake. He thought he'd have to leap over the narrow stream once he found the exit to the real world. He was so sick of all this darkness and gloom, and he didn't have anybody to kiss or hold in a goofy way. All of his body parts and his head had come together while he was alone as he traveled down from level to level. He couldn't really expect help now, not even from Maggie and Mabin.

"I always have to do everything myself. That's all right," he muttered. "I'm too young and I've always gotten along by myself. All I have to do is find the exit, climb out and then go fishing."

The boy walked the entire perimeter, following the flowing stream of good clean red blood, but he did not find the opening to the fresh mountain air and free life that he looked for. He came to the shore of the lake of blood where the stream emptied itself, and he gazed out to where the horizon should be but he could see no horizon or end to the lake.

"Wow, there must have been a lot of bad blood in the world that needed to be cleansed," he said to himself. "How many vampires could there be if they drank all this? A lot, I guess."

He walked, tired of talking to himself, for a few feet along the shore when just above him one of the Outliners flickered to life, its round form nothing but a circle of tiny flames. The boy stopped to look up and smile.

"Hi," he said. "What brings you down here, Natas?"

"I came to check on you. I thought you might have left the fourth level too soon. Are you feeling all right?"

"I'm fine. I can't walk too well just yet, but that's getting better every minute. I didn't want to stay up there with what those two were doing. I thought they needed their privacy and I don't like goofy stuff like that."

"Your health is more important. You should have waited for them."

"I know, but I feel healthy again, thanks to you."

Natas floated down toward him.

"What I mean to say is, thank you," the boy said.

"No need to thank me. If you're well, that's my thanks. Just don't try to go too fast."

"I am well, so I guess that thanks you."

"You're welcome. I think maybe you should return to the bottom of the ramp and wait for Mabin and Maggie. I know you feel well, but you still have some healing to do."

"I'm tough. I can take it. I want to find my way out of here."

"After coming back from what you went through, you should take more time."

"Do you really think so?"

The boy was feeling a little light-headed, so it was easy to agree with Natas.

"Wait for Mabin and Maggie. Then you can decide what you want to do next."

"Should I climb back up to the fourth level and tell them I'm here and alive and in one piece?"

"No! If you climb back up, you revert to what you were on the previous level. Never climb up a level you've completed. It will undo all the healing you've done."

"Oh, crap. Rules like that suck. I like my freedom, so that rule sucks. I guess I just have to wait."

"Yes. It won't be long. Simply wait, and rest."

The boy found himself slowly descending to sit on the earth, as though he was falling asleep on his feet. His eyelids grew heavy and his breathing became full and deep.

"I thought so. You didn't sleep enough on the fourth level," Natas said. "That's why you're not quite healed yet, and drowsy now. You should sleep more if you want to become yourself again."

The boy's head bobbed up and down and his eyelids drooped.

"I think I'll take your advice," he murmured, dropping down and sitting back until he lay on his back staring up at Natas. "I see what they mean ... you ... it's like looking at a circle of stars when I look at you ... thank you ... thank you ..."

He settled down comfortably on the floor.

As soon as the boy was asleep, Natas let his lights die out, but he continued to hover over the boy.

The old soul of the vampire, now a spirit of resurrection, was troubled about the boy. He has far too much confidence for his own good, Natas thought. He knows what he's been through, but he thinks he can do anything after recovering from death.

The thing is, the boy had done the impossible.

He had come back from lifelessness, from being nothing but the parts and pieces of a boy to a complete boy again with breath, a beating heart and a soul.

And he had done it with a great deal of courage and daring.

"This is quite a child," Natas said to himself. "It's a shame, it's a shame what happened to him and what he had to go through."

And then Natas gave the boy the courtesy of darkness in which to sleep, just as he had given that same courtesy to the lovers on the fourth level.

*

Mabin and Maggie descended upon the Great Plain of the fifth level walking hand-in-hand. They were happy to have reached their final destination, happy that their ordeal was almost over and that normal life beckoned to them after exiting this place. Although they had traveled down the ramp from the fourth level in silence, they could not stop turning again and again to glance at each other and smile. There was no need to say anything now that both were fully alive as lovers. Their soft looks of pleasure were enough and said more than words could say.

"What are you thinking?" Mabin asked.

"Oh, nothing. Well, not nothing. I was thinking about a dream I had before I fell asleep."

"Before you fell asleep?"

"I'm not sure. I think it was a dream. I know Tommy is gone, but I thought I saw him. I know that couldn't be, even though Stephanovich and Elsa dropped his remains into your grave. What the black blood did to him was more than anyone could endure. There could be no recovery from that, not even here, in this place, or even in a dream."

"What was the dream you had?"

"Well, I thought I was falling asleep after we gave you back your soul, and I thought I saw Tommy going through the same ceremony, except no one was helping him. I guess I was just feeling guilty for not being there for him and was dreaming his resurrection to make myself feel better, but I could have sworn I saw him taking back his soul in the same way you did."

Mabin stopped and turned to her, but did not drop her hand.

"Where was I when you saw this?"

"You were asleep, healing. I guess I dreamed I was falling asleep and saw him re-inserting his soul through his navel, but that couldn't have been. It couldn't have been. No one could re-insert his own soul. It was just a dream."

"But you saw this?"

"I dreamed I did."

"It doesn't make any difference. If you saw this on the fourth level, whether you were awake or asleep, it meant it happened. All the things that happen on the fourth level are real, whether they happen in dreams or while awake. The fourth level is the level of souls and dreams, where both are real."

"Dreams and reality are the same thing on the fourth level?"

"It's what the Outliners teach."

"So you're telling me I saw Tommy?"

"I think so."

Maggie covered her mouth with her hand to muffle a sob.

"So it was real? He's alive again? Can this place do even that? Put back together those who have been torn apart and died?"

"It can. It did it for me."

"Then we have to go back up there and find him."

Mabin pulled on Maggie's hand to prevent her from rushing up the slope to the fourth level, but her first step back up the ramp made her feel violently ill.

"Don't do that!" Mabin yelled out, reeling her toward him by the arm, gently but firmly. "This is a one-way resurrection. Any step backwards and you're doomed. It's forward, always forward, or backwards to death."

"But Tommy's up there."

"I don't think he is."

"But you said everything is real up there, that –"

"The rules apply to him, too. He knows that. If he's not already down here on the fifth level, he's right behind us. He has to go through everything we went through."

Confused and feeling as though she had been hit on the head after taking a step backwards toward death, Maggie blinked and stared at Mabin as though he was talking nonsense. She looked first ahead, and then back.

"What do we do?"

"Forward, always forward. We'll find him, I promise."

"I'm so happy. Tommy could be alive."

"I'd bet on it. Now come on. One more level and all of us are done with this place and we can go home. Come on. Just one more level and we're free."

Maggie didn't know if she had the patience to wait. She was so overjoyed at how well things were going she was about to burst with happiness and love.

She understood she'd have to be patient.

Any step back would be the death of everything she worked so hard for. She could wait another few hours to assure things turned out right.

16

By the time Elsa and Stephanovich had burned the entire town of Victor and its vampires, night had come on. It was as though vampires made particularly good fuel for burning, because not one of the fires they had set had gone out. If the homes they had put to the torch were burned in the morning, they were still smoldering piles of ash and cinder when the sun went down, with little crackling flames popping up her and there in the ash. If the houses they had set to flames had been on fire in the afternoon, then they were piles of crackling wood and black ash at sunset, with larger pieces of the structures still ablaze. If they had set alight houses and businesses in the evening, then those fires were still in full flame when darkness touched the mountains. The only thing that had ceased was the squealing of the burning vampires. Hundreds of piles of black ash, their remains, were scattered across the landscape. Many of the piles had diminished as the wind lifted the ash and dispersed it, but there was little doubt in their minds that this had been the greatest single day in history of the world for slaughtering vampires, and they were very proud of their work.

"They all deserved this, and more, for what they did to our family," Stephanovich said. "I only wish there were others to burn."

"They deserved this and more. I only wish all this had brought back the children."

"I wish we had counted them as we killed them and written down all of their names," Stephanovich said. "It would have been very satisfying, a big payback."

"That would have taken forever, to keep an inventory of the dead."

"Did we get them all? That's what I'm worried about. We could have compared our inventory to the town census."

"We leveled the place. I didn't see anyone escape. It was a massacre. Either the fires got them or the sun immolated them. I don't think we let any of them escape."

"You know ... come on, let's get into the truck and drive to Mabin's grave to see what we can do there. It bothers me that when the vampires died we saw those rings of small flames rising up off their ashes. I don't really trust they're dead."

"Do you think there might still be hope for the children?

"Maybe. The grave might be open again, and if it is, this time I'm jumping in."

"Into the grave?"

"Why not? What do we have to live for?"

"I think you're being obsessive, but I don't blame you. You just want to make sure of things, make sure they're gone."

"Maybe you're right, but those little rings of fire still bother me."

"That was just a trick of the wind."

"Maybe so, but all of them? I don't recall seeing a single vampire burn without that ring of fire rising off of him."

"A trick of the wind, I say. They're all dead."

"Then I just wish we had time to celebrate," Elsa said. "Let me drive. If we can dig out the children, or free them in some other way, I think we would be safe forever. What can they do to us now, if we get our children back?"

"I'm sorry it took us so long to kill all these things."

"What else could we do? What would be the point of bringing our children back into a world full of vampires? We couldn't have lived like that. I won't bring any child into a world of vampires. I still don't have a lot of confidence."

"I know we did the right thing. I guess I'm worrying too much."

"That's my job."

Elsa let herself be convinced that their work of burning the vampires was done, and she demonstrated that her driving. It was as though they were on a joyride up St. Mary's mountain through the off-road countryside, but that lasted only a short time. While she had no concerns about the vampire genocide they had perpetrated, she was worried about their own situation. The rough incline nearly ripped the steering wheel out of her hands, but she righted the Humvee with two strong hands.

"We're homeless now," she said. "What are we going to do if we free the children from out of this mountain? We can't live in our truck."

Stephanovich considered this for a moment. He had nearly forgotten in what form they had last seen their house.

"I wish we had had the time to retrieve our camping equipment before the vampires blew up our home. The weather's nice. We could have camped out."

"You mean camp out in Vampire Valley? With all the vampires?"

"They're all dead, remember? We don't seem to have much choice. We burned all the homes and motels. I suppose we could start out again in another state."

"It would be the same old thing there, vampires everywhere. Besides, we might not be finished here, now that I think of it."

"I know, I know, we can never be certain of anything concerning those sorts, but once we dig out the children, we'll be free to go wherever we want."

"That's not what I meant. I really fear we might not have gotten all the vampires here. There always seem to be more."

Stephanovich wiped his mouth with his open palm, not because he thought there was something smeared on it, but because he thought Elsa might be right about the rapidity with which vampires proliferated and their ability to endure. A spark of worry lit inside him.

"Let me check something."

Before Elsa could ask what he wanted to do, he leaned down and pulled the Transylvanian Mysteries out from beneath the seat. He grabbed for what parchment he could find and was surprised to clutch and entire handful of pages, many sheets instead of the few he had saved from their exploded home. His eyes scanned the pages of parchment and he gasped with each new page he perused. His gaze danced over page after page as he flipped through them with celerity, and real worry made him slump in his seat and let the thick pile of pages fall to his knee in frustration.

"Ah. Ah. Ah," was all he could say, gasping out each word as he read one page after another.

He held his head in both hands as though it was about to explode.

"What's wrong with you? You look like you're having a heart attack."

"I might be."

"Should I pull over? Is there any aspirin in the truck?"

"No, I'm not really having a heart attack."

"Then what is it?"

"The mysteries ... they're writing themselves again in English. They added several more pages to themselves."

"And you read all that in just a couple of seconds?"

"I didn't have to. Every page says the same thing, page after page, line after line. KILL THEM ALL, KILL THEM ALL, KILL THEM ALL, KILL THEM ALL, KILL THEM ALL."

"I thought we just did."

"Evidently we were wrong. That's the meaning of this. If the mysteries are saying we should kill them all then that means we haven't. There are more of them. We might only have killed the stupid ones, the ones who thought they'd be safe in their homes in broad daylight. There might be many more to worry about. They can be awfully clever."

"Well isn't that just wonderful."

"There is nothing wonderful about it," Stephanovich said grimly. "If there are more to kill, we can't attempt to free the children just yet."

"I was being sarcastic. It's clear the brighter ones found dark places to hide in the daylight or took other forms so we wouldn't notice them, if the mysteries are still telling us to kill them all. We have to go hunting."

"How? All we have left in this world is this truck and our children. We're out of gas. We even lack the chemicals needed to cook up another batch of the antidote to cure the vampires we don't have the resources to kill. I think it might be the other way around now. Once it's completely dark, they'll be hunting us."

Now it was Elsa's turn to gasp at the hopelessness of their predicament.

"I wish we were inside the mountain with our children," she said. "Life might be better in there, for all we know now."

"No place beyond the grave is better. We have to get them out, no matter what, and then we have to go on killing them."

Her hand trembling, Elsa reached out and clicked on the high beams. Ahead of them the forest lit up, but as far as they could see, there was no one lurking anywhere among the pines.

"Do we even have a shovel?" she burst out loudly.

"We have a shovel, one shovel."

"Just one shovel. How high is this mountain?"

"Several thousand feet high."

"So we're going to dig down several thousand feet with one shovel. Honestly, Stephanovich, sometimes you don't think things through at all."

"I wanted to blow up the mountain. You wouldn't let me."

"You wanted to blow up the mountain with the children inside?"

"I wasn't exactly planning on this happening, all our wonderful friends and neighbors drinking the black blood seeping out of the mountain and becoming vampires again so that we have to kill them. I wasn't exactly planning on this."

"Are the mysteries saying anything more?"

"No, even they have gone stupid. Stupid mysteries." He lifted the thick pile of parchment pages to his face and screamed at them: "First you tell me to kill my son, and now all you can say is KILL THEM ALL, KILL THEM ALL. Can't you be a little more helpful than that, mysteries?"

Elsa reached over and pushed down Stephanovich's arm so that the mysteries dropped to his knee again.

"You're acting more than a little crazy. If they're not helping, we have to help ourselves. At least we can open up Mabin's grave again and see what we can do from there. That seems to be our only option at this point."

"And I guess that would liberate more black blood, and if the vampires are around, they'd have more to feast on. Good idea, Elsa."

"Don't yell at me! Do you have any better ideas?"

"Not at this moment. I'm sorry, I'm tired from all this killing. I thought all our problems would be solved if we killed them all."

"Tell the mysteries you can never kill all the vampires. There are always more."

Stephanovich lifted the mysteries to his face and yelled at them: "There are always more to kill."

"Now you really have lost it."

"No, no ... they ..."

Stephanovich was staring at the old parchment.

"They've stopped writing themselves in English. There's one sentence now in Sumerian, I believe."

"What does it say?"

"Wait ... it's been a long time since I've read Sumerian. I'm a little rusty. It says, *get them out of there*. That's all."

"So I suppose we dig. Is that what it means?"

"You just drove over Mabin's grave!"

"What? How was I to know? I was talking to you and the mysteries. I didn't see it."

"Stop here. I'll get the shovel from the back. Just stop!"

"All right! Stop yelling! Why are you yelling at me all the time?"

Hitting the brake hard, Elsa brought the Humvee to a halt and reached out to turn off the engine. Stephanovich's hand stopped her.

"Let go of me."

"How are we supposed to see what we're doing? Turn the truck around and shine the headlights on the grave so that we can see what we're digging up."

Frustrated and angry, Elsa jammed the Humvee into gear and turned to the left, backed up, turned to the left again and finally straightened out the wheel to drive forward to the edge of Mabin's grave.

"Keep the engine running so the battery doesn't die," Stephanovich said.

"Don't worry about me. We'll take turns digging. You dig first."

Each exited into the night and turned to rush to the back of the truck. As soon as they did, they saw they had made a mistake in their hasty exit. Behind them, in the dark, hundreds of the small circles of fire hung in the air, floating on the breezes, flickering and then burning intensely. The small circles of fire wafted among the branches of the pines and the trunks of the trees, or hovered at various levels over the open spaces of the forest.

"I knew it," Stephanovich said.

"Those are the little fires that rose off the dead vampires," Elsa said. "They were souls. They must be. They were the souls of the burning vampires."

"They know we're here to open the grave. They think they can get to the black blood when we do and revive themselves. I might not have translated the mysteries correctly."

"What are you saying?"

"Now that I think of it, the Sumerian said not *get them out of there*, but *get out of here*. I'm pretty sure that's what they said."

As though understanding their mistake and what they should do about it at the same time, Elsa and Stephanovich turned and rushed back inside the Humvee. Just as they slammed closed their doors, they saw hundreds of the little circles of fire diving out of the sky to surround the truck.

"The mysteries were right. We should get the hell out of here," Elsa said. "Those souls must be pretty angry we killed their bodies."

Without hesitation, or waiting for Stephanovich to agree, she slammed the Humvee into gear, stomped on the accelerator and took off on a wild ride down through the bumpy mountain night.

"There must be another way to get the children out of here," Stephanovich moaned. "We have to figure it out. Now. We have to figure it out now."

They fled down the mountain in the night.

17

The mountain shook once and then settled into itself as Mabin and Maggie reached the fifth level.

"What was that?"

"Was it an earthquake?"

"I don't know. The entire mountain shook."

"We really do have to find a way out of here, Mabin. What next? Is the mountain going to fall down around us?"

"It felt like it might."

"I'm not leaving without Tommy."

"Don't worry, I'm not, either. We'll find Tommy and get out of here as quickly as we can."

Another muffled explosion shook the walls of the fifth level. From above, several large rocks crashed down and shattered out on the plain, and beyond that, they could see that the lake of blood was unsettled and roiling, with waves rolling in off its disturbed surface and crashing onto the shore. It was as though the ceiling and walls were uncertain they could stand, and the lake was uncertain it would ever be calm again. After the blast loosened the foundations of floor, walls and ceiling, the cavern seemed to recover on its own. It settled down without collapsing. All was quiet. Maggie moved close to Mabin and put her arms around him with a smile, and he settled an arm over her shoulder to comfort her.

"I don't know if I like the looks of this," Mabin said.

"I thought we were safe now. Are we ever safe?"

"Sometime. Somewhere we'll be safe. I'm not sure this is the time or place, though."

Peace settled over the fifth level, although an orange glowing mist they had not seen in the caverns prior to his seeped out of the far wall like a wisp of colored fog floating through a street lamp. The mist leaked out of a crack in the sheer cavern cliff to their right, formed itself into a twirling fog while retaining its color and radiance and then settled down onto the floor, where it seemed to dance across it before flattening itself out at the stream of blood just ahead of Maggie and Mabin. The fog hovered over the flowing blood, and then the front end curled up to a height of six feet. Its middle and rear followed as though in a line until the mist was an erect column of orange vapor standing in the stream. Slowly, from the top down, the fog transformed itself into a hideously formed vampire, slumped over with a hump on his back and staring with huge red eyes at the blood. His crooked fingers trembled with delight at the sight of the blood, and then he stroked the deeply scarred skin of his face, which retained its orange cast. He gaped with delight at the flowing blood, his head tick-tocking back and forth like a clock as he watched the stream flow by, saliva dripping from his mouth. In human form, he fell flat on its stomach and submerged his face in the blood to drink in ecstasy, his body shaking in paroxysms of pleasure at slaking his thirst with the purest blood any vampire had ever tasted.

"I must tell the others of this," the vampire whispered, when he came up for air, the red dripping off his chin. "They must know of all this blood that is here for the taking."

As soon as they saw the creature drinking, Mabin and Maggie fell to the floor hoping he had not seen them.

"I don't know where that thing came from, but it looks like the vampires have discovered what's in here and found a way in through the crack those blasts created," Mabin whispered. "Is he the only one you can see?"

"So far," Maggie answered. "No, wait. There's something crawling floor toward it."

A small dark figure was making its way across the floor, sneaking up on the feeding vampire, intent on it as though stalking it. The figure was outlined in the reflected orange glow of the creature, and then as Mabin and Maggie watched, it made its way behind the vampire, moving stealthily toward it with a quiet savage energy, a spring wound tight. When the stalking figure was in position, it leaped to its feet, a wooden stake held over its head. It rushed forward, leaped onto the back of the feeding vampire and plunged the stick down toward its heart. With a speed that nearly blurred the creature to invisibility, the vampire slipped out from beneath the attacking figure, avoiding the thrust of the wooden stake into its heart. The stake nicked the creature's shoulder, but there was no blood inside it to seep out. The small figure that had attached the vampire was thrown to the side of the stream and landed in a heap, groaning and unable to move.

"That's Tommy!" Maggie screamed, leaping to her feet. "I know it is. The vampire's got Tommy now."

She shot toward her brother just as the vampire collected itself and sneered at the boy lying in a heap nearby. It took a few steps forward, slumped over and laughing to itself at the ease of its catch and savoring the coming pleasure of taking real, fresh blood from the boy. The creature should never have hesitated to bask in a victory that was not yet his. Maggie flew across the cavern in an instant and slammed into the snickering vampire, falling into a heap with the creature, while she screamed, "Get away from him! He's my brother!" They rolled across the floor, the vampire's breath nearly overcoming her with the fetid stench of rotted black blood that he belched. He had transformed the pure blood to black blood as soon as it hit his lips. Maggie wrapped her hands around the vampire's neck tightly, but the creature's head collapsed like a tower retracting and it slipped out of her grasp. In a second, the vampire turned the tables and was on top of her, pinning her down by the shoulders and staring down at her with hateful red eyes and a grin.

"A boy and a girl," he said, snickering. "Quite a very balanced meal."

"Get away from her!" Tommy screamed, but he was still too battered to get up and join the fight. He had struggled to his knees but could rise no further.

The vampire flared out its blood-soaked fangs in preparation of feeding on Maggie, but then with a whooshing sound, something flew into the vampire and sent it rolling across the cavern floor with a grunt.

While the creature had been faster than sight, Mabin had been faster than thought. He crashed into the vampire and sent him tumbling away.

"Did he nick you? Did he get his fangs in you?" Mabin asked. "Are you all right?"

"I'm fine, untouched. I'm a little rusty fighting these creatures."

As soon as they looked up, Tommy was dashing toward the fallen vampire with a limp, his wooden stake again in hand, screaming at the prostrate creature.

"Don't you ever touch my sister again! I hate all you stinking, red-eyed, blood-sucking freaks," he yelled, again raising the stake to pinion the vampire. "Suck on this!"

With a speed he had not shown in his first attack on the vampire, Tommy leaped forward and plunged the stake downward, this time catching the scrawny bent leg of the creature under the point of the stake as it squirmed away. The stake pinned the creature to the ground, and it squealed in pain, but then immediately freed himself by transforming into a fog. Tommy crashed down on it and was enveloped in the floating miasma, but he still pummeled the mist with his fists, until it rose up toward the crack in the cliff wall and exited the cavern the way it had entered.

"And stay out!" Tommy yelled at the cliff wall. "Don't you ever come back here again."

Before he could move or say another word, Maggie rushed up to him and embraced him, tears flowing over her cheeks. She lifted him off his feet and kissed his forehead over and over, until he yelled out, "Hey! What the heck, Maggie? What the heck? What are you doing? That's enough already. What the heck ... I love you, too."

"I'm just so happy to see you. How did you get here? I thought I'd never see you again."

"Hi, Maggie. Stop it! Stop! Don't kiss me anymore. I got here the same way you did, from one level to another, purifying and putting myself back together again until I was whole. It wasn't easy, but a soul named Natas helped me."

"He helped us, too."

"He's a pretty cool dude, don't you think? Still, it wasn't easy."

"No, it wasn't easy, was it? I can't believe you're here."

Maggie kissed his forehead again, and this time Tommy endured it with an uncomfortable sour look. His eyes widened with pleasure when he saw Mabin.

"Hey, Mabin! You made it, too. Hey, I'm sorry I dug you up too soon."

Mabin gave the boy a big bright grin.

"No harm done. You don't know how happy I am to be out of that grave. I should thank you for that."

"I made you do it, Tommy, and I'm so sorry," Maggie said. "I just missed Mabin so much. I didn't mean to put that much pressure on you to bring him back to me."

"That's all right. I did what I had to do. You might have gone completely nuts if I hadn't done something."

"Now that I have Mabin again, I forget how crazy I was when I didn't have him."

Maggie put her arms around her lover and sank her head down onto his chest.

"Oh, no, not this stuff again," Tommy said. "Can you stop for just a minute?"

Suddenly, there was another massive explosion, this one sounding far closer than the other two. The high cliff walls shook and dropped rocks and dirt down onto the cavern floor. More of the rocks and dirt splashed into the flowing stream of blood, muddying it and clogging the flow. Several boulders rocketed straight down from the ceiling and splashed into the lake of blood, sending flowering geysers of red into the air and unsettling the surface of the lake. Tommy was about to dash for cover up the ramp leading to back to the fourth level, but Mabin grabbed his arm.

"You can't go backwards here," he said. "Didn't Natas tell you that? If you do, you revert to what you were."

"Natas might have said something about it. Yuk. I'd revert to a bloody, mashed-up, headless body? No thanks. I guess I'll stay here and get clobbered by falling rocks instead."

Tommy raised his eyes to the ceiling to check for danger from above, but the cavern had settled down, dark and quiet again.

"Let's get out of here, can we?" Maggie asked. "First, the place shakes with all these explosions and then a vampire shows up. That's enough to make me want to forget this place forever."

"I'm all for that," Tommy said. "I'm glad for what happened in her for us, but I want to go home."

Looking around, Mabin had just one thing to say.

"How?"

"What?"

"How do we get out of here?"

More debris plummeted down from the ceiling as they pondered the answer to that. It crashed onto the cavern floor just twenty feet away. Maggie and Mabin and Tommy covered their heads with their arms and cowered together, huddling close as more rocks and debris fell.

"Are we going to be buried again?" Tommy screamed out. "In here?"

"No, no," Mabin said. "There's got to be some way out."

"There is not."

From the end of the ramp, Natas had spoken. His voice was calm and certain. They turned quickly when they heard him, and the debris stopped falling as the cavern settled down again after the last blast.

"Was there a vampire in here?" Natas asked. "I sensed one."

"He came through the walls in a mist," Mabin answered. "He came for the blood. We fought him off."

"Good. I sensed a disturbance down here, and there is a bigger disturbance going on outside the mountain. I don't know what it is, but there are hundreds of new vampire souls at the top of the mountain, waiting to get in. Something's killing vampires, so we have many more new vampire souls to process and educate."

"We heard explosions," Maggie said. "Did the vampires set them off?"

"There are cracks in the mountain the vampire came through," Tommy added. "I think the explosions might have something to do with that."

"They sensed the blood in here and are finding their way to it," Natas said. "Somehow, they know it's here. This is very dangerous."

"You said there are more souls on top of the mountain?" Mabin asked. "Do they have anything to do with the explosions?"

"I doubt it, but we have to process them before we know. I thought the vampires were under control in this area, but now they know the purified blood is here and they will be after it."

Mabin turned to Maggie.

"It's Stephanovich and Elsa. It's got to be. They killed them. Who else knows how to kill vampires so efficiently, hundreds at a time?"

"I think you're right."

Maggie turned to Natas, who floated closer.

"Can you let us out so that we can help with killing the vampires? My parents might be in danger. I'm worried about them."

"I would let you out if I could, but I don't know how. This mountain is intended for purifying blood only, and then for shipment to where it is needed, but it works if a damaged human enters, as I discovered with the three of you. You three are the first humans ever to survive the process. Once the blood is purified, it stays here securely, because it can not retreat uphill. The same restriction is on you. No one ever thought humans would come here for resurrection."

"Whoa. You mean we have to stay here?" Tommy asked, aghast. "I was just starting to feel better, and now you tell us we're trapped."

"You don't have to stay, but there's no way to leave. I suppose that's the same thing. No exit was ever built in for humans, only small pipes to ship the pure blood out. You would not fit through them."

"So you are telling us we have to stay."

"As fellow Protectors of the Blood. You've proven you can fend off vampires. We'd be happy to have you here to help in our work."

The largest explosion yet rocked the cavern where the three trapped, purified humans talked to the ancient vampire soul. More rocks and debris came crashing down around them as the ceiling shook so badly it seemed on the verge of collapse. With large creaking sounds, the cliff walls cracked in several places, showing long fault lines in the rock, and in one spot a beam of light somehow found its way into the cavern. As the rocks shifted again, the fault that allowed the beam of light in closed again, but then there was a whiff of fresh air as the mountain winds found the way into the cavern.

"Thanks for the offer," Maggie said to Natas, "but I think we all prefer to leave."

"I can smell freedom," Tommy said. "Don't tell us we can't get out if I can smell freedom."

"If we can smell it, we can find it," Mabin responded. "I know it. We have to."

"All of you should take cover until we discover a way out, if you choose in the end to go," Natas said. "This mountain and the National Emergency Blood Bank are no longer secure, and I think it might collapse in on us and ruin all our work. I have to find out what's happening outside, but first I have to let in all the foul souls waiting for purification on top of the mountain, so that they can begin their cleansing."

"Wait. You can't leave us here," Maggie said. "We're not meant to be here. I only came to free my brother and Mabin. I didn't know we'd have to stay for eternity."

"I have no choice. If the mountain collapses, the vampires have access to the blood, and you know what that means. More new, purified souls might be able to help us. I have to do what I must to protect the blood."

With that, the small circle of fire turned and fled up the ramp toward the fourth level, free to move as he wanted, while Mabin and Maggie and Tommy were trapped inside the mountain that threatened to fall in around them.

"This place is no longer secure," Maggie said. "They can get in, and I can sense they're coming."

"I sense it, too. If the vampires are at the gates, we have to be ready," Mabin said. "Find whatever you can among the rocks, any shard of rock or small piece you can use as a weapon. Something like this."

Mabin reached down and held up a piece of rock in the shape of a knife. He lifted it for Maggie and Tommy to see, but their attention was riveted on the cliff beside them.

Through the biggest crack in the rock, several orange and pink clouds of fog were seeping into the cavern. Several smaller faults were seeping other orange and pink mists into the dark atmosphere of the cavern.

Mabin spun around to see what they were looking at. His face dropped with consternation at the number of bright orange mists seeping into the cavern. They seemed to be everywhere along the walls and ceiling, a true invasion.

"I don't think we're going to be alone for much longer," Tommy said.

As they stared at the cliff walls, yet more thin clouds of pink and orange fog were finding their ways through, hundreds of them.

"I think we're going to need more sharp rocks," Maggie said. "Mabin …"

Mabin was already stooped over and gathering extra weapons for the coming fight. He was determined to protect the blood, now that Natas had said they could help in doing so.

"They're not sending me to the grave again," Mabin said, his voice rising with determination. "I'm not going through that again. No. Never."

"Step behind me," he said to Maggie and Tommy. "If I'm the person I was, if I've healed too, I might be able to handle this."

"We can take them," Tommy said, stepping forward to stand next to Mabin. "There can't be more than a few hundred of them. Piece of cake."

18

The full moon provided too much light for the vampires to work their mining operation safely. Protective clothing, black cloaks with hoods, was provided for them, and the cloaks and hoods prevented their skin from sizzling in the moonlight when they had to leave the mine for more dynamite.

Even when they set off their charges inside St. Mary's mountain, the flashes from the explosions were enough to singe their flesh, so they had to run for cover outside the mine as the charges blew. Once outside, they would have to draw their hoods over their heads and take cover to prevent the unpleasant consequences the moonlight might have on their skins. Inside the mine, the flashes from the charges were the danger. Otherwise, work was going well on the mine, with more and more progress being made as the vampires became more adept and expert at their jobs, and soon the tunnel to the hoard of blood contained in the National Emergency Blood Bank would be completed and the blood would be theirs for the taking. With that thought in mind, they worked like maniacs, as the vampire Harkin Davis led them in their efforts. They already had forged an opening you could drive a bus through, wide but not deep. They had extended a shaft for several hundred feet into the mountain.

Davis urged them on with promises of great treasure inside.

"Hurry, brothers, this is what we've waited centuries to find, a mother lode of blood like this for the taking. We'll never go hungry again, never be weak."

"No human can stop us once we have the blood. The fools never should have thought they could keep our blood all to themselves," another vampire piped in.

"Human are greedy. They never think of anyone else," Davis said.

"They deserve to die."

"They deserve to suffer. I wish we could tell them what we're going to do to the lot of them once we're made strong by the blood."

The excited talk accompanied the vampires' work to dig out the hoard of riches inside the mountain, and made them work with more fervor. The rumors of the great stash of blood had traveled around the globe, as the networked vampires used cell phones and social media to spread the word of the coming feast in Montana. Harkin Davis had first placed the invitation to come to Montana to feast on several social network sites, and others had shared the good news that promulgated across the globe. Places like this, secret places, existed, but it was not often they were found by immortals. A mountain full of the purest blood of their holy feast was leaking its secret, and it was ripe and rich for the taking, dirty at the top of the mountain but pure at its base.

Hourly, more vampires were flying in, generally in great clouds of bats that came to assist the vampires transformed to human form who were doing their mining work on the ground. As the bats landed and assumed human shape, they transformed into eager workers immediately in no need of rest after their long journeys, for their inspiration was great. The wonder of a mountain that gushed blood was true. More workers meant more dynamite carried into the new mine and more and more charges set and more and more explosions opening the way to the NEBB. It also meant more and more reckless behavior, as the vampires rushed to mine the riches they could smell inside the mountain but could not reach. The aroma was like fresh meat to a wolf.

"Work as fast as possible," Harkin Davis pleaded, as the new vampires arrived. "They can pump the blood out if they discover we're here, and then our work would have gone for naught."

Once Stephanovich and Elsa had fled from the hundreds of strange circles of floating lights at Mabin's grave, they felt somewhat safe, for the circles had not followed them far down the mountain. Their sense of safety soon dissipated. One explosion inside the mountain blew the Humvee up in the air and nearly flipped them over as though they had hit a huge rock at too high a speed, but there hadn't been any rock and the sound of the explosion was only too apparent.

"My god, what was that?" Elsa screamed out. "Who's blowing things up now?"

"I'm afraid I know what it is, and who," Stephanovich answered. "Oh, hell."

"Was it a bomb?"

"The vampires have found my entire cache of dynamite in our basement and stole it before they blew up our house. I think they're using it to get to the children. Somehow, they know they're inside the mountain and think this is the only way to get to them."

"We have to stop them."

"That's been the plan all along. I had thought we gotten rid of all of them, but I suppose I was wrong. This is what the mysteries meant when they told us to kill them all. The mysteries knew we hadn't killed them all, but only thought we did."

"So they're after the children?" Elsa asked, panic-stricken.

"I'm afraid so."

How wrong Stephanovich had been about the vampire genocide they thought they perpetrated became evident as soon as they descended farther down the mountain. In the moonlight, they saw the vast flocks of bats dropping in their hordes out of the moonlit sky to land at the base of the mountain. The two humans they knew something big was happening. It was as though all the bats of the world had convened in the burned-out town, and although it might have appeared to be a natural phenomenon at first, it soon became apparent to Stephanovich and Elsa that this was anything but nature working its kind, sweet magic of life. When the next series of explosions rocked the truck, nearly flipping it over each time, they understood they had to abandon their ride and deal with the vampires on different terms.

"You were right," Stephanovich said. "Look at all of them. They're like ants. I guess there really always are more vampires to kill."

"Believe me, I'm not happy to be right. What can we do with all of them?"

"Kill them the old-fashioned way, by hand."

"All right. I guess we have no choice."

At least of few of Montana's vampires must have survived and called on others from all over the world to come to assist in the taking of the blood of the children, Stephanovich said, thinking of Harkin Davis. Without knowing that the NEBB was inside the mountain, Elsa and Stephanovich assumed the outsiders had to have come on invitation to feast with their children, but that seemed out of all proportion. As great as they were at destroying vampires, Mabin and Maggie and Tommy were only three, not enough to feed bats in the thousands. And so Stephanovich and Elsa soon determined that the bats were not simply bats but bats on a mission they did not quite understand.

They parked the Humvee near the base of the mountain after coasting down its slopes with the lights and motor off. They quietly exited the vehicle. Stephanovich stuffed the

Transylvanian Mysteries in his back pocket after consulting them once again for instructions. The mysteries simply repeated their tiresome dictum instructing them to KILL THEM ALL, KILL THEM ALL, KILL THEM ALL.

"The mysteries are like a broken record," Stephanovich said. "I think we're going to have to figure out how to do this by ourselves."

"We are in for a long night."

From the vampire ash littering the ground they blackened their faces and hands, and found as many fire-hardened sticks as they could and sharpened them to killing points without knowing how they were going to destroy so many vampires with mere sharpened sticks. They carried their weapons in bundles the rest of the way down the mountain, being careful not to expose their presences to the flocks congealing into human forms at the floor of the mountain. When they were within sight of the landing zone, they saw one great piping conglomerate of bats hover over the mouth of the mine and then gently land as one, transforming into a human mass just as soon as they hit the ground.

"I knew it, it is Harkin Davis," Stephanovich said, spying the vampire leader as he encouraged the new arrivals. He saw they were issued the great black cloaks with hoods, for if they stepped out of the shade of the great pine trees, the consequences would be awful. The newcomers set to work at once, joining the great line of vampires carrying dynamite into the cave. Just as this group commenced carrying the explosives in, another foolhardy group was fleeing their recently set charge. They did not make it out, due to the new arrivals blocking their way. The charge ignited, sending burning, squealing vampires flying out of the mouth of the cave. The newcomers were not deterred at all by this. They simply picked up their dynamite boxes and rushed into the mine past the burning bodies. Now there would be more blood for them.

The dead bodies of the burned vampires littered the mouth of the cave, as no one cared to move them.

"These creatures have no morals," Elsa said, as they watched the vampires work.

"Let's go. We can have no morals in dealing with them. Never forget what they did to our family."

Elsa and Stephanovich crept forward, carrying two sharpened sticks each, one in each hand. They had stashed the rest of their killing sticks in strategic places, should they have to retreat. They had no plan beyond that but trusted in fate to reveal one to them. They also knew they had no choice but to fight.

Another tremendous explosion lit up the night with a fiery belch from the mouth of the cave, and several dozen more flaming vampires flew out of the mountain, squealing as they quickly disintegrated into ash. While this appeared to be a common occurrence, the vampires never seemed to learn how to avoid it. Something else also caught Stephanovich and Elsa's attention, for above the mouth of the mine other vampires were transforming into vapors of pink and orange. The vapors disappeared into the cracks in the mountain, finding a fast way in that the lowly bat-miners could not take advantage of, being made of more substantial stuff.

"They're entering the mountain in any way they can," Elsa said. "What is going on? The children are going to be destroyed by all these vampires entering the mountain if we don't get in there ourselves to help them."

"We better figure out a way to stop these things, and quickly."

"But what are we stopping? How can we know what to do if we don't know what we're stopping? Or how many of them there are?"

"The mining operation has to stop first. Then we'll deal with those vampires in the mist."

Their whispers, even this small break in the silence, did not go unnoticed. As soon as Stephanovich had answered his wife, a pair of red eyes spun around in the darkness to fix on their interruption. The vampire's bottom third had disintegrated into mist as he lowered himself down into a crack in the mountain, and the rest of him was quickly becoming fog. Realizing they had been overheard, Elsa leaped forward in a flash, driving the stick in her right hand into the vampire's heart and tearing the upper, solid part of his body off of the vaporous bottom. As he was torn in two, a great squealing issued from him, and he flailed at Elsa with twisted, gnarled claws.

"Shut him up!" Stephanovich whispered urgently. "They'll know someone is here if we don't shut him up."

Even before he finished speaking, Elsa whipped forward her second sharpened stick, driving it through the vampire's mouth and sending his teeth flying out the back of his head. She pinned the half-creature to the earth by the skull. The vampire twitched but then was silent.

"Let's get out of here," Stephanovich said. "We can't stay now that they know we're here. Get your weapons."

Elsa put a foot on the half-vampire's chest and pulled out her first sharpened stick, and then lifted her foot to the creature's neck and removed her second stick from his head.

"What are we doing to do?" Elsa asked. "We can't kill them all."

"We can try. Come on, quickly. We're climbing up the mountain."

"Why?"

"Because rocks fall downward. If we can find some big ones high up, we can start a landslide and close the mine, at least for a little while. It's the best I can come up with for now."

Elsa nodded, set in her determination, and turned and ran up the incline, the slimy sharpened sticks in her hands nearly slipping from her grasp. She had not run ten feet when another pair of red eyes leaped up and glared back at her. This time the eyes were only three feet off the ground. The vampire had transformed most of his lower half into a vapor and was dropping down through a crack in the mountain, but he still had enough bad blood in him to snarl at Elsa. It was a mistake. He should have disappeared into the mountain in silence. She lunged at him, leading with the weapon in her right hand, and drove it into his closed mouth, again knocking his teeth out the back of his head. It quickly became her favored method of dispatching vampires. The kill stroke was so expert the creature did not have time to squeal. He remained a partial body on the mountains, cut off just below the shoulders. She slipped her stick out of his skull.

"This is not much harder than it looks," she said, grinning back at Stephanovich. "When they're half vapor, they die easily."

Elsa looked up just in time to see two more vampires transform and drop side-by-side into the same crack in the mountain. They had seen their friend destroyed, and wanted no part of Elsa. They quickly escaped to the feast inside the mountain.

"Stephanovich, they're all over the place. What is going on?" Elsa asked, glancing over her shoulder. "Stephanovich?"

There was no need to tell Stephanovich they were in for a fight. He was silently engaged with two fully intact vampires, his sharpened sticks flashing in the moonlight as the two creatures circled around him, trying to gain an advantage that would allow them to leap onto his neck and tear into him with their fangs. Stephanovich kept moving his eyes from one to the other and adjusting as they rushed forward and retreated, parrying toward one to drive him off and then spinning to deal with the other. Elsa leaped down the mountainside, seemingly flying, and led with her left-hand weapon. She drove it into one of the vampire's back, through the left ventricle of the heart, just as Stephanovich pinned the other vampire through the neck, driving it to the ground. He finished off the creature with a strong thrust of his second stick through the chest.

"We're going to have to fight them all the way up the mountain," he said, slipping his now-slimy sticks from the dead bloodless body. He was out-of-breath. "As you say, this isn't going to be easy."

They continued their ascent, their senses primed to their highest sensitivity, careful to look for the blazing red eyes in the dark as a telltale sign a vampire was transforming into mist and dropping into the mountain and therefore vulnerable. The shadows of the tall pines each seemed to hold a secret hiding place where anyone or anything could escape detection. With their senses so greatly heightened and their hearts beating wildly, Elsa and Stephanovich crept up the mountainside, their heads swiveling from side-to-side in anticipation of being attacked. When they finally were accosted, it was with a simple sarcastic expression of gratitude.

"We have to express how much it means to us for you to do away with our rivals," a voice said, almost laughing at them.

They froze. They knew that voice.

"Harkin?"

"It is Harkin Davis. I can see him now."

"Where?"

"Right in front of you."

"Where?"

"Right there, in front of you. Two feet away from you. How did you survive, Harkin?"

"I still don't see him."

"Maybe I can help you distinguish me in the dark. And, oh, I survived your burning of our community by transforming into a bat and waiting in a nice, dank cave until your rampage was over."

With that, Harkin Davis opened his eyes, revealing two large burning red orbs not two feet in front of Stephanovich. The light from those eyes revealed a small curving of his lips, a smile as sarcastic as his words.

Stephanovich immediately lunged and struck out at him, but the vampire knew the thrust was coming and side-stepped it, sending Stephanovich tumbling to the ground. Stephanovich rolled and jumped to his feet, ready to face the vampire again. He held up sharpened sticks to threaten the creature and searched for his next point of attack.

"There's no reason to that attack," Harkin Davis said. "I'm too quick. You can't stab me ... or my friends."

With that, he raised his gnarled hand and a thousand burning red eyes opened in the surrounding night, a circle made of hundreds of eyes burning into them. The vampire circle had closed around them with no path of escape and no possibility of fighting their way out of it. Harkin Davis gave out a squealing laugh as he saw Elsa and Stephanovich's consternation, and then the thousands of vampires chimed in with squealing laughter of their own. The squealing overwhelmed the quick of the night, like the deadly cackles of a million sick geese in an amphitheater.

"Good-bye, Elsa," Stephanovich said, over the din, realizing their time had come.

"Good-bye, my love," she answered. "Let's fight well, for the children. Each one we kill will allow the children to live another hour."

They backed up toward each other until their shoulders touched, and then they craned their heads around until their lips brushed in a kiss for just a second. Then they crouched down and raised their sharpened sticks, facing the vampires determined to fight until their end.

"This touches me, no it really does," Harkin Davis said. "Truthfully, it really, really does. Two against hundreds of vampires, with the two thinking they're going to die fighting and kissing each other tenderly before being overwhelmed. Touching, really."

"We'll kill you first, Mr. Davis," Stephanovich said. "Book it."

"You will? And I was ready to express my thanks again for your help in killing our rivals, the vapors ... is that how you react to my gratitude?"

"This is a strange sort of thanks. Give us our children. Leave them alone and you can have us."

"Oh, I haven't taken your children yet, but the vapors traveling into the mountain soon might, unless you cooperate with us. What we're really looking forward to is your cooperation, not your blood."

"Don't listen to him, Stephanovich. He's lying. They all do."

"I'm not listening to him, my love. If he makes one false move, he'll be the first to die."

"Now, Stephanovich, no one here is going to die."

Someone in the circle of vampires was breathing heavily and whispering unconsciously, as though he could not help himself, "In the neck, in the neck, in the neck."

A chill went up Elsa's spine, and she shivered, not wanting to show fear but unable to control her dread. Unable to restrain her fear, she touched the soft skin of her neck and whimpered.

"Step back!" Harkin Davis yelled at the whispering vampire, who was inching toward Elsa. "We need these two. No one touches these two!" he roared, taking a swipe at the impatient vampire with his clawed hand.

He left two scratches that did not bleed on the offending vampire's cheek. The creature squealed and moved back.

There was a horrible stench in the forest that overwhelmed the sweet pine aroma of the trees. It was the stench of hundreds of unwashed vampires, all of them indifferent to hygiene. Elsa gagged as they moved closer to her.

"We're wasting time," Harkin Davis said. "We need these two humans for slaves, not the fleeting pleasure of their meager blood."

"Us, slaves? We'll never work for you," Stephanovich said. "Ha! Slaves? Us? Never!"

"We're not slaves," Elsa said, her voice quivering.

"There is nothing else for you to do. Time is wasting. You will fill your truck with explosives and drive it into the mountain and deliver the dynamite to our demolition experts, or we will kill your children. Then you will drive back out and pick up another load. We're losing far too many of our kind in this effort, and since we saw you arrive with your truck the solution became obvious. You will get to live until you help all our bats find their way to the blood in the cave, and in exchange your children will live. Too many of the vapors have beaten us inside, and we can not wait for you to decide."

"Both of us, for their leader," Stephanovich said quickly to Elsa, and understanding that he was in danger of being rushed and overtaken, Harkin Davis raised his hand to call in help.

Stephanovich and Elsa sprinted toward him with their sharpened sticks directed at his eyes. Elsa thrust for his face first, but the vampire stepped aside and she tumbled to the ground. Stephanovich screamed out for her and rushed to help her up when he was pelted by what seemed like a thousand handfuls of mud. From out of the trees, Harkin Davis had called down the multitudes of vampire bats to attack but not harm Elsa and Stephanovich, and now those bats were doing their business as best they could, multitudes of them. Soon the two humans were struggling on the ground and overwhelmed in a squirming black mass that pinned them down. There was a thick carpet of squirming creatures fighting hard to get Elsa and Stephanovich under control after knocking them to the earth. They swarmed and flapped their wings by the thousands, and more and move dropped out of the sky to help, a black rain of them. Harkin Davis waded through the bats toward the two helpless humans.

"I hate bats!" Stephanovich yelled.

"Kill them, too! Kill them all!"

"How? How?"

"You will drive your truck for us!" Harkin Davis screamed. "You will be our slaves or the children will die! The vapors will take all the blood if we bats do not make it inside quickly, and only you two among us know how to drive stick shift to get us inside! Carry them off! Carry them off to their truck!"

Then quickly bound shackled with rope and gagged with fetid strips of cloth, they were lifted up and carried off through the air by the multitudes of the bats to the Humvee to do the vampires' bidding.

No one heard Elsa screaming.

19

The vapors had beaten the bats to the interior of the cavern and the NEBB lake of blood, but they encountered obstacles there that suggested that they had some common sense, when of course they did not.

As soon as an individual leaked through the wall or ceiling that individual was confronted by Mabin and Maggie and Tommy in mid-air.

It was not common sense but fear that led them to remain in vaporous form and flee toward the top of the ceiling without manifesting as corporal human beings, for the word had spread of how the children had driven off those who attempted to drink the purified blood. Thousands congregated near the top of the cavern, glowing pink or orange and lighting the entire interior with the glow of their frustration.

Having escaped Elsa and Stephanovich, who had torn only a few in two, they now had to deal with Maggie and Mabin and Tommy, who were capable of kill many more. They chose to remain out of reach high above them.

"They're going to come down and attempt to get to the blood eventually," Mabin said. "The cowards. They won't be able to resist it. I'm just warning you to be ready."

"What are they waiting for?" Tommy asked. "Hey, what are you waiting for? Come on down and get what's coming to you, you creepy blood-sucking morons. Come on, come down. We're waiting. Yeah!"

"You don't have to encourage them, they'll be down soon enough," Maggie said. "They want the blood."

"The sooner they come down, the better," Tommy said. "The sooner they come down, the sooner they'll all be dead and we can find our way out of here."

The light above was eerie, almost sickening in its beauty, for it reflected on the lake of blood and off the rocks and cliffs, mirroring the troubled nature of its sources, the vampire vapors. One brave vampire hovered for as long as he could with the temptation of the blood there below him for the taking, and then it did something foolish, as they knew it would. So much available blood was more than he could bear, and he shot down in a column of orange fog to the shore of the lake swiftly, landing there and taking a human form and gasping at the riches of blood lapping at his feet. The creature was dressed colorfully in a loose flowered top and bell bottoms and scandals. As swiftly as he had fallen, Mabin flew across the plain of rock and expertly picked him off his feet by the scruff of the neck and then twisted his head off as you would twist off the head of a bug. The body fell onto the shore, kicking and writhing in its death agony, but the head bit out at Mabin in frustration, the fangs no where near him as Mabin held out the head by its long hair, but the intention was clear. Mabin crushed the head between his hands and threw it down next to the thing's body. Hovering in the air, he pirouetted while staring up at the cavern ceiling where the other vampires had not dared to try the same thing and seemed disinclined to attempt feeding after this display of strength, despite their great hunger and thirst and lust for blood. Their lights burned intensely, frustrated response to what they had just seen.

When Mabin had spun around in a full circle, he came face-to-face with Maggie, who had flown to him to back him up, as though he needed it.

"Is that something new?" she asked, amused.

"Of course. I learned it while I was dead."

"At least you can fly again. I was beginning to wonder if you'd ever regain your powers, but they seem beyond anything you had before. I don't wonder about you anymore."

"I think I'm healed. I apologize for the weakness I suffered when you first came in here. It's gone now."

Tommy ran up to the body on the beach, looked it over, said "Wow, cool," and then raised his eyes to Mabin and Maggie.

"Showoff. A few days ago you couldn't even walk, and now look what you're doing."

"Don't get too close to the head," Mabin warned from above. "If it drinks, it will increase its power greatly and be capable of doing us harm."

"This thing? This thing can't hurt me," Tommy said. "Piece of crap."

As though to prove he couldn't be hurt, Tommy kicked out at the head, but as soon as his foot struck it, the fangs came out of the crushed head and snapped at him.

"Whoa! Maybe he's not dead yet."

"He will be. Just don't let it drink! Then we might have a problem even though the head is crushed."

Being careful now, Tommy walked around behind the head and kicked it far away from the lake. It settled like an old, rotting pumpkin on the rocky surface, its jaws still working up and down.

Suddenly, with a swiftness they hadn't seen until this point, another column of pink vapor shot down from the ceiling onto the beach, right next to Tommy. It materialized in an instant to a woman of immense girth, so large around that she dwarfed the boy. It was as though a salivating hot-air balloon had landed beside him. The creature had on blue jeans several sizes too small for her, and a large belly hanging over her belt, and her red eyes had hunger in them that matched the sloppiness of her dripping mouth.

"Wow, no wonder you fell so fast," Tommy said, looking her up and down and smirking. He was unimpressed with her as a monster.

"Are you all right, Tommy?" Maggie asked.

"I'm fine. At least she didn't fall on me. Then it would have been a different story. I might have been hurt then."

The large creature spun with difficulty toward Tommy.

"I've killed many little boys like you, and babies, all because they ridiculed me. All were tender and delicious. Don't you make fun of fat vampires, or you're next," she said, sneering. "Body size has nothing to do with how great a vampire is."

She reached out for him, showing real quickness for her size, but he side-stepped her with a speed born of desperation. Still, he could not help but giggle at the ridiculous creature before him. As difficult as it was in her weakened condition, once she saw her brother in danger, Maggie dropped out of air and landed feet-first on the woman's shoulders, hoping to knock her over before killing her to prevent her from getting to her brother and the blood in the lake. The large woman barely budged when tiny Maggie hit her. She turned around and when she saw Maggie behind her smiled and then sneered at her.

"What do you want, twig? Do you think you can keep me from what I need so badly? A twig like you? You think you can keep me away from the lake? Or the boy?"

Almost ignoring Maggie, the large woman took several steps toward the shimmering blood. Twenty feet behind her two more orange columns of vapor descended rapidly from the ceiling in flashes of light. Gathering all her strength together, ignoring the distraction of the two new vampires falling to earth, Maggie smashed the large woman in the face, in the nose above her bared fangs, with a suddenness that sent her sprawling on her back. Struggling to get up, the woman rolled to her side but by then Maggie was on her with a rock that had been chipped to a fine, sharp edge. She drove the stone blade into the side of the woman's neck and then grabbed her curly, greasy hair to stabilize the head. When she had a good grasp on it, Maggie expertly drew the blade through the neck, severing the head with one cut. Without hesitation, she tossed the head off to the side to lie with the skull of the vampire Mabin had killed. It rolled past the first head, still snarling but then finally coming to rest with its eyes closed and its fangs out.

"I could have done that," Tommy said.

"I know you could have, but you were playing around with her. You can't play around with these things."

"It's funny how they don't bleed when you kill them," Tommy said. "If they can't drink, they can't bleed, and it's almost easy."

"I'm warning you, don't be overconfident. Pay attention to what you're doing," Maggie said again. "There are two more behind you."

His eyes widening as he spun, Tommy pulled his sharpened stone from his belt and lifted it high over his head. The two new, foolish vampires transformed into human shape in the flash of an eye, but instead of worrying about Maggie or Tommy or Mabin above, they headed straight for the lake of blood, thinking of nothing but their great thirst after their long journey. Their backs were bent and they could barely walk on legs that were twisted and wobbly, as their age held them back from a feast they could not resist. If ever two vampires were in need of fresh blood, these two were, for each must have been hundreds of years old and showed it. They had ancient black felt suits with holes in the elbows and knees, black boots with flapping soles and almost no hair on their heads. Each look like an inverted J. Fresh blood would revive them, but for now they hobbled along leaning on each other for support.

"Let the old ones drink first," one of them said, to no one in particular. "I brought a cup with me."

"Eh?"

"The old should drink first."

"Oh."

"I always think ahead."

"Eh?"

"I think ahead."

Mabin had no intention of letting even these ancient characters slake their thirst, despite their absurd ideas of what was right and wrong.

"You old ones are just as dangerous, once you're had fresh blood," he said. "You're not going anywhere near that lake."

"Eh?"

Mabin was not going to repeat himself as these senile creatures did. A tremendous explosion rocked the mountain, and many more rocks and much debris cracked off the ceiling and came hurtling down. A huge boulder brushed by Mabin from above as he was about to attack the two elderly vampires and in an instant there was nothing left of them. The boulder pounded them into the sand like a hammer hitting two nails at once. It drove them deep into the earth.

"Cool stuff," Tommy said. "Wow. They're gone. Just like that. Wasn't that cool, Maggie?"

"Watch out!"

As though this latest explosion set off something in them, some fear or desperation to get to the blood before it was too late, the air above them rained down vampires in columns of orange and pink light. The columns of fog settled all over the plain before the lake and instantly transformed into human forms, an army with fangs extended. Despite the deluge that rained down, there were many more vapors hanging by the ceiling that did not dare take the plunge to the three vampire killers below. Only the truly desperate or mad ones decided to rush for the blood. Tommy took the lead in killing these newly materialized interlopers. With a speed he hadn't shown until now, he shot straight ahead through the air, flying with his fists closed around stone knives. With one swipe, he decapitated a skinny, wretched creature whose purple veins showed through his paper-thin yellow skin. The creature's last gasp opened his mouth and exposed his musky, decayed fangs, and then the bald head and trembling body fell to the floor separately. With a back-handed effort, Tommy swiped out again and cut through the neck of a very slow and somewhat stupid monster that was snarling and looking around as though he didn't know where he was.

"Gump," said the creature, just before Tommy's knife sliced through his neck.

"What does 'gump' mean?" Tommy asked, when the creature's head hit the floor.

The head held no answer for him but continued to snap at him.

Maggie entered the fray, flying low through the forest of vampires and cutting the legs out from under scores of them, swiping her two stone knives to the left and right as though felling trees with single axe blows. Mabin worked in tandem with her, expertly slicing through the necks of the falling vampires as they were tipping over or when they hit the ground. Between the two of them, they scythed the vampires like a deadly threshing machine, back and forth across the plain, harvesting the vampires like rotted wheat.

"Keep it up!" Mabin shouted out. "There are so many of them. We can't stop!"

"Who said anything about stopping?" Tommy asked, as he swerved through the vampires with his knives, cutting down any too slow to see their death awaited them.

"Where's Natas? Why isn't he helping?" Maggie shouted out.

"He's purifying souls. He'll be here soon," Mabin answered.

"Yeah, after we've killed them all," Tommy said. "Lousy blood-suckers."

Seeing what was happening to them, the remaining vampires at first retreated with snarls and squeals toward the back of the plain. Some even attempted to escape by running up the sloping stone ramp toward the fourth level, but after a few steps they clutched their throats and collapsed on the stone, where they withered and turned to dust. There was no going backwards in this place. In a last desperate effort to survive, many of the remaining vampires transformed into their vaporous forms and ascended to the ceiling, out of the reach of the children's stone knives.

"Get back down here, you cowards!" Tommy yelled at them, as they flew upward to safety. "We're not finished with you."

"Where did you learn all that?" Maggie asked her brother, landing next to him. "I've never seen you doing the things you were just doing."

"I just learned it."

"But where?"

"Here. It's funny what you think about when you're dead, and what you can learn," Tommy said. "All I could think about was what I was going to do to the vampires if I ever had the chance to get my hands on them. I kept thinking of new ways to kill them, for what their lousy black blood did to me."

Another tremendous explosion, greater than any so far, rocked the cavern. Again, boulders rained through the floating vapors above, crashing down around Mabin and Maggie and Tommy. They covered their heads with their arms, but still glanced around for any vampires transforming to human form. A great amount of dust formed in the cavern and settled over everything, forming a coating on the rocks and a thin layer on the lake of blood.

"Did we drive them off?" Mabin asked, floating by to land next to Maggie.

"They're back up there again. You seem like your old self again. How many did you kill?"

"Not enough."

"They'll come at us again."

"I know, and again and again and again, to get at the blood, and us. We have to be ready."

Out of the dust floating all around, Natas emerged by flying down the slope from the fourth level. His fires were burning hard in a broken circle, as through he was disturbed by the events transpiring all around them. "Oh, no. Oh, my," he was mumbling. The Outliner found Mabin and Maggie and Tommy and flew directly to them, stopping to hover over their heads. He looked over the masses of dead bodies littering the cavern floor, but he was not satisfied.

"This should be good news to you," he said. "You've done excellent work here."

"We got as many as we could before they headed back for the ceiling," Mabin said. "We might be able to hold them back and keep them from the blood."

"There are many more of them on the way," Natas said, barely acknowledging what Mabin said. "We can help you with them once they've arrived. I've called many of the Outliners down here and as many as we can spare are on their way. The rest have to process the dead vampires souls already in line, but we have to kill them down here first of all before we can process their souls above. The more we kill, the more we can purify above, so we get more help from them for our side after they die, but it takes time. Our circle of death has to close before we can win. Each one you kill helps out in several ways."

The first of the group of Outliners appeared behind Natas. About seventy of the round fires hovered in the air over the cavern floor. Then, sensing the situation, they headed for the ceiling.

"Up there!" an Outliner yelled.

"All of us, up to the ceiling!"

It was as though the vapors knew the danger coming at them and panicked. The Outliners rose toward the orange and pink mists, and the mists fled from them to whatever corner of the cavern they could find. Many were too slow. The Outliners encircled them with their fires like nooses around necks and closed the circles of themselves around the mists, snuffing them out with a hissing sound. The fine mists of burned ash fell from above and littered the cavern floor, settling over the dust and bodies of the vampires the children had killed. Above was a melee of Outliner fires roping and destroying the vampire mists, with the action taking place over every inch below the ceiling. It was as though groups of stars were encircling clouds and burning them.

"Wow, that's some really cool stuff," Tommy said. "If there's anything I like, it's seeing those creeping misty things die before they can turn into blood-suckers again."

"We can only do that to them when they're in that form," Natas said. "Once they transform to human form, you have to take care of them."

"What did you mean before when you said more are on the way?" Mabin asked Natas, sounding worried.

"A large cloud of vapors, a thunderhead, has formed over the mountain," Natas said. "They say they're from Asia. Those in here now are from Eastern Europe. There must be thousands more, all waiting to seep through the mountain to get to the blood. We're going to be busy with them for a very long time, protecting the blood, and there are still others on their way from every continent on earth."

"Are you serious about that?"

"I am dead serious."

Natas was about to say more when another explosion collapsed part of the far cliff wall. It fell into a pile of rubble and raised yet more dust."

"Who is trying to blow a hole in the mountain?" Maggie screamed out at Natas, as the debris fell around her and she covered her head to protect herself from the falling rocks. "This is insane!"

"The bats are doing it."

"Cool. This seems like a perfect place for bats," Tommy said. "I like bats."

"You won't like these kinds," Natas said. "These bats are vampires who flew great distances from other parts of the world, Africa and Australia and South America, in that form to arrive here and take the blood. They're competing with the vapors for the blood, but they have to use a different method to break into the mountain. They can't seep through the walls."

"How many of them are there?" Mabin asked.

"As many bats as vapors, maybe more. Great clouds of them have been flying in to Montana all day from all points on the globe."

"I don't like the looks of this," Mabin said. "I don't like the sound of what you're saying to me."

"It doesn't bother me," Tommy said, "although it's kind of creepy having all these things around."

"You will have to earn your resurrection now, both of you," Natas said to Tommy and Mabin. "Now that the word is out about this place, there's no going back to secrecy about it. Every vampire on earth knows about it now."

Tommy grew serious, a look of concern covering his face.

"I have a feeling I screwed up with this again," Tommy said. "I guess I let out word about what's here when I dug up Mabin early."

"We all had a part in this," Maggie said, "but this is happening because of the vampires, not us."

From above, clouds of fine black dust fell as the Outliners continued to corral the vapors and burn them to soot. The Outliners worked quickly, knowing what was at stake, and they worked competently and desperately, floating to surround one vapor after another and setting them alight in a choke hold of flames. It was as though scores of small constellations were encircling the pink and orange clouds of sunset and transforming them to black powder. Just as dozens of the vapors were burned, a dozen more seeped through the ceiling, as Natas predicted. As soon as they seeped through, the Outliners clutched them in their circular fires and eliminated them before they could taste or even catch sight of the blood. So desperate did the situation near the ceiling become that several of the vapors took human form while hovering in the air, just to avoid burning at the hands of the Outliners. Then it was their turn to suffer gravity and plummet downward toward the floor of the cave, screaming and squealing at the prospect of splattering against the rocks there. With sickening thuds, a half-dozen crashed onto the rocks. Many did not die but remained twisted and broken monsters, writhing on the cavern's floor.

Suddenly, another hundred of the Outliners flew down to the fifth level off the ramp in a line and headed directly for the ceiling to destroy the vapors. They trailed clouds of light behind them and further illuminated the twilight of the cavern.

"Wow, more Outliners. How many more of them are there?" Tommy asked.

"Those are some of the newly dead," Natas said, of the reinforcements thrown directly into the battle. "We processed them quickly. I hope they know how to fight."

A new curtain of fine black dust floated down from the ceiling as though in answer to Natas' hopes, as the fresh Outliners flew directly into the battle and eliminated dozens of the pink and orange clouds, as though by instinct. Now the vapors had little choice but to die a horrible death floating in the air or travel back to earth, materialize and deal with the humans decapitating them with sharp stones. As more and more of them seeped out of the cracks in the ceiling, crowding those there into the waiting arms of destruction with which the Outliners mercilessly greeted them, dozens came to the conclusion it was better to seize a fighting chance on earth than die in heaven. Panicked, they descended in columns of pink and orange mist to the cavern floor and transformed into human shapes. Some turned and ran directly for the lake of blood, while others looked around in desperation for a place to hide or die in peace. Several leaped toward Tommy, surrounding him and closing in, but the four of them were no match for the boy and Mabin, who came in swinging and slashing so violently that the vampires' deaths were nearly instantaneous.

"We're doing pretty good, aren't we?" Tommy asked Mabin.

"We're doing a lot better than I thought we might," Mabin answered. "Both of us are a lot stronger than we used to be."

"We can't deal with the human forms," Natas said. "You must go after them. Hurry. Some are approaching the blood. We have orders to fulfill from hundreds of hospitals and wars, and we can't let them steal it before we can ship it out."

Tommy was off again before the words were out of Natas' mouth. He had his two sharpened stone knives clutched in his hands, and he flew with a speed that was nearly too fast for human eyes to see. His stone knives flashed out at the vampires running for the blood, and in their weakened state, they were no match for the angered boy who had come back from the dead with revenge on his mind. One after the other, the vampires lost their heads to his slashing thrusts, and the bodies tumbled down to join their comrades' bodies on the cavern floor. Mabin and Maggie raced through the air to the columns of colors dropping from the ceiling. They timed their slashes to the instant the vampires materialized, catching them as they were half-mist and half-human. It was the best time to slice off heads. One after the other the enfeebled vampires, weakened further by their long travels, fell at their hands before they could take blood and gain strength. Above, the orange and pink vapors continued to die at the hands of the Outliners. The cavern was so filled with their black dust floating down through the air it was as though a sandstorm had blown in with the pitiful creatures who sought blood so futilely. Another hundred of the Outliners entered the fray, flying down to the fifth level from the ramp and heading for the ceiling. Still the pink and orange vapors entered the cavern through the cracks in the ceiling, only to meet their deaths at the hands of the Outliners, their souls to be sent upward to start the purification process as soon as they died. Then as souls they'd return to destroy their own kind as they entered the National Emergency Blood Bank.

"They don't know which is worse for them," Natas said, to Maggie, as she stopped to assess the situation before returning to the slaughter. "Yet they won't stop coming for the blood."

"They are the sickest of the sick, madmen who can't stop lusting for blood, because they know they'll die if they do."

Now the greatest explosion they had yet heard rocked the cavern, and the cliff wall nearest them collapsed, revealing a large mine shaft that had been blasted through the mountain by the bats.

"Oh, no. The mountain has not held," Natas said. "The way in is open and the bats are here. Outliners, after the bats when you can!"

Instead of bats, a dust-covered Humvee crashed into the cavern, nearly flipping over as it sped ahead over the dead bodies of the headless vampires and other debris. It came to a halt suddenly, as though broken down or out of gas, and from its open windows the first bats appeared, huge vampire bats with fangs that could have done in a human easily. With the slaughter of the vaporous vampires going so well above, several of the veteran Outliners saw the dangers below and dove down to confront the new invaders. With flying every bit as expert as the vampire bats showed, the Outliners twisted and pirouetted and slipped their fires over several of the invaders in thin air, and the results were the same for the bats as they had been for the vapors. As soon as an Outliner encircled a vampire bat, it disintegrated into ash and rained down its black dust onto the cavern floor. Seeing what was happening, several of the vampire bats landed and instantly transformed into human shapes. All wore black capes and boots with pointed toes, and had hair slicked back and shining, and their red eyes were larger than those of the vapors. Instead of squealing as bats do, they laughed in a hideous manner, seemingly over nothing. With a hunger derived of their long exodus into Montana for the rumors of an endless supply of food, they flew for the shimmering red lake, got there before anyone could stop them, hovered over the shore and then landed and stooped to drink. Their transformation from weak, white-skinned monsters to powerful, bold creatures was immediate. After several mouthfuls of blood, they stood straight up and screamed out their invincibility at the Outliners, who were murdering their brothers in their expert flames.

"Come for us now and see what happens to you," a large creature with huge hands cried out to the ceiling, raising fists that looked like melons. "We've had our blood now, and your time is through. We can't be stopped."

Having the sense not to challenge a blood-bloated vampire, the Outliners continued their work of burning the vapors and bats they could reach before they transformed to human shapes.

"After they've had blood, I'm afraid these, too, are yours to deal with," Natas said to Mabin. "Our protection extends only so far, and they will be more difficult than any vampires you've faced."

"Just keep the others away," Mabin said, grimly. "If they take blood, they're ours, just as you said. We still might win this."

Tommy did not wait for any encouragement from Natas but immediately shot across the cavern floor toward the vampires that had broken through to the lake and recovered their powers. He did not wait for Mabin and Maggie to fly with him but instead smashed into the legs of three of the four that had imbibed their fill. It was as though their strength never had been. Their feet flew out from under them, they crashed to the floor and slipped across it on the black dust of the dead. Tommy recklessly stopped to appreciate his own work at knocking over the creatures, laughing with the fun of it, but then the standing vampire flashed across the floor and lifted him by the scruff of the neck.

"Well, a little ant," the vampire said. "A very little ant. And I can smell fresh blood in you. Did you drink it or make it yourself? No matter. It's mine now."

The creature opened wide to reveal a monstrously large pair of fangs that were riddled with cavities filled small white worms twisting in them.

"I'm resurrected, and you're disgusting, so you better watch it," Tommy said, slashing out with his stone knives, which could not reach the vampire. "I'm three times stronger than I was."

"A little fighting ant, I see, but still not nearly burly enough, I'm afraid," the vampire said.

With a slap of his hand he knocked Tommy's knives out of his grasp, smashed Tommy on the floor once as though he was a toy and then drew the boy close to him. Tommy's eyes wobbled back in his head, as though he was about to faint. The vampire lifted Tommy's chin slowly, laughing, as the boy partly regained consciousness and struggled to free himself, screaming at the bite to the neck he thought was coming, but then a sudden great wind seemed to decapitate the creature that held him as suddenly as a guillotine. The vampire's head fell from his shoulders just as he was about to sink long fangs into Tommy's neck, with the head seemingly lopped off by a wind. The head fell to the cavern floor but the body remained upright, spewing the fresh blood from the neck that the vampire had just taken from the lake. Behind the vampire Tommy saw Mabin's face where the creature's head had been. With one stroke in mid-flight, Mabin had ended the threat to the boy's life, but with the immense strength the vampire now had from the fresh blood, he was not done fighting as a living monster. His hand still clutched the boy's throat, wringing it so harshly that Tommy gasped from the lack of air.

"Put him down!" Maggie screamed at the creature, as she flew toward him, but that had no effect, just as she knew it wouldn't. She swung the headless vampire around by the shoulder and drove her stone knife into its heart. The vampire's entire body shook in spasms and his hand opened to let Tommy fall to the ground.

Then the creature collapsed in a heap at Maggie's feet.

"Wow. That was a tough one. He didn't go easily," Tommy managed to gasp.

"It's going to take two of us to kill one of them after they've drunk blood," Mabin said. "Don't be so reckless to think you can kill them all alone, Tommy. If we work together, we survive."

"Ah, I had this. He wouldn't have sucked a single drop of blood from me before I bashed his teeth in. I wouldn't have let him get me. I'd have busted him in the mouth and knocked those fangs down his throat."

One of the three vampires Tommy had knocked to the ground jumped up and rushed toward him. Tommy spun away, grabbing his stone knives from the cavern floor as he did so, but the vampire came face-to-face with Mabin, who flashed between him and the boy, but only for a second.

The vampire skid to a halt before him.

"My name is Krispin. We don't care about you," the vampire said. "We only want the lake blood. You can leave in peace if you allow us our food. We came too far to be stopped now."

"No, it's you that will leave, and leave you will," Mabin said, and with two quick swings of his stone knives separated the creature's head from its body. "We will see your soul here very soon."

Behind him, Tommy leaped up and drove his knife into the creature's back, through the heart. The body fell beside the other vampire's headless corpse.

"Is that how to do it with the strong ones?" Tommy asked. "First cut off the head and then stab the heart?"

"You're a fast learner," Mabin said. "But wait for us. Don't rush off after them. Once they drink, they can take any one of us."

"Watch this."

Tommy spun around and leaped on the two other vampires he had knocked over. Swinging both knives at once, he removed the heads but the bodies stood up and swung their arms around, groping sightlessly for the boy. Working in tandem, Mabin and Maggie rushed forward in two straight lines and drove their knives into the headless bodies' hearts.

"You've got to wait for us, Tommy," Maggie pleaded. "Please. You can't simply rush every vampire you see and hope to kill it."

"Just watch me. I could kill them all if I have to. I'm that tough."

The black powder was still falling heavily from above, dusting the three of them with what seemed like volcanic ash. Tommy raised his head to the ceiling to watch the ash fall. He laughed, as though it was winter's first snow, but them there was a loud scream, human scream, from the entrance that had been blasted into the cavern by the vampire bats. The three of them spun around instinctively. Several of the vampire bats had transformed to human shape, and they were dragging two figures across the floor of the cave. The woman screamed again, while the man fought to get to his feet but was pushed down roughly by two of the monsters. The two forms were bound, their hands tied behind their backs, and as soon as the man was roughly pushed to the ground again, several more of the bats took human form and leaped on them, pinning their hands and feet to the ground while they struggled and screamed and kicked out at their tormentors. Two of the vampires, who seemed to be leaders, unbuttoned their capes and allowed them to fall to the ground. With a snarl, they stared down at the two humans on the ground, their eyes glowed bright red, and they flashed out their fangs and dove in for the necks.

"My god! It's Elsa and Stephanovich," Maggie gasped. "They're going to take their blood."

Now Tommy did not have to be told to wait, and he would not have, for Mabin and Maggie immediately shot across the floor, flying low to the ground, as Tommy flashed along behind them, crying.

A second was all they had to save Elsa and Stephanovich from a horrible death.

20

A great chorus of squealing vampire bats filled the air as those outside the mountain realized the way to the blood inside the mountain was open and all they had to do was fly through the mine shaft and the lake of blood would be theirs.

In the second it took to reach Elsa and Stephanovich, Mabin and Maggie and Tommy smashed through a thousand skittering, squealing, blood-maddened creatures flying en masse into the cave. Many of the bats died with the violence of the contact, for nothing was going to get in their way. Above them, as far as they could see, thousands of the vampire bats were flashing through the air, and even below them the bats flew low to the ground, just above the surface. Any airspace they could find they flew through, for it was so crowded now inside the cavern that the air became a near-solid mass of black.

More Outliners, newly purified souls, rushed down the ramp from the fourth level to the fifth level to enter the fight, but their numbers were few in comparison the many bats and vapors now in the cave. However many they killed, another thousand took their places. The air grew foul with the floating black dust of immolated bats and vapors, and the ground was three inches thick with their ash. The ash whirled up around Mabin and Maggie and Tommy in the instant it took to fly across the cavern floor to where the vampires were drinking Elsa and Stephanovich's blood, but their stone knives were ready.

"Get them off their necks first!" Mabin screamed. "Cut off their heads!"

Tommy was so incensed at the vampires that he seemed ready to break into flames at what they had done. He rocketed ahead of Mabin and Maggie. With no hesitation, he slashed off the heads of the two vampires attached at the necks of their parents, but the heads remained stuck with their fangs in the necks, the blood of their victims pumping out of the necks of the vampires as they drank. So great was their lust for blood that the two decapitated vampires barely realized they had been separated from their bodies, and continued to drink. Two other vampires had leeched on to the legs of their victims, and while Mabin and Maggie pulled open the mouths of the vampires on Elsa and Stephanovich's necks to remove them, Tommy cut off the heads of the vampires drinking from the legs. The headless bodies fought with him, but he expertly stabbed their hearts with deep, violent thrusts of his stone knives and sent the bodies falling to the ground, murdering the two of them on his own. Blood gushed from the open wounds on Elsa and Stephanovich's necks and legs, and all Mabin could think to do was scoop handfuls of the black ash up off the floor and cover the wounds with it, forming a paste to slow the loss of blood. Tears flowed out of his eyes as he did so, and they watered down the black, bloody mix he used to stem the flow of blood. Maggie leaned over Elsa when the black-ash paste was set in place, but a heavy weight jumped on her back as another vampire tried for her mother's blood, attempting to push her aside. Mabin slashed off this one's head before it came close to the neck, and Tommy drove his stone blade into the creature's heart. It was dead in place next to their parents that instant. Tommy scanned the perimeter around them shaking with hate and anger, his stone knives clenched tightly in his hands, daring the other vampires to come near.

"Can you breathe?" Maggie asked Elsa. "Can dad breathe, Tommy?"

Elsa gasped, her eyes set on the ceiling in great pain.

"I think I see his chest moving up and down."

"Can you talk, mom?"

Elsa nodded with difficulty.

"I think I can," she whispered hoarsely.

Her eyes were set on the ceiling, while yet more of the vampire bats were entering in a tornado though the tunnel blasted into the mountain. They made a black, swirling, squealing, endless invasion.

"You have to get out of here," Stephanovich gasped, as hoarse as Elsa and writhing in pain.

He coughed, opening the wound in his neck again. Blood dripped out of the corner of his mouth. Mabin covered the neck wound with his hand and pushed the black dust into a paste again.

"We'll fight our way out with you," Tommy said. "We'll drive you out in the Humvee."

"It can't be. Can't ..."

"Can you stand up, mom?"

Elsa's eyes softened, while she continued to stare at the ceiling. Her body relaxed, as though resigned to what fate she knew was coming next.

"Can't stand ... I'm ... finished."

"What? No. Don't say that. No."

"I'm finished. I am. Can't stand."

"We're going to get you out of here. The Outliners will have to take care of the vampires. It's more important we get you out of here."

The bats had nearly filled all the airspace in the cavern, so that they crashed into each other and slammed into the children kneeling over their parents. Tommy brushed them away so violently they each squealed once and then lay still on the floor.

"We ... can't."

"Yes, you can, dad. We'll all leave together. Can you get up?"

"Never."

"What do you mean, never? You have to get up. This is not never."

"Never. Gone. Give me Elsa's hand."

Maggie gently lifted his hand and directed it to Elsa's, where his fingers closed around hers. A weak smile came to his face.

With the way to the lake of blood open, few of the bats or vapors saw any point in remaining in their present forms, and as Elsa and Stephanovich lay dying, the two types of beasts began their transformations into forms that could drink from the riches at the far end of the cave. The vapors dropped in columns of pink and orange through the black dust floating in the air, and the bats dropped down to the floor in a carpet of squirming creatures three feet thick. There simply were not enough Outliners to stop them, although they continued to kill the invaders in their aerial forms. Each of the varieties transformed to human form, crowding the cavern like rush hour on a subway platform but with even more violent intentions. The bats in human form fought with the vapors in human form, tearing at each other with fangs and claws, all in the fight for the fresh blood of the lake. "It's ours!" "No, it's ours!" "Then die if you think it's yours!" "No, you die!" The vampires jammed up against Mabin and Maggie and Tommy as they knelt over their parents crying and had to be knocked back with force. The three of them had to cut out a place to breathe with their stone knives in the crowd, slashing through them and driving the vampires back away from Elsa and Stephanovich, who still lay motionless on the ground holding hands.

"Get out of here! Get away!" Tommy screamed, flashing his knives at anything he could reach, again and again, tears streaming down his face. "Get away from them!"

There were too many to drive off, for there was no space to drive them into. Tommy shot through the air with his weapons cutting off heads and stabbing hearts, but so deeply in lust for the blood were the vampires, fighting among themselves, that they barely noticed when a dozen of their members died at the hands of the humans. They pushed in a mass of salivating monsters toward the blood in the lake while killing each other indifferently but with great violence. Maggie and Mabin also slashed out at the vampires from their knees when they came near, cutting into the mass pushing up against them, cutting off legs and arms and opening huge gashes through the empty stomachs of the monsters. It still made little difference to the vampires, and Maggie and Mabin and Tommy knew they were the only ones who could still feel anything in this underground world. The vampires had little inclination to fight over the blood of the three humans and their dying parents, but they did wish to contest each other for the deep well of blood just across the plain. With a savagery that made human battles appear trite and harmless, they tore into each other with every means possible in the slobbering crowd, with teeth and claws and rocks lifted off the ground. They smashed their enemies' bloodless skulls as they rushed for the lake of blood, all the while ignoring Mabin and Maggie and Tommy in their hurry to get to the lake first. With a kind of natural order taking over, the vapors congregated to the right and the bats to the left, and between the two masses vampire killing vampire continued as the ranks rushed each other.

"Will they be all right?"

Natas had flown over to inquire about the state of Elsa and Stephanovich, but as soon as he saw them, he knew the answer to his question. His lights dimmed.

"We have to get them out of here," Maggie said. "We can't save them inside the cavern, we have to get them out and to the hospital."

"Do what you must for them. All is lost in here," Natas said. "We can't do anything more now that they've taken human form and reached the lake. You must go. If they all drink, nothing can stop them. Many are drinking already. The world is not ready for what will happen once they've been unleashed with full bellies of blood."

"We'll deal with that later," Maggie said. "Thank you for what you've done for us."

"I could do nothing less."

"Let's get them in the truck and drive out of here," Mabin said.

"No!" Stephanovich screamed out forcefully. "No! Never!"

In his weakened condition, it shocked them to hear such a powerful objection. He shook with the pain his scream caused him, as they knelt beside him, confused by his objections.

"But we have to get out of here," Maggie explained. "It's our only chance to save you."

"You ... must go ..." Stephanovich said in a whisper, again so weak that he could barely hold open his eyes.

"Pick him up under the arms," Maggie said to Mabin. "I'll get his feet."

"No!" Stephanovich screamed again, once again with great power. "You must leave me here to die with the vampires."

"We die with them," Elsa chimed in, with a whisper that was barely audible. "When they die, we die."

"No. We're getting you both out of here," Maggie said. "Don't even think of staying behind. You couldn't possibly kill them in your present state."

"Yes we can."

"The truck is rigged."

Stephanovich said this in such a weak whisper that they barely heard him, but they understood at once what he was saying. The explosions that had torn apart the caverns educated them as to what he meant. This world would end with a demolition.

"Then we can't drive them out, if what he says is true," Mabin said, standing up and slashing out at two vampires that came near. "The truck will explode if we do. We'll stay and fight. That's the only way now."

"I'll stay and fight," Tommy said, with tears streaming down his cheeks. "I'll fight them all. I'll kill them all, after what they did to my parents, and we'll all die when they do."

Tommy choked up, and Stephanovich gasped and lifted his head to try to speak to his stepson, but he was too weak and his head fell down to the ground.

"What is it?" Maggie asked. "What are you trying to tell us?"

"The Humvee ... the C4 is packed in the wheel wells ... the vampires didn't know it was there ... I set a timer ..."

A smile crossed his lips.

"The damn fools ... They're all going to die."

"How much longer do we have?" Mabin asked immediately.

Too weak to talk, Stephanovich held up one finger.

"An hour? Do we have an hour?" Maggie asked.

Stephanovich held up one finger again.

"One ... minute," he gasped.

The chaos in the cavern had grown in volume as the two vampire nations pressed closer to the blood and became more and more incensed that they couldn't get to it without murdering their rivals. There was an immense cacophony of squeals as the vampires died, and instead of drinking much of the mass pushed into the lake, only to be swamped and submerged by other vampires rushing into the blood. Vampire tripped over vampire and stumbled and fell into a chaotic tumbling of bloody fools immersed in pure blood.

"What did Stephanovich say?" Mabin yelled out, over the noise of the vampires' deaths.

"We have one minute before the Humvee blows up."

Without hesitation, Mabin took Elsa in his arms and lifted her off the floor, rising over them with her.

"Maggie, get Stephanovich. Tommy, you fly behind us in case any of the vampires figure out what's going on and try to escape. Natas, can you come with us?"

"None of us would last very long on the outside. We are not of that world, and must stay here. We can only visit your world. We will survive, I believe. I will take all of the Outliners to the top of the mountain and wait inside for the explosion. This is our home."

With a nod Mabin said good-bye and Natas shot off toward the ceiling, where he rounded up the Outliners. Hundreds of them flew desperately toward the exit to the fourth level.

Mabin shot off toward the light in the mine shaft, Elsa in his arms. Maggie picked up her father as tenderly as she could, and then she immediately rose a few feet off the ground and shot along behind Mabin and her mother. Just as she was about to enter the mouth of the tunnel, she saw two vampires turn around and watch her go. She could not hesitate. There was no time.

"Are we going to make it?" Tommy screamed at her, as he flew beside her.

"I don't know. Is anybody following us?"

"Shit!"

"What?"

"There are two of them. I think one of them is that Harkin Davis."

"I knew it. I saw them looking at us as we left. They figured it out."

"They're twenty feet behind us. I'll go back and take care of them."

"No, there's no time. No! We could be crushed inside this mine shaft when the bomb goes off."

Tommy looked behind as he flew, but saw that the vampires were not gaining on them, and seemed too wary to approach too closely to them. The mine shaft stretched on and on before them, with only the scant light from the entrance providing any beacon of hope that they would make it out in time. Then there was a flash of light behind them as the Humvee blew up in a tremendous explosion. A massive rush of wind overtook them, pushing them faster and faster toward the entrance, but behind the wind the dust and the smoke and the flames rushed to catch up to them. Maggie heard the two vampires behind them screaming as the results of the explosion caught them in the violence of the event, and Stephanovich muttered to himself his memory of what the Transylvanian Mysteries had told them to do: "Kill them all. All ... of them."

"You're going to be all right," Maggie whispered to Stephanovich as she carried him in her arms toward the light at the end of the tunnel.

He was limp in her arms, his head drooping down to the side, and he did not respond, other than to repeat: "Kill them all."

The rush of wind from the blast threw her up against the wall of the mine shaft, and she nearly tumbled over and Stephanovich almost fell from her arms. She gathered him up again, and flew on as quickly as she could. Dust and debris was tumbling around her. Small sharp rocks pelted her and cut into her flesh, and she gasped for air to breathe.

Then she was out.

Mabin had flown a hundred feet ahead and had gently laid Elsa down on the ground. Maggie flew off to the side to avoid the blast from the explosion that still belched from the mine, but then she flew next to Mabin and lay Stephanovich down next to his wife.

"Is she breathing?" she asked.

"No."

"Is he?"

"No."

Maggie let out a wail as she looked to the sky. Tears were falling from Mabin's eyes. Maggie collapsed on the ground, her arms draped over both Elsa and Stephanovich, and she wept.

"Is there nothing we can do?" she asked.

"I have no ideas. I didn't know things would turn out like this if I came back."

"You didn't cause this. We must be able to do something. We brought you back. We have to be able to bring both of them back."

As soon as the words were out of her mouth, she was aware of two sets of boots standing over her. She looked up to see the leering faces of the two vampires that had flown out of the caverns behind them.

"Mr. Davis, it appears there is only the blood of these two left for us."

"Yes, Williams. I see no alternative now that the lake is gone. Feast on them or die. The two adults I believe are empty."

"Then let's make our feast of them. Do you want the boy or the girl?"

"The girl looks delicious. I'll take her."

"Selfish of you."

One final great scream filled the forest as both the vampires were knocked to the ground. It was as though the mountain had fallen directly on top of them. Tommy lashed out at them as he screamed from the air above and behind them, and he cut through their necks to drop them to the earth and their deaths.

"This is what you've done to them! Harkin Davis! I cut your lawn!" he yelled. "Look at it! Look what you've done! This is what you always do, and then this is what we always do to you in return. Why are you always so stupid?"

The boy was on top of the vampires instantly, finishing the work of cutting off their heads. They still struggled, but not for long as Tommy drove his stone knives down into their chests again and again and again as he sobbed.

"This and this and this and this, Mr. Davis!" he screamed, so incensed that he did not care that the vampires had ceased moving. He pounded his knives into them, time and time again. "And this! And more! And this! And this!"

When he had sliced the vampires to bits he dropped his weapons and turned to the bodies of Elsa and Stephanovich.

"They can rest in peace now," he said, looking at Maggie with soft, tearful eyes. "It's the only peace they'll ever find in this world, with creatures like those two around."

Tommy tenderly kissed Elsa on the cheek, and then Stephanovich. He draped his arms over them, and cried.

The last sounds of the explosion died away, but its filthy dust still filled the air.

21

Their world was in ruins.

As the dark dawn turned to morning, they saw that nothing remained of the town of Victor but burned-out buildings. Behind them, St. Mary's mountain had collapsed to a smoldering heap half its original size, its trees tumbled down and broken like sticks. The vampires inside were dead, but so was human life, save their own lives, over the entire area.

And worst of all, Elsa and Stephanovich lay still at their feet, having passed away on the flight out of the mountain.

Tommy and Maggie and Mabin huddled together in the sunrise, and as the bright light strengthened and warmed the forest, their crying ceased and they relaxed into numbness. They stared down at their parents' bodies with minds made blank by suffering, and not one thought ran through the three of them. They were numbed by what had happened. Occasionally, a tremor shook Maggie to her bones, and Mabin held her closer and tighter to ease her anxiety.

"At least you and Tommy survived," she said, looking up at him. "At least you and Tommy came back from the dead."

"Only because you willed it. I couldn't have come back without you. You gave us both life."

"The mountain helped. Its magic helped. Now look at the mountain."

"Do you think they're all dead inside it?"

"They must be, or all of this would have been for nothing. No one could be crushed like that and survive, no matter how much blood they drank. And if they are still alive, crushed by all that debris, I hope they're suffering."

"It looks as though all the faults in the mountain are sealed. No one can get in or out. The blood is secure, at least. Elsa and Stephanovich would have been pleased with that, at least."

Maggie's beautiful gray eyes welled again with tears at the mention of her parents.

"What should we do with their ..."

"Take them home. They'd want to be at home. They felt most comfortable at home."

"All right. We'll take them home for a little while. We'll let them rest there."

"What do you think the world looks like to them now?"

"Empty. Bright. Safe. Lonely."

"Me, too, it looks that way to me. And you look like the best thing I've ever seen. Thank you for bringing me back here."

Maggie pulled Mabin's head down and kissed him on the lips, and then she buried her head in his chest. He stroked her auburn hair, the hair he dreamed of touching while in the grave.

He backed away from her.

"We should take them home now."

Mabin gently lifted Elsa's limp body off the ground, and Maggie took her father in her arms to begin the journey down the mountain. With Tommy walking in bitter silence behind them, they kept their eyes up and pointed straight ahead, navigating their way through the rocks and between the trees by feel. Never had they been so close to Elsa and Stephanovich, and never so far away as death took them.

"My god," Mabin said, when he broke through the edge of the forest near their home.

"What is it?"

"It's nothing. I see nothing here. I never thought we'd lose our house, our home, Elsa and Stephanovich's home. I thought I had a place to come back to. There is nothing at all left here."

When Maggie broke through the line of trees marking the edge of the forest, she saw what Mabin was talking about. She scanned the area while holding her father in her arms. Their development was as Elsa and Stephanovich had left it, nothing but a burned-out disaster of leveled homes and parched lawns. Their own home, or rather what had been their home, was now a blast crater with remains of the building scattered across the landscape. Pieces of furniture and items from the house, burned and broken, littered the charred lawns around it. Everything that had been inside the house was now outside it.

"What have we come back to?" Mabin asked. "It's nothing. There's nothing left."

"It is ... nothing. What are we going to do? How are we going to live with nothing?"

"Ah, don't sweat it. We'll rebuild," Tommy said, and there was a savage cutting edge to his voice. "At least we're alive and can do things. They're dead. Maybe you two should worry about that for a minute, instead of yourselves."

Both Maggie and Mabin were stunned into silence at the bitterness of Tommy's attack on them.

"We'll take care of them as best we can," Mabin said gently. "It's hard knowing what to do after all this, that's all. We weren't complaining about being alive."

"I've been through as bad as you," Tommy shouted out. "I don't know what to do, either, but I'm not going to let that stop me. We'll do everything we're supposed to do to survive. That's what they would have wanted."

"And what do you think that should be?" Maggie asked, an edge to her voice. "How are we supposed to live now?"

"Why don't you ask those things? Those things always have the answer, don't they? Ask them."

For a moment, Mabin and Maggie grew only more confused as Tommy pointed to Elsa and Stephanovich's bodies. It seemed so harsh of him to say such a thing. He was calling his own parents "those things," as if they were nothing now that they were dead. The tears came to Maggie's eyes at the cruelty Tommy seemed to show toward Elsa and Stephanovich, but then Mabin stepped toward Stephanovich's body and pulled the Transylvanian Mysteries from his back pocket. Maggie suddenly understood that's what Tommy meant by "those things." Mabin opened the folded sheets of ancient parchment and stared down at them.

"They're in English," he said.

"I never heard of that," Maggie said. "Stephanovich always had to translate them before."

"What do they say?" Tommy asked. "Spit it out. Don't just stand there."

"They say, 'The grave is open.'"

"The grave is open? What does that mean?" Tommy asked. "It's English but it doesn't tell us much about what to do."

"Maybe it does," Mabin said. "I think it definitely does."

"Oh, yeah? How is that stupid phrase supposed to help? How is them telling us that there is an open grave supposed to help?"

"Maybe it's my grave."

It took just a second for the instructions offered up by the Transylvanian Mysteries to sink in for Tommy. Maggie gave out a little cry immediately and covered her mouth with her hand, but Tommy took a second before his eyes widened and he said, "Oh. That."

"We're to bury them in Mabin's grave," Maggie said. "It's the only logical thing. That's what they're telling us."

"Wait. Why does that make sense?" Tommy asked, still not wanting to believe what the mysteries told them to do. "We can't bury them. Let's keep them, for just a little while. I don't want to see them go yet."

"We can't, Tommy," Mabin said. "We have to do what the mysteries instruct us to do."

"It might make sense because the mountain might not have lost its powers completely. If you lived through the purification, and if Mabin lived through the purification, maybe Elsa and Stephanovich can, too," Maggie said. "That's what the mysteries are saying."

"Seriously?"

"What else can they mean?"

"Seriously?"

Tommy's face screwed up with thought for just a second, not believing what he was hearing, but then he broke out into a huge, bright smile.

"Well, yeah, maybe that's right," he said, talking very fast. "Maybe if we came down through the mountain after we were so ruined by the vampires and came out all right in one piece, maybe they can, too. It was hell in the mountain, but I'm all right now, and Mabin's all right, and you're all right, Maggie, so maybe in a year they can be, too. It could happen."

"There is a problem," Maggie said.

"What is that? What could go wrong now?" Tommy asked.

"They have no blood. I gave the blood from my heart to Mabin's heart, Stephanovich injected my blood into Mabin's heart because I loved him, but how do Stephanovich and Elsa exchange the blood from their hearts when the vampires have taken it?"

"We'll just use my blood," Tommy said. "I don't care, if it would help them I'd do it."

"Would that work? How? Look at the mysteries. See if they're saying anything."

Mabin gave a quick look down at the ancient parchment, and screwed up his face as though he could not understand what it was telling them to do now.

"It says, 'Use your powers.'"

"What powers? Which one?" Maggie asked, in frustration. "Where do we find a syringe in all this mess? Everything's scattered all over the place. How do we make the blood exchange when they have no blood?"

"I don't know. It simply says 'Use your powers.'"

"Then let's go."

Maggie seemed desperate when she suddenly lifted Elsa's body and rose off the ground, her destination obvious. Mabin did not hesitate to do as she did, lifting Stephanovich's body off the ground and rising in the air.

"I remember where I was," Mabin said. "It's something I'll never forget. Come on. The sooner we get them to the grave, the sooner they can live again."

Flight fueled by exhilaration is the greatest flight, and now they rose in their greatest flight yet, for they were using their powers as the Transylvanian Mysteries said they were to use them – to save someone. They rose high over the trees and shot directly up the damaged slope toward the grave where Mabin had spent a year of this death. Now that his death was no more, he could help those who had helped him. He could repay his debt in full. The spot where he had lain in the earth was too familiar to him, and it was painful to see it again, but it was also joyful to see it again, for now that spot had a good purpose.

Maggie saw the conflict between his pain and his purpose as soon as they landed. He was staring down at the grave.

"It's open," he said. "Just as the mysteries said it was, it's open."

Maggie saw it was true. The grave was open. She knew why it was open and what to do about it and she knew what that grave could do for them. She gently rose to hover over it, and then leaned down and deposited her mother in it. Without hesitation, Mabin laid down Stephanovich beside his wife in the open earth.

They climbed out of the open pit to stand beside it solemnly.

"Where's Tommy?" Maggie asked, after a moment.

"I don't know. I thought he was behind us."

"We should wait for him before we say something and close the grave."

They did not have to wait for long, for as soon as they looked up to see if he was nearby, he came crashing down out of the sky so quickly it nearly knocked them backwards in a rush of wind. He did not land beside them but shot directly into the grave, seemingly on top of his parents' bodies. He bellowed out a scream so loudly they thought he had gone mad. It sounded like the scream of an immense beast with a wound to the heart, and then they saw it was a wound to the heart. Tommy had plunged a huge syringe into his own heart and was pulling out the plunger to draw blood from it, blood intended for his parents. Maggie gasped at what her brother was doing. When the syringe was full, Tommy pulled it out with another scream of immense pain and black anger. Quickly, he plunged the needle first into Elsa heart, where he emptied half of the blood he had taken from his own heart, and then he withdrew the needle and plunged it into Stephanovich's heart, where he emptied what remained in the syringe.

Tommy collapsed in the grave.

Mabin jumped down quickly to pull him out, but it was barely necessary. The boy was awake when Mabin brought him up to stand next to Maggie, but there was a great hurt, along with endless determination, on his face.

"What did you do?" Maggie asked him. "What did you do, boy?"

"What I had to do," he yelled. "Now say the words! Say the words!"

"What words?"

"The words to close the grave. Say them. You have them in your hands."

As if physically forcing them to do what he commanded, Tommy pulled the Transylvanian Mysteries from Mabin's hands and shoved them into Maggie's hands. Then he forced Mabin's hands on top of hers, and yelled it again.

"Say the words!"

Maggie looked down at the mysteries and intoned the words now writing themselves across their surface, "With this end is also a beginning. When two are finished with death and look to live again, those two begin to put an end to the suffering of others. With these words, I am yours and you are mine, forever."

"Now you say the words!" Tommy screamed at Mabin, furiously, his face red and angry.

Mabin took the Transylvanian Mysteries from Maggie's hands and spoke as Tommy commanded.

"Two are gone and two come together, forever and at once. With these words, I am yours and you are mine, forever."

"Good. Now was that so hard? You two are married now."

Speechless, Maggie stared into Mabin's eyes, and he laughed. She returned the laughter to him, as she returned his love, and they kissed.

"Elsa and Stephanovich always wanted to see you two married," Tommy said. "They told me so. Now they've seen it. Now they can rest in peace."

When Maggie and Mabin opened their eyes, they caught one last glimpse of their parents below as the ground closed slowly over them, sending them on their long journey back to life. Both broke out sobbing, and shook, and laughed, and fell to their knees in joy.

Just ahead of them, in the shadows of the tall, dark pines, a broken circle of tiny lights ignited, hovered in the air, and burned for a second for them to see.

Then it flickered out.

THE END

Next is ...
The Haunting of Vampire Valley

1

Maggie awoke sitting with her back against a pine tree, the warm sun on her face. She had never slept sitting up, but felt as calm and rested as any morning of her life after a long night's rest. What was strange was that she was alone in the forest, after just getting married. She expected her husband to be by her side, but Mabin was not, and her brother Tommy was no where to be found. The woods were quiet and empty, with sunlight falling in wide white beams between the tall trees. If a pine cone had fallen to the ground at the top of the mountain, she would have heard it here near the bottom. She had no idea where anyone she loved was and called out with faint trepidation.

"Mabin? Hello? Tommy? Are you asleep, too?"

Not even a bird answered. The sun beams continued to stream down around her and flies buzzed in senseless pirouettes in the uninterrupted columns of light.

"Hello?"

Buzzing loudly with joy, a fly landed on her nose, and she laughed and swiped at it playfully to drive it away.

"Mabin? Hello? Tommy? I guess you're not here. Is anyone here?"

Mabin couldn't be far away, as she knew he loved her and she loved him and it is not usual for two people with such feelings for each other to be separated for long. He would be by her side again soon, as surely as sunlight would always find the earth, and the earth would always open its arms to the sunlight's warmth.

She got up and brushed herself off, which was quite a chore. The pine needles stuck to her back and legs as though she had been lying on top of them. Most of them came off easily, but the rest of the forest seemed intent on remaining somewhere on her person. Her shoeless and sockless feet had picked up the soil from the forest floor, while the recent fires that destroyed the town the Victor had smudged her face and arms. She was perhaps the least pristine bride ever. Even her long auburn hair was tangled and knotted, with twigs and debris clinging to it as though she was a mop that had been used to clean the forest. She and Mabin and Tommy had cleaned up this part of the forest, driving out those who would destroy them, but now that their enemies were gone, it was a little too quiet, even for her.

She knew Mabin would find her, but she got up, thinking she should find him first, and surprise him. She was anxious to see him, and pining for him, but happy and fulfilled now that they had finally been married and could begin their life together. She had lost her parents, but she had reclaimed her husband and brother from death.

"You must be at home," Maggie said out loud to herself. "I guess we don't have a real home anymore, but you must be where it once was. I remember you saying that's where I would find you if we were separated. I'll meet you there."

It was a short walk down the mountain to the burned-out house where she had lived with Elsa and Stephanovich and Tommy, and where she had met Mabin. Almost nothing remained of it. Sudden small gusts of wind lifted the ash into the air and twisted it into whippoorwills and quickly settled down and spread across the earth again. The view across the valley was open, as it must have been hundreds of years ago, for the town had burned to the ground, all of it, and the valley was returning to its pristine state, as nature had made it so long ago. She took in the view for a long time and then spun around slowly to search the valley along its entire length and then take in the view of the mountain above. Everything was as it had been long ago, with nature taking over what had been built over it.

"Did you just wake up?"

Maggie stopped and stood stock-still, closing her eyes after hearing the voice she longed to hear. Mabin was behind her, and she had no idea of how he had snuck up on her while she was scanning the area for him.

"I didn't see you there," she said, before turning around.

"I was watching you sleep," he said. "You were so quiet when you slept I thought you might have been sleeping for a hundred years."

Now she let herself turn around and embrace him, without another word.

"I couldn't sleep that long without wanting to wake up and see you," she said, finally. "I wouldn't want to sleep that long."

He said nothing but held her close to him, his breathing in her ear, her head on his shoulder.

"Is Tommy here?" she asked.

"He's right beside us," Mabin said, sounding surprised. "We both were watching you sleep."

When she opened her eyes, she saw they were as marked by the forest and their recent fights as she was. She hadn't seen either one of them when she spun in a circle looking for them.

"Hey, Maggie, you sleep too much," Tommy said to her, with his crooked grin. "We've got things to do, so I hope you're awake."

Caked blood smeared their faces. Their clothes were in tatters and their shoes and socks had been torn off their feet during the battle. Still, Mabin could not stop staring at his new wife lovingly, since she had never looked so beautiful, with her innocent gray eyes as wide as a cat's and her long waving auburn hair lifted by the breeze, despite all the debris it carried. She was the one who had brought him back from the dead, and risked everything to do it, but it had cost her dearly. It had cost all of them dearly, and left these marks on them. Now they found their town wasted and destroyed, every last building burned and everyone killed. Tommy had performed the ceremony marrying Maggie and Mabin at Elsa and Stephanovich's grave after all that, and then as a honeymoon they sat near the base of St. Mary's mountain in the bright summer sunshine weeping. They were homeless and alone, blinking in the sunlight. That must have been when Maggie fell asleep.

Mabin reached out and took Maggie's hand. He kissed it but was still silent.

"So what do we do now?" Maggie asked, staring into his eyes.

Mabin could not answer as she stared into his eyes, and he seemed too confused to speak. He always had answers for her, and she wished he would come up with them now, and not be so quiet.

"Look at it this way," Tommy quickly said, nervously drawing together mounds of pine needles with his bare feet. "We've got all the time in the world now. It's only three-hundred-and-sixty-five days until we resurrect mom and dad, and by then we should have everything back to the way it was. I'm going to count every day to make sure I don't mess up again and bring them back to life too soon."

"Maggie?" Mabin asked, finally able to talk.

She was staring at the pine needles by Tommy's feet, mute and unresponsive.

"Yes?"

"Are you all right? You were sleeping for a long time and now you're staring at the ground. Did you hear what Tommy said? Only – "

"I heard, I heard."

"We have a lot to do."

"I just miss mom and dad," Maggie burst out. "All of a sudden, I can't stop thinking about them, and how we were trapped with – "

"Oh, leave her alone!" Tommy yelled at Mabin, flaring up and pushing his shoulder. "She's been crying and sleeping for too long and that's why her eyes have that look in them. Just leave her alone. She's not happy about all the bad things that happened to us, and she knows what I said anyway. I promised I'm going to be there to resurrect mom and dad in a year, and I'm going to keep that promise, no matter what."

While still staring at the ground, a small strange smile came to Maggie's face. She still seemed to be elsewhere, and she could barely remember what she had been thinking a minute ago.

"It's all right, Tommy. I guess all of us have to learn how to live again."

Tommy and Mabin had been brought back to life with Maggie's help after dying at the vampires' hands, but in the real world every house and business in Victor had been burned to the ground by Elsa and Stephanovich in retribution for killing their children. There was very little for them to come back to, not even memories, and they clung together, never getting out of sight of one another, back to for safety's sake. Stunned, the three remaining vampire killers could do little but unconsciously sift silently through the ash and rubble, looking for something that could sustain life without knowing that's what they were doing. The light summer wind did nothing to lift their leaden spirits.

Only the love Maggie and Mabin felt for each other allowed them to feel anything at all.

Mabin raised his eyes to the mountain above.

"The trees are left," he said, weakly, avoiding any discussion of what had just transpired, while holding Maggie's hand. "They haven't burned. As long as there are trees, the Native Americans said life would go on. It will go on for us. I promise you that, and I love you."

It sounded strange for him to say that, and there was a silence until Tommy laughed and spoke up.

"Cool. The trees are still her. Cool. We'll live in tree houses for a year," he said. "I never really liked my room in that house of ours anyway. A tree house will be better."

Mabin turned to him with a smile.

"That's not what I had in mind," he responded. "As long as there are trees, there is life."

He raised his eyes to the top level of the forest as though staring at the sky and he was strangely silent again.

"Mabin?"

"There are lots of lodge pole pines," he said suddenly, "and lodge pole pines have always been used to build log cabins. I was thinking the first thing we need to do is build a cabin."

Maggie stared off into the sky as Mabin did, hoping to see what he did, but for much longer than he did.

"So that's still cool," Tommy said to break the silence. "We'll cut down trees and build a log cabin and live in that. That's real cool. I always wanted to live in a log cabin. Now I know why we resurrected you, Mabin. You always know what to do."

Maggie still stared into the sky, feeling disconnected from it all, and they waited until she broke off the gaze and looked into Mabin's eyes and smiled.

"So ..." Mabin said.

Maggie cocked her head to the side and stared into his eyes.

"Let's get to work," Tommy said, and turned away.

The ash of the burned vampires was everywhere. It lay scattered across the ground in a black coating and it coalesced in piles behind rocks away from the wind. Tommy kicked at it as he walked, dragging his feet through it as though playing with it. As soon as a strong breeze kicked up, what remained underneath the ash was exposed. Any whiff of it would gag them, and send them into fits of coughing.

"They're all dead now," Tommy said. "Good. I hope they rot, the bastards. We've got stuff to do."

Without another word to each other, they lowered their eyes to ground and searched for something, anything, that could help them to rebuild their world. They found nothing useful in the first hours of sifting through the burned debris in silence, nothing that could help them survive. They kicked much of the debris and ash aside, only to find twisted spoons or unburned fragments of fabric or the insides of fried computers. The wind always swirled up again and buried those items once more in the vampire ash but exposed others. Even the asphalt of the streets was transformed by fire, changed to black waves between the undisturbed concrete curbs. Elsa and Stephanovich had been thorough in their killing.

It wasn't until Tommy playfully jumped onto a large pile of ash that they discovered anything useful.

"Hey, Maggie! Mabin! Hey! Look at this! Remember when we used to jump into piles of leaves back east? I'm going to get up and jump into this pile of ashes again. Come of with me! It'll be fun!"

"Tommy, I don't know if you – "

It was too late. Tommy, still covered by soot from his first leap into the ashes, flew through the air, hovered over the four-foot pile of smoking debris and then dove down head-first into it.

He immediately screamed out in pain.

"Hey! Crap! What the hell was that?" he asked, flying up out of it with a bump on his head.

"I told you not to – "

"Wait a minute. I see something," Mabin broke in, flying quickly toward the disturbed pile of burned debris. "I saw something glinting in there."

Mabin bent down and dug desperately and soon picked out a blackened chunk of metal and held it aloft for Maggie to see.

"What is it?"

"It still has its edge. It's an axe head."

Choking on the stench of the ruins, he brushed off the implement and stared at it for a few seconds.

"Hey, what about my head? Is that what I hit it on?" Tommy asked.

He broke into a coughing fit after his foolish leaps into what remained of their enemies.

"That or some other piece of metal. I see more things. These vampires must have burned inside a tool shed."

Mabin tossed the axe head aside and dug with care into the black pile with bare hands. Tommy, thinking better of diving in head-first again, returned to the pile of remains and buried his hands into it, searching for useful things.

"Ow!"

He quickly withdrew his hands and shook one of them as it bled.

"What happened?"

"Something bit me."

"Something bit you?"

"Yeah, look at that. A thing bit me." Tommy held up his hand, which had a cut at the base of the thumb and was leaking blood that mixed with the black ash to form a thick paste.

"It doesn't look like a bite to me but a cut," Maggie said. "Let me see it."

"No! I'm telling you, something in there bit me, and I'm not going to let it get away with it. One of those stinking things is still alive in there."

Before Mabin or Maggie could respond, Tommy picked up a thick black branch from a downed tree and clubbed the pile of ash with it. The ash flew up and twisted in the wind, forming whippoorwills that escaped into the forest. Angry, Tommy swung out again at the ash pile that bit him and this time hit something. The branch came to abrupt halt, jarring Tommy throughout his entire body.

"Ha! Got you!"

The boy pulled out the blackened branch from the pile and with it came something that did have teeth, a five-foot metal two-man saw blade with its handles burned off at both ends. The teeth of the saw were stuck into the branch Tommy wielded in the attempt to kill whatever had bitten him. Suddenly, from deep in the forest a hideous cackling of some strange bird broke out and echoed among the trees. Mabin and Maggie and Tommy froze, remembering all-too-well what had happened in that forest beneath the mountain, their many battles, but the cackling dissipated quickly, as though it never existed. Mabin's shoulders slumped in relaxation, but he stared off into the woods with concern weighing down his brow.

"It couldn't have been them," Maggie whispered, unsure if she believed her own words. "They're all dead and buried under the mountain. It couldn't, it couldn't have been them."

"You're right. They're all dead. We don't have to worry anymore."

Tommy scrunched up his nose and stared into the forest.

"Maybe they're not dead," he said. "That sound made it seem like they're not dead. It sounded like a bunch of them."

"If a mountain falls on you, you're dead," Mabin said. "Although ..."

"What?"

"Nothing. They're all gone, and thank goodness. They have to be. We can get to work now that we have some tools. Come on. We'll fashion handles for the axe and the two-man saw and then we'll start cutting down lodge pole pines. We'll build a small, three-room cabin at first, just for shelter, and then we'll build a bigger house after we move into the cabin."

There was nothing to do but agree and get to work rebuilding, since everything had been destroyed and they needed shelter to live. They found an eight-inch knife deep inside the pile of ashes with its rawhide-wrapped handle still intact. Its edge was razor-sharp, and once they had cleaned the blade it was as bright and shiny as a new knife hanging in the store. This was not a new knife, but salvage, but it was of great value and great use to them. Mabin found some low branches on the nearby trees at appeared the right size, cut them down and quickly fashioned handles for the axe and two-man saw. Out of desperation, knowing what it would be like to sleep outside in the elements, they did not hesitate to go to work at once felling trees for their new shelter. Maggie and Tommy manned the two ends of the saw, and after they dropped their first tree, Mabin went to work with the axe stripping off its bark and hacking off its branches. By the time he had finished work on the first log, smoothing it and shaping it, Maggie and Tommy had felled three more, and he worked furiously to strip and smooth those logs in order to catch up.

"They can't find us inside a cabin, they can't find us," Tommy was muttering to himself, but Maggie heard him.

"Look at us, look how ridiculous we look," she said, only half in jest, as she glanced first at Mabin and then at Tommy. She was gasping for breath, and her face was blacked by the vampire soot flying through the air and her soft hands were cut and bleeding.

Both Mabin and Tommy mirrored her condition.

"What do you think we should look like after all we've been through? And I'm hungry," Tommy said. "I don't care, I know there's nothing to eat, but I'm worried about how we're going to live now."

"We'll find a way. We'll live like the first settlers here. There are fish in the streams and mushroom and berries growing everywhere," Mabin said. "The supermarket burned, but I'll bet there're some canned goods in the rubble. We have to shelter ourselves first, or at least begin the cabin, and then we'll eat something, whatever we can find or forage or catch."

Mabin attacked the log at his feet as though making an example of what had to be done to survive. He did not look up, and soon Maggie and Tommy were working the two-man saw again, cutting through a large tree that would be good for a base log for one of the walls of their cabin. They cut as though in anger and pain over the loss of Stephanovich and Elsa, as though working hard would pacify the agony of their deaths. They had cut and stripped sixteen trees before they used their powers to lift the logs into the air on their shoulders and fly to where their burned-out home had been. Without discussing it, that was where they decided their cabin should be, where their old home had been. By drawing a perfect circle on the ground with two stick attached by a string to make an improvised compass, Mabin determined where the northern corner would be. He bisected the circle once and then cut down the center of that line to form the northern corner. He drew a line twenty feet in one direction following the line he had started inside the circle, planted his improvised compass in the ground and drew a circle and cut through it twice to draw there the second corner would be. Then he drew the other two corners in the same way on the ground and had a perfect square on which to lay down the first base logs. They determined which logs would work as the bottom logs, and while Mabin flattened all four logs on opposite sides with the axe, Maggie and Tommy went back to the forest and gathered up the remaining logs and returned with them to what would be their new home, a new safe place.

Mabin had set the four base logs in a rectangle by the time they returned.

"It's a beginning," he said. "Let's find something to eat, and then we'll continue building. They didn't kill us. We're not dead yet, and once we have shelter we'll be all right. Then we can start living again."

They headed for the burned-out town.

2

The great difficulty and effort put into their work was not commensurate with the results of it. By dark, they had raised their walls to the height of just three logs on two sides and four logs on the other two sides, but they had logs stripped and piled in the ashes all over the ground ready for placement. The sunlight intensified all day, with the sky above a blue dome holding in all their pain and frustration at having to create a new life for themselves after the last one had been destroyed. Finally the sun dipped below the mountains and brought on twilight. All they would have to do when the sun rose again the next day would be fit and set the logs to form the walls of their new home, but first they would have to get through the night sleeping on the ground without completed walls around them or roof above them. While silent, each of them thought the same thought as darkness threatened, and they remembered the same things: that just under their feet were tens of thousands of vampires that had been crushed in that underground of death after Elsa and Stephanovich rigged the Hummer with explosives and brought the mountain down on top of them while they feasted on the lake of subterranean blood. With still enough light clutching to the earth so that they could complete their next task, they hurriedly collected soft boughs of pine and lay down a bed of them on what would be the floor of their new home. The found forked branches and pushed their sharpened ends into the earth at the foot of the boughs and then stripped other straight branches and laid one end into the forks and let the other end touch the ground, forming a roof over the soft pine boughs that would be their bed. Then they collected scattered branches that had been stripped off the logs that would form their home and laid them on top of the lean-to, which smelled so sweetly of pine as the dark came on that each of them rushed to crawl into bed and escape the anguish of the dark and all it might threaten, as normal children rush into bed to escape goblins. Exhausted from their labors and everything they had endured with the deaths of their parents and the long combat with vampires, they huddled together as each wept silently and bitterly until sleep finally took them. There would be no bliss for Maggie and Mabin on that the dark first night of marriage.

It was what Maggie saw a short time after falling asleep huddled in Mabin's strong but tender embrace that made her not quite sure Tommy had been resurrected as a human being.

A glowing light awakened her, as though a pretty yellow candle was held before her closed eyes. It was a very pleasant glow, but then a sudden thought flared up in her troubled mind: the forest was on fire. It burned every year about this time from lightning strikes. Lightning must have struck near them, as would be just their luck, and their just-begun new home would burn. She quickly opened her eyes and sat up, but neither a welcoming candle nor a threatening blaze awaited her.

"Tommy?"

She saw that her brother was the source of the soft glow.

Near the roof of the lean-to, just inside it, he hovered while still asleep, floating in the darkness. He was lighted from within. He had taken off his shirt to sleep, and there was no source of the light inside him, as far as Maggie could tell, just a glow but no fire. Everything inside him simply pulsed with light through the transparency that had become his body. Sitting up, she could see through him as though he was made of glass – his beating heart, his expanding and contracting lungs, his stomach and other organs – all working quietly in the glow and visible. His flesh was as clear as a window in the form of a human, allowing a view into his interior.

She nearly screamed, and would have, had it been a stranger and not her little brother who floated over them like a lucid human lantern in the blackness. He snored as though unconcerned with his condition, and rocked gently in the still mountain night air.

"He's dead, he truly is still dead, if this is what he is now," she whispered. "My, god. He did not come back to life, but he is still dead, with a strange thing inside him, and what happens to him now is something I can not say."

While staring at him, with no idea of what to do about the boy, the glow inside the lean-to suddenly intensified, as though someone had turned on a switch to a second light inside the room. The second intense glow came from behind and above her.

She spun on her haunches to see her young husband in the same condition as her brother, a larger lantern floating above her. He was suspended near the roof of the lean-to in a transparent body filled with light, just as Tommy was, his shirt off revealing the same glasslike skin and pulsing interior of light, with his internal organs visible. She saw his beating heart and throbbing lungs. He wavered in midair, as deep in slumber as any of the dead, and as clear and beautiful as the moon on a cloudless night. While she stared at Mabin, a little cry broke suddenly from her lips, for it seemed some darkness descended again, as the light behind her faded. In a panic, thinking that the fading light could mean nothing but that Tommy had died, she spun around again to see that the light had dimmed because Tommy had drifted away of the constraints of the lean-to's roof and was floating farther above her, as though the tall trees of the side of the mountain were calling him and the multitudes of stars were his destination. With her panic deepening, she crawled out of the lean-to and leaped into the air to grab at the ascending body of her little brother, but he was high above and moving away at speed. She was about to use her powers to fly after him and retrieve the ascending spirit, but her powers were nullified somehow and she was as stuck to the earth as any of the tall lodge pole pines surrounding her.

"Tommy!" she cried out. "Tommy? What is happening to you? Can you wake up? Wake up!"

She turned swiftly toward Mabin, but then noticed that the light around her had dimmed even more, and she understood what was wrong before she saw the second oddity of the night. Mabin's clear sleeping form also had broken free from the constraint of the lean-to's roof and was rising in the air, just as her brother's form was rising. Tommy was away over the treetops, and Mabin was just entering the pine-needle canopy at the edge of the forest, following the little boy's trajectory toward the stars as they slept. Again, she attempted to leap into the air to fly after them and retrieve them both before they disappeared into the heavens, but she could not rise an inch out of the dust of the dead vampires. Trembling with frustration and fear, she stood planted in the earth with her neck craned and her eyes staring upward as the two transparent dots of light receded into the sky. For a second, they were two tiny traveling stars high above, and then they disappeared into the blackness, leaving her staring at the constellations and gasping, having lost both of them to the night.

"Mabin ... Tommy ... gone. And dead? Are they dead?"

Panic-stricken, she stared up into the sky, but no change came to it: the two lights of her life did not return, as husband and brother were gone without explanation. She tried again to rise into the sky after them, but now her panic grew greater as she realized she could neither lift her feet off the ground nor move them from where they were stuck in the earth. It was as though some force was pulling her in the opposite direction from her little brother and lover, pulling her down into the earth. She looked up to see if they had returned but then looked down toward her feet quickly and saw in the starlight reaching the earth that they were covered in the black dust and disappearing below the surface. She felt her entire body being pulled into the earth, and she screamed out for the only two people who could save her before the earth swallowed her.

"Mabin! Lover! Tommy! I'm here below! Where are you? Why have you gone away? Come along back to me! I can't live without you! Come back to me! They're pulling me down!"

She raised her arms to the sky, imploring them with an empty embrace not to fade away into the nothingness above, the black nothingness with only stars for company, but to come back to her, who had a warm heart for them, and open arms, and love. She cried out again.

"Mabin! Tommy! This is the last night! We can't live, we can't live anymore in an empty world alone! You must come back!"

She felt the great violent tug first on her right leg, thinking it had been snapped off at the thigh by the great relentless power pulling her into the ground, but then she realized her right leg was still attached when her left leg also was jerked into the ground up to the knee. The tug of that something inside the earth was pitiless, and she could think nothing but that she was being pulled down to hell, claimed by it the ones below she could not see but had condemned to their deaths and punishments.

The ground split below her, opening the way for her descent into fire but encasing her mud and leaving her unable to move. She struggled pointlessly, completely immobilized by the earth, and would not look where she was going. She raised her eyes to the sweet sky, where her life was, where her lover was, before drowning in the earth.

If she would have only one final vision, Mabin would be it.

Her last sight and thoughts would be of the night sky, and her lover, and the stars. Mabin was one of them now.

3

Why there was light in her eyes when she was underground she did not know. It was bright and she could not stand it. She was a creature of sleep deep inside the dark earth and could not stand light, any light. Light illuminated the beasts in her mind that roamed the earth above her present home, those beasts of long, sharp tooth, red eyes and pale skin that had killed everyone she knew and chased joy from the world. She was a creature of the underground and she did not like the light.

Her eyes snapped open and she saw the morning sky. The tops of the lodge pole pines at the edge of the forest were swaying in the breeze like the hair of tender giants. It was an odd way to return to the surface of the earth from the dark inside it, where she had lived she had lived with monsters just a short time ago. She relaxed and let out a long helpless sigh. She would escape her imprisonment inside the muddy earth in any way she could, even if she had to endure the harsh light and the ancient monsters who might be on the surface. The monsters down below were just as bad, or worse.

She blinked and blinked and could not stop. A thunderous pain exploded from the inside of her head but did not blow it apart to pieces, although it felt as though it should have. The pain simply remained lodged insider her brain as though it belonged there forever and ever and would never go away. She thought it was normal that the searing, painful explosion should rest inside her head forever and ever, like the molten core inside the earth.

"Maggie? Are you awake? Why are you breathing so hard?'

It was true. Her lungs felt like two bellows inside her chest, and she blew out air so hard through her pursed lips it seemed to her she was causing the treetops above to sway. After being underground and unable to breathe, it seemed normal to take in as much air as she could. One of the monsters of the light was talking to her, although his voice was pleasant and friendly and did not betray the fact that he was doing to murder her.

"Maggie?"

With one final explosion of breath it all went away. The pain inside her brain receded in an instant. Her breathing slowed to a normal pace and there was no monster anywhere. But still her eyes danced from side-to-side in her head as though powered by a mad energy of their own.

Then everything was still.

She was staring at the wilted branches of the lean-to over her head. She could no longer see the swaying treetops. She had rolled over to hide under the covering of pine, away from day's monsters that were no longer there but had only been imagined.

"We opened a big can of beans for breakfast," Mabin said, from somewhere above. "We left a covered plate for you on a log."

What in the world was he saying? And who was he? She still felt the tight grip on her ankles from last night when she had been pulled down into the mud, and sobbed at the memory. Her shoulders heaved up and down, and once more her lungs felt like two bellows pushing explosions of air out her mouth. Sitting up, she rubbed her ankles where the claws had been, and then the agony of remembrance inside her head eased. She noticed that the toenail on her right foot was cracked and black and blue, an injury left over from being dragged down into the earth by rough creatures. The toe throbbed, and caked brown blood formed a dry coating over the nail.

"What's the matter with her?" Tommy asked. "Her eyes look crazy again."

He leaped down off the back wall of their new house, a wall raised by three more logs on all four sides as Maggie slept. He landed two feet away from her and stood over her, his face grimy from the hard work of building, but he had a big grin.

"I think she was having a nightmare."

"Well, that's stupid. The real nightmares come when we're awake. Sleep's the best time to avoid monsters. I sleep really well."

"She's trembling."

"Hey, Mags, are you all right? You slept a long time. Why are you shaking?"

The explosion might have ceased inside her head, only to be replaced by a thick fog. She could not answer. She realized she was shaking like a flag in a storm. Staring at Tommy and Mabin, she saw that both had scratches and bruises on their necks, and Mabin had a small cut on his cheek.

"She's all right. She's awake now."

"She doesn't look all right. What's wrong with her foot?"

"They dragged me down into the earth!" Maggie screamed, clutching her big toe with both hands and trembling, but that only made the agony in it greater.

Both Mabin and Tommy jumped back, so violently did she protest last night's abduction.

"Who did?"

Maggie glanced up at Mabin with wide, empty eyes.

"I don't know. Someone did. I went down into the earth with someone. What's wrong with your neck?"

"It must have gotten scratched by some branches while we were working. It's fine. I didn't even notice it."

Her mind felt as though someone was stirring it with a big wooden spoon. She tumbled back down onto the bed of soft pine branches and closed her eyes so that she did not have to understand what was happening to her. As soon as her vision was darkened, a huge round face floated quickly toward her out of the dark with its mouth open and its fangs extended and bloody. It came so close to sinking its fangs into her neck that she screamed and opened her eyes. Just as she did so, the face popped like a balloon into rubbery fragments that then melted with the light.

She jumped to her feet.

"I'm going crazy with this!" she screamed out. "Who was that? Who just broke up into pieces?"

"Whoa, Maggie," Mabin laughed, but she grew furious with him as he did so, for her big toe ached terribly as she put weight on it and she still understood nothing. The spoon was still stirring her brain. She stumbled and nearly fell from the pain in her toe and she understood nothing. It was all too confusing, but for no reason.

Tommy grabbed her shoulders to prop her up.

"Who's scaring you, Maggie?" Tommy asked. "Why are you scared?"

Suddenly, the question made sense to her, the first thing that had made sense to her all morning. The mountain air had a delicious pine freshness to it, and a sweet breeze tickled the flesh under her chin and then lifted her hair. Aside from the agony of her toe, it could not have been a more pleasant morning, and she was no longer afraid of anything. Her fears simply evaporated that fast.

"Why do you think I'm scared? I'm not scared."

Tommy let go of her shoulders and glanced at Mabin with a concerned look.

"You looked scared. Now you don't."

"You were shaking," Mabin said. "You were breathing so hard we thought something was wrong with you."

"I was cold. I was just cold. Nothing scares me anymore. I can't remember being scared."

"In this heat you were cold?" Tommy asked. "You were shaking from the cold? It's so hot, I was ready to take a break from building, but then you woke up shaking and gasping."

"No. I'm fine. I was just cold. Don't ever tell me I'm afraid when I'm not."

She stared at Mabin, knowing she was acting oddly, but then she smiled at him, and when she did, he lit up happily to see she was well enough to smile, his concern vanishing and his sweetness returning. There was a cackling in the forest of those strange birds, and then there was a rushing of wings that forced a torrent of wind over them. All three of them glanced into the pine forest, but it was suddenly still as night but filled with the cool, damp shade of morning.

"What are those birds talking about?" Tommy asked.

"Are they talking?"

"I thought I heard them say, 'Come below.'"

"I thought they said 'Help us,'" Mabin said.

"Now you two are being weird," Maggie said. "They're just birds."

Tommy and Mabin had been up since dawn, and the efforts they had put in had paid off in the rising walls of their cabin. They had marked places where they would cut into the logs for windows and doors, and they had prepared all the logs they would need for the first floor. The logs were piled neatly outside the walls and were bright and fragrant in the sunlight, as though they waited eagerly to be stacked into a home. With the birds silent, Maggie felt the protection of the walls, even though they were incomplete, for this unfinished house had already become their home. It protected her like a home already, and it felt like it had memories inside its four walls already. She reached out and touched one of the walls, and it was brown and sticky, like blood drying, but she quickly wiped the substance off onto her jeans. It had to be some sort of sap seeping out of the just-cut log.

"Let's get back to work," Tommy said. "Eat your beans, Maggie. Then maybe we can find something better for lunch, after all three of us work for the rest of this morning."

Nightmares make a bad start to the day, for the way a nightmare makes you feel while sleeping lingers after you open your eyes. You have to make an effort to chase away its feelings long after a bad dream fades. Maggie saw how much work Mabin and Tommy had done while she suffered in her sleep, and on top of the feelings left over from the nightmares, she did not like thinking she had not worked just as hard as they had in making their new home. She would have to make up for it. Despite her disturbed sleep, all her powers had returned, and she was as strong as several men. She notched the longest log she could find on both ends to fit it into the logs that would be below it and above it, and she could not help but notice again that she did have what appeared to be claw marks lining her ankles and feet. The scratches stretched in long broken marks down to her toes, and there were puncture marks in her ankles and in her feet. The blood had scabbed over the marks, but as she moved the pain shot up her legs all the way into her hips. It did not stop her. She finished notching the long log and lifted it onto her shoulder and flew to the back wall of the house, where she balanced herself in the air as she placed the log where it belonged.

"Go, Maggie!" Tommy shouted out to her. "We'll have the house ready in no time, just you wait."

"Do you need help with that?" Mabin asked, as he was stripping another long log on the ground to her right. "Tommy and I had to work together to put a log into place."

"I don't need anybody," Maggie said angrily, but she immediately regretted it, since Mabin looked so hurt. She dropped to the ground, furious with herself for letting out the bad feelings from her nightmare. She quickly notched another log on both ends. She really didn't mean that she didn't need Mabin. She needed him more than ever, and she felt foolish for letting her night-time anger out on him. The bad feelings left over from the nightmare would not leave her alone, even in the bright sunlight.

"I'm sorry," she whispered to Mabin, as she flew up to put the newly notched log into place on the wall.

It was evening before they stopped work, having forgotten about lunch as their need to stop thinking about everything that had happened to them overwhelmed them on that first day back from the dead. What they wished to avoid remembering were the dangers and deaths that had put them in this predicament. They had to start over in life all over again, from scratch, after all had been destroyed. They wanted to forget about what had ruined their world, and they especially wanted to forget the final end of their step-parents, deaths that had bought them the lives they now lived. They simply worked hard to forget it all, and they worked in tears.

The first floor walls were in place by the time the sun crept behind the mountain and brought on the evening. A chill struck them as soon as the light fell behind the curtain of the high peak. It told them it was time to stop work and huddle together against the darkness and cold.

"It's going to be a chilly one," Mabin said. "Maybe we should pile the bed with more pine branches."

"All right."

Maggie could see her breath, and she watched it rise into the night air as she had watched Tommy and Mabin rise into the sky in her nightmare.

Silently, Mabin went about collecting the loose pine boughs scattered around the cabin, boughs that had been cleaned off the shining logs piled onto their new four walls. Maggie watched him in silence, fearing she had angered him by snapping at him, but he seemed content and happy to be doing what he was doing.

"We have to talk," Maggie said, when he walked by her with an armful of the pine branches.

He stopped before her.

"What do you want to talk about?"

"I'm upset that you don't believe I was pulled down into the ground last night. I think it was demons. It wasn't really a nightmare, and it could happen again. It seemed like a nightmare but somehow I know it wasn't."

"So they're still here."

"I think so. We just can't see them now."

Mabin paused and stared off into space.

"Okay."

He stood with his arms full of the branches, staring at the night, and did not move after answering her with the single word. Even the possibility that she had been taken by demons did not move him, and it was so strange to see him like that.

"Is that all you're going to say? Okay? Look at my feet. They're cut to pieces, full of claw marks."

He let his eyes fall to her feet, and he stared at them now.

"My feet are cut up, too. It happens with the work. Tommy's feet are nicked up, too, worse than mine. It doesn't mean demons did it."

"Your feet are not clawed like mine."

"That's true, but –"

"And there's something else. You and Tommy did not stay on earth last night."

"What?"

The word snapped out of Mabin's mouth, as his eyes snapped up to meet hers. The consternation and worry showing on his face made her wish she had not mentioned the strange way he and Tommy had lit up from within and floated off into the sky, there to disappear, for it made her story even more implausible. It sounded crazy even to her. Now it was as though Mabin knew she was mad. If he thinks I'm crazy, it must have been a dream, she told herself, but she knew it wasn't. Somehow she knew it was. It just couldn't have been, it couldn't have been, for it seemed so real to her, even now. His look saying he thought she was crazy and his silence were enough to make her blood boil up. She could not control it, but she felt like slapping him. Stop it, stop it, she said silently, to calm down.

"You're not really alive yet, are you?" she blurted out.

The words burst from her like an accusation, but as soon as they left her mouth she regretted saying them. Mabin gaped at her. He stood before her a fully resurrected being, with heart and soul intact and every part of him functioning normally. Yet what she had seen last night made her certain what she said about him was true. After lying in the grave for a year, he wasn't quite himself, even now. She simply hadn't expressed it well, or sensitively, or kindly, and she was sorry about that. Yet she could not have been more certain that he and Tommy had been altered in some way by their experiences of death and rebirth, and she felt in her bones that they were all in danger because of it.

"Why do you say that? That's I'm not alive?" Mabin asked, in a calm tone.

"Because last night I saw you and Tommy do something no other human being has ever done. You lit up from within like lanterns and floated up into the sky, far up into the sky. I tried to follow you, tried to retrieve you, but I was dragged down into the earth. I could not follow you because I was not resurrected as you two were, and am not quite the same as you because of it."

Tommy slowly walked over to become part of the conversation and stood next to Maggie staring at her with his forehead crinkled up and his eyes narrowed. He, too, thought she was crazy.

"Oh, crap, Maggie, there's still something wrong with you," he said bluntly. "I never slept as well as I did last night. I would have remembered it if I had lit up and floated off into the sky like some Chinese lantern. Seriously, Maggie, does that sound like anything but a dream to you?"

"It was not a dream! I'm telling you something wants me down inside the earth, and something else wants you two up in the sky. I saw it. I experienced it. I know it happened. It wasn't a dream."

Tommy turned away biting his lip.

"Oh, crap. She's gone now, too."

He tapped a finger to his head, and then a tear rolled down his cheek.

"Maggie ..."

"She's not gone," Mabin snapped. "Something is wrong here. Maggie, don't you think something is wrong?"

"That's what I've been saying. I know there is something off here. That's what I've been trying to tell you."

"Let's just think about it for a moment ... I remember I read something ... there was a French writer ... he woke up after dreaming he was a butterfly and after thinking about it, decided he didn't know if he was a man who had dreamt he was a butterfly, or a butterfly dreaming he was a man. Could your dream have done something like that to you?"

"It was not a dream. It happened. I am not a butterfly."

"I – "

"Tell me I'm not a butterfly!" she yelled.

"Jeez, Maggie," Tommy said.

"All right. You're not a butterfly."

With that, Mabin reached up and gently touched her face.

"You have the soul of a butterfly, though, and you saved me with it. That's something I know about you. You brought me through all the stages of resurrection and rebirth."

"Can we please get back to work?" Tommy asked. "You're both starting to make me a little sick. First you act crazy, and then you act goofy with each other. Which is it? Are you crazy for goofy for each other. I'd like to have a house to live in again as soon as possible. If you haven't noticed, ours was burned down and we need to work hard to build ourselves a new one."

"We noticed."

"Then let's get back to work."

Maggie kissed Mabin on the lips, and he relaxed and smiled at her. There wasn't much to eat but canned food with the labels burned off, taken from the grocery store, which had been burned down by Elsa and Stephanovich when they caught the owners slurping up human blood off the butcher's floor. Opening cans without labels meant they didn't know what they were going to get, but they had stockpiled dozens of cans after they made a foray into the burned town. It was potluck. If Mabin used the knife to open a can and handed it to Maggie or Tommy and if they didn't like the contents, they handed it back and asked for something else. Eventually, they found three large cans of beef stew and settled on those for dinner. Eating lasted just a few minutes. Then they decided that Tommy was right and they should finish the side walls of the cabin before it got completely dark, but they did not succeed in that. One wall was complete, forming a perfect peak on which to start the roof, but when it got too dark to see properly, they flew down off the second side wall with it only half-done.

"We might be able to get the roof on tomorrow," Mabin said. "This might be our last night sleeping under the stars."

"If you don't fly off up to them first," Maggie snapped.

She immediately regretted saying it.

"Maggie, what is wrong with you?" Tommy asked, annoyed she had mentioned her nightmare again. "We're doing the best we can. We might have the four walls and the roof done tomorrow. I think that's pretty good work for just three days.

We've got to start living again, and forget the past, no matter how bad it was."

"I'm sorry. I was thinking, do you think we might lay down a floor before we put on the roof?"

Both Mabin and Tommy froze and stared at each other.

"Do you want the floor because you're afraid of what's underground?" Mabin asked.

Maggie nodded.

"Then we'll lay down a floor before we put on the roof," Mabin said. "If you think there's a danger down there, then we'll do what we can to make this house safe. It's too dark now to – "

"That's just stupid!" Tommy broke in. "We need a roof first. What if it rains? The floor won't keep us dry."

He turned away from them angrily.

"I'm going to sleep. Why are we even arguing about this?"

He retreated quickly toward the lean-to in the corner of their unfinished new home and slipped into pile of pine branches, where he disappeared completely into their sweet-scented arms. Maggie was quivering with the prospect of returning to the place where she had been abducted the previous night, and Mabin reached out for her and enclosed her in an embrace.

"You're frightened. You're shaking, but it's going to be all right."

"I don't know if I can take this. Mom and dad are gone, but I thought we were safe because of what they did for us, but now I think there's just as much danger as ever. They're still here."

"No. I promise you, things are going to be all right."

"Really?"

"Yes, butterfly."

"Am I a butterfly again?"

"Yes, I told you that you weren't before, but you are my beautiful butterfly."

He touched his lips to hers, and she truly did feel like a butterfly in a cocoon, a butterfly at home and safe, and she made him kiss her again and hold her tighter. They were all transforming into something better than what they were, she hoped.

"We're two butterflies, new to the world," she said. "Let's forget the old world tonight and be butterflies as best we can, and find all the sweet things."

Mabin drew his wife tightly to him and their wings unfolded into a spectacular display.

4

With all her heart Maggie wished it was the bright morning she saw through her closed eyelids.

In the pit of her stomach was dread at the light, after she was awakened again by the same glow she had seen at this time the previous night. Nestled within the pine-bough bed, she quivered with fear and reached out with her eyes closed to find Mabin's hand. She could not. She reached out again, and again, and would not open her eyes for fear of what she might see. Each time she reached out she clutched air. She feared she had been abandoned, and soon they would reach for her again out of the earth, and drag her down.

"I have to open my eyes eventually," she said to herself. "I've always been crazy, and it will be nothing new if I still am crazy, but I have to know if I've lost my mind or if it is morning. I wish it to be morning, but I have to open my eyes to find out. It's better to know than not know. All right, I will open my eyes."

Something grabbed her ankle and tore a claw deep within it. With a scream she pulled her foot away, which opened the scabbed wounds there to bleed again when she escaped the thing's grasp. Her eyes snapped open naturally, and she crawled across the floor on the pine boughs, but then stopped. Her heart nearly dropped through her body to the ground when she saw the two glowing bodies floating away above her, again lanterns in the night, but she had little time to scream again. The clawed hand was tearing at her foot, reaching up out of the mud, and she had to get up and run. Once again, after she jumped up, she tried to break the bonds of earth and fly up to her lover and brother near the stars, but could not, and more things were reaching up out of the ground to snap at her feet. She ran and could not fly, but she kept her eyes pointing upward to where the same spectacle of Mabin and Tommy disappearing into the night sky toward the stars repeated itself. As she ran through the mud watching them, they became smaller and smaller until she could no longer see them. A hand pinched her foot as she reached the back wall. She stomped down on it with her free heel and clawed her way up the wall, reaching into the chinks between the logs for a grip and climbing up to get away from the hands rising out of the mud after her, all the while gasping for breath. Then she perched precariously on top of the wall in the dark, squatting for balance and thinking she would faint in the thin black air. As she looked below at the mud floor, it roiled with movement, like a thousand snapping black crabs on the ocean floor as the clawed hands sought her feet in blackness of the mud. Eight feet above them, she was safe but trapped. She let her eyes wander to the sky. The two lanterns of her life were gone. She was abandoned again by the only people who could help her, and even though she knew it was no good to call out to them, she did, crying Mabin's name again and again and then shouting out for Tommy. No one answered. She was amazed at how quiet the sky could be when you asked something of it. The stars made no response, and the endless dark was mute and remote and indifferent, and the dark air had nothing more to say to her as the snapping below her intensified. She listened intently, but she heard only the clicking and snapping of the clawed hands in the mud. No one spoke her name, or saved her. She settled onto her back carefully, spent but making sure to balance herself firmly on the top log so she would not tumble off, and then stared at the night sky, waiting for Mabin and Tommy's return.

In a panic, she reached down behind her to grab the two sides of the log on which she lay, to prevent herself from falling. The light had returned to her eyes, but she now believed it was not a good light but the light of her lover and brother abandoning her, as they had abandoned her twice already. Slowly, as she hyperventilated in a hard panic, she came to realized that made no sense. If she saw light again, it meant they were returning from the night sky, not leaving. She opened her eyes but saw no stars, only the pinkish-blue sky of dawn.

The nightmare was over.

"Hey, sis, what are you doing up there?"

Without moving, she continued to stare at the morning sky while holding tight onto the log on which she lay. She was stiff and sore.

"I came up here to get away from them. They came again last night, and you weren't here. You went into the sky again. Both of you abandoned me again."

Tommy stood staring up at her from below.

"Oh, no," he said, his shoulders slumping a little.

"Is she getting an early start on work?" Mabin asked, walking up to the back wall on top of which Maggie lay. He carried three open, charred cans of ravioli which he intended to offer up for breakfast.

"No, she thinks things came out of the ground after her again last night. I guess she slept up there to get away from them. Is that what you did, Mags?"

"It's what I had to do."

"Maggie, did you have another nightmare?"

"You left me again. They were here just as they were last night. It was not a nightmare."

"Who was here?"

"Those hands with claws down there, where you're standing."

Without putting down the cans of ravioli, Mabin looked to the forest floor at his feet. Tommy also let his eyes drop. They saw nothing.

"Just claws?"

"There must be more of them than just claws under the ground."

She clung to the wall above as though it would topple and send her sprawling into the mud, where the danger was.

"Maggie? Why don't you come down and eat something? You'll feel better."

"No, not yet. Tell me something. Where did you two go last night?"

"We were right here, sleeping beside you. We never left. You were snoring away all night."

"Yeah, I couldn't sleep, you were snoring so much," Tommy said. "I kept poking you to make you stop, so maybe that's what you felt. Maybe you felt me poking you and dreamed it was something else."

"I don't think so. If I was sleeping down there all night next to you, why am I up here now?"

"I – "

Mabin broke off his response, confused. He dropped quickly to the ground, nearly falling, and sat there helplessly, despondent at seeing Maggie in such a state.

"Maggie, we need you down here with us. There are no hands down here trying to grab you. Please don't go away like this.

Don't go away to somewhere else. We need all of us with our feet on the ground to survive. Please."

"I'm not the one who went away."

"We were here all night, I promise."

Maggie stared at the mud floor of the cabin.

"Is anything down there?"

"No, I swear. I'm sitting on the ground, and it's safe. I have breakfast."

Maggie hesitated a moment before taking her eyes off the sky and sitting up on the top of the wall. She froze there, still frightened, but then let her eyes drop to the ground below, where Mabin sat motionless staring up at her and Tommy stood impatiently, his eyes red and upset with grief, also staring at her.

She pushed off her perch and slowly glided down to them.

When her feet hit the ground she trembled and looked to the earth. Then she raised her eyes to stare at Mabin, who stood up at once. Her eyes with locked into his, trying to see the truth there, and they rose boring into his.

"We have to work harder," she said.

"We'll work as hard as we can."

"I want to work on the floor first," she burst out. "We have to put down a floor first. We have to. We just have to, or they'll come again at night when you leave."

"All right, Maggie, if it will make you feel better, we'll lay down a floor first. I see you finished off the side wall by yourself already this morning."

"What are you talking about?"

"The final few logs of the wall we didn't finish last night. They're in place."

Maggie looked up. The wall they had not finished last night stood in the mirror image of its opposite, a topping triangle of ever-shorter logs completing it to form the shape for the roof.

"I didn't do that."

"Come on, Maggie. You couldn't sleep so you went to work on the house."

"I did not do that, I did not work on the house in the middle of the night, and you did not, either, since you were not here."

"We were here, I promise you, but asleep, and so were you. It's all right to say you couldn't fall asleep, that things are bothering you, and you went to work to forget about everything. We're all upset about what happened to Elsa and Stephanovich, but they'd want us to build a new life for ourselves and let them go for now, until we can resurrect them in a year."

"I'm telling you, both of you, you lit up from inside and floated off into the night sky, and I couldn't wake you or stop you or do anything to prevent it. I screamed at you, and I cried out, but you just floated away as if I wasn't there, as if no one was there and nothing mattered, and you disappeared into the sky."

"Oh, hell," Tommy said.

"Does that even sound half-right?" Mabin asked her gently. "Think for a minute, Maggie."

"Yeah, think. Get a grip, sis. If we were up in the sky, how did we get back down here? Did we fall? Why aren't we hurt?"

"I don't know. I guess you floated down."

"We floated down ... I never floated anywhere in my life. I don't float. When I want to go somewhere, I go."

Maggie stared at the floor and shivered.

"We've seen so many strange things," she said. "Why can't you believe this one? It must have been the vampires we – "

"They're all dead, Maggie, and I'm glad they're dead and I'm glad we killed them," Tommy shouted, his face growing red with agitation and anger. "I'd do it again. I wish I could do it again, over and over, for what they did to mom and dad, and for what they did to us. I'd like to kill them all a million times if I could."

Maggie dropped to the ground. She fell because she could no longer feel anything, or argue with the only two people who loved her now, and she sat there staring off into space, unable to think or remember where she was or move.

"Maggie?" Mabin asked. "Can I help you up?"

She offered her hand to him, remaining mute and still, and he clutched it and gently lifted her until she regained her feet. She was standing, but still not moving. She simply stared off into space.

"So do you want your stupid floor or not?" Tommy yelled out. "Do you? We'll make your stupid floor, but I miss mom and dad just as much as you do. I'm doing this for you, because you and Mabin are all I have left. But I miss mom and dad, too. Ah, I'm going to start building."

With that, Tommy grabbed one of the cans Mabin had brought for breakfast and dug in with his fingers, while the tears fell from his eyes. So that they would not see him crying, he turned away and walked out the opening made for the door to get to work.

Mabin offered one of the remaining cans of ravioli to Maggie as she stood lifeless and empty next to him, and she did as Tommy had done. She reached into it with her fingers for the poor substitute for breakfast. It was all they had. It was all she could do to eat.

Somehow, work began on the floor that Maggie requested, the floor that would keep the things from grabbing her at night. The three of them labored quickly but lifelessly, going through the motions, but with Mabin's immense strength intact, they managed to cut and split two dozen great logs, fashioning floor boards out of them. There was much cackling now in the forest, as it seemed a flock of the annoying birds had descended on the woods around their new cabin, but they paid little attention to the noise. They cut several smaller trees for the floor beams, and then set them in place by fitting their ends into the logs at the base of the walls. They had no nails but made pegs, two for the end of each floor board, and then with their knife drilled holes into the beams and the ends of the boards and set the flat pieces of pine in place one by one. The pegs secured the floor boards, although there were small gaps between the boards that worried Maggie. Whatever was down there in the mud might not be able to reach her through the gaps, but they could see her, and that was nearly as bad. They dragged their bed of pine boughs back into the house and settled them into place to make their bed. There was still sunlight streaming in through the opening where there was no roof, but the sunlight was broken by clouds racing across the sky and the clouds dropped fleeting shadows over the house.

"I hope you're happy now, Maggie," Tommy said. "Those are rain clouds. We're probably going to get drenched tonight by a big storm tonight because we built a floor first instead of a roof."

"Please don't be mad at me, Tommy."

"Is that all you can say? Please don't be mad? The old Maggie would have told me off. The old Maggie would have kicked my butt. Why don't you kick my butt now? Huh? Why not? I'm being a jerk, so kick my butt."

"We'll build the roof tomorrow."

"Tomorrow we'll all be soaking wet and the house might be ruined. If a house doesn't have a good roof, it's not a good house and just falls apart in the rain."

"We'll be all right," Mabin said gently. "We'll build the lean-to up over the bed, and that will keep us a little dry if it rains."

"A roof would keep us completely dry, if we had the sense to build it," Tommy said. "Why couldn't we build a roof first, like we were supposed to do, Maggie? Why couldn't we?"

"Because we'll all be dead if they get us from underground."

For a moment Tommy was speechless and stared at her.

"Oh, crap, that again. I'm going to float away for awhile, Maggie, because you're just making me mad now. I'm going to go visit mom and dad's grave. At least they understood what we had to do to stay safe from the vampires, who are all dead now anyway."

When Tommy was gone, Mabin turned to Maggie.

"There's still some light," he said. "We can make use of it. We can begin making the things we need for the roof, and then work on it tomorrow. We'll split shingles out of the scrap wood and cut down more trees for the roof beams. That way we can maybe finish the roof tomorrow, if we work hard on it."

"Don't be angry with Tommy. He's been through a lot and doesn't know how to handle things yet."

"I know."

Mabin and Maggie walked off into the woods and worked the two-man saw together, cutting down the trees that would become their roof beams.

They worked in silence until dark. Tommy was still not home.

They fell into bed, too exhausted to look for him. Despite being anxious, fretting about him, they dropped off into sleep before he returned. They were so tired they could not remain awake.

5

Maggie did not wait to determine if the light striking her closed eyelids was morning.

She jumped up instinctively as the first clawed hand grabbed her ankle. She kicked out violently at it three times to knock it off, but the claws had already dug in and drawn blood.

As soon as the first hand was knocked off a second jabbed up at her back and then a third grabbed hold of her neck and closed around it, choking her until she gasped and spit blood.

Another violent flash of light seemed to scare off those who had her tightly in their grasps, for she screamed into the night just as the flash of lightning died way. She awoke in the dark barely able to breath, but her mind was as clear and sharp as day, even though she looked out on the night. Another flash of lightning illuminated the inside of the cabin, and it was with great relief that she realized she was soaking wet from the cloudburst pouring into their roofless home. Rain fierce and steady came down upon her without letup, and only the flashes of lightning provided any illumination of her predicament. She felt the hard floor beneath her and laughed, realizing she had awakened from a dream. The floor had done its job well but they had no roof to do its job. You can't have everything, she said to herself, laughing. If you have bad dreams, at least you can rely on a storm to drive them away, if you're lucky and put off adding a roof to your house.

"Maybe the monsters were a dream, and maybe the floor is keeping them down where they belong," she said, out loud. "I don't know which it is. Mabin? Tommy? Maybe you were right. Maybe I was dreaming there were things underground trying to get me. That's good. It means I'm not crazy, but just having nightmares. Maybe only my dreams are crazy."

She spoke to them, and waited, but there was no answer. She reached out in the dark, first to one side and then to the other, and another flash of lightning confirmed what she had discovered by touch. Neither Mabin nor Tommy was there. She raised her eyes to catch sight of their glowing lanterns floating away above, but the rain pelted her face so violently that she had to cover it with her hand and look down. So intense was the storm that she could see no stars, no trees and no glow of friends above. Her eyes were filled with water and she could barely see, the downpour having blinded her.

"Maybe having a roof isn't lucky."

A bumping beneath her froze her heart in her chest. The floorboards on which she sat jumped up suddenly, as though several hands had punched them from below in the attempt to escape their underworld and grab her, and her body flew several inches off of the floor. She let out a cry of surprise. Bruised, she fell back down suddenly in time to feel another violent punch from below on the floorboards, and she cried out again. When that effort did not remove the boards and expose her to them there was a screeching of claws on the bottom of the boards and a desperate groping at the wood and then a glow of light seeped up through the spaces between the boards as though someone was burning candles beneath them.

"Trapped we are again, no. She's up there, the girl is up there. I smell the blood," a voice whispered. "It is her blood. I smell blood. She has laid a trap over us. We must escape and take her."

A fierce gust of wind lashed her with the rain. She leaped up and looked at the fresh torrent as her savior. It would wash away the smell of her blood, she hoped. She dared not move for fear they could discover her through the sounds of her movements. The lights glowed brighter in the cracks between the floorboards, and the strange thought struck her that perhaps the water would drip down through the floorboards and extinguish the candlelight and the creatures below. Suddenly, the floorboard on which she stood flew up again, so violently that it sent her careening into the air. The board clapped down loudly into its place, doing its job, and even though she knew they could not reach through the floor for her, or destroy it, she regained her feet and made a desperate dash for the back wall. "Get me out of here, get me out of here!" she yelled out. She leaped when she was two feet away from the back wall and reached up to gain a purchase with her hands on the wet logs. They were so slippery from the rain she could not grab the wet wood and then crashed into the wall and then dropped down with a thud face-first onto the floor that was designed to save her.

"We rip her to pieces of fresh flesh," a voice whispered, just below her ear through the wood. "Perhaps she will come down to fight, perhaps she will, and we will have her then."

If she had a rope and a roof beam, she would hang herself, she thought, for it would be better than being alone and hearing what she was hearing and smelling what she smelled through the floorboards, that acrid stench of burned flesh. She gasped at the stench, the rot of a thousand dead bodies left to molder for days, and she could not stand being so close to the rotted creatures below her. She got up and sprinted for the door. Just as she got to the opening, thunder broke above and then a fresh bolt of lightning crashed to earth fifty feet away. It illuminated the entire area for an instant. That split-second of light brought her to a sudden sliding halt at the doorway, for she saw there was no escape. In the mud-bath surrounding their cabin, mud brought on by the unending storm, were thousands of the clawed hands swimming around like fish and reaching up for her and clicking closed when they thought they caught something.

"I am madness," she whispered. "I am true madness itself. There is no escape from me, for sanity is too far away. Perhaps I will go down to them, or find a rope for myself here."

As quietly as she whispered in her desperation, she was not safe talking to herself about her own destruction. She felt a clattering rush of those below her toward her feet. Outside in the dark a splashing of the multitudes of the dead through the mud let her know they were coming for her from there, too, and then the floorboard on which she stood flew up and sent her careening into the air. She managed to maintain her balance as she fell to the floor and the glow from below escaped with the rise of the board, and then she saw the claws clustered like moldy crabs, white globs of fungus growing upon them. They were snapping at her like the directionless dead. She thought of trying to climb the wall again to escape as she did last night, but thought better of it when she felt the rain still pelting her from above. The walls were still too slippery to climb, and the floor was nearly too slippery to walk across. Her only escape was the window, and that escape might only be temporary, since sitting on the open window sill would trap her halfway inside the house and halfway outside, and she was not safe in either place. She didn't know what would happen to her if she sat on the window sill, but she felt her eyes closing with exhaustion and helplessness, as though no matter what she did, it was the wrong thing to do and there was no escape but capture.

"Do something!" she yelled at herself.

She could not remain standing one minute more. She climbed up on the window sill and straddled the wall, trying to wedge herself in the window so that she would not fall once she lost consciousness. Leaning forward, the only position she thought would save her was an odd one. She bent her body nearly in two and reached down to the first space between the logs underneath her. She wedged one hand into the space on the outside of the wall and one hand in the space on the inside of the wall, and then she waited. The rain soaked her long hair and pasted it to the sides and front of her head, blinding her in the dark, and she could do nothing more but cry.

"Mabin, I begged you not to leave again, but you left again and now there is only this for me. Only this. Why would you leave me?"

She spoke out-loud, and the only answer she received was more clacking and splashing.

The light was soft, so soft upon her eyelids, and the air was fresh, so very fresh as she breathed it in. Both things were strange, since she believed there was nothing but rot and decay and darkness now in the world with Mabin gone and these things inside the earth coming after her. Something must be wrong with her senses. Her eyes had gone insane to see such sweet light, and her nose must have twisted itself toward madness to inhale such wonderful air. Such things did not exist in the world of sensations gone insane.

"Why is she sleeping on the window sill?" she heard Tommy ask, quietly and with grave concern.

"I don't know. Don't wake her. All that work must have exhausted her. I bet she fell asleep right there as soon as she was done."

"I feel bad for talking to her the way I did last night," Tommy said. "I didn't know she'd go to all that trouble in the middle of the night, just for me and because I said I didn't want to get wet and the floor was a stupid idea."

"What did you think she'd do? You should know you sister by now. She saved you twice from the vampires, and now she made sure you wouldn't get wet while you were sleeping last night. She'd do anything for you."

"I feel really bad. Sometimes I'm just stupid. I guess I'll wait until she wakes up to thank her."

"I'm awake now."

Despite hearing Mabin and Tommy's voices and experiencing the sweet light and lovely air, Maggie still did not trust the world outside her eyes enough to take a good look at it. She grabbed at her ankles to protect them in case something was about to grab at them, and she tucked her head between her knees to shut out everything.

"Sis?"

"What? Are you Tommy?"

"Sure ... you know that."

"What do you want?"

"Can you open your eyes and look at me? I want to thank you."

"I don't want to open my eyes. They're all around me. If I open my eyes, they'll see me."

"They are? I don't see anybody here but Mabin."

"Are you sure?"

"I'm very sure. I'd tell you if there was anybody here but us."

"What did you want to thank me for?"

"For what you did."

"What did I do?"

"You built the roof in the middle of the night. I know I complained a lot that you wanted a floor first, but you didn't have to get up in the middle of the night and build a roof over us by yourself just to keep us dry from the storm."

Remembering how the storm had drenched her, Maggie thought her brother had gone crazy now, with the talk of a roof that didn't exist, so she slowly lifted her head from between her knees. She blinked to clear the sleep out of her eyes, and then she twisted her head to look first at him and then up at the sky. The sky was no longer there.

She let out a horrified scream.

"I'm under the ground! I am underground. I begged you two not to leave me last night and you did, so now they pulled me underground and you, too. All of us are under the ground again with them!"

Seeing her wide eyes and her panicked expression, Mabin rushed to her and took her in his arms before she could leap down off the window sill and injure herself.

"No, no, Maggie, that's over with. They're all dead, and that's a roof you see above us, not the ground. You built it last night while we were sleeping."

"You're crazy! Are you one of them? I didn't build a roof."

"You didn't?"

"No."

"Then how did it get there? Tommy and I were exhausted from work and dead to the world, and I know you'll do anything for us, so who else could have done it? You really didn't have to."

"Yeah, we would have helped you do it in the morning. I really wouldn't have minded sleeping in a little rain."

"I didn't build it."

Mabin held her tightly in his arms and lifted her off the window sill and onto the floor. As soon as her feet hit the wood boards, she flinched and stared down for the claws to tear at her feet. Her toes quivered in anticipation of what might happen to her if she kept her feet planted on the floor.

"Ah, Mags," Tommy said. "Look up. All that killing and dying under the mountain is over with. They're all dead."

"He's right. You're safe in the house," Mabin said. "Can you remember what we did to the vampires? All of them? They're gone, crushed. They're not coming back. Tell her, Tommy."

"I'm not worried about the vampires anymore at all. I'm worried about you, Maggie. I think something came loose up here with you, Mags."

Tommy tapped his head with his forefinger.

Maggie looked up.

"Is that a roof?" she asked. "Why did someone take away the sky? Or is that a roof?"

Now Mabin glanced over at Tommy with concern.

"We told you it was a roof. You built it last night. Don't you remember?" he said to Maggie.

Maggie pulled herself out of Mabin's grasp with a fierce push. "You!"

"Mags ..."

"I'm surprised you made it back home after leaving me again last night all alone to deal with the vampires. Didn't the roof keep you inside when you tried to float away to wherever you go at night? I was stuck down here in the mud with them while you floated away somewhere in the sky. I don't know how you could do that to me."

The flock of cackling birds resumed their morning song just outside the window when Maggie stopped speaking. For some reason, their cackling hurt her ears terribly, and she clapped her palms over them to keep out the sound. She closed her eyes tightly, but the world swayed in the dark. Mabin gently pulled down on her arms, and as soon as she felt his touch, she let her arms drop. She stepped into his embrace and wept, her eyes wide open now.

"I'm so sorry."

"I'm sorry, too. We can't do this without you," Mabin said to her. "I know it's so hard, after what happened to us under that mountain, but if it wasn't for you none of us would be here. Remember that, please, Maggie. It's only because of you that we're alive. You were so strong then. You killed hundreds of them."

Maggie relaxed into Mabin's arms, and for the first time in hours, felt some sense of calm. She remembered nothing of fashioning the roof over their small cabin last night; she could not even imagine it, building in that downpour. With an odd thought, it seemed to her that the house was completing itself. She realized that was nonsense: there had to be some other explanation for it.

First, part of the side wall had gone up without anyone working on it, and now last night an entire roof had appeared, with no one remembering having built it. It was the sort of thing Elsa and Stephanovich would do. As the cackling of the birds outside their open window continued, the thought stuck with her that somehow Elsa and Stephanovich were still here and protecting them, putting together their new home out of thin air. It gave her great comfort to think so, even though she knew it could not be true. And she still had Mabin. She stepped further into his embrace but as she did so her toe struck something. A sharp pain burned through her leg. Still frightened of everything she imagined around her, she leaped back and burst out with a question before she bothered to look down at what had caused the pain.

"What was that?"

"I don't know what you're – "

"That, Mabin, that! What is that? I just stepped into it."

Thinking Maggie was still not clear on things, Mabin would not let his eyes wander down to the empty floor. He was reluctant to take his eyes off of her in her condition, reluctant to look down and discover there was nothing there. He thought another phantom had flared up to disturb Maggie's raw imagination.

"Look at it!" Maggie screamed, pointing at Mabin's feet.

With that, Mabin let his eyes drop to the floor.

Pressed onto one of the floorboards was an iron ring, innocent and motionless. It was attached to a short iron spike in the floorboard, looped through an eye in the spike so that it could be lifted by pulling it up.

"Did I build that, too?" Maggie asked.

"What is it?" Tommy asked.

"You're standing on it, Mabin. Don't you understand? You are standing on it! They built it! Look around you, on the floor, they built it so that they can come up at night for me while you're away."

Mabin looked first directly at his feet, where the iron ring sat motionless in front of his toes, and then looked down to his left and right.

Cut in a square around him was a trap door. Behind him, its hinges proved it was indeed a gateway to the space below the cabin.

"What are you talking about, Maggie?" Tommy asked, without looking down at the trap door.

"Look! Look!"

Finally, he glanced at the floor.

"Mags, what do we need that for?" he asked, puzzled. "Why did you build that, too? Are we going to dig a basement under the house?"

"I didn't build it! They cut it into the floor last night when you weren't here and I was hiding from them. I didn't build the roof! They did! And I didn't build that!"

Maggie was screaming so loudly it silenced the cackling birds outside the open window. It also quieted Mabin and Tommy, who stared at her with hurt and pity. Mabin stepped toward her, reaching for her, but she jumped away from him.

"Don't get off of it! Don't you ever get off of it! Your weight is holding it down! They're in there, they are in there waiting to come up!"

Without hesitation, Mabin stepped to the side and off the trap door. Maggie gasped and moved away quickly, staring at the door in terror. Mabin leaned down, grabbed the iron ring and lifted the trap door. A cold, damp breeze wafted up slowly from beneath the cabin, like the air rising out of a just-dug grave, but that was all that came out of the hole cut into the floor boards. Tommy stepped forward to peer into the dark hole. He laughed at the emptiness below.

"See? There's nothing, Maggie. The door is even cut over a floor joist, so that nobody could go down or come up if they wanted to. You cut the door in the wrong place, Maggie."

"I did not cut that door into the floor."

"Then how did it get there? I didn't do it. Mabin didn't do it."

"I think we built the house in the wrong place," Maggie said firmly. "This is not the place to begin our new life."

Mabin closed the trap door and stood on it to secure it in place.

"This is where we lived before in our old house," Tommy said.

"They know that."

"Who knows that?"

"The monsters in the mountain. They know we lived here with Elsa and Stephanovich. That's how they found us. That's why they come here at night when the two of you are gone."

"Maggie, we don't go anywhere at night. We're so tired we fall asleep and stay asleep."

"That is not what I see."

"I know, I know, we light up from inside and float away into the sky. Maggie, really? Are you sure that happens?"

"I know it happens, and why it happens."

"If it does happen, then, why does it happen, Maggie?"

"Because both of you were dead and we brought you back to life, but there is still something wrong. There is still something dead about you, something wrong with you, and it comes out at night."

"I still don't understand. I feel fine."

"It happens because you're still looking for the place you should have gone after you died, and you can not find it because you're alive again. There's still something in both of you searching for that place you never found but were supposed to find. At night you drift away to find it."

Tommy screwed up his face.

"So what you're saying is we shouldn't be here."

"No! I want you both here more than anything. Just stay with me at night and we'll find out what's wrong with you."

"But we do stay here. We wouldn't ever go anyplace else and leave you."

"They're here at night. Don't you understand? They're here. They can only be here because you're not."

"Ah, Maggie, I slept all night, but now you're making me tired again," Tommy said. "I don't think we ever left, or that they ever came here. I still think they're all dead."

"So you think I'm crazy then?"

"We went through some horrible things," Mabin said. "Things like that linger in the mind."

"You ass. So you think I am crazy and there's nothing wrong with you. If that's what you think, why don't you just stay away tonight at that place you're searching for and can never find, because if you come back, you know I won't be here. They know what they're doing, and I won't survive them one more night without you two here."

"Maggie, if we can just – "

"No! We can't!"

With that, Maggie stormed out the open doorway, but she had no idea of where she was going. Soon she disappeared into the forest alone.

6

While she was gone, Mabin and Tommy did for her what they thought she wanted them to do.

They found fine, double-paned windows for the house stacked against the north wall. Each one was brand-new, a perfect fit for the openings they had left in the walls, and each one solved the problem they thought they had of having no window frames or glass to put in the frames. Each closed off the building from the outside and provided the protection they would need from the elements. They also found a new door frame and new door hinged to it by the south wall. Again, the door and frame fit perfectly into the opening they had made for it. It was the final piece to secure their tiny cabin from what Maggie feared lurked below and outside.

"She was really busy," Mabin said, when the door was in place. "Roof, windows, doors, and that trap door for the basement. She built them all and I didn't hear a thing all night. How did she get it all done?"

"I was wondering that, too. She's a strong girl, but what she did last night while we slept was a lot, even for her."

"Do you think somebody else survived and helped her?"

"I don't think so. Nobody could have. If there was one thing Elsa and Stephanovich were good at, it was disposing of vampires in a lasting way."

Mabin wiped his sleeve across his forehead and glanced up at the hot sun. He smiled at Tommy.

"I don't mean the vampires, they didn't survive. I know they're all dead and underground. I meant someone normal who might be helping us now but doesn't want us to know, or for us to see him because he still doesn't understand what's going on."

"There was nobody else normal in this town. They all drank blood infected with the vampire virus, and that's why we killed them. It was us or them, so they died."

"Maybe even we don't really understand what's happening. Do you remember being in the cabin for all of the last two nights?"

"If there's one thing I know, it's that you and I didn't start glowing and float off into the sky. I never slept so well. I worry about Maggie when she talks like that, as though her dreams are real."

"What do you think is wrong with her?"

"You see it. We both see it. Something's cracked up there. The whole thing up top might be cracked."

Tommy tapped his head.

"I'm so sorry for it," he added. "She's my sister. It happened just like that. After all we've been through, I'm not surprised."

"She's always been so strong," Mabin said. "I never saw her falter once, no matter how dangerous it got, or who we were fighting. Now she's lost it when we're safe."

"But that's the difference between you and me and her. She's more human, so she has to be stronger, and it shows. She can feel that stuff more than we can, so she has to be tougher than we are so that her feelings don't overwhelm her. Maybe it was different this time. Maybe her feelings got the best of her this time."

"So maybe we can't understand what's going on when she gets like this since we're not like her?"

"No, we're not like her."

"Not at all?"

"We're killers, and she's not. She has to work hard at it. She's too sweet."

With the door in place, Mabin and Tommy found two salvaged cans of food, again with their labels burned off so that they didn't know what was in them. They cut the cans open with their knife, and found ravioli again. The day had cleared as last night's storm clouds scudded away to the east, but new clouds were forming above, vast white billows miles high in the sky, with dark undersides. Another storm was coming, and soon. Mabin and Tommy sat on the ground and pulled the pieces of ravioli from the cans with their fingers and stuffed the food into their mouths.

"We eat like animals," Tommy said.

"We're just settling here. We have to. We haven't put our lives back together. Maggie's missing lunch, not that it's so great. I miss her."

"Should we go find her?"

"I think she needs to be alone. I don't think there's any danger, and she did so much more work than we did that we have to catch up. We can start gathering stones to build a fireplace, or we can dig the basement. Maggie wants a basement, I guess, since she made the trapdoor."

"If she made the trapdoor."

"Do you still think she didn't?"

"I can't say. We've seen some things that nobody else has ever seen. It wouldn't be too difficult to believe there are other strange things we don't know about."

"But she's acting so weird, and there's no evidence of what she says."

Just as the words were out of Mabin's mouth, Maggie came around the corner of the cabin. She was bent over at the waist and peered distrustfully at them, her head lowered and her eyes full of fear. She said nothing but instead gasped at them and then looked into the cabin, eying every in of that side of it, and then turned to them again without talking.

"What did you do?" she asked in horror.

"We set the windows and door you made in place," Mabin said, smiling at her. "We're glad you're back."

"I didn't make any windows or doors."

"But we found them where you left them stacked against the outside walls. We don't have to worry about the weather now. The floor's solid and the roof's on and the windows and doors are in place."

"You should not have done this."

Mabin blinked quickly and glanced at Tommy.

"No?"

"No."

"Why not?"

"Don't you see what they're doing?"

"What do you mean?"

"The house is building itself."

"It's building itself?"

"It is, not exactly by itself, but with their help, those underground, and it's doing it to trap me inside when you're not here. You can always get out at night when you become lights and float away, but I'm trapped in the night. They're telling the house to do this."

"Who is?"

"The people under the floor."

"Ah, Maggie."

"Mags, you'll be able to rest now," Tommy broke in. "You don't have to worry about them any more."

"I can't rest while they're here."

Mabin glanced at Tommy again.

"We know we've been sleeping soundly at night, but you're bothered by what happened to us and to Elsa and Stephanovich and what you saw when we were underground. Now that the cabin's done, and you have a safe place to sleep, you'll start feeling better."

"This cabin is not a safe place."

"With the windows and the door in place, it's going to be – "

"Look at my feet and ankles!" Maggie yelled out. "They grabbed me. In there! Their claws, they grabbed me with their claws but were not strong enough to climb up out of the mud! And you two were no where around."

"Our feet and legs are cut up, too," Mabin said gently. "We can't go barefoot forever. We'll have to find shoes and socks somewhere, or make them, just like the first settlers here did."

"I'm going to show you one more time," Maggie said, in a quiet patient voice. "I'm going to open the trapdoor and show them to you. You'll see."

"There's nobody down there," Tommy said. "We already looked. We looked again when you weren't here."

Maggie kicked open the new front door all the way, violently, gasping with her face contorted and her eyes looking wild with fear and frustration.

"I'm going to show you," she said. "Now come in so I can show you. I come in now. They are down there and have red eyes and they did this to me."

"Maggie, why don't you have some lunch. We ate already, but you – "

Before Mabin could finish, Maggie ran into the house and screamed at them to come to her, she would prove what she was saying was true, but instead of moving Mabin and Tommy stood still staring at the doorway, their shoulders slumped over in frustration. Before they could say anything more, Maggie screamed so loudly from the darkness inside the house that both Mabin and Tommy were jolted awake and shot through the doorway. Another scream and they rushed to her, even though in the half-dark they could not see well. She had opened the trapdoor and was pulling her leg out of it as though something had a hold on the other end of it. She screamed and screamed, until finally Mabin reached her and jerked her away from the trapdoor. He glanced down into it but saw only the cool dark. There were no red eyes staring back at him.

"What happened?" he asked.

"I opened the door and someone grabbed my leg right away. I told you, I told you this was going to happen."

"Who grabbed you?"

"I don't know. That's the point. I don't know who it was, but they wanted to pull me down there."

"Why?"

"Will you look at my leg? Look what they did to it."

As their eyes adjusted to the dark inside the cabin, Mabin and Tommy could see scratch marks and a trickle of blood down the side of Maggie's leg.

"It's not safe in this house, it's not safe here, and I'm not staying inside here another night. We need another house far away from here."

Tommy shook his head resolutely.

"No. I'm not leaving Elsa and Stephanovich," he said. "Not for at least a year when we can resurrect them."

Maggie gaped at him in disbelief as he said it. She looked at the trapdoor and then kicked it shut.

"Do what you want," she said, rushing out the open door. "I'll sleep in the woods before I spend one more night in here."

Then she ran for the forest where she imagined she might be safe.

7

They found Maggie sitting at the base of a tree at the edge of the woods and sobbing. She was clutching her stomach and leaning forward as though in pain.

"I know, I know, I didn't get very far," she said meekly, as they rushed up to her. She was rocking back and forth and shaking. "I'm so silly. I'm sorry, I don't mean to be like this, but that cabin scares me. Maybe you're right. We're going to have another storm, and I don't want to be outside when it comes. Did you hear that lightning last night?"

"I ... maybe a little bit," Mabin said.

Some look flashed across Maggie's face, a look of distrust perhaps at the white lie Mabin told, but then it vanished as soon as he reached down for her and pulled her up into his arms. She could barely get up, but she settled in his embrace with a sigh. Her relief at being near him and the comfort of it made her cling tightly to him. Her legs were wobbling and her head was falling off to the side.

"I don't feel very well."

Suddenly, Mabin jumped back from her as though in pain.

"I ... don't feel very well," she repeated. "I'm not good."

She would have collapsed to the ground, but Mabin held her up. He did not draw her to him, though, and held her at arm's length.

"What's the matter with her?" Tommy asked. "What are you doing to my sister? She asked for help. Why don't you hold her tight? She needs you. Help her."

Tommy rushed up to Maggie and put his arm around her, but he screamed and he withdrew his arm quickly. He stood shaking his hand and staring at her as though he did not understand what had just happened and why he was in such pain.

"She burned me!" Tommy cried out. "She burned my hand!"

"Help me lay her down on the ground," Mabin said. "Quickly. I hope I don't know what's wrong with her, but I think I do."

It was not a difficult proposition to lay Maggie down on her back. Her legs dropped out from under her. She was moaning but unconscious, and as soon as she rested on the ground, her barely open eyes staring at the sky, they noticed smoke on her tee shirt just over her belly. A foul wisp of it curled up and assaulted Mabin's nose. He gasped and choked but he did not move away. Instead, he lifted Maggie's smoldering tee shirt off her belly.

"Oh, my god," Tommy said.

"It is, it is," Mabin said. "Oh, no."

A black patch of skin sizzled on the area he exposed. It was the size of a small plate and was bubbling and hissing, the skin crackling. More acrid smoke arose from the burning flesh, but Mabin put a hand over his mouth and nose to make sure he didn't breathe it.

"Get me the knife!" he yelled at Tommy.

"I don't have it!"

"Then go and get it. Now!"

Tommy did not run but flew the short distance back to the cabin, where he found the knife where he had left it stuck into log. He flew by and withdrew it in one motion and turned to fly back to the edge of the woods. As soon as he did, he saw more smoke rising up off of Maggie's center, and Mabin with his hand still over his mouth and nose, moving side-to-side to avoid the smoke. Tommy was next to him in an instant, avoiding the foul smoke rising off of his sister's midsection but choking on it when the wind blew it into his face. Mabin grabbed the knife out of his hand.

"What is going on? What is that fire on her?" Tommy asked.

"Get back. They're burning her from the inside," Mabin replied.

"Who is? Who's burning her? How do we put it out?"

"We don't put it out? I cut it out of her."

"What? You're not cutting open my sister."

"I have to. If I don't she's finished."

Without hesitation, Mabin pushed the tip of the knife into Maggie's burning flesh, just below her navel.

"What are you doing? Stop it! You'll kill her!" Tommy screamed.

With a deft flick of the wrist, leaning close to make sure of the cut, Mabin slashed open a small half-moon of a cut. Tommy was about to reach for his arm to stop him, but then he saw it, a small brightly glowing bit of stone, red but as bright as the sun, and he withdrew his hand from Mabin's arm. Maggie's flesh was sizzling around the tiny red stone, and with the cut open the smell was an overwhelming combination of seared flesh and sulfur.

"Get it out!" Tommy screamed, reaching for it.

Mabin stopped him by grabbing his arm and holding it.

"It will burn you hand off if you touch it. Step back. I have to use the knife."

Tears streamed down Tommy's face, but he retreated two steps while staring at the vicious little stone within Maggie's wound. With a deft hand, Mabin slipped the tip of the knife under the stone and flipped it out of the wound. It landed two feet away from her on bare ground but it did not extinguish itself. As though angry at being removed from Maggie's flesh, it flared up, sending a column of fire four feet into the air but then seemingly sucking the fire back down into itself. It bored into the earth as though burning through paper and disappeared, leaving a charred and smoking hole no bigger than a half-inch across.

"What was that?" Tommy asked. "Who put that in Maggie?"

Mabin was silent for a moment, staring at the wound in Maggie's belly to make sure there were no other burning stones. He closed the flap of flesh he had cut into her, kissed his hand and then touched the kiss to the incision.

"It was brimstone. I think I know who did this."

"Who was it? If I find him I'll ... you know what I'll do to him."

"You might not be able to."

"Why not? I'm not afraid of anybody or anything, especially if they're messing with Maggie. I'll find him, and then – "

"It was brimstone, Tommy."

"So?"

"Don't you know what that means? It means they've crossed over. They're damned now, damned souls. It makes them all-the-more dangerous. They can do things we've never imagined."

"Screw them. I don't care what they are. After they did this to Maggie, they're dead."

"Tommy, that's the problem. They are dead, yet they did this. Most people can't even see them, but I think we can. I know now that Maggie saw them, even if they weren't there, and I know now they saw her."

"How can you see something if it's not there? How can it be there if it's not?"

"It's not there in a normal state, and if you are in an abnormal state you can see it. They did this to her because she is in an abnormal state and saw them."

Half-conscious, Maggie was moaning, her head rolling from side-to-side on the ground. She tried to get up, even though semi-conscious. As she did so, the birds deep in the forest, far away, cackled so loudly that it reached their ears. Instinctively, they knew something was wrong after hearing the birds. Mabin peered deep into the half-light of the forest, and Tommy turned his head to catch sight of whatever it was Mabin was looking at.

"Why are they so noisy?" Tommy asked. "Does it have something to do with Maggie?"

"I think it has something to do with the dead."

"I wish they'd just shut up."

"They're not going to shut up. They're talking about this, and I doubt that they're even birds. I think all they are is voices. There is nothing left of them but their voices, and even those aren't human. They just sound like birds, but are not."

"If they've got voices, they've got throats, and if they have throats I'll – "

"We should get Maggie back to the cabin. I don't want the three of us out there alone, without a roof over our heads in the night."

"Maggie said they're under the cabin. Do you think it's safe?"

"If they're under the cabin, they're under everything around here. We'll block off the trapdoor, and make a bed for her. I think they'll be a little more careful now that we've cut the brimstone out of her and we know they're here. She'll get better now. The cabin might be the safest place for us."

"I guess so. Maybe I'll go try to find those birds, or voices or whatever they are. If they're bothering Maggie, I should take care of them before anything."

"All you'll find are voices, if you can find them at all. I think it's best we make as little contact with the ground as possible, since we know now what Maggie said is true. They're under there. They want us."

Mabin leaned over and slipped his arms under Maggie, between her body and the ground. He rose into the air with her, and as he did so Tommy mirrored him and rose beside him. Mabin slowly floated the short distance to the cabin, while Tommy went ahead and opened the door to let them in. As soon as they got inside, they noticed the trapdoor was open. Tommy grabbed the axe from beside the front door and lifted it over his shoulder, ready to strike out at whatever came up out of the ground. As Mabin predicted, they were not there, even though it was clear they were, or had been, there. While still holding the axe in the air, ready to strike, Tommy flew over to the trapdoor and kicked it shut and then stood on top of it. He stared down at the floor, looking for any movement.

"It won't do you any good," Mabin said. "You can't sense them in the state you're in. You'll need to look for them in another way before you can see them. You'll need to be in an altered state of mind before you can sense them at all."

"Like Maggie?"

"Just like her."

"So I have to be a little crazy?"

"Yes, just like Maggie. Good crazy."

"So how do we keep this trapdoor closed?"

"We were going to gather up rocks to build the fireplace and chimney. Why don't I do that while you watch her? Stay where you are until I can find some rocks big enough to hold down the door to make sure they don't open it again."

Mabin gently floated over to the bed of pine boughs and lay Maggie down on it, but she did not remain there. Even though unconscious, her eyes still closed, motionless, she floated above the bed and suspended herself in midair.

"She knows," Mabin said.

"What do you mean, she knows?"

"Even through she's asleep, she senses what happened. Now that we've cut their poison out of her, she has her powers in play again, and she knows who did this to her. I'd hate to be them once she encounters them again."

"I think she might already have encountered them," Tommy said.

"What do you mean?"

Tommy pointed to the girl floating above the floor.

"Look at her. You can see something's happening inside her. She does know. You said we have to see them in our dreams to fight them, and I think she's seeing them right now."

Maggie was twitching ever so slightly, but as she did so a small smile came to her lips.

It was a smile of triumph, and confidence, because now while unconscious she knew what she had to do to keep those who would destroy them firmly buried in the earth.

8

She left her body in the cabin and went in spirit to the place where she could find the two people who could help her. She went up the mountain in the night to the spot that had been Mabin's grave and now held her parents, Elsa and Stephanovich.

It was there she had both buried Mabin and married him, and now for the past few days it had held those who had the answers to what she must do to live in this strange empty world, if there were any answers. The forest at night had only the memories of her fears, for they had cleared it of those who would do her harm, yet she knew that the memory of fear is almost the same as fear itself. Both had their roots in the heart, and the memory of fear is as real as fear itself when it dominates one. It had to be fought. If the real creatures who had wished to destroy her instead had been destroyed by her, then their burial under the mountain held the same memory of her fear for her as their attempts on her life had held real fear. They reached up for her from the grave with claws ... That fight with the memory of fear was what she had to overcome now.

She found Mabin's grave, which held Elsa and Stephanovich as its second occupants, among the tall dark pines with a sprinkling of starlight over it. The stars glittered silver on the ground, mirroring the sky, as the wavering pines overhead made it seem as though there was a constant windborne scattering of daubs of starlight falling onto the forest floor. As she descended toward the grave, she looked down at her hands and arms and saw they had the same specks of starlight falling on them. She hovered above the grave and then lay out flat in the air, floating above it, just as her body was floating above the cabin floor now at the same time, and then she descended and settled down onto the warm earth covering the bodies of her parents. Her descent into the earth would be pleasant, since she knew she was about to see again those she loved so much, not those spirits who wished her harm. As she came to rest on the starlit ground and lay there, she felt her body settle onto the pine boughs back at the cabin. Both parts of her were at peace, at Mabin's grave and floating in the cabin. Closing her eyes, she let her weight relax into the soil, and she slowly fell down through the earth, its fragrant arms encircling her, until there was no starlight or moonlight falling onto her eyelids, and she was within the grave. Without opening her eyes, knowing she could not open her eyes and still see what she had to see, she felt her hands grasped by their hands. Quietly, Elsa took her right hand in hers and Stephanovich took her left hand, and she heard sobs.

"You've come," Elsa said, her voice broken and sweet. "We've waited for you, for you know us best."

"Why are you crying?" Maggie asked. "Things will be better in a short while, when we come to resurrect you, but for now I came to see you, but yet I know I can't see you. If I open my eyes, you'll be gone, and so will I."

"We're crying for the same reason. We knew you would come, but can not open our eyes to see you, and never will again be able to see you."

"Then the touch of hands must be enough. Our spirits will talk through our hands."

"It's more than enough for us, who can never be with you and our boy again."

"But in a year we can meet again. Tommy performed the ceremony that the mysteries told you to perform with Mabin, giving his blood into your hearts, and we have only to wait a year to resurrect you once more."

There was a short, deep silence in the grave.

"No," Stephanovich said. "It is not like that, not at all."

"It's not? What do you mean? It worked for Mabin, and for Tommy. This grave has the magic of life in it, and you will feel it."

"It has the magic of life for those who follow the mysteries to the letter, as we did, and Tommy did not follow the mysteries to the letter but acted rashly. He took his heart's blood and injected it into our hearts, but that is not what the mysteries demand we do. He did not think, or consult."

"It worked when you took my blood and injected it into Mabin's heart. Why would it not work with you?"

"Because the mysteries say you must inject the blood of the beloved into the heart of the deceased. You were Mabin's beloved, so it worked when we did as the mysteries commanded. Tommy is our step-son, and we here are each other's beloved. What he did will not work."

"It will not work?"

"No."

"Does that mean you will not come back to life with us? Will you stay here forever? How can you? That can't be."

"We can not come back, and we will not stay here. It is our end."

"But you can't here. You must be in one place or the other."

"No. You know that's not true. There are other options."

"Other options than life or death?"

"Yes."

Maggie felt the earth trembling above her and nearly opened her eyes out of the fear that something was going wrong above them. She had the good sense to keep her eyes closed tightly to retain the spiritual connection with her parents.

"We can never come back."

"No."

"That is simply the way it is. All things have an end."

"That's can't be right. Our loss can not last forever. Our loss has to end sometime and become as things were."

"We understand, and your loss has ended now in a way, but it can not be as it was again, we can't live as we did once," Stephanovich said. "I want you to consult the mysteries and listen to what they say about your present troubles and pain, but you can never tell Tommy what we just told you."

Maggie felt the tears forcing their way out of her eyes under great pressure, but still she did not open them, for fear of losing this moment, for fear of losing her grip on their hands.

"Always listen to the Transylvanian Mysteries," Elsa said.

"Instruct Tommy in them," Stephanovich added. "He needs to understand more than anyone, since he's just a boy. Bide your time. Instruct him. Do not tell him what we told you for at least a year. He can't know our end is final, or it will go very badly for him."

"But what of me? And Mabin? How are we to live if you refuse to come to us again?"

"We don't refuse: we have no choice in the matter. Now let go of our hands, Maggie. Let them go. Keep you eyes closed and know you can see us whenever you wish by closing your eyes and dreaming of us, for that is what we are now. We are dreams within your dream. Our rightful place is in your thoughts, and we will stay there forever."

"Beautiful girl, good-bye."

With that, Maggie felt Elsa's hand slip out of hers. She grasped tightly for it, but it was too late and her mother's gentle touch was gone. She wished more than anything to turn toward her in the warm sweet earth and embrace her, but she was trapped under its gentle pressure. Then she felt Stephanovich's hand slip out of hers, and she tried to clench it into her own, reaching out, but she felt only the damp soil where he now lived. Again, she wished to turn to him but could not, with the earth pressing down upon her. She felt her breath coming hard and fast and the tears filling her closed eyes, but she would not open them, for then she would lose the dream. And the dream of her parents was all she had of them now.

It was not until she heard Stephanovich's faint voice, seemingly coming from far away under the earth, that she returned to her body.

"Open your eyes and fight," he said, in a fierce whisper. "You have been cleansed of brimstone and fear, and now you must fight them to survive, for they wish to return to earth."

She came back to consciousness in her body with a start. She lay gasping heavily in bed in the cabin, the sweet pine boughs soft beneath her, but she was elevated off the floor in the bed that Mabin and Tommy made for her while she visited her dead. Back within herself, she felt free to open her eyes on the world again. She reached for Mabin first. She could tell him what she had just experienced, but not Tommy. Her eyes snapped open like doll's eyes and she turned quickly to look for her lover's body next to hers, but she could not see anyone in the dark. The inside of the cabin was pitch black except for an eerie glow emanating from under the floor near the trapdoor, and she knew then that Mabin and Tommy were not there but that someone else was. She stared at the ceiling while gasping, hoping to see the two lanterns floating above her, but they had already gone as they always did at night, and she still did not understand why. She felt something violating her, a gentle touch of a hardened hand, as clawed fingers moved slowly across her bare stomach where the brimstone had been. With a speed of hand she did not know she possessed, she grasped two of the fingers that were about to rip into her stomach. Then with a strength she knew she possessed but had not felt for days, she snapped the fingers back and tore them from their bony hand.

The monster's scream filled the small space within the cabin, but she was not yet finished with him. A pair of small red eyes, floating in a mist, burned down into her face from inches away. With the palm of her free hand she smacked the creature on the side of the head and pushed him off the bed and off of her. With two lines of red forming where his eyes flew away from her, he tumbled onto the pine planking below like a fog skirting a valley floor at dusk. She was up immediately and chasing him.

He recovered; in an instant he slipped away and dashed to the far corner of the room.

"You are trapped," he said. "Return me my fingers before you die."

"I am never trapped," Maggie said. "I can not be."

"This cabin is your trap," he said. "You knew, yet you came back. You knew we built this cabin as a trap for you, and yet you are here. Perhaps wanting to die?"

"No, I came back to destroy you," Maggie said. "Elsa and Stephanovich told me to."

"You thought you had died when you saw them, didn't you, but perhaps you were dreaming again, Butterfly? Dreaming you had done what can't be done, dreaming you had destroyed us? I am Harkin Davis and I can not die but will be forever."

"Mr. Davis? I saw you die. I helped you die for what you did to my parents."

"That was in your world of dreams. You are acquainted with the world of dreams now, aren't you? And you know now we are from there and therefore can not be ruined in this world."

"Yet I have your fingers in my hand."

"You only think you do. Watch, Butterfly, and dream again."

Harkin Davis held up his bloodied hand, a hand that was barely more than a mist, and with a sudden jerk drew it back quickly. His fingers flew from Maggie's hand and reattached themselves to the bloody stumps protruding from his palm. He opened and closed his clawed hand several times while staring at Maggie and grinning.

"So what are we now, Butterfly? Are we awake or asleep? And why do you think I will let you live in either one of my worlds?"

With the glow from beneath the floorboards affording her just enough light, Maggie quickly looked around the room for others like Harkin Davis. They appeared to be alone. Over the windows were locked shutters that prevented her from crashing through the glass and escaping. The door had a heavy bar across it and a lock to keep the bar in place. All this was new. She was alone with Harkin Davis. She knew that she could not leave, but that he could, for he knew how to navigate the world of her dreams better than she did. Since he had found his way in, he could find his way out. With a slow movement, Harkin Davis circled around her, his red eyes like beacons warning her where he was. She mirrored his movement, circling in the opposite direction to keep him in front of her.

"I came alone, and you know I'm unable to stay for long," he said suddenly, in a nervous, high-pitched voice. He got his voice under control and went on: "I do not need anyone else to do to you what I am going to do to you. In fact, I prefer to do it alone. It will give me more pleasure to tear you to pieces by myself."

Maggie felt a great surge of strength at the threat. He felt no weakness or madness now, but lived in both and accepted both. That gave her power.

"Whatever you are now, you're as foolish as you were in life when we gave you a chance to live as a human being and you chose the way of blood. We killed you then, and I will find some way to do the same to whatever thing you are now."

"Impossible. I am far more than I was, and you are far less than you were. While you slept, I put the devil's stone in you, in your belly, to take away your powers. You are nothing but a girl now."

"Just a girl? Is this where you put the stone?"

Maggie lifted her shirt to show Harkin Davis the burned patch of skin and wound left behind after Mabin cut out the brimstone.

His red eyes widened with fear.

"Mabin cut it out when it started to burn my flesh. Until he did, I had no idea why I felt so strangely. Now I understand, and I think you do, too."

Maggie made a sudden movement toward him but stopped short when he flashed across the room and halted to face her in a corner.

"It doesn't matter," he said. "The devil's stone always does its work. I am not what I was, but better, and you are not what you were, but worse. I will take great pleasure in dismembering you, while you will be able to do nothing about it."

Still uncertain what sort of creature she faced, Maggie knew she had to act. But what to do? Would he bleed if she wounded him? Could he be damaged? Was he a nothing, like a mist, that would dissipate at her touch? While in danger in a dream she knew it was always best to wake up. But was she a butterfly now or a girl? And which one would be the best to be in a fight against this thing? What would she wake up to be? She decided on a butterfly. Instead of rushing directly at him, she fluttered first to the left, and then up, and then down, and then up again into the dark near the ceiling and then directly down on top of him. She crashed down on him feet first, landing on his shoulders so that his knees buckled and he fell to the floor with a grunt. Her weight falling directly on top of him did the trick. When his knees hit the floor his lower legs snapped off like branches, so brittle were the bottom parts of the creature. She tumbled to the floor beside him and swung out at him, hoping his head was as frail as his legs had proven to be, but he swiftly ducked and then picked up one of his legs as she recovered. He swung it at her and she ducked, feeling the whoosh of the misty appendage going past and smelling the acrid stench of his dead flesh. It gave him time to grab his other leg and rush across the floor on his bloody stumps to the trapdoor. He was breathing very hard but the air seemed to pass right through him, as though he had no lungs but holes in his chest.

"Butterfly," he said. "I should have known. I came to fight a butterfly when the girl was gone but the butterfly dropped a great weight on me and I did not expect it. It will not happen again. Next time, thousands of us will come up into this cabin at night after you, after we take more power from the dead."

With that, Harkin Davis transformed into a glow that seeped down through the floorboards quickly, returning to the place of brimstone.

Maggie rose off the floor and fluttered up into the dark air of the cabin. Crossing from one wall to another, then up and then down, she settled onto the sweet-smelling pine boughs of the bed, since butterflies always seek out sweetness, a flower to rest upon, and it was sweetness she found when she thought of sleeping by Mabin's side.

She rested there, waiting for her lover to return, but still trapped by her condition and warily watching the glow beneath the floorboards. She watched in case any other malignant creature tried to force its way up between through the cracks to come calling on her with more tricks in mind.

She no longer feared the dark places of her mind.

9

For the first time, Maggie was awake when her lover and brother floated down through the ceiling on their return from their night-time travels to the stars.

The dawn was near, and its light was returning through the cracks in the shutters that trapped her in the cabin. Mabin dropped down next to her first, settling softly onto the pine boughs of the bed with a sigh, his eyes closed in sleep and a small smile of pleasure crossing his face as soon as he was beside her. When he was resting in bed, the glow inside of him extinguished itself, and his chest heaved up and down regularly, as a human chest will do.

Across the room, Tommy drifted downwards toward a single bed of pine boughs that she had not noticed, a new bed they had built just for him. He dropped heavily the last foot, and mumbled something in protest when he hit the bed, but he remained sleeping. The glow under the floor faded and died, as the monsters retreated from their watch below. Day was not kind to them, Maggie knew, and she told herself to remember that, that daylight could protect her and harm them. Maggie settled next to her husband, at last feeling she could rest, and laid her head on his shoulder. She was too tired to fight sleep, or whatever it was butterflies do to rest, and she did not understand if she was sleeping while in his arms or awake and dreaming she was within his embrace. It was all confusion in this cabin, but pleasant now with him here, and she didn't really care if it was a dream or real, as long as he was with her in one form or another.

"There you are," he said with a smile, when his eyes opened on Maggie beside him. "Are you better now?"

"Much better. I'm not afraid now of any of it."

"Did you sleep through the night?"

"Not a wink. I spent it all in my dreams."

"Then you did sleep."

"No, and you didn't, either. You and Tommy left the cabin again, and only came back a moment ago. You live another life in your dreams, too, you know. You're as much of a butterfly dreaming you're a person as I am."

"I think I remember a little of it, what we did last night. We cut the brimstone out of you and you seemed to be asleep. There wasn't much to do but fall asleep, too, right beside you."

"I don't remember you leaving, but I just watched you come back."

"I feel as though I slept right here beside you all night. I guess that's what my dream is, to sleep beside you always."

"You didn't, though," Maggie laughed. She was about to say she left her body behind, too, to go visit Elsa and Stephanovich, but then she recalled they told her they were never coming back, that they could not be resurrected, and she thought it would wreck Tommy to hear that.

"Harkin Davis was in the cabin last night. He's learning how to haunt this earth, and gaining more power over it. I couldn't get out but had to fight him."

"Harkin Davis ... that's the vampire we killed after what he did to mom and dad," Tommy said. "He's dead. He couldn't have been here."

"He was here, I assure you of that. He's the one who implanted the brimstone in my belly. He thought it was still there and that he had me weak and trapped inside the cabin, but he didn't know what you had done for me."

"What did he want?"

"This cabin is a trap, Mabin. Somehow, they helped us build it to catch us inside while we were sleeping. That's why parts of it were built without our efforts. Somehow, they did it. The door was locked and the shutters were closed tight and I couldn't get out. He came for me, but he was very brittle and it was easy to chase him back down. If he gains more power, I don't know if he'll be a brittle next time."

"Why didn't we wake up?" Tommy asked. "Maggie, why didn't you wake us up to help you fight him?"

"Because you weren't here."

"We weren't? Again?"

"Tommy, you and Mabin are different from me now. Both of you came back from the dead, but I didn't. I think that makes us different."

"How?" Mabin asked. "I sensed that, too, but how?"

"You're not susceptible to them. You've became different types of beings, and I'm still just a girl. At night, you move into the dream world completely, while part of me stays here. Part of me has to, but you've been resurrected and are different. I think when I am dreaming, you are awake, and when you are awake I am dreaming, but we still sense each other, and know we're together."

Mabin took her in his arms.

"I don't feel any different. I want the same things as always. I want you, and dream of you, and I want a regular life with you. If this world was a good world, we would have it. We would have our life together if they weren't here haunting us."

He stared toward the floor.

"You leave at night because you know in your dreams you have to," Maggie said. "I think you're awake in your other world, and only dreaming you're with me. You're not fully a part of this world yet, but went through your death and got to live again in another way. Maybe your death is still inside you and is the part of you in which you're truly awake. It makes both of you different from me."

"I remember a little of last night," Tommy said suddenly. "So you think we're awake in death and dreaming when with you?"

He sat up in bed.

"What do you remember of death?" Maggie asked.

"I remember the stars. It seems like a dream. Is it supposed to? I remember floating high above, like you say we do, Maggie, and I remember seeing all of the stars, and I mean all of them. Somehow I knew I was seeing every star there is and it was incredible. I was very close to them."

Mabin slumped back in bed. He was not quite as impressed by the vision as Tommy was.

"Oh, no. I remember that, too," he said, as though shaken by the memory. "I remember I wanted to be here with you, but I wasn't. It felt wrong not to be with you, and I was struggling to get back here. I knew they were coming for you."

Suddenly, there was a gust of wind and the shutters and windows and door flew open. A strong fresh morning wind brought the clean fragrance of pine rushing into the cabin and carried out the dank muskiness that had been enclosed there all night. The pine boughs shook beneath them.

"Whoa!"

Tommy jumped up to close and latch the front door, but he left the windows and shutters open.

"Did they just do that?" Tommy asked. "Why would they open the door and windows now after keeping them closed and trapping Maggie all night?"

"Maybe it was just the wind," Mabin said.

"I don't think it was," Maggie said. "They can't survive up here above ground yet. Everything that's happening is happening because of them. I don't understand it, but they want the cabin to seem fresh and clean now, maybe to keep us here."

"Then we have to end it, again," Mabin said grimly. "If we burn down this place and leave, would we be safe?"

Maggie laughed.

"Safe? What's that?"

"Would we be?"

"They'd follow us," Maggie said. "The dreams of the dead can follow you. They don't have much power now, but they're clever. Maybe we should be even cleverer. They know you have to leave at night and that's when they come for me, but you can't, Mabin, you can't go if you can help it. I don't know what I'll do if all of them come at once, with more power, and you two are not here."

"Well, I'm not going anywhere tonight, Mags," Tommy said. "I don't care how many of them come or who says I have to go or if I'm really dead and dreaming of this world. I'm staying here with you."

"I don't think we have much of a choice but to go, except maybe to stay awake, stay away from our dreams," Mabin said. "It's as though we're being called when we sleep. You and I are not what we were, but maybe we can understand how to be the people we were before our resurrection."

"We have to stay!" Tommy yelled. "We can't leave Maggie alone! Or forget about mom and dad."

"I'm not saying that, but what are we supposed to do, if we have no control over what we do and where we go at night, if when we're dead is when we're truly awake?"

"I don't know about all that. If they trapped Maggie in here alone, then maybe we should trap ourselves in here with her," Tommy said. "We'll stay awake and make it so we can't leave this cabin, and then we'll see what happens when they come again. Then we won't let them leave, and then we'll see how long they last. I'm not leaving, ever. They've ruined enough for us, and we have to get rid of them once and for all."

Mabin turned to his wife.

"Maggie, you have to tell us exactly what happened last night. You said they were brittle. If you hit them, what happened?"

"They would get injured, just fall apart to pieces, but it was so easy for them to put themselves back together in the dream."

"You have to tell us exactly what went on last night, what you did and when Harkin Davis got scared and ran off. Can you remember?"

Maggie thought back to the previous night in the cabin alone, and she remembered it from the beginning, when she felt the hard touch of claws on her stomach where the brimstone had been.

She began telling the tale with that.

"The first thing I did was rip off his claws when I felt the creature touch me, and then I ..."

Tommy flew across the room and sat down on the bed to listen to the rest of the tale.

"This is going to be fun," he said, settling down beside her. "Go on. Tell me the rest, the whole thing."

Maggie went on with the tale.

10

The recent fresh heavy rains had washed the mountainside clean of most of the black ash that was all that remained of the bodies of the vampires that Elsa and Stephanovich had burned alive while the creatures hid from daylight in their homes.

Seedlings had emerged from the purged bare ground, and the mountainside was on its way to recovering and taking a normal, natural course of life.

What scarred the area was the cabin, a hastily built structure that was the work of three desperate people in concert with many vile creatures that lived their deaths below ground and refused to accept their lot but instead sought revenge on the living in their dreams. It was clear to Maggie that the monsters had come out at night while they slept and dreamed and worked on the cabin quietly and with evil intent. It was a trap. When it was completed, the creatures planned to snap the trap shut and finish them off, before they could finish off the dead vampires.

"All I wanted was a home," she sighed, "with you and Tommy living with me. Instead, I got this."

The cabin was cute enough as it was, built of logs and topped by a shake roof, and with more work to finish it off it could have been a fine temporary home, if not for those below. It lacked a chimney and window boxes filled with flowers, but those touches could be added later, if they killed off the ghosts from below and survived.

To prepare for the night when the others would come, to prepare their own trap, Maggie and Mabin and Tommy examined the outside of the house to see if there were any obvious weaknesses in the structure that would allow the dead souls in. They looked over the sparse mountainside that had once teemed with homes and life and now was reverting back to a strange nature, the feeling that they did not know if they were alive or dead and dreaming came back to them. Everything they had known and loved was gone, as though it had never existed, without a trace of its existence left behind. Only this small cabin remained as a reminder that they were once whole human beings, but even it told them things were not as they had been. Tommy kept pinching himself again and again to determine if he was awake or asleep, alive or dead.

If things were as Maggie described them, with monsters seeping up out of the floor of the cabin and Mabin and Tommy drifting off into the night sky to leave her to face the creatures alone, then they truly must live in a dream, or be mad or dead and not know it. Perhaps they haunted this life, as did the vampires under the cabin. Perhaps they lived in a borderland between life and death and had yet to discover their true new home. Maggie had found that the hurts delivered in dreams can be just as powerful and real as the hurts given while awake, and she had no desire to suffer anymore indignity, in dreams or in reality.

While they walked around the outside of the cabin, Maggie thought back to what Elsa and Stephanovich had told them when she visited them in the grave in spirit. She remembered they told her they were not coming back, not returning to life, and with the memory a tear coursed down her cheek. She wiped it away before Tommy could see it, and she blurted out something just to hide what she was on the verge of telling Tommy: that their parents truly were dead and could not come back. No magic extended that far beyond reality. None could.

"We should consult the mysteries about what's best for us now," she blurted. "They might tell us what to do with these creatures."

Elsa and Stephanovich had promised her the mysteries would guide them, if they remained true to them.

"Every time we consult them, somebody else seems to die, or more vampires show up, or something bad happens," Tommy said. "The mysteries never did me much good."

"Elsa and Stephanovich lived by them, and we should, too."

"Yeah, yeah, I guess so. Where are they, anyway?"

Mabin pulled the parchment out of his back pocket. When he did, the wind kicked up with a sweet smell of pine and the sun broke out from behind the clouds. It seemed to be a sign they were on the right track.

"I hope the mysteries have learned English," Mabin joked. "I couldn't read them if they speak to us in any of the ancient languages that Stephanovich knew."

"Hey, can we go visit the grave today?" Tommy asked. "I just thought of that when I saw the mysteries again."

"Tommy, it's only been a few days," Maggie said. "Remember what happens if we go back too soon. We should stay away from the grave until the time is right."

"I know, I know, I messed up with Mabin, but I won't do that again, I promise. I learned my lesson."

"It says something here," Mabin said, peering down at the mysteries with excitement.

"Does it mention mom and dad?" Tommy asked, standing next to Mabin to read what was written. "Maybe they sent a message to us through them."

"It says, 'All must pass on, and when they pass, they can never return,'" Mabin said.

Maggie stepped up to stand on the other side of Mabin and peer down at the parchment.

"They don't mean Elsa and Stephanovich," she said quickly.

"Of course they don't. Look at Mabin and me. We had to pass on, and yet we came back. They can't mean mom and dad, because I did everything right this time so far and now we just have get rid of these creatures under the cabin and then wait for Elsa and Stephanovich to come back to life again. The mysteries are saying those creeps under the house have to go, that's what they're saying."

"Does it say how we can get rid of them?" Maggie asked Mabin.

"They're writing something ... it says, 'Stand on them. Stand where you are. Never move and all will be taken from them, if you never awaken. Only two of you are free, and one is asleep.'"

"What does that mean? It's gibberish," Tommy said. "Who's asleep? I feel like I'm awake."

"I don't know what it means."

"Do you understand it?" Tommy asked Maggie. "It might as well be written in Sumerian."

"It says to stand on them. That's all I understand of it," Mabin said. "It makes sense, since they're underground. Still, it doesn't sound right. Why can't the mysteries be clear?"

"Because they're mysteries," Maggie said.

"So we're not supposed to go anywhere? We're not supposed to run away? Just stand on top of them?" Tommy asked.

"That's what they seem to be saying."

"That's stupid. Big help they are. I wasn't going anywhere anyway, but that just sounds dumb," Tommy said. "We're got a year to go, so we have to hold out here to bring back Elsa and Stephanovich, no matter what happens."

"So we spend another night in the cabin?" Mabin asked.

Maggie drew in a breath and held it.

"I guess we have to."

"No. We spend every night for the next year in there," Tommy said. "I'm not forgetting about mom and dad. You guys can go if you want to, but I'm staying here."

"I'm just saying – "

"I don't care! I'm not leaving!" Tommy yelled. "You're scared, and I can tell you're scared. Think of somebody other than yourself for once, Maggie."

As though angry with them Tommy burned red in the face and turned from them without another word. He walked around the cabin. They heard the door slam after he went inside.

"He's a little touchy," Mabin said.

"After what we've been through, can you blame him? Elsa and Stephanovich are the second set of parents he's lost."

"I know he doesn't mean it. Mabin, do you feel like yourself?"

"Of course I do. I never felt better, except when I let myself go and think about the bad stuff that's happened. Then I don't feel so good. Why?"

"Because Tommy's different, and you are, too. They've gotten inside our heads. You're exactly the same as you've always been while we're awake, or seem to be awake, but when we're sleeping you're different."

"I am?"

"I know you are, but I don't think you know it yet."

"I believe you when you tell me what happens when we're sleeping, but I still can't remember much of it, and it still sounds strange. Glowing from inside, flying up out of the cabin and disappearing, it ..."

"What?"

"Sounds as if I have no control at all when I'm sleeping, that I am another person, but I don't remember any of it. The next time it happens, wake me. I don't like doing what you say I do while I'm sleeping."

"I've tried to wake you, every time, but I couldn't."

"Try harder. Let's go inside and make sure Tommy's all right, then we'll get ready for the night, when they come. I won't leave you tonight, I promise."

"It's going to be a hard promise to keep."

Tommy was kneeling on the floor, his face pressed to one of the wider cracks between the floorboards, a knife held in his hand. He didn't get up when they entered, but he remained staring through the floorboards at the darkness below, trying to get a look at anyone who might be staring back at him.

"Do you see anyone?" Maggie asked.

"No."

"They won't come out in the daytime," Mabin said.

"I know, but I'm thinking of going down after them," Tommy said. "It's a bad idea just to wait around for them, until they think it's a good time to attack and kill us."

"The night is different, and they're different then and so are we," Mabin answered. "If we went after them now, all we'd find is mud."

"They've got to be somewhere down there. I say we go get them." Tommy insisted.

"We'd only be going after what we can see in the day. What we see at night is completely different."

Tommy got to his feet.

"If that's the case, then maybe I will just stand here and wait for them. I'm tired of their crap, and if we have to wait until tonight to get rid of them, then I guess all we can do is wait and get ready."

"Let's seal the cracks in the floor, find some more weapons and then take a nap. We need to be wide awake all night so that Maggie's not the only one in here when they come. I don't know what we're going to do when they get here, but I think we'll figure it out before long."

Tommy banged his foot down on the floor.

"Hear that?" he shouted out, looking down. "I'm going to stand here all day waiting for you creeps, and then tonight if you come anywhere near us, you're done, finished. This is your last warning. Understand?"

Tommy stared down at the floor, but the only answer was a cool, dank miasma floating up between the floorboards.

And silence.

It was the sure silence of death.

11

The daylight lasted long into the night, as the summer sun refused to give way to the night-time's coming reign over the earth. Without knowing if they would be of much use in their dreams, while awake they had gathered together various lengths of wood and fashioned them into clubs and spears. It felt silly to stockpile the cabin with weapons to use while asleep, against vampires that were dead, but they had little choice but to arm themselves even if the clubs and spears would prove useless against phantoms. As soon as the late twilight came, a wind whipped up that encircled the cabin and swung the shutters closed, and then the open window panes slipped down and closed and latched themselves. There was a click and the lock on the front door slipped into place. All was still. They were trapped, and there was little question who wanted them ensnared within the cabin.

"I think they're coming," Mabin whispered. "Is everybody still awake?"

"I am."

"I'm going to unlock the front door," Tommy said. "We'll need to be able to get out of here if we have to."

"If you move, they'll know where you are and come up through the floor at that spot. I have a feeling the door won't unlock anyway."

"Can they do that? Come up through the floor? Are they strong enough?"

"They might be by now."

"Are you asleep, Tommy?" Maggie asked.

"I don't think so. How could I be asleep if I'm talking?"

"Good. Don't fall asleep. If you do, they'll come in. They'll know I'm alone if you fall asleep and leave with Mabin."

As though not hearing anything Maggie said, in a daze, Tommy curled up on the floor. Immediately, his breathing was deep and slow and a weak light glowed in his chest just under his shirt.

"Oh, no. Tommy, what are you doing?" Maggie asked, in a panic.

"Huh? What?"

"You're falling asleep when I just said – "

"I am. I couldn't stop it. It's dark in here, and I've been up all day, and ..."

The boy's eyes snapped shut with a will of their own.

Mabin helped the boy sit up, but Tommy's head rolled over to the side and his eyes rolled around under his eyelids. It was as though he had been knocked unconscious by a blow.

"Listen to me, Tommy. If we don't do this, Elsa and Stephanovich don't have a chance," he said. "We have to defend this place every night for the next year, and you have to stay awake."

Tommy's eyes snapped open with the mention of Elsa and Stephanovich, but the weak light remained on in his chest and he blinked over and over uncontrollably. It was as though his backbone had given way, for he was slumping toward the floor and could not straighten up as the light inside him grew brighter and brighter.

"I'm just so ... tired."

"Tommy, don't! Mabin?"

"What? Can you help me with Tommy? He's falling over."

Maggie didn't help, but instead pointed to Mabin's chest. Just under his shirt a soft glow matched the glow in Tommy's chest, and he raised his eyes to Maggie in a panic, even while his eyelids drooped down.

"I exhausted, and I don't know what's going on," he said. "I can't keep my eyes open. This is what you saw before, isn't it? This is how you described it."

Before she could answer, she saw a column of fog standing in the corner of the cabin. Red eyes appeared at the top of the column, but then the eyes disappeared and the column of fog dissipated but then re-formed itself as a puddle of white mist on the floor. The white puddle swirled like whirlpool and then seemed to fade away into the floorboards with a hissing sound.

"Did you see that?" Maggie asked. "They're here."

As though in answer, Tommy fell to the floor deep in sleep, snoring loudly and curling up into a ball. Mabin could no longer hold him up, since he was weakening into sleep, too. The light inside his chest glowed brightly now. Maggie felt a cold hand on the back of her neck. She screamed and swiped at it, but it let go of her quickly.

"Don't let Tommy sleep," she said to Mabin. "Someone touched me just now, touched the back of my neck. Don't you sleep, too."

Mabin's eyelids drooped lower and lower, and his head sunk toward his chest.

"I ... won't ... sleep ..." Tommy said, even though he was dead to the world and already gone.

Inside his chest the light glowed so brightly it lit the corners of the small cabin. More small white columns of mist were rising and hissing and dancing and then falling away again into the floor in each of the corners, as though looking for something but not having found it retreating again into the mud. One would rise and then disappear, and then another would do the same. Maggie was wide awake in a panic. "These things, look at these filthy things," she said. The light inside the cabin intensified, and then it was so bright it was as though the shutters had opened and morning had come. Maggie turned to see Tommy was in full glow, with several of the small swirling mists circling around him, and he was already four feet off the floor and rising. One of the mists sharpened itself to a point and with a swift movement jabbed itself at Tommy's neck. He winced and kept rising, but four drops of blood fell out of the wound and splattered onto the floor next to her. She leaped up to reach for her brother to wake him and save him from the stabbing mists, but he had risen to the ceiling and was out-of-reach. The room got even brighter, as though a second sun had arisen, and she knew what was happening before she turned to see Mabin in full glow rising through the air. More of the white mists quickly surrounded him and formed themselves into sharp points that stabbed into his neck and chest and back, cutting him in a dozen places so that the blood flowed down out of him and dripped onto Maggie below. Tommy was bleeding in several dozen places now but still sleeping soundly and floating upward, and his blood dripped down in constant red rain. In an instant, he disappeared through the ceiling and the flow of his blood ceased from above. She spun around and raised her face to the ceiling to see the sharpened mists still attacking Mabin. His blood splattered down on her face in a torrent and she stepped back and wiped it out of her eyes just in time to see him fade away through the roof.

Then the vampire's dead souls turned on her.

She was enveloped in a thick fog as they coalesced around her, stinging her as though she was swimming in a school of jellyfish. "No help, there is no help for you now, and we will bleed you with pinpricks of fire until the end," one of the mists whispered in her ear. "You are the one who did this to us, took away everything from us, all the blood we desired and fed on, so now you will pay with your blood, and we will haunt you until the end. Your blood is of no use to us now, but we will drain you of it anyway."

Maggie swung out at the whispering in her ear, but her hand merely passed through the mist, and it laughed at her and then bit her earlobe. She screamed, and tried desperately to grasp the creature, but it was like grasping hot smoke. It stabbed her hand, seemingly passing through it with a burning agony, and she closed the hand into a fist reflexively but the burning did not stop. With an agony that nearly made her faint, two more of the burning mists burned into her breasts, setting her chest on fire as she fell to her knees and screamed out for help. "Mabin! Tommy! I'm on fire! They have set me on fire!" Another burning mist stabbed into her side, into her liver, and she collapsed to the floor, her breath heaving out of her mouth, her chest and side aflame with the boring burning mists, and then they attacked her bare feet. A dozen of them stabbed into the souls of her feet and burned the flesh and set afire her bones as she screamed in agony. They were twittering like hellish birds around the souls of her feet and pausing only to bore into them with small sharp fires. She cried out and jerked around on the floor in a desperate attempt to get away but she could not escape them, and the only relief she got was the feeling she was about to faint from the agony of this torture. The blood from all her wounds was dripping onto the floor and if this kept up for much longer it would drain down through the floorboards and sate the revenge they sought by killing her. She felt the faintness coming on, and her head bobbing up and down, and her eyelids got very heavy and her tongue felt thick, and then there was the blackness.

Her hands reached out and she felt the bodies on the floor on both sides of her, and when she opened her eyes there was a hellish pink and orange light inside the tiny cabin: it came from the mists that had attacked her. Beside her, she saw first Mabin and then Tommy, and her heart leaped with the joy that they had come back, had not deserted her, but then she gasped with horror to see they were unconscious and that flowing bloody wounds covered their faces and necks and arms. She felt her own cuts slowing seeping blood, but the wounds were already closing and her blood was coagulating into thick wet scabs. She was covered in a body-mask of drying blood. The killing mists were standing back and observing their work, each a column of orange and pink with red eyes topping the columns, and they stared at her and the two boys on the floor, standing still and not speaking, but with their red eyes blazing. She could not understand why they simply didn't finish her off, continue their cutting and burning until she was no more.

"It was too fast," one of them said. "We tried to do her in too quickly, and now she's slipped into her other world."

"I tried to go slow, but it was such ecstasy to burn into blood again I could not stop myself. I wish to burn her again now."

"Step back! Don't try! She's able to injure us now in this world where she's whole again. When her mind shifts to the second world of the dead, then we can have her again."

"I want her now and can not wait."

"No, wait for her to drift off back to where she was. Patience. It's only a matter of time until we taste her again and finish her off. We can not deal with her when she is in this world of real blood."

Maggie was still so faint she could barely understand what the vampire souls were saying, but she thought she was safe now that she was herself again. But what self was she? And in what world was she truly herself? This one? Or the one in which they attacked her? Was this the world of sleep and dreams, or was the other one her sleep and her dreams? In which world could they harm her? Not this one, she slowly came to understand.

"Mabin? I need you now," she said, touching his shoulder. "Tommy? Both of you please wake up!"

They were dead asleep, barely breathing, and she realized the seriousness of their wounds. They might have been driven down by these spirit-creatures, burned from the outside and inside, and now left to die. They had seemed to escape from the vampire souls, seemed to have floated off into the sky again, leaving her alone, but it seemed now that the attack on them as they floated away had been successful. Still, they were beside her now and she did not know how they had returned. They must now be in their second world, too, she thought. She felt her strength coming back as her anger grew. She was the only one left who could contend with these things, they said it themselves, and as her wounds closed in this second world she knew her powers were returning. They knew this, and they stood back, waiting for her return to the first world, where she was vulnerable. Without thinking, with a quickness that was too fast for her to understand, she grabbed the axe from the floor and flew across the room instantly. She brought down the axe on one of the vampire spirits, splitting the mist that formed him right between his piercing red eyes, and there was a horrendous squeal as the mist divided in two and dissipated.

"He is no more!" the vampire spirit beside him screamed out in despair. "I told you we should not stay and wait for her to fade!"

Other vampire spirits squealed out, and it fed her fury. Now I know, Maggie said to herself, now I know. Barely stopping after destroying the first spirit, she swung the axe in an arc parallel to the floor and split two more lengthwise, and they tumbled to the floor and were no more. The remaining spirits scattered to the corners of the room, desperately looking for an escape, and several of them found unsealed chinks in the floor and disappeared through them into the mud below the cabin again. She spun around to see who might not be so lucky and immediately caught another spirit sneaking up on her. She brought the axe down on it, splitting it lengthwise as she had the first spirit. Its squeal sent the others backing away from her and scurrying frantically for the chinks in the floor. Soon the hundreds of orange and pink mists were descending en masse through the floorboards as quickly as they could. Maggie managed to decapitate several as they descended, slicing them just below the eyes, and their squeals were the last thing she heard that evening.

She fell to her knees gasping, the strength suddenly drained from her, and she fainted and dropped forward onto her face.

She had no idea in which world she would find herself once she awoke, but she had no choice but to leave this one now.

12

The sweet morning breezes woke her.

It was the only thing that could wake her, since the dawn's light was blocked out as she lay face-down utterly exhausted on the floorboards. She was surprised she was still breathing, and it felt like pure joy.

Without opening her eyes, she rolled over onto her back and again had to contend with the light on her eyelids. She did not want to know: was it sunrise or was it Mabin and Tommy glowing in the middle of the night, about to leave her again to the whims of the vampire spirits? Mabin's groans made her eyes snap open. Tommy coughed in pain, as though sick, but then also groaned. Maggie felt the sting of her wounds on her neck and face, and when she moved her arms it was as though small fires ignited on them. Fighting the pain, she rolled over to see Mabin and Tommy in a similar condition. They were cut and bruised on their faces and necks, and dried blood covered them and caked on their clothing. Wincing, Mabin turned to her, his eyes widening with alarm.

"Maggie ... Are you hurt? What happened to you?" he asked.

"The same thing that happened to you. They came in here last night and attacked us. You two slept through it."

"We slept through it? How could I have slept through it?" Tommy asked. "I couldn't have slept ... Ow!"

He cried out when he rolled over toward Maggie and the pain from several of his caked wounds stabbed into him.

When he saw her, he asked the same question Mabin had, with the same concern.

"What happened to you?"

And she gave him the same answer.

"The same thing that happened to you. They came in here last night and attacked us. You two slept through it."

"I don't remember any of that. Are you sure we slept through it?"

"You not only slept through it, but you weren't here for half of it. You left me alone again and I had fight them off until they cut me up so badly I fainted, which saved me, and then when I woke up you two were here again but wounded and they were afraid of me. They cut you as you were leaving, but left you alone when you came back."

"Are they here now?"

"I think it's morning, so we're safe for now."

"I can't remember any of it," Mabin said, looking down as though exasperated.

"You can see now I'm telling the truth. Who else could have done this to you?"

Mabin looked down at the wounds on his arms.

"I know you're telling the truth. I don't question that now. I just don't know why I don't remember anything and why we leave you alone night after night to deal with them. You know if I understood that, I would never leave you, especially with them living under this house."

"I think it was the resurrections that made us this way," Maggie said suddenly.

"Our resurrections?"

"I think so."

"But they brought us back to life," Tommy said. "We're the same as we've always been again, and we're in the same world we've always been in."

"Then why are you two so different and I'm the same?" Maggie asked.

Mabin hesitated before answering. His eyes held a deep knowledge that made Maggie believe he finally understood.

"Because you never died, Maggie. We did. That makes us different because we did and you brought us back to life. Is that what you're saying?"

"It's the only explanation. The dead are different from the living. Just look at the vampire spirits. Then look at yourselves."

"But we're not dead anymore!" Tommy burst out.

"You are, but you don't know it. You're in the two worlds of the living and the dead, one foot in one and another foot in the other. You're resurrected, but that doesn't mean you exist in the same way you did before, in one world only. Parts of you were left behind, and that's why you can't stay with me at night. You have to go back."

"So we move between the worlds, between the living and the dead, when we're awake or asleep? Is that what you mean?"

"I can't see any other explanation."

"How do we make this, and only this, our world again? It's what I'd like to do, to stay with you always."

"I don't know. It's the riddle of the girl and the butterfly again, only this time you two are the dreamers, not knowing what you are. When I sleep and dream, you return to your second world."

Tommy flopped back down on the floor.

"I really messed things up again, didn't I?" he asked. "Now I'm alive and dead at the same time."

"If anybody messed them up, I did," Maggie said. "I couldn't live without you and had to have both of you back after you died. Elsa and Stephanovich had to have you back. The mysteries told us how to do it."

Mabin took Maggie's hand and held it in both of his.

"We have to come back to you completely. I love you too much to be partly in one world and partly in another."

She kissed his lips.

"We have to figure out a way to do that. We're haunted by the vampires we killed," Maggie said. "They know what our problem is and are taking advantage of it. Maybe if we get rid of them we can be free of your deaths, and be together the way we're supposed to be."

"How do you kill the spirit of a vampire who's already dead?"

Maggie stared at Mabin and there was a cold hardness in her grey eyes.

"By fighting them in the world of the spirit, when they invade it. Last night, I had no trouble killing them when I was asleep, but when I was awake they tortured me. When you entered your other world of dreams, they attacked and hurt you."

"So all we have to do is be asleep when they get here and then we can kill them?" Tommy asked.

"It's more complicated than that."

"This is crazy. What do you mean, Maggie?"

"I think when I am asleep, you are awake to your deaths and leave this world, and so then you are asleep you are awake to another life. Our worlds are crossed."

"So that's why we leave when you're asleep? Because we're awake to death and you're not?"

"It's the only explanation."

"So what do we do?"

"We have to get control of our dreams to stay in the same world at the same time."

"How do we do that?"

"We work on the house. This house is where they found us, and where they've trapped us. If we make the house our own, we make our dreams our own. We close off this world to them. We make a home here."

Tommy didn't seem to understand what having a home meant to controlling your dreams, but he nodded, still looking skeptical.

"What more can we do to this place?" he asked.

"I always loved window boxes with flowers," Maggie said. "Flowers keep away bad thoughts. And we need a fireplace where we can have fires and drive out the night's chill, to make it cozy in here. We can cook in the fireplace, too. If we build another bigger house soon, they'll just find their way into that, too, until we can close it off and make it a home."

"So that's all we have to do? Make this our home?"

"It's the last thing they want, for us to be safe and secure at home."

They could not work quickly enough, once they had decided that having a true home where they could control their dreams and destinies was the solution to their haunting. It was that simple. Houses are haunted because of the evil things that happened inside them, but houses that have just been built are haunted from outside influences and are secure once they've been established as solid homes, capable of securing dreams. Maggie went to work on her window boxes, splitting logs carefully to form boards to nail together and hang below each of the windows. While she was doing that, Mabin and Tommy gathered together rocks from the stream and carried them back to the cabin to begin work on the fireplace and hearth. The flat rocks they formed into a hearth on the floor next to the north wall, and then they cut through the logs for an opening for the fireplace and extended the hearth outside as a base for the chimney. All three of them could sense the seething frustration of those below the house, those who knew they would be denied entrance and revenge once the home above them was completed. The vampire spirits could do nothing to stop them, since while they were awake Maggie and Mabin and Tommy controlled their dreams in this world and could exorcise from it the demons from outside. When they night came on, this little cabin, their home, would secure them, and they could rest easy. Keeping the haunting out was as simple as controlling their thoughts and dreams about it, controlling the world they lived in, and they could do that if they were safe while they slept dreamed.

"I still want to kill them," Tommy said. "I think that might be the only real solution to this haunting."

"It's hard to kill ghosts if half of you is a ghost, too."

"Well, yeah, I admit that."

After filling the window boxes with the good rich forest soil, Maggie walked up the mountainside alone to find wildflowers. She dug lupine and Indian paintbrush from a place not far away and quickly carried the native flowers back to the cabin before they wilted and transplanted them into the window boxes. She carted water in an old burned metal bucket up from the stream for them, and the flowers seemed to approve of their new homes, for they grew as straight and tall as they did on the forest floor. Her bare feet made her feel as though she was rooting into the soil of this place, as did her flowers, and she felt stronger than she had in a very long time.

"I'd like to have a garden once we're done with the house," Maggie said, "a nice place with vegetables and flowers. We'll grow our own food and have everything we need right here, once they're gone."

Mabin and Tommy built the fireplace inside out of clean round rocks from bottom of the stream and then squared off a five-foot log for the mantelpiece. With mortar they mixed from lime and sand and clay, they worked to build the chimney up the outside wall where the smoke from their fires could travel skyward and up into the clouds, as they had before they had a secure home. If there is one best way to get rid of the evils of the past, it's to make a good new home where lives could be lived as they pleased and loves could be lived as they desired.

"I think this is going to work," Mabin said with a grin, as he was suspended in the air above Maggie, about to place a flat rock near the top of the chimney. "I haven't felt this good in a long, long time."

"It's fun building your own home," Tommy said, floating up with two rocks under his arms for Mabin to place next on the chimney. "It's not big enough for all of us once we resurrect Elsa and Stephanovich, but we've got almost a year to build a bigger place for all of us and secure that, too."

As they worked, their wounds from the attacks of the vampire spirits the previous night slowly healed, until they could move without pain. When the work was complete, they cleaned up the cabin inside and out, and then went to the stream to bathe away the dirt and blood that had accumulated on their bodies. Tommy skipped off to a pool of water downstream he did not want to share with Maggie and Mabin, saying "See you later," and when he was gone they decided to wash their clothes was well as bathe. They found their own shallow pool and sat in it side-by-side, touching each other tenderly as they smoothed away the grime and dried blood, and the waters washed away what remained of their wounds from the night before and they kissed tenderly again and again.

"I think if this works we can finally live the way we want to," Mabin said. "It's been such a long time, and such things happened to us that – "

"Don't call them up again now," Maggie said, touching her fingers to his lips. "All this is so that we can forget what happened and live only for the future. If our past wants to come for us, it will find we've escaped into our future where it can never catch us. We can't give our past any power over us."

They rinsed out their clothing quickly, wrung it out and placed it on a nearby rock. Sunset was near. With the dusk hanging on only by a few stray rays of the sun shining through the trees parallel to the earth, they turned to each other, still sitting in the pool of water, and found the day and their move into the future had smoothed their skins to the touch. Mabin thought he was touching velvet as his hands ran over Maggie's body, and Maggie gasped under his touch and reached out for his hard smooth wet back to draw him into her.

"At last ..." Mabin moaned.

As night was coming on, they dressed in their wet clothes and returned to the cabin. As they came near, they smelled pine smoke and then saw that their fireplace was working. Inside, Tommy had built a fire and piled enough logs on the floor to keep the blaze going the entire night. He was drying himself by the fire, his clothes already nearly dry, for he had washed them, too, and he had a pot filled with ravioli sitting by the fire and heating up.

"You guys will get cold if you stay outside in those wet clothes," he said. "If you're hungry, I'm cooking tonight. Come sit by the fire and dry off. Then we'll eat. I can't wait. It'll be just like home."

Mabin closed the cabin door behind him while Maggie sat down by the fire, hoping that they had done enough to keep those creatures under the floor down in the mud where they belonged, forever.

They ate their dinner and laughed and laughed, until total darkness came on.

13

Before she knew what she was doing, Maggie opened the door at midnight after hearing a knock and saw the ghost of Harkin Davis standing before her.

Half-awake, she thought she had heard someone calling her. It must have been this demon from below the house.

"What have you done?" he gasped, in utter frustration. "What have you done to all of us? To my friends?"

He was barely more than a column of white mist with his face etched into the mist near the top of the column. He floated just outside the door in the dark, his red eyes boring into her with hate, his feet planted in the ground. Maggie barely remembered waking and walking to the door, let alone opening it to the night when she knew what was out there. Behind her, the embers in the fireplace were twinkling like red stars on the floor. She panicked when she thought Mabin and Tommy had deserted her again, flown off, and she was there alone to deal with the spirit of Harkin Davis, but then Tommy coughed in his sleep and Mabin turned over in bed of sweet-smelling pine boughs. She sighed in relief.

"Are you going to answer me?" Harkin Davis barked out. "We can't move beneath the house. We are trapped in the mud, but I found a way out, thanks to you. I am the strongest."

Maggie was finally awake enough to understand there was no profit in arguing with a ghost that wished you harm. She tried to slam the door in Harkin Davis' face, but her arm was frozen to it and would not respond to the order from her brain.

"Asleep or awake, Butterfly?" Harkin Davis asked with mirth at her predicament. "What parts of you work when awake, and what parts work when you're asleep?"

Maggie tried once again to slam the door, but gave up when she could not move her arm.

"It doesn't matter. There's nothing you can do anymore. The cabin you thought would trap us is our home and safe from you. You're forever doomed to a half-existence underground."

"That is what I thought, but look."

Harkin Davis pointed into the dark night behind him. Maggie saw there were more columns of mist with blinking red eyes, hundreds of them arrayed in ranks, one after the other, all with their feet stuck in the mud. They floated to and fro near the cabin but the breezes did not lift them from the muck. Maggie again attempted to slam the door shut, but her arm still did not function.

"We escaped the mud, thanks to you," Harkin Davis said. "More are coming every hour, although we must always return to the mud, again, many thanks to you. What lovely flowers you have in your window boxes. It's a shame the flowers will prove your doom."

With her eyes adjusted to the darkness, Maggie could see the lupine and Indian Paintbrush covered with dew in the nearest window box. She did not understand what Harkin Davis meant, until she remembered she had dug the flowers out of the mountainside, the same mountainside under which the vampire spirits swirled together inside the mud. She had pockmarked the land with shallow holes when she removed the flowers, but it was enough to allow an escape route for the damned vampire souls.

"I can see you figured it out," Harkin Davis said, managing to pull his feet from the mud and float toward her. "It's not such a bad place to be, in the mud. You should visit us."

"Maybe I will, but if I do, you won't like it."

When Maggie looked away, a misty piece of him snaked out for her, but only the cold sharp claws at the end of the spirit's arm managed to brush her neck. It was enough to send chills through her entire body as the claws nicked her flesh so that blood dripped down to her chest. She stepped back quickly. If they could injure her now, she knew she was awake and not dreaming this, but that meant that Mabin and Tommy were asleep and in their other world of death and therefore vulnerable. She had to protect them first of all.

Harkin Davis was a step ahead of her.

"Give us those two while they sleep," he said, with as pleasant a smile as such a creature as he could muster, rising a foot off the ground. "Carry them to us from out of the cabin, and you can stay safe inside. We will let you live, for this night, if you give us the two of them while they sleep."

Maggie stared into Harkin Davis' eyes, as though contemplating the offer. She let her eyes seem dazed and wide.

"It seems fair," she said, after a moment. "Let me give you the boy first, and only the boy, so that I can watch what you do to him."

With that, she turned and walked toward Tommy's bed. She lifted him in her arms as he snored and returned to the cabin door, where she laid him down on the floor just inside. She remembered they could hurt her while she was awake, but she also knew that she could hurt them.

"Repeat the terms for giving up the boy," she said, while still leaning over her brother. "You allow me to stay safe for tonight, is that correct, if I give up the boy?"

"I said both of them, but we might settle for the boy for this night, and take your husband tomorrow night."

"I don't know."

"Take this deal. There are too many of us, and more rising out of the mud every minute. We're making a very generous offer."

Maggie looked beyond him and saw that it was true. Columns of mist topped with red eyes seemed to stretch off into the distance.

Harkin Davis came as close to entering the cabin as he dared. He was quivering with excitement that he might be handed over a good resurrected spirit, vulnerable in his somnolent world of death, to do with as he pleased, and he came too close. He was used to killing, but was not as adept at it in his present state, and got very excited that he might be able to indulge himself in it once again. Maggie sprang up, the knife from Tommy's belt clutched tightly in her hands, and she flashed out at Harkin Davis where she believed his neck to be. Aghast that he had been tricked, he hesitated for a split second, but then retreated in a flash into the black mountain night, out of her reach, in his zone of safe passage and out of hers. She had to stop just short of reaching him and slicing through the tall column of mist, and the beady small red eyes widened to the size of burning coals.

"A trick? You tried a trick on me?" Harkin Davis asked. "This will not go well for you now."

Maggie stepped forward.

A moaning that sounded like a low group howl rose out of the vampire spirits in the dark, and hundreds of the red eyes glowed brighter when they thought Maggie might give up the invulnerability of her home and venture outside into their midst. She stopped at her doorstep, and withdrew the knife and her arm from the blackness just outside the cabin's walls. She was used to killing, too, and in her disappointment slumped there, her shoulders sunk down.

"This is a bad decision on your part," Harkin Davis said, as the other spirits gathered around him and they advanced on Maggie, who was frozen in the doorway.

She knew they had no power over her in her home, so she did not move.

"Hey, Maggie, what the hell?"

She heard Tommy's voice behind her. It stopped the vampire spirits in their tracks and they froze as Maggie had frozen when they realized Tommy had awakened out of his dream of death and was no longer vulnerable to them. The spirits flitted about nervously in consternation.

"You opened the door, Maggie? Are you crazy?" Tommy asked, standing up. "We're safe with the cabin closed up, but they can come in if you let them."

"I don't know what happened," Maggie said. "I think I was sleep-walking and heard a knock and someone calling my name. It must have been them."

"That's still no reason to do this. Maggie, you can't do this sort of thing."

"I know, but I couldn't stop myself. I was not awake. I was asleep and not able to think."

"Well so was I asleep. I was enjoying my first good night's rest in a long time, and now I'm awake, because of these things again."

Tommy pointed outside toward the vampire spirits in disgust.

In one quick motion, he grabbed the knife from Maggie's hand and flew out the doorway into the darkness. As soon as Harkin Davis saw him shoot through the air toward him, he chose the safe place to be and immediately dropped down into the mud, like white steam retreating back into a kettle. The other vampire ghosts scattered, with some flying off up the mountainside and other fleeing downhill. Many did not stay out of their safe environment for long and retreated into the earth once again as had Harkin Davis. Tommy caught up with one of the uphill spirits and immediately sliced it lengthwise, laying out the two slices of mist onto the ground, where both pieces sizzled and dissipated. Each of the red eyes stared up at him until they too blinked out and transformed to a reddish-brown liquid that seeped into the earth. Another vampire spirit foolishly flew past him too closely and was immediately hacked in half. Both pieces of him tumbled downhill as they melted and then seeped back into the earth.

"Is that the end of them?" Tommy asked. "How many forms can these things take before you kill them for the last time? If it wasn't so much fun killing them, I'd be getting tired of it."

The last of the vampire spirits disappeared into the ground and Tommy saw it was safe to return to the cabin. He flew over to Maggie quickly and landed just outside the doorway where she stood. As soon as his feet hit the earth, Maggie noticed the slight glow of orange and pink light under them. As she watched the glow grew brighter, until Tommy saw it lighting her face and looked down.

"Oh, what is this again now?" he asked.

"You better come inside," Maggie said.

"I thought they couldn't harm us in our home," Tommy said.

"It's not glowing inside. Come on step inside. It's all they can do to light up the earth beneath us."

As soon as Maggie pulled her brother into the cabin by the hand, the ground around their home glowed red-hot, as though turned to molten lava. A stray pine branch ignited twenty feet away, having fallen to earth in the storm. It burned to ashes in an instant, so hot was the ground, and there was a great rumbling and shaking outside as steam rose out of the ground and climbed into the air hundreds of feet above their heads. An area a hundred feet around the cabin was glowing hot and shooting up steam, and the ground swirled around the tiny home as though it was lava, bubbling up and hissing as it transformed into noxious steam. Maggie and Tommy were coughing and choking so severely they could not slam the door closed.

Tommy pulled his arm from Maggie grasp and turned to stare at the show outside.

"Come on, Tommy," Maggie shouted, even though Tommy was right next to her. "I've got to get this door closed."

"What is going on?" Mabin shouted above the din.

He had awakened and rushed to be just behind Maggie and Tommy. He grabbed each of them by the arm and pulled hard to bring them inside, and then he kicked the door closed and bolted it. The burning ground ignited the closest trees and the fire engulfed the pines so quickly it was as though they were giant matches. Several crashed down, unable to stand firmly in the molten soil, their roots igniting like witches' hands as they were exposed to the open air. Through the open window they saw the mountainside burning as though the sun had come down next to earth and licked it with flames.

"The vampire spirits found a way out," Maggie said. "They found a way. They knew you were vulnerable while asleep and I was vulnerable while awake, so they chose the perfect time to come. They couldn't get in, but they tried to lure me outside and give up you two."

There was a gigantic crack outside and then a whoosh of air as a Ponderosa pine crashed down and broke into burning pieces when it hit the ground next to the cabin. It burned so quickly that it was gone, turned to ashes, within a matter of seconds.

"Are they doing this?" Mabin asked.

"I think so."

"Should we get out of here?" Tommy shouted, above the din. "Is the cabin going to burn?"

"I don't think it will," Mabin said. "I think we're still safe here, at least safer than outside. They're burning the trees from the bottom up. The same thing would happen to us if we went outside. They'd burn us from the feet upward."

A cavalcade of cracking trees came crashing down to the ground as the mountainside turned into a cauldron of fire around the cabin. The trunks bounced once, the burning branches cushioning their fall, but the heat was so intense on the ground that the trees did not last more than a few seconds. The inside of the cabin grew so hot it was as though it was on fire, but the logs resisted the blaze outside with some force they did not understand. They only knew everything would be all right as long as they stayed inside, that safety existed only in this home they had constructed with their own hands and with the devious help of the vampire spirits.

"God, it's hot in here!" Tommy said.

"It's better than outside," Mabin answered. "Who knew they were still capable of doing something like this?"

"They're not so easily done away with by simple killing," Maggie said.

In an instant, the fires outside were extinguished and darkness fell over the cabin. A cool breeze wafted through the interior, and from an existence inside an oven, they now felt as though they were inside a cooler.

"Okay, it's safe to go outside," Tommy said. "Let's go get them."

"Are you crazy?" Maggie asked.

Tommy shrugged.

"Well, yes."

"Let's stay inside for the night," Mabin said calmly. "We survived that fine, and we don't want to push our luck."

"Well, why are we fine now when we might have burned up another time?" Tommy asked.

"Because you two are actually dreaming," Maggie said quietly. "You're dreaming in your resurrected state, now that you woke up from death."

"What?" Tommy asked. "When we're sleeping we're actually dead?"

"It seems that way, in this world, anyway. When I'm awake I can deal with them, but when you're asleep from death, or dreaming from death, seems to be the only time you can deal with them."

"Well, let's go do something about them now that we're all in a condition to do so, now matter what world we're in now," Tommy said. "If I'm awake from my death now, resurrected, and you're awake from your dreams, I say now is the time to go after them."

"How?"

"What do you mean, how? The same way we always do. Just go after them and kill them with knives. Cut their misty asses to pieces."

"Go underground after them again? I don't know if I want to do that," Mabin said.

"Do you have a better idea?" Tommy asked.

"I'll think of one. For now, I think we should stay awake all night, and watch over Maggie as she sleeps. They won't come in here if we're awake from our deaths, and if Maggie's asleep she can deal with them in her own way."

Tommy glanced out the window, where a few embers were bright enough to light the night.

"They ruin everything," he said. "Just when we were getting some rest, just when we have a nice home, they come along and ruin everything. I'm going to think about it all night and find out some way to get rid of them once and for all."

"Get rid of ghosts?" Mabin asked. "Good luck with that one."

Suddenly, Maggie felt an utter exhaustion overcome her. It was as though someone had encased her in a cloud of sleep. Without saying good-night, she lay back on her pine-bough bed and dropped off into the other state of the butterfly.

14

This time when she dropped off into sleep, the bright lights did not bother her.

If it was dawn, she knew she would be safe, since a haunting by the vampire spirits was nearly impossible for them to do in the daytime and she was inside their home and therefore safe. If Mabin and Tommy were transforming into their other light-state of being, then she knew she was still safe, since their home was secure without them.

She opened her eyes not knowing what world she was in but unafraid. It did not matter. She had hoped it was dawn, knowing that was the finer time for her than the middle of the night, but she was disappointed to see that both Mabin and Tommy were glowing from within and had begun their ascent out of the cabin. Their good sense as resurrected creatures was to flee this woeful place for a better existence above, to escape the mud and evil of this world for another glorious world where they belonged. It was the instinct of the chosen that led them to rise away. It did not mean they did not love her or were abandoning her. It was simply the natural state of their beings to rise above this world after it had destroyed them and she had brought them back, but even now the world harried and beset them. It was a great comfort to her that they always returned to her. They came back for her, for the love of her, and could not stay away. In a sense, they were ghosts, too, having died, just as the vampires had died, but they had made their way back to earth with her, and she knew they did not want to leave her and would always return to live with her in this world that was now half-strange to them.

When she got up out of bed they would not know if she was awake or asleep, for they had drifted up through the roof, leaving her alone in the dark.

If she was asleep, she would not be vulnerable to the haunting from below, but if she was awake she would be vulnerable but powerful. The only way she would know if she was conscious or slumbering would be to notice their condition and derive hers from it. But Mabin and Tommy were gone and she could not do that, she could not know for certain in which condition she found herself.

Butterflies could not know that.

She sat up and hung her feet over the edge of the bed. Through one of the windows at the back of the cabin, she could see the ground glowing from below. It pulsed with orange and pink, and it meant that the vampire souls were active again. They had only one purpose now, she knew, and that was to put an end to those who had put an end to them.

It was simple.

Destroy the ghosts below, once and for all, or they would destroy the three of them, once and for all.

There was no other choice for her, whether she retained her powers or not.

"It's me and only me against them," she said. "I have to think that's fair, or I won't be able to do this."

She wanted a home, like everyone else, and she knew she could not have one as long as they chased and harried her from below, chased her even beyond their deaths. She had to have a plan to end this haunting: if she did not have a plan, she would fail. She quietly dropped to the floor and stood up, noticing with satisfaction that the haunting was no longer glowing below her feet but was limited to the outside.

"I could stay inside our home and be safe, but that wouldn't be right. I couldn't live with myself if I did that."

If she was going to develop a plan, she had to find out what the vampire spirits were up to, and to do that she had to go to them. As quietly as she possibly could, she shuffled across the floor to where the pile of large rocks held closed the trap door in the floor. She lifted the top rock off of the pile and gently laid it on the floor off to the side, and then she went back for another of the large rocks. Without making a noise, she lifted one rock after the other off the trap door and moved each to a spot on the floor where it would not hold down the door. Each of the rocks felt like a large chunk of ice and her fingers cramped and froze as she lifted them. She planned only on gathering information about the vampire souls, not fighting them, but she grabbed the large knife off the kitchen table that Mabin had built and clenched it in her fist, in case it would come to a fight. Then she returned to the trap door and stared down at it, her heart racing at what she was about to do.

"I have no choice," she whispered to herself. "They'll never leave us alone, and if I don't do this now, I don't know if we'll have time to form a plan before they come for us again. If I want a home with my husband and my brother, I have to find out what they're up to. I have to learn how to kill the ghosts."

Clutching the knife in one hand, she bent and lifted the door to open the way into the vampire souls' domain.

Before she knew what was happening, she heard a wind howling and pulling at her, as a vortex formed around her and sucked her down through the opening into the earth. She could not resist it and let out a silent scream as she gasped for oxygen and the force pulled the air out of her lungs. It was utterly dark as she spun around and around, her hair whipping her face and the wind nearly pulling the knife from her hand with the force of the gale. She managed to look up and saw a faint twinkling of light where the trapdoor remained open above her, but then the door slammed shut with a bang. She was in a free-fall, not in the mud, but down through some new opening beneath their cabin.

The violence of the swirling wind increased, and then suddenly she came to rest on a very soft spot on loose earth, still gasping. Despite being dizzy from the spinning fall, she looked around to see where she was: there was no question about it: she was underground. Above, she saw that the hole she had fallen through was barely wider than she was, and that it led directly upward through an eight-foot-high mud ceiling that seemed to go on forever in darkness. In the distance she saw the same orange and pink glows that she had seen when looking at the ground from her cabin just moments before, but now she was underground with the soft lights, instead of above them on the earth. She knew she had to remember this spot for her escape, but in the dark there was no mark or monument that could guide her back to it. She bent and quickly drew a circle around her feet that corresponded to the narrow hole above her. If she survived and came to this spot again, she just might be able to find her way home again, if only she could reach this circle.

"Welcome," a voice whispered to her.

She spun around expecting to see Harkin Davis leering at her through the darkness, but it was as though the rocks had spoken to her, for there was no one there.

Something touched her shoulder, some piece of ice.

When she spun around to face it, holding the knife ready before her, there was nothing there but darkness.

She had come down into the earth to reconnoiter the activities of the vampire souls: she had to move on to discover those activities without letting her mind play tricks on her. The whisper she thought she heard must be nothing but that: another whisper that no longer existed. The icy touch she had felt had to be nothing but that: another trick of the mind that darkness plays. Maybe the whisper was the voice of one who was dead and buried, and maybe that voice was the only thing that remained of the dead person whose person now had faded away completely. She knew that our voices could live on after us. Maybe that was all the whispering welcome had been, the last vestige of a once-living human being, a being restricted to nothing but a whisper and an icy touch.

She stepped out the circle that defined her escape. She chose a random direction, since she appeared to be directly in the middle of a large circle with its outskirts defined by the orange and pink glow of the vampire souls.

She crouched down, thinking if she made her form smaller they would be less likely to see her. As she walked away from the circle she had drawn in the mud, a sick feeling grew in the pit of her stomach: she might never return to it and the earth above. This could be her burial.

"Welcome home," the voice whispered to her. "Do what you can for us."

She spun around, certain that she had been detected but once again she discovered no one. In the distance, she sensed motion, a vast swirling circle at the outer edges of the underground world in which she walked. A glob of mud dropped onto her shoulder and she jumped off to the side, raising her knife to defend herself. Mistaking the mud for a hand, she cried out and slapped out at it but discovered it was only the wet loose earth from above. Small gobs of muddy earth were falling all around her. The wind still blew over her from the vortex at the edges of the underground world. The wind must have loosened the globs of mud and dropped them around her.

Carefully, she took a single step forward.

Her foot came down on a slimy lump moving across the mud floor, an animal or a soft piece of rock, and when she looked down she saw a hand reaching up for her. Her heart raced and she stepped back quickly and slashed at it with her knife but missed it. It was nothing, nothing alive, that is. She was relieved to see it was a stiff hand and not a grasping one sharp with claws. It did not try to take hold of her ankle as the vampire souls would. It was moving toward the outer edges of the cavern at a slow pace, as though being dragged, and then she recognized an arm and a torso and a face with bared yellow teeth staring up at her lifelessly. All were barely attached to the hand that had touched her. What could she expect to find underground but a corpse? All pieces of the body were sliding in the mud toward the outer edges of the circular cavern, and formed one poor cadaver disturbed in its grave. She watched the dead body sliding away in the mud, its mouth still gaping open as though laughing with pain at her. Then something else bumped into her feet as she watched the first corpse sliding away. Another body brushed by her, this one, as was the first, covered in mud as though pulled from a grave, but it was a woman's body in an old, mud-splattered gingham dress, a dress she had been buried in that had been beautiful once, but now barely more than a large rag being dragged through the mud. She gasped at the predicament of the disturbed bodies, but could do nothing about them.

"This is what is."

The whisper came from behind her, and she spun around with the knife before her ready to stab out. It was as though the corpses were speaking to her. She was still spooked by living inside a grave. In the extreme dark she saw many dead open eyes on the ground, staring up and reflecting the orange and pink light emanating from in the distant swirling fog. They floated in a steady stream by her toward the swirling lights in the distance, hundreds of dead bodies being pulled in the same direction. Stiff arms brushed by her and tumbled over in the mud. One large man crashed into her, and his great stiff weight nearly knocked her down into the mud with him. Once he had crashed into her, he simply slid onward toward the pink and orange glows in the distance without pardoning himself.

The bodies were talking to her, silently, and she realized the voices were in her head. The dead can not speak to anyone except in imagination.

"Why have you come to a world where you don't belong?"
"Get out while you can."
"Help us, please!"
"Will you go with us to where we have been called? Beware."
"Such a young girl ... why did you die?"
"It's best to fade into old age, if you can choose."
"Help us!"
"Why did you select this end, to be here now with us?"
"Go home, before you see our end and can not prevent your own."
"Help us!"

With her eyes adjusted to the dark, Maggie fought with her thoughts and the voices, tying to forget them. She had to keep her focus on what she had come here to do, to find out how to rid this place of its ghosts. She looked into the distance and saw that masses of bodies were being pulled away from the center of cavern, thousands of bodies, toward the pink and orange lights of the vampire souls. The bodies popped out of the mud near where she had started her journey like fish breaking the surface. Then they floated toward the perimeter, toward the swirling lights. This was sea of mud filled with every kind of human being in a decomposing state – men and women and girls and boys but also horses, many horses, and sheep with their white fur matted with dark mud, and even foxes and wolves. The bodies were being pulled in all directions from the center of the circle toward the spinning lights at the edges of the cavern. From the circle she had drawn in the center of the cavern in the mud, bodies were popping to the surface and then sliding in each of the three-hundred-and-sixty degrees of the circle toward the rotating circumference of vampire spirits.

"If you must die, lie down among us and come with us to our final end. They have taken us."

"They will take you."

"Who will?" Maggie shouted, forgetting herself. "Who is doing this? All of the dead taken? Are all of you dead? Why have you been taken from your graves?"

There were sickening slurping sounds all around her as the bodies were being slid by her in the sticky deep mud of the cavern floor. There was the smell of rot, but there was no voice outside her head to answer her question. The only voices were inside her head. Two more bodies crashed into her legs, nearly knocking her over, and she realized that the crush of bodies moving across the muddy floor was growing thicker, as more and more of the dead appeared from underground and joined the procession toward the ring of pink and orange lights at the outer edge of the cavern. She could barely remain upright. A hand reached up to her, stiff and half-closed, but to avoid falling she took hold of it and let it pull her along. She had to see where this journey ended if she was to discover anything about the dangers beneath their home. If she had to travel among the dead to do so, she would.

As she floated over the mud among the dead, her heart crying out with pity for them, for their disturbed rest, she sensed the forward rush of the dead toward the swirling vampire spirits was slowing down. When she was within twenty feet of the orange and pink mists rotating like a giant wheel on its side, she let go of the body that had pulled her along. She lay still among the dead, whose progress stopped. As she lay there watching the wall of vampire souls spinning by, she realized they were in a resting state, perhaps sleeping and dreaming as they had when they were human. Their red eyes had dulled to a soft pink, as though misty eyelids drooped over them, and there was a great sense of peace among the tumbling mass. Slowly, the muddy slough of dead human bodies began to move in a circular motion, following the movement of the sleeping vampire souls. The body next to her suddenly stiffened, as though in a death spasm, but since it was long dead Maggie knew it couldn't be a death spasm but had to be something else. With another jerk, a white column of mist rose out of the body's mouth, its soul finally leaving the body after so many years waiting for resurrection, but this was not the resurrection it expected. The white column of mist exited the mouth and then immediately flew by Maggie to join the twisting, rotating swirl of vampire souls, who immediately took it in and grasped it tightly. As the dead bodies joined in the circular motion of the vampire spirits, more mouths opened and more souls exited those mouths and flew into the orange and pink circling vampire spirits. When the while columns of souls were grasped and taken by the dead vampires, they remained white, so that their presences dotted the orange and pink wall rushing by. There were cries of pain and distress from the taken souls. A dead little girl, her hair still bright blond, tumbled by Maggie in the mud, and as she did so her mouth opened and her white frail soul came pouring out. For a moment, Maggie thought she saw the little girl's face contorted with panic and fear, and she thought she heard a weak desperate voice cry out to her for help. "Don't let them take me from my parents. Don't!" Maggie reached out, but the frail white mist flew by Maggie and entered the chaos of soul-thieves rushing by, and soon it was gone from sight, digested by the tangle of corrupt spirits. The little one's weak cries faded in the distance as the rush of orange and pink lights continued to tumble by the one live human being watching from the mud.

Like worn-out socks of white mist reduced to a thin fabric being stripped away from their owners, thousands of blameless souls continued to be pulled from their decaying bodies as they followed the circling, swirling mass of orange and pink lights above them. As one of the dead vampires raced by her, its red eyes snapped open and seemed to catch sight of Maggie among the dead victims below it in the mud. Maggie closed her eyes quickly to feign death, and she froze in place. The awakened vampire soul raced away in the mass of his friends, and soon he was out of sight. Now that she knew what she had to know about this place, Maggie tried to think of some way to escape the circling mass of dead bodies that were having their souls stolen and return to her home, but the force of the many dead in the mud kept her moving with them beneath the pink and orange onrushing wall of corrupt souls. Around and around the wall went, and although she might have been detected, Maggie could not think of a way out. She had to help the dead, but she could not imagine how to do that at this point, and she had reached her breaking point. She could not stand one more minute in this hell of mud and decay and spirit-theft, could not stand its stench and horror, and she tried to lift her legs out of the mud to run back to her place of escape. As she did so, the awakened vampire soul who had first spotted her rushed by, taking care to stare down at the place he thought he had seen her before, and as she struggled in the mud his eyes blazed in recognition of her. The wall in which he was traveling was moving so fast that he was by her in a moment, but she knew he had seen her. She jumped to her feet with great difficulty, her heart bursting with pity at those she had to leave behind, but she knew she could not save anyone if she did not save herself. When she was on her feet, she saw that the awakened vampire had stripped himself away from the mass of his fellows and was staring back at her from a hundred feet away. Maggie knew she had to march over the bodies of the dead if she wished to live. She held tightly on to her knife as she raced away, stepping on backs and bellies and faces as she did so, crying with regret at having to do so. She glanced behind her to see that the awakened vampire soul was coming after her.

She leaped into the air to see if her powers were intact in this underworld of twisted intent, and she was relieved to see she did not fall into the mud but flew very quickly toward the circle she had drawn on the ground so very far away. As fast as she flew, the awakened vampire soul flew faster, closing the gap between them. He was at a disadvantage in that he did not know where she was going, but Maggie also was at a disadvantage since she had to find her place of exit and could only guess where it was as she flew. It was no use. As she dashed through the fetid air, she looked over her shoulder and saw that her pursuer was just feet from her, its red eyes practically staring at the soles of her feet. With an expert movement, she turned quickly to the side and stopped, floating above the mud and bodies. The one who chased her flew past but then also came to a sudden stop and spun about to face her.

"We have a living one," the vampire soul mused to itself. "You are of great value here."

"And you are of no value to me, so I don't think I'll stay."

"That choice is not yours. We can make you stay."

"We'll see. Were you a man or a woman?"

From the way the soul stiffened with indignation, Maggie could see the spirit was offended to have his manhood questioned. As though responding to the insult, he raised his hand and spun it around in the air. Immediately, the twisted souls in the wheel at the edge of the area increased their speed, and the wind whipped up, drawing Maggie toward them as it drew the pitiful dead innocent souls being dragged through the mud toward them at a faster rate.

"As I said, we have ways of making you stay."

Maggie resisted with all her might, and held her place. If she could simply find her exit, she could get away, but with the winds howling and swirling around her it was difficult to see or think clearly. The dead souls beneath them in the mud were dragged quickly toward the outward wheel of vampire spirits, and in the distance she could see the white helpless mists being sucked out of their bodies and consumed. The large wheel of vampire spirits spun faster and faster, increasing the wind, as they received the power of the dead souls into them, and Maggie thought she could not hold on much longer but would be taken by them. The effect the vampire spirit had hoped would take place with Maggie now afflicted him, as the winds took him and flung him back toward the outer rim of spinning spirits. He was thrown back into the mass, but after he crashed into it, it slowed to a stop. Maggie knew what had happened: he had told the others she was there. The winds died down, the dead bodies stopped in place in the mud below and one by one the vampire spirits awakened and dropped out of the mass spinning around the underground cavern.

"I guess they all know I'm here now. The exit ... I have to find the exit."

Hundreds of blazing red eyes turned her way. They spotted her, and without hesitation they shot through the air toward her. With the tornado around her deafened, Maggie turned away from them and shot through the air, staring downward for the circle of escape she had marked. As soon as she turned, she saw a dozen pairs of the blazing red eyes racing through the air directly toward her. With a quick change of course flew up and over them.

"If we catch a live soul, we can increase our power a hundredfold," one of the spirits said, wheeling around to pursue her. "Get her, trap her, and take her soul! With it we can enter the world again!"

All around her the vampire spirits in the huge spinning wheel of mist were awakening, dropping out of it with their red eyes blazing awake and then entering the chase after her. She avoided several by dropping down below them as they flew, and then flew high over several others. She twisted and turned in midair to escape the thousands of grasping claws. It would be impossible to keep up this pace for long. She screeched to a halt as a wall of the vampire souls stood before her blocking her way and quivering with anticipation at taking her. She spun around desperately and looked down.

She was hovering over the circle in the mud.

From all sides they dashed at her as one mass, closing the trap around her, their eyes so bright they lit the cavern with an eerie red light. The light showed her the opening through which she had dropped, and just as they clutched at her with their claws,

Maggie shot upward without thinking of where she was going. She just wanted out of there, wanted to get home to safety.

She remembered the trapdoor had slammed closed just after she entered. She flew upward in complete darkness, but she knew they were following. Looking down, she saw the blaze of many pairs of red eyes rising toward her, and she prepared to slam into the trapdoor, and then back off and fight before being taken.

Suddenly, she was in the cabin, hovering in the air in the firelight. Behind her, the trapdoor slammed shut, and Tommy dropped one of the heavy rocks on top of it, and then Mabin added two more. She did not stand still but instead fell to the floor and pushed several of the boulders onto the trapdoor in desperation.

"My god, Maggie," said Mabin, looking at the covering of mud smeared over her.

"Maggie, where were you? We woke up and you were gone and we saw the rocks were taken off the trapdoor and we just opened it now," Tommy said. "You popped out, just like that."

Maggie was pressing down on the rocks, staring at them and not moving. Some of the mud had dried and caked already, and pieces of it dropped off of her onto the floor.

"What was down there?" Mabin asked. "How did you break through the earth? How far did you get?"

To add her weight to the rocks holding down the trap door, she sat on them, gasping and unable to speak, so out of breath she was wheezing.

When she could finally say something, she babbled.

"All the dead souls ... and the dead ... they were taking them ... I couldn't do ... a thing to ... stop them ... they want all the dead ... all of them."

15

All was quiet in the cabin, but outside the birds were singing. Somehow, Maggie knew that they were the same birds that had cackled out in the forest so often to warn her what was about to happen. Why they were singing sweetly now Maggie didn't know, but she did know why things had been going so very wrong, after her visit underground. Somehow, the birds had known what was going on underground and had been trying to warn her.

"They want to capture us down there, too," Maggie managed to say. "The spirits ... there are thousands of them, and they want to take us, too."

Maggie was staring off into space, looking at neither Mabin nor her brother. It was almost as though they were not there and she was below the earth again, trapped among the blameless dead in the mud.

She curled up into a ball.

"So the spirits of the vampires we killed are trapped down there?"

"Yes, and they've claimed the bodies of the innocent dead that still hold their souls and haven't moved on. They're stealing the innocent souls to make themselves more powerful."

"Well, that's got to stop," Tommy said, offended. "Let's go back down and protect those people, the dead people, I mean."

"No!"

"Why not?"

"You don't know what its like down there."

"It's what we're supposed to do, protect those who can't protect themselves. If we don't do it, who will?"

"There are so many of them. They're not very strong yet individually but they can still do us little hurts, and thousands of them doing little hurts to us can kill us. They're gaining strength from stealing the souls of the dead, and then I think they're coming up here."

"So? I don't care," Tommy said. "Let them come. They never got the better of us before."

"There is something different about them now. They're ... blank, with nothing to them but anger and revenge, and most of them are not individuals any more. Vampire souls aren't even souls, but just anger and revenge and not much else, all wrapped in a mist."

"We killed the rest of them, right? Their stupid bodies, I mean," Tommy said.

"We did, but as bad as they were, the worst part of them is left."

"And they're desecrating the dead?"

"It's as though they're eating them. They've created a giant whirlwind down there, and are drawing the bodies closer and closer to them out of the earth until they can pull the souls out of them."

Maggie described how she had been sucked down through the opening below the trapdoor when she opened it, and then told in detail about the thousands of bodies in the mud, and how she hid among them as they were being drawn toward the giant wheel of spinning vampire souls. She told them there was no respect paid to the dead, not even if they were children or old women or the weak and the lame. There was no pity. Their souls were simple sucked from their corpses for the nourishment they could provide. Just as the vampires had taken blood to survive while alive, they now stole souls to survive.

"What do they want with us then, if they can eat the dead souls?" Tommy asked.

"We have fresh souls, live ones," Maggie said. "That's what they need more than anything. I think when they believe they're strong enough they won't have to stay underground any more, but would be strong enough to come up here and take anyone's soul they want to take for nourishment."

Tommy gave a little, impish grin.

"Can you burn underground vampire souls?"

"I don't know," Maggie said, despondently. She stared at her feet. "Maybe if we could get a blaze going down there, they'd get what they deserve. That would be hell for them, and hell's what they deserve."

"Hey, Mabin, what do the mysteries say about that? Can we burn old vampire souls?"

Instead of removing the Transylvanian Mysteries from his back pocket, Mabin reached out gently for Maggie's hand and helped her down off the pile of rocks holding closed the trapdoor.

"I don't know if we can," Mabin answered, pulling Maggie to him and holding her to him his arm around her shoulder. "Are you all right?"

"I think so. I just hated it down there."

"Well, see what the mysteries say," Tommy said. "Ah, the heck with it. Never mind. I'll do it myself."

Tommy reached out and pulled the Transylvanian Mysteries out of Mabin's back pocket. He stared down at them.

"Wow," he said. "Look at that."

"What is it?" Mabin asked.

"Won't we ever be done with them?" Maggie asked, looking up at Mabin. "I thought we were finished with them, but we can't seem to get rid of them. Once we kill them, they come back in another form. It's endless."

Tommy looked up from the Transylvanian Mysteries.

"Hey, it says here we can burn them, I think."

"What do you mean, you think we can burn them?" Maggie asked.

"Well, remember that stone we cut out of you?" Tommy asked. "It was brimstone, right? I think it says brimstone will burn them."

"Let me see it," Mabin said, reaching out with his free hand for the parchment but holding on to Maggie tightly.

Tommy handed it over and then stood silently as Mabin read.

"It says, 'From the top down, the final end comes when brimstone is set to fire on those below, if they agree.'"

"If they agree? What does that mean?" Maggie asked.

"I think it means if they want to die in the next world, we can oblige them with brimstone. Where do we get brimstone?"

"I barely know what it is, except for that piece of it they put in Maggie," Tommy said.

"Does it say anything else?"

"No, that's all."

"I say we just go down and kill them," Tommy said. "We know we can. Just use the knives on them like we already did, slice them in two. I think brimstone might be too hard to find."

"There are so many of them, and it's different down there," Maggie said. "I didn't feel right down there, it's different."

"How?" Tommy asked.

"It feels like it is hell, but hell without fire. There are so many of them they might have put the hell-fire out so that they don't have to burn."

"Then I guess we'll just have to take some fire down there and light the place up again like it should be."

"What if they come up here again once we burn up what's down there?" Maggie asked. "They came up once but were weak and we chased them back down. What if they get strong enough to stay up here?"

"Then I guess we'll have to burn down all of Montana," Tommy said. "They already tried to, so we might as well try to, too."

"I know where we can get brimstone," Mabin said.

Both Tommy and Maggie turned to Mabin but they were silent, not quite believing what they were hearing. They waited for him to tell them where the brimstone was, but he simply stood there biting his lower lip.

Finally, he spoke up.

"This mountain is made of it."

"Saint Mary's mountain is brimstone?"

"That and silver, lots of silver. What isn't silver or dirt or pine is brimstone. It's everywhere. It's why this place is such a power spot for the vampires and those like us with powers. The silver balances it out, so that it's harmless to normal people, but the silver negates the influence of the brimstone for the vampires. If they can find pure brimstone and avoid being burned by it, they become more and more powerful. It's the reason we have powers here, too, since we have such strong tendencies toward becoming vampires but fight it and refuse blood. The vampire virus is dormant within us, and only needs the blood of others to flourish. But it gives us our powers."

"Well, let's go dig some brimstone up. What does it look like?"

"It looks like that."

Mabin let go of Maggie and turned to the fireplace, where a weak fire was licking up from a pile of burned-out logs and ash. He pointed to the stonework.

"Every rock in it is brimstone."

Tommy rushed over to the fireplace with a grin on his face and touched one rock after another with wonder. He laughed as though his hand was tickled by the rocks, and then he spun around with a big grin.

"So why doesn't it ignite if we burn fires in there?" he asked.

Mabin turned away from him, seemingly upset at the question. He looked at Maggie helplessly, unable to speak.

"What's the matter with you, Mabin?" Tommy asked. "We've got these rocks that we can use to burn the vampire spirits, so why don't we just do it? If we burn them, then we're done with them and can just go on living."

"There aren't enough rocks. We need a lot more than what we have in our fireplace."

"Well let's go get some more," Tommy said. "We know what it looks like now, so if it's all around here we should be able to get plenty of it."

"It's not that simple."

Again Mabin turned away from him, bothered by the question, and again he looked at Maggie helplessly.

"What is the matter with you?" Tommy asked. "We know what to do to solve this problem, so let's just do it."

"Because it makes too much sense."

"What? Of course it makes sense. That's why I said it. We'll just throw plenty of brimstone down in the pit and set it on fire and that will be the end of them."

Mabin walked to the trapdoor and stared at the rocks holding it down. He did not answer but continued to stare at the rocks.

"Mabin?"

When Maggie spoke his name, he turned and looked at Maggie again, his face so filled with hurt that it appeared he might break out into tears.

Finally, he took a deep breath in preparation.

"These rocks are brimstone," he said.

"Good," Tommy said. "That's less we have to collect."

Mabin spun around and grabbed his head with both hands.

"No! No! No! Why do you think hell is not burning anymore?" he asked, his entire body shaking with indignation.

"I don't know," Tommy said. "Because the vampire spirits put it out?"

"How? How did they do that? How did they put out hell-fire? Just by wishing it? How do you put out an eternal fire by simply wishing it? You don't understand."

"Well something put it out," Maggie said. "I saw it down there. It wasn't burning."

"It's not something that put it out, but the lack of something," Mabin said. "The fires are out because they lack something they need to burn."

"Well let's just get that thing and then get the fires going again. What do we need to make the brimstone burn again?"

Mabin stopped in place and stared at Tommy, horrified.

"Come on, tell us what we need."

Mabin turned away.

"What do we need, Mabin?" Maggie insisted.

He turned to her, so stricken he almost could not speak. He finally managed to say it.

"We need blood."

Tommy grew solemn and looked over at Maggie to determine if she understood. She held his look for a moment, but then turned to Mabin as though confused.

Mabin exploded with anger. His face reddened as though on fire itself, and his hands flew up in the air.

"Why do you think the fires of hell have gone out? Think about it? There wasn't a single trace of flame down there, was there? No. And why? Why? Because brimstone needs blood to burn, human blood, and we killed all the vampires that were supplying it. You don't think they were taking all that blood for themselves, just to live, do you? They can get by on very little. They were taking the blood to keep the fires of hell burning, to continue to escape the fires themselves and burn human souls, and now that they can no longer take the blood of humans the brimstone can no longer burn. The fires of hell went out when we killed nearly every vampire on earth, and now that the spirits of those vampires can no longer burn in hell, they want to return to earth in another form. Do you see it now? Do you see it?"

Tommy walked up slowly to Mabin, his eyes lowered.

"Wow, I didn't know," he said softly. "We can give the blood. If we need blood to get the fires going again to burn the vampire souls, we can give it. I don't care. I can give all the blood we need. I'll give as much as you want."

"No!"

Mabin flew into a rage again, stomping across the floor and then returning. He walked back to Tommy and stared into his face.

"You still don't get it!" he screamed. "You don't understand!"

"Well what is it? Why can't we just give blood and burn those monsters up the way they're supposed to burn up?" Tommy asked.

Frustrated, Mabin flew into a greater rage and stomped across the floor to the table, where Maggie had laid the knife after returning from underground. He lifted it and in one motion made a deep cut across his wrist.

"Look."

The cut was dry. No blood flowed.

"You see, I'm different," he said. "I've been resurrected, which means I might seem human but I'm not. I'm something else. I have no blood because I'm on another life."

"Well, wait a minute. I've been resurrected, too. Does that mean – "

Before Tommy could finish, Mabin took his hand and made a small cut on his index finger. It was dry. No blood flowed from Tommy's small wound.

"Oh, no," the boy said. "This is a surprise."

"Don't you see why I'm upset? I'm upset because the only one among us that still has blood is Maggie," Mabin said. "And if you think I'm going to spill her blood to burn these vampire souls, you're crazy. I'd never do that to you, Maggie. I love you too much."

Stunned, Maggie walked silently up to Mabin and took the knife out of his hand. With the tip of the knife, she nicked her index finger and walked to the pile of rocks over the trapdoor. She turned over her hand and let a drop fall onto the top rock. The rock hissed and smoked, and then a small flame flickered up and died.

"I can do this," she said, staring at the smoking rock.

"It will take a lot more blood than that to start a blaze going," Mabin said. "And you're not going to give it. We'll find some other way. There's no way we're opening any vein in you just to make hell burn again. We won't do it. We can't."

Still silent, Maggie walked to the table and returned the knife to its place on top of it. She squeezed closed the nick in her finger and stared at the floor.

"How much blood would it take?" she asked.

"Too much," Mabin said.

"How much?"

Mabin closed his eyes in agony and threw back his head.

"All of it. It would take all of your blood. We're not going to do it. We're not. No. Never. That's the last drop of blood you're ever going to spill to make brimstone burn, I guarantee you that. I won't let it happen."

Maggie sat down on the bed and stared at the floor without speaking, too stunned at what she had seen below and at what Mabin had just told her to be able to form words.

If you cut a dream, it does not bleed.

She could feel her heart beating fast in her chest, pumping the blood they needed to burn the vampire souls once and for all.

16

As evening came on in silence the vampire spirits rose by the thousands out of the earth like thin columns of cool, foul steam.

Still too weak to remain on the surface for long, most of them quickly dropped back down through the mud, but their intentions were clear. They intended on returning to their rest in the spinning wheel of damned spirits underground and steal more innocent souls to gain enough strength to inhabit the earth again. All those thousands ascended from beneath the earth for a whiff of fresh air and freedom. They hovered outside the tiny cabin in legions as Maggie and Mabin and Tommy watched, and then after a short time they dropped down below the earth again, only to be replaced by others who took their turn in the haunting. As the evening darkened, their red eyes glowed brighter and brighter, as though millions of pairs of ugly red stars had fallen from the sky to hover in the clearing around the cabin and in the forest beyond. One was barely recognizable from the other, but all had they same intention. They rose through the earth for a taste of life and freedom, and descended with the aim of stealing souls to obtain permanent residence on earth.

"So what do we do?" Maggie asked.

"We might only be able to do what we've been doing and keep fighting them, although I hate the idea of living with them," Mabin said.

"No! I'm not living with them, not after what they did to mom and dad," Tommy said. "I still say we just go down there and kill as many of them as we can. Maybe we can kill all of them, and that would solve that problem."

"And what if they kill us, and we're not here in a year to resurrect Elsa and Stephanovich?"

"Oh. I didn't think of that. But they can't kill me."

"Are you sure only blood can ignite the brimstone?" Maggie asked.

"It's been that way since the beginning of time," Mabin answered. "It's what human beings have always fought against. It's why we try to be better than we are."

Mabin stopped and thought a moment. A huge smile crossed his face.

"That is, if I'm still human," he said.

"You're human," Maggie quickly said, embracing him. "Everything about you feels human, not like them at all."

Suddenly, there was a face at the window in the growing darkness. Its red eyes announced its presence, but it had more form than the others, indicating it had seized more power from the dead souls, for its face was very recognizable. It was nearly ready to haunt the earth: it was Harkin Davis. He reached out and drew his claws down the glass, scratching that could be heard inside the cabin, to announce his presence. Maggie shivered, and Tommy immediately raced to the table for the knife and flew to the window, but Harkin Davis retreated from it instantly and disappeared into the dark.

"What's that creepo want?" Tommy asked.

Maggie walked to the window.

"He wants me," she said. "I should go out to talk to him."

"You're not going anywhere," Tommy shouted, "but I am."

He rushed toward the door, but Mabin quickly moved to block his way.

"We can't go out there, none of us can," Mabin said. "It's not like it was before when they didn't stand a chance against us. There is something very different about this haunting."

"I don't care! What can they do to us? We're not like we were, but that only means they can't hurt us the way they used to be able to do. I'm going out after that creep that was looking in our window at Maggie."

With a quick, expert movement, Mabin took the knife from Tommy's hand.

"We have to figure out how to get rid of them without any of us getting hurt or killed," Mabin said. "That's what we have to do now, not just rush outside after them. That's what they want."

"So what do you say we do?" Tommy asked.

"I don't know."

"We need my blood to burn the brimstone, don't we?" Maggie asked. "That's the only thing that will work."

"I told you, that's not going to happen," Mabin said. "You're not going to die to save the rest of us."

"I don't think I have to."

"You can't live without your blood."

"I know, but I can live without some of it."

"It won't work, just using some of your blood. Even if we take all of your blood, I don't know if it will ignite enough of the brimstone."

"We take all of it, but we take it slowly."

"What do you mean?"

"I mean, every day I give a pint or two of blood and we save it. My body will replenish it in another day or two, and then we take more of my blood. Then we keep repeating the process until we have enough blood to burn all of the brimstone and all of them."

Tommy laughed.

"Hey, cool, sis. That might work," he said. "I think that's a good idea."

Mabin knitted his brow as though he was considering the proposition, but then he turned away quickly.

"I don't know if it would work."

"Why not?"

"I don't know if we could get enough of your blood before they take enough souls to become powerful enough to haunt the earth. We'd have to take too much of your blood too quickly, and then you'd die."

"What else can we do?"

"Hold them off. Maggie, there's something wrong with the world we live in. You know it and I know it. Tommy, you know it, too. Sometimes you just have to live with the things you don't like about the world, as bad as they are."

"That's not the point," Tommy said.

"What is?"

"The point is that if they become strong enough, we're done for. They're not going to come up here and become good neighbors and all that stuff."

"We can't take Maggie's blood. It's out of the question."

"What else can we do? Tell me. What else can we do?"

As though giving up, Tommy threw his arms up in the air and sat down on his bed, barely able to keep his eyes open. His head fell forward as though about to fall asleep sitting up, but then he forced himself to look up. His head fell down toward his chest again, and then Mabin sat down on his bed and mirrored Tommy's actions. Maggie had seen this before and did not like what was happening. She glanced at Tommy's chest and through his shirt saw a light glowing inside him, and she knew what was about to happen. Just as the vampire spirits rose out of the earth, these two good souls rose from the earth toward a better place. She turned quickly to Mabin and saw the same phenomena through his shirt. His chest glowed with a soft light that pulsed and grew stronger, and despite everything, despite all the danger, he was falling asleep. Tommy had already settled back on his soft pine-bough bed, and his breath came slowly and evenly.

"Tommy! Not now!" Maggie yelled. "Mabin!"

"What's wrong with us?" Mabin asked, barely able to mouth the words, since he was so sleepy. "We can't go now. No, not now. Tommy? They're outside, and it's night. Wake up. Wake me up. We can't go now."

With that, he fell back on the bed asleep, and Maggie rushed to him to lift him by the shoulders and beg him not to leave her. Outside the window, the vampire spirits were drifting across the ground toward the cabin, knowing what was going on inside, knowing that Maggie would soon be alone.

"I can't ... stay ... awake ... not supposed to ... be here ..." Mabin whispered. "I am one of the dead?"

"What do you mean?" Maggie yelled at him. "This is exactly where you're supposed to be! Why do you say you're not supposed to be here?"

"Dead ..."

The light inside the cabin intensified as Tommy lifted up off his bed and floated toward the ceiling. It seemed to be a signal for the corrupted souls outside, since more and more of them crowded around the windows to look in. Their red eyes made hideous constellations just outside the glass, and as their eyes struck the glass there was a tapping as though glass was striking glass. Some scratched the panes with their frail claws, increasing their insistence, and then as Maggie watched the vampire souls crowding the windows from outside, the light inside the cabin grew even brighter, as though the sun had risen inside. Mabin had floated up off of the bed, rising in sleep toward the ceiling as Tommy was, the light inside him growing brighter and brighter. Tommy rose through the ceiling, his foot lingering inside before disappearing into the night above the cabin. Maggie grabbed for Mabin above her head, but it was as though her hand slipped through him and he continued his ascent. Soon he joined Tommy in the night sky above the cabin, and the only light inside the four walls came from the dying embers in the fireplace. Its logs were cackling and popping as they burned out reluctantly. The only company remaining for Maggie was the continued scratching at the windows, which intensified as they stared at the girl alone in the cabin. Maggie let a sob break from her, but then she picked up the knife off the table, angry and determined. She was safe inside her home, she knew, but with such creatures in such numbers outside she realized that safety could be compromised at any time if there was a chink or opening anywhere in her small fortress.

There was a scratching at the door, and then a tapping.

Someone wanted to come in.

"Really?" Maggie shouted loudly. "You really think you're coming in here."

With her brother and husband gone, a quivering fury grew inside her that she directed at the tapping on the door. "I'll open up, but you won't like what happens once I do."

She raced across the floor, half-insane that the final two best people in her life had been taken from her again and incensed at the intrusion on her grief. Without hesitating, she threw open the door and brandished the knife before her, intending to slice lengthwise any orange or pink mist that attempted to barge in.

When the door flew open, Harkin Davis stumbled backwards quickly.

After he composed himself from the fear Maggie's sudden attack put in him, he managed to sneer at her and grin.

"They left you again, didn't they? We both knew they would."

"It doesn't matter. There's nothing you can do about it, and they'll be back. I know I'm safe in here."

"Are you sure? You know, there will come a time when they can not come back, no matter how much they want to. They will be beyond your reach and ours, truly resurrected, and you will be never be with them again."

"That will never happen."

Maggie slashed out at Harkin Davis, who had floated too close to her for comfort, but he deftly slipped backward and away.

"Oh, but it will happen. It has to. Just as we will lose our battle for existence if we can not steal enough souls, they will remain forever lost to you if you do not join them."

"Why would I join them? They'll come back."

"You still do not understand? You must join them in death to stay with them. That is the only way for you, freedom through death. Let us kill you. I promise you can keep your soul and join them when you wish. It will be a comfortable end at our hands."

"You'll have to forgive me if I don't believe you."

"Maggie ... I once was an honorable man. I believe I can be honorable once again, if I simply have a second chance at life here on earth. You have our word. Don't you think I deserve a second chance? Won't death be a relief? About this you can believe me. I wish to be good again and will kill you to be good again."

"It would be comfortable to be with them ... I can't live without them. It's all I want."

"Then come outside and let us get this over with. We'll be gentle. It will be a good death, and painless."

With tears streaming down her face, Maggie nodded and took a step toward Harkin Davis, a step out of the cabin and safety.

"That's better. That's good, good for you! Come on now, a few more steps ..."

Hesitating at first, Maggie took another step and was completely outside her door, still weeping and seemingly resigned to her fate. She knew she had to die to be with Mabin and her brother. Suddenly, she stooped down and picked up a rock. She stepped back quickly, just as a dozen of the vampire spirits were about to converge on her, and found the safety of her cabin again.

"What are you doing?" Harkin Davis asked. "You said you would die for us. Do not abandon your husband and brother now!"

Suddenly, all around him, several hundred of the vampire spirits opened their eyes, their red pupils blazing in the night. Maggie saw what trap she had narrowly escaped.

"What am I doing you ask?" Maggie asked. "I am doing this."

With a slow motion, Maggie made a small cut in her little finger.

"Wait! Wait! There's no need to kill yourself," Harkin Davis said. "Such a cut will not do it. Let us. We are the experts."

"I know you are experts, but there's something else I know," Maggie said. She lifted her finger into the air and let a few drops of her blood fall onto the rock she held in her other hand. "I know this is brimstone, and I know what happens when human blood meets brimstone."

The rock immediately smoked and became so hot in Maggie's hand that she knew she had to let it go, drop it or throw it. The vampires surrounding Harkin Davis appeared greatly disturbed to see the ignition of the rock and cackled as the birds had been cackling for days in the surrounding trees. The rock burned in Maggie's hand. Harkin Davis' beady red eyes enlarged to the size of fists. Maggie drew back the flaming brimstone over her head and hurled it forward, missing Harkin Davis but catching three of the vampire spirits with glancing blows. In an instant, the corrupt souls were aflame and screaming as the fire consumed them. There was not much to them: they disappeared in whiffs of smoke. The rock bounced and rolled away down the hillside, and as it rolled and bounced it caught several more of the vampire souls and engulfed them in flames. As soon as they could, the myriad others retreated through the earth to their prison below. There were thousands of sucking sounds in the mud as the earth reclaimed the dropping, fleeing souls who did not wish to burn at Maggie's hands.

"Betrayer! We will not forget this! Come visit us soon," Harkin Davis said to her, with another sneer. "We have a much better use for your blood and your soul."

With that, he dropped through the earth and was gone.

Maggie thought it best that she take up his invitation. She had seen what she could do with blood and brimstone, and she knew that to resolve this situation and be with Mabin and Tommy forever in a fresh and new country cleared of these foul spirits she would have to destroy what was going on underground. She closed the door behind her and latched it, and went immediately to the pile of rocks over the trapdoor.

"It's brimstone, it's all brimstone," she mumbled to herself. "If I have enough blood I can kill them all ... and then I will die. I don't want to die. Do what you can, and live if you can."

She rolled the top rock off the pile and found their axe in a corner of the cabin. She returned to the rock she had separated from the rest and lifted the axe over her head and swung it down. On impact, the rock shattered with the force of her blow, breaking up into many smaller stones that scattered across the wooden floor. She gathered up as many as she could and stuffed them into her pockets, being careful not to let any of the dried blood from her cut finger contact them.

"Now all the other rocks, now I move all the other rocks," she said to herself out loud, half-mad and very disturbed at what she had to do. "And then I go down the hole."

With a strength and energy she did not know she had, she dragged the rocks one by one off the trapdoor, until only one remained. Slowly, with great care, she pulled that rock off the trapdoor, being careful to remain behind it since once the door was opened the vortex would again suck her down into the hole so powerfully she might not be able to resist. With the last rock just next to the trapdoor, she removed the knife from her belt and opened the cut on her finger. She was too quick to cut herself and the blood spurted out and onto the last brimstone, immediately setting it smoking and hissing, about to ignite into full flame, so she rushed round it and flung open the trapdoor. The swirling winds from below nearly pulled her in, but she used all her strength to fight her way back to behind the hissing, smoking boulder. She pushed on it as hard as she could and the vortex took it and pulled it down through the opening. A huge flame shot up off of it as it fell, and it nearly singed Maggie's face as she watched it go tumbling down. It impacted in the mud below and shattered, breaking into pieces that got caught up in the wind drawing the unfortunate souls below toward the vampire spirits. She watched as fiery pieces of brimstone shot out in all directions below, and they quickly flew across the mud floor. She heard screams as the burning brimstone got caught up in the whirling mass of damned souls, and she knew she had to attack now while they were on the defensive and vulnerable. She stepped forward into the opening to the cavern below and was immediately sucked down into it. She landed within the circle she had drawn on her last visit to this place but knew she could not stand still. The darkness was now light, as the whirlwind of spirits at the edge of the cavern had caught fire and was ablaze in many spots. The dull red eyes of the sleeping spirits were set on fire and immediately turned brown and fell down to ashes on the muddy floor. Souls were still being stolen from the innocent bodies being dragged through the mud by the vampires, so Maggie rushed forward and reached into her pocket for a rock of brimstone. As soon as her gushing finger touched the first piece of brimstone, it hissed in her pocket and she knew she had to withdrawn it immediately. She pulled it out of her pocket and hurled it across the cavern and into the whirlwind of spirit thieves. It caused a circle of fire to ignite in the corrupt spirits, as though gasoline had been poured into them, and more of the orange and pink vampire souls fell down to foul burned ashes in the mud. She did not hesitate. She reached her bleeding hand into her pocket and pulled out another hissing piece of brimstone and flung it into another spot in the whirling corruption of souls. Again, it blew up into a huge round circular fire in the wall of fouls souls, but she did not stop to watch. She removed one hissing shard of brimstone after another from her pockets and stood in one spot flinging them into the whirlwind. She circling wall of vampire souls did her work for her, as more and more of them came rushing past and were attacked by the burning rocks tossed into them. The entire whirlwind was alight, but she was not foolish enough to think all the vampire souls were burning. Mabin had been right. She did not have enough blood. There were so many she could not dream of destroying them all with a few slivers of brimstone. Watching the whirlwind rushing by on fire, feeling its heat, she felt dizzy. The fires were spreading among the foul souls but some were already exiting the swirling mass to discover what was going on. She was so light-headed she nearly dropped to the ground, but she flung the last of her hissing pieces of brimstone into the slowing mass around her. Then she knew she had to flee. Gathering all her strength, she turned and flew just over the bodies in the mud to where she believed her exit to be, but she was wrong about where it was and disoriented and she had to fly around and around looking for the spot that would afford her the safety of her cabin above. The orange and pink spirits had located the source of their affliction and some were awake and recovered enough to rush toward her. They were weak, too, but not from a loss of blood, as was Maggie. They were weakened by what she had done to them. They were weakened by the flames they had flown through while in a resting state. One came near her and lifted its claws to scratch her face: she sliced it in two, top to bottom, with a single parry of her knife. Another stiffened and slowed as it reached her, afraid now that it had seen what happened to its compatriot, but Maggie had no mercy on it. With another strong arc of the knife, she cut in it in two, the top and bottom halves dropping into the mud with the dead human bodies, where both halves were still. Its red eyes died like embers, and Maggie continued her search for the exit. Suddenly, she understood it was best to fly against the wind, since that would take her back to the hole in the earth leading upward to her cabin. She cut through the vortex, gauging the middle distances between the walls of the whirlwind, and soon found the exit upward to the light. The wind was blowing fiercely downward through the hole, but she gathered together her strength and shot up toward safety. She broke through into her empty cabin, but she knew she was not finished with the raid. As she turned around to gaze down at her work, she saw several pairs of red eyes gazing up at her from the bottom of the hole, so she rushed around one of the boulders of brimstone and in one motion scraped her bleeding finger across its surface. It ignited into a fire on its surface at once, and with a great push she shoved it down into the hole. Just as she did, one of the orange and pink spirits poked its red eyes over the edge of the hole: the burning rock dragged the vampire spirit back down with it into the pit, and the screams of several other vampire souls, all burning in the attempt to invade her home, told her the ploy was successful. She slammed closed the trapdoor and pushed the remaining rocks over it to re-establish safety in the cabin.

She collapsed onto the floor, but she knew the floor was not the safest place. She still did not know for certain what those below were capable of, so she dragged herself across the floor and climbed into bed. The room was spinning, and in the fireplace an ember cracked and popped.

There was very little light, and her throat was dry and she felt drained of strength.

"I have to find a way to make more blood inside me," she whispered to herself, as she was dropping off to sleep. "Mabin was right. I don't have nearly enough blood. But I got a lot of them. I killed hundreds, with just a pint or two. There are thousands more down there. How can I make more blood? How can I do it? Brimstone ... brimstone ... alone."

It was as silent as new-fallen snow in the cabin. She knew it was dangerous to be alone and unconscious, but she had to risk it.

She had lost so much blood she had no choice but to drop away unconscious despite the thousands of vampire souls seething with anger and thirsting for revenge below her.

As she fell asleep, she knew they would never be satisfied with the simple revenge of killing her.

They would want more.

17

When the light returned it was even more difficult to wake up than usual, since she was weakened by her blood loss.

She was hopeful it was dawn's light that softened her eyelids, since dawn meant Mabin and Tommy had returned from the night spent in the sky above and she could feel secure in their presence. Although awake, she let the soft light relax and warm her eyes, for she hoped to see only good things when she opened them. She stirred, but only slightly, since she felt very weak. Moving her arms and legs was difficult. She never enjoyed killing anyone, even vampires.

"Maggie?"

Instead of answering, she smiled. She remained silent, pretending to be asleep, with a smile for Mabin.

"I don't know if she's dreaming," he whispered, not to her but to Tommy. "At least she's happy. What do you think happened to her last night?"

"I can guess."

"What do you think she did?"

"She probably did what I would have done. She went after them by herself. Some of the brimstone rocks are missing. What's wrong with us, Mabin? First, our blood dries up. We have none, but we're still walking around and talking. I feel fine. But then we can never be here for her when she needs us. I don't know if I'm even human anymore. This is not how a good brother should act with a sister who saved his life."

"Did you wake up while we were away?"

"I did, for the first time, and I didn't know what anything around us was. That's when we started dropping back down here, as soon as I woke up."

"It was the same with me. I woke up, up there, and didn't know where we were but then we started dropping until I saw the cabin below. It wasn't easy. Maggie was right, though. She wasn't sleeping when we left her. She was wide awake and we were the ones who were unconscious, or living in another world and dreaming this one."

"This sucks. I don't want to be in another world without Maggie."

"I don't want to be without her, either. I can't be."

"But when we go, we have to go. We can't stop it. What does that mean?"

"It means were really are different from her. We died and came back. She brought us back. How could we be the same after that?"

Instead of listening to more of their conversation, Maggie groaned comfortably, glad to know how much they loved her, and stretched in bed. As she did, she felt a sharp stinging in the finger where she had opened the deep cut for blood. She winced, but the pain made her think of the mayhem she had inflicted below, of how she had weakened the vampire spirits and bought them more time here above to understand their situation. It seemed Mabin and Tommy also understood a little bit more of what was happening to them now. Before opening her eyes, she took one last look at her memories from last night, of how she had set the pieces of brimstone ablaze with her blood and tossed them into the whirling wall of foul souls. She saw them burning and falling to earth, their dull red eyes dropping into the mud like dull broken marbles. It made her smile. So maybe she did enjoy such work ...

"I know who's here now," she said, still smiling.

She opened her eyes wide, sure she would see Mabin smiling back at her. Instead, she saw the beautiful boy standing over her frowning and distraught, beside himself with concern.

"I'm so sorry, Maggie."

"Sorry? About what?"

"We said we weren't going to leave you last night and we did, didn't we?"

"Yes, the same way as always. I kind of expected it."

"I didn't mean it to happen, Maggie. My god, you were all alone with them. What did you do? What did you do?"

"Ah, she did all right," Tommy said. "Don't bug her. She probably kicked their butts again, didn't you, Maggie?"

Maggie tried to sit up in bed, but she was too weak at first and could only rise on her second attempt.

"Are you all right?"

Mabin took hold of her arm to support her, but she shook out her hair and spoke in a strong voice.

"You gave up your blood, didn't you?"

"I'm fine, and you were right about the blood and brimstone. With blood, the brimstone burns like gasoline."

"It does? Cool. How many did you get?" Tommy asked eagerly. "Damn, I wish I still had my blood."

"Not enough. I got hundreds, and they'll never bother us again. But there are tens of thousands more we still have to contend with."

"You went down there, didn't you?" Mabin asked. "Without us."

"What else could I do? I wasn't going to wait for them to come after me, but you were right about not having enough blood."

"Ah, Maggie, you shouldn't have risked it. I know you. You'll overdo it every time. You would have used every drop you have if you thought it would kill them all."

"Well, now I know I can't kill them all with my blood and the brimstone. We're going to have to figure out something else."

"I'm sorry we left you," Tommy said suddenly.

"I know."

"We can't help it. We never can. I don't know what happens to us, but we're not all here. We can't control it, and it's not right."

"We have to figure out why you go."

"There's something wrong with us, that's what it is. We should be able to help you, but instead we fall asleep and drift away."

"Where do you go?"

"We don't know," Tommy said exasperated. "I only saw where we were last night for the first time, and I didn't understand any of it. It's like we were in another world, where none of the rules apply. I saw things, but it was as though my eyes didn't work and I can't say what they are. I saw things but I didn't see them. Then we fell back down here."

"At least you're safe."

"Do you think so?"

"I think they've given up on capturing you and are only interested in me now," Maggie said. "They know you're beyond their reach."

"Now I really think we have to do something," Mabin said. "Promise me you won't try to go after them alone again like you did last night."

Maggie stared straight ahead.

"I can't."

"What do you mean, you can't?"

"Everything depends on getting rid of them. If we don't get rid of them, we can't move on the way we're supposed to and live our lives the way we should. We can never have a home and a life and children if they're around. We have to get rid of this haunting in any way we can."

Mabin turned away.

"Then all of us have to go down there."

"Can we?" Tommy asked.

"Why not?"

"Because every time there's a fight coming on, we fall asleep and drift off. What if that happens when we're down there and Maggie's alone with them again?"

"We have to try."

"Well, sure, I'm up for that. We can try. I'll fight them anytime, anywhere, for what they did to mom and dad."

"Maggie, can you describe exactly what it's like down there? I might have an idea of what we can do," Mabin said.

She began with telling them about the whirling vortex, the fierce gale that blows from the power of the tens of thousands of vampire souls swirling around in a great wheel at the edge of the huge cavern. She described how the pull their motion created drew the dead up out of the earth, and how when she opened the trapdoor in their cabin floor she was sucked down inside the cavern. They were drawing all to them to steal their souls and claim their power so that they could return to earth.

"I took the knife, so that I could cut myself, and I had broken up the brimstone into smaller pieces so that I could throw the burning pieces like grenades," she said. "I didn't count on seeing so many dead bodies in the mud, but I kept close to them to stay near enough to the whirling wall of vampire souls to ignite the brimstone and toss it into the souls speeding by."

"But there's no burning that they're capable of?" Mabin asked.

"No, they seem incapable of that. I know they're supposed to burn, and when I threw the flaming brimstone at them it destroyed them. There were just so many ... I couldn't get them all."

"We might have extinguished the fires of hell when we crushed so many inside the mountain," Mabin said. "What a pity."

Maggie stared at him, her mouth agape at the magnitude of what he had just said.

He met her glance and stared back at her for a moment, his expression set and hard.

"That's what's at stake," he said. "If they can regain any of their powers, they might be able to deliver human blood once again, and hell would burn once again. Maggie, do you have any idea of just how big the cavern is below?"

"It's big, a couple of hundred feet across."

"But exactly, can you say exactly how big it is?"

"I'd say from the center of it below our trapdoor, it's about two-hundred-and-fifty feet to the wall of dead vampire souls."

"So altogether it's about five hundred feet across?"

"Yes."

"Come outside."

"Why?"

"Because we have to find the perimeter of their circle if we're going to deal with them in the way I want to."

The soles of Maggie's feet were hardened from going without shoes for several days. When she jumped out of bed, she felt no pain in her legs from her adventure of the night before, but her blood loss made her dizzy. She shook her head, smiled at Mabin and took his arm to remain upright.

"Can you stand?" he asked.

"I'll be fine. Let's get this over with. If we can finish this and I can rest, I'll be fine."

As soon as they opened the cabin door and fresh mountain air swept in Maggie felt her lost strength return. Her vision became as clear as the air, and she thought she understood a little of what they were going to do. Mabin walked with his arm around her and she felt so happy and well being close to him that she did not want to admit she was no longer groggy. He might let go of her. To make sure he did not, she put her arm around his waist and pressed up against him tightly.

"Husband ..."

"My wife."

"I love you," she whispered into his ear. "Whatever happens, I love you."

He kissed her, and they stopped to embrace and kiss again.

"I've always loved you," he said. "You know that. I've loved you always."

"Will you two stop this?" Tommy asked. "This is so frustrating. I thought we were going to kill the vampire spirits, not mess around and kiss each other. We don't have time for this."

"There's always time for a kiss," Maggie said. "If there's not, what's a life for?"

"Okay. Geez. You're right. Keep on kissing while they steal more souls."

Mabin laughed out loud.

"I think I will kiss Maggie again," he said. "While we're busy kissing, why don't you pace off two-hundred-and-fifty feet in that direction and mark the spot with a rock, brimstone if you can find it. Then turn around, go behind the cabin and pace off another two-hundred-and-fifty feet in the exact opposite direction. Mark that spot with another rock."

"Oh, okay, I get it. I get to do all the work while you two have all the fun. I almost wish I had a girlfriend so that you two could see how gross it is to watch other people kissing all the time."

Tommy turned to walk away quickly, counting off steps as he did so. At first they laughed, but then Maggie felt so stricken by her little brother's loneliness that she turned to him and said the only thing she could.

"You'll have a girlfriend someday."

He stopped, stared at the ground and clenched his fists.

"Ah, now you made me mess up my count. No, wait, I remember. Just let me do this and don't talk to me anymore about girlfriends, okay?"

Maggie turned to Mabin again as Tommy walked away counting to pace off the distance.

"Is he going to be okay?"

"He'll be fine. I've never known a tougher little guy than him. He understands what we're doing. He's just giving us a hard time."

When Tommy had marked off the two spots that marked the underground circumference of the circling vampire souls below, Mabin mentioned they had to find some shovels, and when he said that his intentions became clear. They flew off to the burned-out hardware store and sifted through the ashes for shovels. After a few moments, they hit the jackpot. Among the ruins of the store they found a trove of a dozen shovels that had been displayed on the walls for sale but had been trashed in the blaze Elsa and Stephanovich set to destroy the town's vampires when they were still in human form. The handles of the shovels were no more than ashes, but the shovel heads were sharp and intact. They gathered up four of them, more than they needed, and when they were kicking aside the ashes to retrieve them, found the heads of several pick-axes. They took two, and then flew back to the cabin to fashion handles for their new implements before they could begin digging.

"I'm going to dig at the uphill spot, since it's probably a little farther down than the downhill spot until you reach the circle of vampire souls," Mabin said. "Maggie, do you think you can gather up as much brimstone as you can find and bring it to Tommy and me as we dig?"

"Wait a minute," Tommy said. "I can dig the uphill hole. You don't have to give me the easy job just because I'm a kid."

"Believe me, this is not going to be easy, wherever you dig," Mabin answered.

"In that case, okay. If I have to dig a shallower hole to get to the vampires souls first, then I can start doing away with the creepy things faster. Good deal."

Mabin began fashioning stout handles for the two pick-axes, working as the sun rose higher in the sky and baked the mountainside. Tommy gathered up straight and strong poles in the surrounding forest for the shovel handles and brought them back to the cabin. By the time he returned, Mabin had carved the first handle for the first pick-axe and was pushing it into the opening of the axe head to finish the job.

"There you go," he said, handing it to Tommy. "Swing that down into the earth and you'll loosen up a good chunk of it. You can get started digging if you want while I make the handles for the other tools."

"I'll start on your spot," Tommy said. "It's only fair, since you're still carving the handles. It wouldn't be fair if I started on mine first and got to them while you were just starting to dig. You'd miss out on all the fun of killing them."

"That's fine. The handles are the easy part. The hard part is going to be the digging down and what comes after."

While they worked, Maggie scoured the countryside looking for brimstone. She found lots of the blood-flammable rocks and carried as many as she could embrace back toward the two dig-sites. She dropped the first pile beside Tommy as he swung the pick-axe into the earth to loosen great chunks of it, and then she flew back into the forest to search for more.

"Hey, remember to drop some of those rocks where I'm going to dig," Tommy said. "I'm going to bomb the hell out of them once I'm finished with this hole and done with mine."

Maggie embraced another cache of brimstone she found piled in the forest and brought it back to deposit it at Tommy's dig-site. He had moved from Mabin's dig and started on his own. He swung the pick-axe furiously at the innocent earth and broke great clumps of it with each blow. When Maggie dropped the rocks nearby, he stopped and picked up his shovel, which had a brand-new handle, expertly made.

"Hey, Maggie," Tommy said, as she was about to fly off for more brimstone. "Mabin told me to tell you that when one of us breaks through to the cavern, we have to be careful. Once we do, the wind is going to try to suck us down in, and we have to be prepared to resist it and fly up out of the holes we dig and start throwing the rocks down on them. Don't be pulled down by the wind, he said."

They hit rock. It was not the flammable kind but hard shale that resisted the blows of their pick-axes and slowed their progress. Sparks flew off their tools as they struck the rock over and over to break through it, and Maggie worried a stray spark might ignite the brimstone. As though angered by the resistance of the stone, Tommy swung the pick-axe faster and faster and harder and harder, sending more and more sparks up out of the hole.

"Come on, come on!" he yelled at the earth. "I don't care how tough you think you are, I'm tougher."

Maggie found Mabin battling the same type of rock that Tommy was, but he was making greater progress. He broke up the rock into pieces with fierce blows of the pick-axe, and then quickly shoveled it out of the hole, tossing it up over his shoulder onto a pile that grew faster and faster. He had dug down so far only his head showed over the rim of the earth. His hair was covered in sweat and gleamed in the sunlight, and dark smudges marked his face. He smiled up at Maggie as she approached.

"Are you getting close?" she asked.

"I'm getting dirty."

Maggie laughed. "We all are."

"I think I'm almost there. I can almost feel the rumble of them whirling round and round below the soles of my feet. If I had shoes, I could work faster. How's Tommy doing?"

"He's working like crazy, but he hit rock, too. It's slowed him down."

"Tell him it's important we finish at the same time. If he starts to break through before I do, tell him to stop and wait for me. We have to attack them at the same time."

Mabin paused to stare downhill to where Tommy worked, and as he did Maggie turned around to see how her little brother was progressing, too. It was as though a volcano had erupted at Tommy's dig, as earth and rock flew up into the sky in fast spurts from his shovel.

"I better let him know not to break through on his own," Maggie said. "It looks like he's going crazy down there."

"After you tell him, get some more brimstone if you can," Mabin yelled after her. "We can never have enough to burn these guys."

Maggie paused to fly over Tommy's dig and shouted down the instructions Mabin had given her. Wait until both digs were ready. Don't break through until the attack can commence at once from both spots. Tommy nodded to her but continued to shovel earth and rock furiously. Maggie easily found two more armfuls of brimstone and returned with them, distributing the flammable stones evenly between Tommy and Mabin.

Tommy jumped up out of his pit and waved and shouted to Mabin.

"I'm right on top of them! One big rock pushed down there will break through!"

"Good!" Mabin shouted in return. "The same here!"

Instead of giving the signal to set the brimstone on fire, he hung his head and walked slowly down the mountainside to where Tommy and Maggie were waiting. He did not let his eyes meet theirs until he was a few feet away. Then there was great concern in them. He hesitated before speaking.

"I know I said you shouldn't give your blood, Maggie, but –"

"I don't care. I've known all along what we were going to do, and I knew I'd have to cut myself again to do it."

"I still don't want you to."

"I know, but what choice do we have? Either I cut myself, or our life here is done."

"Ah, who's afraid of a little blood?" Tommy broke in. "Maggie's not afraid. We're not going to let her bleed to death or anything. We just need a few drops to get things burning down there, and then we'll be free. I want to be free."

Mabin had dropped his eyes to the earth, and it was clear he had some unspoken dark thought in his head.

"I hate this," he mumbled. "I hate it, but I guess we have to do it."

"All right!" Tommy said. "I have this big mother of a rock ready right here on the edge of the hole, and all Maggie has to do is set it on fire with a few drops of blood, and then I'll push it in and that will be the end of them."

"Wait for me to do the same thing," Mabin said. "We'll get your rock burning and then Maggie and I will fly to my dig and set one of my rocks flaming there. We'll push them in at the same time, on my signal."

Tommy moved behind the big rock of brimstone and placed both hands behind it in preparation to push it in the hole. Maggie lifted the knife out of her belt and held it over her healing finger.

"Ready?"

"Now!" Mabin yelled.

Maggie closed her eyes and opened the small incision again. She felt no pain but could sense the blood dripping out of the wound onto the brimstone, which heated up immediately. When she opened her eyes, the rock was smoldering, about to break into flames. Mabin took her uninjured hand and pulled upward on it, and in a second they were airborne and flying toward the second dig. As soon as they landed, Maggie held her magical blood over the large rock Mabin had prepared and watched this time as it set to smoking. Looking downhill, she saw that Tommy's brimstone bomb had already burst into flames, and he was leaning backward to avoid the heat but staring up at them for the signal. Mabin's brimstone showed a small flame and he waved at Tommy.

"Push it in now!" he shouted.

With a strong shove Tommy launched the brimstone into the hole. It dropped quickly, crashed into the ceiling below and then sent a huge geyser of flames shooting up out of the dig. Then the geyser of flame dropped down and Tommy leaned in to see its effect.

"It broke through!" he yelled.

Immediately from inside the hole came the screams of the burning vampire souls as the huge rock of brimstone fell into their midst and ignited in all directions, sending fire through their ranks. Mabin's brimstone burst into flames and without hesitation he mirrored Tommy's action and sent the burning boulder down into the hole, where it disappeared but then also sent a tower of fire shooting up from the dig as it hit the ceiling below and broke through.

"Maggie! I need more blood!" Tommy shouted. "We've got them now! We've got them! We can't stop!"

Without hesitation, Maggie shot down the hill and provided what Tommy requested, squeezing her finger to drop its blood onto the next brimstone bomb. The rock ignited at once, and Tommy pushed it into the hole with a shout.

"All this trouble you caused us! We'll it's over! You're done now! We did away with you, and now we're doing away with your souls!"

Maggie did not wait but took to the air and shot uphill to where Mabin waited behind a huge boulder of brimstone. Without saying a word, she dropped a stream of blood onto it, realizing if she could get this rock to burn it would decimate the vampire souls below. It was smoking and hissing in an instant, and Mabin pushed and it descended down the hole as a huge ball of fire. She watched it hit the whirling circle of depraved souls below, but she had to withdraw from the edge of the hole quickly when a column of burning embers shot up.

"We've got to burn all of them," Mabin shouted. "We've got to get the entire wheel in flames so that not one of them survives.

They're trapped and can't get away. Are you all right to go on, Maggie?"

"I'm fine."

She lied. She was already feeling a little light-headed but the prospect of ending their long battle with the vampires wouldn't let her stop now.

"I'm going back down to Tommy. There must be thousands still spinning around and stealing souls below us."

She shot downhill where Tommy had another rock ready to roll into the pit below. Again without hesitating, she milked her swollen finger for more blood and dropped it on the brimstone. It smoked and hissed but Tommy did not wait for it to ignite but pushed it so that it fell down smoking. When it smashed into the wheel of vampire souls it ignited like a bomb and sent flames flashing in all directions below them.

She turned without touching the ground but her light-headedness made her pause before flying uphill to give more blood.

"Are you all right?" Tommy asked. "You look a little pale."

"I'm fine. I'm not stopping until they've all gotten what they deserve."

She rocketed up to Mabin and prepared to drop blood on the next batch of brimstone.

"Wait a minute," he said. "You're breathing hard. Hold on until you catch your breath. This might be too much for you."

A stream of blood shot out of her finger in response, as though an artery had suddenly opened, and so much of it painted the waiting brimstone that it broke into tall flames immediately. Mabin had to kick it into the hole, and Maggie fell to earth clutching her finger to stop the flow.

She fell to her knees and her head bobbed up and down as though she was about to faint.

"Just hold on. Rest for a moment. You might have given all you can give," Mabin said.

Maggie did not answer but remained on her knees as her chest heaved up and down quickly to take in as much air as possible.

"Are they burning?" she finally managed to ask.

"We've re-ignited hell."

Maggie dropped her head with a smile but still her breathing was forced and it appeared she might topple over at any moment from the lack of blood.

Then suddenly she looked up at Mabin with her eyes wide and frightened.

"My god. We forgot," she said.

"Forgot what?"

"There are hundreds of innocent souls downs there. We're burning them along with the vampire souls. We can't! We can't do that!"

She struggled to her feet and tried to lift herself up off the ground, but she was too weak.

"Maggie, you have to –"

Without listening to what he was about to say, she ran downhill toward the cabin and threw open the front door. She had only one hand that was clear of blood, so she had to use that to push the brimstone over the trap door aside or set the inside of the cabin on fire. Holding her bleeding hand off to the side so that the blood would not ignite the brimstone, she pushed one rock after the other off the trapdoor and lifted it open.

"Maggie!" Tommy was at the open door. "You can't go down there! It's hell! You'll burn up!"

Maggie stared down at a true description of what Tommy said. Below her, a bright conflagration lit the bottom of the pit, with flames licking up the sides of the tunnel leading down. She tossed her knife to Tommy.

"If any of the vampire souls try to escape, use this on them," she said. "I'm saving the others."

There was no vortex of wind drawing her down, since the fiery brimstone had halted the spinning wheel of vampire souls. That meant the innocent souls were no longer being sucked into it for power. Maggie dropped feet-first down the hole and landed in the middle of the inferno, right within the circle she had drawn there. Columns of flame rose off the floor of mud, which was now caked and dried, but in it the bodies of the dead still awaited their fate. Looking around without an idea of what to do, she noticed these bodies were from long ago, the women and girls in long dresses and petticoats and the men in loose pants and white hemp-fabric shirts and cowboy boots. In the distance, she saw some of the vampire spirits had escaped the fiery wheel and were bending over the dead, opening their mouths and sucking out their innocent souls.

Suddenly, a white mist rose out of a little girl in a gingham dress.

"I don't want to go with them," the mist whispered to Maggie, and then saw a lovely innocent face form in its mist. "I saw what they did to the others. Burn my body, but don't take my soul."

"Then leave this way," Maggie said, pointing to the opening above her. "I'll stop them."

The little girl's soul hesitated for a moment, but then it floated across the mud, touched Maggie and then rose to exit the burning inferno.

The vampire spirits were too busy greedily stealing what souls they could before expiring and did not see Maggie at first.

She stepped forward out of her circle and spoke to the dead bodies on the mud floor.

"Any of you, do what the little girl did. This is your time to be saved. If you wait, they will take you and you will burn with them. Rise up out of your bodies. Rise and be free. Follow where the little girl went."

As though hearing and responding all at once, hundreds of the innocent souls slowly abandoned their bodies and ascended from the mud and came together so densely they formed a fog. The fog of innocence moved steadily away from the vampire spirits that still collected the unwary souls from the dead, and when the vampire spirits saw what was happening and that they were about to be starved and burned they looked around and caught sight of Maggie. A thousand pairs of red eyes blazed at her. In a white stream of mist, the innocent souls flew past Maggie and ascended through the opening toward the light. They flew upward in a quickening stream that increased in speed as more and more souls entered it. The vampire spirits were chasing them down, picking off a few of the stragglers and consuming them on the spot. Maggie looked around desperately and found what she needed. She stooped for a handful of smoking brimstone, set it ablaze with her blood and then flew directly at the horde of vampires closing in on the innocent souls. When she was within feet of them, she flung the burning rocks among them and ignited hundreds at once, their screams filling the cavern. They retreated as the innocent souls increased their pace toward escape to the upper world behind Maggie.

Suddenly, from her right something shot at her and she ducked just in time as it flew over her. She spun around to see who it was and the spirit of Harkin Davis stood motionless, its red eyes aflame and staring at her.

"So you have done it," he said. "We have no chance now."

"You should never have tried to take them."

"As though we had a choice ..." he said bitterly.

"You did, but you made the wrong choice long ago."

"Will you kill me now?"

"I'll leave you to burn with the rest."

"You would ... you would. I should have expected nothing less."

Behind her, the last innocent souls were exiting through the opening in the ceiling. Harkin Davis stared bitterly at them as they left, and then the last one disappeared. All around, all through the cavern, one vampire spirit after the other was falling to the flames, their red eyes dropping into the caked mud and fading out.

"If you won't kill me, I won't die like this," Harkin Davis said.

"You have no choice. You're not coming to the surface, ever again. You're burning down here as you deserve to."

"Then burn I will!" he screamed.

With a last look at Maggie, his red eyes blazed intensely and then he flew directly into a burning column of brimstone to end himself among his brothers. The fire took him and burned his soul to ash, and he was no more.

Maggie held closed the wound on her injured finger. She turned and hovered over the floor of the cavern and looked around.

The bodies of the innocent were caught in the flames, but it was all right, for they had been long dead and their souls were saved.

The last cries of the vampire spirits faintly reached her as she flew up and out of this hell.

She was never so happy to see the light above as she was when she reached the small interior of her cabin and home.

It was one light she did not fear.

18

"Close the trapdoor. Slide the brimstone on top of it. They're done and can't get out, but I'd like to forget what they did to steal all those souls down there as soon as possible," Mabin said. "I wasn't right, it just wasn't right."

Maggie had just returned to the world when Mabin spoke of his disgust for the vampire souls who were now burning below them. Maggie settled onto the floor of their little cabin, drained of emotion, her body nearly empty of blood. She still held her damaged finger in a tight grip, but Mabin opened her grip and brought the finger to his mouth and kissed it. The bleeding stopped immediately.

"It's over," Tommy said. "We won."

"I know. It's over, or at least this part of it is over. Their bodies are no more, their souls are extinguished. We are free of them," Mabin said. "We've done all we could and are finished this part of our work."

Maggie collapsed backwards onto the floor, staring at the ceiling, and Mabin scooped down to pick her up in his arms. He carried her to their bed and lay her down. Her head rolled from side-to-side in delirium or happiness.

They had lost so much, but had achieved a great deal.

"Is she okay?" Tommy asked.

"She will be. She's done everything asked of her. She can do no more."

"Hear that, Maggie? You're going to be okay. They're all dead and gone. It's no longer Vampire Valley."

"I know. I saw them die."

She couldn't help but smile and take Mabin's hand. It felt unusually cold in her grip as she pressed it and brought it to her lips. When she looked into his eyes, they could not have held more hurt and pain, and tears formed in their corners and flowed down his cheeks.

"What's wrong? You should be celebrating. They're dead, aren't they?" Maggie asked. "Even their spirits are gone and the world is clean again. You said so yourself."

"Yes, I said so. The world is clean."

"Then why are you crying?"

"Because it's the end."

"The end? No. It begins now. It's always beginning again."

Mabin reached out and took both of Maggie's hands.

"Can you get up? Are you strong enough to come outside?"

"Of course. I was just a little faint with relief. I'm plenty strong now that they're gone."

"Then come on and see those you saved."

As they made their way out the door Maggie caught a whiff of rancid smoke that made her cover her mouth and cough once. There were two columns of black smoke rising out of the two holes Mabin and Tommy had dug to bomb the vampire souls with burning brimstone. The underground cavern still had plenty of fuel to burn, and even heated the ground below their bare feet as the summer noonday sun did. The smoke from the conflagration under them rose straight up into the sky, and as she watched it seemingly escape all the way up into the blue, the smoke turned pure white, as white as angel's wings. The thick black smoke continued to pour out of the two holes in the ground and change to white above, and just as Maggie brought her eyes down to earth again, she saw a collection of white souls hovering over the earth. They were little more than mist, but they each had a separate appearance, as though the souls were still individuals. There were women in long skirts and bonnets, and men in overalls and boots with cowboy hats on their heads. Small children were standing among the taller souls, each of them holding hands with a parent or stooped grandmother or grandfather. The little girls were in simple gingham dresses and the boys in rough linen shirts and loose-fitting pants and caps and boots.

"Are these the innocent souls from below?" Maggie asked.

"They're all free and ready to move on now that you helped them escape the vampire souls below," Mabin said. "They've been waiting a long time for this day, trapped in their bodies and afraid the vampires would take them if they dared attempt an escape."

"But some of them are so young, so many of them are young," Maggie said. "Even most of the men and women are young."

Mabin stared at the gathering of freed, innocent souls hovering above the ground, a deep concern on his face.

"They died before their time, unjustly," he said. "There was a massacre very near here, with much blood spilled, and they've been waiting in their graves for the time they could be free again and rise to their just place without fear of those we just burned."

"It took them that long to escape?"

"It's been nearly a hundred-and-fifty-years," Mabin said. "It took us that long for us to free them."

"But now they can move on?" Maggie asked. "Now they don't have to fear anyone and can leave?"

"Yes," Mabin said, and then hesitated before going on. "And Tommy and I have to go with them."

Maggie wasn't certain she had heard her husband correctly. She objected immediately.

"No, you mean they move on and you stay here, right?" she asked.

"No. I meant what I said. I'm sorry."

"But what about what we fought for, to make a life for ourselves here, free of those we killed. I can't do that alone."

"They can't move on without us, and they have to move on. We are their guides."

Maggie was about to object again that she and Mabin and Tommy were free to live again and the spirits were free to go their own way, but when she looked at Mabin to speak a sick feeling overcame her. His inner light had begun to glow and pulse, in a way she had not seen before. The light inside of him was more gorgeous than any she had ever seen, and it was fragrant with a freshness so great she might have stepped outside on the first day of the world. The pulsing light inside him grew greater and faster and lovelier as she watched him and the glow inside him increased in intensity. She knew what this meant and had never thought it would happen again now that they were free. If they were free, she thought they would be together. In a panic, she looked over toward Tommy and saw the same thing was happening to him. His inner light was bright and strong and growing brighter and stronger as she watched.

"Maggie, we never came back to life again, never as human beings, at least," Mabin explained, seeing her panic at what was happening.

She was speechless as the white souls surrounded Mabin and Tommy.

"No one can come back to life, real life, once dead," Mabin went on. "We were resurrected, you helped resurrect us, but we came back to our souls and not to our flesh and blood."

"But wait, I saw you come back to me, to come alive again as we went through the steps to resurrection inside the mountain. I saw you came back and become my husband of flesh and blood. You are flesh and blood."

"I am your husband, but I am not flesh and blood," Mabin said firmly.

"And I am your brother, and always will be your brother and love you," said Tommy. "But I am not flesh and blood. I know this now."

"But you have to stay, both of you have to stay, no matter what you are. I can't be here alone, without you both."

"We would stay with you forever if we were living human beings," Mabin said. "I am not, and Tommy is not. We belong above, with them, and have to go. I'll always belong to you, but can't with be you."

Maggie fell to the warm ground.

"Ah, Maggie, I don't want to go," Tommy said, tears splashing his face. "But I don't belong here. As Mabin said, I died and you helped bring me back, but not as a true human being."

Even as he talked, Tommy rose a foot off the ground, the pull from above becoming too great for him to resist. In a panic, she turned to Mabin, who had also risen a foot off the ground to join the white souls hovering there. Tears were splashed all over Mabin's face, and he was shaking as though freezing.

Maggie rose and rushed to him and embraced his legs, but he was so unsubstantial that she barely had anything to hold on to. With as much strength as she could muster she pulled hard on the armful of light hovering above her and managed to pull Mabin back down to earth.

"Maggie, don't!" Tommy yelled. "You could kill him if he says where he does not belong!"

"It's all right, for a moment," Mabin said.

Mabin's tears splashed down on Maggie and joined those washing over her face.

"I have to kiss my wife good-bye."

"No! I won't kiss you if you're leaving," Maggie screamed. "You have to stay. I will not let you go, no matter who needs your help or says you have to leave."

The spirits Maggie had saved were not listening to what she said, and had already begun their journey to their destination above.

"Maggie, you know I love you and have always loved you, like no one I ever knew, through all time," Mabin said. "It is impossible for me to leave you, but impossible for me to stay."

"Then stay if both are impossible. We've always done the impossible."

"This is the most impossible of all things, for if you love a dead man, you live in the past."

"It is impossible for any living woman to live and love in the past," Tommy said.

The tug on Mabin's being was growing stronger and stronger as he was compelled to rise above this earthly existence by forces much stronger than any of them. Maggie felt it. Gathering all her strength together, she held on to him fiercely, weeping, and raised her lips to his, just managing to touch them to his as he was torn from her arms. His light grew brighter and brighter as he rose above her, but she still felt his tears falling out of the sky and onto her face.

"Good-bye, good-bye," he whispered to her. "We are for always."

All around him the hundreds of white souls congregated in the air, and then she saw Tommy's bright light among them. The congregation floated higher and higher into the blue as Maggie sobbed below, unable to lift her human body off the earth, even an inch, unable to fly as she had flown so often with Mabin. The gathering of souls rose higher and higher, forming a distant white cloud with two bright lights within it, and then it disappeared into the blue.

The sky was empty.

Maggie tumbled back onto the ground and fainted away.

It was the only thing a human being who had just lost everyone and everything she had ever loved, finally and forever, could do.

19

The first thing she thought when she saw the light was that it was the light of the damned that assaulted her eyes, for she thought she had been damned to lose husband and brother all at once.

The light turned to darkness and then to light again, and the only reason she knew to open her eyes was that it might somehow be Mabin and Tommy coming back to her. But no. They were beings of light, and gone forever. There were only shadows here. The light turned bright again, but then dark, and she thought if she had to face this darkness alone forever she would not flinch but fight it. She would fight this darkness of being alone with all her might, just as she had always fought darkness, and she would begin the battle now.

She opened her eyes.

"She does seem to be alive," a woman's voice said above her. "Perhaps you were right."

"What a poor excuse for a girl, though. She must have been through a great deal, with no shoes and torn clothes and that dirty face."

Even with her eyes open, the light turned to darkness again, for the two figures standing over moved to shade the sun from her eyes. One of them leaned down and peered into her eyes and the bright light of the sun again assaulted her vision as the woman bent down.

"Yes, I believe you're right. She is alive, but what a dirty mess she is. What happened to you, child?"

Maggie broke out in hysterical laughter. How could she possibly tell anyone what had happened to her? She laughed on and on at the absurdity of it, for all her efforts to love had led her only to loneliness and heartbreak, a life alone in the wilderness.

"Is she laughing or crying?" one of the women asked.

"I think she's laughing, but why would she, in her condition? Perhaps it is laughter brought on by an excess of pain."

"Perhaps it is. Let me help you up, child. Can you get up? I think she is crying, or perhaps she is mad."

Maggie was still so weak from the loss of blood that could not think properly or form any words. She simply babbled in a cracked voice. She felt hands lift her under her arms and before she could object and say she wished to remain on the ground, alone, staring up at the empty sky that had deserted her, she was brought to her feet.

"The others are below. Let's take her down to them. The Reverend will know what to do."

"Are you all right? Can you walk?" the second woman asked, but they were nearly carrying her down the mountainside and did not give her a chance to answer.

She was too weak either to walk or talk properly, and merely stumbled and whispered.

"I love him," she managed to say. "I have always loved him, and he is gone."

"Why, she can speak. She said something about loving a man. Are you married, girl?"

"Yes."

"And did he leave you?"

"Dead ... both dead ... and my brother ... gone ..."

"My goodness. Both your husband and brother are dead? Were they killed? Was this your cabin? Were you attacked?"

Maggie could only manage to nod. Her legs fell out from under her and she nearly toppled down to the ground, but the women were strong and managed to keep her upright and moving.

"We'll help you, child. We're good people, and when we see someone in need like you are, we do all we can to return her to a blessed state."

"You need food and care and to be cleaned up like a proper girl. You'll receive all you need from us."

Maggie was being led down the mountainside by the two portly, strong women and could do little to resist. Her heart was aching and she constantly tilted back her head to stare up at the sky in the hope of catching one last sight of him. While she was staring up into the blue, she heard the snorting and neighing of horses, many of them. Her head fell down to her chest. She was barely able to lift it, but when she managed to lift it she saw a scene that confused her beyond all confusion, a scene that did not allow itself to register in her mind because it made her think she had no mind left. Stretched out on the valley floor was a line of horses and Conestoga wagons, seemingly going on forever. There must have been a hundred of the wagons, and around them were people, not real people she thought, but people like the dead she had just seen rise into the sky. There were women in long skirts and bonnets, and men in overalls and boots with cowboy hats on their heads. Small children were among the taller souls, each of them holding hands with a parent or stooped grandmother or grandfather, or running around in play. The little girls were in simple gingham dresses and the boys in rough linen shirts and loose-fitting pants and caps and boots.

"Dead, you're all dead," she murmured. "I see you and you are the dead who left with Mabin."

"Why, no, we're not dead," one of her benefactors said. "Whoever killed your husband and brother did not get us, you can be sure of that."

Maggie forced herself to open her eyes and take in the scene around her. She had not hallucinated but had seen exactly what she saw now. Conestoga wagons pulled by horses. A wagon train with men and women and children in antique clothing. She nearly collapsed to the ground again, and heard a refrain in her head.

... *if you love a dead man, you live in the past.*

That is exactly what appeared to be before her now. She was living in the past. A desperate, absurd laughter broke from her, the laughter of hysteria.

"I love a dead man. He is dead. I am in the past because of I love a dead man."

Before she could fall all the way to the ground again a pair of strong hands caught her around the waist. Someone had taken her by the waist and prevented her collapse.

"Thank you, Joshua," one of the women said. "The poor girl has been difficult to bring down off the mountain. We wish to save her, but we don't know how. Help us get her to the Reverend to find out what to do with her. He'll know. He knows all."

Again, Maggie felt herself held up as she stumbled across the valley floor along the line of wagons. People stared at her in wonder, the women holding their hands to their mouths in horror at her terrible condition and the men stoically staring at her, their rifles held to their chests. So strong were the arms that held her that she knew she could not fall, and she relaxed into her new terror, this new life in the past.

"There's the Reverend ... Reverend! Reverend! We found a girl all alone up on the mountain. She says her husband and brother have been killed."

A man in dressed all in black turned around directly in front of her. She saw only his black pants and shining black boots, for her head was lolling down on her chest. She felt a rough hand lift her head by the chin, and then staring into her eyes with a severe judgment in his was someone she knew very well.

"This is the Reverend Harkin Davis," one of the women said. "He is a good, godly man and will decide your fate. He is the leader to all these pilgrims, a true saint among us, and has saved many a one of us on this trip to our new lands."

As weak as she was, Maggie managed a scream. She kicked out at Harkin Davis and her foot caught him in the shin. She pulled one arm free and shot her hand out to tear the man's eye from his head, but he pulled back and she merely managed to draw her fingernails violently down his cheek and scratch four lines of blood on his face. There were gasps of horror all around.

"She's mad!" Reverend Harkin Davis screamed. "See the mad girl! I don't know, and will not know until further inspection of her, but she is perhaps possessed, too, but I know for certain now that she is mad!"

More gasps of horror rose up from the crowd assembled around her, and the strong arms she had broken free from were thrown around her and embraced her so that she could not attack the holy man before her again. She struggled mightily as she tried to attack the vampire she found again in his flesh, the vampire that had destroyed her family and lover, but the arms holding her back were too strong.

"Take the child and bathe her and feed her, Mrs. Mabin, to see if she calms down from her torment," Reverend Davis said. "She seems a child of the devil, but perhaps she can be saved. I will decide overnight what to do with her, and in the morning she will discover her fate. Have your son let go of her and take her. Joshua, let go of her, I'm fine now, and let your mother bathe and feed this child."

She felt the strong arms around her loosen her grip, and she was too weak to attack Harkin Davis a second time. The two women who had brought her down off the mountain again gripped her by the arm. She did not have the strength to break free and attack Harkin Davis again, but the name she had heard made her focus her strength elsewhere.

"Mabin!" she cried out and spun around to break free of the women's grip.

She caught sight of that face she loved, shaded by the wide-brimmed hat, but still it was the face she loved. It was the pure, clean face of a young man, and not the grave concerned face that that risen into the sky just moments ago.

... *if you love a dead man, you live in the past.*

"That's me, miss, Joshua Mabin," he said with a grin. "And who might you be?"

Before she could say she was his wife, she felt something crash down on the back of her head with great power.

Darkness slowly descended over her.

The Reverend Harkin Davis had hit her over the head with his thick black Bible for speaking out-of-turn.

"Now she is calm and manageable," he said. "That will learn her to interrupt me. Mrs. Mabin, take her and bathe her, as I said, and feed her once she is awake. By all appearances, she is a child of the devil, but I will make final judgment on her this evening. Now take her away and do as I bid you."

*

"Miss, Miss, are you awake?"

The first words she heard were his. She could tell even with her eyes closed. The light he brought was dimmer now, but it was his light. She would recognize it anywhere. It was his light and his voice.

"Mabin ..." she murmured.

"Yes, Miss, I'm Joshua Mabin. You have to wake up now. We have to get out of here."

Maggie could not wait to open her eyes to see him. With a joy she could not hold back she opened her eyes and saw him again, that same boy she loved, that same face, partially hidden by the wide-brimmed hat. He was holding a lantern to light his face, and she was in a pile of blankets below one of the wagons.

"Husband ..."

She reached out to touch his face.

He took her hand gently but urgently before it settled on his cheek.

"Listen to me! Please! We have to get out of here! Now! We have to go. The Reverend Davis is going to make a blood sacrifice of you in the morning. He says you have shown yourself to be a child of the devil, but I know better. I could see you're not of the devil when you looked into my eyes earlier today and smiled. You are not of the devil, no, but a beautiful girl who's been injured, that's all. He wants to make a blood sacrifice of you in the morning! He's done it before and will do it again, to you, so we must go. I won't let him do it to you."

Maggie knew right away the truth of what Joshua Mabin was saying, and would do anything he said at this point. She climbed out from under the pile of blankets and wished only to be held in his arms again before they fled.

He helped her up, and they stood face-to-face, and she rushed forward to embrace him and break into tears.

"If you trust me, I'll take you away from here," he said, his arms wrapping around her. "I'll save you first of all, and then we can figure out a way to save the rest of these people from him. Do you trust me? Will you go with me?"

Maggie pressed up against him and tightened her grip on him.

"I'll go with you anywhere. I entrust you with my life and soul."

"Good. I am a trustworthy fellow, you'll see. I'll be good to you, because I can see you're good, and a beautiful soul, and not like that phony pastor back there these foolish people have chosen to follow."

Joshua Mabin set down the glowing lantern and closed off the flow of oil to the flame.

When everything grew black around them they ran off, barefoot and hand-in-hand, into the endless Montana night.